THE SPECIMEN

Martha Lea

WINDSOR
PARAGON

First published 2013
by Canongate Books Ltd
This Large Print edition published 2013
by AudioGO Ltd
by arrangement with
Canongate Books Ltd

Hardcover ISBN: 978 1 4713 2582 3
Softcover ISBN: 978 1 4713 2583 0

British Library Cataloguing in Publication Data available

Printed and bound in Great Britain by
TJ International Limited

Part I

PRELUDE

HELFORD PASSAGE, CORNWALL. SEPTEMBER 8, 1866.

THE TIMES, Thursday, September 6, 1866.

MURDER AT HYDE PARK.

ON the morning of Tuesday, 7th August, the body of Edward Scales (38), late of Helford, Cornwall, was discovered at his Hyde Park residence in London. During the inquest held on the body by Horatio Moreton Esq., Coroner, and attended by Dr Jacobs of the London Hospital, it was made known that the body of the deceased bore the marks of ligatures to the neck, and that the contents of the stomach of the deceased had been found to be largely full of brandy. After lengthy examinations of witnesses, a Mrs G. Pemberton (26) of Richmond, Surrey, was later charged with the Murder of Mr Scales and committed for trial at the Central Criminal Court.

Never is a newspaper read more intently than when it is about to be put to some other use. Their names came in and out of focus. For a few blessed moments her mind was utterly quiet, and she waited for the shaking to subside before tucking the slip of newsprint away. She ripped the next square from the string, and the next and the next until she was done. Outside the privy she leaned on the closed door and breathed the damp morning air.

There was just a hint of rotten autumn settling in but nothing very definite.

As she went back to the house she tried to remember what she had been doing on that Monday a month before. She tried to remember, because she didn't want to let her mind gallop around, gathering thoughts about how many people in the country over the past two days had already seen the information hiding up her left sleeve. People on trains and at news-stands. At breakfast. On park benches, and waiting on street corners.

She was standing now in front of the bureau in the study. For such an imposing piece of furniture, its lock was a pitifully small mechanism. With the need for an actual key now positively redundant, she took up the poker from its place by the empty grate. It was simply a matter of precision and determination. The bevelled point of the poker slipped the first time and gouged a scrape through the walnut. On the fifth attempt she was able to force the poker into the space between the locked-up lid and the body of the bureau. She levered her weight onto the poker. The crack of splintering wood and the lock giving way brought Susan to the room.

'Ma'am?'

'That's quite all right,' she said. 'I shan't require any assistance. Except, of course, that I shall be going to London today and will need to pack.' Then she turned her attention again to the bureau and set about finding the name and address of the late Edward Osbert Scales' solicitor.

Seven Years Earlier

CHAPTER I

HELFORD PASSAGE, CORNWALL. APRIL 1859.

The sun lay heavy on his clothes making him tired, and he had to stop for a while and rest against the rocks. They were thrust up on the beach, it seemed to Edward Scales, like wrecked ships. Hulls keeled over, encased in barnacles. A seam of white crystal pressed between layers of dark grey was caulk jammed between planks. He didn't see the rearing layers, contorted, extreme pressure distorting and forcing the horizontal to the diagonal and vertical. Only ships. He knew that they were not, could not ever have been ships, but his mind rested on that thought because anything else was too immense to confront.

The succession of small beaches on the Helford were each enclosed by high cliffs, pocked with shallow caves. Strewn with sharp, jagged rocks, the ground in between was made up of grey, white and ochre pebbles from fist-sized lumps down to number eight shot. At low tide on the Helford the bladderwrack clung to the rocks, and draped like crowns of slick hair. Not an easy terrain to walk over. He could have come by boat, but he hadn't thought of that. And he could have stayed there, too, in the shade of this wrecked ship turned to stone, to take the boots off his aching feet. And if he had done this, he might not have bothered going further. But Edward Scales moved on between the broken ribs to the other side, and stepped into her view.

Gwen Carrick was almost ready to go back up to the house when she saw him. She recognised the profile, the gait. She'd seen this man on a couple of occasions earlier that month, but he had always been in the distance, retreating, scrambling between the rocks. Now she stood up and had a better look at him. His boots were new: stout, nailed things and uncomfortable-looking; and she noticed that his calves were wrapped with gaiters.

When Edward turned again he saw the young woman standing, shielding her eyes against the steady pulsing light on the brackish water of the Helford. And he saw that this was to get a better look at him. His hat was buckled to the side of his knapsack so he could not raise it to her. Instead, he lifted his hand in a half wave. She mirrored his action, and did not move. A good sign. As he clambered up the steep shelf of shingle on the little beach, Edward wondered what he might say to her. When he stumbled near the level part of the beach she came forward still shielding her face, bunching up her skirts with her free hand. Her strides were big, confident. He saw that her hands were tanned against her pale skirt. She had the unconstricted movement of a woman not wearing a corset, though she held herself straight inside her riding jacket. Her waist was tiny over an ample—he tried not to think of what lay under her skirts. They met with a yard of pebbles between them. She was tall enough to meet his gaze without having to tilt her chin. She was bareheaded. Edward calculated the length of her hair from the size of the neat coil piled up.

'Are you lost?' she said. She could see that his jacket, a hairy tweed, was new and probably still in its first season.

It was not what he expected. He answered her slowly, 'No, I don't believe so.'

'Sometimes people get lost.' The Cornish swirl embedded in her vowels, curling on the edge of her consonants, was very slight.

The air was still between them, and he caught a scent of her, the curious effect of sunlight on skin and hair. She smelled of herself. Not masked by soap or perfume. It was neither sweet nor stale. She was waiting for him to speak.

'I'm sorry to disturb you, Miss Carrick.'

'You have the advantage, sir; have we met before?'

'Edward Scales.' He bowed very slightly.

'Should I remember you, Edward Scales?'

'It is neither here nor there.'

She nodded at this, and Edward felt relieved. She said, 'Do you live near by, or—' She waited for him to fill in the gap.

'I have rooms in Falmouth. I have been walking.'

She raised her eyebrows. 'Really? All the way? You must be exhausted.'

Edward caught something in her expression which looked like amusement. Was she flirting? 'The distance is not so far.'

An ornament in her hair flashed in the sun. She saw him looking and she pulled out a thin stick. 'My paintbrush.'

Edward was unsure of how to answer; she seemed to be challenging him. He said, 'I've kept you from your painting. I am getting in your way.'

'You're entitled to rest after your walk,' she said. 'But I would like to finish my picture. If you go and stand where you were by those rocks I'll put you in.'

Edward relaxed. 'How long shall I stand?'

She was already gathering her skirts in her hands. 'Give me a quarter of an hour,' she said. 'No, twenty minutes.'

As she made her way back to her things she turned her head, smiling, tugging her bottom lip in with her upper left canine.

Edward saw in that gesture of hers a childish glee and a suggestion of self-containment. He couldn't help being stirred by it. Neither could he help being confused by her. But, of course, she had been making things easy for both of them by pretending not to know him. Her poise had been immaculate when she had refused to acknowledge that she already knew his name. Yet there was something in the way she had spoken. The frankness of her. Almost as if she were a different person entirely. Edward retraced his path down to the rocks by the tide line marked out by a thick rope of seaweed. Taking out his pocket watch he leaned back against the rock. It dug into his shoulder.

* * *

Gwen sketched the figure of Edward Scales into her painting. She wanted to put him in the picture, it seemed to her an absolute necessity, to paint him into her watercolour landscape. Not just for the sake of its composition. It gave her a space to think without him searching her face. Because the painting was already finished, his figure on the paper became a dark shape, without features. Yet, his awkward posture was recognisably his, and this pleased her. Whilst they had stood opposite each other like that she had wanted to evade his look, which seemed to seek some sort of confirmation from her. He would not get it.

Sometimes people get lost. She'd said it for something to fill the surprise of seeing him. But it hadn't been the best thing to say. Now it was there again, going around in her head as she mixed the darkest shade of Payne's grey. The argument was two years old, but it was as raw as ever in her mind.

'People don't get lost here,' she'd almost shouted at her sister Euphemia. 'The sea is on one side and the land is on the other. There is a path, you walk along it.'

Euphemia's expression had been blank, her voice very calm. 'Mother got lost.'

'She can't have, Effie, she can't have.'

And then Effie's voices had started. Mrs Fernly, their aunt, had tolerated the voices for as long as she could. It was never said out loud. It was never mentioned in a very direct way, but Mrs Fernly, it was widely known, couldn't abide young creatures who made deliberate exhibitions of themselves. But much more than that, and more importantly, Mrs Fernly had no time under any circumstances, for the jingling bells and rattling tables or anything else in a Spiritualist's parlour, least of all the Spiritualist herself and most especially if the Spiritualist began to talk in voices in Mrs Fernly's own parlour without prior warning.

Gwen and her sister had been moved back into the empty Carrick House only three months after their mother's funeral. It was fair, thought Gwen, that it should have been decided—unilaterally, by Mrs Fernly, that it was time for Gwen and Effie to cut short their stay at the Fernly's and manage at their own house. There were after all two of them and they would have the maid, as well. Gwen had felt nothing but relief. She could put a door between herself and Effie at last. And not only at night. Gwen spent most daylight hours out of doors, away from her sister. Euphemia did not exert herself at all during the day; she stayed inside the house, to preserve her complexion. If Euphemia wanted to look at a view for a moment, she made sure that it was through a north-facing window. They embarrassed each other with their habits, but there existed between them a delicately preserved understanding.

* * *

Painting in the figure of Edward took much less time than she had asked for. When the time was up he picked up his stick and bag. His second approach was much more sure-footed. He came deliberately, slowly. When he was a few feet away, she patted the shingle beside her and he sat down.

'I'm glad we have met like this,' she said. 'Being outside makes you much freer. Here, I have your image immortalised on paper.' She handed him her sketchbook, and watched his face as he looked at her work on his knee. 'Would some Power the gift to give us to see ourselves as others see us.'

He smiled. 'You know Burns, then.'

'Burns? No, it's just something, a saying. I didn't know it was a quote.'

'It's from the end of a poem: "O wad some Power the giftie gie us, To see oursels as others see us! It wad frae monie a blunder free us—"'

She laughed. 'I like that. From many a blunder free us. What's the title of the poem? I shall have to find a copy.'

Edward coughed. 'It is called, "To a Louse", and its subtitle is, "On Seeing One on a Lady's Bonnet at Church".' He looked sideways at her. She was smiling. He said, 'I hope I haven't offended you.'

'You haven't. I'd like to hear the rest.'

'I'm afraid I don't know it thoroughly. I wouldn't want to murder it before you had read it for yourself. You needn't search though. I'll send you a copy if you like.'

'That's too kind of you.'

'It would be my pleasure.' Robert Burns would not have been his first choice of poet to send to a young woman, whether he had only just met her or not. He cringed inwardly at the thought of her reading Burns' more bawdy efforts.

She cut into his thoughts. 'Your accent was very realistic to my untuned ear.'

'I spent a lot of time in Scotland as a boy. It's not a genuine accent. Only gleaned, borrowed inexpertly from my playmates.' Edward felt suddenly perilously close to the edge of the dark chasm he had so far been successful in avoiding. He studied the young woman's profile with every bit of concentration he could gather. 'To which address should I send the poems?'

'I'll write it down for you.' She took the sketchbook back from his knee and turned the page over. He watched her write her full name and address in soft pencil. She tore off the page and handed it over. He looked at it. She also noticed that he looked at the paintings revealed by her tearing the top page out. Studies of bright red Cardinal beetles studded the glaring white of the paper Gwen instinctively held to her chest.

'I will be pleased to send the poems to Miss

Gwen Carrick. May I keep this? I shall pay the artist, naturally.'

'No payment is necessary, Mr Scales, you are welcome to it. Well. Now my paints are dry and I'm finished for the afternoon. Will you come up to the house?'

Edward didn't want to do that, for all kinds of reasons. He asked her if she would like to have a picnic with him. He felt himself becoming very nervous and he worried that she would see how agitated he really was. How disconcerting. The more he worried the more he was certain that she could read his thoughts. But then the sun shone brighter on the water, and she had to shade her eyes as he produced the food, so she probably did not see his reddened face after all.

Edward brought out of his knapsack two bottles of ale, a large piece of cheese wrapped in a cloth, and a small loaf of bread. He took a small knife from his pocket, and began to carve off chunks of bread and cheese. He weighed the bottles against each other and gave Gwen the heaviest, having already begun to drink from the other. 'I hope you like ale. It is quite a strong one.'

'It looks like you have enough. At least I shan't worry about depriving you.'

'I always take more than I think I'm going to need. Once, in Dorset, I met an old vagrant who asked me for something to eat. He looked so wretched, I gave him what I had but he insisted on sharing the beer I had given him. I only had one bottle. I spent the next month convinced I'd contracted something.'

'But you didn't.'

'No, I did not.'

'Dorset is a long way from here.'

Edward took the smooth pebble he had been carrying in his knapsack and laid it down by his side. Gwen Carrick did not notice, she was utterly absorbed in cutting more cheese and bread with her own pocket knife. One edge of the grey stone partly revealed the ridged arc of an ammonite. Gwen held her bottle between her feet. Edward saw that she was not wearing the clumpy old boots from the time before but fine brown leather shoes with a low heel and a strap, fastened by one button across the arch of her foot. It made him think of something Charles had once told him. But he could see that the eroticism of the action was entirely unintentional.

'I couldn't help noticing, Miss Carrick, those red beetles in your sketch book. To my eye, they looked quite delightful.'

'More so than the study I have just given you?'

'I wouldn't say that. They startled my eye. They interest me in a different way, that is all.'

'When a young woman makes a picture of a pretty red beetle, Mr Scales, it is called 'Delightful', put into a frame and a husband is found for the artist. When a young man makes an anatomical study of a Cardinal beetle, he is expected to know that it is the Pyrochroa serraticornis, and he is bundled off to university so that he can one day add to the body of scientific knowledge on Coleoptera.'

'I see.'

'Do you though, Mr Scales? I don't want you to admire my skills for the wrong reasons. My work is not bait; I am looking for the truth. In all things.'

'I'm sorry. I didn't intend to disparage your gift.'

'Gift? My talent is not something handed down from God, Mr Scales. It is hard won.'

'Of course; I can see that you are very dedicated. My words were ill chosen. I meant no offence.'

'But you don't offend me, Mr Scales. If I were a man, would you apologise, or would you debate the talent of an artist as divine gift, as opposed to something instilled by regular practice?'

'I suppose I would do neither. I would have entered into a conversation about beetles without complimenting the rendition on paper.'

'In which case, I can tell you that I was surprised to find this particular beetle so early in the year, they are usually out in May, June and July. And it does startle the eye, doesn't it?'

'I'm sorry to have intruded, Miss Carrick. I think I have trespassed into a world in which I have no right to be. When I listen to you I see that my own existence is very dull indeed.'

'I am sure it is not.'

'I can assure you it is.'

'Even though you may wish to see yourself as others do, it can never be done, and so I think that you may as well not try.'

'You seem, despite your talk, very content with your life, Miss Carrick.'

'I am content to be alive, Mr Scales, but I do not possess the quality I think you must see in me. I am quite discontent, in myself. It has been driven into me.'

He caught her gaze and held it for a moment with a question in his own, but Gwen would not elaborate further. 'The last time I saw you, Miss Carrick, there was something I had intended to say to you.'

'I beg your pardon? Mr Scales, have you been spying on me?'

'I—I *have* been here before.'

'I must confess I have seen you before as well, Mr Scales. Don't look so alarmed. I have seen you from afar, out walking once or twice, always walking away from here. I have since then wondered who you were, where you live. I must admit I have wondered what you looked like, too. It struck me you had some kind of important intention to your walking.' She wanted to say that she had thought he looked at first like a tourist who had no idea of where he was, but that after a while, she could see that he did possess some passion in his stride. That a stranger, seen from a distance, could sometimes make an impression on the mind, and could work away to become something of an obsession; she had wanted to admit this to Mr Scales. There was something about his manner that told her he would understand her meaning. The puzzle of the man had struck her from time to time, and she had wondered if an opportunity to talk to him would ever present itself.

Edward was outdone by her talk. He realised that it was useless to try and broach the subject which could not be touched or coloured by any choice of word. What he had begun was more complicated than he had imagined, and as he listened to Gwen, and saw the uncomplicated manner of her evasion, he thought he understood her more completely than anything he had ever known.

He could see now that Miss Carrick was quite young; how young he couldn't guess. He knew that he must move away, that he must leave her alone. If he felt he had made an indecent intrusion previously, this seemed just as bad. Her tact, and the straightforward approach she seemed to have over something he had been unable to rationalise, made him cringe at his own rough attempts to smooth over his indiscretions. And so he knew also that he would come back, in spite of what he had promised her before, in spite of his own conscience. He'd come back again, and he would not hesitate, in his need to speak of everything, and plainly, to the creature who wished to keep her red beetle studies a secret.

*   *   *

Gwen came to a halt at the south wall of the kitchen garden. A bonfire had been lit and its smoke curled over the wall. She'd smelled it on her way back up from the beach. It had none of the earth or wood tones of a garden fire. Now that she was very close, she could see flakes of black drifting in the air and coming back down, too heavy to be carried far. She walked quickly now under the wall following it around the corner until she came to the gate. No one was there to watch over the fire. It hadn't been banked down; flames leapt from the heap and parts of its bulk fell away. Its position was odd; she couldn't think why Murray would have told the lad to make a fire right under the south wall where the fruit trees were trained into their tortured forms. While she was thinking about this, another part of the fire fell off the heap and her attention shot to it. Now that she could see how the fire had been constructed she lunged towards it. Sandwiched in the middle of garden prunings were books; her father's library. She saw her old friends, Bell's *Anatomy*, Duncan's *Beetles,* Mrs Mantell's engravings of Strata and Fossils, all turning back into their base element. She spun about looking for something to help her. A large spade had been left against the north wall. Gwen ran to it, not caring to stay on the paths. She felt her chest tighten with anxiety and purpose as she hauled her skirts in her arms and made her loping strides more efficient.

She attacked the heap, letting out a yell, beating the burning books with the heavy spade, her striking unwieldy and misdirected. Pages and half-scorched volumes tumbled onto the soil and continued to smoke as she turned to retrieve everything she could manage and then hurl clods of earth at the rest of the fire, still beating and yelling in between shovelling.

'What the bloody hell?'

Gwen didn't stop when she heard Murray. He took the spade from her hands mid-swing and finished the job. 'Well, you've put that one out, miss. You can have a rest.'

'Murray—' She had to bend over and cough.

'I'll have to have words with the lad. I thought he was a good choice, but I was wrong.' Murray nudged the remains of a burned cover with his toe.

'It wasn't his fault.' Gwen gasped, retching, and grabbed at Murray's sleeve. 'He wouldn't know.'

'He's a ruddy, half-witted goose is what he is, miss. You may as well take that as given.'

'It's done, Murray. At least I found it.'

'You did. What'll you want done with it?'

Gwen picked up one of the less charred volumes. The spine curved the wrong way and the now partially browned pages spewed forward and then curled in on themselves, as if they had known themselves fey and beyond saving. The leather on the spine was brittle and had bubbled in places to form strange scabs; the gold leaf had burned away in places making the title illegible, but Gwen knew the book by heart. The irreparable damage was sickening to see. She'd spent hours in the company of Lyell's four volumes, poring over his maps and folding them carefully back into place as she'd moved through his *Principles of Geology*.

'I don't know.'

Gwen surveyed the mess across the earth and saw two of the other three Lyell volumes. She picked them out and tried to brush off the dirt and still smouldering remnants of other books and garden clippings. They made an awkward stack in her arms as she walked slowly back towards the house, the stink of bonfire clinging inside her nostrils, catching the back of her throat. Instead of going in by the kitchen, she took the long way round and let herself in through the front door.

The library door was closed but not fast. Gwen kicked it with the flat of her shoe and stood in the doorway hugging the charred books to her body. She supposed she must have looked deranged. She regarded her sister; so immaculately dressed, so tightly laced, gathering books with delicate soft hands off the shelves into a wheelbarrow.

She wanted to move into the room but felt herself stuck there. Euphemia in turn stopped. Neither of them said anything for a moment. Euphemia paled. Gwen heard her mother's voice very clearly in her head then. It was not, as some said of the recently dead, as if the person whispered into her ear, or stood at her shoulder. It was more a feeling that her mother was in the middle of Gwen's brain, and that the voice she heard was simply her mother's thoughts.

'Of course, I know what he says, darling Gwen. But why should I let him know? After all, he would only do himself an injury. There are some things it is better we keep to ourselves.'

Gwen straightened her back and continued to stare at Euphemia who had been about to place into the wheelbarrow another book, but now she took the smallest breath and turned around, and put the book back on the shelf. One by one she placed the other books back on the shelves and never met her sister's eye. Gwen settled into her heels, and as her sister reshelved books she simply watched and waited until the last book was back in its place. Only then did Gwen move into the room. She placed the ruined three volumes of Lyell's *Principles* on the wide empty shelf they had come from. She poured herself a glass of water from the carafe on the desk and then taking up the wheelbarrow handles trundled it out of the room.

At the door, Gwen said, 'Have you any idea what I am thinking?'

'No, because it is impossible to tell what a traitor thinks or feels.'

'You admit, then, that I have feelings.'

'And you admit it, finally. That is what you are, you can't escape it.'

Gwen went out of the house and back to the kitchen garden. As she bumped the wheelbarrow down the steps, along the paths, pushed it past unclipped bushes, her anger at herself made her clumsy. She should never have allowed Euphemia to draw her into the old argument again, but the previous evening over dinner she had been unable to contain her contempt for her sister's dogged belief that the fossils in their father's collection were all remnants of the Great Flood. She had stormed out of the dining room and fetched *Strata Identified by Organised Fossils,* by William Smith. The book had landed on the table next to Euphemia with an almighty thump and had sent an empty wine glass to the floor where it had smashed. Gwen blamed herself now for having been influenced by the wine. The glow it had given her sense of righteous certainty over Euphemia's stupidity had given Gwen's tongue free licence to vent her derision. She opened the book at the place where it was marked and pushed it under Euphemia's nose.

'Are you really too stupid to understand what the words say? Yes? I'll read them to you.' Gwen recited a passage, barely needing to look at the page. The words had danced in triumph—now where were they? Euphemia had tried to burn them out of existence. But they clung to Gwen, and she to them: '. . . organic remains peculiar to each stratum . . .' She pushed away the memory of her jubilance at having committed those words to memory for her father. Of having found herself standing at his desk, trying to talk to him the way she imagined he would have allowed had she been born a boy. It didn't matter. The knowledge was not his alone to keep.

Gwen rounded the last corner and stopped the barrow next to Murray. 'We have miscalled the lad, Murray. This was nothing to do with him.'

Murray turned and looked into her eyes, and she returned his hard stare. His eyes flickered as she saw him understand her meaning. Together they set about pulling the books from the dirt. Some were not very badly damaged on the inside and could be saved. But Smith's volume had received special attention from Euphemia, and Gwen began to find small fragments of the pages torn by hand from their binding and ripped bit by bit beyond repair. Here was a corner bearing the partial remains of an intricate illustration of an ammonite. Every book in the bonfire had been part of Gwen's armoury, as she had come to think of it, against the blinkered and determined stupidity of people like the vicar who had the intelligence to recognise the truth but turned his eye from it, and Euphemia's gaggle of black-clad visitors who shunned the truth completely in favour of spirits and their messages from the other side. Euphemia called her a traitor. A traitor to their mother and her faith. Gwen knelt down and let the pain of her grief enter her body; she let it snake through her, probing its tongue into each dark crevice.

She told herself after some minutes that it didn't really matter that the books had been burned. They were, in theory, replaceable, and the truth of what had been contained in them, the spirit of them, still lived in her head and in the heads of others. What mattered was the vicious nature of Euphemia's spite. Gwen chided herself for bringing Euphemia's desire to take possession of the house to the fore, to eradicate every memory of their blasphemous father who had detained Reverend Sparsholt in loud debate on the steps of Helford Church on the day of their mother's funeral. 'She had her time in Heaven while she was alive.' Gwen remembered the passionate grief in her father's voice. 'Now her flesh will rot under the soil,' he said, 'And that is *all*, Sparsholt. That. Is. All.' And so every trace of his sinful library was to be purged from the house, in order that Euphemia could fully dedicate and fashion the place to the memory of their mother. Gwen saw now that Euphemia was also attempting to annihilate Gwen's sense of herself, and her right to belong to the place. Euphemia wanted, she could see, to deny the house and its contents any hold on Gwen.

There was one thing she had now though, which Euphemia did not have, and did not know about: her new friend, Mr Scales. Gwen recalled the fossil in his hand as they had spoken that afternoon. She went over and over their conversation. Parts of it had become lost, but most of it she could remember, and its urgency. The intensity of the conversation had soon eradicated all the usual formality and convention. They had not made polite enquiries about each other's history; they had existed fully in the moment with no regard for the past or the future.

Gwen tidied herself up, smacking dirt and ash from her clothes while Murray pushed the barrow of books to one of the potting sheds and she followed behind. Murray left her to it, and Gwen began the ordeal of assessing the damage in detail. As she examined each part of Euphemia's essay on destruction, Gwen knew that she would never mention Euphemia's existence to Mr Scales. There would be no poisoning the air with the mention of her, of what she had done, of the way she had made Gwen feel.

CHAPTER II

The Spiritual meetings held at Carrick House attracted a plethora of bizarre people. Like a bundle of strange insects, Gwen thought, batting at the glass in the door, blundering around the dimmed lamps. She couldn't bear it; she hated their sweaty hands and, in their wide hopeful eyes, that grateful admiration of her sister. No spirits, though, had ever come into the drawing room to divulge their secrets, to deliver their messages or even to assuage some kind of guilt of their own or of the living. It tugged at her conscience, and the knot of disdain grew in her stomach. She watched them arrive. In bundles of four they plopped out of carriages on to the drive. This Monday evening there were three carriages, and two clients had walked up the drive on foot, flapping blackly with the setting sun at their backs. 'Pity help them,' she said, and drew the curtains.

Gwen's absence from the meetings was enough. Euphemia did not need to be told how much her sister despised her gift.

And what Gwen got up to in the evenings, whilst Euphemia held the Spiritual meetings, was of no concern to her. Her ladies (and some gentlemen) were attentive and appreciative of her talent. Some, like the Coyne woman, Penelope, came to Euphemia in fear of a loss not yet happened. The tremble in Penelope's lips was never quite still, always expecting the wash of her son's far-travelled drowning or some other likely misfortune to be revealed to her in those meetings. Connoisseurs, some of them, and full of stories about the charlatans of the profession, who performed nothing more than parlour tricks. Euphemia did not have a repertoire of tricks, only an inexhaustible supply of voices, which could dance across the room and whisper into her clients' ears. There were never any rappings in Euphemia's drawing-room, nor tinkling bells. She did not have a table with a wobbly leg apt to rock uncontrollably in the gloom. The only glistening things were her clients' wide and thankful eyes, and after they had gone, the coins in the discreetly placed dish. And most gratifying of all was not the counting out of the coins and the entries in the book she kept, but the fact that she had never once solicited custom. Never placed anything so vulgar as an advertisement in a paper. In fact, Euphemia considered herself more than a little apart from other clairvoyants. On the rare occasions when an introduction to another Medium looked as if it might have been in the offing, she was quick to discourage without appearing ungrateful or rude; though she did often feel incapable of hiding her feeling of condescension. Her isolation seemed to induce a certain kind of expectation amongst her clients. Her talent was unsullied by the riffraff. Like those young girls in Europe who suffered from visions of the Virgin, she was pure and she wanted to keep it that way.

It was a mixed bunch tonight; too many for the table in the drawing room. Many new faces, which always gratified her. Euphemia began with her induction talk. She didn't like the way her voice sounded in the dining room but there was nothing which could be done about it now.

‘We must remember to keep in mind the fact that the spirits are sensitive,’ she said. ‘And for this reason, of course, we will only refer to ourselves by our Christian names.’ She paused for a second. ‘There will be no communication from the other side for a “Mr Smith” but a spirit may wish to talk to “John” or “Harry”. And the spirits, of course, make no promises other than to speak to you if your heart is open and free of doubt.’

Naturally, Euphemia was always ‘Miss Carrick’ to these people; how on earth would she manage to remain in control of the event otherwise. Her gaze travelled around the table and settled for a moment on a young man whose complexion, temporarily ruddy with excitement, was sickly. He licked his lips and his hands trembled as the introductions flowed around the company, the hush punctuated by the hesitant voice of each new client saying their name out loud. Euphemia smiled. They all looked at her and told her their names; the rest looked at the one speaking. It was all ticking along, but she kept the young man in the corner of her eye. As it came to his turn, she could see that she had been mistaken; he was not so very young after all. She looked into his eyes.

‘Ch-Charles. I’m Charles. Hello.’ He looked up at the ceiling and searched in the air above their heads.

‘Welcome, Charles.’ She noted him as difficult, perhaps an unbeliever, and moved on to the woman sitting next to him.

‘Good evening, I am Penelope.’

‘Welcome, Penelope. So lovely to see you again.’

CHAPTER III

HELFORD PASSAGE. APRIL 1859.

Paths meandered down each side of the cleft in the garden crowded with old rhododendrons. Palms, which had once been ships' ballast, now sprouted rich fronds of growth. Camellias flushed a pink frothiness into the wet green of spring alongside the magnolias' burst of waxy petals. Stands of bamboo, once tidy and slim, were now out of control, pushing their spiked shoots throughout the grounds. Bisecting the garden, a stream fed unkempt pools for carp where none swam; along its banks the formidable gunnera leaves pushed up from their hairy crowns. Edward saw all of this in his mind because the night sky was especially overcast. The day had begun well, with a clear horizon over the sea, but the bank of cloud now obscuring the moon and making his progress difficult had come and built up its volume as it moved over the sea towards this part of the south Cornish coast. He doubted, now that he had finally met Miss Carrick in daylight, that she would be there waiting for him for a second time in the dark chill of the summerhouse. She had made him keep a promise, and already he had broken it. He had come back again hoping to redeem himself, to explain that he couldn't have kept away in daylight, that he couldn't possibly have let the chance to see her face pass. Her manner on the beach had encouraged him. And yet he was nervous, so much more nervous than he had ever been about anything in his life. And he was exhausted. The seven miles had tripled. Early that morning, he had set out intending to do something very different. He had walked to the boundary of the small Carrick estate, intending to call at the house and present himself. He had turned back. When he had arrived at his rooms in Falmouth, he had caught sight of himself in the mirror above the wash-stand. He'd stripped to the waist and passed a frenzied minute washing himself before putting a clean shirt on his damp body and setting out again.

There were times on that walk as the gloaming turned to pitch when he thought he would fall over the cliff edge. And deservedly so, he told himself, deservedly so. You have behaved irrationally towards Miss Carrick and too bad for you if you fall over the cliff and never discover her feelings. Too bad for you if you never have the opportunity to declare your own feelings. He had stopped at several points to strike a light, but the pathetic flare cupped in his hands had been blown out almost instantly by the gusts coming in off the sea.

How easy it was to allow events to overtake one's former intentions. It was a relief to discern the shape of the red brick summerhouse coming out of the mist, the wet dark slate of the roof almost a comfort to Edward as he rounded the corner on the steep path. In the far corner, he settled into the old armchair and pulled the musty blanket on it around his shoulders. It smelled strongly of tobacco smoke and the kind of smell Edward associated with cellars.

* * *

At five-thirty the crescendo of birdsong woke him

briefly and he drifted back into the remnants of a dream. But he was cold and he woke again, the memory now of the real Miss Carrick stronger than the wisps of what he could recall of his dream. He looked at his watch and saw that it was almost six. He took another mouthful of whisky and decided that he would stay a while longer. He unfastened his breeches, pulled himself free and allowed the warmth of the whisky and the memory of Miss Carrick in the sunshine to run through his body.

* * *

By the time Gwen had been down to the beach and back up again, the mist had not lifted. The garden remained wet and veiled. The tips of her fingers inside her gloves felt a little numb. She could have a small fire in the summerhouse. It would likely be laid, and waiting for a match. She turned off the main path and made her way under the trees. The door had been left wide open. She could see that it had not been Murray opening the door. A man she did not at first recognise sat next to the unlit fire in the chair which Murray usually occupied to unknot string when it rained. For a second, she wondered if Murray had sent some younger chap in his place, but this man was not a gardener. Gwen's heart thudded. At first sight it seemed as if Mr Scales was asleep. His head tipped back in the chair, his eyes were shut and his mouth hung open. And she could see from the slight twitch in his arm that he was caught in a dream. His breaths though were not those of someone in a restful sleep: they were rapid and laboured. Gwen hovered in the doorway, unsure of whether she should make a noise to wake him, or leave him to sleep.

Down at his feet on the floor of the summerhouse was his old knapsack of heavy canvas with leather straps; the only worn-out thing apart from Mr Scales himself. Gwen wondered briefly if Mr Scales had been there all night. A sharp whiff of stale sweat hung in the room, even though the door stood open. As she was about to leave, Mr Scales stirred in his seat—but he did not open his eyes or close his mouth. Nothing about him changed but for his left arm, which began again to twitch. Perhaps he was suffering a fit, like the ones which had eventually killed her mother. In which case she ought to do something. He didn't appear to be unconscious though. She stepped quietly inside the room, her view slightly obscured by the blanket draped over the arm of the chair. As the whole of him came into view, she saw that his breeches, the same ones he had been wearing when she had shared his beer, were open and pulled down around his thighs.

* * *

The drag of her heavy skirts was like the wash of a strong tide against her legs. By the time she reached the house, her back was studded in sweat, and her gloved hands were very hot and moist. She stood in the hall, listening to the ticking and grinding of the clock which struck the quarter hour. It was still only six-fifteen. Her gaze came to rest on the coat-stand. A large, old overcoat was hanging there, and on the tiles, next to the skirting, a pair of old boots she hadn't worn for a while. She was still standing there thinking about the last time she'd worn the boots when Euphemia bounced down the stairs at six-thirty.

'Oh, are you back from your wandering so soon? I didn't hear you come in.'

Gwen flexed her fingers. 'The mist hasn't lifted yet. I'll go out again later.'

'Are you going to have breakfast?'

'No, I'm going upstairs for a while.'

*   *   *

Gwen relaxed behind the closed door of her bedroom. Slowly, she began to undress. She traipsed over the carpet towards the adjoining bathroom. She stood shivering in her chemise beside the large white tub and turned on the tap. She watched the level of cold water rise, concentrating on its growing depth whilst trying to imagine what it was that Mr Scales had been doing to himself. She tugged the bell-pull to let the maid know that she needed a bucket of hot water, turned off the tap and sat on the edge of the tub to wait.

*   *   *

Susan did not look to see which little bell was pinging away on its spring. She'd watched Gwen coming up the path to the house. She liked to think she could anticipate what either Gwen or Euphemia might want next, and it was a bath for Miss Gwen. She'd come hurtling up the path at just gone six that morning, tugging her outdoor things off, all puce in the face from the effort.

Susan calmly put a damp cloth over her bread dough then took up the padded mitt and lifted the kettle. She poured the steaming water into a bucket, refilled the kettle and set it back on the stove before taking the hot water up the back stairs.

Susan had not told her mother about the bathroom at Carrick House. She knew that the idea of long mirrors in a room just for washing yourself would make her mother think unfairly of the Miss Carricks and the late Mistress.

Not long after the funeral, when Mr Carrick had gone back to America, and the girls were staying with the Fernlys, Susan had taken a bath in the long white tub with the mirrors glinting at her from all sides. Susan had set the copper boiling and then emptied it quickly into buckets so that she might have a proper good hot soak, like the Mistress used to.

Breathing in the emptiness of the place with just the ticking of the tall clock for company gave her a jittery feeling under her ribcage. If Mistress Carrick had died in the house Susan would not have agreed to go back there on her own. Susan thought about her sometimes. About her being grey and cold out on Rosemullion Head and no one knowing; the liver-coloured bruise as they'd turned her over. They said a fox had pissed on her, but Susan didn't want to believe that was true.

* * *

Gwen sat on the edge of the bath tub, the skin on her arms like a plucked songbird and her face pinched. Susan put the bucket of hot water down and went to close the window.

'Thank you, Susan. I was very hot, but it is cool enough in here now.'

'Would you like an extra bucket of water, ma'am—I mean, miss?'

'That's all right, Susan. I'm sure you've got better things to do.'

Susan expected this answer, and knew it had nothing to do with what she had left to do. 'Let me help you off with that chimmy, miss. You're all fingers and no thumbs.'

Gwen let Susan help her out of her underwear. Susan said, 'You've let yourself get too cold this morning.' She lifted the bucket and poured the steaming water into the bath. Gwen climbed in, totally unselfconscious of her naked body. Gwen's breasts were firm and rounded; they did not swing or fall with her movements. Susan turned to go, picking up the empty bucket.

'Stay awhile, Susan, will you? Perhaps you could talk to me. I feel I should like to talk to someone.'

Susan put the bucket on the floor again and clasped her hands in front of her. She could not avoid her reflection so stared at her feet.

'Move those things from the chair and sit down, if you like.'

Sitting down meant that Susan had to face Gwen washing herself. 'I won't stay more than a minute, miss. I've got bread rising.'

'I won't keep you, Susan. I wanted to ask you something.' Gwen soaped her leg with her foot propped up on the edge of the tub. Susan looked away as she caught a glimpse of pubic hair. 'I wanted to ask you, because I know you have brothers and you are older than Effie and I. The thing I want to ask you—' She stopped washing and looked directly at Susan. 'You mightn't know the answer, of course.'

Susan stared at the soapy foot and then at her own hands. 'You'd better ask the question, miss, or I'll not be able to answer one way or the other.'

'Whilst I was out this morning, I came across something. Someone. I'm sure now that what he was doing was meant to be private. But, having seen it, I want to know whether you think it might have been rather unhinged.'

'Are you telling me you saw a madman this morning, miss?'

'I don't know. I don't think so.'

'What was he up to?'

Gwen lathered her other leg. 'I'm not sure I can describe it properly. He was in the summerhouse. I thought Murray might have sent someone. I thought he was asleep at first.'

'A tramp?'

'No, I'm sure he wasn't a tramp. In fact, certainly not a tramp. Susan, is it usual for a man to do . . . things . . . to himself?'

'Did this man do something to you, miss?'

'No. He didn't even see me. And when I saw, when I realised which . . . part . . . of himself was in his hand, I came back.'

Susan bit her lip. 'Maybe you should keep that summerhouse locked up.'

'What *was* he doing, Susan. What did I see?'

Susan breathed in deeply, and let her breath out slowly. 'Some would say what you saw was an awful, horrible thing, miss. But I'm sure it's no sin telling you I reckon it's a normal enough thing for a man to do sometimes, if he's not got a wife.' She glanced at Gwen.

'But *what* was he doing?'

Susan looked down at her hands in her lap and told her.

'Whatever for?' Gwen began to wash the rest of her body.

'For the relief of it, I believe.' Suddenly Susan envied Gwen's ignorance. It seemed peculiar to her that someone could read Latin, and not know about *that*.

'It looked quite brutal,' said Gwen. 'He looked uncomfortable or even that he might have been in pain. Do you think it hurts, to do that?' She was lying down in the bath now and splashing water over her flat stomach.

She's still like a child, thought Susan. Anyone else might think what she's just asked would be some sort of trick, some sort of tease. But she's asking me like a child, Susan thought. Who else might she ask anyway? It isn't the sort of stuff you could talk about politely.

Gwen said, 'I'm glad I'm not a man, Susan. Aren't you?'

'Well, you couldn't change it, miss, even if you wished it.'

* * *

After that, Gwen had avoided going to the garden so early in the morning, waiting long enough to be sure that she would not come upon him again in that way. She was uneasy with her intimate knowledge of Mr Scales' personal habits. It seemed impossible to reconcile the sight of him, the deep mauve of his—she didn't have a name for it, a word for it and this also made her perturbed. Of course, she knew the biological term for that appendage, that necessary organ to the male, from the beetle to the horse to the man in her summerhouse. But the purely biological was not enough, did not explain the emotion she now felt. The smell of him had worked its way into her dreams and tonight she had woken drenched in sweat, a noise from her own throat bringing her awake. And the rippling of that sensation. Yes, it was there, still there, but ebbing away as she lay in her sweaty sheets, coming awake. She brought her hand up to her face, listening intently to the quiet of the house, to the distant chiming of the clock in the hall, telling her that it was about to strike the hour. Gwen counted the twelve chimes and threw back her sheets. She had gone to bed just before ten and to be so wide awake at midnight disturbed her; she knew that she would find it difficult to go back to sleep and that she would have a bad temper in the morning. It put her on edge to be tired in the day when she wanted to be busy but found herself stupid and clumsy. Gwen got up and went to her bathroom to wash her hands and wipe her neck with a cold sponge. She did not take a light with her, feeling her way instead with her feet and her hands outstretched. Back in her bedroom again, she went to the window and pulled back the curtains. She raised the lower section of the window quietly, the sash cord working smoothly as she put her weight to the task and felt the cold draught against her thighs and stomach. She crouched on the floor, her face level with the open air, and listened to the night. The familiarity of the garden was made alien. She listened, cupping her hands behind her ears, to the very distant sound of the waves breaking on the beach and the play of wind in the trees. Below her she heard the crunch of careful footsteps on the gravel path as either Euphemia or Susan made her way to the privy. Gwen left the window open but pulled the curtains back together again.

CHAPTER IV

Edward Scales had sent Gwen a letter, and it was in her pocket, but she hadn't opened it yet. The thrill of seeing his handwriting for the first time had made her nauseous with excitement. Euphemia had again slept in very late and her usual habit of being first to sift through the morning post had been abandoned.

Taking the letter from the table in the hall, Gwen had felt an intense lurch, then a tightness in her shoulders threaded its way through her torso, down to her thighs, and back up again to the back of her skull. But she hadn't wanted to hear his voice in the hall where she stood resisting the urge to rip the letter open. She had met him first on the beach at the foot of her garden, and that seemed the most appropriate place to read his letter.

On the beach Gwen lay down on her stomach. She didn't linger to examine the seal as she broke the wax in half and pulled out the stiff laid paper. She felt her body thrumming to the rhythm of her pulse against the pebbled ground, heard the crash of the waves behind her, saw the bright sunlight on the paper, registered the unsteadiness of her hands as she straightened the single sheet, bending its crease back on itself; all of this crammed her senses as she began to read his letter. His handwriting was singularly awful. A great deal of care had gone into the addressing of the envelope, but the letter itself was a different matter.

'My Dear Miss Carrick . . .' Gwen studied the stroke of his pen, the urgency of the formations, the haste, the going over of certain letters where the ink had run dry, the fine spatters from the nib. On the corner of the paper there was a smudge of fingerprint.

The contents of the letter were very formal; he promised that he would send a copy of the Burns poem as soon as possible and that he admired the watercolour painting very much. He also told her that he was writing from his address in London, and that he would be travelling back to Cornwall within the month. He hoped that she was in good health and hoped that it was not too much to hope that he would have the pleasure of meeting her again. There was something touching in his repetition of the word 'hope' and the fact that he had been in such a hurry to write to her he had forgotten to write his London address. His feverish scrawl affected her more than she had expected. To know that while she'd been anticipating his return to her beach, he had in fact all the while been in London, made her grab a large stone and place it on the letter, haul herself from her position and walk to the water's edge. She let the waves come to her feet and run over her toes several times before she stepped back out of their reach. Within the month, he had said. He had left her no option but to wait for his return and whilst she did very much want to see him again, she felt trapped by her emotions, by her personal geography. Her world was this place, this brackish river from the shore of which she could stare out to sea. Her beach was officially part of the Helford river, but its waters were that of the wider ocean. He could come and go as he pleased. He could choose his place. She returned to where the letter lay and folded it back into the envelope. She walked up and down the beach from one end to the other until she could not face taking another step. In her exhaustion she sat down on the pebbles again and let herself weep. Nothing came but dry sobbing. Her lungs and ribs ached, and she swayed back and forth as if in a state of intense grief, yet there was nothing but lightness inside her.

* * *

On her way back up to the house Gwen saw a familiar young man come slithering down the shady path towards her in finely tailored clothes and a shiny top hat. Freddie Fernly batted at the overhanging ferns with a lacquered cane. She hadn't seen her cousin all winter and spring. He was as dapper as ever. His voice rang out as he noticed her.

'You know, it's an absolute bore having to chase after you all the way down here, Gwen. Mother has been waiting up top for at least an hour and your dear sister hasn't yet deigned to emerge.'

'Freddie. How lovely; I didn't know you were coming today.'

'Hello, old thing.' He took off his hat and gave her a kiss on each cheek. 'You look wild,' he said, 'like a tempestuous creature from a novel.'

'Idiotic fellow, you look expensively over-dressed.'

'Vulgar, as always. I have so missed your

tenacious wit.'

'And I yours. You should have told me you were coming.'

'And if I had, you would have put us off.'

'How is your mother, Freddie? Is she well?'

'There must be another way back up without having to go through all this verdant jungle.'

'No, there isn't.'

'Oh. Well, you know, I am her biggest frustration, and having given up on me for the time being, she thought she would make an impromptu call on the most eligible young lady in all of Cornwall.'

'I'll see if I can persuade Effie to come downstairs.'

'Not her, you gorgeous goose. You know Mother's opinion of ghosts and rappings and shaded lamps well enough. You and I are now at the top of her list.'

'But she has given up on you.'

'In a manner of speaking.'

'I see. Ask me quickly, Freddie, so that we can get it over with.'

'This suit is brand new. Mark my words, I am not getting down on bended knee in the mire.'

'Ask.'

'Gwen Carrick, will you be my wife?'

'Certainly not. Never in my life, Freddie Fernly.'

'Thank God for that. Well, let's go and tell Mother the good news.'

'I can't believe she really thought it would come off.'

'No. I think it's a mark of how desperate she has become to get rid of me once and for all. She has already been through every possible candidate this season and I have refused every single one of them. We are back early because she is in a fit of pique.'

Gwen laughed. 'You should just tell her, Freddie, in simple words that even she can understand.'

'What? Dearest Mother? It would finish her off. In any case, I am glad to see you more cheerful.'

'I'm not unhappy.'

'What tosh. You've turned yourself into a veritable hermit. No one can be happy living like this. Which reminds me, we are having a little gathering, Tuesday week. Do say you'll come.'

Gwen had no desire to spend an evening with Mrs Fernly, despite her affection for Freddie. They arrived at a level path, halfway up to the house, where they stopped to get their breath back, Freddie more than Gwen.

'Euphemia won't be able to call off her engagements for that night.'

'I know, that's why I fixed it for a Tuesday. I found out, you see, which nights your sister entertains her ladies.'

'So very wicked of you, Freddie. There are male clients, too, just occasionally.'

'Pooh to them all! So, now you will accept?'

'You won't let your mother make me sing, and you won't let some horrid crony of hers corner me.'

'I promise that Mother won't even be there. It will be fun. And perhaps you can wear that lovely blue silk, because it will go very nicely with my new waistcoat and everyone will leave us both quite alone, because we shall strike such a stunning effect.'

'I don't have it, Freddie. I sold most of my gowns.'

'You do know that you have committed a mortal sin? That blue was heavenly on you. Never mind, whatever you shall wear will be irrelevant. You are truly the most eligible young lady in the entire county.'

'If it weren't for my so-called hermitism and the fact that I can't sing.'

'That and your love of stones. If you would just love the shiny kind.'

'I do, just not in that way. And you've forgotten something.'

'Of course. I am sure there is a perfect match for you out there. If some gentleman were to present you with a big shiny beetle I am sure your heart would melt at once.'

'Don't tease. I can't think of anything more hideous than handing over my future and property to some—'

'Pax! I won't tease you any more. Do come Tuesday week.'

They moved off again, going slowly up the steep path arm in arm; Freddie cajoling Gwen until she agreed that she would go to his party.

'Ha! I knew you would,' he said, as they reached the house. 'I'll send you a lovely present—but you must promise not to sell it. At least wear it once.'

'You mustn't do anything extravagant on my behalf, Freddie.'

'Not at all. I have something perfectly exquisite in mind.'

'Your mother will have entirely the wrong impression if you send me gifts.'

'I don't much care if she does. I want you to sparkle and be happy. I've neglected you, old thing; I want to make reparations.'

CHAPTER V

London. May, 1859.

Edward had suffered a long and uncomfortable journey; dirty, tired and hungry, he'd been so dispirited on his return that he had considered booking a room somewhere for the first night back in London. He wished that he had decided after all to tear up his ticket and stay in Cornwall.

He had been back in London for about ten days but he had lost sense of the exact date. During this time he had witnessed his wife miscarry her child. The pregnancy had been troublesome; Isobel had lost blood on and off throughout, both from her womb and through leeches on her arm, courtesy of some quack in Edward's absence. She had been determined it would go to the full term and had neglected to continue the treatment he had secured for her. Now, Edward found himself organising a minute coffin and a funeral to go with it while also sourcing the right concoctions to dry up the milk which now leaked from her swollen breasts. Already it was all becoming too much again. He didn't know how many days he would be able to stand it.

After his supper, Edward took a cab to Leicester Square. To walk and to think—or rather to lose himself in the cacophony of sounds and smells, to see the sights, and be thoroughly revolted by all of it, so that he could go back to the miserable house and try to find something living there, some small remnant of the positive feelings he had once harboured for his wife.

He stood on the left-hand flight of steps leading to the entrance of the insalubrious Saville House. Beneath its three storeys of shabby late-baroque grandeur, Edward recalled snatches of his times with Natalia Jaspur. The memories of her person, her voice, and the physical presence she had. The way she owned the air in the room. Edward hesitated on the steps. Should he go up to the door and go in? What kind of tricks would he see there now? Would she still be there, or would she have moved on, as she had promised she would? There were few who could deny the quality of her voice. She was the kind of person to somehow always find a way of getting what she wanted. Notoriety of the right kind would surely fall her way. And what about him? There was a time when he had believed that Natalia Jaspur's medical condition was going to provide him with the evidence to make his name. That the condition had already been scientifically described had not prevented this belief for a while.

There was loose change in his coat pockets and in his trouser pockets. He couldn't remember putting the coins there. Some was change from the cabby. Some must be kept for the ride back home. Edward advanced a couple of steps higher but found himself clinging to the newer memory of Gwen Carrick, both in the summerhouse and on the beach. Such an extraordinary woman; so complex, so intuitive and so angry about the world. Why could he not have told her more? Did he really have to know her deepest passion and she his? He knew the answer to that. Edward looked up and tried to focus properly on the crowd of night-time revellers, the shadows from the lamplight making their faces ugly, every one of them.

Edward pushed his way down through the people now crowding up the steps to Saville House. They were welcome to their cheap entertainment. He found a cab and gave the address of his club. There he found Alexander Jacobs looking morose and staring into the fire, swirling a full measure of whisky, his half-bald head catching the warm glow from the grate. When he saw Edward he perked up, stood to shake his hand and offered him a drink.

'Hell, Scales, where the devil have you been hiding yourself? I was beginning to think you must be either dead or in the West Country.'

Edward tried not to recoil. 'I'm very much alive, as you can see. What makes you think I'd be in the West Country?'

'I didn't, not really. It's just that a lot of people have shot off there at the invitation of that Fernly.'

'Who?'

'Don't know him? I thought everyone did.'

'But you didn't go.'

'Christ, no. I have my patients to consider. What *are* you doing with yourself though, Scales. When are you coming back?'

Edward was grateful for the fact that Jacobs had pretended not to know what had kept him away from London for so long. He couldn't remember if he had ever talked to Jacobs about his interest in the West Country, or that he'd considered looking for a small property there. Never mind if he had or had not. The fossil hunting was common knowledge.

'I don't think I shall. I've been considering a change of scene.'

'But you've *had* a change of scene. You ought to

come back and finish training. I always said you'd make a damn fine surgeon. We could fix you up in next to no time. Damn sight more talent than Jeffreye and I have put together.'

'I don't know about that; rather late in the day. I don't think I shall ever elevate myself beyond general practitioner.'

'Nonsense! This is unwarranted modesty. You still have youth and your health on your side. Jeffreye's gone off for that Fernly's Ball, you know; wanted me to join him. Had the devil of a time myself trying to persuade him not to go.'

'Indeed.'

'By the look on your face I can see that you two are still not reconciled. I don't know what your quarrel was, but if you'll take my advice, you should patch things up. It's a terrible thing to lose a true friend over a squabble.'

'It's no simple quarrel. No doubt he's gone off in search of another self-indulgent medieval dose. Pity the unsuspecting in the West Country.'

'Of course, I'm intruding where I've no business. It's between the two of you. Have another?'

Edward accepted a second whisky and decided not to mention Isobel. Now that the drink was loosening his wits, he didn't trust himself to remain neutral after Jeffreye's name had come up.

Jacobs moved the conversation on and went along quite happily without much contribution from Edward. He talked about his horses and his dogs, and invited Edward to dinner the next week so that he could show them off. Then he talked about a difficult skin case at the hospital, and tried to elicit some advice from Edward on the matter. It was an attempt to try and prove to Edward that his proper place was by his side, at the hospital, that his talent in medicine was being wilfully squandered. But Edward was noncommittal, and kept the talk moving without promising Jacobs anything definite. The pair talked until after one in the morning and Edward took a ride back to Hyde Park in Jacob's carriage.

'Good night, then. Give my best to your wife. How's she coming along?'

Edward jumped down to the street and steadied himself, clinging to the cabin door. 'Isobel lost the child a few days ago.'

'Oh. Bloody bad luck.'

'Yes.'

'Still, early days yet. There'll be others. Don't give up.'

'No.'

'Good chap.'

'Good night, Alex.' Edward shut the door and the cab pulled away. He took his shoes off in the entrance hall. In the dark, he twice missed the peg on the stand before his coat found its place. He blundered as quietly as he could, but his head was thick. He found a lamp and managed to light it after rummaging a long time for the box of matches in his trousers. He hadn't smoked in a long while but kept up the habit of having matches about him. He came to the bottom of the winding flight of stairs and gripped the turned end of the banister. He put his foot on the bottom step but then changed his mind. He didn't want to go and lie in bed wide awake. He just didn't want to go upstairs at all. Edward went to his study and turned the lamp up full. He poured himself another drink and pulled open the drawers where he kept his case-study papers. Perhaps Jacobs was right; he'd allowed himself to wallow for too long. He had once believed in himself as much as Jacobs now pretended to. He shuffled through them, looking for the file he'd kept on Natalia Jaspur. He could not find it; his mind was fixed on the naked body of Natalia Jaspur, and the extraordinary effect it had produced in him. He'd felt his whole being punched alive; a spark, a jolt, something unexpected. The revulsion he'd anticipated, and had been prepared to hide from her, had not been there. The sight of her naked body, so completely covered in hair, had caught him so sharply, so intensely that he had been afraid of his own desire. The papers were gone. He had no recollection of having destroyed his work, but, then again, he had not been terribly well. He could not settle. Seeing Alexander Jacobs again had caused the feelings he'd buried to migrate to the surface of his mind. When he closed his eyes he could not fully conjure Miss Carrick's face; the restorative effect she had brought to him was obscured by the too-familiar throw of the lamp's shadows in the room and the memory of Natalia Jaspur, the countless hours he had spent in her company, and then the striving to release himself from her hold. Meeting Miss Carrick had opened up something better in him—something he now knew that he valued above everything, and that he had never thought to own. There was no word nor expression that matched what he felt for her, and so he let the nameless thing exist without trying to pin it down. The torture he had minutes ago felt in remembering Natalia Jaspur dulled, and he fell asleep in the chair at his desk.

When he woke in the morning he was still drunk.

He roused himself and looked at the chaos of paperwork he had strewn about the night before. He knew he could be better than the sum of these papers. It was just a matter of finding his own truth. Miss Carrick seemed to be aware of her own truth; she seemed to have a clear sense of purpose and a fierce determination, in spite of the hand that had been dealt her. He went upstairs to bed where he slept until late morning. Waking for the second time he threw himself out of the covers. He stood still for a moment at the bedside and reeled at his hangover, determined not to throw up. The pressing thought that he must find the Burns poem before he went back to see Miss Carrick was clear in his mind. As he splashed water on his face at the wash-stand he knew, suddenly, what the inexplicable feeling was. The thing he had been unable to name was simple. He was in love.

CHAPTER VI

'They are taking advantage of your vulnerable state, Isobel. These people are the lowest sort.'

'Then you should be happy that I shall find myself in suitable company, Edward.'

'Those are your words, not mine. What is done is done, but this will only serve to compound your unhappiness, not cure it.'

'I am not looking for a cure, Edward, I am looking for my child.'

'We buried him. Two days ago, we buried him; you know where his body lies. Wherever his tiny spirit has gone, I can guarantee that you will not find it in some spinster's *parlour* overstuffed with horsehair, velvet and threads of manipulation tied to hidden china bells.'

'They say the spirits sometimes bring gifts from the other side. The Enderby sisters say—'

'All of it is nonsense, Isobel, and if you were not in this unfortunate state you would say the same yourself, without any doubt. Pure nonsense; it is nothing more than cheap trickery.'

'And, of course, you are an authority on that particular subject. Why can't you let me grieve?'

'I wish you would grieve, but this is no way to go about it.'

'You are punishing me because of the child.'

'I have no wish to do any such thing.'

'And yet, had he lived, I think you would have punished me more.'

'Isobel, you are not yourself. Let me take you home.'

'No.'

Isobel's comment about his authority on trickery had pricked him, but he felt it unjust. Spirits quite simply could no more be conjured than congealed blood be made liquid and life-giving. Life was governed by the function of a body. Its deterioration to the point of cessation of functioning parts stopped the flow of blood. It—the flow of blood, that ordinary substance in veins—this in Edward's mind was where the spirit lay. Blood became infected with disease, and the body still living could exist for a time with the process of decay. He glanced at his wife, whose expression was unreadable. After the last breath, thought Edward, blood congealed, and then decayed. Once the body was dead, the spirit too was dead. He had watched, in his observation of patients' deaths, for evidence of the departure of the spirit. He could not attach to the process of a human death the sentiment enjoyed by those zealous purveyors of idiotic lies.

Their carriage came to a stop and Edward opened the door for her. He got out and helped her down. She was pitifully weak on her feet.

'We did not bury my child, Edward. You had him put in a box lined with lead and locked him into a cold, dark place. He will not be happy, and I need to let him know that it was not me who put him there.'

'Your father and I did what you yourself asked us to do. You did not want him to be under the ground.'

'I did not want him to be dead; I did not want to let him go anywhere. At least allow me this.'

'I will be here again in one hour.'

He took her up to the house and surveyed its facade with distaste. The afternoon light made the masonry glow, and a blackbird sang in a branch somewhere above his head. It was very ordinary. In spite of everything, he did not want to leave her here, but he did not stop her. He reached up for her and knocked on the door and watched her go in. My God, he thought, this is ridiculous. And where was Charles, in all of this? In Cornwall, in exactly the place Edward wanted to be. Edward felt he had more right to be in Cornwall at that moment than any other man. He told the driver to take him to the park.

'Which one, sir?'

'Oh, just any park, I don't care.'

'Right you are then, sir, won't take five minutes.'

When he went back to collect Isobel he could see

that she had been weeping. They travelled in silence. He didn't know how to tell her that he would be returning to Cornwall the next week. She went to her room and he followed her.

'Isobel, I can't stay here and watch you do this to yourself.'

'Don't use pity for myself or my child as your excuse, Edward.'

'I am sorry. I must go.'

'Curiosities again, is it? Or some other brilliant new *idea* of yours?'

'I know that it might seem—'

'Edward, stop now. I am tired.'

CHAPTER VII

FALMOUTH. MAY, 1859.

A Masqued Ball. If he was trying to make up for having neglected his favourite cousin, Freddie was doing it in the only way he could manage. His house in Falmouth town was overspilling with guests when Gwen arrived in the carriage Freddie had sent for her. Freddie leaped down the front steps of the house to greet her, wearing a grotesque *papier-mâché* grimace on the top of his head and waving an elaborate feathered mask in his hand.

'No one but I shall know who you are. There will be no introductions, no ghastly formalities. We are going to have so much fun. No singing for those who don't want to. No polite trivialities.'

'This isn't a little gathering, Freddie.'

'I've a wicked mind, dear Gwen. Do put this on.'

He tied the tapes at the back of her head and admired her hair. 'The beetle looks lovely on you.'

'It is too extravagant, Freddie. I can't keep it.' The brooch he had sent her, a brilliant green beetle, was stunning in its design and the delicate craftsmanship of the goldsmith. Freddie had no regard for the amount of money he spent. It was only money, he always said. Happiness and love are more valuable. But Gwen knew that the money Freddie spent so easily was minted from the sweat and degradation of human beings he never had to see and never chose to dwell upon. It was the only subject which they could never discuss. If they did, then they would lose each other irrevocably.

'Such rot, of course, you shall keep it. No one else could wear it with such an audacious charm. Besides, it was made for you. Now, come with me. All these people think that they have abandoned London mid-season for a bit of riotous sensational whatsit, so we had better give it to them.'

'You've been planning this for weeks.'

'Months, if we must be truthful. I have missed you so much, and I know how you hated the way those half-wits swooned over you at my mother's gatherings. But I know you too well to know that you can't actually like the way you've gone and cut yourself off from the whirligig of life.'

'Don't let's get into that again.'

'But this fixes everything! You can say whatever comes into your head to whomsoever you choose. No one can form an opinion of your opinions, if you get my drift.'

'I think Effie would be better at this than me.'

'Your sister has chosen her own amusements. She prefers mothballs to masqued balls.'

Gwen laughed, and Freddie pulled his own mask down onto his face and put his arm around her corseted waist.

Some of the guests had already spilled out onto the lamplit lawns of the garden and were having a treasure hunt among the topiary. The drawing room was set up as a gambling parlour and was a clamour of noise—music, the rattle of the roulette wheels, the chink of crystal and money, and shrieks of laughter. Everyone was playing Freddie's game to the letter and wore a mask of some kind; even the musicians.

Freddie spoke into her ear as they walked past a roulette table. 'You see, dear cousin, we all need a mask to be our true selves. Look at them all, having such fun. In two days' time they will be back in London; the last thrill of this mid-week excursion to the precipice of debauchery will be the rattling speed of the express locomotive, and when they alight at the station they will pretend it was all just a dream. Now, come and trot a *gavotte* with me.'

Three men sat at one piano playing the music to which Freddie and Gwen began to dance among the crowd of guests. Freddie's mask was the embodiment of the frustration Gwen knew he suffered in real life; the mask he was forced to wear and could never remove in the company of those who believed they knew him so well. Gwen was whirled about and lifted from her feet by Freddie's exuberant interpretation of the music. She felt herself swept along in thrall to his enthusiasm. She glanced at the other masked guests in the confusion of costumes around them and recognised no one at all though she knew there must be people in the room who were known to her besides Freddie.

When the *gavotte* came to an end another man took Gwen around on the next dance until someone else cut in halfway through. Over the next hour, Gwen drank punch and danced with more strangers; she lost sight of Freddie. The mask's feathers stuck to the sweat on her face. She eventually went outside to find a private place to take it off and cool down. Others had the same idea, and there were several ladies wandering about fanning themselves among the tightly clipped hedges. She couldn't find anywhere private enough and so kept her mask on.

'Marvellous stroke of genius, wasn't it?'

Gwen turned to face the man who had obviously crept up behind her. 'You refer to our host's flair for entertaining.'

'I do, indeed. I've been trying to work out which mask is Fernly's ever since I arrived. Dark fellow.'

'I think you mean that he has entered fully into the spirit of the evening.'

'Absolutely. Yourself likewise. I may not be permitted to ask your name, but may I bring you some refreshment?'

'A glass of water, thank you.'

He left her, and Gwen finally lifted her mask away from her face and craned her neck up to the night sky. Some of the lanterns hung about the garden had burned out; where she stood, another guttered its last as she waited for the man to return. She heard the approach of a voice and put her mask back on, even though there was not enough light now to make out more than the outlines of figures backlit by the bright windows of the house. But it was not the man bringing her a drink. She heard Freddie's voice and was about to come out of the shadows to greet him when she heard that he was speaking to another man. She pulled her mask off again and stayed out of his sight. The punch had made her woozy; away from the swirl of the company of others she felt it more acutely. She tried to listen to what Freddie and his companion were saying on the other side of the hedge. It seemed that at last Freddie had found someone with whom he could wear his ideal mask. Gwen leaned against the thick hedge, slightly jealous of his romantic success and his utter disregard for rules. Freddie and the other young man moved further on into the deeper shadows where they would not be chanced upon by anyone.

Gwen retied her mask, but, unlike Freddie, she didn't want to go through life feathered up in an elaborate disguise. She loved Freddie for his sincere and elaborate efforts to make her happy despite his own deeply melancholic nature, but he didn't understand her desire to be treated with respect when she spoke openly about the things she cared for most.

The man who had gone off to fetch her a glass of water now came holding it out in front of his person, his view of the ground limited by his mask. He picked up his feet and raised his knees in a very comical way. Gwen thought he looked like a grey heron.

'I am very much obliged to you, sir.' She took the glass and drank all the water.

'The lamps are going out. I'm afraid I left you standing alone in the dark longer than I anticipated.'

'I didn't notice. I was looking at the stars.'

'Ah, a romantic nature. Much like myself.'

'Actually, I was reflecting on the fact that I so

rarely take the trouble to study the night sky, and that I can't distinguish between the stars and the planets.'

'I don't bother about it myself. They all twinkle, and they are all a very long way away, so I understand.'

'Yes. A long way away. Perhaps tonight is not the time to be thinking about the planets.'

'They are playing a waltz, madam. Would you do me the honour again?'

Gwen was disconcerted that she hadn't remembered dancing with the man and that he had taken the trouble to seek her out in the garden, but she agreed to dance with him again. As she waltzed she wondered how long Freddie would spend out in the dark with the other young man and whether either of them would take off their *papier-mâché* masks. She thought of Edward Scales and wanted to know what he was doing at that precise moment. The sudden thought that he might even be there, at Freddie's Ball, gripped her mind and would not leave her, even though she was convinced that a place like this was the least likely venue in which she would ever find him.

CHAPTER VIII

It was seventeen days since Gwen had received the letter from Edward, and she had heard nothing more from him until this morning. His short note told her that he would be taking a walk and begged for her company on the beach. Gwen picked up Freddie's beetle brooch and fixed it into her hair;

then she took it out again and put it back into the velvet box. She changed her clothes again, swapping her good dress for the things she had been wearing the first time and looked at herself in the long mirror. The feathered mask she had worn at Freddie's ball hung by its tapes from the frame of the mirror. She unhooked it carefully and found some tissue to wrap it in. She placed it inside a hat box with some sachets of cloves and rosemary. When she picked up her jacket, her hands were shaking.

*   *   *

'I know I promised to send the poems to you by post, but I wanted to give them to you myself.' He presented the book wrapped in paper to her. She opened it.

'Thank you.'

'I hope you haven't minded the wait too much.'

'It's a very handsome volume.' In fact, it was a very tiny volume covered in a loud, blue-and-green tartan silk; it slipped into her pocket very easily.

Edward was relieved and sighed through his nose as he opened up his knapsack and began to spread out on the beach a lunch better prepared than their first picnic. The giving and the receiving of the gift was over. It had troubled them both, and they were both glad that it been done. The pebble containing the ammonite was still there in the bottom of his bag; he took it out and tossed it up and caught it, before putting it down next to the bottle of wine and the corkscrew. Gwen picked it up and ran her finger over the ridges.

He opened the wine and unwrapped wine glasses

from newspaper. Gwen was touched by the effort he had gone to. He had brought delicacies and silver cutlery and starched fine linen serviettes.

'Tell me why you like fossils so much, Mr Scales.'

'They intrigue me. They are a conundrum. And I like to discover them, to uncover a creature never before seen . . . At Lyme, in Dorset, it was possible to pick up glorious specimens from almost any random part of the cliff or the beach. Yet, here in Cornwall there seem to be no fossils at all.'

What he had really wanted to say was that he believed he could find something new, and that he constantly hoped for this because he wanted to name a creature himself. He'd even gone so far as to write out invented names of half-imagined curiosities. They came out as badly as the shapes he couldn't quite fix in his mind's eye, always ending with 'scalesii'. He burned the scraps of paper afterwards. It would be as mortifying to be found out at that as—no, not today. He concentrated instead on Miss Carrick's voice, the pleasant breaking of the waves, the sun on her skin.

'Yes, they *are* very rare so far to the west,' she said, 'though not entirely absent. It is possible to find trilobites, for instance, at a place further west from here, but I would be surprised if you were able to find one after six months of searching. But, surely, it isn't so much of a conundrum, Mr Scales, since the geology of Dorset is quite different to that of Cornwall.'

'Now you have stoked my attention, Miss Carrick. I was under the impression that your area of interest was the live flora and fauna of the region.'

'But one specialism cannot exist without its

complementary subjects, Mr Scales.'

'Although, a creature like the ammonite, long since made extinct by the Great Flood, surely has but a slight connection to the live creatures with which we now inhabit the world.'

'Mr Scales, I do hope you are being deliberately provocative.'

'I am not insincere, Miss Carrick. I am impressed by your scope.'

'You misunderstand me. I meant that I hope you don't really believe that Noah's Flood was the agent responsible for the distribution of fossils?'

'I take it you do not.'

'Mr Scales! Good heavens. People once believed that the earth was flat and that the sun moved around the earth. Scientific thought, experiment and deduction always bring us closer to the truth. Have you not read Mr Smith's *Strata*?'

'I have not. I wish that I had.'

'I would lend you my own copy, if my library had not recently suffered fire damage.' Gwen had not been able to stop herself. She was aghast to find that Mr Scales' interest was based on the assumptions she so despised in her own sister.

'I'm sorry to hear about that. I hope no one was hurt.'

'The damage was limited to a small area. It was caught in time.'

'But, still, it must grieve you.'

'It does. Books may be replaced, though. And you may find a copy, I am sure, quite easily in London.'

'And when I do, I shall send it to you immediately.'

'There's no need, Mr Scales, though your offer is

very kind. I would rather you read the book for yourself. It is a revelatory volume.'

'I will make it my priority, Miss Carrick.'

'I'm glad. But, Mr Scales, you must have had cause to wonder about the geology of this place, as opposed to that of Dorset.'

'Your knowledge of rocks is superior to mine. I must confess that, before this year, I have never had reason to study them in the way you obviously do.'

'I have lived with these rocks all my life, Mr Scales. Perhaps my advantage is unfair.'

'But I think life cast you an unfair disadvantage, Miss Carrick. I have thought about what you said to me about the beetles you study and paint. If you had been born male, you would have been sent to university. You would have had an even greater advantage. Yet, that also would have been to my great loss.'

'I wouldn't wish to be a man, Mr Scales. Only that I should have the freedom to expand my knowledge of the world at first hand without attracting derision from all sides.'

'All but one, Miss Carrick. I admire you a great deal.'

'Thank you, Mr Scales.'

'One very rarely meets a person like yourself. I consider myself extraordinarily fortunate.'

Gwen could think of nothing to say to this. She was annoyed with herself for having been harsh with Edward. His ignorance was perhaps not his fault. Why should a man have cause to stop and wonder about the strata of rocks when he had, as she assumed Edward must have, spent his life in the city. And now that she had told him he would be unlikely to find any more fossils in Cornwall, he would have no reason to visit again. He said he was glad to have met her, but she knew that he must have a life of some kind outside her own world and that he would not be able to accommodate a passing interest at the expense of his other commitments, whatever they may be.

All of the food and most of the wine had been consumed. Gwen was drunk. She let Edward pour her a last half glass of wine.

'I consider myself fortunate, too, Mr Scales. I hope you will write to me again when you return to London.'

'I have no need to return to London for a good while, Miss Carrick, though that shall not prevent me from looking for the title you recommend.'

'I expect that you shall return to Dorset and continue your search there.'

'Indeed not. I believe I have finished my search for fossils, at least for the time being. There are only so many one may find room for in a cabinet.'

'But your collection from the south coast of England will be incomplete. Perhaps I can help.'

'Miss Carrick, you have already inspired me more than you can know.'

'Rubbish. I have told you to read a book. Anyone could have done the same, and you would probably have found Mr Smith's *Strata* without my help.'

'It is by no means a certainty. What I have been trying to say, Miss Carrick, is that my interest in fossils has been supplanted by a much greater passion.'

'Then you must pursue it, as fully as is possible. There is nothing worse than a pursuit for knowledge left to wither and atrophy. I think it sinful.'

'I wouldn't dream of letting it happen.'

'That is good to know, Mr Scales.'

'Please understand me, it is my passion for you which overshadows everything else.'

Gwen stood up; Edward scrambled to his feet.

'Stay a while longer,' he said. 'I have wanted to tell you this—please don't reject me. I want so much to prove to you that I can be more than the person you must think I am.'

'I'm not leaving yet. The tide is coming in, we must move further back up the beach or we shall be cut off here and have to climb the cliff, which I wouldn't recommend, the topsoil of the overhang is—'

The energy contained in his kiss, the taste of his wine-tainted saliva on her tongue and the force of his grip as Edward put one hand behind her neck and the other around her waist pulling her close to his body so that she smelled his sweat—wasn't this what she had tried and failed to imagine after she had seen him in the summerhouse that morning? His own lungs seemed to be sucking the air from hers. His eyes were closed, and the image of his left hand working away at himself flooded her mind. The vivid colour of it. She found herself fighting for her breath, and he stopped the kiss but did not release her.

'Will you reject me, Gwen? Will you tell me to go away and leave you alone?'

'No, I don't want that. But my feet are getting wet, and so are yours.'

Edward picked up his knapsack, which was also wet, and put it over his shoulder, carrying the two wine glasses in one hand. Gwen lurched up the beach, hauling herself in sodden skirts, trying to gather them all in one hand, Edward holding her by the other. The wine bottle, the corkscrew and the empty caviar pot and serviettes were all left to the incoming tide.

Edward and Gwen collapsed side by side onto the pebbles beyond the high tide mark. They watched the advance and retreat of the abandoned picnic articles. The waves churned the serviettes into the seaweed and they were lost from sight.

'I'm sorry about your dress, and your good shoes. The salt will have ruined them.'

'Yours, too.'

'Yes, never mind it.'

Edward's second kiss threw Gwen off balance, and he clasped her so hard that she could do nothing to stop herself from being made to lie on her back. Edward's mouth pressed to hers as the mussels stuck to crevices in the rocks. It did not frighten her. She felt that she was somewhere above her body, looking down at what they were doing. Just as suddenly as the kiss had begun, Edward finished it. He kept his face close to hers, so close that she was unable to focus, and after a minute she pushed him away, smiling at him. Her bottom lip had split and she tasted her blood.

'I've made you bleed. I'm sorry.'

'It doesn't matter. But talk to me now.'

'What shall I tell you?'

'A secret.'

'I have none worth the telling.'

'Everyone has a secret. Don't be miserable about it. Tell me something about your distant past if you like. Then it won't matter.'

Edward looked at her and was stumped. He didn't want her to become bored but what on earth could he tell her? He cleared his throat.

'When I was nine, perhaps ten, my father took me on an expedition. Days of travelling. I was quite ill by the end of it all—the suspension of the carriage, the rocking and jolting. It was almost this time of year. There was hawthorn blossom in every direction. The scent of it; such a simple thing, but in such profusion. My father was a keen angler. He had a box of the most exquisite flies, which he made himself from feathers. I was clumsy as a child. Nervous. I wanted to please him. My feet were unused to the loose pebbles at the riverside, and my boots slid. I upset the box, almost crushing it, and the flies were scattered amongst the pebbles. I ran away down the riverbank after he had chastised me. He did not strike me. I ran away to the shade of some alder trees and brooded there.

'And my eye came to rest on a strange thing: an insect, quite large, but almost completely transparent in a pool of sunlight, clinging to the overhang of a large rock by the water. I leaned down to look. It did not move. I don't know how long I was like that, watching it. Eventually, I put out my finger to touch it, and it partly came away from the rock. I realised that it was not alive. I bent closer, and saw that it had an opening on its back. For some reason the thing frightened me.'

Gwen sat up straighter. 'You had found the empty skin of the mayfly.'

'Yes, I understood that much later.' He had been about to tell her the rest and then held back how he had taken the thing between his fingers and crushed it. Over the years, Edward had remodelled this memory; telling it now with only his father and himself in the frame made the recollection easier to live with.

'I don't think I would recognise you if I were to meet you as you were then,' said Gwen. 'Children can be so strange, can't they?'

CHAPTER IX

THE TIMES, Tuesday, October 2, 1866.

MURDER TRIAL AT THE OLD BAILEY.

IT is anticipated that The Crown v. Pemberton will prove to be a most interesting case to observe. Mrs Pemberton (26) is accused of murdering Mr Edward Scales (38) on or around the 6th of August. The gallery in court was swamped with a surfeit of spectators by 8 o'clock this morning, some of whom had to be removed in the interests of public safety and decorum. The prisoner, when asked to declare how she pleads at the opening of the trial, said, 'Obviously, I shall plead Not Guilty, my Lord. I may say I had supposed I would not plead at all, as I am affronted that I should even *be* in this position, and I do not wish to give one iota of credence to the charge by answering it. However, I feel even more strongly that I must dissociate myself from this dreadful affair by stating the plain fact that I am Not Guilty. I do not know what else I can say to support my case other than to look every single person here in the eye and say that I did not have a hand in this awful deed.'

Detective Sergeant Gray, of the Metropolitan Police Force, gave evidence of his discovery at the Hyde Park residence where the body of Mr Edward Osbert Scales was discovered.

'I attended the property of Mr Scales, on the morning of Tuesday, 7th August, accompanied by Constable Winters, and by Mr Pemberton, the husband of the prisoner at the insistence of Mr Pemberton. On entering the property, Mr Pemberton advanced before myself and my Constable, and began to open doors of the rooms and call to Mr Scales, whom I presumed to be still living at that time; that he must come out and answer for himself and that his time was up. Well, we soon after that found the deceased Mr Scales lying in the middle of the carpet in the morning room. Mr Pemberton spoke loudly to the tune that Mr Scales had better wake up. Constable Winters went to Mr Scales and turned him over whereupon it was obvious that the man was some time since passed away. Around the body were various bottles of spirits and spilled decanters of red wine. The room itself was in a state of great untidiness. At this moment, I had no reason to believe that Mr Scales had succumbed to anything other than a natural death. I sent Constable Winters for a doctor, and standing then in the hallway of the residence, I became aware of someone standing halfway down the main staircase. This person said he was Mr Morrisson, and that he was valet to Mr Scales and how could he help us. I informed him of his employer's demise, at which he did not so much as blink an eye. He came calmly down to the hallway and proceeded without hesitation to the very room where Mr Scales lay. Asking him how he could know where the body lay, Morrisson answered that Mr Scales had kept to that room all the previous day and night, and had not moved from it.'

Mr Probart asked why the prisoner's husband had insisted the Police attend the property of Mr Scales.

A: 'It was some domestic matter, which did not seem to make any sense to me, and so to straighten it all out, I agreed to go there.'

Q: 'Could you be a little more specific as to the nature of this domestic matter?'

A: 'I believe it was some quarrel that had occurred. Mr Pemberton made an accusation against the man regarding his wife's—the prisoner's—honour, sir.'

Q: 'Which part of the dispute did not make sense to you?'

A: 'Mr Pemberton seemed to think that a murder of some sort had been committed.'

Q: 'Which, it so happens, had, in fact.'

A: 'Aye, sir. Unfortunately, it turned out to be so.'

CHAPTER X

HELFORD PASSAGE. JUNE, 1859.

There hadn't been a single moment when Gwen had found herself thinking that she ought not to carry on. She did know, really, that this sort of encounter, might, in certain circumstances be dangerous but she didn't care. He was more than she could have ever hoped for. Better than that, he made her feel—without sliding into cliché, she thought to herself, as she slipped on the steep path between the bamboo thicket and grabbed at the yielding green poles—alive. It made her laugh, to think of all the ridiculous introductions she had been through under the gaze of the Fernly household. Pointless, all of them. Apart from the fact that she had used the money from the sale of her gowns to buy the microscope. Freddie would never have understood her attraction to Edward, and she was glad that she hadn't told Freddie about him, though there had been several times when Gwen had found herself almost on the point of confessing her secret.

No one was watching her. No one knew. No third party expected anything, and nor could they disapprove. He wasn't exactly any kind of romantic hero. For one thing he had the most peculiar sticking out pale hair she had ever seen and his skin was pale: freckled under his shirt and blotchy where the sun had caught his forearms. She stopped where she was amongst the stands of bamboo. This garden, she thought, we're hardly managing to keep abreast of it. In fact, there were parts of the garden which were virtually impenetrable. Murray and his lad, they kept the paths down to the beach clear; and they kept the top lawns well. But still, more than three quarters had run wild. She was trying an experiment with two goats, tethered under a massive magnolia. They looked like stupid animals and by the end of each day they had managed to get themselves tied in knots under the tree but they did eat everything. There was a sort of scruffy clear patch now. This was where she was heading, along a winding path which took her in a zigzag of steep gradients to the place where there had once been a lawn, nestled in the scoop of a valley. It was sheltered from the wind but rather too much goat manure had spoiled the ground, so they couldn't sit down.

Last time, they'd moved the goats away from the magnolia and tethered them in a very wild patch, so that they'd been hidden. Only the goats crashing about and their silly bleating disturbed them for a while. They'd talked, exhaustively, about the stupidity of goats until the animals had settled.

He'd pinned her against the tree, because of the ground being so littered with the dark pellets. Well, not pinned exactly. More supported. He'd kept her there anyway (perhaps, yes, she had been pinned, now she thought about it, because of her skirts being pushed up and to either side of her); and his head, she'd gripped his head to steady herself. None of it seemed wrong. The thrusting and the panting and the wetness between her thighs afterwards. He explored her with his fingers, running them back and forth until she was slippery and pliant in his hands and eager for anything that he would do, that he might think of doing; and then he would slip himself between her thighs. Make her keep them together, very tight, and he would delve there, and moan words in her ears that she hadn't heard before she'd met him, and still didn't know the meaning of.

She didn't like the smell. The runny then glutinous liquid which came out of him. It was too earthy. It caught in her throat like the smell of hanging poultry, and reminded her of certain flowers which attracted flies.

As he tightened his grip on her, and breathed into her, Gwen remembered one of the young men she'd been introduced to. His own body odour had been strong. They had been dancing and even out on the balcony in a stiff breeze she had smelled his sweat. The pressure of Edward's body reminded her of how the young man at that Ball had leaned in close; his breathing had been almost exactly like Edward's was now. What hindsight was, indeed, she thought.

'I was sorry to hear about your mother,' he had said to her, and she had pretended not to hear, but he had carried on. 'I had the good fortune to have been introduced, once.' Still she had pretended not to hear, as the orchestra was very loud. 'I am not one of those—' here she lost his words in the crescendo of the music '—you know, Miss Carrick.' She had thanked him for his company and had never spoken to him again. She couldn't even remember his name. Charles somebody. A nobody.

Edward clamped his mouth over a tender part of her neck near the collarbone and sucked hard. Gwen looked up into the branches of the tree as she tried to twist her neck out of his mouth. Edward's groans were muffled; he let go briefly and then clamped his mouth again onto her neck, at the same time thrusting between her legs more furiously. Gwen concentrated on the sharp pinpricks of sunlight bursting through the leaves above her as they shifted in the breeze and made different patterns.

Edward released her. He said, 'I have found a place in town. I mean to establish a practice.'

'A medical practice?'

'Yes.'

'You're a *doctor*.'

'The idea disappoints you.'

'It surprises me.'

'Oh. I had hoped to be able to see you more often. I hope I soon shall.'

Gwen walked away and brushed down her skirt, buttoned up the collar of her blouse. She was upset that Edward had kept the secret of his life from her until this moment. How could he do this? One instant to be spilling himself between her clamped thighs, the next to be discussing some business arrangement. She had once asked him for a secret and he had told her some *thing* about a mayfly. He's made himself out to be ignorant about science, she thought, and yet he must have spent years in his medical training. Edward came after her, tucking himself up.

'I should have introduced myself in the proper way. For that I am sorry. It has been on my conscience. I would like to make amends.'

'Why did you not?'

'I have never thought myself particularly worthy of the title. Call it self-doubt.'

'And now you are confident.'

'My mind and attitude have altered considerably

since meeting you. You must know that you have had a great effect upon me.'

'I am disappointed by your secrecy, Edward.'

He slid an arm around her waist. 'I am sorry to have hurt your feelings.' He kissed her while he grabbed at the fabric of her skirt and pulled it up, slipping a hand underneath. He let his fingers rest, poised until he was sure of his impact through the kiss, and delicately drew her forgiveness from her as inevitably as the yolk in a blown egg must burst though the tiny aperture made by the pin.

* * *

'We simply can't afford anything so ridiculously extravagant. What on earth possessed you?' The irony of her own words were not lost on Gwen who looked at her sister across the breakfast table with cool fury.

'He's a gift.'

'What? Oh, that makes it so much better. For heaven's sake. As if it wasn't already—'

'Yes? You were going to say "bad enough", weren't you?' Euphemia's lips were parched and cracked and as she pursed them into a thin line of satisfaction, Gwen saw a beading thread of blood ooze over the papery skin.

'You are making us ridiculous, agreeing to have a pastry chef, of all things, in the house.'

'I'm sorry, Gwen, to arouse such passion in you, but I can promise you that Mr Harris will do his best not to appear to be ridiculous under this roof.'

'What kind of person, or mayn't I ask, sends a, a *dwarf* pastry chef to a household such as this?'

'An appreciative client. I knew it was his size

which irked you, and not his culinary expertise.'

'An appreciative—who exactly, which of them would—'

'I have not the faintest idea.'

'He'll have to go back then; he'll be poisoning us at the first opportunity. We simply can't.'

Euphemia threw back her head and shrieked like a herring gull. Gwen leaned over the table to slap her cheek and felt the smarting of it in her palm. Euphemia straightened up, instantly silent, glaring at her sister.

'He comes with the highest recommendation,' she said. 'From the housekeeper of a very good address in London.'

Gwen regarded her sister in mute defeat for a few moments before telling her, 'You appall me.' She left the table, snatching up the daily newspaper and stalked out with it, rolling it into a baton as she went down the passage to the kitchen to inspect this new servant.

CHAPTER XI

Helford Passage. July, 1859.

'Let us be clear from the outset, Mr Harris—' Euphemia had invited him into the morning room to compliment his pastry, but a fever had lodged in her mind between the invitation being issued and her reading the letter Fergus Harris had given Susan for the post box that morning. It had been addressed to Mrs Isobel Scales in London. 'Whilst you live under my roof, you are part of my household. You do not answer to anyone living in the establishment at which you were previously employed. Do I make myself quite understood?'

'Ma'am.'

'You will not write letters of any kind to my clients.'

'No, ma'am.'

'And you will not make secret reports of any kind to any of my clients, nor to anyone else, about the private lives of people living in this house.'

Fergus Harris looked up from where he had been staring at the floor. Euphemia saw no register of change in his expression as he replied that indeed he would not.

'Furthermore, you will not accept gratuities from any of my clients nor from anyone else, for any such undertakings. As you have so far surmised, we lead ordinary lives here, and there is nothing so remarkable about us bar that which is already known and appreciated by my clients.'

Fergus Harris said, 'No, ma'am. But is this you telling me to pack up and go?' Euphemia set her jaw and drew out the document she had prepared. 'This is a new contract of employment, which you may read now and choose to sign. If you sign your name there, you will abide, absolutely, by everything which is set out, in plain English on that paper.'

Fergus took the contract from where she had placed it on an occasional table beside her. She watched his eyes run over her tidy script. Here and there in his concentration he raised an eyebrow. When he came to the end he said that he would sign. Euphemia stood up and asked him to follow her through into the library where the ink and blotter were ready at the desk. Fergus Harris signed his name with the same flourish he had used to sign his letter to Isobel Scales. He rocked the blotter over his wet ink and handed the paper back to Euphemia.

'Thank you, Mr Harris. You are a most valued addition. Remember where your loyalties now rest and we shall all enjoy a peaceful, harmonious existence in this house. And, I almost forgot, your pastries are indeed quite excellent. That will be all for now, Mr Harris.'

Married. Of course, he was married. His hand was practised; his touch was sure. Bella. The exceptionally quiet one. She could not credit the woman with such an extravagant habit. But there it was. She turned her attention to the pile of letters brought in from the table in the hall. The usual drift of thank-you notes and exclamations of gratitude. Among them a letter to Gwen in a hand she did not recognise. She put it to the side, and attended to things in an orderly fashion. Every now and then, between replying to her own letters, Euphemia's hand went out to touch the envelope addressed to Gwen. She picked it up, and turned it over and put it back down again just as her sister came into the room. She jammed the door wide open with a wedge. She brought the outside into the room with her.

'Effie, Susan tells me there is a letter for me this morning.' Her whole self smelled of the hot weather. Of dust and pollen. And wine. Gwen came over to the desk. 'Have you got it? Yes, there it is.'

'A commission?'

'Perhaps.'

'You were expecting it.' Euphemia smelled the

gritty earth on Gwen's hem as she swept around the back of Euphemia's chair.

'Hope for everything, and expect nothing, Effie. Isn't that the best way?'

'You have been taking our wine into the garden.'

Gwen had been about to leave but she turned back again. 'Honestly, Effie. It is such a glorious day, please don't try to spoil it for me.'

'I hope the commission is a good one.' Euphemia thought, I despise this buoyancy of yours. Please leave.

'If that is what it is, then so do I. It's very stuffy in here, Effie. You should go outside once in a while. More often than when nature calls. You go to bed too late and get up too late. You miss half the day. In fact, you have missed the entire summer. We may not have many more days like these.'

'I miss nothing I do not wish to miss, much less than you might imagine.'

*   *   *

Gwen went into the dining room to find the carafe, picking it up and then replacing it before going to the cellar instead. On the way down the path past the top lawn, she wiped the dust from the bottle on her skirt, holding the letter from Edward in her teeth. Edward, not Susan, had told her that there would be a letter waiting for her that morning. He had begged her not to rush off and fetch it but to read it after his visit. Seeing Euphemia with that pile of dull letters from her clients and her own placed there beside them had made Gwen suddenly sick. What if Edward one day forgot to put her full name on the envelope as he addressed it in a hurry.

Miss G. Carrick. In a hurry, a 'G' could be scrawled badly by Edward to look like an 'E'. The eleven o'clock sun was fierce out of the shade, and Gwen hurried back along the paths, under the wall of the kitchen garden and under the beech trees where she continued along one of the higher paths, past a wasps' nest and on to the boundary of the Carrick estate where she could look out over the fields if she chose, or out over the water where tall ships cut across the horizon of the glinting sea. Gwen opened the bottle; bending over, holding it between her feet. The noise of the cork coming out of the neck was satisfying in her solitude. She twisted the cork slowly from the screw with the letter laid across her skirts.

Dearest Gwen,

I am so happy with you. Does it seem like a monstrously obvious thing to say? To lie with my head in your lap and listen to you talk so seriously—these things matter enormously to me. You have no idea what a refreshing blast of goodness you have done to my soul. I have often wondered how any man could be content to loll in acres of petty small talk and twiddle flowers between thumb and finger when there is a universe of feeling to be communicated on all things—and you do so in such a fine and generous manner that it makes my whole self weak in admiration for you. Can you bear to read my inadequate missive? Perhaps you may think my words empty or second-hand when I have told you that I am inspired by you. It might seem too much to say, and yet I cannot say it enough—you must believe me when I say that there is no other person in this world near to you in your capacity for the extraordinary.

Do you see that full stop? I had to put down my pen and take a walk into town to prevent myself from spilling a torrent of cliché onto the paper. This is because there is no arrangement of words in any language which may adequately express the depth of my feeling—it gives me a sorry pain to try to make my brain and pen work in harmony. You are an inspiration and yet inspiration renders me speechless. Perhaps it is a mark of the truth of my feelings for you that they cannot be expressed in words. Would that I could kiss your mind, taste the light on your furrowed brow, swallow your every thought . . .

Gwen took a swig of the wine and wiped a drip from her chin with the back of her hand. She looked at the letter again and laughed. Edward, she said to herself, you are utterly incorrigible. He had engineered the manner of their meeting that morning so that when Gwen read his letter the two would match exactly. He had steered the conversation. Gwen had been talking about ordinary things: Murray and his arthritis, and how she didn't want to have anyone else, but knew that he was finding the work too much. Edward had teased her mind away from that, by talking about Eden. It was not a subject she could remain quiet about, and he had known it. So, while she had talked about her ideas on the impossibility of a species derived from a limited source, he had lain his head down in her lap and relished her impassioned speech. But the letter did not mention how after a while with his head in her lap, he had blown hot air through the fabric of her skirt, his mouth firm against the layers of cloth at her crotch, his hands gripping her at the hips so that she could not move. Yes, thought Gwen, there were some things which could not be written down.

CHAPTER XII

AUTUMN, 1859.

He had been to the summerhouse only twice since the spring of that year. Between those visits Euphemia had waited there for him every night. Each of those times he had come, she had failed to accost him with her findings. Frost underfoot. Rime touched the edges of every leaf on the ground. As she left her mark on them, treading clumsily in the old boots she had slipped her bare feet into at the back door, she thought of the wasted hours she had spent waiting for him to arrive when she could have been sleeping. It was all made worse by the fact that what Gwen had said was true. She had been sleeping away the best of the day, every day, because of this man. No more humiliation on his account, then, she told herself. His wife may come to her meetings again, if she chose. Euphemia would not approach each evening with dread, hoping that the woman would not arrive to taunt her. She could give the woman what she wanted with a clear head. Mr Scales could scuttle off to wherever he had come from.

'If he is not here tonight,' she said, 'you will never come back to this summerhouse after dark.

You will keep better hours and no one will have cause to scorn you. You will stop punishing your health over this man.' And yet she still could not prevent her mind from skipping back to the details of those visits.

The first time she had met him in there she had been practising Gwen's voice. Euphemia had made the most of her awkward situation; it had been dark enough not to have been recognised. At first she assumed it must have been Murray, and after the surprise of finding him there, she managed to talk with him as carelessly as if she might have done in broad daylight. She knew that on the days he came, the gardener spent a great deal of time in the summerhouse. It had seemed entirely logical to Euphemia that the man should still have been there at midnight because he spent so many hours in the old chair sucking on his pipe. Murray didn't like her, she knew that. He suspected her of being a fraud. But he liked Gwen because she spent so much time out of doors scratching away in her sketchbooks and collecting murky water from the ponds.

'I'm sorry to have disturbed you, Murray,' Euphemia had said. 'But you are aware that it is midnight?' She had been delighted at the way Gwen's voice was coming on and she smiled in the dark.

'I am the one who should apologise; I don't know who your Mr Murray is. I fell asleep in here, I hope you don't mind—there was no one here before. I must introduce myself; I am Edward Scales. You won't have heard of me, I shouldn't have thought.'

And so the confusion had been eliminated. But Euphemia had enjoyed masquerading as Gwen and prolonged his stay. Letting Mr Scales believe she was someone else extinguished her sense of propriety altogether. It was just the way it was in the dark with the ladies and the spirits. She could do and say anything that came into her head. Mr Scales had advanced towards her as he introduced himself. He had obviously wanted to take her hand, politely, but they were standing closer to each other than he had judged. His hand touched her breast through the thin fabric of her nightdress where the overcoat was not buttoned down. Euphemia had remained absolutely still for a moment because, on touching her breast, Mr Scales did not take away his hand but kept it there. In the dark, in those slight seconds, Euphemia felt the pulse from his heart beating down his arm and joining itself to her own body.

Euphemia had thought that she had begun to see how her talents could be employed beyond the confines of her drawing room; that she would take her ability out into an altogether different sphere of experience. Some of the words he had spoken into her ear as he'd touched her on those other visits were not to be found in any dictionary. He had opened her eyes to the true meaning of delirium. But, in her craving, she had found that she was in control of nothing, and now, finally in his company again, Euphemia was determined to straighten everything which had become crooked. She had been feeling cold, but now she found herself at a perfect temperature.

'Who's there?' Edward's voice was uncertain, but his tone was proprietorial, indignant.

'What audacity, sir. This is my property, and you are the trespasser.'

‘Miss Carrick? My apologies, to you and your companion. I meant to startle no one.’

‘There is nobody here but me.’

‘Then, I—Gwen, are you quite well?’

Euphemia paused at the sound of her sister’s name on his tongue. Images of the summer cantered before her eyes like the flicker of a daedalum. The memory of what he had done with her there suddenly sickened her. The slotted drum of illusion spun around in her mind. She heard her own heavy breath as if it did not belong to her. And it did not. What on earth had she wished for? If she met this man in daylight, she would not even know him until he spoke.

‘This charade cannot go on, Mr Scales. Whatever would your wife have to say about your behaviour, should she know the truth of it?’

‘I cannot say that I have not expected the event of this conversation.’

‘There is no conversation.’ Euphemia began to walk away from him and heard him take a few steps out of the summerhouse to follow her along the path.

‘Gwen, please stay and listen to me. I must explain.’

‘There is nothing to explain, and nothing I wish to hear from you. I am glad I will never have to look into your eyes and see the arrogance there. Shame on you.’

She left him standing in the dark and walked quickly, the cold in her lungs a relief. Physical exertion and pain were a liberation. To get away from him, to leave him there. She would go straight to bed and in the morning she would rise before her sister and this would end.

CHAPTER XIII

CARRICK HOUSE. CHRISTMAS, 1859.

Whilst Euphemia's meetings went on in the drawing room almost every night, Gwen vanished to parts of the house where she could not hear her sister communicating with the departed on the 'other side' in various odd voices. She went, despite herself, with a plateful of sweet almond pastry and pored over Darwin's text, getting sugar between the pages, finger marks on the green cloth covers. Some of it she did not understand, and she read again until she thought that she had it. Not that she believed any of it at first, she was merely trying to comprehend the argument. She believed that to believe in anything she had to be true to what she saw as her duty of doubt. To try to comprehend evidence from every angle. This was difficult because the evidence had been collected by this man Darwin, not by herself. And the arguments he put to her were from his head. She always came up against this problem, of having to assimilate the ideas of others, always other men without ever having the opportunity to question the man who spoke to her from the page. She did not want to be lectured to; she wanted to have a conversation. But in between trying to grasp whatever Darwin was talking about and hiding from her sister's clients, she agitated over Edward. He came and went as he pleased. Over the summer and into the autumn her life had been turned inside out, and yet on the surface nothing had altered. She made her studies and kept herself to herself.

Once, on a November morning, he had surprised her with an outburst of anguish, and it had taken some hours to persuade him that nightmares were only nightmares and that they meant nothing, and that whatever he had dreamed in his sleep could not possibly have been real. Here they were, she had said to him. Were they not happy together? Of course, they were. But still she felt that she might have been consoling him against her better judgement. The pain of being apart from him was real. He had seemed to read her thoughts, but then his absences were more protracted than ever. I will find you something extraordinary, he had told her. He brought her books, including the Darwin, as though it was enough. As though it would sustain her through the uncertainty of his long absences. She chided herself for being pleased when he did come, yet, she was pleased, she really was. The pleasure of finally seeing him standing under the big magnolia, after weeks and weeks, almost choked her. Knowing that it was childish to say that it wasn't fair didn't make it any less so. Freddie had almost given up trying to persuade her to quit her quiet habits and become the lively, sociable creature he wanted her to be. His invitations had become much less frequent. Sometimes, Gwen had wanted to go away, spend a week in London with her cousin, but the thought that she might miss one of Edward's visits while she was out riding with Freddie, or going to the opera, kept her to the confines of her own garden.

This, she thought to herself, is what women do. We wait, seemingly endlessly, without complaint, and without adequate solace, for men whose lives are too busy, too full, for them to stop and consider what degrees of frustration they heap thoughtlessly upon us.

CHAPTER XIV

CARRICK HOUSE. MARCH, 1860.

'Oh, please, not this again.'

'I didn't tell her "yes" outright, I only hinted.'

'I'm not doing any more blasted portraits of that overfed lapdog.'

'I think Miss Lotts has her nephew in mind.'

'Exactly so.'

'It will look bad if you don't at least come down and say hello.'

Gwen narrowed her eyes at her sister. 'Five minutes and not a second more. But, please, do not bother to introduce me to any of your clients. I will only be tempted to snub them and that will make you feel worse than me.'

Gwen was becoming increasingly agitated by Edward's absences, which left her feeling hollow and without purpose. The thought of being forced to mingle with her sister's clients for the evening, while Euphemia proceeded to tie her to promises to paint pug dogs or nephews on cushions was too infuriating to handle with decorum. She felt sure that she would offend someone in the next thirty minutes.

They were mostly middle-aged women that evening, and Euphemia, for once, did not try to introduce Gwen to any more of them. Some of them clucked around one of the newest hopefuls, down from London, mid-season too; and the *petites bouchées*, a particular speciality of Fergus, were gobbled up appreciatively before the proceedings began. The sour-faced lady, in her late twenties, perhaps, seemed to take an especial interest in the tiny pastries but was the only one of the clients who did not sample them.

Gwen made polite conversation with the dreaded Miss Lotts, trying to undo the promise Effie had made on her behalf.

'I must apologise, Miss Lotts,' she said. The woman took her arm and began to walk a few steps over to the large oval table where there was a gathering hush.

'Oh, call me Fanny. I am Fanny this evening, my dear.'

'My diary is already very full, Miss Lotts. I have a very busy few months ahead of me. Now, if you will excuse me I—'

The lamp had already been turned to its lowest flame, and sputtering feebly, it went out. Gwen peeled Miss Lott's fingers from her arm in the sudden dark, thinking, I don't care if I offend the old bat.

Someone said, 'Oh, that's a pity.'

Euphemia cleared her throat. When the shuffling of expensive cloth let up, Euphemia began to go into her trance. The lamp going out was a great disappointment as the clients liked to see her eyes roll whilst the spirits took possession of her body.

Gwen squirmed in the dark and closed her eyes as her sister spoke in various pinched baby voices before settling on the one which a lady recognised.

'I'm here, my little dumpling,' the woman called out.

Gwen's heart thudded; she didn't want this. It wasn't right. But she wasn't going to be weak about anything this evening.

It took some time, as there were a number of obstacles in her path. When at last she reached her sister's side at the head of the table she put out her hands to feel for her. She took a large handful of hair and tugged it. Gwen had been wondering what she could do to stop Euphemia's performance. When it had no effect at all she grew angry. She pulled very hard this time, and Euphemia let out a squeal, but continued to talk in the baby voice. Completely enraged, Gwen pinched her sister's arm through her silk shawl. As Gwen held on to her flesh, Euphemia cried out and in a pathetic voice murmured, 'Stop. You're hurting me.'

A low wail began from the lady's direction. The wail was punctuated with sobs and half-uttered, unintelligible sentences.

Gwen let Euphemia go.

The woman slid off her chair in a faint.

Gwen fumbled for the matches. As the wick took the flame the scene came into view. Someone ministered a bottle of smelling salts to the already recovering client who heaved herself back up onto her chair. Satisfied, soothing noises came from all directions. The evening had been a success. The woman, whose name was something like 'Bella' was moved to a more comfortable seat where she could be crowded and petted some more. Gwen whisked up the decanter and went off to fetch fresh water, saying to no one in particular, 'If she hadn't had herself so tightly laced then there wouldn't be all this fuss.'

Euphemia was still at her place at the head of the

table, apparently in the last stages of recovering herself from the trance.

Did this woman do what she had once done? Euphemia shivered, remembering the sensation of cold air on the soles of her feet and the warmth then, between them, as this woman's husband had pressed his hands against her arches, the insteps slippery in that particular brand of intimacy. Was that, and the other thing, what married women allowed their husbands to perform on them? Or were those things especially reserved for another kind of woman? She remembered the taste. The pungent saltiness and the slime in her throat. How idiotic she had been, to have imagined herself any different from the kind of woman she knew she had imitated. Euphemia made another little groan. She had been surprised to see Isobel again, and immediately reminded herself that nothing should be surprising any longer. She had been right to end it. Trust no one and nothing but your gift, she said to herself, and Euphemia opened her eyes.

CHAPTER XV

JUNE, 1860.

Gwen's face turned up into the deluge of rain and her long hair, undone, loose at last, was plastered over her naked body in thick strands which trailed off over the ground.

She stood up and peeled her hair from her body to plait a dirty rope, then wrapped it up in a shawl, a turban of silk dirtied and wet. They were both suddenly aware of the cold summer climate now. The rain continued to pour down through the trees and landed large droplets onto her clavicle and onto her breasts, which were firm and rounded on her chest. He pushed away the question of her age as he brushed at the leaves stuck on his own thighs. Oak, elm, ash. He gathered her up into his arms and kissed her neck, sucked at the rain which pooled on her collarbone but the moment was gone now, and she was cold, reaching for the damp blankets. He hated this parting. He both loathed and loved this weather.

Gwen was laughing now, as she dried herself, her jaw juddering in spasms. 'I don't know how you can stand there,' she said, wrapping the blanket tightly around herself, shutting out all sight of her body. She craned her neck, holding the weight of her hair with one hand and gazed up into the latticework of branches, then closed her eyes. The sensation of the spattering rain on her face.

When he had days like this, he could imagine himself doing something unthinkable, just so that he could have her to himself, all the time. For a split second, he held the image of Isobel, drowned at his hands in her rose-spattered bathtub, and this girl forever in his arms. A moment of intense ecstasy, which made him hard again, and which he did not bother to hide as he reached for his own grey blanket.

He ached to pull her onto the ground with him then, and just as she let her head down again and opened her eyes, the words spilled out of his mouth. He couldn't stifle them.

'I want you. I want to take you. I want to do, to do other things to you. I need to, I need to so very badly, to have you for my own and I can't—I'm—it's all impossible and horrible and wonderful all at the same time.'

He saw her face collapse in disgust.

'Don't spoil it, Edward. Why do you have to spoil it now? There's no need to make excuses. I can well imagine.' She was rubbing herself more thoroughly now and struggling with the inconvenient reality of being naked and filthy wet in a hidden spot of her garden, trying to rub some warmth back into the numbed parts of her. 'I've known long enough and only too well that you and I would never cross paths in normal life. We occupy different spheres.' She gave up trying to talk and manage the task with dignity.

'I'm sorry.'

'Don't ever be sorry; I couldn't stand it.'

They both rubbed their bodies in silence and then walked a short distance up a steep path to the old schoolhouse where they had left their piles of clothes forty minutes before.

It was a tiny building, once used for summertime lessons a dozen years before, disused now and crammed with old bits of garden furniture, bird baths, broken tools, mouse-traps and garden machinery. A gin-trap hung from the wall, its crushing teeth feathered with spider-webs. There was a small, wooden dovecot in there, and a perfectly good, sturdy table which had been cleared of broken plant-pots and brushed clean and now had a striped blanket over it. This was where they had laid their clothes. Gwen had found a serviceable chair amongst the tat and used it sometimes to watch the rain from the open doorway.

They shut the door now, closing themselves into the peculiar stuffiness of the schoolhouse. Something small scuttled in the rafters. They looked at each other. Her mind was empty except for the thought that she needed to wash herself. The rain came down around the schoolhouse, falling onto the old thatch and pouring off in noisy splashes. It was as well that there was some kind of noise for them both to focus on because neither had said anything yet. Edward was trembling. She couldn't tell whether he was overcome or just plain cold. She certainly felt clammy. But it was impossible for her to leave him there yet; he had a vacant look in his eyes and seemed rooted to the spot.

'Edward,' she almost whispered, afraid now of what was happening.

'I have failed you,' his voice cracked.

She stepped up to him, careful not to crush his naked toes under her shoes and grasped him with both hands. She felt annoyed, suddenly, that the aftermath of this event, which had come to its conclusion only ten minutes earlier, had opened a chasm between them that she alone was now compelled to dispel. She shook him slightly, not caring if it seemed odd. 'I'll see you in two weeks.'

'Tomorrow,' he said. 'I want to see you tomorrow.'

'Tomorrow I'll be busy. I'll be just the same in two weeks' time.'

'The day after tomorrow—will you see me then?'

She let go and turned away. She put on her ankle-length coat and finally unwrapped her hair, and put her hat on before taking up her bag of sketching things and paints and her old umbrella.

She let herself out into the rain without looking back, pulling the door shut behind her with her head bent against the drive of the rain and wind.

Gwen made herself stay calm. It was nothing. It was everything. For more than a year she had lived in perpetual waiting. The ache in her groin spread down her legs and she powered them forward and up along the overgrown, meandering pathways until she reached the tended areas of garden nearest the house.

It would come the next day. There would be nothing until the morning except this growing ache, like a goblin's fist in her muscles, here and then here; reducing her by degrees to a knotted heap of pain and subdued only slightly by bags of hot wheat. She could never have agreed to see Edward in that state. Sweating and rushing to empty her bowels every half hour. Sometimes when it came, she vomited, doubled over the chamberpot. It came alternately less and more. The last month it was less. She braced herself now. Whatever it was, that had made Edward react in his peculiar way could wait—and she certainly didn't intend crying herself silly over it.

A hot bag of wheat clutched to her belly, she remembered the flash of bizarre scientific inspiration which had occurred to her as she'd lain on the blanket. She placed a glass trough on the table in her room next to her microscope. She squatted, rummaged with her fingers and then wiped the result into the trough. Quickly she put the trough into position and looked through the microscope at her specimen, focusing in disbelief at the frenetic movement of undulations in the tails, like eels of an indescribably small size.

CHAPTER XVI

JULY 8, 1860.

She said, 'You probably fell asleep, and dreamed it. You'll have to tell me what you think you've already asked me.' Her heart pounded, in a way which made her feel nauseous, which made her feel like an idiot female. He'd never asked her anything. This was what it felt like, she supposed. Or did it? The wind was getting up again in the trees; its sound crammed her ears and knotted her brain. She knew that she would accept, having never dared to even think of this kind of conversation happening between them. She watched his face; he looked so confused.

'I am quite certain that I came here, two days ago. We met in that very heavy storm. You were hurrying away and I caught up with you. I can't have dreamed it, Gwen. I was soaked to the skin. And you had forgotten your umbrella—you were wearing that huge hat. Rivers of rain fell off you, as though you were a—'

'I didn't go out that early, Edward,' Gwen spoke slowly, tried to keep the anxiety out of her voice.

'Well, in any case, let us not argue over it. I was inconsiderate to ask you in such a way in the first place. But you must have received my letter by now? I sent it the same day.'

'No, I haven't had your letter. Ask me again, Edward. It isn't raining yet. Besides, you must know by now that I'll accept.'

'I have been making preparations,' he said, 'to go to Brazil, and I would like you to consider accompanying me, as illustrator of the natural world there.'

Gwen's heart thudded in a different way. Don't let him see, she thought. But she fixed her gaze on his face, and as she did, she knew that she didn't want the thing she'd imagined. It was only vanity, and it made her cringe to think of it. 'You are asking me to go with you to a place that is very far away. I have lived all my life here. I would leave my sister alone. It is a large house to be alone in. There are other things to consider, besides.' Inwardly, she leaped in excitement. Stuff the silly thought that he was going to ask for something different. Now her garden seemed to be a gate, not the prison she had resigned herself to. She would be with him every day, and those interminable weeks of waiting to see him would be over—perhaps for years.

'These are not insurmountable obstacles.' He faltered. A sister? She'd told him that she lived alone, hadn't she?

'This has come out of nowhere. Why Brazil, of all places?'

'Because of you. Because when I visited the Glasshouses at Kew, I was constantly reminded of you, and this place. You *in* this place, and you painting away at your beetle studies, and what you said, about beauty and science.' He did not say that it was also because of something she had once told him about there being more insects in the world than any other kind of creature. Edward had discovered, during a conversation with Jacobs one night, that some believed most of the world's insects had not yet been named. He thought if he was to stand any chance of finding an insect as yet unknown to science, then the Brazilian forest seemed the best place to begin. He had begun practising his *scalesii* inventions again.

'You want me to run away.'

'Think on it,' Edward said, his voice flattened. Their meeting was over. He began to move away. Five paces. He stopped, half turned. 'I have already bought the best-quality artists' paper and some vellum. Sketchbooks. I would rather it was your work filling the pages than that of some stranger.' He felt inside his jacket, brought out a folded document and held it out to her. 'Look.'

Well, that's still not good enough, she thought. Can you not tell me now that you love me, after all? But she held onto the papers for long minutes, reading off the list of provisions and equipment. So many different items. Her brow wrinkled in concentration. 'What are the numbers, the codes beside each entry?'

'Let me see. Ah, yes. It is to indicate which crate each item shall be packed into.'

'This,' she said, her finger on a line of script. 'Surely, this is not right.'

He came closer to her, and she smelled the sweat of him in his ungainliness.

'Oh, yes. That is quite right.'

'*Such* a size. Will that be necessary? What on earth could one find to preserve—or is it meant to be used the way one packs fruit, I wonder?'

'Well, one never can quite predict, but that is the thrill. Don't you see?'

'The weight would be almost immeasurable.'

'I had to have it. I went to the glassworks and there it was, and it—well, it inspired me. Yet not half as much as you.'

* * *

Half an hour later, he was getting ready to leave again. He picked up the lacquered bamboo sticks which had held her hair in place and handed them back to her. He turned away while she twisted her hair into a knot.

'Did you hear that?' Gwen touched Edward's sleeve. 'I thought I heard it before; I'm sure I'm not mistaken this time.'

Edward looked at her, and as their eyes met, they both heard the noise, louder this time and undeniably there. 'Some kind of animal? Perhaps a weasel with a rabbit,' he said.

'No,' Gwen shook her head, and looked away into the middle distance, scrunching her eyes into slits as though that might make her hear better. 'No,' she said again, the blood gone from her face. 'It's more human.' Gwen was yards away from Edward, before he realised that he was running after her.

* * *

Edward did not want to go into Carrick House now. He'd thought about what it might be like in there often enough; conjured up a picture of something extraordinary, even though he knew that in all probability it was the kind of house you would not remark upon except for its occupants. Now he had discovered that his wife had been there. Spiritualism and hokus pokus; Isobel was mocking him again. He'd been so sure that she had been lying, calling his bluff. He knew for certain that Gwen was not a Spiritualist. The very idea that she would indulge in that particular abomination was so preposterous. He'd laughed in Isobel's face. But she'd described the house in such detail. What was he to do? He thought of Gwen with her furrowed forehead scuffing the ground with her foot and imagined that he knew what it must be like, to be her. Waiting for him to appear. Looking under the tree, not letting herself hope that he might be there. And then the chill from the ground penetrating their bodies. No wonder she was guarded, angry. She was besieged by his long absences, and now Isobel, too, with her silly games. He'd meant to ask her to come away with him in a different way. He'd meant to use different words, but they'd rolled around at the back of his throat. His apology for his inconsistencies; it was a bolus refusing to be anything but that.

The house appeared from behind the screen of tall laurels: red brick, amongst so much green. Edward stopped in his tracks to admire it. Gwen caught his arm and pulled him forward into its shadow. 'This house,' he said to her, 'it's barely twenty years old, is it?'

'What? Oh, yes. The other one was demolished to make room for it. I'm told it was a scandalous thing to do. At least they left the garden—'

* * *

It began to rain. Hard spittles smacked the windows at his back as Edward suppressed his desire to flee the place. Gwen turned to the bundle propped up in the chair. 'Mr Harris, help is here now. I'm sure Mr Scales will be able to get your eye open.'

Edward hesitated, concentrating on the pool of

light at the table.

Gwen went outside and pumped a jugful of water. She brought it to the table with a glass. Edward looked critically at the dwarf. His eyelid was swollen, and where Euphemia had stitched the lids together, there was a general crustiness of blood mixed with yellow secretions. Edward glanced at Gwen, wishing that some of her apparent calm would settle on him.

'I can remove these, but, as for the rest, I am no specialist. I will be as careful as possible.'

'I'd be much obliged, sir,' said Fergus.

Edward said, 'We'll have to bathe it first. Some boiled and cooled salty water would be best, I think.'

As Gwen moved around him organising things, checking the water was at the right temperature, spooning salt into it, Edward wondered at her composure. Bed sheets tied around a man, pinning his arms to his sides, fixing his head still—he couldn't imagine the terror of it. He couldn't imagine why this man had not been able to save himself. Did she pounce on him? Did she trick him? Somewhere in the house Euphemia was locked safely away in her room. Edward recalled Gwen's face as she'd led Euphemia away from the scene. Euphemia bedraggled and wild-looking, slumping into her sister's arms, letting herself be moved away. Madness. There were all kinds of madness. Perhaps this was what Gwen had meant when she'd told him that there were other things to consider. Not the shame of being the mistress at all.

As he worked gingerly at the threads of silk, Edward's own eyes pricked with exhaustion and he battled to keep them open. Gwen stood behind

Fergus with her hands on her servant's shoulders, her body pushed up against the chair.

No one said anything. The atrocious task in front of him seemed to demand an equally atrocious silence. Here I am, he thought, picking thread from eyelids. It was all too much of a mess, yet he had to find some way of persuading her to accept his offer. His hands fumbled. He thought of the wasted hours young women like Euphemia spent bending over needlework; it'd be enough to drive one to madness, perhaps. He wiped his face on his sleeve. If he could have bright daylight he could get this done much quicker. But the lamplight made everything uncertain. Was that silk thread or was that a bit of flesh? He had to decide. The blood oozed out of the puffed-up lids, and Fergus sat tight, bracing himself against the back of the chair. He'd be a mess in the morning. Gwen was watching Edward. He wanted to know what she was thinking. Was she making her decision, or was she lost in some other place not connected to where she stood? Edward cleared his throat several times just to make a noise. An hour passed and he wanted to rest, but it was better just to get on and finish the job.

CHAPTER XVII

THE TIMES, Wednesday, October 2, 1866.

MURDER TRIAL AT THE OLD BAILEY.

ON the second day of The Crown v. Pemberton, a veritable rumpus was observed outside the Central Criminal Court, as members of the public, keen to obtain entry to the gallery, had gathered in large numbers.

Witnesses for the Prosecution were called after the opening. The first, Mr James Morrisson, said, 'I was valet to Mr Scales since the date of his first marriage up to the time he went away. I was never given notice to leave the house, and I carried on there until the present time, or near enough.'

Q: 'And how did you become aware of the untimely passing of Mr Scales?'

A: 'I heard the noise, downstairs, in the morning. As I came down, I came upon the three men that I know to be the two police constables and her husband.'

Q: 'Do you mean Mr Pemberton, the prisoner's husband, Mr Morrisson?'

A: 'I do that.'

Q: 'You had been at the deceased's residence the night previous to this?'

A: 'Yes, and most of the day as well. Mr Scales was in town, and I knew that he'd be in need of my services. As it turned out, his wants were not many, and I had not much to attend to, so I retired. I was aware of his having visitors—a lady. I saw her enter the house about three in the afternoon. From an upstairs window I saw her approach the house, and Mr Scales let her in himself. He'd already said that he wouldn't want to be disturbed at all should he get a visit from anyone, so I kept to the back of the house until I heard the door bang shut about seven or so. He did not ring for me all night, so I did not go near his room.'

Mr Shanks for the Defence: 'Is it not the case, Mr Morrisson, that you were not wanted by the deceased Mr Scales in the days leading up to his death, but that you forced your way into the property, in your own words, "to make his life a misery"?'

A: 'I never said so.'

Q: 'We shall see, Mr Morrisson.'

Other witnesses included staff from households neighbouring the Victim's address. Mrs Peters gave her evidence thus: 'I have been housekeeper at the property adjoining the Scales' residence for some years and have always noticed the quantity of visitors, or lack of them, going into that house. On the morning of the last but one day of July this year I saw a man approach the house and I heard his knocking. I remember this quite clearly as it was so persistent. I also recall it in detail as I remember wondering at the time that a person should knock so when the house was empty. Then, on looking out more carefully, I saw who was there, and, of course, I was surprised to see Mr Morrisson returned after such a long absence. Well, naturally as his banging and knocking was a nuisance I sent out Smythe, my footman.'

The footman, Mr Smythe, then later gave his evidence: 'I am Smythe, footman to the Picard household, and on the morning of July 30th I was instructed to go out and tell the gent making the racket that the house he was banging on was empty. I went out and I said to the man, who I knew to have been valet there long since but knew not on common terms, "Here, the place is empty, sir." In reply, he said to me that he knew Mr Scales was in there for certain and that he was d—d if he wasn't going to get in there and have words. He was very agitated and of a very high colour in the face, and persisted with his banging. I stood there some minutes and tried to persuade him that his racket was useless, when, all of a sudden, the door opened, and I saw Mr Scales himself. Mr Scales did not seem at all pleased to see who was stood on his doorstep. 'What the D— are you doing here?' he says to Morrisson, and Morrisson says back to him, 'More to the point, what the blazes are you doing here?' except stronger words than that was used, sir. 'I've more right to be in this property than you,' says Morrisson to Mr Scales, and then he pushed his way over the doorstep, and Mr Scales done nothing to stop him. I asked Mr Scales if he would like me to assist and he said he'd deal with the matter himself. Just before he shut the door, I heard Morrisson telling him he'd stay there whether he liked it or not and that he'd make his life a misery while he was at it.'

Doctor Alexander Jacobs gave his evidence: 'I attended the body of Mr Edward Scales at around ten o'clock on the morning of the 7th of August. The body had been turned over, but, other than that, had not been moved. Evidence of the body having lain face down on the floor for some time was immediately apparent. Because of this effect, it was not at first obvious that any trauma had occurred to the body. However, on detailed examination later in the day, it became clear that death might have occurred through strangulation by application of a ligature to the neck.'

Cross-examined by Mr Shanks:

Q: 'You said just now, that "death might have occurred by strangulation". And yet you were not so reticent when you stated at the inquest that you were of the "firm opinion that the man had been strangled to death". Are you saying that you have changed your mind? Or that you were not really sure in the first place?'

A: 'In retrospect, sir, I conclude that the amount of alcohol present in the body of the deceased could just as easily have caused death to occur. I do not, in retrospect, believe that the marks to the neck, which were slight, corresponded with other, more conclusive, cases of death by strangulation that I have attended during my career.'

CHAPTER XVIII

CARRICK HOUSE. JULY 9, 1860.

Edward woke to the sound of a mistle thrush. Its song just beyond the window joined with the last of the dawn chorus. Lying there, listening to the burbling melody, he remembered a comment of Gwen's one morning; that the dawn chorus must be a wave of birdsong, as it moved from east to west, following the break of day in a relay of sound all over Europe, perhaps even the world, as it turned on its axis; and then, at nightfall, the sound coming back as a kind of inverted echo, west to east, the pinking and chipping sounds announcing the end of the day. Can you imagine, she'd said, if one could *see* it, as God must. It would be a tidal surge of sound, moving in an endless ripple of song across the globe.

His body felt clammy and cold; he shifted around under the covers and tried to plump up his pillow. He'd asked her where she had read this theory. Damn. That a mere girl should happen upon a thought as profound as that. He'd taken her rather too roughly some minutes afterwards. And then when he had left her, he'd written down everything she had said in his notebook, suffused with a surge of love.

There was the most God-awful smell in the room and the fust of mildew. The blankets felt heavy. He felt around underneath his hip for the hard object pressing against his skin. It slipped around in the folds of the rucked-up bed sheet. Edward listened to the thrush for a short while, turning the object in his fingers, wondering about the best thing to do. He did not turn his head to the left where he knew Gwen's servant, Harris, lay sleeping next to him. By God, of all the things that had happened to him, waking up next to a dwarf had to be one of the most novel. The object in his hand was about the size of a robin's egg, its surface both smooth and pitted. He couldn't think how a marble could have wound up in bed with him. But then, by the smell of the room it had not been in use for a long time. He couldn't stay there. He heard stifled strokes of a clock somewhere striking five. Getting into his clothes haphazardly, Edward skimmed over what he could remember of the night before. He stuffed the marble into his waistcoat pocket. In the dim light he tried to check his own time against the chimes he thought he had counted. Edward sighed heavily. Gwen would not be swayed, he thought, now that this had happened. The situation was only slightly better than if her servant had been dead.

As he tiptoed towards the door with his shoes in his hand, Harris spoke out from the bed. 'Much obliged to you, sir, for all that you have done.'

Edward paused. 'Ah, yes. Don't mention it. Take care of that eye,' and out of curiosity, he stepped back onto the square of carpet and moved over to the bed to peer at Fergus. 'Look here, um, Harris. About this business.'

Fergus hauled himself up and spoke as if he'd rehearsed his lines all night. 'She hadn't slept for about three or four days by yesterday, and I ain't no medic, but I'd say that was half the problem, sir.'

Edward sat down on the end of the bed, keeping his face turned away, so that he would not have to breathe in the rotten air expelled by Fergus. He felt sure his own breath smelled just as bad. He needed to spit and gargle.

'Has she suffered from insomnia—I mean to say, been like that before?'

'Not since I was at the house, sir.'

'And do you know by any chance what the other half of the problem would be?'

'A romantic involvement.'

Edward frowned. 'You know this for certain?'

'I do.'

'How unfortunate that she should take it out on you.'

'It was an accident.'

Edward was about to ask what kind of accident could possibly have resulted in the man having his eye sewn up when Fergus said, 'You've your own romantic involvement, as well, sir. Though I think you've picked the more sensible of the two of them.'

'What? Don't presume to speak to me of things you know absolutely nothing about.'

'Well, I doubt Miss Gwen is ever likely to try sewing your eyes up and leaving you in a cellar to freeze half to death, now is she?'

'Have a care, Mr Harris. You've no business speaking about Miss Carrick like that. And I'll thank you not to speak of her in those tones again.'

Fergus shifted against the bolster. He breathed deeply through his nose. 'South America's a long way to go.'

Edward narrowed his eyes, 'Watch your tongue, Harris.'

'So, did you never finish your *special* medical studies then? Last time I heard, you was going to be a famous doctor. Writing some big paper, she said, all about her. And then *pouf!* No more. Now, correct me if I'm wrong, but I don't think you abandoned Miss Jaspur for lack of interest. So, as I say, South America is a long way to go.'

Edward stood up. 'Who in hell's name are you?' He reeled, felt himself sway.

But Fergus had not finished. 'Not saying I blame you, mind. Natalia snared all her men, including me. Don't know though, what Miss Carrick would think about that.'

Edward found himself grasping the little man's neck and squeezing. 'Tell me how you know these things.' Fill his vile little mouth with feathers and let him choke. He released the pressure, eased himself back. 'How dare you.' Edward forced himself not to shout. 'How dare you speak that woman's name in the same breath.' He stared at Fergus. He's lying, he thought, he's lying. He must have said something to Euphemia; he must have done something, known something. Perhaps he'd been taunting Euphemia with information about her sister's reputation. He'd infuriated Euphemia and she had acted on her anger. Edward breathed heavily, waiting for the impulse to grind Fergus into nothing to subside as the extent of Isobel's involvement became clear. Edward knew he'd be a fool not to recognise it. Waiting for him to answer when he could see that he would not. 'I should kill you now,' he said, 'but I'll not be a murderer for her.' He glanced at Fergus. 'Yes. I know. I can see it.' He lowered his voice so that it was barely audible. 'My wife sent you here. But mark my words, whatever she's promised you, she will never honour it. You are out of your depth, and you'll do well to keep your mouth shut. By God, you will.'

The door handle turned, followed by a faint knocking. Edward went and put his ear to the door before opening it a crack.

Gwen pushed open the door and pulled Edward into the corridor. 'How is Mr Harris? Is the swelling very much worse?' Gwen's own eyes were dark-circled and bloodshot.

'It looks worse than it really is. A lot of bruising, that's all. Your poultice has helped enormously.'

Female hysteria, he thought. Common enough. Easy to handle that. Get some sedatives into the girl. But, by God, who was he trying to fool? He needed to get Gwen out of the house, away from everything. Isobel's hand was all over this. Her poisonous tendrils had spilled over the boundary he had constructed and were threatening to choke everything. He turned the object around in his fingers, not realising that he'd taken it from his pocket. He could still persuade Gwen to go with him to Brazil. He felt Fergus' presence in the closed room behind his back and he dropped the object into the folds of his pocket again and bent to tie his laces. As he straightened up, he saw Euphemia running at him. She had on a soiled nightdress and was screeching as she wielded a knitting needle in her hand.

'For goodness sake, Euphemia,' Gwen bellowed, adding to the din. 'Pull yourself together and stop behaving like such an idiot. This really is too much. Especially before breakfast—'

As Edward stepped neatly aside to avoid Euphemia, he stuck out his foot and tripped her up. Her face was stuck all over with matted strands of hair, glistening with fresh mucous; and her features swollen and red-blotched from weeping. Her nightdress was unbuttoned down to her navel. Edward looked away as Gwen bent over her sister to try and tidy her.

Edward helped Gwen take Euphemia to her bedroom. There was a strong smell of shit-filled chamberpot in there; it shrouded them in a clinging gossamer of stink as soon as the door was opened. Shafts of light hit the heaped chaos of clothes and torn papers. Gwen made her sister get into bed. Edward watched her tuck Euphemia into the covers as though nothing much more than a cold in the head had aggravated her temper. She'll not come with me, he thought. I'll not be able to drag her away from this.

Gwen pulled the window down on its cord, letting in a gust of fresh air.

'You didn't by any chance mention my travelling plans to that Harris, did you?'

Gwen picked her way over the mess on the floor towards Edward. (She stooped to pick up a visiting card. The photograph showed a beautiful, clean-shaven young man. She turned the card over. The printing was scratched out.) Distractedly, she said, 'No, I never discuss private things with—Why?'

'Oh, nothing. He was mumbling something last night, probably just talking in his sleep. I may have got the wrong end of the stick.'

'Susan will deal with all of this.' Gwen waved her arm over the mess, letting the card drop. 'Let's go downstairs now.'

'By the way,' Edward said, 'I came across this in your guest room—an artefact from your childhood, perhaps?' He took her wrist gently and put the marble into her hand. Puzzled, Gwen glanced at it briefly before shutting the door behind them.

* * *

Fergus heard the commotion outside the bedroom door but did not pay much attention to it. He had drawn the curtains wide open and pulled back the covers from the bed. It must be hidden in a fold. He turned both pillows out of their cases and shook everything. He scrabbled around the mattress like a terrier looking for its rat. Then he got down and inspected the underneath of the bed. He lifted the carpet at its edges. He shook out all the bedding piece by piece, and folded every sheet and blanket in turn. Not an easy thing to do. His arms ached. He tussled with the panic bubbling in his throat and sat down on the heap of folded bedding to get his breath back. He began to doubt the memory of putting it under his pillow in the small hours before dawn. Mr Scales had been snoring like a drunk. He had not imagined it. He had fallen asleep with the balas diamond in his fist. He got up off the pile of bedclothes and began to unfold and shake out the sheets again, though he knew it was now a waste of time. His tears stung, and they blocked his already impaired vision. He poured the salty water from the jug into the bowl Gwen had set down and then put on the clothes which had been laid out for him the night before.

It was time to reassess his situation. This bit of theatre was over; there were better things to worry about. Bugger. He had to find it. He couldn't leave without it.

* * *

Edward looked about him in the library where he was waiting for Gwen to return after speaking at length to her maid. It had become clear to him that Gwen's sister had chosen the maid's one night off in the month to cause her havoc in the household. His own brief first appraisal of Susan at Carrick House that morning had been that she was not the kind of woman you would want to have about the house if you chose to misbehave in such a manner. Her hands were large and square. And she had an attitude he would never seek to cross in a month of her days off.

The library was at the front of the house and its window had an excellent view of the drive; the fields either side of it with their crops of barley and flax were full of flowers; swallows skimmed low for insects over the heads of the colourful blooms and ripening seed heads.

Gwen shut the door behind her, and Edward turned away from his gazing. He had been lost in his situation for a moment, but now he tried to guess what Gwen had to say. He waited for a moment and when she said nothing he asked if there was anything more that he could do to help. She shook her head. 'I'll go with you to Brazil, Edward. You need not worry that my sister's hysterics will detain me here.'

'Thank God. Thank you, I hardly know what to say.'

'I am sure you're tired, and want to go to your own house and sleep properly.'

'You are exhausted.'

'Yes.'

'But you are sure that you want this?'

'I am. It is not because of what my sister has done, or only partly. It has become impossible for me to live with her, but it is also impossible for me to continue to live the way I have been since the day I met you. I want to be with you every day, and I want to expand my scientific knowledge. So, yes, I am sure I want this, because I want you.'

Edward lunged across the room and smothered her in a tight embrace. 'You can't know how glad that makes me.'

'I can guess.'

'I have almost seven weeks to make the last arrangements. I must return to London for a short while. I have been given the name of a gentleman who will verify and buy specimens and I must meet with him to discuss terms. And there are other matters to tie up. But these things are routine, I should be able to return in three weeks' time. Our ship embarks from here.'

'You mean from Falmouth?'

'Yes. I thought that if you did decide it was something you wanted, then you would not want to travel all the way to London or to Liverpool.'

Gwen nodded and closed her eyes. She was sure that this was what she wanted. It frightened her more than anything and it gave her a thrill it was difficult to conceal. It was worth enduring the next weeks, no matter what kind of hysterics and difficulties Euphemia devised, when afterwards she would be able to be true to herself and to be with Edward.

'This is what we were always meant to do,' he said. 'Our joining together, in this way, is more divine than anything ever imagined.'

Gwen opened her eyes again to find that he was

leaning in; before she could speak he had clamped his mouth around her partly open lips.

CHAPTER XIX

HELFORD PASSAGE, CORNWALL. SEPTEMBER, 1860.

Susan stood with her hip against the kitchen table in Carrick House and rubbed at the brass key with her apron. Fergus watched her bring the key up to her face and blow the last bits of soil from its crevices. She was calming herself after all the bother with the large crate of glassware which had arrived that morning from town. There had been some wrangling, but Susan had managed eventually to persuade the deliveryman and his lad to get the thing down the outside steps to the cellar. She eyed Fergus over the jumble of things on the kitchen table. He had been emptying another cupboard, and was halfway through examining the contents. The stone jar of flour was half sifted into a large bowl and a white layer of dust covered everything else. Susan cleared her throat and rubbed harder.

'I usually do that kind of thing in the springtime, Mr Harris,' Susan met his eye, 'and that flour was only bought very recent, as you well know. You won't find no grubs in there.'

'I ain't looking for grubs, Miss Wright.'

'Then what are you up to? It's making such a mess.'

Fergus put down the sieve with a resigned huff. 'I'm sorry, Miss Wright. I thought, with all the house being so upside down, I might have found—'

'Yes, Mr Harris?'

'You've been at this place a while, Miss Wright. Do you think—I mean, does this business seem out of the ordinary to you?'

'I never do the spring cleaning like that, if that's what you mean, Mr Harris.'

'No. I mean the thing with the key. Her hiding it all over. And the other things, as well.'

'You mean has Miss Euphemia done this before?'

'It is her, then? Not the other?'

Susan pulled out a chair and sat on it, holding the brass winding key in her lap. She looked at him square in the face. 'Mr Harris, Miss Gwen would never do anything to annoy me, she'd never do anything to upset me and she'd never ever make extra work for me. I know that girl. She's as true as the day is long.'

'And what would you have to say if I was to tell you that Miss Gwen has been making plans to go away?'

'Don't be daft now, Mr Harris. Where would she go?'

'I ain't being daft, Miss Wright; she's going,' he lowered his voice, 'to South America, Miss Wright. Yes,' he said seeing her expression change, 'Brazil.'

'I swear, Mr Harris, you shouldn't tell tales on people like Miss Gwen. It's not nice.'

'Maybe, but it's true.'

'How come you know all about it?'

'Walls and doors have lugs, don't they?'

'Why? Why would she do that to us, leaving us with her batsy sister?' Susan covered her mouth with her hands still holding the key. 'I never said that.'

'Yes, you did. And it's right enough. She is barmy.'

'We'll never manage her in this house on our own, Mr Harris. I'll have to have words with Miss Gwen.'

'You won't change her mind.' Fergus laughed under his breath.

'I might; she's a good girl. She's not like most people.'

'She's running off, Miss Wright, with a man. The man what sorted this out,' he gestured at his bad eye, still very much bruised and sore. Fergus closed his good eye, and he sighed deeply. He felt so bad this morning, awful. His head throbbed. He knew that a fever was building up. He poured himself a drink of water and wiped the sweat from his face with his sleeve.

'I never heard anything so out of character in all my life, Mr Harris. Are you sure?' Susan put the brass key on the floury table and stood up to tower over Fergus. 'You don't make no sense at all today, Mr Harris. I reckon you've got this all wrong. I reckon what you heard is that Miss Gwen is having her sister put somewhere for a while. Though it would be a shame for the family, it wouldn't be no shame for this house. I could do without all her ghostly visitors, all them ladies in their black lace and musty taffeta. Now that *is* extra work, having them in the house four or five times a week. Wears me out—I never sleep when they've been.'

Fergus gave a wry grin, and stopped himself from swaying. 'You should have told me before, Miss Wright; I'd have set your mind at rest.'

'How's that?'

'Ghostly visitors, Miss Wright? It's nought but a

trick. Well, maybe a gift, in her case, she does it so well.'

'And what would you know about ghosts, Mr Harris?'

'Nothing; but I know a damn, pardon me, fine ventriloquist when I see one. And not just that, the voices, my word, she does the voices.'

'But that's just it, Mr Harris. The noises that come out of her, they don't come from this world.'

'You're right there, Miss Wright. They come straight out of another world. I've often wondered where she learned it. I mean, I've seen it done often.'

'At meetings, in that big house you was at, in London?' Susan sat down again and shoved some of the jumble of jars and bowls to the side to lean over the table and fix Fergus in an avid gaze.

Fergus shook his head. 'No, Miss Wright, nowhere as nice as that house. No, I saw it done in Saville House, in Leicester Square, years ago.'

'At a Spiritualist meeting,' Susan said.

Fergus laughed through his nose, shaking his head; his brain felt as though it was coming loose. 'Saville House was a den of infamous beings, that's what they called it. I used to go there, I used to go there an awful lot.'

'You saw spirits there, Mr Harris?'

'Oh Lord help me, no. What I saw was—' His tone softened, seeing Susan's expression. 'What I saw was all kinds of trickery, Miss Wright. Like Miss Euphemia does, with the voices. Some was so lunatic you wouldn't believe it.'

'Mad people?'

He smiled. 'It was mad what they believed they was paying for, in some of them rooms. Learned

Pig was one. There was a pig kept in a cellar that was supposed to be able to read and write. And the lady who had her head cut off, every night, every half hour.'

'Oh, my word, how awful.'

'But you see, Miss Wright, it were a trick. There was two of them, the same, or almost. But see? I almost told you how it was done, and I ain't supposed to.'

'Who'd know?'

'Me. Or take the Horned Lady. She was a friend of mine. She wouldn't mind me telling you, she showed me her scars on more than one occasion.'

'I'm not sure I think you should be telling me anything about that, Mr Harris, if it's all the same to you.'

'She weren't no lady friend! She was a pal, like. Like you and me.'

'Are we, Mr Harris?'

'Well, I should hope so, Miss Wright. See, what I'm saying to you is, there ain't no need for you to bother about ghosts, and what have you. It ain't real.'

'I'm sure I want to believe you, Mr Harris, but on the other hand, I'm not so sure. It might be nice, in a funny kind of way, to think you could get messages, from the other side.'

'But the dead can't talk. Once you're gone, that's it.'

'This has turned very gloomy indeed all of a sudden.'

'Then we shall talk of it no more, Miss Wright. I shall undertake to divert, delight or charm you in more light-hearted ways.'

'Mr Harris! Whatever shall I do with you?'

The bell pinged and bounced on the wall. Susan started, half jumped out of her seat. She gathered the tray of breakfast things and hurried out of the room with it. Fergus gave up the search in the kitchen. He felt very bad. He felt that he needed to lie down, and so he did, right there on the floor. The cold stone was like a balm to the fire that now engulfed him. He hadn't the strength to loosen his shirt; he just let the weight of his head press against the cold floor and waited for Miss Wright. Fergus wasn't sure if she would come in time. He let his mind sink a little further as his temperature raged. Here was something to hang onto. Something real, something that had been good in his life.

London: May, 1858. He'd been at Saville House in Leicester Square, that den of infamous beings which changed like the weather. He'd been there, as usual, to look out for an interesting angle, a new trick to add to his own tired repertoire of regurgitating objects from his stomach at will. Saville House: it could send your head into a spin if you didn't know what to expect. If you wanted, for sixpence, you might watch a lady have her head cut off and suffer no ill effects. You could go to the North Pole in another room, or see a diorama of gold-diggers in California. From dingy corners, ventriloquists would send a whisper into your ear, making you jump half out of your skin. Jugglers were two a penny. Fergus saw living serpents wrapped around a lady's naked body. And another lady whose enormous snake might have swallowed him whole. Its huge body rasped as it moved slowly over her skin and between her thighs. He saw her muscles quiver at the feat of holding the beast up for so long, but she was not at all afraid of it. This was the place where he met many other people who were like him, though he never spoke to any of them. They acknowledged him in the staircase and in the corridors. A nod, a pat on the shoulder, a quiet bustling family of strangers. No one asked Fergus for his money. His size was his ticket in Saville House. He moved unseen through the hall and down the cellar steps to see the learned pig, which seemed to have lost the will even to grunt. Once, he had seen hens' eggs being hatched out in a steam-filled cage in one room up the stairs, while in the adjacent chamber the lady was having her head cut off again. Above the disgusted gasps and muted shrieks he heard singing. Distracted, he had watched the exhausted chick still with its shell stuck to its rear end. It panted heavily. The singing was so light and airy it sounded to him like a nightingale—how he imagined a nightingale would sound. He watched the chick roll onto its side and flex its tiny legs. He didn't wait to see what happened next. He knew it already. The feathers would not dry out in the steam. He walked away from it.

The Horned Lady was having a break. A bright, jade-coloured turban of silk covered the lumps on her forehead where the ivory had been pushed in under her skin.

'Hello, my sweetheart,' she said from behind her thin cigar.

'Madam, good evening.' He bowed low, making her laugh.

'You little ones are a caution.' She drew heavily on the cigar and blinked her eyes through the thick smoke. 'You're always on the lookout. You lost somebody?'

'Who is that singing?'

'Mysterious Lady. They say she's so flippin' ugly, she'd turn you into stone, so she keeps her face hid—well, she ain't so much ugly as just covered in hair. Sings like a lark, though. As a matter of fact I was meaning to go and have a proper word with her. See if she wanted to pair up. But you know how it is.' She took another long draw on her cigar and tapped off the ash, spilling it over her silk gown. 'Looks like she's worked her spell on you.' She blew smoke over his head and grinned. Her perfect false teeth gleamed in the lamplight. 'Go on, I don't mind. Upstairs on the right. Now, I'll have to get this off my head and earn the rent.'

It was late; almost chucking-out time. Fergus climbed the stairs. Narrow and steeper than the staircase leading up from the hall, they curved as he followed the sound of her singing. There were so many bodies crushed into the small room Fergus couldn't get a peep, but her voice wound over heads and through legs to reach him.

'Look at her shoulders, then. That little lady is hairier than what I am.'

'Show us yer face, love.'

'Shut up, I'm listening to her singing.'

'Show us yer bits then, luvvie.'

'It'll no' be a lassie at a', maybe.'

The singing went on, unwavering through all the catcalls until the room began to empty a little. Fergus found spaces. He wriggled his way to the front, squashed next to the wall. The singing was pure and light, unchanging. The black veil over her face fell way below her chin. It billowed when she took a breath. The song finished, and she remained in position, with one leg stretched out, toe pointing.

Fergus dawdled his way down the staircase.

Saville House was now closed to the public, but there were still plenty of punters milling around in the larger rooms downstairs and the main gallery. The sounds of their voices permeated the rest of the building. Fergus looked through the balustrade on the first-floor landing and surveyed the scene below him through a thick haze of tobacco smoke. One man stood out from the rest. His coat was long, almost touching his unfeasibly shiny shoes, and he stood right next to the main entrance. He looked as if he was waiting for a cab. People less conspicuous pushed past the man now and then, and he was obliged to make way. Every so often he took out a large handkerchief to wipe his top lip. Either he was suffering from the effects of overdressing for the occasion, or he had smelled something disagreeable. Both seemed likely to Fergus. He couldn't see much of the gentleman's face behind the upturned collar of that long coat. After a couple of minutes another man approached him on the step. Fergus recognised Miss Jaspur's assistant. The two men exchanged a few words whereupon the gentleman took off, turning on his heel so that the hem of his long coat flared out. As he turned, Fergus could see that the gentleman carried a large leather bag.

'He has come this night, asking for me again, the man down there at the door, the Doctor Scales.' Miss Jaspur's voice lisped; Fergus noticed that her breath smelled faintly of aniseed. 'Mr Scales wants to interview me. I cannot decide whether to make him wait a few more nights or put him out of his misery tomorrow.'

'Would you like my opinion, Miss Jaspur?' He wondered if she had been sucking on a bon-bon, or drinking that French stuff—what was it called?

'It would do no harm.'

'Make him wait, Miss Jaspur, for a week. If he's a genuine type, then he won't give up. Whereas if he is looking for a quick—if his intentions are less than genuine, he'll move on sure enough.'

'Well, I should think his intention is genuine; that is not the question.'

Perhaps she had been drinking after all and had suddenly grown tired of the charade. Only a few people now were left to be shepherded out of the building.

'If you have far to go, I should be happy to take you in my cab. It is waiting for me.'

'But you barely know me, Miss Jaspur.'

Her throaty laugh rang out too loudly. 'I don't suppose you will prove troublesome, will you?'

'Wouldn't want to put you to any trouble. I ain't got far to go. Only just a couple of streets.'

'Forgive me, but you are not a very tall man, and at this time of night there are all kinds of unmentionable, horrid people out there. Come.' And she slipped her arm through his. Fergus was swept away down the wide staircase amidst the flurry of Miss Jaspur's rustling cape, her forearm jammed up inside his armpit.

*   *   *

'You'll tell me everything he says, Susan.'

'Yes, ma'am.'

Euphemia sat up with a posture of renewed force, 'Everything; I won't stand for any mishaps with your memory, Susan. None.'

'No, ma'am.'

Susan told Euphemia about Saville House, but not the part about the trickery. Euphemia sat back a little and waited for her to finish. Eventually, Euphemia sighed with impatience.

'Yes, I know all about Mr Harris' low beginnings, Susan. Did he tell you nothing else?'

Susan said that no, there was nothing else Mr Harris had told her.

When Susan went back into the kitchen she didn't see Fergus on the floor. She thought he had gone off to create another bit of chaos elsewhere in the house, and she cursed him silently for leaving all that mess on the table. He'd had long enough to clean it up. Miss Euphemia had kept her back for an hour. Everything covered in a shower of flour. She began to clear it up. When she moved to the sink she tripped, and the armful of crockery she carried flew into the air as if time had stopped. Later, she didn't think that she could remember the sound of the breaking things all around her. In the instant before they hit the ground, Susan Wright turned her head just a few degrees and saw that she had tripped over Mr Harris. He was gone.

CHAPTER XX

SEPTEMBER, 1860.

In the last moments of daylight, Gwen wrote hastily.

September 27, 1860.

Dear Effie,

I feel no compunction in my leaving, as I think it would do more good for me to do so. You must see now that your efforts to thwart my plans will go no further—stealing and hiding my correspondences from Mr Scales will not help you at all in whatever scheme you may have devised. But I will not admonish you further.

On a purely practical note, I suggest that you take on another servant. I cannot say more, Effie, as I write in haste, other than to say that as your sister I have to forgive you, as I hope you will be able to forgive me. I remain, forever, your loving sister,

Gwen.

The tide had long since begun its climb up towards the place where she sat when Gwen heard Edward's approach over the pebbles. In the last of the gloaming she had stared intently at the place he would appear from, and regretted not asking him to come earlier. The failing light played tricks, and once or twice she had started, thinking that a shadow among the rocks was his human form. Now it was unmistakably him.

He greeted her and wanted to hold her, but she asked him to stand still. Suddenly, she was breathless. She didn't want him to understand her surprise until he could see it. She didn't want to let him anticipate what she was about to do. The waves lapped gently, hardly making a ripple as they hit the shore. Gwen could not have hoped for better conditions.

'Are you ready?'

'Yes, though I hardly know what it is I should be ready for.'

'Close your eyes.'

'But it is dark.'

'Close them in any case. Do it for me.'

'Will you tell me when to open them?'

'Count to ten very slowly, facing the water, then open your eyes again.'

Edward began to count too fast. She flung off the coat she had been keeping wrapped about her and ran into the water. She let out a gasp as the chill touched her thighs but she plunged on further into the water up to her shoulders.

'Gwen! My God, what has happened?' He had run to the water's edge.

'Be calm, Edward. Look at the water. Look at me.' She ducked her head under and resurfaced, beginning to swim back to the shore. The pinprick sparks of unearthly light, grouping in thousands, flaring in the water around her body like waterborne fireflies had silenced Edward in his cry of panic. Gwen thrashed the water and lunged, throwing up armfuls. 'Can you see it, Edward. Do you see?'

'Yes,' he said. 'I am dumbstruck. I have never seen anything like it in my entire life. You have brought the heavens down into the water. There are entire constellations falling from you. You are lit up, like a miracle, like Venus.'

'Take off your clothes, Edward.'

'What? Oh, no. I couldn't.'

'Yes. Take them off, come into the water.'

'But the vision of you is so lovely. I don't want to spoil it.'

'Rubbish. Come in!'

But he would not be persuaded. Gwen swam out in the dark, where the water was colder and where the lights no longer burst so readily about her. It gave her a thrill to be utterly suspended in the dark water, with the dark night above her. She turned on her back and looked up at the stars coming out in the sky, then, suddenly too cold, she began to swim hard, back towards Edward. The eerie, bluish lights in the water began to stream into life about her again as she neared the shore, and as she stood up, her legs weak, gravity pushing her down, she laughed as Edward caught her in his arms, wrapping his own coat about her, pulling her into his warmth.

'I have a towel, Edward. There is no need to make your clothes wet.'

'Look, the light is still falling from you, from your hair and, my God, it is truly astonishing.'

He cannot swim, she thought. That is why he wouldn't come in, why he did not rush into the water after me.

Part II

CHAPTER XXI

OCTOBER, 1860.

Gwen leaned on the rail of the ship and held her head over the water, the spray stinging her eyes. She tried to imagine what it would be like to lean over a fraction more and then more—and then she tightened her grip. What was she thinking? That she had come unprepared for the boredom as well as the enervating effects of excitement. And where was her travelling companion? She saw him once or twice a day gripping the rail of the ship with a grim face, and the desperate character of him got on her nerves. That he was so sick at sea seemed such a miserable outcome. His greenish pallor had settled after a week to a general debilitation and waxiness. It was not fair. The bilious nausea she felt herself on waking was soon dispelled by rising and taking exercise on deck. When the captain asked after Edward at the dinner table in his scruffy quarters the compulsion to ridicule Edward almost overtook her sense of loyalty towards him. She looked down at the stained tablecloth and tried to make herself remember how much she had felt about him that had been revelatory in a very different way. Her recollections made her blush at the table, so that the captain imagined that his conversation was too much, and became solicitous, which made her agony even worse. Trapped in the conversation she wished herself outside. Outside she dreaded seeing Edward being ill over the side of the boat, the force of his vomiting not strong enough to get past the updraft, sending his expulsions back up to his face. This had happened only once; but it was the way she pictured him now at every hour of the day. It wasn't fair.

If she had been his wife she would have asked the captain for advice; or she may have felt obliged to stay at his side. She did neither.

Under her blankets at night the press of the vast water bothered her sleep. The groans of the ship, and the activity of the men who marshalled the wind to her sails and got her across the unimaginable depths swam with her jumbled memories. She went in and out of sleep each hour, and once she thought that Edward had come into the tiny room. She thought that he had heard her muttered misgivings, but she couldn't face him and turned her back to the cramped space and buried her face in her hammock. When she next saw Edward he seemed slightly better. He met her in the sunshine and blustered out something, but she misheard, or thought that she did, and so they tried to talk until the embarrassment of having nothing new to say to each other was overtaken by Edward's embarrassment at having to excuse himself.

When they arrived in New York and spent the day and night there together, Gwen's spirit was repaired by Edward's brief recovery. For the rest of the voyage she tried to hold on to the memory of those hours. But having to dine alone at the captain's table every evening did test her.

* * *

Swithin knew he was ugly. This woman was lonely, and he liked to see her smile. Her husband was in a bad way. Swithin couldn't get much of a hold on his character. You couldn't tell a man's character from the way he wrote a letter or through the woman he chose. There were moments when Swithin almost became jealous of the fact that this pair were newly wed. But this eased off, and his sympathy for Gwen came back again.

* * *

Gwen had spent as much time on deck, away from her own cramped quarters, as possible. One hour into the voyage she had begun writing in her journal.

> *This barque is primarily a vessel for goods, for things; & I think that I am but a very small thing amongst the boxes in this makeshift cabin. Despite staring out to sea for much of my life, the fact of its vastness had somehow, somewhere slipped from my imagination: now I am surrounded by this ever moving, ever changing & never changing grey swell of fathomless water, without the security of a rock at my back. The wind, a different animal out here, tugs from all sides—and I had never imagined how swift the shift in temperature might be. A penetrating salty chill to the air, even on a day so warm on land—Land & the people upon it seemed so insignificant & small very rapidly as we drew away from everything solid & still. The elements rush us all along on this unknowable voyage. Level with the Manacles & I spent a quiet moment in contemplation and prayer, strangely wordless, but more prayer than I have ever made, for the souls, past & future whose lives*

were & are yet to be lost there. Past the rolling breakers, crashing over the hidden treachery, I could not turn to look at the last view of our small river; instead determining my gaze on the horizon I saw a host of white gannets plummet one after another into the waves at tremendous speeds. Our course altered very slightly & as we neared the birds, the glistening bodies of dolphins broke the surface all around us, leapt along the rolling push, & I am sure I could spy as much joy in their dark eyes as there must have been in mine . . .

Edward read this passage two days after it had been written. Looking for Gwen one morning, and finding her little space empty, he'd put his hand into the neatly folded blankets in her hammock. Perhaps, he told himself, to feel some of the warmth her body might have left behind. His fingers discovered her journal and closed in around the newness of the leather binding. How could he help himself from opening it? He'd only wanted to see some part of her. And so it was in that cramped space he had first seen that Gwen was happy to find a substitute.

And now at the end of this journey he watched Gwen with the captain. He was tutoring her on the correct way to use a telescope. Edward watched how Gwen covered one eye with her hand and gave the captain her full attention.

'The city of Pará is seventy miles up the river of the same name,' The captain spoke with his face close to her ear—he brushed Gwen's elbow. 'Although, as you will have noticed, there is still plenty of wind to carry us along.' Edward thought of moist breath on her earlobe: the captain's, then his own.

'Then where is the Amazon river, Captain?'

'In the simplest terms the Amazon proper is two hundred miles, or sixty Spanish leagues from here.'

She fingered the leather pouch at her neck and appeared agitated. Perhaps, thought Edward, she is recalling the scene she had imagined waiting at her destination as described to her by Swithin. Faced with the enormity of scale, he felt painfully aware of the smallness of the life she wanted to discard.

'The largest river in the world,' Edward forced a cheerful note. He grasped the rails, inhaling deeply and leaning back, trusting his weight. 'Good morning, Swithin.'

'A good morning to you, sir. I trust this day finds you well?'

Gwen murmured a greeting and did not look at Edward as he stood beside her.

'Perfectly, thank you.' Edward's hand slid along the rail and as he clasped her hand briefly, he noticed the appalling state of her kid gloves; they were stained with salty watermarks, smudges of dark stuff and paint. He suddenly felt that he should have thought of something as simple as gloves. He'd only thought of getting her enough good paper. And then, in New York, trinkets; he couldn't remember what. He'd never thought of the look of her hands, only of what they might give him.

Now that they were beyond the reaches of the open sea, Edward felt his nausea vanish. It was strange to be beside her on deck again. It had felt as though they had made the journey across the Atlantic on different boats.

'You must excuse me, madam. I will leave you in

the capable hands of Mr Scales.'

'Your telescope, Captain.' Gwen offered it back, but Swithin put up his hand, glancing quickly away and then back to her. Edward noticed how the captain's gaze flitted back and forth, landing on anything except her face. Edward revelled for a moment in Swithin's discomfort.

'I have another; don't be concerned. In any case, this part of the river contains no surprises which may be detected by telescope. Besides, that kind of event is to be avoided, I should hope, by the skill of our pilot there.'

Edward caught her eye and saw the look on her face. He saw the satisfaction in Gwen as she breathed in the knowledge that land was not an impossible distance from her.

The wind dropped slightly for a moment, and Gwen shut the telescope. She opened the small bag at her feet, putting the telescope in there for safekeeping, and took out her paint-box, brushes and sketchbooks. She sat on a coil of rope and began to make a sketch of Edward's profile as he leaned on the rail. He let her think that he was oblivious to her endeavours, but he noticed how awkwardly she sat.

Captain Swithin approached them again to tell them that the *Opal* must wait awhile as the customs officer cleared it for docking. Gwen stopped drawing Edward and held the telescope out to Swithin, but he declined again, saying, 'Please, I would like you to keep the glass.'

'I couldn't possibly steal a piece of equipment from you, Captain.'

'Please,' Swithin insisted. 'A memento of your first voyage across the Atlantic.'

'Jolly decent of you, Captain,' Edward said. 'A most essential piece of equipment, indeed. I'm sure it will prove very useful.'

Gwen flushed. 'Thank you, Captain. I hope you realise that I will have developed a squint by the time you make your return.'

'That may well be; but I tend to think—and you may agree—that one should always have an alternative view at one's disposal.'

CHAPTER XXII

PARÁ, BRAZIL. LATE OCTOBER, 1860.

Just look at him. Seeing Edward prancing about among the crates being landed was something of a shock. It was a wild, bare-headed, leggy kind of dance under the flattening sun. All trace of his debilitating aversion to open water was miraculously vanished. Only the spikiness of his frame, his bony wrists, jittery as a cranefly, gesticulating at everything and nothing, spoke of his month-long ordeal on the Atlantic Ocean between Cornwall and here.

Gwen thought, Great men, great thinkers, have suffered the same; and look at him, he's well again now.

Edward grimaced against the glare and picked his teeth with a long fingernail. Gwen turned away. The telescope in her hands slipped. Her palms were slick against the warm metal; its topmost section came to a slithery halt as she tightened her fist and sat down on one of the crates.

It was a vast array of collecting equipment—Edward's announcement of his unfailing enthusiasm and faith in himself and everything he turned his hand to. She remembered the list, four columns deep and two pages long. Inside the crates were Wardian boxes, elegant insect frames and cabinets, glass jars of all different dimensions. Gallons of formalin. New books.

But Edward's optimism was infectious, too. And as she watched him again, the pale hair flaming from his scalp, she remembered the lick of fire in her bowels and gut. She stood, feeling her petticoats clinging to her sweating thighs. Someone, a man, came up to her.

'Grindlock,' he said. 'Consignee of the *Opal*.' Mr Grindlock grasped her hand as if she were a man and pumped her arm. Grinning like a lunatic, he let go of her. Oh, God, let him not be a lunatic, she thought.

'Mr Scales!' Mr Grindlock lurched towards Edward and clapped him on the back. Edward flinched in pain.

Gwen said, 'Mr Grindlock, I was about to buy some oranges, I wonder—'

'No need to waste your money, good lady. There are fruit trees aplenty at my humble abode. You may pluck as many oranges as you fancy.' He ushered them away from the quayside up to his townhouse, talking all the time about how wonderful it was to see them. 'My home is, of course, at your disposal. Consider yourselves most welcome whilst we look for something suitable in the suburbs—it being more convenient, I'm sure you'll come to agree, for your collectings. Do you have a particular area of interest, Mr Scales?'

They followed Mr Grindlock and tried to keep pace with his banter. She felt her underwear becoming soaked with sweat and then, by degrees, the rest of her clothes. Struggling to keep up, she bumped her parasol against several people; one of them was a priest.

'I beg your pardon, Father.' Drips from her forehead ran down between her eyes and off her nose.

'*Senhora*.' The priest barely turned. He touched his wide black hat and disappeared.

By the time she entered Mr Grindlock's cool house, every part of her body was running. Her clothes clung and dragged, and she felt as if she was drowning. Edward and Mr Grindlock were both drenched. Their host wiped his square, flattish face vigorously with a large handkerchief and kept the soggy material in his hand. Several children shouting, '*Pai! Pai!*' ran up to Mr Grindlock as they walked in.

'Hettie,' Mr Grindlock called into the gloom of the house, over his children's heads, 'I have brought two fine young people to keep us entertained.'

One of the smaller children tugged on Gwen's sleeve and spoke to her in Portuguese.

'Remember to speak English to our guests, Pippi. It is polite. Now, here is my good wife. Hettie, I have brought Mr Scales, a naturalist, and his lovely wife. Mr Scales wanted to oversee the unloading of all his boxes of equipment, but I've put one or two of my men to the job.'

'Another scientist!' Hettie clasped her hands in front of her large bosom. 'Mrs Scales, you are the first lady I have heard of to accompany her husband. And I don't blame you. If Mr Grindlock had to travel again, we should all have to go with him.'

Hettie's skin was mottled with a blue tint and quite dry. Gwen was conscious that her tendency to stoop was becoming more pronounced. She was a good head taller than Hettie.

'But Mrs Scales is an *artist*, my dear.' Grindlock's words echoed off the cold walls. 'Very sensible of Mr Scales to bring her along. Keep it all in the family, much the best way. Now, let's see about something to drink. We almost lost Mrs Scales in the market for the sake of an orange but what about some cold tea?'

'Don't worry, Mrs Scales,' Hettie said. 'It's not as bad as it sounds. We have it weak, with a slice of lemon. I have never acquired the habit of coffee. Mr Grindlock is partial to a cup in the morning, but I find it compounds the heat somewhat.'

Hettie took Gwen by the arm and guided her through the hall and into the drawing room. Pippi was still hanging onto Gwen's other sleeve. The house and its people were swallowing her; this unconditional acceptance and the solid ground made her dizzy. Gwen could not catch what Pippi was saying; the child was asking her something. She smiled down at her, and the girl scampered off.

'Very cooling, you'll find, Mrs Scales,' Mr Grindlock said. 'Come and make use of the coolest air, over here.' Gwen looked up at the ceiling where she saw the contraption. She followed its cords away into a corner where a man sat working rope pedals with his feet.

The children were all over the place; on and off the chairs and up and down off their parents' laps. Mrs Grindlock was doing her best to be firm.

'Mrs Scales will not appreciate it. Take it away.'

'But, Mama, I have it on a string.'

'A monkey?' Edward asked.

'A spider. They are taking it away. Aren't you?'

'A spider monkey, now that is something I should like to see,' Edward said.

'No, no, Mr Scales,' Hettie said. 'A spider.'

'Well, I am interested in all creatures.' He walked across to peer over the huddle of children's heads. 'Ah, goodness me, quite a monster.'

'I think, for the sake of Mrs Scales, these little revelations must come by degrees. Children, I really am going to become quite stern with you. That is better.'

But Gwen's attention was still drawn to the fan working away above them all. The man, half obscured by a screen, silently pedalled, as if none of them were in the room with him. Gwen tilted her face upwards and closed her eyes, feeling the currents of air stroking her neck.

* * *

Later, while everyone in the house dozed, Gwen was alone in the room where she and Edward were to sleep. Edward was below her in the citrus courtyard, writing. She stepped away from the window. She'd been spying on the way he hunched over the papers perched on his knees, his ink positioned precariously on the tray at his side. She couldn't see anything of his face; he was wearing a straw hat with a wide brim. She could make out the faint, feverish scratching of his pen mingled against the peculiar and penetrating scrapings of insects. The noise of them got into her head and stayed there. Grasshoppers and hearth crickets would be as whisperers now.

There had been a package waiting for her on the cane chair beside the wash-stand. Earlier, when Edward had been in the room very briefly, she'd made a point of not acknowledging it.

'Better than you thought. The arrangements suit us.'

She'd gaped as he turned his back and left her alone in the room. She eased off the string and paper.

It was a small, half-bound volume of tan calf and marbled paper with a swirling amber and bronze design flecked with touches of black. Gwen turned it over in her hands, reading the gold lettering on the spine. She ran her finger over the words indented slightly into the surface of the leather: *Eternal Blazon*. She frowned; it wasn't a romantic novel, was it? Sent by her sister as some kind of pathetic joke. It would suit her sense of humour; the carefully blocked name on the packet label which was only half her own, with merely, 'Pará, Brazil' as the address. Gwen flicked the pages casually and found them unslit. Holding it away from her body, she read the frontispiece: 'Eternal Blazon, or, Confessions of a Nondescript'. So, not one of her sister's books after all. Who else? She blanched at the thought of Edward giving her a book with such a title. Whenever he'd given her a book, he'd given it into her hands and watched her face intently for whatever it was that he hoped to see.

Two-thirds of the way down the page there was a line which read 'Printed and Bound for the Author, London 1859'. Rather strangely, there was no mention of who had provided this service. Gwen's stomach flipped, and she snapped the book shut. She worried at a tiny flap of sore flesh inside her mouth until she tasted her blood. *Eternal Blazon*—Eternal Truth. She knew it from somewhere, but her wrung-out brain wouldn't let her place it. It'll come, she thought.

Sunlight slashed the room in half, and a small, brown lizard spread its body against the wall and sunned itself. Gwen watched its barely perceptible breaths and dropped the book silently onto the bed to fetch her drawing things. She worked several sketches over the page, making enlarged details of its mottled, nubbly skin, its head and its feet. The lizard moved every now and then, allowing her to make studies of it from different angles. And then, it was gone. Shooting out of her sight, along the wall and over the edge of the window frame as quick as a bird. Gwen tidied up the sketches, adding areas of shading, giving more weight and substance to the creature. She put her things away and stretched. Hearing someone's footfall outside the room Gwen shoved *Eternal Blazon* along with its packaging into her sketching bag.

The girl with the pet spider—Pippi, was it?—came into the room, and Gwen scanned the floor around the girl's feet in case the spider had come in with her.

'Shouldn't you be resting?' Gwen didn't feel comfortable alone with the girl; she didn't really know how to speak to her, or what to say. The girl shrugged her shoulders and jumped onto the bed. Gwen watched as Pippi sprawled on the covers, rumpling them, and then pulled herself to the edge, hung her head over, arms falling down by her ears.

'I lost Hercules. He likes to hide in dark places.' She raised herself up with a solemn look on her face, but then broke into a grin. 'Your face is a picture.' She laughed. 'You're scared of spiders. Most people from home are scared of spiders.'

'But you have an affinity with them.'

'What's that?'

'You like them, as a friend.'

'Almost.'

Gwen relaxed a bit and sat down on the cane chair. 'Almost. Then why do you keep the spider?'

'To watch it.'

'And how do you watch it?'

The girl narrowed her eyes and frowned. 'Like this.' She put her elbows on the bed and supported her chin in her hands and opened her eyes wide.

'I see. I like to watch things, too. In fact, I was watching a little brown lizard a few moments ago. Here.' Gwen pulled the sketchbook out of her bag and flicked the pages to the right place. She held the book out for the girl to see.

'Gecko.'

'Is that its name?'

'Yes. You shouldn't keep your things in bags like that. Hercules might crawl in. It needs to have a tight string or lots of buttons. Hercules can do this . . .' She made her hand into a tarantula and lifted the edge of the bed clothes before making her hand crawl under the sheet.

Gwen's body jerked quickly, in a shudder of revulsion. 'And what would be your advice, if I should meet Hercules, or one of his kind inside my bag?'

'Don't squash him.'

'And after I haven't squashed him?'

The girl rolled over and stared hard at Gwen. 'Find someone who isn't scared of spiders.'

CHAPTER XXIII

Edward wrote in his small pocket diary by the light of a single candle, so as not to disturb Gwen's sleep.

The relief of being finally on dry land again, for both of us, is unquestionable. This evening I felt it as a palpable entity. The landing of all my equipment will take a few days at least, as the ship is anchored some distance from the port due to the fast currents and the silting bottom of the river. The landing stages seem hardly fit for the purpose they were made, but I must trust to those with greater knowledge and experience in these matters for the time being. Meanwhile, we are commodiously accommodated by Grindlock, merchant of cocoa and other such goods. His family and house being large and almost as riotous as the auditory assault emitted constantly from a plethora of faunae so new and alien to us. That is, the house does seem to have its own character, if that is possible. Everything about the place excites me. My brain is overloaded with senses, questions, possibilities, desires. I wish I could say the same for my ~~concubina~~ companion. I would not have imagined her to be so beset by an apparent misery. Perhaps it is merely the heat and humidity—it can be a shock if one has never experienced it before. However, a niggling doubt creeps, and I suspect that it is more deep-seated than that. On arrival, we were introduced to the entire retinue of the Grindlock household including giant forest spiders, and a small monkey which bit Grindlock on the hand (he made very light of it saying that the creature has never liked him). Also the servants. I did wonder that the lady of the house did not discreetly offer my companion a chance to freshen herself. We were fairly dripping with sweat from head to foot. We drank some cold tea, which I gathered was offered quite genuinely in place of a bowl of water and towel. Gwen hardly touched her tea. She kept looking up at the ceiling fan with quite an addled expression and stared at the negro fellow operating it for so long that I thought she would draw attention to herself. I made a buffoon of myself with the children, and so Gwen was for the most part left alone. There was an absolute downpour after a light lunch of cold ham. Some of the children ran out during the rain into the courtyard where there are growing several different kinds of citrus. The Grindlocks indulge their progeny somewhat. Gwen ate two oranges and a few other fruits which we do not see in England, their skins quite deformed with uneven knobbles, their colour quite unappetising. Her mood was lightened a little, I think, watching the children getting drenched, and she was more the person I left England with for those few moments. But on our ramble about the town (escaping the Grindlocks' offers of attendance with good grace), the mood darkened again. I did my utmost to cheer her spirits. I fear I annoyed her a little, or perhaps a lot. It is so difficult to know how to behave with her. ~~Sometimes I think perhaps I made a mistake.~~ There are certain fundamental aspects of her character ~~which I know nothing about.~~ The attraction of this state of affairs is no longer a sufficient basis for our project here. Coaxing her along the crowded streets was almost akin to cajoling a reluctant and grumpy child. It occurred to me this afternoon that I have no firm idea of how old she is. This thought kept me preoccupied for such a length of time that I did not notice when she fainted at my feet on a street none too salubrious, to say the least. Some of the natives living in the hovels there procured a cart and we arrived back at the Grindlocks' abode amidst much fuss (to the apparent amusement of all the small Grindlocks). Thank God, none but servants were there to greet us. We have managed to pass it off as an adventure, citing sore feet, which, I believe was not untrue. When she took off her boots, Gwen's feet did seem to be in a hideous state, and I have put cushions underneath them as she sleeps to drain the fluid. It would seem to work.

Now, I am concerned for her. Gwen has never been the type to faint; she even said so herself. She tried to dismiss it as a reaction to the heat, but the heat had passed; the air was much fresher after the rain.

Swollen feet and fainting do not bode well though; am I to have to search for another assistant before we have even begun? Perhaps it will not come to that.

Edward snuffed out the light with spit on his fingers

and, having no blotting paper, waited for the ink to dry in the dark, listening, for the first time, to Gwen's breathing as she slept.

CHAPTER XXIV

Apart from a limited and limiting wardrobe, Gwen had brought with her two sets of watercolour paints, several good brushes of different sizes, leather-bound journals of good paper to paint in bought by Edward in London, as well as her smaller sketchbooks, and her most treasured possession, her microscope. Edward was convinced that the end result would bring some reward. There were already some studies: good likenesses of Edward reading on the boat—on the rare occasions when he had not felt ill, and there were a couple of impressions of Pará, done before the lighter had been ready to take them.

However, she felt no inclination to begin work right away. The idea of kudos did not greatly concern or excite her. She was perplexed by her own reaction to having arrived, which was so different to Edward's. She was aware of a vagueness, as if she saw everything through a mist. I am suffering from apathy, she thought. It puzzled her.

Mr Grindlock had found them a *casinha*, a little wooden house in the suburbs. Finally inside it, with her things around her again, Gwen wanted immediately to lie down. It had been a very strange experience, that first night in the Grindlock guest-room, where being suspended was forsaken in favour of more solid furniture. The enormous bed had allowed her to sleep, eventually, without having to touch Edward. In the dark of the room with only a light coverlet over their bodies, she'd sensed Edward's heartbeat: it had reverberated softly through the mattress. Being flat on her back had not dispelled the sensation that her body was still at sea. As he'd fallen asleep Edward had begun to snore. Gwen had sighed loudly and plumped her pillows vigorously, banishing all thoughts of eerily articulated and oversized arachnids roaming free of restraining tethers. Even so, she hadn't slept well after the first night. Bad dreams had woken her, the details hazy but still disturbing as they persisted, festering in the hot, damp space between Edward's body and hers in the foreign bed. She had seemed to keep her sister company all night.

*   *   *

A verandah encircled the whole building of four rooms under wide eaves. Here, as the cookhouse was not yet ready for use, Gwen found Maria. She was already boiling water for tea on a small stove.

Gwen thought she would like this woman. She was glad that Maria had none of the deferential habits of Susan in Cornwall. If anything she had been relieved to get away from the 'Yes, ma'am' and the bobbing Susan insisted on, even though she had been told not to.

Bearing the tea tray in front of her Maria said, 'There are people in the town who could build a bed quickly.'

'I'm not sure if our budget extends to large pieces of furniture,' said Gwen; a proper bed was too much of an extravagance, and she didn't know whether she preferred the idea of big spiders hiding under her bed-covers or not.

Maria poured the tea and flicked the leaves from the strainer out over the verandah palings. 'Wouldn't cost much.' She poured two more cups of tea, drinking one before Edward left his unpacking and came out to join Gwen.

'Mrs Scales,' she said, before Edward was within earshot, 'I know how you Europeans like to have your babies.'

Gwen laughed. 'We are certainly not planning to start a family here, Maria. We have work to do. And, in any case, a bed would take up far too much space.'

Maria looked her up and down, and said nothing.

No, Gwen definitely didn't want to share a bed with Edward. A bed was far too much like a statement of subservience, somehow. Gwen still felt uneasy about her status. She felt that she had to find her own way of existing in this set-up. It was a game, after all, what they were doing. Some of the rules had been foisted upon her, but the rest were unwritten, unspoken, unknown. She could pretend that she was his wife, but she didn't think it was necessary to have her sleep disturbed at quite such close range.

In the night, Gwen was woken by a thump from Edward's study and a faint trickle as he relieved himself over the edge of the verandah. She listened to geckos moving across the walls, and tucked her muslin net in about her more securely. The strange lizards were a delight to her; it was the large hairy spiders, whose nests she had seen under the eaves, which bothered her. Knowing that the ones living under the eaves were now secured in labelled specimen jars did not help. Edward, still unfailingly exuberant, had enthused about the proximity of nature in all its variation. And where a vacancy existed, she had reasoned, it would immediately be filled.

'Such a small creature,' he had said, and laughed.

'I would say it was anything but small.'

'It's smaller than you. It isn't poisonous . . . All the best houses in town have them, you know. Think of the Grindlock children.'

'I would rather not.'

'Well, this one is dead now. You can come out of the mosquito net. Besides, if it fancied biting you its fangs would go right through that muslin. Sorry, that's not at all funny.'

'If it wasn't poisonous, then why did you use a pencil to poke it, and not your finger?'

Gwen's skin crawled; she was embarrassed for Edward because he didn't quite know how to behave with her. Standing next to him, looking at the revolting spider, and listening to the rising pitch of his voice, she wondered if he had ever really known how to behave with her. Before settling down to sleep again, Gwen made sure that there was no part of the muslin which touched her; she had already lined the rest of the hammock with a thick blanket. Dear God, she thought, but the rest of her plea was wordless.

Alone and naked in the dark, Edward listened to the sounds of the night. He shifted inside his hammock, aggravated by the image earlier that evening of Gwen with that thing at her neck. It was already very grubby. Like a sickly fetish. She touched it, fiddled with it, could not seem to leave it alone for a minute. Though the temperature had dropped considerably, it was still too hot for his blanket.

He could not help but recall the effect of a similar pressing heat. For much of that indelibly marked, and unseasonably hot week in May 1858, the closed stuffiness of the little rooms kept by Natalia had produced in him a state of lazy and surprising contentment.

God damn that woman. But even as he thought it he retracted it. He could neither resent nor condemn her, only his own stupidity. He got out of the hammock clumsily and went to relieve himself.

CHAPTER XXV

Carrick House. October 17, 1860.

Euphemia woke at six in the morning and sat up remembering where she had stuffed one of Gwen's letters in a hurry the winter before. Its place in the library was too tantalising to ignore, and in the dark she reached for her dressing gown. While Euphemia lit the lamp in the hall, she heard the barely perceptible clatter of Susan riddling the grate in the kitchen. Holding the light to the bookshelves Euphemia let her fingers run along the spines until they came to the place. She pulled out the thick volume, made very slightly thicker by the papers she had hidden there. Her fingertips lingered for a moment over the broken seal before she pulled the letter from the envelope.

November 13, 1859.

My Dear Gwen,

I have made, already, several different drafts of this letter, which have all found their way to the fire. I feel that I owe it to myself, and, of course, to you, to write this letter to you, and to send it. Please, when you receive it, do not keep it. After you have read it as many times as you need to, please destroy it in the fire. I could not bear to think that the words I am about to put down on this paper should lie in a drawer as a testament to my failings.

I know that I have not behaved properly with you. I know that I have not been the gentleman that I would have wished to have been with you. You were absolutely right to be angry with me. But can you believe me when I say that I am more angry at myself than you could ever be? In time, I hope that I may be proper and chivalrous towards you, as you deserve nothing less. You are the most extraordinary person I have ever met, and I would like you to know that in being my friend and my secret companion you have saved me from a certain kind of madness. Gwen, when I am with you I am whole and unmarked by my past.

You have been so very patient with me and most extraordinarily kind in every way imaginable. You have accommodated me in your splendid grounds without complaint. And the few nights that I have spent with you, when we have come together in the most secret of places, I have been beside myself with joy. I know that it is impossible for you to take pleasure in these particular meetings, but I wish you to know that I am most humbly grateful for them and that I will never embarrass you, as you have requested, by ever mentioning them to you again. They remain, those nights, our most secret and most blessed times.

But I must now speak of my past and indeed of my present. I am husband to a woman called Isobel—but husband in name only, as the marriage is not, has never been, consummated. It is for this reason that I have tormented myself over our friendship. I have omitted to reveal myself in my true colours, and for this I remain deeply ashamed. If you can bear to read it, let me tell you now that preceding our first meeting, I was entangled with another person. A female whose personal attributes I cannot bring myself to describe but for whom I was nevertheless bent on destroying myself. Please be assured that she was nothing compared to you and that my wife is nothing compared to you.

Truly, I feel that I have been saved by you and that you are the one person, the only person whom I should ever be able to call my own. You, and only you, have shown me what it means to be a whole man, unfettered by the ridiculous, stringent constrictions of our society.

If you still feel, after reading this letter, that you are able to allow me to continue to see you, then you must do no more than behave as if you have never received this letter. I hope that you will still accept me, as you have done so far, without judgement. If you will still allow it, let us meet, in darkness, as we have done before when no words have been needed except those which feed my all-consuming desire for you.

I seal this in haste, lest I should again waver over my conviction that I may remain, for ever,
Your Own Edward.

With a shiver of intense and exquisite satisfaction, Euphemia slid the letter back between the pages of the almanac.

CHAPTER XXVI

Each time he went out with his insect net, Edward seemed to come back with his collecting tin full of specimens he had already collected. For he would take not just a male and female specimen of every possible species, but several, arranging them in rows to show off minute variations in pattern and colour. And then there were those which did not make it into the collection but were discarded for slight lack of lustre or a small section of wing which had been broken off. There was a midden heap under the house outside his room. In varying stages of rapid decomposition, butterflies, spiders, beetles and other small fauna Edward did not wish to transport back to England soon became indistinguishable in a friable mass.

But her painting things stayed untouched; she worried vaguely that the humidity might be bad for them but she did nothing about it. The scents from the flowers in the garden and the undertones of decay were quite overwhelming; in part she blamed it for her inactivity. Sometimes, she would realise that she had been reading the same sentence over and over in a loop which made no sense, the magazine almost dropping from her hand. She felt herself sweating into her clothes and waiting for Edward to come back with his tired but joyous step and full of it all. What is wrong with me? she thought. She got up later than usual one morning, and was cross. It is absurd, she thought, that I should be here and not see for myself the walks he tells me about. She spent the rest of the day with the sticky shadow of an ill temper and hardly spoke to Maria.

When Edward came back she jumped up. 'At last,' she said.

Edward frowned, and then smiled. He put down his heavy bags. Bottles inside it clinked. He blew his nose through his fingers onto the ground and then after wiping his fingers on his trousers, he looked at her, holding her out at arm's length by the shoulders. She felt uncomfortable in his gaze, imagining herself as him, coming up to herself through his eyes to see that he hadn't thought of her all day. He never thought of her during any of his rambles. Since they had stepped off the boat he had been on the edge of something approaching ecstatic rapture. Gwen was aware that her eyes were staring and wide, and she bit her lip. Edward put his hand to her chin, and he squinted at her mouth where mango fibres were trapped between her top front teeth. 'Has something happened?'

'No, no, nothing, nothing at all.' She disengaged her chin from his fingers. 'I should really like to come out with you tomorrow.'

'What about your feet? Hmn? I thought we agreed that you should keep those ankles up.'

She shrugged off his hands but she recovered her attitude, slipping her arm through his. 'I'm not suggesting that I should be out with you all day. Perhaps a short walk.' Do not treat me like an imbecile, she thought.

'Well, I had rather imagined that you would like to make a start on some of the specimens I have collected so far. But I can see that you are restless. It's understandable, of course. Nothing too taxing.'

Gwen struggled to hammer down her frustration and fury as they went into the house.

* * *

Edward chatted for the entire ramble the next day. They had agreed that they would go out early, before breakfast. This is not what I had meant, she thought, as she listened to his incessant commentary. From the humidity (which she was already familiar with), to the height of the trees (which she could see for herself), to the insects in the leaf litter under their feet. Edward filled the air with his voice. They stopped once or twice, and she dutifully craned her neck to admire the height of the canopy. Edward took out his pocket knife and gouged into the side of a fallen tree to show her a beetle grub.

'See how its fat body writhes so slowly in my hand, Gwen. It would have stayed inside this rotting log for years, perhaps, before finally pupating. It's one of the longhorn beetles. I'll find one for you.' My God, she wanted to say, I know a beetle larva when I see one. Who on earth do you imagine you are talking to?

She tried to hear the forest around them under the sound of his voice. It seemed incredible that a man who had not even known the Cardinal beetle in his own country should now be telling her about exotic Coleoptera. The morning chorus had calmed some time ago, but around them here and there were isolated bird calls and the ever present hum of insect life in the air. Gwen played a game with herself. How many things could she spot before Edward pointed them out to her. She knew other people used these paths. There were villages deeper into the forest, though what she regarded then as deep forest would be as nothing by the time she would have finally left Brazil. It would not be unusual to meet someone, even though they had not, so far. I am being silly, she told herself. But the sensation that she was being observed, like the squirming fat larva in Edward's hand, would not leave her. She watched, rather repulsed, as Edward put the larva into a small vial of preservative and straight into his collecting bag; its final moments dismissed to the dark pocket of red leather.

She could not believe what he was doing, treating her like some silly young girl out for a walk in the park, pointing out the greenness of the grass or the song of a blackbird. How could this be the same man she had wanted to spend all her days with? She wondered what it would take to have been able to make him understand her desire to see everything around her in the same state of awe that he had enjoyed. His being able to name some of the flora and fauna was a clever kind of trick, but she couldn't see that it served any particular kind of usefulness to his understanding of the place. The flora specimens they took were identified, housed and despatched to England in the Wardian cases. The butterflies not for his own collection were wrapped in triangles of paper and sent off to be set by others and placed in private collections. No, she thought, in naming these things, in speaking their names, he is claiming them. As they stood on the high ground and looked down into a swampy hollow filled with huge arums she tried and failed not to mind as Edward's tremulous voice told her that they were standing under a Cassia tree. A surge of desire rushed down through her legs, but it was undirected and confusing. It was not Edward she desired. The heat prickled her neck and back, and her head felt hot in irritation. She grasped his arm, and he patted her hand saying, 'Time to go back? Better not overdo it.'

She clenched her teeth and watched where she trod, and noticed little more than the mango trees lining the road. The feeling that she was being watched disappeared slowly. Perhaps it was just a monkey, or some animal like that.

* * *

After a couple of days, Gwen followed the road again away from the direction of town. She went alone, taking herself into the nearest edges of the forest. She did not tell Edward about her plans. She told Maria that she was off for a little stroll, that she would not be long. A rush of excitement came over her, and as she turned off onto a path leading into the forest itself, butterflies danced in the patches of sunlight around her.

Now the light changed; a diffused green was cast over everything. She dared to look up into the canopy. She was at the bottom of a pond and she reeled. Her bowels fluttered. She bent over and took deep breaths, and stared blinking into the shadows, which somehow contrived to surge before her eyes. The white tips of wings danced in and out of the islands of shade, the rest of the insects virtually invisible to her unpractised eye. They never went very high. It was, she thought, as if they were pretending to be moths. Upside down, some rested beneath wide, waxy leaves and she put out her finger, almost touching their closed wings before they took off again to settle out of reach. She retraced her steps back onto the sunnier main path through the forest and was mesmerised by the sight of several different blue Morphos. There was a very leisurely, luxuriant pattern to their flight; the way they seemed to know where the warm air would facilitate their desire most effectively. They would twist, mid-glide, like a seagull. No wonder Edward came back so frustrated sometimes. The changing hues of iridescent blue flashed in the sunlight as if they were taunting her. It was lovely to see these things in their proper context, and she was more than sorry for the burgeoning collection of butterflies in the wooden cases. And yet she wanted to hold one, to see it as closely, she thought, as the Creator in that moment of inspiration. And then she checked herself, remembering Darwin's theory. Her feelings and thoughts and learning were tangled and knotted, so that she didn't know what she should think or feel, confronted by the magnificence of everything surrounding her. How was it possible to believe and doubt at the same time, to see connection and disconnection in every object. She was completely overwhelmed—and burst into tears.

And now there was that suspicion again that someone was watching her. She had tried to dismiss it as a benign sensation in her brain. But she felt it more in her back; not only out here on the forest path but around the house she felt it sometimes. Some days, it was more acute than others. She could not talk about it. Every time she had felt like saying something about it, there had been the notion that Edward would not take her seriously or think that she was, after all, of flimsy character; a silly female, unable to function satisfactorily in this new environment, suited only to exist on the banks of the Helford in Cornwall. And sometimes she allowed herself to think that this was true. It must not be true, and yet while she was in awe of her surroundings she wanted to escape them. She found herself wishing that she would not have to speak to Edward when he returned. Already his voice grated in her mind and tipped her nerves. I am just his facilitator, she thought. He would not be here without me; no self-respecting man would have agreed to my unequal share in this endeavour. She wondered if this was the real reason she had been reluctant to begin her part of the bargain here.

*　　*　　*

She unlaced her boots and tossed them into a corner, pulled off her silk stockings and rubbed at her ankles, then she went barefoot through to Edward's room and rummaged in his closet. Maria's voice at her back remonstrated, and Gwen froze, her hands clutching at the waistband of Edward's trousers. 'You can't wear a man's clothes, Mrs Scales. I've got a better idea.'

CHAPTER XXVII

THE TIMES, WEDNESDAY, OCTOBER 3, 1866.

MURDER TRIAL AT THE OLD BAILEY.

MR Probart for the Prosecution addressed the Jury: 'The prisoner is a woman, as we shall see, whose enthusiasm for immorality in her younger days persists into the present. Following her ill wonts has led her here: Murder. Gentlemen, why are we never surprised in this city when foul murder is committed by a female of low morals and even lower reputation? Perhaps it is because these two thrive together. Be not deceived by the prisoner's apparent stature, by her—notable—command of language; and nor yet by her insistence of guiltlessness. This, gentlemen, is a wily female cornered, who would stop at nothing to get what she wants.'

At this last, Mrs Pemberton leaned forward. 'I will have you retract every last slanderous word, sir,' before she was reminded by Mr Justice Linden that she must, 'internalise her outbursts, however well founded she believed them to be'. The Clerk was not asked to strike the prisoner's remarks from his notes, and nor were the members of the Jury advised to ignore them.

In response to the Prosecution's statement, Mr Shanks for the Defence said: 'Observers of this case may be forgiven if they have thought, up unto this moment, that what we are trying to set out for examination is a simple case of a lovers' tryst gone horribly, murderously wrong. The murder victim, the late Mr Scales, as you will come to see, treated the prisoner, Mrs Pemberton, with deviousness and subversive intent from the moment he laid eyes on her; this, you will see, is true. He lured her away from her family home, from the security and safety of her known world under false pretences. We know this to be true, for we know that Mr Scales was already a married man, and having no intention of enlightening the young Mrs Pemberton to this fact, allowed her to believe that in travelling with him to Brazil, she would eventually become his wife. It is a familiar tale, but in finding herself unwittingly cast in the tawdry plot, Mrs Pemberton, her passion high, one might assume, would, one might assume, seek revenge at the most convenient time and not, Gentlemen, wait, wait, wait and wait more long years until she was under the gaze of the entire City of London to commit a murder she might so easily have done many years before. Think on it, if you please, Gentlemen. In attempting to untangle the ghastly threads of any murder, one must cast his mind in the role of the perpetrator. A cold and calculated act, from a person as level and as intelligent as the prisoner, Mrs Pemberton—would it result in such an obvious mess? Would she have allowed herself to have no alibi? The obvious answer, of course, is that a woman as level and intelligent as Mrs Pemberton is not the murderous type. The crime, Gentlemen, does not fit the accused, and it does not fit the accused in such an obvious manner that I wonder, like the prisoner herself, and indeed many others, that she was charged with the crime—if there was a crime—at all. Life, real life, is not always as neat as we would like it to be. Mrs Pemberton was unfortunate in her acquaintance with Mr Scales from beginning to end. It seems that, even in death, Mr Scales has contrived to leave his mark upon her. Mrs Pemberton happened to have called upon Mr Scales on the day preceding the night he was, allegedly, murdered. This small fact has cast such aspersions on her—and why?'

Witnesses were then examined before it was stated that the Jury should be taken to see the house where the body of Mr Scales was found.

CHAPTER XXVIII

Gwen could barely breathe in the only evening gown she had brought with her. It had seemed such a ridiculous thing to pack into her trunk. It dug into her armpits, and her bosom was pressed painfully inside it.

'Mr and Mrs Scales! Marvellous! Hettie will be so pleased that you have been able to come to our little gathering.'

'Mr Grindlock, good evening. We could hardly not have come; it was very good of you to invite us.' Edward's speech was as stiff as his collar.

'Not at all, it's a pleasure to see you again. How

are you finding your feet? Getting the feel of the place yet?'

'Absolutely, yes, absolutely.' Edward cast a sideways glance at Gwen and placed his free hand briefly under her elbow. 'Collecting's been most productive.'

'Mrs Scales!' Hettie's voice floated in a sing-song warble over the room, closely followed by the woman herself, diaphanous and fluttery, in a muslin confection with a silk stole. She beamed into Gwen's face and prised her away from Edward's hands. 'Do give Mr Scales a drink, Tristan. Mrs Scales, do come with me, and meet the ladies of our little amateur operatic society,' she said, steering her away. Leaning into her she said, 'It's such a pity my brother can't be here—I hope he will be with us by Christmas. I'm sure you'll adore him to bits. Tristan,' she called over her shoulder, 'you did say, didn't you, that Marcus Frome will be coming tonight?'

'Indeed, indeed I did, my dear,' he said, 'many, many times.' He caught Gwen's eye and gave her half a wink. His wife caught the tail end of his action, and he hastily poked a finger to his eye to brush away an invisible fleck. It was misjudged and he injured himself. Hettie admonished him from across the floor with a hint of a frown.

'Someone for your husband to talk to, my dear girl. Marcus Frome is a doctor of medicine, poor man. He has been travelling to the interior, back and forth, back and forth. We could never pin him down—so committed to his work, you see. Always writing up his papers. Lost now, of course. Here we are. Ladies, you must make our newest member very welcome.'

They had arrived at the far end of the room, where a gaggle of pouchy-looking ladies opened their huddle and drew Hettie and Gwen into the circle.

The names were rattled off like a peculiar mantra, and Gwen regarded each one in turn with a polite smile.

'What are you, Mrs Scales? Wonderful, to have a 'Mrs Scales' in our society.'

'I paint. I'm an artist.'

'Oh, yes, we know all about that,' one said with a dismissive air. 'But what are you—contralto, soprano?'

'I'm barely passable, is what I am,' said Gwen. 'I don't think I would make a very useful addition—quite apart from my, from our routine being very rigid. Though it is very kind of you, of course. I am very flattered.'

'Oh, but all the ladies from home are in our society, Mrs Scales.'

'I'm sure I—'

'Marcus Frome has arrived at long last, the dear soul!' Hettie exclaimed and clapped her hands. 'Ladies, do let us give him an impromptu musical welcome.'

Gwen did not know where to look. She could sense the hilarity of the situation unfolding as the gathered ladies began to twitter like syncopated chickens whilst they decided which piece would be best. She moved herself a little apart from the group and then, sure that she would not be missed, went back to where Edward stood, still talking to Tristan Grindlock and now the eagerly awaited Mr Frome.

'Is everything all right?' Edward asked.

'Yes, of course.'

'Mrs Scales,' said Tristan Grindlock, 'may I introduce you to Marcus Frome, who is just regaling us with his tale of woe.'

Marcus Frome looked to Gwen like a toad. She gave him a pleasant enough smile and let him take her hand and press his lips to her fingers, glad that she had worn the lace cotton gloves after all.

'Enchanting wife, you have, Scales,' he said with a wet smile on his lips. 'Enchanting.'

'Mr Frome,' Gwen said, unable to find anything pleasant to say to the man as she felt his saliva soak into her glove and between her fingers.

'Frome, poor chap, was just telling us how he's lost everything in a gale,' said Tristan Grindlock.

'Yes, I'm making arrangements for my passage back to Liverpool. Can't get the stuff, see, out here.' He rolled on his heels. 'Got to hop back and stock up all over.'

'How terrible,' Gwen managed to say without irony.

'Yes, it's a blow.' He turned away from Gwen to address the two men: 'Two years' work sunk. Capsized, see? Not enough ballast. I expect you, Scales, I expect you've seen to it that you're properly kitted out?'

'Properly, indeed!' said Tristan Grindlock. 'Took a week to land all those crates. Well, near enough anyway, eh, Scales?'

'Entomology? Almost my line.'

'Indeed, Mr Frome?' said Gwen, still put out by the saliva which lingered on her glove.

'Yes, Mrs Scales,' he said, very deliberately turning to address her, but finding that he had to look straight into her eyes, lowering his gaze to her bust and addressing her there. 'Mosquitoes.' He turned away again to speak to the men.

'Mr Frome!' Hettie floated herself up to him. 'Do forgive us, we are ready now.' Quite unselfconsciously, Hettie Grindlock took his hand and pulled him to a sofa where she made him sit down. Ranged in front of him now were the ladies, some of them breathing too rapidly to be able to sing effectively. Gwen thought, I do hope this turns out to be truly dreadful; he certainly deserves a good blast of bad notes.

Hettie ushered everyone else into seats, and Gwen noticed that all the Grindlock children were now present. Her eyes widened in search of creatures on the ends of strings. There were none.

'A little bit of 'Lucia', we have decided upon, in honour of Marcus Frome, who will soon be leaving for England, and will be very much missed. We give you 'Spargi d'amaro pianto',' Hettie declared.

It was as Gwen had hoped and more so. She revelled in Mr Frome's discomfort and, when it was over, stood up to give her very enthusiastic applause to the ladies. She beamed at them all with genuine smiles of appreciation.

Edward muttered in her ear, 'You do know that was a dreadful rendering. A cat, a dead one, could have done better.'

'Of course,' she said, still smiling. 'It was most extraordinary, and I would not have missed it for anything.'

'Are you sure you are quite all right?'

Gwen didn't have time to reply; they were called to dinner and spliced to different parts of the table. She was happy to note that Marcus Frome was nowhere near her and that she wouldn't have to speak to him. Gwen was amongst the ladies, who having delivered their masterpiece, now wanted to know all about the young couple. They began to quiz her in earnest. Gwen gave vague replies and picked up her glass of wine.

'French,' nodded a woman called Mrs Trisk, whose top notes had been delightfully grating. 'They have it shipped twice a year. Royal stuff, royal.' Mrs Trisk gulped at her own glass. Gwen sipped and felt a rush of energy swoop down her arms and rest in her elbows. My God, she thought, I'm absolutely drunk on one mouthful. Her plate of meat and fruit danced on the table, and she gripped the edge of her chair with her free hand. She took another sip and the same rush powered its way to her elbows, but she steadied and let go of the chair.

'Eloquent, isn't it?' said Mrs Trisk, studying Gwen's reaction.

'Very.'

'So, do tell me again, your family are Cornish?'

Gwen sliced at a bit of meat.

'Why, that's extraordinary good luck!' Everyone at the table stopped talking or eating to look up and direct their attention to Marcus Frome who had just shouted the words out and was standing up to lean over the table and shake Edward by the hand. He pumped his arm as though he would never stop.

'Mrs Scales, you were saying?'

The noise of resumed conversations rose to fill the air again, and Gwen couldn't catch what Edward had said in reply to Mr Frome's outburst.

'My family? My family is my sister.' Gwen did not want to get further drawn into the conversation.

'And she is married, too?'

'No, she is not. What do you know about Mr

Frome?' Gwen looked past Mrs Trisk towards Edward and strained to hear how his conversation was developing. His words were muffled, but Mr Frome's were not.

'Absolutely, my dear fellow! One cannot allow these matters to flourish. In my opinion—'

'Not married?' Mrs Trisk engaged her again. 'How on earth does she live?'

'Quite well, as a matter of fact. What do you make of Mr Frome?'

'Oh? Ah. I am sure I am not as well acquainted with Mr Frome as our dear Mrs Grindlock.'

'But why do you think he must go back to England, when, surely, all he needs to do is send for whatever he requires?'

'But, my dear Mrs Scales, the man lost everything, everything, you understand. He had not even a full set of clothing on his back when he was rescued, you see.'

Gwen pushed the food around her plate, slicing it up into ever smaller and smaller pieces until it resembled something indescribably horrid. She stabbed a flake of meat and put it into her mouth.

'Can't let them loose amongst such dangerous subjects,' Mr Frome said, and Gwen tried to hear the rest. 'Consequences dire, I may assure you.'

'Is he married, Mr Frome?' she asked Mrs Trisk, 'Is he perhaps returning to see loved ones?' The very idea struck her as unimaginable.

Mrs Trisk tucked her chin into her neck and tried to sip her wine. 'I think he is a confirmed bachelor, Mrs Scales.'

'Really. How interesting.'

Later during the meal, Gwen heard Edward's voice raised. He was being too loud because of the wine. She heard him say, 'Of course, the country offers a vast opportunity, as you yourself are aware, Frome, to make one's mark, to secure one's place in the annals of history and scientific endeavour. And, in entomology, especially so.'

'And what of the opportunities of the land itself, eh, Scales? What do you make of the fertility of the place?'

'Obviously, the verdant nature of the forest points to all kinds of opportunities, indeed it is so. If one were to cultivate the land in the civilised way—'

Gwen listened to Edward's talk with a growing sense of disbelief. Everything they had talked about before they had come here was being flayed. Knowledge for its own sake, not kudos; the value of pristine nature and its role in the search for that truth which was as yet incomplete. In her bleary, tipsy state she saw Edward in a moment of intense clarity, and she hated it. She blanched and then felt suffocated as the talk went on. Edward's voice pitched over the clusters of babble going on around the table.

'From what I have seen so far,' Edward was now saying, 'the local way of cultivation is very primitive. These fellows don't seem to take much pride in their kitchen gardens; weeds choking things, nothing in any discernible order, a hotchpotch. From what I have been able to gather, the attitude is just the tip of the iceberg—'

* * *

The evening had to end, and it did, and Gwen was very glad of it. She couldn't wait to get back and take off her clothes, breathe again, eat something, empty her bladder. Stop talking, stop trying to both hear and blot out what the men were saying. To just get away.

'There'll be a slight change to my routine tomorrow,' Edward told her as he unfastened her gown, his breath hot on her neck. 'I've invited Frome for breakfast. Well, he's invited himself, actually. Nothing I can do about it now, of course. Still. So, formal for breakfast. Apologies.' He let his hands fall away from her.

Gwen stood still for a moment, and then without a word went to her hammock and dropped her clothes to the floor, too tired to care about what might crawl into the folds of it all.

*   *   *

In the morning, she chose from between the layers of tissue and mothballs in her trunk a good dark skirt. She struggled to fasten the skirt's topmost hooks and eyes. As long as I don't sit down, she thought. She undid the last four fastenings and tied a sash over the gape, its tail hanging down over her hip. To make up for it, Gwen fixed her hair into the neatest, most severe style she could manage on her own, using every pin and comb she could lay her fingers on.

'You won't mind if I don't wait for Mr Frome,' Gwen said as she took up a cup of pale tea and stabbed at the lemon slice with a small fork. 'Only, I didn't eat last night.'

Edward coughed, and Gwen froze, looking up at him.

'Carry on,' was all he said.

Marcus Frome was an hour late. They received him on the verandah where he arrived in a burst of noise. Gwen wondered how anyone could be so consistently obnoxious.

'Capital morning, Scales!' he said. 'Capital morning! My God, I've hardly slept a wink all night. I've been revising everything. Up to here I am, up to here,' he said, his hand jabbing at the air above his head.

'Good morning, Mr Frome,' Gwen said. 'May I get you something?'

'Enchanted again. Enchanted.' He turned to Edward. 'Listen, old chap, I can't tell you how much I appreciate this.'

Gwen moved towards Marcus Frome with a cup. 'Your coffee, Mr Frome.' She put it into his hands so that he had to take it from her or risk scalding himself. Marcus Frome was also forced to acknowledge her. 'One gets frightfully jungly,' he said, looking her over, 'but that's to be expected. Shall we get on with it, then?' Marcus Frome put the cup down untouched and walked off into the house. 'Ah yes,' he said through his nose, 'standard set-up. Though, of course, with me, there were no females to complicate the situation. Through here then, is it?' He busied himself into Edward's workroom and stalked about, surveying the room and its contents, touching things with an offhand flutter of his fingertips.

'It's, er, not exactly. No, not in this room at present,' Edward said quietly as he followed him.

'So, let's see the thing then, shall we?' Marcus Frome's eyes widened in impatient expectation.

Gwen stood in the doorway and leaned against the timber with her arms folded. Edward turned to her, his face pale. 'Gwen, I wonder, if you would mind very much, if Mr Frome were to have a look at the—at your microscope?'

'I beg your pardon?' Her arms unfolded.

'Microscope, Mrs Scales; not a plaything but an instrument of science.'

'I'm fully aware of its function, Mr Frome.'

'Let's have it, then, Scales old boy, and I'll see what I think of it and write you out the note.'

'Would you mind stepping outside for a moment, Edward? Do excuse us, Mr Frome.' Gwen trod heavily to the verandah and turned on Edward. 'What is going on? What does the man mean, 'Let's have it'?'

'Gwen, I was meaning to—I would have liked to have had more opportunity to discuss the matter.'

'I'd like very much to know what there is to discuss.'

'Nothing to discuss, Mrs Scales.' Marcus Frome had appeared behind them and picked up the cup of coffee to blow noisily over it, grinning at them. 'Scales is selling me his microscope, see. But I can't very well buy the thing if I haven't seen it first.'

'Mr Scales doesn't have a microscope to sell,' she said, not taking her eyes off Edward.

'Ha! What did I tell you last night, Scales, eh? Got a pair of trousers on under that skirt have you, Mrs Scales?'

'You'll kindly leave at once, Mr Frome.' Gwen's voice was level. 'Good day to you.'

'Sorry, can't do that. See, Scales here made me a promise.'

'Mr Frome! You appear to have been labouring under the misapprehension that Mr Scales is at liberty to sell my property without telling me and without my say-so. Allow me to divest you of this misguided notion.'

'The modern woman, eh? Well, let me tell you, Mrs Scales, when you made those vows, you relinquished all rights to your property; Mr Scales is your protector and keeper. He has promised me a microscope, and, by golly, I'll have it.'

'You are not having my microscope, you impudent toad of a man; get that plain fact into your fat head.'

'Gwen,' Edward's voice was quiet, 'perhaps if we take a moment to discuss the matter—'

'I'll be discussing it no further, Mr Scales.'

'For God's sake, Scales! See to it that your obstreperous woman here understands her obligations.'

'This man is offensive, Mr Scales; invite him to leave immediately.'

'You see, the fact of the matter is this. Frome was in the middle of some very—' Edward's manner was irritatingly calm and reasonable, and it stirred up a turbulent fury just underneath Gwen's breastbone.

'Will you, or will you not, tell this person to leave?'

'He was telling me about his undertaking some research, you see, into malaria, and—'

'Malaria? He said that he was interested in mosquitoes.'

'Madam, I most certainly did no such thing. I—'

'Mr Frome, I am not stupid, and I am not a liar. You told me your interests lay in mosquitoes.'

'I didn't! I said no such thing at all. I assure you both on my life that I am not interested in mosquitoes and I have no reason to be interested in mosquitoes. I am not an entomologist. I am a medical man; I am a doctor of medicine. It was not mosquitoes, not at all.'

Edward and Gwen both regarded Mr Frome with great interest as he gave his fast, stuttering speech on his lack of interest in mosquitoes. Gwen was the first to cut into the silence which followed.

'I believe, Mr Frome, that you are indeed, very, very interested in mosquitoes.' She paused, expecting him to deny it further, but his chest heaved as he drew out a grey handkerchief to wipe over his forehead. 'And I shall tell you what else I believe, shall I? I think that you lost your last chance in that squall to complete whatever research you were engaged in. I believe, Mr Frome, that you are penniless now, and that in returning to England you will be permanently terminating your secret relationship with the mosquito.'

'Preposterous!' A shower of spittle caught the light, but his protest was feeble, and Gwen continued regardless.

'However, hearing that Mr Scales and I had recently arrived in the country, fully equipped for entomologising and so forth, you sought immediately to make our acquaintance with the sole intention of stealing some instruments of science from us. From *me*.'

'Absurd woman, your mind is no doubt affected by the humidity, I—'

'You know, Frome, I don't think Gwen's mind is affected by anything at all but good sense. I am inclined to agree with her. It does seem a trifle strange that you have not chosen to resupply yourself with a microscope by the more reasonable, by the more *usual* process of writing off for one to be shipped out here to you.'

'Are you to tell me, sir, that you will stand in the way of a major scientific breakthrough? The biggest medical discovery of this century?'

'Well, I suppose, given that I only have your word for it,' said Edward, rather thoughtfully, scratching the back of his head, 'it rather looks like I am.'

'You what?'

'I concur; I'll not let you have that microscope. You'll be obliged to locate another or return to England.'

'There is no other! There is no other microscope in this place that I might have.'

'Oh, come now, Mr Frome,' Gwen said wearily, sitting down, tired of it all now that Edward was on her side again. 'I'm sure there are other, more gullible people in possession of a microscope whom you may yet endeavour to hoodwink.'

'No,' he spat, 'there are not!'

Gwen laughed and kicked off her fancy house slippers, leaning back to put her feet onto a footstool. She wriggled her bare toes.

'Then we must, Mr Scales, declare this breakfast party over and done with. I do hope, Mr Frome, that your return voyage to England is uneventful.'

'You sly bitch.'

'How dare you!' Edward shouted. 'Apologise immediately, sir, or I'll see you.'

Gwen sat up, astonished at Edward's swift change in tone and, moreover, dumbfounded that he—had he?

'Edward,' she said, standing up and putting a hand lightly on his arm, 'I don't think it very wise.'

'No, you are quite right,' he said, relaxing as

Frome backed away clumsily. 'He is no gentleman; I'll just fetch my whip.'

'Are you threatening me, Scales?'

'Indeed, I am, although I perceive you are something of a coward, and I may not have to act on it.'

'You'll regret this, see, you will.'

'I doubt it most wholeheartedly.'

Gwen and Edward watched as Marcus Frome marched away from them, turning back every now and then to glance over his shoulder to convey what they supposed were meant to be sneers of contempt. Edward put his arm around Gwen and raised his hand in farewell. As Marcus Frome disappeared from their sight she rounded on him.

'Hypocrite,' she said separating from him. 'You're as unspeakable as that wretched man.'

'It wasn't as it seemed, Gwen. I made no promise of anything.'

'Don't make things worse. I am not an idiot.'

'I know that.'

'Then please do me the honour of not behaving as if you didn't. Furthermore, I wish to make it abundantly clear that my few possessions are mine and mine alone.'

'Absolutely; Gwen, please forgive me, I should have given you fair warning.'

'And you had ample opportunity; but whatever promise that Frome man thought he had extracted from you last night, you were too much of a weakling to put him right.'

'The Bordeaux was very—'

'It was certainly far more 'eloquent' than you. Don't ever let anything like this happen again, Edward, or I shall follow that odious creature back to England.'

'You can't possibly mean that.'

'Can't I?' she sat down, loosening the sash at her side and breathing out.

There passed some minutes where they would not look at each other. Edward paced up and down the verandah, and Gwen put her slippers back on her feet. She fiddled with them, slipping them half off and on.

Presently, Edward came to a halt. 'I have excused your behaviour this morning for two reasons. The first being, as you quite succinctly surmised, Marcus Frome is an odious creature—of the lowest order. The second being that I excuse you on account of your condition.'

Gwen's slippers fell to the floor. 'I beg your pardon?'

'Which part?'

'All of it! I can't believe what I've just heard. *My* behaviour? Have you forgotten, Mr Scales, that I am not, in fact, your wife? You have no business excusing or not excusing me. Almost selling my possessions. You have no business treating me so—'

He caught her up by the arms and pulled her close to him. 'Haven't you understood? At all?' His eyes roved her face. 'You're tied to me, whether either of us likes it or not, by your *condition*. And I'm not asking you, I'm telling you now. Don't make a fool of me again.'

'If anyone has made a fool of you, Mr Scales, it is only yourself.' Gwen picked his hands off her and sat down, utterly livid.

In the aftermath of Frome's attempt on her microscope she couldn't sustain the bravado she had felt in his presence.

I just don't have a single thing to say to him, she thought. And she slithered down into a capsule of loneliness. A crushing wave of homesickness came over her. All she wanted to do was stamp off and tell her sister what a thoroughly annoying and bumptious man he was; that perhaps she had been right to try and stop her from leaving Cornwall. She couldn't think how Edward might have arrived at the conclusion that just because she had agreed to this *condition*, as he called it, to be his mistress, he had the right to fume over her with his idiotic words.

The humidity gathered around Gwen and Edward; they were deadly silent with each other until Edward left with his nets and other equipment. I am leaving, she thought, watching the stiffness of his gait as he walked away from her. I shall go home. She pictured herself packing up her few things, nesting the microscope in its box amongst her clothes. Infernal man, she muttered, but she made no move to do anything except kick her fancy slippers across the floor and let down her hair. Slowly, she began to plait it into a thick rope, and when it was done, she spent a long time wrapping the rope of it around her wrist and along the length of her forearm.

* * *

Soon after turning in that night, she heard the shuffle of Edward's bare feet on the floorboards as he scuffed his way towards her in the dark. She lay still in her hammock and did not speak.

'I must apologise,' he said. 'Everything I said

before, in England, everything I told you, it still holds true. Please forgive my unutterably dismal attitude today. I couldn't bear it if you went away. There would be no point.' There seemed to be a moment in which he intended to tell her what, exactly, there would be no point to. The space for the words was there—and then it closed. She heard him turning blindly in the dark of the room and his retreating footfall to his own hammock.

Gwen lay awake for a long time wondering to which conversation in England he could have been referring. After a while, she heard the alarming, deep choking rattle of Edward's snoring. She muffled her head with a blanket and tried to sleep.

CHAPTER XXIX

PARÁ, BRAZIL. OLD YEAR'S NIGHT, 1860/1.

Of course, she had known. She must have, mustn't she? No, she still didn't think so. The knowledge sickened her and tore at her. She felt shredded and raw under Edward's gaze and Maria's solicitations. And fat. And stupid. And desperate. What was to be done about it? Nothing. Her half-formed plans to return to Cornwall were as substantial as a drop of ink in a barrel full of water. And so she'd started work.

Gwen arranged the first insects she intended to paint into her book. Very delicately, she reached into the middle of the wooden case and tugged a pinned butterfly free from its base of cork. An afternoon breeze caught the edges of the stiffened wings and the insect twirled around on its axis like a vibrant miniature windmill. Cupping her hands over the insect she brought it away from the main thrust of the breeze, and she stuck the pin into another piece of cork set onto a wooden wedge.

She began to sketch out very lightly the outline beginning with the bulbous eyes and delicately furry thorax, down to the abdomen, which was as brightly coloured as the rest of the butterfly. She imagined it alive, its fat pulse. It was now thin and pinched, the result of its handling. Edward did not collect every single insect himself. Sometimes children came to the house with things they had caught. One of them said he had collected for another Englishman a few years before. He brought Edward some specimens which he said the other man had not been able to catch.

Gwen stared hard at the butterfly. Making the thing properly, *scientifically* symmetrical was a challenge in itself. At home, she'd always accepted her slight mistakes as part of what it was to spend time staring so hard at one creature or landscape. Now, she felt entirely useless. She lightly sketched out the first half on the left of the insect. She shifted in her seat. Her internal workings were not her own. There seemed an awful lot of wind to pass, and at frequent intervals. And she had become terribly constipated. These things were easy to deal with when Edward was not at the house. She put down her pencil, got up and expelled a lot of wind loudly. When he was there, she spent as much time on the verandah as possible; it gave her the most dreadful stomach ache, trying to hold it all in. Maria had told her to eat lots of fruit from the garden. The mangoes were very sticky and drippy.

Maria laughed at her complaints, saying that as it was she had an easy time of it.

*   *   *

Maria sat with Gwen, it seemed to Edward, for most of the day. When he left the house after breakfast and his first morning ramble, they were sitting in hammocks slung under the verandah; when he returned, they were in exactly the same place. Yet, he knew this could not be true because each evening there would be a new set of studies in her painting book. The first time he leafed through her paintings he had been beside himself with expectation. He had put off looking because she had not offered to show him anything yet. He was disinclined to ask her while the prickliness of the atmosphere over Frome and the microscope had not quite been smoothed over. But, one evening, she said casually, 'Did you see what I have done today, Edward?' and continued to swing in the hammock with her eyes closed.

So, after he had organised his day's quarry—he fiddled about with the mangled bird he'd shot for quite a while—he stepped cautiously over to her workbench by the window as if the insects inside the pages might suddenly detect his presence and fly off.

They were better than he expected. Better than he had hoped for. He took a pocket magnifying glass and held it to the page. She had painted the individual hairs on the thorax of a butterfly. It was modelled in gouache so that it seemed to stand proud of the paper, even hover just slightly above it, the tips of the wings coming down to touch the paper. He went out onto the verandah with the book in his hands.

'Gwen, these are magnificent.'

'I wish there was a way of painting them to look the way they do when they are alive. Feeding on nectar or floating along.'

'These are marvellous things.'

Edward had worried that she might not be up to the task, or that her condition would become her priority. She seemed these days to be as focused in her work as a man might be. The sheer body of it was testament to that. Her condition seemed to be irrelevant to her.

* * *

Gwen had been learning Portuguese from Maria. Keeping her feet in the air, propped up inside the hammock made her restless. As the heat gathered between eleven and three there was little she felt like doing, anyway. As the temperature soared, the silence of the place was absolute, only punctuated now and then with the odd penetrating whine of an insect.

Every day, it was as if the oppressiveness had been only a part of her imagination as the rain, suddenly released, poured down to enliven her spirits, and sharp cracks of thunder erupted overhead. And every afternoon, she doubted the relief which was to come. In the stillness, she doubted the ability of the birds to start up their calls again. And over each new tree bursting into bloom in the morning out of the blanket of green she was as surprised and delighted as she had been the first morning she had seen it.

'You are fighting, fighting all the time.'

Gwen looked up from the letter she was trying to write. 'What?'

'The heat, Mrs Scales. You have to let it through you. You have to let it soak you up.'

*   *   *

Maria observed the Christmas festivals in the town, leaving Edward and Gwen to themselves. They did not exchange gifts, and they did not attend any services at any of the churches. Without Maria, they got on with each other as well as they could. In England Edward had once remarked that he couldn't imagine Gwen inhabiting an interior. He couldn't imagine, he had said, what it would be like to see her contained within four walls. And he still could not, for there had not been many occasions when he had been inside a building with her. And that seemed as if it was another life, anyway. He looked at Gwen and at the rain falling off the verandah roof. The clothes she wore concealed her shape. They were an odd combination of styles. Maria had brought some items to the house, and together the women had connived and contrived to transform Gwen's appearance, slowly. Now, when he looked at her properly he would easily have mistaken her for—what? Not quite a native. Her skin had changed, too. He pictured the dark line of melanin, which he assumed was marking her belly, and almost wanted to take her there where she stood. She wore her sleeves short. The slippers he had bought for her spent most of the day under the hammock. The sight of her toes and their new colour drew him out under the eaves. She loved listening to the noisy frogs and toads. Pointless to try and talk, even with the shutters closed inside the house. The frogs had released them both for the time being of the arduous business of making conversation which did not include references to the past or the future. This had been one such evening. Edward had gone into his room to try and write up some of his notes but he'd been unable to concentrate. His jagged writing skittered and meandered over the page; the ink was blotted badly, and there were smears made by his grubby thumbs. Out collecting, if he had a thought to put down he'd get distracted before the words were formed on the page. He'd found himself, some days, trying to write with the insect nets still gripped in the same hand, his fingers contorted.

Edward looked at Gwen. Why shouldn't he just go to her now? No words would be needed. He felt a familiar drawing in, as though he were a hawk moth, in awe of her scent, unable to resist. He came up close to her, his fingertips touching the bare skin of her arms, and she gave a half jump, half shiver of surprise.

'Won't you let your hair down for me again?' He spoke the words right into her ear and pulled the thin, ebony rods from the coils piled onto her head. The rope of hair fell heavily down her back, but she hardly moved, barely gave any indication that she had heard him speak or that he had touched her. After half a minute her head turned in his direction. He saw her lips moving, the words lost in the amphibious chorus.

'In London the bells will all have rung out.' His lips touched her face. 'Loosen your hair for me again. This rain is perfect for it; do you remember what you said?' He grasped at her and fumbled underneath her clothes.

'Do you think about England that much?' She pulled away from him, detaching his fingers like so much sticky cobweb. 'What is that?' They were roaring at each other now. The moment, if it had indeed been a moment, was gone. They both strained to hear. Edward cupped his hand around his ear, and made out two distinct male voices, one Scottish and one American.

The Scot was saying, 'I keep telling you why it's Old Year's Night, and yet you still insist on calling it New Year's Eve, which any reasonable man would agree is tomorrow night—tomorrow being the first day of the new year.'

'Oh, indeed; just as you like,' came the other voice.

Gwen and Edward both tensed at the sound of the heavy treading on the boards of the verandah. What must we look like? she thought. 'Give me those,' she said and took her pins back and piled up her long plait, jabbing everything into place. She tried to alter her features into something resembling a welcoming gaze. But still, she thought, we must look like two startled rabbits. The men careened around the corner.

'Ah. A Happy New Year's Eve to you good people both.'

'I must apologise for Mr Coyne. He means to wish you a good Old Year's Night.'

Their arms were draped around each other's shoulders; it was impossible to tell which man was being supported or if the stance was of mutual benefit.

Inside, with the shutters closed, it was just about

possible to converse properly. The younger man spoke first; he wore a pair of spectacles designed to shade his eyes from the sun. The glass was tinted Madonna blue, the frames sparkling slivers of silver. They gave his eyes a most astonishing aspect. Gwen had to acknowledge the effect, even though it did seem a little bit affected.

'Vincent Coyne, glad to make your acquaintance, sir, ma'am, on this fine New Year's Eve.'

'Gus Pemberton, also pleased to meet you, madam, and sir, on the last night of the Old Year.' His voice was playful, like a rolling sweep of cool air.

'Scales. As a matter of fact you are both wrong.'

'Wrong? Hey, we got the wrong day. Ha! Sorry to bother you. We'll just go squish some more of those toads and come back tomorrow.'

'No.' Gwen said. 'Don't go now that you are here. We just meant that clocks at home have already struck the hour.'

'Have you been to every house in the neighbourhood?' asked Edward, a little warily.

'Oh, no, sir, indeed we have not. We have been sent by your friends in town. Mrs Grindlock is a fine, fine lady, for whom I have the very highest regard.'

'Excuse him, he isn't always like this.'

Gwen said, 'That's perfectly all right, Mr Pemberton. I'm sure half the population of the town is in much the same state.'

'I can assure you the numbers amount to more than half.'

Edward breathed in through his nose. 'Perhaps some coffee.'

Gwen looked away and grimaced inwardly at

Edward. Mr Coyne slithered into a lacquered cane chair. Pemberton turned to Gwen. 'I'm sorry we startled you. We did call out but the frogs—'

'—drowned us out.' Vincent tried to sit up. '*O da Casa*.'

'O of the house?'

'It's the proper thing to do, in the jungle you know.'

Gwen suspected that Vincent was suddenly not quite as drunk as he had been outside. She smiled at him. 'I haven't been into the jungle yet, so I am still ignorant about that kind of thing.'

Vincent's eyes made an unabashed tour of her person and stopped at her middle, just for a second, before slewing his gaze around the room. 'You speak the language, not quite so ignorant.'

Mr Coyne was extraordinarily beautiful; he wore the whiskers on his chin clipped to a neat point, rather than cultivating the bushy side-whiskers, which, Gwen thought, made most men who wore them resemble guinea-pigs. Not handsome. Mr Pemberton was handsome; Gwen registered it. The two men were like a pair of elegant butterflies, opposites but perfectly matched; whereas Edward, in comparison, was like the longhorn beetle grub. She watched his squirming accommodation of the unexpected guests with cool fascination.

Pemberton cleared his throat. 'You really don't have to trouble yourselves with the coffee.'

'Please, it's no trouble.'

'We don't like to impose,' said Pemberton.

'You are not imposing. Really, we have made ourselves such hermits; of course, we must offer you something. It is the thing to do, in the jungle, I believe.'

Gus Pemberton laughed. 'Yes, indeed, Mrs Scales.' The chorus from outside almost swallowed his words completely.

'Mrs Scales,' Vincent sounded very serious, 'I have had a letter from a good friend of mine who tells me that—'

'Later, Vincent, later,' Gus Pemberton said.

'Here we are then, gentlemen, a pot of coffee for the weary and travel-worn.'

'That was very clever of you, Edward.' Gwen couldn't help it, but he didn't seem to notice.

'I had made it before, and, would you believe it, the pot was still hot.'

Thank God for these people, thought Gwen. She studied Mr Coyne's profile. I feel that I know him; or rather, that I am meeting him at last. Mr Coyne's blue spectacles glimmered in the lamplight as he pushed them up the bridge of his nose. A beautiful young man—but for all his show, perhaps a bit nervous. The air between the four of them felt charged with something alive. Gwen felt its invisible form move between them, sinuous, shifting, elemental. She thought, this is the creature which has been following me and watching me. It knows my heart, and it knows too that my heart is leaving Edward.

CHAPTER XXX

They were still drinking coffee, and Edward had grown tired of his guests. Still, he listened to the conversation to which he felt he could not contribute.

Gus Pemberton took out a fat cigar and asked if anyone minded if he stepped outside to fumigate the frogs.

Gwen watched Gus Pemberton and Edward go out onto the verandah. Then she said, 'Mr Coyne, you mentioned a letter earlier.'

Vincent cleared his throat. 'I believe we could be of mutual benefit to each other regarding the person you wish to find.' He lowered his voice a little and glanced in the direction of the verandah where Gus Pemberton had managed to get his damp cigar to light. In a confiding tone, he said, 'I have only mentioned to Gus half of what it could mean. You've read Darwin, most likely a given that you are aware of his sparrows.' He paused, and Gwen nodded, mentally correcting him, unsure of how finches could have any relevance. He continued, 'It all has to do with isolation. I have been paddling through the forests, and to cut it rather short, Mrs Scales, I believe it is perfectly possible for an isolated tribe of a type of *pre-human* people to exist within.' Gwen raised her eyebrows but remained silent. It was beginning to dawn on her that perhaps Mr Pemberton's friend really was mad, as he had jokingly suggested. She wanted to ask whom the letter was from. She remained politely and silently attentive, but she didn't want to appear complicit, and certainly didn't want to prolong the discussion.

Vincent took her silence as a cue and continued, 'With no contact hitherto from the outside world, what's to say that a missing link can't in fact be found right here in the Amazons?' Clearly, he expected her to say something.

'Mr Coyne, are you saying that you think there

exists a living example, a specimen of *proof* that human beings are descended from apes?'

'Yes! that's it,' Vincent almost squealed. 'Wouldn't it be the most fantastic discovery? Darwin provides the theory; and Vincent Coyne provides the proof.'

Gwen swallowed. 'Mr Darwin, if my memory serves me correctly, has not exactly, not quite yet, at any rate, proposed the theory you suppose he has. And, in any case, I am sure you are aware that others have already said it. The person, for instance, who published *Vestiges* almost twenty years ago.' Vincent stared at her. He seemed baffled. Gwen thought, He doesn't know about that book. In fact, she hadn't read it either; she only knew about it because of a similar but less personal discussion with Captain Swithin. She said, 'Perhaps it was not available in America.' Vincent seemed not to have heard her.

He said, 'It is only a matter of time. Everyone is aware of what he is getting at. Everyone is talking about it. He's testing the water. He's making little amendments here and there with every new edition. Eventually, when he thinks we've had time to adjust to the idea of natural selection—he'll put in a new chapter about Man.'

'Mr Coyne, I think if and when that chapter is written, then it will be proposed, as I understand it at any rate, that you cannot prove the theory by finding living specimens. I think that, perhaps, in time, Mr Darwin may suggest that apes and humans have what we might call a, a common ancestor, who has long since been laid down in the stones of time. As far as I can see, during the process of natural selection, if you choose to take up the theory in earnest, the links are changed with each generation, so that we are a long line of descendents and ancestors. We cannot live at the same time as our ancestors, Mr Coyne.' Gwen felt herself becoming breathless. 'An isolated tribe of people, however primitive-seeming, cannot be our ancestors; they would merely be an isolated tribe of people with certain attributes, probably attributable to external circumstance.' Gwen felt that she had tied herself up in a tangle of theory she knew little enough about, but she hoped that Mr Coyne would understand that she wanted no part of his plan. He was unnerving her. She threw up her hands in feigned defeat and looked to the verandah to see whether Mr Pemberton was coming back inside.

Vincent Coyne laughed, and Gus Pemberton stepped into the room saying, 'He at least had the sense to do that.'

CHAPTER XXXI

CORNWALL. FEBRUARY 16, 1861.

Euphemia's meetings were reduced to two or three evenings a week. Isobel Scales came once a month. The unbridled and undiminished audacity of the woman. Once a month Euphemia's Spiritualist meetings morphed into a game of Cheat; only two of the players were aware of the game or the lack of rules and the other players concealing tricks or double bluffs. Euphemia's contacts with the other side were leaving her uncharacteristically ravaged with fatigue.

Isobel Scales brought with her a variety of new clients in various states of mourning and others with a nose for something a little sensational. She had a reputation for punctuality and preciseness in everything. So, it was with some bemusement that Euphemia found herself entertaining Isobel Scales at ten-thirty in the morning in the middle of the week. It was shocking to see her so garishly dressed. She wore the front of her skirt flat in contrasting layers of mauve and yellow silk, whilst her rump displayed a voluminous puff of satin and taffeta ruffles in alternating rosettes. The whole thing jarred on Euphemia's eye, and she wondered what kind of imbecile could design such an outrage.

'I'm disturbing your reading,' Isobel perched her puff, settling herself into the nearest chair. Euphemia followed her gaze to the book lying splayed open on a small card table. She took it up and closed it, not bothering to mark the page. The polished calfskin felt cool.

'It's just a trifle. I haven't managed to get along with it yet. Epistolary novels!—I have it on loan from Mrs Coyne. She was anxious to hear my opinion of it.'

'Mrs Coyne, you'll have to remind me if I have made her acquaintance, I—may I?'

Euphemia pretended not to have noticed Isobel's request and kept the book in her lap, covering it with both hands.

'Oh, but you must remember poor Penelope Coyne.'

'Perhaps I do. I must confess that I have an ulterior motive for calling on you like this.'

Euphemia relaxed and her fingers stopped palpating the embroidered hem of her napkin.

Perhaps Isobel would soon go away. She hadn't taken off her gloves.

'I have a little occasion to organise at our London house next week and I wondered if I might borrow your cook. Of course, we can come to some sort of agreement; I would be happy to do a fair swap, if you are willing. It is just that none of the staff have your cook's particular talent in the art of *petites bouchées*, and I did so want something a little more extraordinary—though all of my kitchen staff are quite excellent in their own ways.'

Euphemia did not know whether to be flattered or outraged. Instead, she sat in a fug of agitation and listened to the cranking internals of the hall clock mark the half hour. If she did not manage to get the tonic into her tea in the next ten minutes she would have to excuse herself. Her fingers tapped out a syncopated tinkle on the saucer.

'I have no need of a confirmation immediately, of course. Has your cook ever been on a locomotive, to your knowledge, Miss Carrick? I am afraid it inspired in me a fit of terror the first time I stepped up into a carriage. Heaven knows we should be used to them by now.'

Heaven knows a lot, thought Euphemia, putting her hand into her pocket and fingering the stopper on the bottle of laudanum.

'My dear, don't rouse yourself on my account. There is plenty of time, after all.'

'I have a cramp coming on in my foot; the exercise will get rid of it.'

'Oh, that is a nuisance, isn't it? Why don't you walk up and down?' Isobel got up and put her arm under Euphemia's elbow. 'You seem a little clammy, if I may say so.' Looking at her closely she said, ‘You are in a state, Miss Carrick. I think I will go and find that girl of yours—Susan, isn’t it?

‘Now, wriggle your feet whilst I find some brandy, I won’t be long.’ She peered at Euphemia’s eyes. ‘You look ghastly. I always used to get the cramps down my legs. Of course, all this sort of nuisance just disappears when you get married and—’ She gave a nervous giggle. Perhaps it was a snort.

Euphemia closed her eyes and clutched at the bottle. Isobel Scales was already at the door. Euphemia watched in fascination as the train on her mauve and vivid lilac skirt with the yellow trimmings whipped out of sight.

When Isobel came back some fifteen minutes later with the brandy bottle (not the decanter which would have been easy enough to locate in the dining room) and a couple of glasses (not brandy glasses), Euphemia was almost back together again. She accepted the glass of brandy and drank it quite cheerfully.

‘I do apologise, Mrs Scales. How dreadful of me.’

‘Let’s not mention it. I’m not in the least perturbed by these mishaps. We are all human and subject to the whims of nature. And I think we are well enough acquainted by now, not to let that sort of thing embarrass us, are we not?’

And you are fairly well acquainted with my kitchen, thought Euphemia, as Isobel Scales sipped at the brandy she had poured for herself and fully occupied the chair.

‘After all, I myself have fainted in this very house. If you don’t mind my saying so, you lace yourself rather tighter than fashion absolutely dictates, Miss Carrick. I have always striven for the nineteen; you on the other hand really have no need to be so fierce. My husband, when I was first married, was constantly arguing the case for a more 'natural' figure. His head was full of scientific this and medical reasons for that. To be honest, I did not care for his arguments at all. Being looser around one's torso is in no way indicative of one's morals, Miss Carrick.' Isobel Scales was in no particular hurry to leave. She gave another nervous snort. 'This water is gone tepid, shall we ring for some hot? Then we can discuss my little plan to steal your dwarf away for a few days. Isn't this fun?'

There was no doubt in Euphemia's mind that Isobel Scales was having fun of some sort. She found herself unable, finally, to keep it up any longer.

'Mrs Scales,' she said abruptly, 'Harris has departed this world. It was quite sudden, and unexpected, some five months ago.'

Euphemia watched Isobel's face moving. Flakes of powder fell from her face; spittle glistened on her teeth and made silvery strings as she opened her mouth silently and shut it again. Her hair was dressed so tightly that the skin around her temples forced her expression into something which was not natural. It was interesting to see her in daylight, and alone. Euphemia found herself wondering if Mrs Scales ever took her hair pins out.

Mrs Scales had satisfied her appetite for brandy. She dropped the Angel's fingers she had been holding to the china. 'And so whom must I congratulate for those?'

'Susan, of course. She made a point of learning the craft very quickly.'

'Quite so.' Isobel Scales rose unsteadily to her

feet.

Euphemia forced herself out of her chair to see her out. She did not want Mrs Scales wandering the wrong way.

Isobel Scales thanked Euphemia for the interview, but as she turned to leave what little colour there was in her face drained away. Euphemia was fascinated to see the grey skin clouded under the flaky powder and, sidling a little closer, waited to see what would happen next. Mrs Scales began to say something but it was incomprehensible; she raised her hands in the form of some gesture as the words refused to come out in the right order. Euphemia frowned. One moment there she was upright, the next moment she had fallen onto the carpet in a swoosh of silk and a small thud, which was made by her head, banging on the floor.

The fresh air assaulted Euphemia on the doorstep. It went into her ears and up her nose. It travelled along her sleeves and slipped into her armpits. Mrs Scales' driver got down from the coach when he caught sight of her. Euphemia said, 'Fetch this doctor from this address. Are you literate, or do I need to read it out to you? Very good. Mrs Scales is gravely ill—do not come back without the doctor.'

The coach bounced on its springs as he stepped up and settled himself, slapping the reins. The two horses touched noses and tossed their heads. The gravel beneath hooves and wheels crunched.

'She seemed all right before, ma'am,' said Susan, who had managed without Euphemia's assistance to get the conscious but immobile Mrs Scales onto the day-bed and into a comfortable repose while they waited for the doctor. 'But just because someone seems all right, doesn't mean to say that they *are* all right.' Susan dabbed at Mrs Scales' forehead with a cool damp muslin and felt her pulse. Both of them were thinking about Mr Harris' sudden demise but neither wanted to admit that they feared a repeat performance.

'What on earth are you doing?'

'Taking the lady's pulse, ma'am. I learned it years ago.'

'And what good will that do?'

'It won't do any good at all, ma'am, but it tells me how strong and fast her heart is beating.'

'And how does she do?'

'She's in a bad way, ma'am. Like a bird that's been mauled by the cat.'

'Oh, for heaven's sake, Susan.' Euphemia got down onto her knees and spoke to Isobel in a businesslike voice. 'The doctor will be here very soon, I should think. But, in the meantime, would you please let me know if there is anything you need. Is there a particular remedy, Mrs Scales, which you have been prescribed of late?'

'I don't think you'll get no answer from her, ma'am.'

Isobel's breaths were shallow and laboured; her eyes were open and the lids flickered a little as she tried to focus on Euphemia. Under duress Susan took a pair of scissors to Isobel's corset after unbuttoning the silk jacket of her dress.

'Don't fuss, Susan; it can't possibly do any harm and it may do some good.'

Cutting the linen tapes made no difference and Isobel's paralysis remained unchanged. Susan continued to dab at Isobel's forehead and now also at her chest with the damp muslin. Isobel continued to breathe but just as badly. Euphemia got up and went to stand at the front door. Isobel Scales' penchant for games had taken a turn for the worse.

* * *

Euphemia smoothed the already smooth covers on the bed in the guest room Susan had prepared in a rush while the doctor had examined the patient on the day-bed downstairs. Mrs Scales had been carried up to the room in the arms of her driver. She had recovered from her three hour-long episode enough to talk, though Euphemia wished that she would go to sleep. It had been a difficult day. Isobel slurred as if drunk.

'When I am dead, I want you to invite my husband to your Spirit conference. There are conversations I was unable to have. I would like you to help me.'

'Your time is not now, not even close. The doctor has said so.'

'That doctor is wrong.'

'As you wish. I will do my—whatever I can.'

Euphemia could think of nothing more horrible than being witness to whatever conversation Mrs Scales had in mind for her errant husband. She shuddered to think of it. The idea of the intimacy appalled her.

'It doesn't really matter how long it takes for you to accomplish my request. I will not mind waiting. Though I am concerned for your sister, Miss Carrick.'

Euphemia drew back and released Isobel's hands from what she had been hoping conveyed tenderness or at least polite sympathy. 'My sister conducts her own affairs in the way she has seen fit. I have no influence over her.'

'She can't have known what she was committing herself to.'

'Don't tire yourself, Mrs Scales.'

'I have been battling with this—*malady*, for years, Miss Carrick. I am tired, indeed, of keeping up the pretence. You know what I speak of. My concern for your sister. Troubles me. I did what I thought I must. I tried to help. I have gone to lengths.'

'It is so cold in this room, I must apologise.'

Euphemia went to the small fireplace where the flames were failing yet to throw any heat into the room. She put a lump of coal into the middle of the fire. Euphemia pulled the cord to ring for Susan, and when she came, Euphemia told her to bring another bed-warmer for Mrs Scales.

'The cold does not trouble me. Death will be cold; I will have an eternity to get used to it.'

'That's no way to talk, ma'am,' Susan said. 'I won't have you catching your death over the want of a bed-warmer.'

Euphemia looked at her desperately ill guest. At least it is winter, she thought. As long as she dies soon, I will be able to send her body back to London. I won't have to see to her buried here.

The light went steadily from the window. The day had become duller and duller, the grey of the sky thickened, and in the gloaming, as Euphemia looked out of the guest bedroom window, she saw fat flakes of snow. Her heart sank.

* * *

That evening Euphemia looked for the book which had arrived months before, without a note. Penelope Coyne had not loaned it, but Euphemia suspected that under the quiver on Penelope's pout, there was a taste for something sensational. Certainly, a woman like Mrs Coyne would not forget to scribble a line or two when sending a book. Euphemia searched under all the cushions. Susan must have tidied it away. She sat down in the chair Isobel Scales had occupied that morning and closed her eyes. A vivid image of Penelope's son came to rest under her eyelids. It didn't matter that her communications with him had come to such an abrupt end. She trusted that he would make new contact with her whenever he was able and give her some positive news about the progress he must surely by now be making with her sister.

* * *

Susan checked on Mrs Scales as often as she was able that first night. She made the fire hotter and replenished the bed-warmers and found an extra eiderdown. She covered Mrs Scales' shoulders with a fur stole and made the lamps bright in the room. Susan did everything she could to banish death from the house. Every night and every morning for the past five months, kneeling at her bedside, Susan had begged forgiveness for her part in Mr Harris' lonely passing on the cold kitchen floor. She closed her mind to the rest.

Mrs Scales had eaten nothing of the syllabub but had taken the honey from the spoon; she had refused the tincture left by the doctor, describing it as an evil poison and told Susan that the doctor was an incompetent fool, that all doctors were incompetent, and that she should never trust them, especially those who were the most trustworthy of all. Some of her talk was certainly muddled. At times during the evening, Mrs Scales drifted off to sleep propped up on the pillows. Then, she would open her eyes suddenly and begin to talk again. Twice, Susan had come into the room with a hot bed-warmer to find Mrs Scales having a conversation with the empty room. Susan did not like this. It was her firm belief that those close to death were able to see ghosts. In this case, she determined to make the room too bright and too hot for any ghosts to find agreeable for very long.

'When they lock my body away, in that horrible vault,' she said to Susan, 'you must make sure that the name carved is my maiden name. Fetch the ink and paper to me.'

Susan filled the nib and wiped it carefully against the neck of the ink bottle and passed it to Mrs Scales. She spent some time over it. The pen had to be passed back and forth to be refilled, and Mrs Scales' hand was not steady.

'This is an instruction to be sent to my solicitor. I have put his address there.' She asked Susan to sign her own name at the bottom of the paper as witness. 'I had meant to do this. I have been forgetting and remembering too much all at once.'

'I'll see that it's delivered, ma'am.'

'I am very grateful.'

Susan put it aside to dry as there was no blotting paper. Mrs Scales lay back again on the pillows and closed her eyes. Susan checked the time. It was almost ten at night. Susan was reluctant to do the usual things and leave the room. She looked at the messy scrawl and tried to decipher Mrs Scales' line of thoughts on the paper and was doubtful over it. She filled the nib again and wrote out on a clean sheet what she could make of the instructions.

At half past eleven Mrs Scales woke Susan who had fallen asleep in a chair near the bed.

'Miss, I'm sorry, I don't know your name. Will you tell me where he went? I came here to find him, but he wasn't here. I can't remember your name. Will you fetch Mr Harris? There is something I have wanted to ask him.' She made a feeble attempt to throw back the covers from the bed and to get herself up. 'I think he might be out there.'

'No one is out there this time of night, Mrs Scales. Not in the weather we're having.'

'Nonsense, it is the middle of summer.'

'It's blowing a gale of snow, Mrs Scales.'

'That's not my name. But, my manners, what do they call you?'

'I'm Susan Wright, ma'am.'

'Very pleased to make your acquaintance, Susan Wright. I am Isobel Armstrong. Did you know that?'

'I saw you write it down, ma'am, and I signed my own beneath.'

'So you did. They won't call me after him. I don't want his name after all.'

'Ma'am, please let me put the covers back up.'

'Did you just say it was snowing?'

'I did, ma'am.'

'Isn't that a curious thing to happen in the middle of summer.'

'We're in the month of February, ma'am.'

'I see. Tell me about your sister.'

'I have only brothers, ma'am.'

'Of course, I remember now. And what about Mr Harris? Who has him now?'

'The Lord keeps him now, ma'am.'

'Goodness, how the little man has progressed! Do tell me—Lord whom? Oh, never mind. The next thing we shall hear is that he has been employed to spy on the Queen.'

Isobel sank into herself as she closed her eyes again. Susan turned away and busied herself with the coal bucket; she didn't want Mrs Scales to hear her weeping.

CHAPTER XXXII

THE TIMES, Thursday, October 4, 1866.

MURDER TRIAL AT THE OLD BAILEY.

WITNESS for the Prosecution, Mrs Fernly surprised the court with her statement. It was and, indeed, still remains unclear whether the Counsel for the Prosecution had prior knowledge of its content: 'I have known the accused since the day she first smiled at a handful of May blossom with not yet a tooth in her dear head. What I shall say of my account of the accused shall be this: the dear child [the prisoner] was never an immoral person. Never. And nothing [pointing her finger towards the heavens] will induce me to say that she is an immoral person now. Her conduct throughout her life has been exemplary; her manner with all those around her fine and true, and she never acted on impulse or unkindly. Indeed, she took it upon herself to educate the children of the poorest families in the village, devoting many hours to Bible study with those little souls. To elope is not immoral—misguided in some cases, perhaps—but not the deed of a bad person as has been suggested here. In taking passage to Brazil with that man [Mr Scales], she believed that she was eloping—that she was deceived by him and others is no fault of hers. Her family, *and* the Pemberton family have a good standing, and I believe will continue to do so, once this ridiculous business is over. Murder! For goodness sake, I never heard anything so outrageous in all my blessed days [crossing herself flamboyantly] and I hope that the Gentlemen of the Jury will see good sense and find in Mrs Pemberton's favour.

CHAPTER XXXIII

CORNWALL. MARCH 6, 1861.

Susan showed a small, dark-veiled figure into the morning room. Euphemia sat with her back to the sun; the room was warming up already. The little woman positioned herself neatly opposite Euphemia. Both of them waited: Euphemia waited for the woman to lift her veil; Natalia Jaspur waited for Miss Carrick to speak.

When the carriage had drawn up outside, Euphemia had been pretending that she had not been up all night. She had begun eating a soft-boiled egg as Susan had rushed excitedly into the dining-room.

'Visitors, ma'am.'

'Are you sure? It's barely eight.'

'It's a right grand carriage, ma'am. Four-horser.'

'Horses, Susan.'

'Shall I ask them to wait, ma'am?'

'No. I'll receive them in the morning room, whoever they are.'

* * *

Euphemia had bolted the last bit of egg and now it was repeating on her. Natalia Jaspur was the first to speak.

'I am sorry to disturb you, Miss Carrick, at this hour, but I have spent a good deal of time trying to locate you and I do not have much left.'

Euphemia strained to hear every syllable correctly; the woman's voice seemed to be a hotchpotch of different influences. She cleared her throat quietly. 'My usual hours for Contact are more frequently held in the evening, but I am sure if we were to draw the curtains—' Her hands had become clammy.

'I am not interested in Spiritualism, Miss Carrick. And, if I were, there is no one I would wish to contact. No, the reason I have looked for you is this.' She produced a piece of flimsy paper from a small beaded pouch hanging at her wrist. 'It was discovered by one of my staff and brought to my attention. I see from the look on your face you are a little confused. It is a personal advertisement from the pages of the *Evening Standard*. It bears my name, and also the name of a person I was once in acquaintance with. This is quite old.' She flapped the cutting. 'My housekeeper likes to waste nothing; it was packaging, but that is not interesting to you at all. I made enquiries to the offices of that paper which has eventually led me here.'

Euphemia's mind was in turmoil and her stomach threatened to dispose of her egg. 'You believe I may be of assistance in some way?'

'The person mentioned along with my name on this paper—that person was not the person who placed the advertisement. It is a delicate matter. I wish to contact the person who did.'

'Being?'

'Miss Carrick, I do not have time for obfuscation. I would very much appreciate it if you would let me know the whereabouts of Mr Edward Scales.'

'I did have the pleasure of meeting Mr Scales on one occasion, some months ago—just before he departed on a trip, an excursion overseas.'

'Very good. You will give me his address.'

Euphemia swallowed. 'Mr Scales left no forwarding address. Perhaps his family—I believe they reside in London.'

'I have been there. It is shut. Someone in that house died. The rest have gone.'

'Then I, I can help you no further.'

'Miss Carrick, if you please. I do know, for instance, that Mr Scales went to Brazil to catch butterflies and put snakes and other creatures in bottles, and I know that your sister, Miss Gwen Carrick, is an artist who travelled with him. I know that, despite differences, your sister will have sent a letter by now detailing her particulars of residence in that country.' Natalia Jaspur breathed heavily after this, and her thick black veil moved a little. 'I have no time to play any games with you, Miss Carrick. I am sure your sister is an honourable woman. I will leave you my card, in case you remember where you have put your sister's letters.' She stuffed the folded piece of newspaper back into her purse and produced a small, white card, which she placed with a snap onto an occasional table. 'Now, if you will excuse me, I must leave this moment to be in good time. The drive back to Exeter is tedious. I will see myself out.' She stood up to leave. 'Good day to you, Miss Carrick.'

The sunshine had brought out a sweat on Euphemia. She wiped her face and neck, and waited until she was satisfied that there had been a crunching of wheels and the woman had gone. She eyed the card left by Natalia Jaspur for a few seconds then picked it up and took it to the study where she chose a book at random and slipped the card between its pages. That this strange, dark little woman had been right there in the morning room was not in itself the most extraordinary thing. If only she could find that missing book; Euphemia felt, for the first time in her life, that she had been speaking to a ghost. *Someone in that house died*. She went to look for Susan. The kitchen door was wide open to the morning, and Susan was on her knees cleaning the flagstones. Euphemia spoke to Susan's backside as it wagged back and forth with the effort of scrubbing.

'Spring is here then, Susan.'

'Yes, ma'am, and about time, too.' Susan did not stop scrubbing.

'I'd like a cup of tea, and some more toast. You can bring it up to my room.'

Susan's shoulders sagged momentarily, but she did not stop scrubbing.

CHAPTER XXXIV

Edward awoke in his hammock one April morning not knowing if he should concern himself over Mr Coyne's attention to Gwen. God knows, he thought, how physically lacking in seductive charm she had become in her present state.

Edward had seen Mr Coyne coming away from the house and walking down the road towards the town. He'd waited for her to mention it, and when he'd asked her how her day had gone she'd said that it had been quiet enough. Gwen still did not mention Coyne over the next couple of days, and he decided to leave it alone.

Sometimes, he imagined himself telling her that he made it all up. It was different each time. Sometimes, she laughed, and said that she knew and told him not to be a silly. Other times, his mind played out something violent. Gwen threw objects. Ripped up her work. Shouted. Or she packed her things quietly and calmly into her small trunk and left. When his thoughts ran this way he fixed on telling her the moment he next saw her. Things got in the way. She would be talking to Maria, or asleep.

Gwen did not talk about Natalia Jaspur to Edward. He was thankful for this. The idea of the two of them discussing her at length was too disturbing to contemplate. Edward thought that he must remove himself from the torment of it and the painful silence of avoidance in the house during the evenings after Maria had gone home to her own family.

Pemberton had told him about a small place, a village one day's walk away where he would find Morpho rhetenor. Perhaps, he reasoned, he should go there for a while. The thought of the rhetenor's alluring blue metallic sheen quickened his stomach.

He'd lingered longer than usual over his coffee and biscuit. As he readied himself, Maria arrived with the day's provisions and handed him a letter.

'I've brought you some American pork, Mr Scales, it came in yesterday. Won't you eat before you go?'

Edward wavered on the threshold at the thought of bacon. 'Thank you Maria, but it will be better for the waiting, I should think.'

'Letter from home, Mr Scales?'

Edward looked at the postmark and the writing. It was addressed to him and was from Cornwall. The hand was not his wife's, though certainly female. There were careful flourishes all over the envelope. He inspected the seal on the reverse, which was also flamboyant and depicted a ship with a 'C' curled around it. He put the letter inside his knapsack next to the killing jars waiting for the post-breakfast entomological ramble. He hitched his collecting bag over his shoulder, picked up the birding gun and bid his perfunctory farewell to Maria. Gwen was still asleep.

*   *   *

Waiting for Maria to cook the bacon, Gwen noticed Edward's knapsack on the verandah. She picked it up, imagining it slung over her own back. Tucked in with the jars, she saw the letter and pulled it out. She looked at the fancy handwriting which she recognised at once as Susan's. Her fantasy evaporated.

Gwen had often found discarded or forgotten lists of things to do and things to buy, scrawled carefully by Susan. Sometimes the lists were personal, and sometimes for the house. She turned the letter over, thinking how long Susan must have practised to get her handwriting so neat. She looked at the seal. Susan must have been rummaging in the library bureau to have found that old thing. Gwen smiled at Susan addressing the letter to Edward, in an attempt to be proper. Gwen knew that the letter inside would be meant for her.

She tapped the letter on her knuckles before deciding not to open it. She would wait until Edward came back. She left the knapsack on its proper hook on the wall and replaced the letter inside. All through breakfast the thought of Susan's letter took precedence over everything else until Maria asked her what was wrong.

* * *

Curupíra, the wild man of the forest, mysterious being with various attributes: Edward recalled Gus Pemberton's description as he headed down the road towards the forest paths. He stopped himself from turning to look behind. Sometimes, he heard noises which he supposed might be attributable to the *Curupíra*. Gus Pemberton and Edward had discussed the propensity of primitive peoples to find unnatural causes to occurrences for which they could not account. Or, rather, after the disagreeable beginning to the conversation, Edward had listened to Gus Pemberton's ideas whilst trying to listen with half an ear to what Gwen had been saying to Vincent inside and wondering at the extreme effrontery of the man in turning up like that.

Now, though, as he walked, he heard only Natalia: 'You are as curious to me as I am to you. Sometimes I have asked myself: why does a man with a pretty blonde wife spend so many of his hours here? And before my question is finished I answer myself. The two sides of my head in conversation.' She breathed deeply at her own convenience which coincided with Edward's hand slipping between her thighs. 'Because I remind you of what you are not and what your wife is not. It is simple, I think. You confirm our own place in this world by putting yourself inside me. You say nothing. This is because I am right. It is the same with all the people who must come to hear me sing and assure themselves. Your curiosity has never been any different to those faceless people, dropping coins, dropping their jaws at me. I am a freak; yes, I can say this word; but are you not a freak also?'

At the window a fly had buzzed; Natalia had risen from the bed and crossed the room to kill it. Edward watched her. Her backlit outline glowed in the dirty room at three in the afternoon. He had not cared that she mentioned his wife. That she knew her hair colour did not concern him. Perhaps one night he had told her, after too many glasses of stout. It did not matter, Edward was immersed. Natalia climbed back onto the bed with her fist closed over the fly. Its muted buzzing against her skin sounded in Edward's ear as he pushed her legs apart with his knee.

Now, the insects in the forest air butted his conscience, the high-pitched whine mirrored the protracted death of the bluebottle in Natalia's fist.

In the next moment, Edward's brief return from Lyme Regis to London filled his mind; the pile of letters, opened at random and scanned through, revealing nothing but that which he knew to already have been said or not said, left burning in the grate of his attic room at the hotel.

The surprised astonishment, embarrassment, and later, the disgust betrayed by Isobel's face.

Edward had arrived at his home in London at nine-thirty in the evening. His manservant still on extended leave as Edwards' had not been due back for another week or so, he brushed aside the feeble attempts made by some maid (whose name he did not know and forgot as soon as he learned it) to help him out of his overcoat and remove from him his travelling bags containing all his rocks and fossils. His intention had not been to see Isobel immediately, but the rather peculiar noises and furtive looks from the maid persuaded him to go straight to Isobel's rooms.

Edward had stood unobserved in his wife's bedroom as he watched her receive the attentions of his best friend, Charles.

He had assumed it was Charles; whose face was hidden between his wife's pale thighs; whose hair was being twined into knots by her dumpy fingers (he did not remember Isobel's fingers as ever having been dumpy). Edward thought that he would step out of the room as quietly as he had entered it, but the play of lamplight on his wife's skin kept him there. He saw Charles move his head up from between Isobel's thighs and over her belly, slowly licking her skin in a line up to her chin where she caught his mouth with her own. In quiet fascination Edward watched Charles take possession of Isobel, his eyes fixed on Charles' buttocks, reminding him of the young woman with the flushed pink cheeks in the hotel room below his at Lyme Regis.

He did not wait to see it end. He let himself out, allowing the door to make a noise, and returned downstairs, still grimy from his journey, where he poured himself a gin and drank it neat. He stared at a portrait of Isobel hung above the fireplace, whilst another servant whose name he had no intention of learning fussed over the fire which had been allowed to get low. Half an hour, perhaps forty-five minutes later, he heard someone leaving the house. Edward poured himself another gin and went back upstairs in the manner of someone who has only just that moment arrived to greet his wife.

She was sitting at a card table, wearing a green silk dressing gown, embroidered down the front with pale yellow butterflies. She was dealing herself a game of patience. She had dabbed cologne on her wrists, which did not mask the smell of Charles' own distinctive hair pomade, nor the acrid linger of his cigars in her silk. And as he looked at her he saw how plump she had become. A loose sentence from the pile of burning letters skipped in his mind: 'We have a new addition to the kitchen; he does not take up much space and so does not incur the wrath of Cook, but the best thing is that he makes the most delightful pastries.' What pleasant words of greeting there might have been were obliterated by what had happened next. The shouting, and the bath water. Forcing his wife to wash herself, his hand gripping her neck and her fine pale hair coming loose. The way the bath water wicked into his dirty clothes as he rammed her head under. Hurt her, Isobel, his wife. And her placid face all the while despising him; her eyes open beneath the surface, bubbles escaping from her nose, just waiting for him to finish.

He let go of her when he saw her hands. The palms flashed up at him revealing the brown rash. He stepped back from her, as if that would have made any difference. Very slowly, Isobel got out of the bath, drew to her skin the green silk which clung and darkened against the contours of her. There, around her middle, obvious now, the swell in the candle light.

'You are finished,' he'd spat out at her, pointing at her belly. 'If that doesn't kill you, then those marks will.'

'What are they?' she'd whispered.

'Hasn't he told you? A medical man. I suppose he thought to get himself a nice easy cure. Bit more palatable than mercury but, unfortunately for him, utterly useless.'

'What is it? What do they mean? Please, tell me—' the whisper barely audible.

He'd backed further away from her, wiping his hands on his clothes. 'I'll get you—' His voice fragmented and he struggled to contain the pieces. 'I'll see to it that you receive the best treatment, but it's probably too late. For God's sake!'

'Please, Edward?'

'You have syphilis, courtesy of Mr Charles Jeffreye.'

He'd turned and left her there, deaf to her calling him to come back. He'd rung for a maid, any maid, and told her to bring him some carbolic and hot water.

Afterwards, he'd gone and looked for Natalia, but he'd not been able to find her that night.

* * *

And how could he ever have thought of mentioning Natalia's name to Gwen? He cursed himself for it; and then he cursed Gwen for passing on the lie, for making others become entwined in a moment which had been so intensely private, tenuous and desperate between himself and Gwen. As he turned the thing over in jagged thoughts he remembered that Gwen had made such a play of not remembering that second rainy day in her garden. He could not fathom her game.

Edward took the letter from Cornwall out of his collecting bag and ripped it open.

Mr Scales,

My Mistress being unwell, it falls to me to write to you with the grave news that your wife, Mrs Isobel Scales, died here at Carrick House on the 21st February in the year of Our Lord, Eighteen Hundred & Sixty-One. Mrs Scales visited here & she was taken ill. She did not recover well enough to return home nor leave her bed here. I am sure it would be a comfort to you to know that your late wife was well cared for &

wanted for nothing except to be able to speak with you at some time in the future, when, as she conveyed to my Mistress & to me, she hoped that you would attend one of my Mistress' Spiritual Evenings in order that she could talk with you. This was her dying wish.

We had a big fall of snow here, & we were not able to get a carriage through to take the coffin back to London. It must be my duty, also, to tell you that your late wife was buried here, at our church.

Another person has been here who was very interested to know where both yourself & also the late Mr Harris had got to. She payed my mistress a visit not long since & not so long after Mrs Scales had come here and passed away. This person said that she had spoken to your wife previous, & I thought that all in all you would want to know this as well.

Yours Truly,
Susan Wright.

CHAPTER XXXV

If this is what happens to every woman who becomes a mother, thought Gwen, then it is no wonder men want as many offspring as possible. A woman continually pregnant would make her forever stupid to the world and to her own thoughts. To her own self. Gwen thought of Edward, of his silly, purposeful stride, boxing up his specimens, busy, his mind uncomplicated by the kind of emotional demands her own body made of her. She thought that she could see his purpose in getting her with child. She did not need to *think* to be his illustrator; he did not want her as his assistant in the true sense. He had brought her here to be the skilled labour. She was becoming a kind of base animal, full of maternal instinct and nothing much else. It was a struggle to find herself each day, to carve out an inch of motivation. It was a battle of wills: her own and the will of nature. If I was not in this state, she thought, if I was not tied down by my 'condition' as Edward had referred to it, then I would leave. The fact that she could not possibly leave pressed a weight of almost unbearable discontent into her being. She steeled herself against it, washed her brush and carried on with her painting. All thought left her. She lost sense of where and who she was as she entered the topographies of the creatures before her.

Gwen looked up from her half-finished study of a large green caterpillar and met the amused gaze of Vincent Coyne. She regarded him for a moment, allowing a smile to curl the corner of her mouth, and then went about the business of putting the object of her study away. Here, at least, was another chance to take her mind out of the spiral of self-pity she had allowed herself to become absorbed in that morning. The defoliated citrus twig went back into the cage with the caterpillar. She wiped her paintbrush on a cloth, and then wetted her fingers with spit to make a point on the sable hairs. Gwen had not been expecting Vincent. He had sent her a note a few days before, telling her that he would not be able to come and visit. He had apologised and described how Mr Pemberton had been struck with a fever. Now, he leaned over the open windowsill.

'How can you do that when he doesn't keep still for one minute?'

'Oh, it's simple enough. Far more agreeable than being presented with an empty skin.'

'People actually stuff those things?'

'Sometimes. Thankfully, Edward is far too busy.'

'So, you've got him trapped in there, food plants on your doorstep. Will you let him go free, or is your plan to observe the whole transformation and then stick a pin through him?'

'No, I couldn't do that.'

Vincent brought up his closed fist and dropped a pale green pupa attached to a leaf onto Gwen's workbook. 'I have no idea how old it is, or if it will hatch, but I think you'll be pleased with it if it does. I believe that the mush in that thing is pretty damn impossible to catch with a net.'

Gwen eyed the gift without picking it up. 'Are you an expert on lepidoptera?'

'Is that what you call it? Well, you learn something new every day.'

Gwen took up the leaf and pupa and held it up to the light. You are getting too familiar, she thought, but I like you. 'You can include moths in the order, as well. Thank you for this, Mr Coyne. I'll keep it on my desk.'

'I'd like to see Mr Scales' face when it hatches.'

'That is probably unlikely since he has taken himself off on a little excursion. He should be back in a couple of weeks.' Why on earth did I tell you that? Gwen blinked and avoided his gaze while making a show of examining the pupa more thoroughly.

'Are you comfortable, alone here?'

'I'm not alone,' she said quickly. 'I have Maria; she stays at night. I have no reason to feel uncomfortable.'

'No, of course not. So. I'll let you continue.'

'And what of Mr Pemberton, is he well enough?'

'To tell you the truth, I think he is malingering.'

'The fever has eased off?'

'Some days it seems like he's just about himself again, and others he is the picture of woe. I'm convinced he eats hot peppers while I'm out to make himself come out in a sweat.'

'But he has enough quinine?'

'Enough? He's using my supply now. We won't be able to make another excursion until the next boat comes in. Our search for your mysterious lady has been put back somewhat.'

'These things are out of our control.'

'May I come in? Where is your maid, by the way? I've been all around the house.'

'I asked her to take a letter for me. I expect she has stopped to visit her family.' Gwen felt suddenly uneasy; there was a kind of suppressed determination in Vincent's voice, which made her want to shrink into herself, like the mimosa leaves at the edges of the forest paths. She tried to make herself sound careless, but her own voice was now stretched with a breathlessness. 'Do you know anything about Oxbow lakes? Edward is determined to find one.'

'Is that where he has gone, to find one?'

'No.'

'Just as well. Easy when you know where to look. They happen when the river changes its course.'

'Have you seen one? Perhaps when Edward comes back you might show him on a map.' Please,

please, she thought, don't start on again about Darwin. She certainly wasn't in the mood for another convoluted conversation about the gigantic scientific discoveries Coyne believed he could make or prove.

'It's a possibility, certainly, but, you know, these lakes dry up. It may be that by the time Mr Pemberton and I are able to travel again, the lakes I know of will have turned to swamp. Of course, if Gus decides to malinger for much longer I may have to review my situation.'

'You don't mean that. I think the pair of you are inseparable.'

Vincent picked up the telescope from its resting place and extended each section. 'Now this is something I never had the brains to think of acquiring. Perhaps I have gotten a little complacent and ought to put myself in the shoes of a novice, or semi-novice, and learn something.'

'That spyglass actually had nothing to do with foresight. It was a gift.'

'Then I wish I had friends like yours.'

'It was a gift from the captain of the *Opal*. If I hadn't asked to use it so much, he probably would not have given it away.'

'Ah.' Vincent put the telescope back on the shelf and seated himself on one of the cane armchairs. 'Don't mind me. Just carry on as you were; I don't want to interrupt you. I promise not to disturb you.'

'You won't disturb me. I ought to move around a little, anyway.'

'You look remarkably well, I must say. And your innovative style is rather becoming.'

Gwen was suddenly annoyed at his candour. 'Let me bring you a little something. I think we still have a drop of *cashaca*, or I could make some fresh coffee.'

'No, no thank you. I don't need anything.'

'Are you sure? What about some fruit? I am going to have some. Will you take an orange, Mr Coyne?'

Gwen went out to the next room and came back with two oranges. She sat in the chair opposite Vincent Coyne and began to peel one, dropping the peel into a handkerchief. Vincent played with his orange. He prodded it all over and sniffed the skin. He dug his nail into the zest and scraped off a tiny amount.

For goodness sake, she thought, just peel the orange. When Gwen had eaten half of her segments, he had still not begun to peel the fruit, nor had he said anything. Gwen noticed that a dullness had come over his expression. She let him be for a few minutes more and then asked if anything was the matter.

Vincent sighed. 'Rust.'

'Pardon?'

He leaned forward, his fist tight over the orange. 'Tell me honestly, do you have any problem with rust?'

'I don't quite understand. Rot, insect damage—these a little, perhaps. We manage to keep on top of it, just. The problem of rust is no more or less trouble.'

'You admit that rust is a problem though. You must beware of rust.'

She laughed, uneasy at his serious face, thinking that he was far more peculiar than she had imagined. 'We keep everything well oiled, you may be sure, Mr Coyne.'

'You do understand my meaning?'

'I think I do.'

'Fine then, that's settled.' He peeled his orange. 'Mrs Scales, I would have loved to see you in English society, hosting one of those "at homes" which people seem to go in for.'

'I doubt you would have enjoyed yourself, Mr Coyne, even if I had. I think you would have found yourself in rather boring company.'

There followed an awkward pause and then he said, 'What do your family make of your leaving England for such noble causes as art and science?'

'I have only a sister. She thinks very little of any of it.'

'I'm sorry. I didn't mean to open wounds.'

Gwen had been avoiding his gaze; now she glanced at him, 'You haven't.'

CHAPTER XXXVI

The morning was fresh as they set off along the road. Gwen tucked her arm into Maria's and they walked like that all the way.

Maria bought bread, dried saltfish, bacon, a jar of oil, tomatoes and peppers. Gwen stayed at her side trying to catch phrases and words of what was said, but she was distracted. Being part of a crowd again after her quiet months with only Edward and Maria for company made her edgy, alert. She was thrilled at the variety of different faces, all absorbed in their own errands or conversations. Her gaze darted, unable to rest on a single thing or person for very long. Her arm was growing tired from holding the basket of Maria's purchases, but there was nowhere to put it down safely. The ringing of church bells filled the air as it had on her very first morning in Pará: some festival was going on that week, Maria had told her. Would she like to go to one of the services? Gwen had been unsure but now she thought that if Maria mentioned it again perhaps she might, after all.

'Mrs Scales, may I?'

She started at the sound of his voice and turned. Gwen looked up into the smiling face of Gus Pemberton. His pale linen jacket, newly pressed and reflecting the light, made her shade her eyes with her hand. She let him take her basket.

He said, 'Are you here alone?'

'Mr Pemberton. How well you look. I came with Maria, I fancied a walk.' She was conscious of herself beginning to babble. She was blushing. She teetered on the heat of it, and chided herself for being so pathetic.

'I always get the day's provisions myself. I can't be sitting around in the morning waiting for my breakfast. I'd much rather go out and buy it myself.'

Gus Pemberton's talk was easy and he smiled again. She felt stupid under his gaze. Gwen saw that he had some packages under his arm. 'I was under the impression—' She felt confused; he didn't seem like someone recovering from an illness at all; certainly not the malingerer that Vincent had reported. She said, 'I mean, it's very lively, for such an early hour. We have a rather more sedate existence.'

'Yes. I do prefer it after the detachment of an excursion. Will you have breakfast? You can enjoy the scene from my windows without having to be in the middle of it.'

Gus Pemberton's apartments were on the corner of a long row of imposing but dilapidated buildings near the port. Its first-floor windows gave an aspect out over the port and across the streets. Gwen looked down at the market vendors in the sun and the sharply contrasting shade cast by the buildings. She could see how easily Mr Pemberton would have spotted her parasol in the crowd; how quick he might have been in going down there to buy himself a loaf of bread before accosting her. The smell of toast, bacon and coffee mingled with Mr Pemberton's cigarette smoke and drifted around her. It was not an acrid smoke but pleasingly sweet; not the tobacco smell she was used to. Gwen's stomach rumbled loudly. She was glad that he had no servant. His preference, not a circumstance. His preference then, had given her the opportunity to compose herself.

There was something about his unspoken experience which left her feeling even more intimidated now that she was alone with him. And she did not want to admit that Vincent had been to see her. She looked over her shoulder towards the open door. There was nothing about the man to suggest that he was capable of malingering. He was whistling a tune. Though perhaps malingerers whistled: she did not know. Something complicated, and too high for his mouth and tongue to register. Perhaps it was part of an aria from an opera; and a giggle rose uncontrollably in her throat as she recalled the amateur operatic ladies' performance. She was reminded suddenly of the surprise she had felt, a long time past, it seemed now, when she had learned that female voices could break. And the remembered surprise could not be dissociated from the look of bewilderment on her mother's face. Gwen let her mother's face slide away. She had not said yesterday to Vincent that her mother would have revelled in her daughter's desire to travel; nor had she said that her mother would have made it impossible to leave Euphemia behind. She told herself Euphemia would never have come with her, even had she been asked. Had she been different.

She would have liked to ask Gus Pemberton things that she had not thought to ask Captain Swithin. But, in between sips of coffee, black and punchingly bitter, she was still paralysed by this shyness. He smiled at her. Gwen consumed her breakfast in a state of extreme hunger. It was difficult not to appear ravenous as she bit into the crisp toast and salty bacon. He squeezed oranges over a greenish glass tumbler on the table. He pushed it over to her. 'Mind the pips, you can spit them out onto your plate.' Gwen gulped the juice, swallowing the pips.

He said, 'I admire your tenacity.'

She laughed, dispossessed finally of some of her shyness. 'For not spitting?'

'For not staying in England; for following your husband in his work. And, I may say, for your reputation. It precedes you, Mrs Scales.' Gwen blanched a little at the connection of Edward to work. It had not occurred to her that what he was doing was associated with the word. A vocation. 'Of course,' he continued, mistaking her discomfort for something else, 'it is yours as much as his. I have known couples whose combined efforts would have amounted to nothing without the female part of the equation.'

‘In our case that remains to be seen.’

‘Forgive me, that did not sound as I intended it. I don’t mean to cast any doubt over your husband’s own tenacity. But do not take this the wrong way. As amateurs you have set out on an equal footing. You have an enquiring and, I believe, determined character, Mrs Scales, that I know already. And talented as you are with the paint-box, I cannot imagine that your part of the venture will ultimately be restricted to such.’

‘Mr Pemberton, may I ask you a personal question?’

Gus leaned back in his chair, and crossed his ankle over his knee.

‘Have you ever had malaria?’ She watched his face for a sign.

He uncrossed his ankle and reached for the coffee pot. ‘Fortunately, not for a long time. You mustn’t worry about contracting it here, if that is what the question is about.’

She watched his hands and then met his gaze. ‘It wasn’t.’

‘I was wondering if you might mention the rather famous tussle over your microscope.’

‘Famous?’ Gwen was at once mortified and confused.

‘Oh, perhaps not famous—you mustn’t worry about it. You are held in very high regard here, you know, for standing your ground. Marcus Frome was never an easy person to get along with.’

‘You know him?’

He paused. ‘Ah . . . not as such. I don’t think anyone could ever have known him, really.’

‘Well, I am glad that he went back to England.’

‘Mrs Scales, did your husband not tell you? I’m

sorry to have brought it up. I thought you knew.'

'Knew about what?'

'Marcus Frome went missing from the ship. No one can be sure of the precise point of the voyage, but, two weeks out, some other passenger was in need of a doctor and—he simply wasn't to be found.'

Gwen gazed at Gus Pemberton in mute disbelief. It seemed too ridiculous. She'd thought of him sometimes, and wondered if he really had been as desperate as he had seemed. 'Mr Pemberton, I'm—thank you for telling me.' Gwen sat in stunned silence for a moment.

'I came with the news on Old Year's Night,' he said gently. 'I had thought that your husband would have wanted to tell you as soon as possible.'

Gwen recalled the excuse Mr Pemberton had used to get Edward to go outside. Fumigating the amphibians.

'A lot of news escapes my attention, Mr Pemberton. *The Times* frequently has sections missing before it comes to me.'

'That's—regrettable.'

'I can't believe that a man would do such a thing over—such a *dreadful* thing to do, Mr Pemberton, over a microscope of all objects.'

'Please, you must not think for a minute, Mrs Scales, that it was for want of a microscope that the man threw himself overboard.'

'Well, whatever am I to suppose? He made it very clear that he believed—'

'What Marcus Frome believed and what was fact did not always sit harmoniously; you must not dwell on it.'

'I can't help but dwell on it. Mr Frome was

convinced that he was on the point of a momentous discovery.'

'Suppose then, that he had been. Giving him your microscope would not have helped him. He would have needed to borrow everything you have, and more.' He leaned forward on the edge of his seat, resting his elbows on his knees. 'And, frankly, Mrs Scales, he was not a lucky man. Do set your mind at ease.'

She wanted to change the subject. 'I have been—' she said, her voice rising. 'I was led to believe that you were very ill.'

Gus threw himself back into his chair, 'Ach, this is about Vincent. I knew he had been to see you yesterday. I think you came into town to find me?'

Gwen shrugged her shoulders. 'Perhaps I did.'

'Whatever he has told you, you mustn't feel let down by his inconsistencies. He means well, I can assure you of that.'

'You are not hurt that he has lied about you.'

'He meant no harm by it. But I feel I must be straight with you. He and I have come to blows over the direction of our own travels. We have agreed to go our separate ways.'

'Then why did he not tell me that?'

'It may have been my fault. I told him to say what he liked about me. That he only cites me as being ill is reassuring.'

'Your disagreement was serious.'

'In the light of day, on a morning such as this, it would sound petty in the retelling.'

Gwen was surprised that a man like Gus Pemberton would admit to describing a disagreement like that. His openness pulled her in. 'I feel deceived. I feel now that I have spent hours talking to an actor.'

'Well, we are all actors, Mrs Scales—whether we think it or not. Even as our truest selves, even when alone with our thoughts.' Gus Pemberton took up a piece of rind and nibbled off a small portion. He played it around his mouth for a while. Gwen waited. After some time, he said, 'In essence, it was about our authority, as outsiders, to disregard boundaries. I, I should say no more about it.' His smile was apologetic.

'I'm sorry.'

'Ach, no need to be.' Gus Pemberton paused. Then, 'He and I were not simply exploring. We were prospecting. Diamonds, gold. That is our business. Partnerships like ours, they come to blows sooner or later.' His tone was light. 'It is no great tragedy.'

'What will you do now?' Gwen felt small in the light of his candid speech. A man can be more than one thing if he chooses, she thought. He does not have to define himself by his means of survival.

Gus said, 'I am undecided. There is some property in Scotland, which I must dispose of, and then, after a suitable period, perhaps take my stick to pastures new. Maybe New Zealand.'

'And what do you think Mr Coyne will do, without you to guide him?'

Gus Pemberton hesitated. 'I think he should go back, precarious as times are. Perhaps in twelve or eighteen months he will be ready to return if he wishes.'

'Mr Pemberton,' she said.

'Gus, please. Call me Gus, won't you?'

'Gus. Mr Coyne has said that he will help me find someone.'

'Indeed, he has.'

'I don't know how to put it, but I don't wish to find anyone. And I don't quite understand how.'

'How?'

'I have never mentioned anything about finding any person, ever, to anyone at all. Not a soul. And as far as I know, neither has Edward. And so—'

'He's talked to me, on occasions, at great length about this. I have understood that it has been widely known.'

Gwen's hands fluttered at her throat and then fell back down to twist in her lap. 'Mr Pemberton, Gus. If I tell you something, I believe you will preserve the integrity of that thing. I don't know you at all, but I have to tell you that this person, the search, is just a fabrication. No one needs to find her. In fact, I don't believe she even exists. At least, not in the temporal world.'

'I can see that it upsets you. Would you rather not speak about it?'

'I merely wanted one other person to know.' She searched his face for any glimmer of amusement. There was none. 'Gus, how could Mr Coyne possibly have come to believe anything so ridiculous and so specific?'

'That, I can't pretend to know the answer to.'

'He is your companion. You must know each other very well.'

'Mrs Scales, please understand. I will keep this to myself, I fully comprehend your anxiety—but Vincent, he . . . Look, we met, quite by chance, some few years back in Australia, and I took him on. He had a letter of recommendation from a fellow I used to know. We travelled, prospecting, and then later here, in Brazil and after, we parted ways—I had thought for good—until we met again, quite by chance in the spring of '59 and—it really isn't important. What is important is that Vincent will be leaving again, quite soon, and so you will have no need to bother about anything but your work.'

His face was open, eager for her to be appeased. He leaned towards her and took her hand. His speech became low, a whisper. 'Don't let him travel with you, under any circumstances. Say nothing; he is here. I saw his shadow.' Before she could say anything, Gus had planted a kiss on her lips and pulled her towards him. She resisted him as she felt her big belly making contact with his body, but he made her stand up, still firmly connected by the kiss and then ushered her into his small sleeping quarters where he closed the door behind them.

'Forgive, please forgive me, Mrs Scales. I didn't have time to think,' he whispered.

'Will he go away now?'

'Yes, I think so. We'll let him have a few moments.' They looked at each other. Gwen tried not to notice that Gus Pemberton favoured a firm bed over a hammock or that the impression from his head was still left in the pillow.

* * *

Leaving Gus Pemberton, Gwen wondered how much influence he held over Vincent Coyne. What kind of influence was it that allowed one man to send another back home? Despite everything, and in spite of herself, she still liked Vincent. Or was it just that she liked him to speak to her. His attention. To look at him, he was so beautiful; that he was mad did not always seem to matter. Conversation with Edward was not stimulating, only irritating. In conversation with both Mr Coyne and Mr Pemberton they had both treated her as if her opinion mattered, as Edward had once done.

The rain came down so forcefully in the afternoon that each drop seemed to have its own precise destination. The first drops fell on the leaves like fleas against newsprint gathering in numbers exponentially, swelling rapidly to a fully liquid sound.

Gwen felt that the weather's exactness was sharpening her senses; she let herself believe this for a while and revelled in her indulgence. What is there to stop me? she thought. Who is there to accuse me, if I never speak of it? The rain plastered her hair to her skull, and she felt the drops mapping its surface, washing all trace of Gus Pemberton from her skin.

* * *

During the night she woke and thought that Gus Pemberton was beside her, somehow, in her hammock. She put her hand out into the dark of the room; a pair of frogs called to each other. She heard the soft snoring of Maria in the next room and closed her eyes again. But the image of Gus Pemberton was still in her mind. His words, the pattern of his speech, the touch of his hand on her sleeve.

'Don't worry, Mrs Scales. I'd never ask you to compromise your integrity, but I'd like to let you have my address. Please, you must write to me, tell me how things progress, regarding everything.'

'I will.'

She shifted in her hammock, smiling to herself that she would be able to write to Gus Pemberton and ask him to explain properly the things he had told her about Marcus Frome and the mosquitoes, and his own thoughts about how it might have been connected to Frome's research—his great discovery. She relaxed back into a sleepy state, but then suddenly became wide awake again. Gus Pemberton had not given her his address at all, not asked her to write to him. And they had not, she realised now, talked in any detail about Marcus Frome's mosquitoes.

CHAPTER XXXVII

THE TIMES, Thursday, October 4, 1866.

MURDER TRIAL AT THE OLD BAILEY.

HUSBAND of the prisoner Mrs Pemberton today gave evidence in the form of a statement read out to the court. The body of the statement was in effect heavily redacted by repeated objections from the Prosecution, all of which were upheld. Being frustrated in his attempts to read out Mr Pemberton's account of his involvement in the case as a witness, Mr Shanks called Mr Pemberton himself, to the great surprise of the court.

Mr Pemberton said, 'I wish to make it known to the Jury that important information pertaining to this case has been omitted from the evidence so far submitted or allowed by this court. As the first person to enter the room where Mr Scales' body was found, I can tell you, Gentlemen, that it was not an ordinary scene, if any scene of supposed murder may be called ordinary. What Detective Sergeant Gray and Doctor Jacobs failed to communicate to both the inquest and this court I shall now divulge.'

Mr Pemberton went on to say that upon turning over the corpse, all three men noted that certain mutilations had been done but that there was no evidence of profuse bleeding, which, Mr Pemberton surmised, indicated that such mutilations had been carried out either post mortem or in some other part of the house at the time of, or close to, the time of death. Mr Pemberton went on to state that he spent some time searching the house for signs of such mutilation having occurred, and that although he found no direct clue, he did notice that the large table in the kitchen had been recently scrubbed clean, and that a copper full of articles of clothing was in the process of being boiled. Mr Probart for the Prosecution made objection to the nature of Mr Pemberton's evidence, but the Judge overruled, and Mr Pemberton was permitted to continue. He said, 'My wife's clothing from the previous day had not yet been laundered, as I found to my relief when I returned home. Her clothes had not a single sign of blood spatters on them anywhere; this fact will be corroborated by my servants whose attention I called to this fact in a discreet manner. Therefore, I must ask the question of all assembled here: that perhaps some other person was responsible for those mutilations. Some other person whose motives, however obscure to us now, may soon become clear. I put it to the court that whomsoever perpetrated this ghastly detail upon the body of the unfortunate Mr Scales was also the perpetrator of his murder.

'I might add further details of the general scene, if I might, of the room in that property. There was, attached to the back of the door in that room, a substantial hook, the screw of which being very long protruded an eighth of an inch to the other side of the door. The hook was a crude one, and its presence there was incongruous with the rest of the furnishings. On close inspection I found traces of fresh sawdust on panel beadings directly below its point of entry. I made several and exhaustive notes on everything I witnessed in that house the same day, which I shall be happy to submit to the Jury for their considered inspection. I feel that such details are pertinent to this case and that without them no true conclusion can be made.'

Mr Justice Linden allowed that such a diary may be submitted in its entirety with the redacted statement for the

Jury to consider, with full copies to himself and to the Prosecution.

CHAPTER XXXVIII

Gwen lit a lamp and paced the rooms in her slippers and then kicked them off. Marcus Frome had actually thrown himself overboard. But why? Why am I anxious about it, when it is already done? The man has been dead for months. I am the last to know about it, when I—. But he was an obnoxious toad of a man, she reminded herself, and did not deserve my microscope, not at any price; even if he had been able to pay. But, she asked herself now, would I have let him take my microscope if I had known that he would do such a stupid thing. Was it stupid, though? How much courage does it take to throw yourself over the side of the ship?

Stop it, she told herself. But she kept running over the things Gus Pemberton had said and realised that he had been trying to allay any doubts she may have had about her own part in Frome's final act.

As dawn broke she got back into her hammock, wild through want of sleep, and she did sleep for a while.

Fitful on waking, she tried to work but found herself dull-fingered. She made errors which ruined whole pieces, and had to give in. I can't go and visit him again, she thought.

*   *   *

In town, she made no pretence of wanting to hang about at the market and went instead straight to Gus Pemberton's apartment. In her purse she had folded a piece of paper with a message, asking Gus Pemberton to come and visit her as soon as he was able. If he is not at home, she told herself, I will leave this. But she could not decide. She stood at his door with her hand at the bell pull. She was acting too hastily. He would think her demented. She turned her back on the door and leaned on it, facing out towards the bustle of the market. The sharp light stunned her eyes and she had to shut them tight. I'll go and find Maria, she told herself. She leaned more heavily on the door to propel herself forward and the door gave under her weight. She turned and pushed on it, stepping into the instant cool and quiet of his vestibule. She retraced her steps, remembered from the day before, to the rooms Gus Pemberton kept. She paused, nervous suddenly of her assumption that it would be perfectly fine for her to walk into his rooms unannounced. To her great relief, the whole place felt empty, and she made to leave, pulling out her note to drop at the threshold. A noise made her catch her breath. A hard slap of a hand on solid flesh. It was quite unmistakable. Then something softer, and with it this time a gruff voice. Gwen stood there, unable to remove herself from the scene of something she immediately knew was very private. Gwen's throat pulsed hard with the beat of her heart and with it the repeated noise and what she knew were moans of pleasure. You fool, she told herself, you were completely taken up with your nightmare and you have delivered yourself into another.

'You want her, don't you?' The voice was unmistakably Vincent's.

'Just shut up.' The words of reply belonged to

Gus Pemberton, but they were hardly his; they were strained and hoarse.

'Say it. You want, her, so much. That—belly of hers. You're. Thinking. Of. It. Right. Now. Aren't. You?'

Gwen clasped her hands over her mouth and turned to leave in a hurry, knocking into the doorframe, hearing Gus Pemberton yelling, 'Shut up, shut up, shut up.'

Remove yourself, she told herself. Get out, before you are discovered.

* * *

She woke streaked in sweat, gasping, fingers digging into the flesh of her palms. Maria stood over her. Gwen struggled to compose herself. 'What was I saying? Did I speak in my sleep, Maria?'

Maria shook her head, 'No, you were fitful, that's all, Mrs Scales. I thought I should wake you.'

Gwen rubbed her face with her hands as though she had come up from under water. 'I have to go into town again today, Maria. I must call on Mr Pemberton.'

The baby turned over in her belly; putting her hand to the unfathomable, undulating writhe of it, she remembered that in her last dream, there had been no child inside her.

* * *

In Gus Pemberton's apartment Gwen was breathless, hot, thirsty. Gus looked at her for a second but didn't do what she dreaded him doing.

He didn't treat her as a flustered and confused woman standing inside his door, clutching at the huge belly she bore.

'Who, exactly, is Vincent Coyne?' She had thought about how she might phrase this as the cart had trundled along the road, the bumps hurting her so much that she had asked the driver to stop so she could get out and walk instead.

'In what way do you mean?'

'I mean where is he from? Because he isn't actually American, is he?'

Gus raised his eyebrows and jerked back his neck in surprise. 'I am not sure that I understand you.'

'How can you be so sure that he is exactly who he says he is?'

'I met him through an acquaintance.'

'And this man introduced you to him personally?'

'Yes, in a letter.'

Gwen breathed, in raising the bulk of her belly. 'But he isn't from America, I am sure of it. I am sure he is something else.'

'*Something* else? That sounds interesting.'

'It isn't really. Has he gone?'

'Yes. He will leave this morning. He isn't here; he has gone out to say his farewells. I am simply waiting for his return and then we will take his trunk down to the—'

'I need to see it. You warned me about him yesterday.'

'Well, yes, but purely for selfish reasons.'

'Gus, please, let me see his trunk.'

It had been left open; Gwen got down on her knees to look at the things inside it. A man not expecting someone to come poking about among his things would not conceal his paperwork, she thought, and her eyes travelled over the pockets on the inside of the trunk lid. Her hands patted the satin and then rummaged into the opening. She pulled out a small bundle of letters and untied the plain cotton tape holding them together. She felt Gus at her shoulder, watching her, but she did not stop, either in embarrassment or in panic at the idea of Vincent's return. She no longer cared if he knew about her suspicions. Her body sagged a little when she did not find any familiar handwriting on the envelopes. She had almost given up, and was on the point of stuffing the letters back into the satin pocket when the last envelope, unmarked, came to the top of the small pile. She delved in and brought out a collection of calling cards. For a moment she was baffled. Vincent Coyne's whiskerless face in a fine photographic representation stared out at her from the flat of her palm. On the reverse was his name, nothing more. She put it back with the rest and replaced them. She tied up the tape and after putting the letters back heaved herself up off the floor.

'I knew that I had seen Mr Coyne before. The first time I met you both, I had the oddest feeling—the feeling that you have lived that moment before and that everything you see and hear is, in fact, just a memory.'

'I know the feeling; there ought to be an expression for it.'

'But it was not in the normal way. I felt it only when I looked at Mr Coyne. I felt a peculiar connection to him.'

'You found him attractive; well, that is understandable enough.'

'No, it was because of that card,' she gestured at the trunk.

'I can't say that I have seen it before.'

'But I have. On the floor of my sister's bedroom, just before I left. Do you see?'

'Perhaps.'

'Yes, perhaps? Yes, certainly. He knows my sister. He has let tiny things slip. Things which I would not usually have noticed if it had been only once.'

'Can you be sure of—what is it that you *are* sure of, Gwen?'

'That my sister has sent him on some errand to drive suspicion and enmity between Edward and me. She has sent Mr Coyne with false information, which she hopes will destroy this venture.'

'You are talking about this phantom woman, the one who does not exist.'

'Yes, some hideous thing—I don't know, I can't even imagine what she can have concocted. She isn't sane. I mean to say, she isn't a lunatic, but my sister was always jealous of everything I did, of everyone I saw, of everyone who wanted to speak to me—though latterly there were very few, if any. I left my home, a place I have loved, to get away from the stifling atmosphere my sister created. And yet I can travel thousands of miles, and still she persists. I sound ridiculous to you. I must be pathetic to you, standing in here, going through these belongings. Like a thief.'

'I led you to this room, remember. But Vincent is leaving, Gwen. He has not succeeded, even if your suspicions are correct. Neither Vincent nor your sister have driven anything here to destroy your marriage.'

Gwen turned away at the mention of that particular lie. She hid her face from Gus for a moment, then said, 'It was his blue spectacles, as much as his whiskers. He never takes them off, and they altered his features just enough to have thrown me.'

'Oh, well, that he probably didn't mean to do. He has sensitive eyes. I've never seen him without his spectacles.'

'And you will be going away as well?' She couldn't say what she needed to express. That one afternoon alone with Gus had changed her beyond her own comprehension, that to see him leave—she felt that she would not be able to cope in his absence.

'But we can write to each other,' he said. 'You can give me a regular report on every new insect and bug that you find, and their peculiar habits.'

'Gus, I am afraid. I am afraid of—I didn't come here to have a child. I came here to work.'

'Maria is the best person in the entire world you could hope to have in the house. Trust her.'

'It isn't that. I'm afraid of the pain.'

'She will help you.'

Gwen wanted to say that she was afraid of death. That she was afraid that the child would die, or that it would be born some kind of monstrous creature, that she herself would die, that she would bleed to death in that little wooden house on the edge of the jungle. That her blood would run through the floorboards and the insects would consume it. But she kept quiet. She let Gus hold her and stroke her hair and lead her away from Vincent's emptied room into his own.

*   *   *

Lying on her side, with Gus curled around her awkward, naked, pregnant shape, she wanted him to beg her to leave Brazil with him. She waited on every breath he took, and listened for the change that would come in the deepest part of his chest. But his breathing was regular and easy, and she knew that he was too good a person to try and take her entirely away from the man he thought of as her husband, no matter what else he may privately have thought of Edward. Gwen had to resign herself to the fugitive nature of their time together and the fact that she would never be able to tell him the truth. And while she lay there with Gus, the trickle of his semen running down the inside of her thigh and cooling on her skin, she couldn't even bring herself to ask if he would ever come back to Brazil, or if he thought that they would ever meet again.

CHAPTER XXXIX

Pará, Brazil. June, 1861.

Edward was carrying a brace of limp parrots over his shoulder as he leaped up the steps of the house. He had been out since seven. Gwen saw the blunt grey tongues caught between the open beaks and turned away. Edward didn't see her revulsion; he was too excited. The birds were a pair, a fine pair which had been flying together, and he had brought them down without needing to reload his rifle.

It had become apparent that skinning creatures near the house was contributing to the ant problem. No specimen or part small enough was immune to the ants' own predilection for collecting. Maria had smeared bitter sticky stuff on the table and chair legs and the ropes suspending the food-sacks. The birds he carried were already empty of their internal organs. He was so pleased with himself he whistled an improvised tune as he dusted the skins and wrapped them in paper. He thought of his waiting breakfast, and the thick coffee. Killing the birds so cleanly, and being able to retrieve them on his own, made up for the terrible experience beforehand of trying to secure a monkey. Nausea fingered his throat. Why had he done that? Monkeys of virtually any kind were easily obtainable in the city. But then there were the parrots. When he saw them, all the sickening guilt over the ruined and wasted monkey fell away.

His boyhood days spent skinning and stuffing crows were paying off. He finished the parrots, and packed them away. Gwen would not paint them unless they retained their living form. Squawking, defecating, flapping and intent on destroying everything with their beaks. Gwen seemed quiet this morning. Perhaps it would be better not to talk about parrots. She was not even talking to Maria. He was glad. All that Portuguese being spoken in the house made him feel more keenly that he was on the periphery of the world that Gwen constructed about herself. He slurped noisily at the coffee and looked out across the garden. It was so fantastic to have fruit growing right there. He'd found a use for them. Every day he took the discarded skins to the same part of the forest, a sunny glade where he had first seen the large blue Morpho butterflies. His idea was to create a kind of feast table, to attract them. So far he had collected an incredible number of different lepidoptera species from that one spot. He finished his coffee and called out his farewell again to Gwen. Her reply came to him as an offhand mutter. He took up his insect equipment and bounced out of the house.

* * *

By two in the afternoon his tin collecting boxes were full. He rested his insect nets carefully with the rest of his equipment in a heap on the floor of the verandah. He had come back an hour earlier than usual, full of excitement, eager to show Gwen what his boxes contained. He finally had an excellent specimen of a male Morpho rhetenor, which had eluded his net during his solitary two-week trip, and a slightly less brilliant but no less exciting pair of M. Menelaus, caught as they'd tasted the banana skins.

One by one, the birds gave up their noises, trailed by the scraping of the cicadas. They stopped and started, stopped and started again, like a partially jammed clockwork toy. The bellies of the clouds amassed overhead were bruised with the swell of rain. As Edward stepped towards Gwen, he felt the first rustle of wind, signalling their release.

There was an extra stickiness about the house, and the pungent smells of childbirth hung in the air. He felt light-headed, knowing that this scene of the simplest domesticity was a world away from his old life. He stepped closer to see the small jaw, the half-extended tongue, fluttering in sleepy rest against her breast. He tried to imagine himself, for a fleeting instant, making the place where he stood his permanent home. The wind grew stronger, making the slack leaves in the trees talk. He had an impulse to step out into it as the thunder cracked. The child opened its eyes, and he thought it perceived him. It had Gwen's mouth and nose; Edward's forehead and brow in miniature wrinkled back at him. A tiny fist had come loose from the cloth bindings and he went to touch it, drawing back at the last moment, remembering his ramble through the forest. He wiped the imagined traces of butterfly onto his trousers. He knew that Gwen loved this time of day best; she would often come out onto the verandah and stand motionless to see it all pouring down off the thatch overhang.

Gwen woke up; the child began to feed again. She didn't notice him standing there. He couldn't bear it; he felt he must break the silence. 'Is it a girl, or a boy?'

Gwen dragged her gaze away from her child, but she was not really seeing him. 'A girl.'

Edward breathed out. Had he been holding his breath all this time?

She smiled at the child; its jaw worked away drawing the milk down. That strange sensation, that strangest thing which Nature had provided for. She felt sure that she would never get used to it.

He bent over her and she accepted his kiss on her forehead. When he took his mouth away, she kept her head tilted up as though she expected more than a simple peck on the forehead. Her eyes were closed. He quickly checked the corners of his mouth to see that no dried spittle had collected there before bending forward again to kiss her on the mouth. He had taken too long. She was moving her head back to a more natural position. Damn it. He kissed her anyway, on her cheek. It reminded them both of a place almost forgotten, that bumbling botchedness which had passed for passion in the beginning.

He would bring back some of those moody birds from the dingy parts of the forest in a cage. She would paint them, and he would let them go again.

He needed to wipe himself down, and change. He could feel bits of forest caught inside his shirt and ears. He always checked for ticks; he couldn't stand the way their heads would bury right under the skin. He'd found that a well-heated specimen pin applied to the abdomen did the trick. He gathered himself together, 'Have you thought of a name. Perhaps a family name?' How strange, he thought, for her to blush at such a simple question.

'Augusta.'

'Augusta,' he repeated, trying it out on his tongue. 'It seems very severe. But it has a certain quality about it. Is it a family name?'

She shook her head. 'I just like it. I thought something would come to mind when I saw her face, and that came to my mind.'

'You know,' he said hesitantly, 'if I could have foreseen this moment, that first night I spoke to you in your little summerhouse, I would have arranged our passage the very next day.'

Gwen's forehead wrinkled in concentration. He could not tell whether she had heard him properly until she spoke. 'We met on the beach, Edward. In broad daylight.' Her eyes were still fixed on the face of her child; it was as if she spoke to the baby, not

Edward. 'I never spoke to you in that summerhouse. I have never told you, but I found you there one morning. You were—you were asleep, and I thought you looked so exhausted I did not wake you.' She laughed. 'At first I had thought you were some kind of vagrant; in point of fact, I was a little afraid of you.' She turned her face up to his and met his gaze.

He said, 'But I remember it so clearly; we spoke for some forty minutes. It was midnight, and you were wrapped against the chill in a very thick old coat and boots which were too big for your feet by far. You mistook me for your gardener. But you were very different from the way you were the next time we spoke on the beach. And I *distinctly* remember being glad, that next time on the beach, that I could see your face properly and that your attitude towards me was much lighter, much more natural. And I remember thinking what a fool I was to have avoided that part of the coast, fearing that I had offended you.' Edward watched a wave of realisation sweep across Gwen's face as it dawned on her what he was saying.

'You could not have known that I had a sister whose most prized possession was her ability to impersonate any being, living or dead, animal or human, including myself.'

'Gwen, I—'

'It doesn't matter; not now.'

Again, she was speaking to him but looking all the while intently at the baby. He almost backed into Maria. He'd totally forgotten about her.

He opened up his collecting tin and paused, remembering his jubilation at having the specimens in his possession. He wavered, half turning, deliberating over whether he should not show them to her anyway. As he picked them over, looking for flaws in the iridescent patina, that shocking, crackling blue, he let the knowledge of what he had done with Gwen's sister that dank morning, and, he now admitted to himself, those other times, wash over his conscience. He'd wanted it not to have been so, and therefore it had existed in his mind as something malleable as putty. A memory reshaped; a physical act becoming a conversation; one person becoming another.

He looked down at his hands and saw the ruined Morpho butterfly wings spread as dull dust across his fingers. And he knew that Gwen was innocent—she did not know about Natalia. He was safe. He found the key to the writing slope and opened it up. There was the letter from Gwen's maid lying on the top of his papers. He walked out onto the verandah on the opposite side of the house from Gwen and their child and Maria. He struck a match and set light to the letter, holding it by the corner so that it drooped down and the flames licked up the words. A mimic. He did not know whether Euphemia's talents extended to mimicking others' voices on paper, but as he could not be sure, he felt it was better to burn it. He had made a note of the date of Isobel's death. He still felt lighter in the head when he reflected on the fact that he was now free of her. He dropped the charred paper to the floor of the verandah and stamped on its glowing fragments. No more recriminations, no more hysterics, nothing of that; even in his absence she had tried her damnedest to reel him in, through the pity of strangers. But she had failed. There was nothing more Isobel could do to him. She was silenced for all time.

CHAPTER XL

As the months went on, Gwen was submerged by the routine of feeding her baby. It would latch onto her breast with a mouth as wide as a cat fish and just as strong. It sucked the juice from her, and Gwen felt herself shrivelling. The clarity of the last two months before the birth left her; she was befuddled and dazed, propped up half conscious. She was either feeding the baby or being woken to feed the baby or falling asleep feeding the baby.

Her world had diminished to her breasts and whether or not the baby was sucking on them. It was so boring. It was everything she had not wanted or asked for. The initial euphoria of having survived it, of having this miraculous tiny human come from her intact and also alive, had evaporated. The momentary surge of warm feelings for Edward had receded, too, as quickly as they had come.

She looked at her drawing things in a state of listless exhaustion one afternoon. The baby was cradled in the crook of her arm; its head moist with her sweat, the bright fuzz which passed for hair, dark and slick against the skull. She caught sight of the fontanelle pulsating on the top. That thick membrane stretched over brain. Maria had told her to make sure it never dipped into the skull; if it did, she'd told her, the baby was not getting enough to drink and might die. This information both fascinated and distressed Gwen. She'd pass her fingers over the patch of soft head and hold her breath.

With one hand she pulled the things out of her bag to air them and to check for signs of mould or insect damage. She wiped over the surface of her books which had been treated with kerosene. It kept away some of the insects; others didn't object to the stink and burrowed holes into her pages. Then there was the novel, still unread. She'd treated that as well, and now idly she checked for insect damage. She shook the book, knocked it on the surface of the workbench. The baby stirred and fell asleep again instantly, her eyes rolling glassily.

She opened the book wide, so that she could look along the hollow of the spine and knocked it down on the bench again. A single beetle fell out, something small and brown. Before, she would have caught it with a pooter and then trapped it in the live box for observation under the microscope. Now, she watched it, her naked eyes stinging with fatigue as the beetle trundled off and hid itself in a crack on the bench.

The book had creaked a greeting at her. The fanning sections had kissed the air, the open lower edges sucking in space. When she closed the book with a disregarding flick, the cover said *fphphphf*. Gwen no longer cared who had sent her a novel to read. She kept the book in good condition because that was what you did with books. And if she never read it, then someone, at some point, might want to; she would have been ashamed to own an unslit book which was falling to bits. Unslit books had once excited her beyond the limit she believed they ought. As a child she had loved slitting pages more than eating, or sleeping between fresh sheets. More than her paint-box, even. More than her sister, sometimes.

She had owned a paper knife made from a very thin piece of bone. She'd loved that instrument, too, until she'd overheard what it was really made of. Then, she had taken it to the kitchen and opened the range door. The smell of the burning slave's rib had escaped into the room and she'd run away to be sick in the pantry.

Gwen doubted now that it had really been a human rib; much more likely, she thought, to have been a sliver of ivory, or something more prosaic like beef shinbone. The baby's head lolled and slipped a bit in the pooling sweat. Gwen fingered the binding on the novel and stared some long minutes at the swirls of colour on the marbled paper.

Edward had bought her a letter knife of carved horn in New York. She hadn't thought to take one with her. It pained her to think of the two of them; awkward strangers seeing the sights, buying trinkets.

Her scalp crawled, the beading sweat masquerading as a legion of lice, and she thought, Where did I put that letter knife? She didn't think, I'm going to slip the knife in and hold the paper firm as I slit it through.

The letter knife was an awful-looking object; it had a pattern of roses, a sort of grim and mawkish posy on the handle and an attempt at a thorned stem along the spine. He'd bought her a pair of combs, as well, but she'd made a show of liking the plain ones. Edward had wanted to shower her with gifts: useless articles, or garish, horrible American hats. She'd needed gloves. All the time, it had been so obvious, she had thought. Perhaps gloves were too mundane. Too ordinary. Too intimate. Too much like a thing to buy for your wife. She couldn't imagine wanting to wear gloves now.

She held the ugly letter knife in her palm. It wasn't nice to handle. It was as if the person who'd carved it had never opened a letter with anything other than their fingers. Or never opened a letter at all.

Gwen laid the baby in the hammock. She slit the first page, and the last page. Her rule was, had been, that if the first page of the book was terrible, she was justified in skipping to the last, just to see how it ended. If the first page was any good, the last page would taunt her. But she had grown out of that kind of nonsense now. She slit the pages, one after another. Everything about the construction of the book screamed money: the calf, the extraordinary marbling, the thick, creamy pages of Dutch paper which behaved so beautifully under the knife, the green silk headbands, which seemed an odd choice of colour. Everything about the book made her want to read the first page.

CHAPTER XLI

Eternal Blazon
or
The Confessions of a Nondescript
Volume I.

I am, in all outward appearances, the antithesis of you. You know this; you know that I am not beautiful to look at. My body is not silken soft in the same way as yours, and it is not as pale as veal flesh, as wan and ghostly as mare's milk. Have you ever wondered over the fact that your husband might want—need—to plunge himself with such force, such consummate desire, at a woman whose body is dark with hair. Whose face, bearded and defiant, stares out at you from the *carte de visite* you so unfortunately found amongst your husband's possessions. My image is everywhere in certain circles. I am scattered on the dirtiest streets of the most unwholesome districts of this city. My face is hidden by respectable men, whilst their good, honest, faithful wives are awake, and then it is taken out to be slavered over in the darkest places, in the deepest part of night.

I am not sixteen any more, yet that image of me as I was then still circulates. As I cover my face with thick veils in public places, my image is there to be appropriated in any which way, by anyone who may choose to do so. I was sixteen. My voice had not thickened with regret; I knew nothing. I believed those who told me when I arrived in this dreary country that the paying public would not care what I looked like; that it was my voice they came to hear. I could not understand, on my first night at the Empire Theatre, why so many people who had paid good money to hear me perform my repertoire should be so noisy. I expected hushed silence. And that I did get: a hushed silence of awe and repulsion. I managed that first night to sing despite the crowd. I never imagined that I would ever have to sing like that; to fold in on myself; to forge my voice into a steely thing. The liquid slipped away.

Will you let the tarnished liquid of your life slip away in your state of ignorance?

*   *   *

When the concert was over, on that horrible night, I was taken by a man to his shop. A man who had sat brooding over my countenance during the concert, his mind silently acting out the delicate, intricate manoeuvres his hands might make if only I would come away with him. The price surprised him. My 'chaperone' allowed him a small discount, enough to pay a cab fare. I was taken out by a side entrance of the Empire Theatre, used only by the rat catchers and the night soil collectors. My chaperone, Mr Helson Blackwater, told me nothing. He avoided my gaze. He handed me over like a skinned rabbit at Smithfield's, and wiped his hands on the tails of his coat.

He did not speak to me, this man who took me away to his shop. He sat opposite me and studied me in the dark interior of the cab as we jolted over the streets, the doors shut to the outside. The cab seats were not quite clean. The floor was grimy. There was a faint odour of vomit, and I put my shawl to my face, thinking I might not be able to control my stomach, though it was empty, as I had not eaten that day through nervousness and excitement.

He leaned forward as our bodies jarred on the cab seats and he touched my free hand. The heat from his fingers seared through our gloves; his hand closed around mine, pushing my knuckles against each other. He slipped over to sit beside me, and I tried to wrench my hand free.

'Do I hurt you?' he whispered. 'I don't mean to hurt you.' His voice was soft, his breath fragrant with caraway seed as he lowered the shawl away from my face. 'I shall not ever do anything to cause you to hurt, my dear.'

But he still held tight to my hand, as though I might fall from the cab, as though he feared that someone bigger than he might jump up to the window of the cab and snatch me away into the horrid night air. I sparkled in his mind, Isobel. My knuckles ache with the memory of it.

* * *

The name of this man was Mr Abalone Wilson Tench. It was written in gold lettering above the door of his barbershop. It glinted in the sputtering gaslight, but I could not read it then. I could read and write only in Spanish when I was sixteen. I did not know that I was being led into an establishment that specialised in the removal of facial hair. Not at once. He lit a taper from a tinderbox, and proceeded to light a lamp and several candles.

I had till now imagined that the man was large only in my imagination, swelled by my own fright to a giant. His chest was wide, and his shoulders broad as a buffalo. I could see now that he had removed his coat and jacket his waist narrowed, like a dancer's. His hands were finely shaped, the skin and fingernails well cared for. He took care not to burn himself or get soot on his hands. He clamped the stove door shut and opened the vent to get the fire raging and hot.

'You are wondering, my dear, what on this earth you might be doing in a barber's place.' His voice barely rose above the guttering of the candles and the hiss of the wet coals inside the pot-bellied stove.

‘Well, I shall tell you in good time.’

He looked at me the way other men of his kind would come to look at me. Including, Isobel, your husband. It was a look of tenderness mixed with desire.

‘I was sore angry at the way you were received this night, my dear. What animals live in this city. Rats, dogs. Horrible beasts.’ He spoke my name. ‘Natalia.’ Only once. He uttered it with such profound sensibility, his tongue lingering on the middle syllable.

‘But I am forgetful of my manners, my dear,’ he said. ‘I will provide you with refreshment, you must have a little something to drink. You must look after yourself. I see that your lips are dry. We must not let you become what they call de-hydrated. Do you know that word, my dear?’ He did not pause to see whether I did. ‘To hydrate, my dear, is to wet something. And so it follows, or, *ipso facto*, as they say in those places what are higher than this, that to dehydrate is to become too dry.’

Though I felt ill with hunger, I could not face the thought of eating; but I needed something to occupy me. I drank the stuff he’d given me; it burned my throat and my nose. My eyes watered, but he did not notice my discomfort. I fought back the urge to cough.

‘My dear,’ he said to me, ‘are you comfortable enough? Have you want for anything more?’ I shook my head. ‘Miss Jaspur,’ he said, sounding perplexed, ‘if you do no more than shake your head I shall not know whether to assume that you have enjoyed an elegant sufficiency or rather if you are not yet fully satisfied.’

‘I do not need anything more. I am very

comfortable, thank you, sir.' Though if the truth be told I was far too hot. Under my bonnet I felt the tickle of perspiration begin to agitate my scalp and I longed to tear out my pins and ruffle my hair with my hands, shaking my head between my knees as I had been able to do every evening before this.

His face had become very grave in the flickering light. 'You must know by now, Miss Jaspur, that I am a barber by trade. I cuts the hair of gentlemen, and I shaves their faces. It is my passion, this trade. I might have been other things, a different kind of man, but this trade called on me the way a man of the cloth is called upon by the Almighty. I don't mean disrespect to them what's holier than me and there is plenty of them. My dear, I wish to impress upon you that this is not just a thing that I do to earn my keep. It is my life. When I puts my hands on a gent's head, when I lays my fingers against his cheek, all hot from my towels, I sometimes see great things. Sometimes the things I see ain't so nice. Now, I don't believe in no hokery-pokery. You must not get this wrong. I have thought hard about it for twenty years or more. A man gives himself away when he surrenders himself to the barber's hands. He is, what you might call, vulnerable in a special way. He lets his soul speak to me. I see it, there, a flash in his eyes, here, in a twitch beside his nose. The way his hands fall onto his chest as he lays back in my chair. The rest is what you might call elicitation. I knows how to make the gents speak. They think I am simple. They think themselves safe. And mostly they are. But your Mister Blackwater, he come to me not two weeks ago. And all he gives me, my dear, it is pure gold. I takes my time; I go slow, careful. He's telling me about a young lady. I gives his cheeks another, closer shaving. I works the soap up into a big, feathery lather, and then I hold his head.' Mr Tench made a shape in the air with his body and his arms, his hands held the absent head of my chaperone and I shivered to see it, Isobel. I shivered because I suddenly heard Blackwater speaking about me.

Mr Tench became solemn. 'You must feel liberated, Miss Jaspur, my dear. Liberated. Your Mister Blackwater, and believe me he is of the blackest, foulest, murkiest water what ever flowed through this city. Blackwater, he thinks one thing of my paying for you, and well I know it to be another. You have your freedom, my dear. I will transform you. I will release you into a better life with my razor and my scissors.'

* * *

'I see structures. I have studied the human skeleton in great detail both living and defleshed, and bleached in the anatomist's cauldron. And I see beauty hid behind your mask. If you will allow me, I will reveal you for the hidden beauty that you really are, my dear, my lovely, my precious, precious jewel.'

I heard Mr Tench move around lighting more candles, refreshing those that had almost burned to nothing. He brought out another lamp. Gradually, the room was filled with an amber hue; I could sense shadows slinking back to the furthest recesses of the shop, and I opened my eyes.

Mr Tench smiled at me in the mirror. His sleeves were folded back meticulously to his elbows. He wrapped my face deftly, gently, without saying a word. He then took up a razor, its handle made from a deep chestnut turtleshell, inlaid with delicate silverwork. He grasped the bottom end of the leather strop, as though he was restraining the beast the hide had come from and slowly began to whisk the opened blade up and down the length of the hide. He laid the honed razor carefully down on a clean cotton cloth on the work shelf and walked the few paces across the room to the pot-bellied stove. He moved softly across the room, carrying out his preparations as though he was performing a religious rite. I felt myself being tipped back in the chair and discerned his breath again close by.

He worked quickly, finding the contours of my face, mapping the structure of my jaw through the round handle of the brush. Mr Tench curved around me, his hands splayed, making my skin taut as the blade moved over, guided by his instinct. In a very few minutes he had finished with my jaw and neck and was engaged in marking a new hairline on my forehead. He separated my eyebrows with one miniscule flick above the bridge of my nose. He rubbed something sweet-smelling into my skin.

'Almond oil,' he told me. 'With something of my own. A little secret that I have been working on for just this moment.' He caressed my newly exposed face, my never seen cheeks, my until now hidden chin. He pulled himself closer to me pushing his belly against the top of my head so that I could feel the heat of his blood through my hair. I heard him sigh again and again. He moved around me fondling my face as though it was the first and last thing he might ever behold in this life. His hands on my face spoke of an aching desire I could not have imagined. I thought that he was done. But he was not finished in his work yet. He spoke to me, his voice cracked and strained. 'I must let you up, my dear,' he breathed in a tiny breath and held it in his chest as if he felt a great pain. I was confronted by a strange girl in the mirror; a girl with pink cheeks, glistening with the sweet almond oil. Her eyes were wide and I watched them fill with tears. Quickly, Mr Tench wiped my eyes with a pocket handkerchief.

'Now, my dear, what say you to this? You have seen my work. You have seen how I have the ability to transform you into a wondrous creature. Let me do more. Allow me to continue. And if your modesty is likely to be offended I will practise my art on the rest of your body with a blindfold. You may even tie it to my eyes yourself.'

I felt my skin ripple in horrific anticipation and yet I knew that I would not be able to leave this man until I had allowed him to do what he proposed. I must expose my naked body in all the truth of its condition in order to satisfy this man's unfathomable desire to swipe his blade over my belly and breasts, over my arms and legs, even, as I was to discover that night, down to the hairs which grow on my toes. He was not a man to be dissuaded once he had set his mind on something. I cowered at the thought of this man thinking of me in such a way; not for a fleeting moment, something which might spark before the eyes and then be dismissed out of hand, but each day. Planning, mixing his special oil. Well, Isobel, what would you have done, if you had been so unlucky as to have been me?

There was nothing I could say.

As I lay there, Isobel, I found myself slipping into

a trance, being conscious only of the sensation of those hands moving the blade across my skin; the quick, sure rub of his thumb where the hair had been removed and then moving on again, working around my arm in a spiral pattern from my shoulder down to my wrist. He wiped my arm slowly when he was satisfied that he had been thorough, and then embarked upon the right arm, after covering my left side. At this moment, Mr Tench spoke to me. 'Are you well enough, my dear? Do you feel the air too cold? I must keep you warm, you see, for, if not, your skin will raise bumps like a plucked goose and I will not be able to continue.'

In fact, I was roasting under the cape and the towelling. It was one of those nights when the air never finds its coolness, and there is no relief from the smothering atmosphere. I felt trickles of perspiration running down my sides, and I knew that my underarms were beginning to let loose the odour of stale sweat. But he was already employed in removing all the hair from under my arms.

*   *   *

You are blonde, Isobel. I wonder if you can sympathise at all with the story I am relating to you. You perhaps have used a weak solution of arsenic to make your underarms silky smooth, ready for your evening gown. Perhaps you have even used it on your long, slender legs. There is nothing I shall not tell you Isobel.

Your husband once told me that he liked the sensation of going from one extreme to the other. So, I assumed, as I still do, that your own body is as naturally hairless as mine is naturally covered in (the words of your husband) 'a thick luxurious mane, a sumptuous, luscious, glossy fur'. He would come to me after those tortured nights with you, in your enormous, bug-free bedroom. He would leave your house while your servants were sleeping, perhaps one boy still awake, polishing your husband's riding boots. He would carry his shoes and his clothes down the hall and go into his room to change into different clothes.

Afterwards, he would wash himself carefully with his own soap and his own washing cloth, which he kept in his doctor's bag along with the morphine and the smelling salts and the callipers and the glass suction cups and the jars of leeches and the speculum and the tweezers and all the other instruments of his trade which he was to abandon in favour of rocks and fossilised forms. But that was to come.

*   *   *

When Mr Tench came to that place between my legs he said, 'This is a place where a woman should have hair aplenty. This is the place I vow I shall never ever touch with my razor.' And he kept his promise. Do I shock you with these words, Isobel?

He smothered my entire body in the almond oil, the scent of which was overpowering now. Its cumulative effect and the lack of sleep made me very tired. I had not dared to fall asleep before, but now all I wanted to do was curl up and let myself fall into a deep and intense slumber. I felt I could sleep for a whole day and not feel refreshed on waking. But the man had to be satisfied. He worked his hands over my shaven body. His hands moved over the lubricated surface of my body in swirls and he began to knead my flesh like you must if you have suffered a cramp. His hands pummelled my body; my muscles at first felt soothed by it, but as his hands continued their journey over my newly revealed form it became more and more uncomfortable. And as the discomfort turned into something more sinister, Abalone Wilson Tench began to groan again. He squeezed and kneaded my skin and flesh as though it was dough on a baker's table. He began to push his weight into my shoulders. He lingered so long over this that he needed to apply more of the almond oil to my skin. The groans became longer and longer, more noisy and abandoned. The room was awash with his feral grunting and I thought that I would faint from the pain, which had turned into such an agony that I barely knew that I was still alive. He began to slap my body; lightly at first, and only with each new application of oil. I felt the palms of his hands burning into my unprotected skin and still I kept silent.

He stopped abruptly. My body was sore. My muscles protested as I slowly moved away from Mr Tench. With my back to him, began to dress myself, pulling on my stockings and my underclothes which clung to my bare skin. As I dressed, I listened to the room. I could not tell where he had gone. I had not been aware of his leaving the room. I did not try to look about me. I kept my eyes from straying into the mirror, and attended to the rest of my clothes. The fabric felt unfamiliar on my skin. As the daylight began to filter through the blinds, and the noises of the streets outside became more lively, what had happened to me seemed to become unreal. I allowed myself to look again in the mirror to fix up my bonnet, which was limp and bedraggled. I avoided my gaze, concentrating only on the business of hiding my unruly hair under the bonnet as well as I could. There was a hairbrush, silver-backed, right by my hand, but I did not like to pick it up. I did not want to touch anything connected with Abalone Wilson Tench. Whilst I looked in the mirror and tied the ribbons under my chin, my hands knowing the form but being surprised, all the time I did this I let my eyes dart about the room behind me. As my body became used to its new state, in all its hurt, in all its injury and its shaven state I noticed that I was hungry again. I looked at the door leading to the street. People's shadows flitted past under the small gap where the blind on the door did not reach. I studied the door for some minutes, remaining with my back to the rest of the room, unable yet to discover by listening whether I had been abandoned, even if only temporarily. My heart beat hard. I had only to walk three paces and turn the key, open the door and step out onto the street. I hesitated, my head in a frenzy of indecision before I felt my hands fumbling with the key, the door swinging open and my feet on the pavement outside. I pulled the door shut, leaving Abalone Wilson Tench inside, neither looking to see if he watched me depart nor waiting to wonder whether he might call me back or try to haul me back into his shop.

The sunlight was bright in my eyes. The stench of the night still hung on the air but it was as a sweet reality to me, then. I did not care to smell anything properly perfumed. I started walking, trying to find my way by keeping the sun on my right. My slippers had worn right through before I found a cab.

*   *   *

And so, as I sat in my room, scrubbing my skin which plagued me with the discomfort of the re-emergence of my hair, I thought of myself as a ghost who was no ghost. And yet unremarkable, Isobel. You will know this feeling. You, too, have harboured the desire to stare and take in your fill. I spent a long night contemplating my future, and with the first light on a chilly September morning I knew that I would have to turn to Leicester Square, not as a sightseer, but to investigate the place as a means to my survival. So, Isobel, I come to the question to which I already have the answer; and it is not so out of the ordinary that one might be shocked. Yes, if I were to ask you, you would admit, perhaps after a little hesitation that you believe that the spirits of the deceased can manifest themselves in this world. I have not been entirely honest with you.

How did you feel when you faced the mirror image of your husband's newest mistress? You went there to Carrick House in search of your dead children, and you sat in the parlour, in its darkened state, waiting for Euphemia Carrick to drift into her trance. What were you hoping to see? What were you thinking? I could have told you that Euphemia was nothing like her sister. That you would not find Gwen. For what is the mirror image but the opposite of that object which you seek?

How can I know these things, if I was never there to see them myself? How can I know that Euphemia Carrick spoke in many tongues—

incomprehensible gibberish which the newly bereaved allowed themselves to believe were the tangled thoughts and messages of those struggling to contact them from the other side.

And you fainted, Isobel. The spell worked on you. No bells tinkling, no table rattling, no pointer on a board twirling magnetically, no glass tumbler of water tipping over. No gifts dropped into your lap from the other side. Only Euphemia, Gwen's sister, babbling and burbling like the babies you once held in your arms whose lives were the briefest of flames, their sickliness only the fault of your loneliness.

You were never your husband's wife, Isobel, and neither I. The impossibility of perfection festers and cripples his mind. You hoped in the end that your presence at the table would be enough to stay the cycle of disaster. But, faced with those sisters, your efforts came adrift. Let a different wind fill your sails, Isobel, as you make that final journey. Not an abrupt end for you, Isobel. I cannot imagine that you would follow the cowardice of your *closest* friend, Dr Charles Jeffreye.

* * *

Forgive me, Isobel, for I get ahead of myself.

Should I go straight to the part now where I met your husband? Shall I describe what he did, or would that be too distasteful?

He came to Saville House one evening. The place was thick with tobacco smoke. People were leaving. It had been my first week there as the Mysterious Lady, though there was not much mysterious about me it seemed—other than whether or not it was me singing and whether or not I was a lady at all.

That night, I would not consent to see him. He gave me his card, or rather he sent it up to me, telling me that he was an admirer. I did not want to see another admirer. I fancied there was another Abalone Wilson Tench down at the grand entrance to that Den of Iniquity. No. That night, I took the advice of a little man called Fergus Harris. I think the name may be familiar to you, if you are the sort of woman who keeps track of her servants' names. Certainly, you will have remarked him; his size set him apart. I liked him instantly. He was direct; the only person in that stinking, louse-infested room who had come to listen to my singing. My voice captivated him, and he was persistent. I did not think that he would prove very troublesome if I invited him to dine with me—people like us, we cannot stand on ceremony, we must behave all as equals and not simper behind Japanese silk fans and parasols. I do not believe in a second sense; I never have thought that one human being may read the mind or thoughts of another, but there was something uncanny about that evening. A prickle shivered down my neck when I spoke to Mr Fergus Harris. It was I for once who felt that I must not let another out of my sight—and it was invigorating. I was exhausted after my long performance, but a new energy came over me.

Fergus Harris was very deferential towards me, though it soon became clear that his personality would have fit inside a body as large as Abalone Wilson Tench's. And so he became my eyes and ears in your house. When you finally became aware of his talents you sent him on his way to Carrick

House. You were able to persuade him with a bigger purse and the promise of cleaner air; an easier life but a more demanding role. He took the challenge, he took it to his heart because he had something to prove and because he enjoyed the irony. He has proven his weight, Isobel, but do not forget that his loyalties will change with the prospect of better weather. His ambition is no brother to duty and the rewards for his endeavours cannot be measured in guineas.

CHAPTER XLII

Observations.
Pará, Brazil. 1861/1862.

Underneath, she was floating.

Her eyes followed the things around her before her brain had a chance to catch up. She managed, in ways which were not too strange, to look after her baby.

I didn't come all this way, she heard herself thinking over and over, just to be his unkissed mistress, to have a child, hidden away in the jungle under lies, swaddled in deceit. To think about Gus Pemberton was too painful and so she tried not to.

On the surface, she was still.

She watched her baby, whose name was Augusta—yes, she remembered that, though other facts were difficult to retain. She watched Augusta watching her with unfocused eyes.

First, the baby was like a grub; pale, and startlingly basic in her needs. Gwen learned how to anticipate the bodily functions of the grub, the baby, Augusta. There were no mountains of soiled napkins to launder or send away for laundering. Maria taught her things; and there was a small dog which came to live in the house and which removed mishaps from the floor.

But this creature was not interesting to Gwen. She never called the dog by its name or petted it in any way. Sometimes, Gwen saw Edward going through her things. He would stand for an hour, perhaps more, unaware that she was watching him read the notes she had made alongside the work she'd so far put into her sketchbooks. Occasionally, Edward would shuffle into his own room with her sketchbook in his hand and then write things down in his own notebooks while referring to hers. She didn't know whether he was transcribing or what he was doing; it was curious behaviour to her and only mildly interesting.

Gwen was aware that she did not speak. When he was out of the house, Edward couldn't hear her whispering to Maria.

The grub learned to roll over. The baby smiled. The baby became mobile. Augusta rolled and rolled across surfaces until she came to an obstacle and then looked about her, unable to roll back the other way.

By the time Baby Augusta had learned to crawl, and dribbled and began to eat plain things, like bananas and rice, Gwen had read the book six times.

There must be a hidden message, she thought, and I have to find that message, and understand it. But all there was to understand was that she could not understand him.

There are certain books, Gwen wrote feverishly, *which are all well and good for the lay-person vaguely interested, one rainy afternoon, in finding out about the secrets a microscope might offer. But they do not illustrate properly, or investigate fully, or show such possible investigations that they might, and which I think that they ought. By which I mean that the secrets of the microscope will remain secrets largely to the entire population of the civilised world, other than those with the time, means and inclination to investigate for themselves. This cannot be right. I do not feel that it is proper . . .*

My own purpose, then, is to create a kind of Atlas of the Insect World.

How frustrating, it is, as I know through my own experience, to see, 'a fly leg' illustrated, for example, in amongst other, unrelated bits taken from other creatures and laid out prettily, *without being able to ascertain from which fly the leg came and which leg it was which happened to be illustrated in isolation.*

It is my opinion, which I am free to expound in the privacy of this journal, that there should be available to any adult person or intelligent and inquisitive child, the kind of Atlas that I mean to create. Moreover, in creating such an Atlas it should, in part, remove the need for the intelligent and inquisitive child (or adult) to plunder *nature so* unnecessarily, *and with such* careless *attitude in the pursuit of elementary scientific enquiry and knowledge.*

Of course, I could never speak of this to anyone. On the surface, my idea is to produce something which is instructive, as well as being a work of Art. I wish to make my work appealing to both the scientist and the art lover.

I think this Atlas might take up the rest of my days

here. I cannot continue to make lovely representations of insects set in their ranks and be satisfied.

We cannot understand the truth of a creature and its place in nature, through the singular fact of its carcass.

And so I wish to say: let us be done with this obsession for collecting variations in a specimen to the last available insect, to be pored over by but a few and left forevermore to the darkness of the cabinet. (Is this Science? No, it is Vanity.) Let us try to understand Nature in a way that does not deplete Her, or ravage Her, or decimate Her. Because I think that this attitude which leads a man to take as much as he can, without thinking with due care for the result of his actions, will lead that man to no good purpose, and ultimately waste his whole life in the pursuit of false knowledge. I do not mean that Darwin's idea is false; I mean that for others to pursue what he has already proved is stupid. We do not need to replicate his work; we need to find other ways if we are to progress. I cannot condone wholesale capture in the name of vanity.

I have thought very much on the ways of the ants here. They are everywhere and there are many different species. We have had to protect our equipment and our food against the attentions of these enterprising insects from the outset, and must always be vigilant against their ingenuity.

Recently, I have been trying out an experiment involving the enticing of a small colony into a large specimen jar which I had prepared. After a frustrating start, I discovered that the ants will only begin anew where there is a Queen to serve, and that the colony is not merely a collection of individuals, but a collective; an organism made up of other organisms, with their beating heart, their Queen, at the centre. I now have a system of cords leading in and out of the jar, which are suspended by treated cords from the ceiling. I have taken the extra precaution of standing the specimen jar in a large bowl of water.

The most marvellous thing that I have found is that these leaf-cutting ants, which we had both assumed were consuming the leaves, are not. A kind of midden heap is prepared by the ants, and it is the resulting fungus growing there on the leaf cuttings which the ants eat.

I have not read anywhere of other observers of these creatures having come to the same conclusion. Of course, I would not claim to be the first to discover the true nature of their foraging habits and their purpose, however, I am still excited by this idea—of the ants' apparent knowledge of, or at least their harnessing of, the basics of horticulture.

I am still much given to spending long hours of thought on the subject of Mr Frome. His remarks, and his wildness, and his claims, and his final deed, seem, on the one hand, to mark him out as a singularly disturbed individual who perhaps spent too much time with his theories and not enough in the common pursuit of friendship and good humour. (Of course, I am an expert on this.) On the other hand, I wonder if, in his madness, there was some kind of logical reasoning. I have gone over it so many times.

Gwen stopped writing, remembering Edward's reaction to her experiment with the ants. He had stomped into her room, and she had listened to him quietly. The quieter she was, the more infuriated he seemed to become.

'There is not the room here, Gwen, for your school-room antics with these pests. Whatever you think you may have observed in these jars is irrelevant and highly likely to be wrong. Just stick to what you came here to do, namely, illustrate *my* findings. And clear up this dreadful mess. We'll have the blasted things in our food.'

Who did this man think he was, to instruct her, to try to remove the one thing which allowed her to reconcile herself to this situation? Gwen did not clear away her ants in jars. She did not stop writing; her efforts were redoubled in the face of his attempts to obstruct her observations.

She began to keep her notes locked up in her trunk.

CHAPTER XLIII

THE TIMES, Thursday, October 4, 1866.

MURDER TRIAL AT THE OLD BAILEY.

MR PROBART for the Prosecution called as witness a Mr Harpe, who said, 'I am a bookseller in this city and I am well acquainted with Mrs Pemberton, the prisoner in this trial. She has come to my shop on many occasions, asking for a certain title.'

Q: 'What is the title, Mr Harpe?'

A: 'The prisoner has always asked for *Eternal Blazon*, sir, and when I have told her that no such title has come my way, the prisoner has always spent a deal of time lingering over other titles on display. Sometimes, she has bought a copy of obscurity, and most other times, nothing.'

Q: 'Curious, would you not say, for a lady to be perusing the shelves of an establishment such as your own, Mr Harpe?'

A: 'Perhaps, at first; I wouldn't often get a customer such as the prisoner, but I came to expect her, sir, after a while. You never can tell what kind of reading matter a person will have in their house, sir, from appearances alone.'

Q: 'Please tell the court, Mr Harpe, exactly what kind of reading matter it is which lines the shelves of your shop.'

A: 'Everything I sell is absolutely legal and above board, sir, in my bookshop. Titles are of a mainly scientific interest, a specialist interest, not novels or any such matter.'

Q: 'And yet, Mr Harpe, the volume which the prisoner, by your account, was so keen to obtain, it does in fact fit loosely the description of 'novel', does it not?'

A: 'I believe it does, sir.'

Q: 'And yet you do not have any such 'novels' on display in your shop?'

A: 'No, sir.'

Q: 'But if I were to pay you a large sum, perhaps to obtain a certain title, then you might be able to oblige?'

A: 'There is no doubt that just about anything is obtainable in this city if the seeker is determined enough, sir.'

Q: 'Please tell me, Mr Harpe, what is the title of the last volume you sold to the prisoner?'

A: 'That's easy enough, it was called *The*

Book of Phobias, and I sold it to the prisoner on the 4th of August, the Saturday before the murder.'

Q: 'A novel, Mr Harpe?'

A: 'A scientific book, sir. By Dr Charles Jeffreye. It is about certain maladies of the nerves and so forth.'

Q: 'Maladies of the nerves. Thank you, Mr Harpe.'

The unfortunate fate of Dr Jeffreye, who was crippled by a fall from his horse and later died, was briefly discussed. More witnesses were questioned—all booksellers—all of whom said that Mrs Pemberton was a regular patron who always asked for a particular title. Mrs Pemberton had visited the establishments of each on Monday, 6th August.

Mr Shanks for the Defence then addressed the court in respect of the evidence given by the various booksellers: 'Mrs Pemberton does not deny having been a regular customer at many bookshops in the city. Nor does she deny having sought a particular volume mentioned earlier. Her motives, however, for having devoted so much time and effort in her search were entirely honourable. The volume mentioned, was, some of you will be aware, of ill-repute. What you may not be fully aware of is the fact that within that novel lay certain unsavoury accusations against Mr Scales. Mrs Pemberton's brief was simple: to locate any surviving copies of that title and to destroy them. Why? Because she wished to eradicate foulness, however false, against her former companion. Why? Because she had forgiven him his falseness against her, and wished to do him well, not ill. This determined effort, sirs, is not the kind of sustained action of a murderess.

Furthermore, the other volume, entitled *The Book of Phobias*, was obtained for the same reason. Spurious and lewd claims were made by its author against Mr Scales' reputation. No one, who had travailed so long, in such a manner, would then murder the very person whose name she desired to clear.'

CHAPTER XLIV

PARÁ, BRAZIL. MAY, 1863.

Gwen, hunched over a pot she had just taken from the fire, was utterly absorbed in her task. The stench coming from the pot stung Edward's eyes. Augusta, unwatched by her mother, poked a stick into the fire—in and out—and then jabbed it inexpertly into the ground and tried to make a hole, immersed in the serious business of finding out what was possible with a stick. Gwen sat with her feet planted apart in a squat as though about to defecate. She stirred the foul brew, which Edward now realised was a broth containing fish skin and bones.

'Soup?' he ventured, little expecting any response; her muteness towards him was absolute. Gwen seemed not to have heard him, and so he continued to watch Augusta should she fall into difficulties with her stick, or the fire, or both. Then Gwen reached to her side and held a tatty book up and waved it, only a slight twist from her wrist. Edward didn't know what to make of this latest peculiar enterprise, but, at least, he had managed to get some kind of reaction from her, which might, at a stretch, be interpreted as communication.

Gwen's post-partum melancholia had been sudden and severe. It had not affected her ability to function as a mother, which surprised him, but she had suddenly one day taken ill and refused to speak or paint. She would spend long hours walking the perimeter of the *casinha* with the baby in a pouch, native style on her back. Or she would suddenly take instead to lying for days on end in her hammock. The malaise had not affected her appetite too badly. She seemed to be aware of the need to fill her stomach in order to nurse the child. She sang to it, whispered lovingly to it, but she would speak to no one else; not even Maria, who told Edward, without his asking, that European women always had some trouble of this kind and that he should keep an eye on her but stay out of her way. Edward resented the inclusion of Maria in their number, but knew that hiring anyone else would probably result in the same deluge of un-asked for advice. Sometimes, he did wonder if it was something more. He wouldn't put a name to it; he wouldn't call her mad. It was like no kind of madness he had ever seen. His entomologising rambles became truncated as a result. He scrutinised her, from a suitable distance, for signs of a change in her condition, either good or not so good. He couldn't even bring himself to use the word 'bad'. There seemed to be nothing bad about her. Occasionally, she appeared to be staring intently at something far away, and so absolute was her concentration, that Edward, more than once, fetched out the telescope to discover her object of interest.

During all this time, Gwen read and re-read a book. He was not permitted to see it. He knew that she kept it inside her painting bag, modified within the first week of their arrival to exclude tarantulas with an interest in art. If Edward came within twenty feet of the open book, it was snapped shut and tucked under Gwen's arm or inside the tight folds of the pouch across her breastbone.

Edward was sure that the tatty article she had just waved at him was the same volume which had received such intensive attention. It had a curious title: *Eternal Blazon*. He'd vowed to get at it one day and see what could possibly be written there which could be so consuming.

* * *

Augusta let a trickle of urine, travelling part of the way down her chubby legs, fall to the ground. She stamped gleefully in the wetted earth and squatted again to poke at it with her fingers. Edward cast a glance towards Gwen. She opened her blouse and placed the book next to her skin. Edward backed away as she got up and removed Augusta from the mess and took her away to clean her, murmuring that she was a rascal, in a voice so quiet no one else would have recognised it as speech. Gwen left the child with Maria and returned to the pot. Edward fetched his gun out to the verandah and began to clean it, taking extra care over each section. He was far enough away now, for Gwen to carry on without hindrance. She turned her back to him again and spent an hour doing something which Edward was not allowed to see. Eventually, she stood and stretched, and with the book in her hand went inside.

Edward went over to the pot. The concoction was beginning to congeal. It looked, for all the world, like glue.

CHAPTER XLV

PARÁ, BRAZIL. JULY, 1863.

The last of Edward's specimens had been packaged carefully and crated up, ready to be shipped back to England. Some were to be sold; the rest were to be kept safely in storage until their own return. Edward had decided that this was the best way to do things. They would now quit the *casinha* and take a boat up into the country to search for specimens as yet unknown to science. The Grindlocks had told him that Coyne, now back in the country, was interested in taking part in the expedition. Edward knew he needed a guide and so agreed to take him on. All this had been arranged, and Gwen had not spoken. Her manner was curiously ordinary despite the muteness. He had taken her silence to mean that she agreed with his plans wholeheartedly.

* * *

Now, she had broken her silence. Edward's mouth hung open, she thought, in quite an idiotic way. What was there not to comprehend? She waited whilst she folded the last of her moth-bitten clothes into her trunk. The only things which were not packed into it were her drawing things, and her tin of paints.

'What do you mean, what plan?'

'I have always intended to leave, Edward, when the child was big enough to stand the journey.'

'But,' he said, 'if she is big enough to stand the journey, as you put it, over the Atlantic, then she is big enough to take part in this excursion. It is what we came here for.'

'It is not the excursion, Edward. It's me. I don't want to stay here with you any longer. I have had my fill. I cannot continue.' Perhaps, she thought, this is more arduous than the voyage I face, and she drew comfort from that.

'Who have you told? The Grindlocks, have you told them?'

'No, why on earth would I do that? I'll make my own arrangements. I can explain my return in terms which will cast no aspersions on you, if that's what worries you.'

Edward threw his arms out, and Gwen stepped back, unsure the gesture was nicely meant. But Edward began to grab at handfuls of his hair.

'You have to come with me. I can't do the thing—not on my own. Those two weeks, remember, when we first came here. It was hell without you. You. You are—necessary.'

'I'm not. You can collect things without me.'

'We had an arrangement. An agreement. I trusted you, for God's sake.'

'To do what? To keep on lying? To keep on pretending that we have some kind of affinity? We don't. Nothing binds us.'

‘Our daughter, Augusta. She binds us. She would be fatherless.’

‘She already is. It makes not a jot of difference.’

‘You can’t take her. I won’t allow it.’

‘You don’t have to allow it. We are not husband and wife.’

‘The law favours me, as her father. You count for nothing. Nothing!’

‘You have no interest in her. You can’t collect her.’

‘I have every interest in her, and I will not permit her removal.’

‘We’ll see about that. In any case, Edward, I can’t be a part of this excursion whilst you persist with the idea of including Mr Coyne.’

‘I had every impression that you were rather taken with him.’

‘I’ll not get on a boat with him, under any circumstances. He is altogether a menace.’

Edward swivelled on his heel to face her, and his hands dropped away from knotting his hair. ‘Since when have you ever regarded Coyne as a menace?’

‘From the moment I met him.’

‘This is just bluff. You had something with him, and now you want to hide it.’

‘Don’t be absurd!’

‘That is exactly the answer I would expect from a guilty party.’

‘Listen to yourself! You’ll drive yourself mad over nothing if you keep this up. I’m going home, Mr Scales, and I’m taking Augusta with me.’

Edward pressed his eyes with his fingers and for several long moments did nothing but breathe heavily through his nose, which made a dry whistle with every intake. Then he spoke from behind his hands: 'Will you at least come and see us off?'

Gwen suddenly felt sorry for him. He looked, and sounded, so pathetic, 'Yes, of course, I will.'

'You'll want to have your luggage sent on to the Grindlocks, I suppose. I shall see to that for you.'

Gwen gave a small nod.

'Gwen,' he said. She was moving away from him, but he caught her by the arm. She stood and waited for whatever was to come next, but all he said was, 'I do love you. You know that, don't you? Above all else.'

At last, she gave another small nod and he let her go.

*   *   *

Vincent Coyne's blue spectacles flashed in the sun; his teeth seemed yellow beneath them in the harsh light. He strode up and down the deck of the two-masted boat, slapping its sides and slapping the crates of Edward's things like tethered beasts which had previously irked him. Still, Gwen looked on the scene with a glad sense of detachment. It was nearly over. She must have smiled as Vincent Coyne looked up and saw her.

'Hey,' he shouted, throwing a clenched fist high in the air, his gaze fixed on her. 'She's here.'

Edward appeared from underneath the awning. He looked harassed. Augusta leaned precariously off Gwen's hip where she had been sitting quietly. She flung her arms out towards Edward.

'Bring her on board, just for a minute,' he said.

'No. We'll wave from here. Here will be sufficient.'

'Don't you trust him?' yelled Vincent, vicious,

playful.

'We don't need to complicate her day.'

'It's not complicated, Gwen,' said Edward. 'Just let her have a little inspection of the boat. Bring her aboard for ten minutes.'

This will be the last thing, she thought, that he will make me do. In half an hour the boat will be setting sail, and I will be able breathe freely again. She relented and carried Augusta onto the boat.

Edward took her into his arms and held her high up above his head.

Had that been the signal, thought Gwen later, for the men to cast off? Around her, the scrambled activity, the sails filling, the ropes thrown, the men jumping here and there with careless concentration, calling to each other short words of affirmation: they were leaving.

Her heart pumped with hatred as she saw that it was useless to make a fuss, or to demand that she be allowed to alight. He had devised this, and she remembered now his warning to her after Frome had walked away; that she should not make a fool of him again. I'll wait, she thought; there'll be some chance later. I'll use this time to think of every possible pitfall. But the hatred surged through her like molten glass; its colours twisted and settled in her breast, hardening her resolve to one day be absolutely free of this man. She walked to the stern and faced away from him, alert all the while, to the presence of Vincent Coyne.

Edward wrote in his diary:

We resemble I don't know what as the boat goes along at a spanking pace. The wind smacks the canvas with a cheerful bite, and the child leaps about the place, her little eyes bright with expectation; and I dare say there is a hint of something similar in my own. All that has gone before was mere preparatory work. The child puts her fingers into anything she can. She investigates any available surface, or drawer, or book, with avid enthusiasm. Her presence adds another dimension to the excursion, which will be no less the richer for it.

In the absence of any practical measure to prevent it, and in the light of the perceived advantages of such a coalition, I have been obliged, after some lengthy discussions, to accept, under the unwavering and hearty recommendation of Mr Grindlock, the returned Mr Coyne as an addition to our party. The regrettable absence of Maria, who must return to her former duties at the Grindlock household, will be felt most keenly by the female members of the party.

Edward emerged from under the awning with an ink-laden pen in his hand. Gwen watched him with a certain amount of satisfaction as he gripped the rail and reached over to be sick before staggering back. And now, as she trailed her gaze back to the open water, she saw her trunk, tucked in with some of the crates.

Vincent Coyne stood at the bow, his arms pounding the air in time to a song he was singing. The wind caught it up and shredded it, the words lost as soon as they left his lungs. Phrases from the now unreadable volume preyed on her mind yet again. It was not only that the ghastly details of his past had been concealed from her but read about by others, nor was it that he had kept his marriage to himself—perhaps she could have found some way to reconcile herself to these things if it were not for the fact that her own name, and that of her sister, and of her family home had been so casually thrown into the pages of the book while Edward himself had never been named. In the whole damn compendium of confession, it was Edward whose identity had been protected. Gwen turned her face into the wind.

CHAPTER XLVI

LOWER AMAZONS. AUGUST, 1863.

They were unpacking boxes properly for the first time since they had left Pará. Before this, they had worked and lived on the boat, stopping in a place for three days, a week, or ten days, and then moving further on, so that Gwen was never able to make any arrangements to get away. Now, she was in a small house rented from some person or other whom Vincent seemed to know. Setting up tables and trying to keep Augusta in sight, Gwen turned around for the umpteenth time to find that she had trundled off again. Following Augusta's trail of discarded objects, and piling them into her arms as she went, Gwen found herself confronted with the spectacle of Vincent rummaging through her field bag, as she had come to think of it.

Immediately enraged and finding herself incapable of finding the right sequence of words to whip out at him, she simply stood, with her arms full, waiting for Vincent to notice her. Outside, she heard Edward speaking to Augusta. She watched Vincent's hands.

He pulled out the stuck-together book, and Gwen made an instinctive move towards him, dumping her armful of things and stretching her arm out towards the book.

'That is mine,' she said. The firmness, the tripping anger in her voice thrummed on the bare walls. 'As is everything else in that bag.'

Finally, lazily, Vincent looked up; his expression masked, as always, by the blue tinted spectacles which she had so loved when she had first seen him. But there was a fever over his top lip.

'Where'd you get this?' His question, demanding, arrogant. The way he held her property in his fist. He began to flick through the book but, of course, was frustrated. He knocked the stiff brick of glued paper against his knuckle. 'What's the point in keeping a book you can't even read?' Tremulous, his voice wavered between incredulity, annoyance and laughter.

'I never throw books away,' said Gwen, her voice gentle, its tone massaging Vincent's shoulders into a droop. She heard Augusta with Edward in the next room and stepped forward, taking the book from his hands as well as her bag. 'Even when I have no intention of reading them again.'

He pinched the bridge of his nose where his spectacles had made red dents on the surface of his skin. 'Dumb name for a dumb book, anyway. What kind of dumb fool'd think up a name like that?'

'Shakespeare. It's the Ghost in *Hamlet*.' She paused. '"I could a tale unfold whose lightest word would harrow up thy soul, freeze thy young blood, make thy two eyes, like stars, start from their spheres—"'

'Is that so?' His posture changed. He pulled himself straight and clicked his tongue at her as though he was speaking to a mare, pushed his blue spectacles up to the hilt of his brow and strode out of the room.

* * *

Gwen's gaze took in her child's pale ringlets and her eyes, which had miraculously changed from the deep obsidian of a newborn to the scorching light blue of her father.

Gwen squared the writing paper lying on the table in front of her, and gave her daughter a spoiled sheet of paper and a pencil to play with. She had not discussed the letter she was about to write. She was still furious and didn't know what to do with her anger. She avoided Edward, and her play with Augusta now came out as false jollity. She couldn't say anything without it coming out badly. The child's puzzlement at her mother's sudden ill temper made it all so much worse. Augusta had begun to draw in the middle of the page. Gwen noted with satisfaction that the child held the pencil correctly. A tight little scrawl of individual shapes began to emerge. Augusta's stomach was flat on the floor and her feet were in the air. Twirling feet.

Gwen cleared her throat as if she were about to address her sister in person, and dipped her pen into the ink. She knew she would not be able to send the letter. Everything in it bore resemblance to the truth—to some degree. A man had lost his life to an alligator in the dark but he had not been going for a swim. The other man had escaped unhurt. Missionaries lost in the jungle. Well, that was true, Gwen reasoned. They had visited a village where the people filed their teeth, but the missionaries had been missing for about thirty years. Edward's pet leech was already dead, and Edward was convinced that the mysterious fish did not exist.

But she couldn't deny that Augusta was her own child. She just couldn't. She couldn't add another lie to whatever she might have left with Edward. Lies can so easily dominate, she thought. Deceptively benign in their first instance, they leach the life out of you as they grow, like a tumour on your good intentions.

She folded the letter and stowed it away amongst her things. She looked at what Augusta had drawn, and wondered if she had been speaking out loud as she had written the letter. Augusta had scribbled a tangle of things, which might be fish, and she had made shapes which vaguely resembled alligators. The child could barely utter a few words but she could draw.

In the days that followed there were new varieties of Morpho butterflies, which had become something of an obsession for both of them: for Edward, because they were so impossible to obtain; and for Gwen, because of the impossibility of rendering in paint the magnificence of that lustrous blue in flight. Their rigid corpses captivated her, but no other did now. The specimen boxes were filling up with an astonishing array of Coleoptera. Edward's interest in beetles grew steadily. Easier to catch and observe than butterflies, he said, and less easily damaged in transit.

* * *

Gwen and Augusta set off along the shore, stopping every so often to look at the drifts of butterflies feeding amongst the thick carpet of flowering shrubs. They had stolen away from that other leech, Vincent. He was making it his own little parlour game to know exactly Gwen's intentions for every moment of every day and to be there, to advise her. As Augusta slithered down off her hip, and stumped about barefoot, Gwen looked back over her shoulder for a glimpse of the man. Gwen had tried to teach Augusta not to grab at things. Plants had poisonous sap and thorns. Broken twigs might reveal legions of ants. Vines were sometimes a snake. Yet these dangers to her daughter's small chubby fingers were only part of Gwen's concern. She did not want her child to grow up believing that the natural world was her plaything. Now she smiled, as the chubby fingers cupped a flower. Their owner looked up for approval. This was a game, too. Everything was a game.

* * *

Later, when Edward had returned from his ramble, and with Augusta asleep, Gwen began to chew a piece of tobacco. Neither of them remembered encountering quite so many ticks as in the area around that village. Naked to the waist, Edward waited for Gwen to spit the juice onto his back to loosen the ticks; he was conscious of the effort she was expending.

*   *   *

Edward had referred many times in his field journal to his 'assistant'. He felt slightly uncomfortable in omitting Gwen's considerable contributions to his work but could not bring himself to name her, either. He had thought on it quite often, changing his mind every time. She was as competent as any man might have been in the tasks she set herself. She familiarised herself with everything, and her observations were meticulous. If she had been a man, he mused to himself, he would have been envious.

*   *   *

Edward sat at his makeshift desk, constructed from crates and rough planks, and opened his journal. On a fresh page he wrote:

A heated discussion on the very first day that lasted into the small hours has culminated in an unfortunate but illuminating incident. The main thrust of my argument that first night was that if a parasite caused its host to die and in the process its own extermination, then the species would not last long enough to establish itself as a viable Link in Nature's chain of Life.

In the days and weeks which have followed, the discussion regarding the candiru fish has re-emerged and re-ignited passionate debate several times. Until today, I believed strongly that the tales bandied about by the local inhabitants regarding this fish were entirely apocryphal.

It would seem that Mr Coyne has indeed

proved his point by using his own body as example. Of course, now I see the inadequacies of my argument, but this would hardly merit such a blatant lack of regard for his own self-preservation.

Edward read over what he had just written and scored through it all, beginning again, incorporating what he could remember of Gwen's observations and conclusions.

The candiru is a phlebotomist, attracted by the urea of larger fish, excreted at the gills. The candiru would seem to follow this trail of urea in the water and attach itself to the inside of the gill belonging to the larger fish. This in itself does not cause the fish to die. When the candiru has had its fill of blood it detaches to digest its meal, functioning in much the same manner as the leech, with which we are all most familiar.

The rather stronger allure of human urea passed in water was attractive to such an extent that the confused candiru navigated Mr Coyne's trouser leg in pursuit of the source. The candiru is in possession of fearsome barbs which assist its attachment to its more usual host. I was able to remove the candiru from the patient's urethra by means of a two-inch incision, thereby limiting damage.

The patient has ~~successfully~~ passed water since the operation, but this caused loss of consciousness. The local rum has proved useful not only in the preservation of specimens, including the rather poor specimen of the candiru, but medicinally it has been of great importance.

I admit freely that, until the evidence before me is irrefutable, I am disinclined to alter my position, and remain sceptical of apocryphal tales. I claim no responsibility, for one must question such intractable determination on the part of the patient and balance it against an apparent underlying inconsistency of rational thought.

Edward closed his journal and set down his pen. Now his attention was drawn to the heaps of unsorted lepidoptera. He took up his pen again.

Infection, followed by fever, in circumstances such as these, is usually followed rapidly by a glissade into unconsciousness from which the patient is most unlikely to recover. The patient has indeed spent two days in a delirious state (curious, indeed, how, suffering from the effects of the barbed fish, the patient began to speak in various tongues). However, frequent and assiduous attention to the wound may have contributed to the patient's remarkable recovery; although much weakened, the patient is able to sit up and converse lucidly.

During Vincent's fever, Gwen had tried to talk to Edward about the practicalities of finding a way to separate themselves from Vincent and continue their journey without the air being filled with the sound of his voice. From sunrise to sunset. It was almost impossible to find quietness, to be able to think. Even when Gwen and Edward retired behind their makeshift screen to deal with the various parasites—or to pretend to, as they had begun to do—Vincent was audible. He'd sing, if he couldn't think of anything to say, and when he'd run his limited repertoire thoroughly ragged, he'd make up his own verses.

'We must leave him,' she said. Her clear voice quivered, but Edward said, 'Irritating he may be, but the man is on his deathbed.'

'I don't think so.'

'It is out of my hands.'

'Will you not consider an early departure from this place, without Mr Coyne?'

'We have much to do here yet.'

It was torture trying to speak to him. Gwen's chest rose and fell with short and rapid breaths. She looked over to the hammock where Vincent lay as another tirade of strange, uninhibited utterances issued forth from his mouth. The blackest water, she thought.

Over the course of the next month, Vincent recovered fully, as Gwen had known that he would. By the beginning of September he was back on form; Gwen thought even more so. She had resented the respect she felt for the way he had used his own body as a subject for scientific study. She knew it had come from his madness, and she regarded it now as coincidence that his madness had manifested itself in such a logical fashion.

* * *

Edward heard her step and continued sorting his butterflies. 'I do like collecting on the *campos*,' he said to her, with his head still bent over the setting boards. 'The thrill of being able to walk in an open space again is exhilarating.'

Gwen waited for a moment to see if he would say anything else. She went over to the table to look at the butterflies. How strange it is, she thought, that we can continue to discuss insects in such a casual way. The accident had no place at the setting table, but she knew that she must speak. She said, 'We have been very fortunate, Edward.' He nodded, and she could see that he thought she was referring to his morning's entomologising. 'But until today I did not appreciate our fortune. I have never considered my own mortality. Our mortality.'

'Has something happened?'

Gwen said, 'What will happen to Augusta, when we go back to England?'

Edward stood up straight and looked into her face. She saw thoughts of classification drop away from his mind as he comprehended her.

'What I mean is, Edward, if I were to die I don't want her to be near Isobel.'

He stared at her incredulously, that woman's name on her lips. 'I can't see that ever being an option, no.' He half turned back to the specimens on his work table, and then looked at Gwen again. 'Isobel was dying when we left England. I had word of her passing away not long after we arrived in Pará—and so, in any case, that person should no longer concern you.' He studied her chin, and Gwen instinctively wiped it with the back of her hand. He licked his thumb and pressed it to her face.

Gwen waited for him to say more. I've finally been able to speak her name, she thought, and you brush it aside carelessly, as if I had known of her all this time. 'Edward,' she said, taking hold of his wrist and moving his skin away from her face. 'You had a wife, called Isobel?'

He did not flinch. She observed him minutely, only the glimmer of a ghost across his eyes. She dropped his wrist. 'You left her to die alone, and put me in her place?'

'You promised never to mention her name.' He did not so much whisper the words as breathe them out over his tongue.

'Now I know it for certain. You have deluded yourself completely. If I had known that you were already married, I would have stopped meeting with you. Immediately.'

'I put that letter into your hand—' But even as he said it, Gwen could see that he knew that it was not the case.

'No,' she said slowly, eliminating any passion from her voice. 'Even Miss Jaspur, especially her—' She couldn't go on. 'What manner of deceit have you created, Edward? What kind of trouble have you peddled with your lies?'

As she came out of the room she walked into Vincent, but this time she did not care if he had heard it all. 'Mr Coyne. At a loose end, again?'

'No, I'm wondering—' He looked past her into Edward's room and quickly back at her again. She knew that Edward was watching them. 'I'm wondering if the Oxbow excursion is still on for tomorrow or—' He looked past her again. '—if plans might have changed?'

'Nothing has changed at all, Mr Coyne,' she said. 'You may assume that everything will go according to plan.' She swept up Augusta and placing her on her hip walked out of the house.

CHAPTER XLVII

Pará, Brazil. November, 1863.

'Mr Edward Scales!' Tristan Grindlock grasped him by the shoulders with a happy grin. 'How long have you been back? Hettie will be delighted. Come in, come in. Do they follow on? Are they waiting somewhere? Let me send someone for them.'

The cool enclosure of Grindlock's house, the resonance and gaiety of the man's voice on the walls—Edward remembered his first entrance to the house with Gwen and knew suddenly that in a moment he and Tristan Grindlock would be surrounded by a clamour of excitement. He must say it now. He met Grindlock's gaze and stared unblinkingly into his grey eyes. Grindlock was no fool. Edward needed, in the end, to say nothing. He did not have to declare it in words. Tristan Grindlock pulled Edward into an embrace the like he could not remember having received since the very earliest days of his boyhood. The man was strong and did not let go for many minutes. Edward felt the sobbing from Tristan Grindlock spread through his own body. He was wrapped up in the man's grief and condolence in one never-ending squeeze and was enormously touched.

Later in the evening, after a faltering start, he told Tristan and Hettie Grindlock how he had left bait for the alligators and had stood ready with his guns primed. He had registered the broad, flat snouts on the huge beasts and had not been afraid of their enormous length or their girth, or the rows of teeth which he later hacked from their stinking gums. He had no regard for his own life in those hours of killing and butchering as he had searched for the remains.

‘But you know the way they consume their prey, they rip and churn; I could not discern from the mess. The abomination of it was too much. I did not pause in my quest for twenty-four hours, but then I was overcome. I had to leave the place. I brought their belongings with me, and I left everything else.’

He could not mention the fact that he and Gwen had spoken words that could never have been undone. That she had chosen, suddenly, to go with Augusta in the second canoe with Coyne, leaving Edward to search for the black caiman with the hired men.

‘I should have insisted that they stay behind. I told Coyne to look for hatchlings only. Something for—’ He had been going to say that he’d thought the hatchlings would be harmless and easy to secure with a woman and a child as company. ‘Coyne stayed on, when I came away, to continue where I left off. He would not hear otherwise. He claimed responsibility.’

‘Of course, he did,’ said Hettie. Her face had not lost the ashen complexion it had assumed.

‘I want to take a passage as soon as possible.’

‘Trust everything to me,’ Tristan said. ‘I’ll find you a good ship.’

* * *

Edward valued Tristan Grindlock’s blunt empathy, and the softness with which he had listened to

Edward's guilt-ridden ramblings. But now he knew he was making Hettie and Tristan uncomfortable. In their position, he might have felt the same. A mammoth obligation surely, to console a man who has lost his wife and only child when one was literally surrounded, overrun with one's own progeny. The pressure of so many children at such close proximity did not disturb Edward. They were not Augusta.

He tried to project himself a few months forward, sitting at home, attempting to make sense of his collections. But he could not even picture which home that might have been.

'Regret,' Tristan Grindlock broke into his thoughts, and yet again Edward was grateful. They were standing together watching Edward's few belongings being ferried over the water to the ship. 'Regret. There is no point to it, no usefulness to be had from it. If you give in to it, it'll drain you till there is barely any part of you not smudged by it. But, I tell you this for nothing, I'd hop on that boat with you in a trice.'

'Your kindness has been immeasurable, but I couldn't let you part with your family on my account.'

Edward smiled at Tristan Grindlock weakly and briefly. They were standing on almost exactly the same spot where he had greeted Edward so effusively. Edward caught something odd in the man's eyes.

Tristan patted Edward's shoulder. 'There's no need to worry. I wouldn't burden you like that.' His hand stayed on Edward's shoulder, and neither man said anything more as the time came for Edward to be taken across the water. The pressure of Tristan's hand on Edward felt immense.

Edward sat facing away from the steamer. He knew the sunlight glinting off the water into his eyes would make his smile seem grim. Tristan Grindlock held up a hand, half salute and half farewell, before he turned and walked away. Edward promised himself that he would write to the man, as soon as he felt able, on his return to England.

Part III

CHAPTER XLVIII

THE TIMES, Friday, October 5, 1866.

MURDER TRIAL AT THE OLD BAILEY.

EXTRAORDINARY scenes were witnessed at the Central Criminal Court today as the Prosecution called for Miss Natalia Jaspur to give evidence. Miss Jaspur, once notorious for her appearance alone, is well known these days for her vocal virtuosity as a soprano, having appeared in a number of operatic performances last season and due to do so again this year.

Mr Probart: 'Did you know Mr Edward Osbert Scales, Miss Jaspur?'

A: 'I did know him. I met him eleven years ago, when my life was hard. Life was difficult for me then. I took my living however I could. Mr Scales was trying to be a doctor. I let him make observations of me. This led to many meetings with Mr Scales which grew sentimental, and eventually an attachment was formed between myself and Mr Scales. However, he was married, and his wife, a very beautiful creature, hated me, and I saw him no more.'

Q: 'Did the prisoner know of your former attachment to Mr Scales?'

A: 'I do not know.'

Q: 'Were you aware, Miss Jaspur, that a novel had been written about you, in which details of your affair with Mr Scales were laid out?'

A: 'I do not pay attention to rumours, though to be quite correct, I do not believe Mr Scales' name was ever mentioned.'

Q: 'But you freely admit that you had an affair with Mr Scales which lasted—how long did it last, Miss Jaspur?'

A: 'I saw him last seven years ago.'

Q: 'Two years, you say?'

A: 'Simple subtraction suggests it.'

Mr Probart then thanked his witness before going on to say that the so-called false allegations made against Mr Scales in the books Mrs Pemberton had been so keen to locate and eradicate were, in fact, true, and that, therefore, Mrs Pemberton was well versed in calling the truth a lie and then attempting to cover up the truth with more falseness.

CHAPTER XLIX

LONDON. FEBRUARY, 1864.

On the ship to England, Edward had taken a grim pleasure in the special violence of his sickness. His berth had a bucket, which he slopped out only once a day. He took his meals in his cabin and never once took a turn on deck.

In the first days back, the extreme change in temperature, which had begun on the voyage, settled into his head. The cold winter air seemed to compress his skull as he walked and slipped on the frozen shit and mud on the streets. He had arrived back in England in the most shabby state imaginable, but he had not realised this until he was among his own countrymen again. He affected strangers in a different way. He had assumed it was because of his own misery—that others did not want to be infected with it—but catching sight of himself in the glazed shop-fronts he understood that it was because he looked like a vagrant. His face was shaggy with untamed beard, and framed with a mass of unkempt, dirty hair. His shoes were coming apart again because the string which had held them together had rotted and worn away. His bare toes were visible with every step he took. His clothes hung from him. He passed his nights in a cheap hotel, and the company of bed bugs had kept him from sleeping. There was something so vile about the bugs in the hotel bed, which burrowed into his consciousness as well as his skin; they were far worse than any of the leeches, ticks, biting flies or mosquitoes they had endured in Brazil. The thought of these bugs biting strangers in that same bed drove him out, and Edward finally returned to his own house. Scratching his bug bites as he looked for a cab, Edward saw a shimmering black edge to everything in his path, and everything else around him. And as the wind bit his face and gnawed at his exposed feet and gloveless hands, he was aware of an aperture opening in his torso, which grew with every step and let in the cold air. Fist-sized to begin with, now as he neared the rank of cabs it felt large enough to admit a small dog. He was embarrassed at this, and hoped that the driver would not say anything about it. The black line around the edges of the man fizzed, and as Edward saw the frightening bulk of the horse gush its steamy piss onto the ground, simultaneously dropping its manure, he wanted to dive under it, make it rear up and bring its hooves down on his head, and break his spine. But the thought of what miscalculation might entail stopped him. Edward got into the cab. As soon as they moved off, Edward fell asleep, the dullness of his thoughts being composed of nothing more or less than the knowledge that he would never be able to put his name next to anything definite except the death of Augusta and Gwen.

Many hours later, in his own old and unfamiliar bed the hole in his torso had gone, but the black lines remained. He took himself to a barber as soon as he could.

He knew that a letter would never do, but he still composed them with the thought that he could pull it off, and not have to face her. But the more he left it, the worse he knew it would be when he finally did manage to get down to the business of breaking the news. The bag containing the few things he had rescued from the wreckage of the day he had lost them lay untouched. He took it with him everywhere; he could not let the bag out of his sight, because although he had not the courage yet to look inside, it had slowly begun to dawn on him that Gwen's notebooks contained his only chance of gaining some measure of scientific celebrity. Edward packed an old overnight bag, musty from the back of a wardrobe. He took a cab to the bank and then to the train station, where he bought a third-class ticket to Falmouth. It would not do for this journey to be remotely pleasant.

CHAPTER L

HELFORD VICARAGE, CORNWALL. FEBRUARY, 1864.

'You feel that the air around her is filled with an essence that, once it has touched you, some small part of you, will forever be there to determine the course your life will veer down.' Edward glanced at Reverend George Sparsholt who in turn repressed the urge to look at his pocket watch. 'You have to imagine her as you would a large gilded moth under close scrutiny. The closer you get, the less of the initial attraction you see, yet still she pulls you in, inviting you to observe every scale. Under the microscope, the lustre disappears and yet you seek the brilliance that you know is there. She holds an illusion you must step back to appreciate, all the while longing to bring her up close to your face.'

Reverend Sparsholt studied his cuticles; stiff and bored, he was not really paying attention to what Edward said. What little he had heard, he had not understood at all. When he spoke, he was alarmed at his own volume; it was almost a bark. 'Moths! What wonderful creatures they are. I never tire of watching the hawk moths on the verbena just outside the study during the summer months.' He took a swig of sherry and sloshed it between the gap in his front teeth before swallowing it. He knew it was not good for his teeth but he could not help himself in the company of this man. It was nervousness, and he stuttered a little. 'In the late hours of a July evening, one can be induced into something almost resembling a trance; I have never yet been moved to still one, however. This may seem contradictory to a scientist like yourself, but I always feel that to stop one (he did not like to say 'kill') would somehow diminish it, would remove some of the magic of our Creator's imagination. That is not to say I disparage your work in the least, I merely wish to say—'

Edward interrupted. 'Reverend Sparsholt, I have managed to contrive a mess—an unintentional mess which I don't know how to untangle.'

'That is hardly surprising, but you must not be disheartened. You must disentwine yourself in order that you may step back and view the situation from a more dispassionate standpoint, to which, I think, you were alluding. And, really, I cannot see how you come to lay blame on yourself when you were a thousand miles away.'

'But that is precisely what I have tried to explain.' Edward's voice began to rise. George began to sweat. Feeling the moisture accumulate on his top lip, he wriggled his nose and mouth, and raised his eyebrows in what he hoped was a sympathetic gesture. He was flummoxed. Edward went on. 'It is all connected; it is all because of me.'

George stood up and placed his sherry glass on the mantle-piece where gummy stains and other telltale rings marked the marble, now blackening with dust and a fine film of dirt. He caught sight of his reflection in the mirror above the fireplace. The mass of wiry greying hair he had tamed with grease that morning had become unruly, and fell into his eyes. He pushed it back and wiped his hand on the seat of his trousers.

'My dear fellow, Miss Carrick is, I am assured, merely suffering from a heightened sensitivity which is self-induced. I do not claim to have any knowledge in medical matters, but it seems pretty obvious to me that her problems are nothing a few months' rest won't see to. Ah, notwithstanding, of course, the, ah, period of mourning, which, understandably—'

'No! No! That is not it at all. I am to blame for the most part. Oh, God, I wish I still had Susan's letter.'

George Sparsholt wished that this twitchy, blasphemous man was not taking up space in his study. It had been something of a relief that morning to realise that here, finally, was another to take an interest in Miss Carrick. He had waved aside a disinclination to invite the man in; his Darwinist views and his adultery and his wild look—despite being clean-shaven—should not be impediments, not that morning, anyway. Now, it was afternoon, well into the afternoon. The sun had not only moved out of his study, it was beginning to set, and Mr Scales was still galloping through his sherry. He had missed lunch because of this man. Whatever had been intended would be served up cold for dinner. The man was obtuse. George wished Mr Scales would vanish like the lustre on the moth wing. But he would not. His eyes, rather disconcertingly, were glittering, and the prospect of George being able to relinquish some, if not all responsibility for Miss Euphemia Carrick now appeared to diminish by the second. George was now responsible; he now had two persons under his roof whose normal faculty for straightforward reasoning had abandoned them, or was severely depleted. With a feeling of hopelessness and a need to be in his kitchen where he might get some food, he grasped at the mention of Susan.

'Ah now, Susan. I know exactly where Susan is. She is with Mrs Brewin. I will go and fetch her.' This piece of information seemed to shock Mr Scales out of his private reverie for a moment. He looked up at George, and George thought if he had told Mr Scales that the queen herself was in the kitchen, he would not have looked more horrified. 'Well, I shan't be a moment then. Perhaps some tea, also. So, if you'll excuse me.'

George swung open the door. He could not get out of the room quick enough. He was not sure whom Mr Scales had been likening to a moth. He had assumed that there was only one female now in the equation, but it would be better if he stopped assuming anything at all. Mr Scales' willingness to lay himself open, to disgorge his most secret, intimate feelings for a woman made George uncomfortable. It was too much. The nearer he got to the kitchen and its pleasant smells, the less irritated he became.

Mrs Brewin and Susan had their heads together over a large book on the table in the middle of the room. Every surface was sprinkled with grains of sugar and punctuated with drips of pulped fruit. Ranks of gleaming preserving jars were lined up, warming near the oven and a flupping, plopping sound came from the giant preserving pan on the hot-plate. He cleared his throat twice to get the women's attention. 'Ah, there you are, Susan. I wonder if I might extract you for a moment. Mr Scales is most anxious to speak with you.'

'Is he still here?'

'Yes. Yes, indeed, still here.'

Mrs Brewin glanced at him, but there was

nothing in her gaze except matters pertaining to jam reluctant to set. George liked his housekeeper a great deal. She was young but plain enough for George not to desire her. And he did not have to worry about losing her to another. She was faithful to the memory of her husband, lost in the Crimea. Initially, George had worried that this fact might inflame Miss Carrick, but Mrs Brewin had told him quite bluntly that she didn't go in for all that murmuring and nonsense. She was pleased, she said, to have Susan to help her; she was a good girl and pleasant company.

Whilst Susan washed her hands and put on a clean apron, George made a pot of tea and fetched the biscuit tin. Mrs Brewin was quite used to him bumbling about in her kitchen and ignored it, but Susan was perturbed by it. Susan tried to take over, but all he would let her do was fetch a small jug of milk. She had to follow on behind down the passage towards the study as he bore the tray in front of him. It had crockery for three. George could feel her alarm and agitation at his back. He had a large stride and the china rattled.

Edward Scales was poking the fire and adding another lump of coal from the wrong bucket. There were two buckets next to the fire: one with the wet stuff, and one with the dry. The fire belched thick, greenish smoke, and as George came into the room the draw from the doorway caused the smoke to guff out into the room. When Edward turned around with the poker in his hand, George had a strong impulse to reprimand his guest, but he did not. He asked Susan to bring up another chair.

'Yes, sir.'

Susan wanted to rescue the fire but didn't. She

watched the gobbet of smoke unfurl along the ceiling from the corner of her eye.

CHAPTER LI

Mrs Brewin was a religious woman but she did not believe in divine retribution. She felt a great deal of sympathy for Mr Scales, even though he had committed the sin of adultery. She did not believe in an Almighty who, having given Mr Scales the gift of a child, should then take it and its mother in such an horrific way. Accidents could happen, and these accidents had nothing to do with anything except extremely bad luck. Certainly, Mr Scales seemed to be a luckless man, if not perhaps perfectly stupid, as well. It wasn't clear whether Mr Scales was a bigamist; he had referred on more than one occasion to his wife, meaning the late sister of Miss Carrick upstairs, and not the late Mrs Scales who had lived in London and was now buried in the Reverend's churchyard.

Mrs Brewin and Susan had taken turns all morning to listen at the study door. If she had not heard it herself she would not have believed it. She had seen pictures of a crocodile once, and she imagined that an alligator was much the same thing. The crocodile pictures were in a large heavy volume belonging to Reverend Sparsholt; it had been left open on the settee, of all places. The vision she had then of George Sparsholt with a heavy book in his lap did not sit comfortably with the way he stood at the lectern in his study to practise his sermons. The picture now fullest in her mind of Mr Scales killing all those creatures and emptying their guts in search of his loved ones appalled and inspired her.

It went against her principles, to eavesdrop. She had always looked down on others who indulged and divulged, as she called it, yet it had been she, not Susan, who had started it that morning. As a result, there was no hot meal for the vicar and Miss Carrick, only some runny plum jam from her stock of bottled fruit, which should by now have set.

She had been George Sparsholt's housekeeper for some years. She liked the position; it was not taxing. He did not notice dust, and she had time to read novels. She had never done that when her husband had been alive. And though the sermons were boring and she was obliged to go and listen every Sunday (as well as through the week in disconnected dribs and drabs), she did at least get to sit in the pew usually reserved for the vicar's family (as he had none), and so did not have to spend the time looking at the back of people's heads.

Now, she felt herself somehow infected by the sudden rash of activity in the vicarage. Susan's enthusiasm for melodrama bubbled over. There seemed to be a surfeit, and Mrs Brewin absorbed it readily, like a sponge sopping a puddle leaking in under the back door. Poor Mr Scales. He'd spent the first hour of his interview with Reverend Sparsholt weeping. Mrs Brewin had never heard a man cry like that before. From the stuffy confines of George Sparsholt's study had come the sound of heaving sobs and hiccoughs. She thought it a very sorry state of affairs, that Mr Scales had felt compelled to remove himself and his mistress to such a remote corner of the world. She'd heard of Romantic Couples going off to Italy; surely, that would have been better. Elizabeth Brewin felt sure that the waterways of Venice were safer, being riddled not with alligators, but handsome gondoliers.

An hour had passed since Susan had been called into the study and she had not yet emerged.

Susan had told her all sorts of tales about the actual, Mrs Isobel Scales, and her visits to Carrick House. She'd nodded knowingly when Susan had mentioned the vast quantities of tonic previously consumed by Miss Euphemia Carrick upstairs. Elizabeth Brewin had suffered with the stuff herself for a short time—whilst her husband had been alive.

Now, she stood at the study door again, aware of the scum forming on the fruit pulp back in the kitchen but not moving to do anything about it. She heard Susan's high voice laughing nervously behind the door, and the rumble of Reverend Sparsholt's church voice. When the Reverend's voice vaulted through the keyhole Elizabeth Brewin retreated down the passage to the kitchen.

Among the mess of her jam-making on the kitchen table she began to draft a reply to a letter from her brother. The letter had been a little distressing, to say the least, and Mrs Brewin still felt that, compared to camels and mysterious Black Brethren of the Australian desert, life at the vicarage was unmentionably dull. Her brother's admonishing words filled her with sorrowful vexation, and she pictured her small letters of the previous months; how those small packets had braved tumult and tempest to arrive at last in her dear brother's hands, only to disappoint him. He'd said that her letters made him lonelier than ever. She dipped her finger into the pooled jam at her elbow and pushed it along. The jam made a wave at her fingertip and then settled back to its puddle without showing any sign of a skin. Not the slightest little wrinkle. She sucked her finger and began to write.

Dearest Brother,
How I dread to think of you alone in that tent all those long and strange nights. What you told me of the stars vexed me, and I can't stand to think of you under the peculiarness of that odd sky, like as if you were in another world altogether. If the stars are upside-down, then does not the blood rush always to your head? Since last I wrote to you two souls more bide here at the vicarage. Miss E. Carrick from the big house on the river, and her girl, Susan Wright, who is fine company for me; and I often speak of you to her, and I know that you would find her a fine person as well . . .

Elizabeth Brewin considered what she had put down, and thought that it didn't much matter that the way it came out sounded like matchmaking. Her brother would likely laugh about it; for a person like him was never interested in taking a wife nor would he let anything of the kind pass through his mind. Certainly, he wasn't the sort to entertain beneath. It was true he thought himself better. And what was it that he had written? '*Here, a man may be anything or anyone he chooses to be as long as he minds his way.*' Her thoughts ran to the way her brother had been as a child. She remembered the particular habit he'd taken a liking to, of clearing his throat before speaking. He'd been a very dry little bodkin, even then, and it pained her to think that he'd wandered so very far from her. She looked about her and heard the tinkle of the bell, and realised that it had been pinging for a while now. All this jam. If she could just get the stuff to set, she could send a pot of it to her brother. She would pack it tight in a box of straw. She was sure that Susan would think it a fine idea. Very fine.

She looked up when she heard the click of the kitchen door opening and Susan coming back in. Down the hall, the Reverend's voice could be heard indistinctly.

'I'm to go up, and fetch Miss Carrick,' Susan said.

* * *

Edward waited in the study, and the Reverend rocked back and forth on his heels, his hands clasped behind his back, until Susan came into the room with Miss Carrick, and then vanished.

'Miss Carrick,' Reverend Sparsholt said to her, 'do make yourself comfortable. This gentleman whom I believe you have met once before, erm, has come bearing some grave news.'

'Edward Scales.' Edward bowed to Euphemia who stood apart from the two of them and refused to sit on the settee. She inclined her head to Edward.

'Susan has told me that you have come to tell me that my sister is dead, Mr Scales.'

‘I wish it were not so, but I must beg your forgiveness, Miss Carrick.’

They each looked into the other’s eyes. Then she said, ‘I am sorry for your loss, Mr Scales. I understand there was a child, also.’

Edward hung his head. ‘My daughter, Augusta.’

‘That must be hard on you. I expect she was very lovely.’

He could not think how this had happened. He felt insubstantial in the presence of this woman he had known so privately and so intimately. He realised how different she sounded from Gwen. He had been afraid of hearing her voice, but Euphemia looked and sounded quite different. Her movements and the clarity of her diction were a little slurred from a recent dose of tincture, but she was not as he had feared. And perhaps it was this which changed everything.

CHAPTER LII

TWO YEARS LATER.
CARRICK HOUSE. JUNE, 1866.

A hot day in the middle of June. Swifts flew overhead, almost clipping the man’s wide-brimmed hat as he walked over the scorched gravel of the drive. The windows were all open in Carrick House, and a warm breeze lifted the edges of papers on the library desk. Susan watched the man make his progress up the drive. The rustle of papers distracted her for a moment, and she patted the paperweight holding the pile of letters and bills in place.

The screeching of the swifts cut through the air as deftly as their scimitar wings. Susan left the room, giving it a cursory glance, and went to find her mistress. It would not be difficult, she had only to follow the sounds of the children playing. With all the doors in the house propped open, she followed the children's noises and their mother's voice through to the playroom. Mr Scales had insisted on the playroom being located downstairs with direct access to the garden. Susan had thought it strange. The new French windows let the twins career in and out at will. They had not employed a nurse or a nanny. Euphemia spent all her time with the children. She was sitting on the floor surrounded by snippings of paper and string. The twins ran clumsily up and down the room trailing kites in each hand. Susan eyed the mess with distaste.

'Ma'am, there's a gentleman coming up the drive. Shall I show him into the library?' Euphemia turned and stood, still smiling at her children, not looking at Susan. 'Yes, show him in. I'm not certain when Mr Scales will be back, but it can't be any more than half an hour. Give him something to drink.' She clapped her hands. 'Let's fly them outside now, yes?'

As Susan stepped into the hall the bell sounded and she ran to open the door.

The man stood straight, clasping his hat to his crumpled, linen-clad chest. He was so tall. He bent down courteously. 'Is this the home of Mr Edward Scales?' He gave Susan his card, but she did not look at it. She put it in her pocket.

'Please come in, sir. Mr Scales'll be back dreckly

from his afternoon walk.' She took his hat, but he kept his walking stick. He followed Susan into the study and accepted a brandy. There was something about his manner which made Susan want to stay in the room. 'We're having such a blast of hot weather, sir. I hope you haven't had to come far.' She put the glass next to Edward's armchair, hoping the man would sit down in it. The warm wind shouldered the smell more or less out of the room. Susan felt her spine ease. The smell from the cellar had come and inhabited the rest of the house; intruder that it was, greeting all at the doormat and on the stair carpet. It was the brother of mothballs and sister to the worst kind of sin.

'You're not so easy to find, out here on the river, are you?'

As if it was she, and not Mr Scales, he had come to see. 'Depends on whether you're local, sir.'

'Ah. Well, I'm not local.' He sat in the chair and motioned for Susan to sit in the other. She remained as she was. The man swirled the brandy around in the glass and looked into Susan's eyes. 'You say he's out for a walk. Does he take a walk every afternoon?'

'And every morning, too, sir. Since he come back, he's not able to—break the habit.'

'No, I should think it would be hard. Is he well?'

'Very, sir. Thank you.' Susan shifted, left to right and back again. She excused herself, dipping a curtsey, and left the room.

Alone, Gus Pemberton paced a circuit of the room, and stopped at the bookshelves along the back wall. He let his eyes wander along the titles without paying attention to them and then turned to look back into the room. It seemed dead. He faced the bookshelves again and made a couple more paces. He stopped again at a slim door set into the wall of books. The papers on the desk behind him rustled as he tried the handle and the door swung open under his fingers with the faintest of clicks. The smell of mothballs and some other kind of clinical taint he'd noticed pervading the air when he'd stepped into the house was now a suffocating fug of determined preservation. He whipped out a handkerchief.

Here then, were the things he had expected to see. A display cabinet, waist high, half timber, half glazed; it bisected the length of the room.

The walls were lined with cabinets and cupboards. Gus opened a drawer and looked down at the ranks of pinned butterflies: luminous, metallic, unearthly blue, shocking in their vivacity. He couldn't remember ever having seen them in flight. He remembered something Gwen had said about Vincent taking her a gift of a pupa. He'd never been much interested in butterflies. He understood that they were beautiful to look at. And, yes, they were like jewels; but no more or less significant to him than a cranefly or a wasp. In another set of drawers, he found bird skins. Hyacinthine macaws. Miniscule hummingbirds. Bright green things. More parrots. All the eyes padded out with cotton wool, the empty bodies stuffed so much like feathered lozenges. A milliner's wet dream, he thought. He closed the drawers.

Gus paced the room, his fingertips skimming the surface of the central display cabinet. He stopped short. There laid out were Gwen's belongings. A pair of filthy kid gloves, which he had never seen on her hands. A pair of combs he had seen her wear on a couple of occasions, which had not suited or complemented her colouring. She'd worn them very deeply, probably aware of this fact. He remembered her hair had fallen heavily when he'd pulled the things out. A truly ghastly letter knife. Her paint-box, opened; the mixing tray still cupped the dried traces of her last study done in South America. There, next to it, her paintbrushes laid out in neat ranks like the insect specimens. Gus felt a wave of sickness and pity and guilt wash through his gut and end in his throat. What could it have been like, to have been Edward Scales? Was this an embodiment of his guilt, his grief? Was it here to ward off madness? Ghosts?

More; and worse. Scraps of paper, scribbled on by Augusta, precocious, of course, with such a talented mother. A tiny smock was laid out, still slightly stained with mud and clay around the hem and around the neck and down the front; the evidence of some dripping fruit, messily consumed. It was too horrible to contemplate, the care with which these artefacts of loss had been laid out. No labels, of course. These things were not meant for visitors. Gus felt his neck prickle.

At the far end of the room was a single armchair; an old thing, covered in worn, frayed and light-damaged watered silk with stains snaking here and there. Delicate structure. He went and stood next to it. He could see that it had once been a good piece. The chair was flanked by a pair of identical cupboards; deep-bodied, they seemed ill-matched to the rest of the room. Gus imagined rails full of Gwen's clothes hanging there, falling apart and still musty with the residues of the forest. He turned a key and opened one of the doors. It swung out fast on its hinge and Gus had to step back. At the same time he caught sight of the contents.

He swore sharply out into the empty room. A crude word to match the raw sight. And then, more softly, 'Jesus.' He cleared his throat and peered into the chamber. The specimen jar was huge. He stood for some moments regarding the thing critically, and then had to look away as he composed himself. He turned again to the body in the jar. It had sunk down to the base, the feet turned in horribly under itself and one side flattened against the glass. The features of the face looked slightly swollen.

He found the edge of the cupboard door, pushed it home, turned the key. He left the room smartly and pulled the door closed. He wiped his teary hands on his balled handkerchief and his trousers, and poured himself another drink. The screaming of the swifts sliced the hot air. With the first mouthful of his drink, his pulse began to return to its normal and steady rhythm.

Gus Pemberton closed his eyes. It's all right, he told himself. It's all going to be fine now. But he knew that couldn't be true. All could only become much more complicated. He still had to speak to Edward Scales. He'd been prepared for it this morning. He wasn't so sure he was still prepared for it now.

* * *

'In a hurry again, Susan?'

'Gent to see you, sir.' She gave him the card, aware that the man could hear her every word.

'He's not been waiting very long. I gave him a

brandy.'

Edward said quietly, 'Good Lord, I wonder if it can really be him, after all this time.'

'Madam said I was to give the gent a drink.'

'It's quite all right, Susan. You did the right thing.'

Susan followed Mr Scales down the hall and, taking her duster from her pocket, began to flick it at the stairs and banisters, climbing up a few steps where she knew the sound of Mr Scales' voice would still reach her.

'What the devil are you doing here?!' Susan heard Mr Scales kicking the wedge away from the study door. He slammed it shut.

Susan thought how odd it was, that a person could say what he was thinking but cover his meaning up with the way that he said it.

* * *

Gus stood up. 'Been availing myself of your hospitality again, Scales, as you can see.'

'My God.' Edward shook his hand and clapped him tentatively on the shoulder. 'What on earth brings you to Cornwall?'

'You, as a matter of fact. I've been sent to see you; I've got a bit of news.'

CHAPTER LIII

CARRICK HOUSE. JUNE, 1866.

Edward stared at Gus Pemberton. The sound of his two small boys crashing about in the hall and playroom was muffled; audible, the sound of his wife's laughter.

Helpless in the face of Augustus Pemberton's news, he sat quite still. Gus, seeming to have anticipated this confusion, also sat quietly, moving now and then to take a sip of his drink and to cast a sidelong glance out of the window.

'Where is she? Did she come with you?' Edward pushed himself up from his seat and went over to the window.

Gus turned, half rising, to speak to Edward: 'Gwen and the child bide in Richmond. She didn't want to come here. She and her sister—there are, shall we say grievances—'

'Does she know? Does she know? Christ.'

'Come and sit down, man.'

Edward's shoulders drooped, and he stood immobile. Gus got up, led him back to his chair and poured some more brandy into both their glasses.

Edward said, 'When I came back to England everything was in turmoil without and within. There had been so much loss, so much death—there was a feeling, a need—in both of us, Effie and I, to salvage something.' He rushed to qualify. 'Of course, my own conscience, but also to do something good for its own sake. At first our own private griefs bound us, but it is so much more than that; especially, since the twins. My wife—my first wife—had been quite ill. An obstruction of the bowel. A rather twisted turn of events.'

Gus Pemberton said, 'Yes, I know. But your deed was an act of chivalry few would contemplate, let alone carry through.'

Edward looked up at Gus questioningly and said, 'It was not a simple case of finding comfort in shared grief. Euphemia was on the precipice of madness when I found her at the vicarage. Amongst so much confusion, the least I could do.'

Edward began to shiver slightly and then his body shook, in quiet convulsions; he hugged himself to try and stop it.

'Have a drink,' Gus said. 'It's the shock, that's all. I should have written first, if I could have been sure that you'd have received it.'

Gus waited for the shaking to subside, not allowing Edward to speak until he'd downed at least half the brandy in his glass.

'I've been alone with it. With how she is—potentially. I'd never, I couldn't ever have expected anyone else to understand the complicated nature of her. I've felt responsible, at every level. Will she want to, to see me, at all; what does Gwen say? Did she give you a message?'

'I can arrange for a meeting to take place, if that is what you would like.'

'Say nothing of it to Effie. This, it will tip her over. I have to think of the boys. I can't have them being—' He was going to say 'ruined', but let his sentence peter out.

'I'll be discreet.'

CHAPTER LIV

THE TIMES, Friday, October 5, 1866.

MURDER TRIAL AT THE OLD BAILEY.

MR SHANKS, for the Defence, called the prisoner's doctor, Dr Rathstone.

Q: 'You were called to the Pemberton family home on the morning of August 7th, were you not?'

A: 'Indeed, that is quite so. I was summoned to the aid of Mrs Pemberton. I put off another call, as this call was urgent, but the nature of the call only became apparent when I examined the patient, Mrs Pemberton. It was rather a delicate matter. The patient was in a considerable deal of pain, and unable to rise from her bed unassisted. It was immediately apparent that Mrs Pemberton had suffered injuries to her torso, limbs and to her head and also to her face. There were abrasions and bruises which I tended first. But, as I suspected a broken rib and further examined the patient, I questioned her in earnest about the nature of her injuries. At first, she was reluctant to reveal how she had sustained the bruising and so forth, but after an hour or more, I learned that Mrs Pemberton had been beaten severely the night before. Of course, I did not want to press for further details, but Mrs Pemberton was anxious for the reputation of her husband. She asked me to pass the

Good Book, lying at her bedside and told me, with her hand upon it, that her husband had not harmed her. She was most anxious about it. Then she asked me if I had spoken to her husband. When I told her that I believed he was out of the house, she became very agitated, saying that she thought Mr Pemberton must have gone to see the man about it himself and that the thought of the two men fighting over it was worse than the injuries. Mrs Pemberton said over and over again that she didn't want her husband to come home battered or worse.'

Q: 'It was Mrs Pemberton's impression then, that the person who had harmed her on the night of August 3rd was still alive?'

A: 'Without a doubt, sir, indeed it was. She feared for her husband's life.'

Q: 'And she seemed in genuine distress over this last?'

A: 'Sir, in my long career, I have seen many women make a sham over some thing or another, but I have known Mrs Pemberton some years now, and no doubt is in my mind that the fear she felt over her husband's safety that morning was genuine.'

Q: 'Please, Dr Rathstone, if you can, would you tell me what her exact words were?'

A: 'She said, "He'll kill my husband, I know he will." She said it many, many times until I could persuade her to take a sedative.'

Q: 'And did Mrs Pemberton give you the name of the man who had injured her and whom she believed would harm her husband?'

A: 'She did not; she was in great distress and

would only repeat what I have told you.'

CHAPTER LV

CARRICK HOUSE. JUNE, 1866.

Euphemia laughed, showing all her teeth. Gus Pemberton smiled, joining his face to her laugh, but he could not meet her gaze. Trout. He attended to the food on his plate. Done very nicely by Susan, gutted earlier by himself and Edward, Susan quiet by the sink waiting to deal with the guts and cleaned fish. The task of taking the trout from the pool (it was not large enough to be a lake, not really) could hardly have been less satisfying. As Edward lowered the landing net into the water, Gus had heard the gentle breaking of waves, fifty yards beyond the garden wall. An unsightly and abrupt end to the amble down the paths. In his mind, he vaulted the mortar and stone, and stood looking out at the scene Gwen had once described to him. The wall must be new. She had never mentioned a wall. The innards spilled neatly, releasing a muddy taint into the air.

Gus Pemberton found Gwen's sister charmless. He tried to discover something he could like in Euphemia's character, so that he would not find himself being false with her. He thought that if he'd found himself married to such a creature, he would have spent twice as much time out of the house as Edward Scales.

Initially, he had been struck by her appearance. How like Gwen she was, in that first instant, despite the obvious difference between the sisters. He could see how Edward would have fallen at once into tying himself to this woman, rather than striving to extricate himself—and then forever regretting it.

Gus felt the tension creep down his back as Euphemia said, 'You never did say, Ted, how the two of you met.'

Edward's reply was a little too studious. 'We have an acquaintance in common. A Midlander, now living in London—'

'What? Mr Coyne is Cornish—and he certainly isn't—'

Edward's cutlery clattered onto his plate. He placed his hands flat on the table. Gus had his fork midway between his plate and his mouth; pink fish flesh dropped with an almost silent splat back onto his plate. He looked from Scales to Scales' wife and back again.

Euphemia said, 'What I mean to say, is—'

'Take the boys, why don't you, Euphemia, to the kitchen, where I am sure Susan will be only too happy to give them their milk pudding,' Edward said quietly.

'But the thing is, obviously—'

'Take them, Euphemia.'

Both men were quiet after the corralling had been accomplished.

Gus said, 'Would I be right in assuming that your wife's comment just now came as much of a surprise to you, as it did to me?'

'If she had made that comment before I'd had your news, I would have wanted to know what she meant by it immediately. As it is, I can wait. And I am even more convinced that your news should be withheld from Euphemia, for the time being at least. She has not been very calm these past few days. Her chirpy facade seems egg-shell thin.'

* * *

The next morning Gus held Gwen's notebooks in his lap. Looking into them by the open window of his room, he'd expected to see her watercolours and sketches laid out on the page in much the same way as the specimens themselves. Ordered by class, neatly labelled, a border of white paper between each regimented subject. No. Her pages were, to the uninitiated eye, a jumbled, mixed-up mess. A morass of things, jostling for space. Her written notes meandered around her work: lines, arrows, and dates seemingly confused, overlapping; nothing was chronological. These were her private thoughts and impressions layered year on year. Gus supposed that her intention had been to sort through and make fair copies of the best of it. It was obvious that she had never intended these notebooks to be used by anyone but herself. With this in mind, he looked more carefully. He got up and went downstairs to the library to find a magnifying glass. He could not read her tiny handwriting without one. The house seemed deserted. Edward, out for his morning ramble. No evidence of Euphemia and the children: perhaps they, too, had gone out. Gus stopped to crane his head at the landing window and studied the sky. If Euphemia had ventured out like her husband, she would get wet very soon. The pallid grey of the early hours had begun to transform into something much more forbidding, though the air was still. On the cusp of something, thought Gus, waiting for the telltale sign, and the rush of wind in the treetops. Always expecting something grander than British weather could produce; he hoped that Cornish weather might prove a little different.

He went on down the stairs and to the library. He took a moment on the threshold. He had not noticed much about it the day before. It had been so terribly hot out, and he'd been so tired, so glad to be in a cool place, and only thinking of how he might tell Edward about Gwen and Augusta.

Edward had wasted no time in giving the heap of Gwen's sketchbooks to Gus.

The room seemed to say that its owner had gone out of his way to make it utterly unextraordinary, bland.

Gus found a magnifying glass on the desk and putting it into his jacket pocket made to leave the room. Susan was standing just inside the door with her hands behind her back, as though she had just shut herself quietly in with the guest.

'Good morning, Susan. I'm just stealing a magnifying glass. I'll not get in your way.'

'It's all right, sir, I don't do this room today.'

* * *

Later, he picked up the sketchbooks again and opened a page at random. A portrait of a girl wearing black and red face paint, bordered by a trail of crimson passion-flowers and studies of Heliconid butterflies and their larvae, as Gwen called them; not caterpillars. The sight of the girl brought a knot into his stomach. She was smiling, her gaze turned away from Gwen, unlike so many portraits of indigenous peoples of far-off places. Gwen's portrait of the girl had caught her in a moment. It was perhaps as contrived as any other portrait; no one could paint that quickly. Gus could sense that, to the girl, this had not been the most important part of her day. Something more engaging had caught her attention, and the viewer was not allowed to look into her eyes. On the same page, Gwen had painted the leaves of the tree from which the red dye had been extracted. There was an unfinished study of a miniscule yellow and black tree-frog. Gwen's tiny script edged around it all, and Gus peered through the magnifying glass at her pencilled in words: '. . . each variant would seem to support its own kind of insect. A curious thing, for these relationships to be so specialised. On each plant stem there are tiny nodules, different on each variant, positioned half an inch or so below the leaf and sometimes around the edges of the leaf itself. The nodules vary in size from the almost invisible to the size of a pimpernel flower-bud. These nodules, I have come to realise, are almost exact representations of the ova belonging to the particular Heliconids which rely on the plant as its food source. It is unclear in my mind whether these nodules serve to act as some kind of attractant, or a dissuasive measure. Is the plant attempting to repel the butterflies by announcing that there is already a crop of ova about to hatch and thereafter devour the food ahead of the new additions. Or is it a reminder to the butterfly to lay her eggs? Either way it is a remarkable example of a plant imitating its parasite. I cannot help but speculate that in some cases at least, nature is indeed perhaps as C.D. suggests, working independently of its

Originator . . .'

Gus smiled to himself at Gwen's younger self and her tentative words. She was much more direct now, and unwavering in her conviction. The open window brought in a rush of cooler air and the first raindrops began to spatter the glass. With his gaze fixed in the middle distance through the gathering rain, he thought of her speculating, her imagination ignited by such tiny things as the almost invisible bump on a passion-flower stem. Gus spent the remaining hours of the morning lost in the pages of her work.

Eventually, he heard nearby the commotion of Euphemia coaxing the children, filthy by the sound of it, from exploring the midden heap, into being scrubbed before Susan took them off to have their lunch in the kitchen. Gus heard the resonant clang of an enamel bowl put down on the flagstones and a cloth being dipped and wrung, punctuated by aggrieved noises from both parties.

* * *

Two days after Pemberton's stay had come to an end, Euphemia was high-pitched and overly loquacious. There was a worrying shimmer in her eyes.

A darkening bruise spread out on the horizon casting a dull beginning to the day. As the sky turned a deeper hue of slate, the sea became pale and luminous under it. The wind frigged with Edward's clothes, and he decided to turn back before he was blown off the path. The house, which only a few days before had been open at every window, was now battened down, and seemed to be as hunched as he was as he came in the back door. He kicked off his boots and shoved them under a chair, fully expecting Susan to appear from somewhere and tell him off. She didn't. Edward poked around for something to eat, and finding nothing that wasn't rising or steaming in the deserted kitchen, went along, still wearing his outdoor things, to the library. He kept dry biscuits there. It wasn't exactly an appetising thought, and he was just considering the possible ramifications of ringing for Susan when he saw his wife.

She didn't see him; Euphemia was standing with her back to the door. She was busy searching for something to read. Edward waited for her to sense him there. She was leafing through a book; he could tell from her posture and from the tune that she hummed that she was unlikely to realise he was there unless he made a noise. He stayed perfectly still for a moment, enjoying seeing her absorbed in something so simple. The tune that she hummed was one that she had been practising on the piano very recently. The mistakes that she made over and over again on the keys had corrupted her memory of the piece so that she was humming it wrong. The wind hit the house in a smack of squall, rattling the windows. Edward took his cue and moved into the room, making a noise as he went.

Euphemia turned and let out a yelp like a puppy being trodden on, her eyes widening in alarm. Almost immediately, but not quite soon enough, she said, 'Ted, you quite startled me. Goodness, a storm.'

Edward waited patiently as she fiddled, putting the book back into the case. His wife slammed the doors shut over the books, standing defensively—protectively? Edward couldn't decide—with her back to them, her arms splayed out at her sides.

'What a silly goose I am. Are you wet? I think I can hear one of the boys; he's calling me.' She walked across the room briskly, intending to go past Edward without another word. Edward stepped in her way, and she bumped up against him, recoiling fractionally. Hardly at all, Edward thought, but it was there all the same. Now, he thought, whilst I don't mind about it. 'There is something I have been meaning to speak with you about.'

'Well, I shall look forward to it over dinner, Ted.'

'It is a private matter. A matter of great importance, which—'

'I must get on, Ted. We can speak later.' She pushed him aside, and he let her go. As she left him, she gave him a parting kiss as an afterthought, her top lip beaded with moisture. There was a tang of ripe underarm heat in the space she left behind.

Edward swore under his breath and locked the door after her. Since the arrival of the twins—no, since the very beginning of her bearing them—she hadn't needed any medicine. The glitter of her eyes, in the first days of his taking her on, as he had come to think of it, had vanished. Her demeanour had changed. She was lighter; hadn't cared about his insistence on her not taking clients in, for those evenings to cease altogether. That part of her seemed to have been smoothed right away.

Edward couldn't be sure when this edginess had come back. It was not easy to pinpoint. He thought that perhaps he was being too hard on her. But then there was the comment she'd made about Vincent Coyne; she'd avoided answering his questions, despite his attempts. He didn't want to think about its possible implications. There were far too many little things that he wanted to avoid dwelling on.

He rummaged for his dry biscuits; cramming one into his mouth, he sloped over to the bookcase Euphemia had been rifling through. He didn't mind, on principle. The books there were as wallpaper to him. Certainly, he'd never read anything from those cases. Never even considered it. Euphemia had transferred her edginess; she'd left it in the room and it hovered right there at the bookcase. Don't be a stupid ass, Edward told himself, as he scanned the shelves. He made himself assume an idleness and was about to shut the doors again when he saw it. A book not aligned with its neighbours or the shelf, its lower edge hovering. Edward slid his middle finger into the inch of darkness and grasped the top of the spine with his other hand. The book was wedged tight and when it came out it spewed papers, which drifted in all directions to the floor.

Edward instinctively dropped to his knees to gather them up. It was as well that he was so near to the floor when he saw whose handwriting covered the papers. He read them hungrily, feverishly, spreading them all out on the carpet, sorting them into columns finding the chronological order, finding the extent of Euphemia's game.

Dear Euphemia,

I write this letter to you in haste, much weakened by a lengthy ordeal which had me laid down very low with a case of the ague. I would have travelled back instead of this letter but for my young companion, who has fared much worse than I with the fatigue and the debilitating effects of the ague. I shall wait here, in Pará, as a guest of some friends here whilst my companion recovers. Do not concern yourself, dear sister, I am all in one piece. But there was some confusion, to put it mildly, when I became separated from my party. I have learned since my return that it was believed that all members of my small party had perished.

Mr Scales has returned to England still under this illusion. I know that he would want to visit our house in person, to deliver this erroneous piece of news.

Please relieve him of this misapprehension as soon as the opportunity may arise either by letter or in person.

I hope to be able to travel home one month from now . . .

—

. . . I have managed to find a place to stay—temporarily, until I have sorted out my financial affairs, and until I am able to manage the final leg of the journey home. The voyage has taken much out of me, and, again, I am able to take advantage of the kindness of friends. I will need you to send me a cheque as an interim whilst you sign over the full amount of my inheritance to me. Please send it as soon as you are able . . .

—

. . . I have spent several days since your letter arrived redrafting my response. But I am now of the opinion, having had time to think on everything, that there is no response which would adequately encapsulate all that might reasonably

be committed to paper. There was no need to include the cutting. I read the papers daily from cover to cover. At least, I know now that he is alive, safely returned to England, and that you are not unwell. Your timing, as always, is impeccable . . .

—

. . . Will you at least send on my work? I don't presume to ruin your happiness, as you claimed in your letter; I wish only to allow him to know that I did not perish, as he and everyone else had previously thought. Don't force me into the ridiculous indignity of having to beg you for something which would normally be given freely, without thought or preamble. I will be contacting the Bank, again, in due course.

—

You MUST inform your husband of my whereabouts. It is the only thing that I wish for, nothing more. I cannot see that any benefit can come from his continuing to believe that I am dead . . . As it would seem that I am virtually penniless, may I now, please, at least, have my work returned to me? There are a number of notebooks and sketchbooks which contain important notes in the work I carried out in Pará on some species of ants. You would find this dull, but it is most important that these books are returned to me.

—

Euphemia, you are and always will be my sister, but you leave me in an impossible position . . . Please be advised that I am not prepared to put up with this charade any more. Do what you will, and I shall do the same.

There were thirty-two letters in all, ranging in length, detail and tone. In none of the letters did Gwen mention anything of Augusta save for the mention of her 'young companion', which he knew Euphemia would not have passed over lightly. Edward buried his head between his knees and rocked on the floor until he almost passed out. He wanted to smash things. If only. If only. If *only* he had stayed just a week more before leaving for England. He banged his head on the carpet until his vision was nothing but sparks of brightness, pinging back and forth, up, down. He didn't have the vocabulary to curse the woman. All words had gone from his head. All was vacant, leaving only sadness and regret and self-pity. And fire. A burning gripped his heart, and squeezed at the life of him as the possibilities of his future seized his imagination. He gathered the papers up to shove them back into the book, taking up another document thicker than the rest, which had slipped from its resting place. His own hand stared up at him: November 13, 1859.

He didn't need to read it. Snatches of phrases rose to the surface of his mind before he could stop them: '. . . *please destroy it in the fire . . . a testament to my failings . . . be assured that she was nothing compared to you and that my wife is nothing . . .*'

He screwed up the letter and threw it into the empty grate, scrabbling for matches, falling painfully to his knees at the hearth. Striking, striking, striking. The stink of the unwilling matches curling in the air.

When Pemberton had given him the news that Gwen was alive, that Augusta was alive, there had been a feeling of weird levitation—of his not really being a part of the scene. Reality, as Edward's father might once have said, had not yet jumped up and bitten his arse. Now, he wanted to go. Take a train to London, and find her. But he stayed rooted to the carpet, crawling, placing his hands on her letters, spreading them. In some, she asked for nothing: she gave Euphemia an account of a walk in a park, which Edward thought he recognised. She told Euphemia about a visit to the gardens at Kew, and her impressions of the Glasshouses. In another, she detailed a visit to the Zoo, with intimate observations of other visitors, which were both funny and poignant. Edward knew that there would have been a small hand in hers; that these were not solitary excursions. Some letters were posted all on the same day—and then there would be a silence which would last for months before the next letter.

Edward felt deeply ashamed at every mention in her letters of her missing work. It was his fault. He'd locked her things into cabinets, made a museum of her. He'd let Pemberton look at those sketches and paintings, and then he'd taken them back, locked them away again as if they still belonged under glass. The embarrassment of his having to be asked for them again, so that they could be returned to their owner. He might have pissed in his shoes for the shame of it if he hadn't busied himself with wrapping them in parcel paper and slipping in a note. And her lost money. Christ, her lost money. Euphemia had spent vast amounts refurbishing the house after the death of their father, and he'd never thought on it. Installation of the gas and a new bathroom with hot water. She'd employed an army of gardeners and had ripped out everything that was overgrown. And his extension to the library—her wedding gift to him, she had said. And he had accepted it. Too keen to believe that it was anything other than a romantic gesture.

And in amongst all of this extravagant activity she had steadfastly refused to allow Edward to erect a memorial to Gwen. Always claiming that she knew that she was still alive somewhere. Her genius; the simplicity of it.

He'd married Gwen's sister so that he might hear Gwen's voice again. It had been for the facsimile of Gwen, as conjured by her sister. And this was the only thing which had kept him from falling over the edge—a black pit in his mind or a real edge; he could have picked one of many along the coast. All he needed to do was go to her bed.

She wouldn't call him Ted. If she did, he shrivelled, and there was nothing to be done for the rest of the night.

He went to her room without a light, and slipped between the covers, pulled the hot body, stumbled into her. Re-enacted fragments of time spent with Gwen on damp ground, under trees and always in uncomfortable places. He pulled the body to the floor, or he made her stand, awkward against the corner of a piece of furniture. Or he'd just manage to pretend, for as long as he needed to, that this was her, this was Gwen's arm, hot against the cool, smooth sheets. This was her thigh, yielding under the pressure of his fingers. This was her, pushed up close to his face, her sea-salt, crusting on his fingers. This was her, the way he had always wanted her to be. The way she had been before she'd known anything about him. He held her and buried himself in her for as long as he could bear it.

He wouldn't ever have to go and do those things again. He wouldn't have to see, or puzzle over, her triumphant face in the morning.

Pemberton's promise—that he could arrange a meeting if that was what he wanted. Edward had said nothing at the time. If? Why should there be, how could there be, an 'if'?

He rose unsteadily, and opened all the shutters in that little mausoleum. He shunted the windows open, each one a fraction to let in the air, the sound of the rain, and the sound of a thrush singing. He opened the cabinets where he'd laid all those things of hers, and removed them. The paint-box and her brushes. Living things again, because of the knowledge that her eyes would look at them again, and her fingers could turn these dry cubes of dust to life again. Everything was not as it had seemed. He laughed at the absurdity of it, that she could have come back from a certain death. That her mouth could speak. Yes, there was that. Her mouth could speak; her hand could write. He pressed his open hand to the filthy gloves she'd worn on the ship, which he'd never thought to replace. How could he scrape the pieces back? He was trying to stem the fury now. Trying to press back the need to destroy things and to cause physical, irreparable damage to the woman he must call his wife, who should only ever have been his sister-in-law. He hated her with every single cell in his body. He wanted to kill her.

CHAPTER LVI

LONDON. SATURDAY, AUGUST 4, 1866.

In all endings, there are beginnings.

In this place, he looked so different. The years spent away from him had drawn him very differently in her imagination; and, of course, she hadn't yet managed to find the courage to look at her sketches of Edward to remind her of particular days or minutes she'd spent staring at him. In her imagination, he'd roamed faceless for so long. A peculiar ghost; even the vivid corona of pale fire had grown dim.

He'd spotted her first, so that she'd been caught looking past him until he'd been so close that she'd begun to move away from the man obscuring her view.

She couldn't ever have dreamed of him looking so—old; and tamed. She moved her hand to get a smut out of her eye, and he grabbed it, thinking she was going to embrace him, in this very public place, where no one would bat an eye at a man and a woman embracing on a station platform. His clutching instantly startled her and also reminded her of why she had liked him so much in the beginning, before she had known.

But what did she know, now, that would have made any difference to her back then? Everything, nothing; she mustn't let herself forget any of it.

Sulphurous pong, smuts, bodies pushing, elbows, smoke, whistles, shouting. I shouldn't have agreed to this, she thought. And then, but there was no other way. Edward held Gwen clasped to his chest, and she felt the thud of his heart through their summer clothes. She braced herself in the stiff shoes she still found so impractical and uncomfortable to wear.

'Edward,' she said, pulling herself out of his grip enough to breathe, 'perhaps we should get a cab.'

He wouldn't let go of her. She hadn't imagined this kind of fever. She hadn't imagined anything at all beyond the simple fact that she would see his face again. He gripped her hand as though Vincent Coyne was about to abduct her again, even though it was absolutely and utterly impossible and quite silly.

Somehow, they both got into the cab, and the door was shut without trapping the yards of her dress. Straight away, Edward fell into a gush of sobbing. This is horrible, she thought. How can I get him to stop? But, she patted him, anyway, all the time looking over his shoulder out of the cab window.

By the time they reached the gardens, Edward was in a better state and only looked as if he had a mild case of hay fever.

They wandered aimlessly, Gwen knowing that Augusta was quite happily spending the day digging up an ants' nest in the garden with her long-suffering nanny. The thought of her daughter's interest in ants brought to mind the moment she had discovered what Edward had done with all her own work. The work she had done with the ants and which he had taken such pains to disparage at the time in Brazil had been written up in a paper and presented to the Royal Society under his own name. She had been denied recognition for her work. She had been denied the chance to prove that a woman might be a person of science in the field of Natural History.

She looked at him, and wondered if she still felt the same anger. She didn't know whether the time for accusations and recriminations was yet past. She had thought she would know it, finally, if she could have the chance to look into his face again. Now, when she looked at him there was nothing she could find of what she had thought of as his devious attitude; his features were a new canvas and he was so much the stranger to her that she felt some of the weight of fury lifted from her.

They came to the water-lily house.

'Shall we go in?'

'Won't you find it, the heat, rather uncomfortable?'

She laughed, 'Come on.'

But they both became very quiet as they walked in, perhaps both of them remembering Edward's exultation, that first day on landing at Pará.

It's just like the tropical Glasshouses, at Kew, wouldn't you say?

And her reply: *I wouldn't know, I've never been.*

It was nothing like it, of course. They faltered on the threshold and then they ignored the stifling, humid air and forged on. But neither of them bargained for the effect it would have.

* * *

Outside again, they walked until they found a niche to sit in.

'Those lilies, they were everywhere.'

'On that day. Yes, I know.' She almost took his

hand and sat back, holding her gloves in her lap. They stayed there, like that, in silence until it was time for Gwen to go. Before she stood up to leave she said softly, 'There is still the small matter of the birth certificate. You brought it with you.'

'The— No, I'm sorry. I forgot.'

* * *

Two days later, on Monday, Gwen took the omnibus to the address Edward had given her. She'd committed it to memory at the gardens, torn the slip of paper to shreds as soon as she'd been out of sight of him.

The house had the closed-up, musty smell of a place left alone for too long. Gwen wondered whether she would take the smell of it away with her on her clothes.

Edward opened the door to her himself and led her into the bowels of the place. In the morning room, a daybed was covered with blankets despite the heat. Under it lay glasses and plates. In a corner of the room, a pile of dust sheets which Edward had not bothered to have taken away.

'Edward,' she faltered, shaken by this scene, 'haven't you, have you no one here, to see to things? To look after you?'

Gwen made herself look at Edward in his pathetic state. He hadn't washed or changed his clothes since she had last seen him. His face was covered in rough stubble. From his mouth, a fetid cloud of breath which hung in the musty air. His lips were stained with streaks of dried red wine. Crusts of sleep at the corners of his eyes and amongst his lashes.

This man is stuck somewhere else, she thought; he's neither at the end of something nor yet at the beginning of anything.

'Tell me what you plan to do here, Edward.'

He regarded her blankly, and then with an expression which asked Gwen why she was asking such a stupid question, he advanced closer to her. She had to move her head to the side and hold her breath. Gwen let Edward put his arms around her, let him put his face to her neck and snuffle into the delicate collar of her dress.

Then she pulled out of his grasp and stood apart from him again. 'Edward, I think you need to make some changes here.' She tried to sound comforting, though it resisted her.

'Changes. Yes, everything must change now,' he said slowly.

'In the wider sense, they inevitably will. But, Edward, I'm talking about practical matters. I mean, for instance, that you must attend to your toilet; change your clothes. Have a hot bath—though if you have no one here, that may have to wait. Find a barber. Open up more rooms. You need to be in a fit state, Edward. I can't talk to you when you are like this.'

'Like this?'

'Edward.' She couldn't take it; she hadn't imagined it would be quite so unpleasant. 'You stink. Your clothes. Your breath is offensive—when was the last time you drank a glass of clean water?'

Edward stared at her. 'I—you say I stink?'

'I'm sorry, I shouldn't have.'

'No. You're right; I probably do. I must apologise.' He swept a hand through his hair. 'What you must think of me.'

'I think you have had a shock. I am standing here, with you, when for years you have imagined that I was, that both Augusta and I were dead. I think, when you saw me at the station and at the gardens, it wasn't quite real for you. There were so many things we thought of saying and couldn't say any of them. I think both of us are wondering where on earth we should begin; what should remain unsaid and what should not.'

'You seem to know exactly what to say, and I—'

'I've had years to think of it, of this meeting, Edward. You have had only a matter of weeks.'

'You might have written to me.' His voice was thick with emotion and a sudden thirst. 'I found your letters, to her.'

'I did write to you, Edward,' Gwen spoke very carefully. 'I wrote every week for a whole year until I was certain that they were being intercepted.'

'You could have,' Edward grasped at the air as though it would offer him some comfort, 'you could have sent him sooner.'

Gwen watched Edward begin to pace the room. How dare you, she thought. How dare you blame me like this, as though it was all down to me. You should have done more, she thought, when Vincent told you I was dead. You should have noticed how mad he was, how crazed, how false he was. You should have done more to find out the truth of it, of what happened that day. You should have been able to find us, she wanted to scream, you should have been able to deduce what had happened in an instant. But, you were as useless as I had always suspected you were, and now you lay all the blame of your own hurt and misery on my shoulders.

Gwen said quietly, 'You'll know her ways now,

Edward. And you have those two boys. I think you know, really, that I could never have acted on impulse.'

Edward stopped and turned, then he let himself slide into a leather reading chair, giving gravity the final decision on how he should land. 'Her ways. Gwen, I am lost. The boys, yes; I think they are everything to her. Yet other times, when I see her, some days, it seems she hardly knows that they exist.'

'Mr Pemberton told me that they looked like they were very happy, healthy children. Edward, I could never have acted selfishly.'

'Why not? She has.'

'That's always been her way, Edward. My sister has never done anything which did not benefit her. The rest of us, we have to negotiate through whatever she lays down in our path. Let's not talk about it until later. Why not show me the rest of your house? I'll help you draw up a list. I can help you find staff.'

And yet all the time she was thinking, I must leave, I've made a mistake. I must go from here.

He brushed her words aside with jerking flicks of his hands as he advanced towards her. 'Pemberton, Pemberton. Why was it him? What else, what did he tell you? To your face? In a letter? What kind of cosy discussion did you have, the two of you?'

'It's irrelevant.'

'Look at me. No, somehow I don't think that it is at all irrelevant. It appears to me now, very odd, indeed, that a man you met *but once*, should be the one to come and deliver such devastating news.'

'You're devastated that I am alive?'

'No.'

'There was no one else; no one who had known us both. Honestly, I have tried to do the right thing.'

'But where did you pluck him from? You don't know him!'

Gwen looked away. 'He is Hettie Grindlock's brother. I thought you knew.'

CHAPTER LVII

RICHMOND. MONDAY, AUGUST 6, 1866.

Gwen's hand hovered over the blank page for so long that the ink dried on the nib. She loaded her pen afresh and closed her eyes as she wrote: *I killed him*.

Opening her eyes, she looked down at her words. They were skewed and slanting, black and shining. She pressed the blotting paper to them; they had authority now. She added something to the sentence, gave the full stop a tail: *I killed him, the man called Vincent Coyne.*

So the letter became:

I killed him, the man called Vincent Coyne. One of us should have done it sooner or later, and since you were not there, the onerous task was left to me.

I can't say I undertook such a ghastly task lightly. It only sounds so, when you write it down.

He came back, to where he had left us. He came alone, and, of course, I never thought he intended to rescue us, or remove us to a place of safety after that first night. After those two days without shelter or food, perhaps he imagined a greeting different to the one he received.

Faced with such an intimidating prospect—left alone to perish through starvation or thirst, I never let myself believe that this was a certainty. I had Augusta to protect. I had the flint and the pocket knife, which Mr Coyne did not know about. He took everything else from us, as you know. But we were not weak with hunger. The place we had been abandoned to was favoured by the river turtle. We ate hatchlings roasted in their own shells for those two days. A happy coincidence while God had been averting his gaze.

Augusta slipped out of my hands, came out from our hiding place, running. He picked her up too roughly. He shouted that I should come out.

'Where is Edward?'

'My conscience is saved. However, you're still alive.' His face for a second looked stupid with incomprehension. But he recovered himself.

'Mr Coyne. Two days ago, you told me that you would be gone for one hour, and that you would bring Edward here. Where is he?'

'You think he respects you. Do you really suppose that a man like Scales could ever respect a woman like you the way he respected Frome? And do you think by not being his lawful wife, you have elevated yourself to some higher position? Think.'

'What? Put my daughter down, and tell me where Edward is.'

'Go on, think. What promise did Scales ever make to you? No one is ever quite what they seem to be, are they, Miss Carrick? You should know that more than most.'

'Augusta is innocent. You can talk to me, but put her down.'

'Think, Miss Carrick. Thinking, working things out. That is your gift, isn't it?'

'Yes, it is, Mr Coyne. Please put Augusta down; you are frightening her.'

'Miss Carrick. Which one of you did he really fall in love with? Do you think he really fell in love with you? Or was it the woman who would never question his authority, who would never be able to put his own intelligence in the dock? Which woman, Miss Carrick, do you think Scales really fell in love with—you? Or was it Euphemia?'

'Your mother was one of her clients. If you suppose that you surprise me, Mr Coyne, with your little revelation, you do not. Augusta, please, give her to me now.'

'No. Euphemia hated you enough to employ my assistance. But I don't believe she would bear a grudge against the innocent party. Scales' bastard child is coming with me.' Augusta, my child, the only light I possessed. To hear that ugly word used to describe my beautiful daughter. He turned his back on me and went to put Augusta in the canoe.

These things are done without thought.

His guard was down for a second. Just a second.

I had been walking slowly towards him over the sand but now I ran. I fixed my loose plait round his neck in a quick tourniquet. He dropped Augusta. He tried to shake me off, and in his confusion, and in the struggle, he and I fell.

He, face down in the sand; myself, landing on top of him. All of my strength was taken by the determination not to let him free of my throttling.

Augusta stood at the water's edge and screamed for her father. Over and over. Bright macaws took off from the trees and called over our heads.

After a while, he became still; I don't know if he meant to fool me or not. I wrapped both ends of the tourniquet around my left hand and brought out my pocket knife. And then a new vigour, I didn't know whether he was trying to throw me off or if these were his death throes. My knee in his back. All of my strength.

Being a mother, protecting Augusta. These were the things on my mind as I pressed the point of the knife into his neck, just below his jaw, turning the blade handle, driving it deeper. And I thought of the stillness of oppressive afternoons as I dragged the knife across his neck, messily, inexpertly, towards the other side of his jaw. I thought of never having to wonder what he would do next. What the next insane plan he might concoct in his addled head or conduct on behalf of my sister would be. I shushed Augusta. I waited.

When I rolled him over, I saw that his bladder had emptied. I am ashamed now to say that I scraped a handful of sand and let it drop into his open eyes; to verify his death, only to know, not out of malice for the corpse. I washed my hair, face, hands in the river.

Her hands shook, her body convulsed, she poured with a sweat that went cold on her skin. Her vision was blurred, the image of his spectacles slipping down into the river, released from her fingers. The silver frames and the blue glass catching the sunlight so briefly before being covered completely by the black, tannin-stained water. She wanted to run; her legs felt twitchy, and yet they barely supported the weight of her. It was impossible to think that it could have happened. Should a letter like this contain every detail, she thought, it loses its purpose.

We drank some of his water, we ate some of his food. I covered him with sand. We got into his boat. I paddled.

We came that night to the place where we had stayed. We were ghosts. But ghosts who were clothed and fed and looked after.

You know the rest of it already. And now—

Gwen read it through. She was tired. Behind her on the bed, Augusta shifted in her sleep—her legs and the sheets tangled, her arms thrown wide. Gwen wanted him to know the depth of it. Had to get rid of him herself; no one else was there to do it for her. Gwen put the letter onto the table. She folded it up. She unfolded it. She read it again. She cut it into flaccid spills and fed them into the flame of her candle, letting them drop, brittle, grey flakes of her confession, onto the rim of the candle-holder. The top half of the window was open behind the thick, heavy curtains. Gwen listened to the stillness. She looked over at Augusta. She'd agreed to take her to the Zoo the next day. It would be a day to make up for her long absence today, just the two of them. She crawled gingerly onto the wide bed, as though it were a trough of sinking sand, not wanting to disturb her daughter, spreading out her limbs, waiting for the tincture of morphine to work.

The afternoon she'd spent with Edward at his house drifted in and out of her mind as she tried to push it firmly out of reach so that she might be able to sleep.

Time and again, Edward had tried to pull her into an embrace, and each time she had evaded him he had become more determined. Eventually, stepping back, putting a physical distance between them, she said, 'Because I don't love you, you see. And because I can't begin to love you. I know too much. Yes, once I was gullible, Edward. From before the moment you met me you were already hiding things, but I am not that girl. I have a different life now. The person you knew no longer exists. I'm sorry. I'll go.'

Edward had made a show of intending to see her out, but at the door he was more insistent than ever. 'A different life? What different life?' He grabbed her hands, pulled off the fine gloves, painfully tugging at her fingers, forcing them into his mouth where he sucked drily on them. She felt his teeth closing on her bones.

'You have no different life now,' he said. 'You are the same, just the same and more; you still wear that cheap ring I gave you. You can't bear to take it off when you put on your gloves. It looks better than I remember. It grows well on you. It used to slide between your knuckles, but now—'

Gwen tried to close her fist, get her fingers away from his mouth, pull free.

He pressed his cracked lips to her mouth and drew breath from her lungs. 'Say the words,' he said. 'Tell me what you used to say.'

In her corset, bound and stiff, she was unable to gather the wit of her strength to block him. She pushed her face aside, nauseated, gasping. 'I can't remember any words, Edward. Let me go now.' She reached out for the door handle, but he grabbed her wrist, holding her painfully, pressing skin to bone.

'Tell me about the weather. Make it the way it was.'

'What?' She twisted her arm in his grip. His determination was manic; rub turning to burn.

'The rain, that we've been having this week. Say, 'This rain, this rain', say it to me.'

'Edward, you must let go of me, you must stop this. I am married. Gus Pemberton is my husband.'

'Whore.' Edward shoved her against the wall and spat into her face. Her anger dug at her as his hands scrabbled at her clothes tearing a seam in the silk. He pushed her back along the dingy hall into the room across the floor and down. She lost her footing in her heels on the rucked carpet, and knocked her head against some part of the daybed as he thrust a hand up under the heaps of expensive silk, his fingernails scraping her, his grotesque heaving panting, shoving her into a corner of the bed, her legs parted now with the full weight of his hips bearing down on her. She took hold of his neck and squeezed. He slapped her across the face. A raw, flesh-stinging swipe, catching her lip against her teeth. She felt the swell of it, the butcher-block taste of it.

'Tell me about the foul weather, Mrs *Pemberton*, you obstinate bitch.'

'I don't care to.'

There came an enormous crack from somewhere. Gwen realised that her hearing had failed, and just as the black edges began to close in around her she knew that the crack must have come from her own head.

She woke face down. Her head throbbing, hanging over the edge of the daybed. He wasn't finished. She made no sound, her eyes fixed on a plate of half-eaten food, a glass half full of claret gone to vinegar. For a long while, it seemed, she simply couldn't believe that it could have happened so suddenly, and without warning.

* * *

She remained immobile as he gripped the flesh on her thighs and pulled himself away from her. Thumbs pressed in, he ground the meat of her as he followed the contours of her lower back to her buttocks and hovered there.

'Do you realise,' he murmured, 'that I have not fucked you since that horrible day when I had to unpick your sister's needlework?' He seemed not to mind that she made no answer or that she might be unconscious. Perhaps he wished it that way. Gwen felt the wet and cooling weight of him resting now between her buttocks. He pulled himself closer again.

'No,' she coughed, and tried to right herself.

'I've always wondered,' he said. And Gwen

thought that he spoke through gritted teeth. She tried to edge away from him. He caught her up and pressed down on her back. Gwen yelled, angry at her incoherence, as he spat at her again; a great gobbet of phlegm landing on her buttock.

She twisted herself around, and flung her arm up, elbow jagged, catching him somewhere soft.

'Stop.' She managed to get the word out as she heard Edward grunt in pain and swear, before he hit her again and pressed her back down into the daybed. 'Don't, Ted,' she said. 'Ted. That's what she calls you now, isn't it? You have a different—' The thump from his fist into her side winded her completely. A searing pain rent through her as he drove into her and thrust harder, harder, shouting, 'Tell me about the rain, you bitch,' until his shouting became incomprehensible, the words catching in his throat until they became one long yell of anger.

He pushed her aside as he rose and left her, walking to the end of the room. She heard the cold, clear ring of crystal meeting crystal as he poured.

'Ted,' she murmured, inaudible to him. She thought for the first time of her sister being his wife, letting him into her bed. She wondered what room Effie had now. Was it her old one or the one she had always wanted? She thought of Effie doing as she was told, and saying the words. Of Effie refusing and of her lying as she was, thinking as she was, that he might have cracked her rib. Concentrating on the bones. Just the bones.

The light had almost gone from the room. Her view of the floor, tipped on its edge, saw Edward's trousers and shoes pacing over the floor, coming to the fringe of the carpet and swivelling on the first inch of wood before turning. The different kinds of pain she felt astonished her. Her right arm was caught up underneath her ribcage, a dead limb. I can't leave, she thought. I shouldn't even move, until I have my arm back.

'Drink?' he said. 'You've got to tell me now, how did you survive? You were thrown from the canoe. The river was teeming with alligators.' Edward did not seem to be talking to her now, and when she replied, Gwen was not sure that he heard her.

'Vincent Coyne was a parasitic lunatic,' she said, and studied the pattern in the carpet as she felt with her good hand for her hair. He was a lunatic, she thought. But you, Edward, are just a disgusting parasite. Letting her hair down slowly, the pins collected in her fist as she unwound the coil.

*   *   *

As she began to fall asleep, the pain of it played over and over in her mind, ghastly and dulled now by the tincture, still present and livid in her mind. She wondered in her stupor on the nature of pain embedded in the memory, trying still to distance herself from the thing which kept her from sleeping.

She'd waited a long time for Edward to get drunk enough to become enfeebled. And for the life to come back to her arm so that she could begin to plait her hair.

Her mind had been clear.

*   *   *

Gus Pemberton smiled at his wife as she lay

sleeping with her daughter on the big bed. He'd come in and drawn back the curtains. The window had been left open a little all night, and the room was only slightly fusty with their sleep. He bent over to kiss her forehead and stopped. There was a large bruise above her nose, and the swelling had spread down, puffing up her face. Her lips were misshapen and dark with the lively purple of trauma.

Gwen opened her eyes. Seeing him standing over her, she moved without remembering and winced.

'You've suffered some kind of injury,' he said. 'What on earth has happened?'

'I stumbled,' she said, her voice masked with a dry tongue.

Gus passed her a glass of water. 'Tell me,' he said quietly, helping her to sip it.

'I lost my footing. On the omnibus. People were very kind. I ripped my dress. It wasn't so bad at the time. But—'

'You'll be feeling it now. Oh, dear, poor love. My poor dove.' He cupped her cheek with a soft hand, and she closed her eyes. 'I wish you'd have said yesterday.'

'It seemed just so silly. I didn't want to wake you.'

'Here, let's get you sitting up.' He tried to ease her into a heap of pillows. She tried to keep the extent of her injuries hidden from him but she couldn't stop herself from crying out at his touch.

'Don't move me, please.'

'No Zoo today. Not for you, anyway. I'll send for Rathstone.'

'Don't bother Dr Rathstone, I don't want to see him. I just need to sleep.'

'But, surely, just to see that nothing—' He

stopped as she shook her head.

'I look as if I've been knocked rather badly, I know, but don't waste money on it.'

'Hell! Who cares about that?'

'Just a drop of tincture.'

'That will not do, you know it. See sense, let me send for the doctor.'

'Bring the scissors from the table, will you please? I'm so hot, and my head hurts.'

Gus put his hand on her forehead. 'Now, why on earth do you want the scissors?'

When she told him, he wouldn't do it.

'But it is matted, and I shan't be able to dress it; no one shall. It is better to cut it off to my shoulder. My head aches with it, the weight of it is too much.'

'When the doctor has seen you, you will feel differently.'

'I don't think I shall.'

Gus glanced at the sprawled child who was beginning to wake. He scooped her up as she became instantly conscious. From the child's hand he saw a pale grey, pearlescent sphere drop to the folds of the sheets. It was a very good example of a balas diamond, the best he had ever seen. He had no idea how Gwen had come about it. She had never said that she knew what it was, and had given it to Augusta to play with a long time ago. Gus jollied Augusta out of the room, making trumpeting elephant noises. It had always been on the tip of his tongue to say that she had given her daughter a small fortune to play with.

Now, as he looked at his wife in her state of distress, just as during the voyage back home on the steamer, he knew it was better to drop all thoughts of probing her deeply over things he could see she did not want to discuss. He knew that she must have spent the day with Scales again; Gwen taking the omnibus was unusual. But here she was, home again. And he knew that whatever she did, wherever she went, she'd always do the right thing. But he couldn't bring himself to cut her hair.

He handed Augusta over to the nanny and sent for Rathstone. While he waited for the doctor to arrive, Gus went back to his rooms to inspect the map of New Zealand he'd recently acquired. As he took the map from its paper casing, he remembered the way the servant girl at Carrick House had shut herself in the study with him.

'You're a detective, sir, aren't you?' she'd said. 'From Scotland Yard.'

'I'm sorry?'

'Aren't you, sir? I thought you was.' Her shoulders sagged hopelessly.

'Oh, I see.' He'd wanted to be kind but he'd wanted to laugh so very badly, as well. The girl had spilled out her speech anyway, ending with, 'I do what I can, sir. But my mistress, she's married him, and I can't look out for her all the time, if you see what I mean.'

He'd said that he did see, and that he understood her to be a very loyal kind of person.

'I always thought it were funny peculiar, what happened just before Miss Gwen went away. He's always made it seem like she was afflicted. But I've known them girls longer 'n anybody. There's nothing mad about her. It's all just to hide what's happened, see. Because of her not being able to say now.'

Scales' words then had come back to him, that Gwen would know what to do. And he had no doubt that she would, if he were to tell her. But, whatever they were, he knew she would keep her conclusions to herself, as would he. A servant's ravings were hardly a sound basis for such a serious accusation. Scales, for all his faults, was after all, a scientist, and scientists were in the habit of collecting macabre objects of interest.

He put his forefinger to the map and traced the lines of the mountains, the contours of the coast. He paused, the servant girl's words trammelling his head: 'I can't look out for her all the time, if you see what I mean.'

'God's sake, I'm an ass. An eejit of the first order,' he said out loud. He rang for the maid.

'Tell Cook hot porridge for Mrs Pemberton. I want you to take it up to her as soon as you can—tell Mrs Pemberton.' He tapped the map on his desk as he thought it through.

'Would you please convey my apologies to my wife. I have to go out for a couple of hours; no more than that, I am sure.'

* * *

The sun moved more fully into the room. Gwen sipped her water slowly. She thought, And still the birds are able to sing. She remembered the sharp clarity of everything her eye had rested on that next day in a life which had seemed so distant from this one. She held her empty glass, waiting for Gus to come back, as he always did, with her breakfast tray.

Effie, she thought, but nothing more than that.

The sun glanced off the mirrors, and a fabulous light ricocheted into the room.

CHAPTER LVIII

LONDON. OCTOBER 5, 1866.

Gus Pemberton felt empty as he watched the Jury stand up and file out of the courtroom to consider their verdict. He knew that had the Defence been conducted by his first choice of man, the case would have been thrown out of court by the Judge, or that the Judge, at least, would have made his direction to the Jury in Gwen's favour. As it was, he couldn't imagine that anyone present would be confident in guessing the verdict. All week, his fingernails had dug into his palms as each witness had been called up by the Prosecution. With each new name, Gus had wondered whether this would be the person to give the most damning evidence of all. When they did, for he was sure that such a person would have been found by now, he knew that he would not be able to stand it. Bettlesham and Bettlesham had kept their distance from the whole proceedings. Henry Bettlesham Senior had said to Gus, with a tone of regret the night before the first day of the trial, that he thought it best if he kept the lowest profile in England.

Gus now wondered if his approach had been all wrong; if there had been, perhaps, some other way of persuading Henry B. that either himself or his son could act for his wife. There was a low hum in the courtroom, shuffling, and much fidgeting as the spectators wondered how long they would have to wait or if there was time to go and empty their bladders. Gus stared up at the ceiling, as he dared not catch anyone's eye. He didn't trust himself not to lose his composure. That first conversation with Henry B., after he'd received Henry's astonishing letter, played out again in his mind. There had been no witness called with the secret information, but still Gus felt his body throbbing with worry that somehow, even at this late stage, this unknown person might still be produced.

Gus had paced about in Henry B.'s rooms, unable to contain his anxiety long enough to park his backside on the chair offered. He'd sucked and puffed on the cigars he'd taken up again since Gwen's arrest and waited for Henry's response.

Henry had said, 'I'm sorry, Augustus. This is quite embarrassing as I am sure you will appreciate.'

'Oh, come off it, Harry. I don't see how there can't be a way around this. If you won't do it then I won't have anyone but your son to represent my wife.'

'It's not a question of won't, but can't; it's simply out of the question. Henry Bettlesham Junior is a fine lawyer, I will admit, but Shanks is his equal. I haven't yet released the details of the will and shan't, of course, until the whole business is concluded. There was no one besides myself at the interment, in any case; such a drab affair. And it is a maze of complications. But the implications for yourself and your wife could be—indeed, would be—very severe.'

'You'll put it about that Scales was intestate?'

'I can't exactly do that, you know; not explicitly. But matters can be alluded to, should they crop up. I should hope they wouldn't. So should you.'

'I know nothing about this Shanks fellow.'

'He's first rate. You couldn't look for a better man.'

'And he doesn't know about the will?'

'Good Lord, no. I must assure you; it hasn't gone beyond myself, Henry and now yourself. There were no copies which left these offices, either then or since.'

'I can barely think why he came to you.'

'You mustn't let it impinge. But Scales thought he was making provision for someone practically destitute. And, of course, he was under the impression that your wife was *not* married. As long as your wife was truly unaware of the change to Scales' will before his death, and as long as it remains undisclosed—suffice to say, we'll keep saying our prayers.'

'But his widow came to see you yesterday. Surely—'

'I told her nothing. Of course, she was deeply distressed and presented some difficulties. She is very—'

'Accomplished. You'll remember I have met her.'

'Quite so. Rest assured, she had nothing from me except my deepest condolences. She won't know the worst of it until it is all over, and she may attempt to contest the will, of course.'

'I don't doubt it, though there may well be no need.'

'Do not give in to the ogre of despair. The most important subject for now is your own wife and the ordeal she continues to face, and I do believe that Shanks is the best man to—'

'Save my wife from the noose and eternal infamy.'

'Shanks is very competent.'

'I don't want competent; I want extraordinary. I can't have some bastard come into court to reveal at the last minute that Gwen has inherited every last damn bit of Scales' estate.'

'Dear man, do compose yourself. It will never come near to that.'

* * *

Gus did not believe in tempting fate but he wished that Shanks had been a different kind of extraordinary. Perhaps he was being uncharitable but he felt he couldn't be held accountable for his feelings towards the man. When Shanks had failed to harangue Morrisson over his flaky evidence Gus had struggled to keep himself from getting up and doing it himself. The triumph he had felt at convincing Gwen's aunt to change her evidence at the last minute had been sweet but brief. The days had been relentless, and now the ticking of every bloody pocket watch in the courtroom seemed amplified in his brain as the minutes ticked on into eternity. As he brought his gaze down from the ceiling, two things happened. First, he made eye contact with Euphemia Scales, whose presence in the courtroom he had until that moment been entirely unaware of. Then, the Jury began to make their way back in.

CHAPTER LIX

CARRICK HOUSE. OCTOBER 5, 1866.

Susan had known that it had been awful of her not to have told her mistress about the murder at Hyde Park. She had tried to look for a sign, a solution. She had gone to the Reverend for advice, but it had been Mrs Brewin who had said that it wasn't really Susan's responsibility to make sure her mistress read every square inch of the daily paper, and that if it had been put on the pile in the scullery, well, that was it done with. Mrs Brewin also pointed out that there were other ways the widow would find out, sooner or later. So, Susan had made peace with her troubled conscience and cut and strung the lavatory paper as usual.

Susan had followed the trial meticulously while her mistress had stayed in London. Running the house and taking care of the boys wore Susan right out, and she'd had to enlist the help of Mrs Brewin, who had been very quick indeed to down pots and pans at the vicarage. In turn, the Reverend had realised at some point that unless he wanted to live off old beef dripping, runny jam, pickled beets and no bread to put it on, he had better walk the three-mile round trip to Carrick House every day and eat his meals there. He couldn't say it was a disagreeable arrangement, and he found that the rigorous, out-of-doors exercise helped him to think clearly and was more conducive to the composition of sermons than the pacing of carpet his study afforded.

He liked the little boys, who said amusing and mainly incomprehensible things, and who did not seem at all perturbed by the extended absence of their mother. He also noticed that there was a keener brightness to his surroundings at Carrick House. His preparations for his sermons, whilst rather different in tone and timbre to those he'd made for years at the vicarage were rather pleasing to his sensibilities. The surfaces of the furniture gleamed at him and seemed to cast God's light about the room in a rather fairylike manner. The windows seemed not to have been glazed at all until his head bumped up against the glass when he tried to peer at the view up the main drive further than the panes would permit. Over the first week or so, the Reverend gradually began to realise that the house was simply very clean. Mrs Brewin, firmly ensconced, took it upon herself to engage through an acquaintance in town an illiterate but excellent cook whose skills in preserving were exemplary.

The Reverend had followed the trial. Everyone he knew had been following the trial. He had tried to keep Mrs Pemberton's identity to himself, but the impossibility of that became clear as the trial had progressed. After all, Mr Scales had not taken a whole *harem* of lady watercolourists to Brazil.

Today, they were all waiting for the paper to arrive, each avoiding the other's eye. The Reverend peered again from the window at the view of the drive and stifled a release of digestive gas behind a clenched fist.

*　　*　　*

Waking to a dry mouth, bodies pressed against

Euphemia as the shroud of an uncomforting sleep slipped away. The empty carriage she had chosen at the beginning of her journey had since quickly filled. The train gave out its final shudder of stopping at a station and the dent in her forehead from taking a sleep against the window frame began to make itself felt. The usual stink of such confinement—stale tobacco, boiled egg, old sweat, camphor, lavender, naphthalene, rotten tooth, fart, wet wool—made her sit up straighter and look about without looking at faces, to see who had travelled with her, who had witnessed her sleep. The embarrassment of the dream she'd been taken from was still fresh in her mind, and it was possible that she had been calling out in her sleep. Euphemia turned her face to the window. There was a wasp, late for its winter nest or tardy in its dying. It butted against the window, and the screams from the guard's whistle masked out its tiny noise.

Before boarding the train, Euphemia had bought herself a newspaper from one of the stands. There were many things, many activities, according to some, which a female of certain rank should not do, should not indulge in, should not permit herself to enjoy. Buying a newspaper was one of them but Euphemia had given up caring what other people would think of her. She had been there to see her sister vilified all through those sweltering days and stuffy hours of the trial. Euphemia had been incapable of restraining her curiosity.

Euphemia had not opened the paper. She knew what the report would say, so she kept the paper folded away in her travelling bag as she reached in for her flask. There were hours yet of this journey to endure, and Euphemia took a very tiny sip, just enough to wet the sour taste on her tongue. Then, she brought out the tin of sweets she had paid for along with the newspaper; she put one of the sugared violets into her mouth and stared again out of the window at the rushing by of the land and let her mind empty, of everything, just for a few moments.

CHAPTER LX

THE TIMES, Friday, October 5, 1866.

MURDER TRIAL AT THE OLD BAILEY.

THE PRISONER has held herself well erect in the courtroom each day of the proceedings, and today was no time for the prisoner to deviate from her usual attitude. Her dress was quite impeccably attended and sombre. A thick veil half obscuring her face, the prisoner kept up a surreptitious knotting or sliding of her fingers against each other, slotting them together in a constant bid to make sure that her gloves were without wrinkles. When each person spoke, she attended to what that person had to say with silent acuity; to the reaction of others in the room, the prisoner seemed alert to every nuance of tone. She has betrayed no emotion during the last session of the proceedings. There has been nothing in her manner which could have been interpreted as that of a guilty party or otherwise. Her attitude has not, apart from the constant adjustment to her gloves, demonstrated that all of this bother has been centred around herself or that her life has been in the balance. Mr Probart for the Prosecution examined witnesses, during which time the Defence made several objections; some were upheld, others were not. However, by the end of the Defence cross-examination it was clear to all assembled in court that Mr Probart's witnesses served only to strengthen the case for the Defence. From the gallery a veritable hum of consternation and excitement could be discerned after the summing up by the Judge, Mr Justice Linden. The Jury retired and deliberated for more than forty-five minutes before they returned the verdict: the prisoner was found Not Guilty, the Jury concluding that the death of Mr Edward Scales was accidental. At which declaration, a roar of appreciation emitted from the gallery and rose to the roof, after which a general hubbub of whistles, cheers and cries of 'Bless you, Mrs Pemberton' were audible amidst the noise. Mrs Pemberton was helped away from the courtroom by her husband and others.

CHAPTER LXI

Carrick House. November 1, 1866.

The Book of Phobias
by
C.R. Jeffreye

'The exercise of combining two emotions, so as to bring out a third different from either, is not intrinsically arduous. Everything depends on the facility of assuming the elementary feelings.'

Bain, 1855.

(i) And so we come to the most singularly intriguing case which has been a subject of my exploratory studies of the mind and its peculiarities under inspection. We shall call the specimen, [censored], or *X*, hereafter.

X first came to my notice some years ago. The spouse had called to my attention, in my capacity as a Gentleman of Medicine, the distress caused to both parties on the occasion of the pinnacle feat of the nuptial requirements. This would not in itself cause undue concern under normal circumstances. My advice to the unhappy spouse of *X* was that Time would Unravel the Mysteries, and that All Would Be As Expected. The dysfunction, dissatisfaction and, moreover, disappointment over the lack of potential progeny continued, however, for several months, and the spouse sought my counsel once more. On this occasion, I was privy to further details, thus: *X* was unable to consummate his marriage due to an aversion to the follicular protuberances of his wife's [cut].

I delicately suggested the obstacle of consternation might be solved by a simple act of removal. This, she informed me, after many floods of tears and blushes, had been attempted without success. The renewal of such follicular emergence, before the next attempt by *X*, was in all senses, quite apart from being wholly distasteful in practical terms, more disastrous than the original state of affairs.

My suggestion then, was to allow a certain amount of time between our meeting and the next attempt, to allow for Nature's Replenishment of that which had been depilated. I suggested that I might have an interview with *X*, to which, after Gentle Persuasion, the Lady agreed.

(ii) In earnest conversation with *X*, his inhibitions loosened medicinally, he unfolded his version of the sorry affair.

X began by relating to me the fact of his ignorance of the way nature has endowed the anatomy of the female. *X* stated that the sight of his naked wife on his wedding night was an absolute shock, his having come to expect a perfectly smooth creature, as portrayed in any tasteful work of art. After jovial reproach, I asked him to expand upon his reaction to this 'discovery' of his. Utter revulsion, was his reply. He did not, could not, desire his wife in any measure from the neck down; that he regarded her as a grotesque freak of Nature.

I earnestly implored him to take the not uncommon measure of approach from afar. That completion of desire, could be attained, I assured him, by stealth. If the marble-like surface was what he desired, and nought else, a route from a different angle entirely, might ease his desire to a more satisfactory conclusion, i.e., that he must [deleted] at all. That he must approach her in this manner every night for a month, and, rather than try to force the issue, remain apart from her and regard the beauty as though a work of art were before him.

X went away much lighter in attitude and I fully expected to hear no more about it.

(iii) Two months later I was again in earnest confidence with *X*. The solution had, to a degree, been successful in that he had managed, after a number of weeks, to stand to and not lie asleep in his wife's presence. However, at the merest touch of passion, all was lost, and unrecoverable. *X* was utterly despondent and, alas, allowing this most private part of his life to overshadow everything in his path. In short, he was a most frustrated mess. At this point, I was quite at a loss as to how to proceed, if indeed it was possible to proceed.

Then, a moment of inspiration struck. I brought into the room a small fur, concealed behind my back. I asked *X* to close his eyes and to put out his hand. I laid the fur into his hand. He seemed puzzled, but not at all vexed by the article. So, I surmised to *X*, that it was not a case of pelts *per se*. No, he concurred; in any case, he said, this sable was like silk. His wife's [removed] resembled his beard: wiry and manly and unladylike. I assured him that the [erased] he so desired could be found within, if only he could overcome his aversion to the fact that all women, not only his wife, were so endowed. That he must make himself familiar with his wife at all costs, as his health demanded it. The next suggestion I made was that in [section expurgated]. In this, I assured him, he might be so satisfied that he may climb to the next ridge of the mountain and thus from here admire the vista.

(iv) Unhappily, *X* was to confide some while later that the weather was not at all suitable or conducive to mountain scrambles. I then suggested to *X* that he should familiarise himself with the true meaning of Freak of Nature. He accompanied me on an excursion to witness the various exhibits at Saville House where I had heard one particular hirsute lady performed.

X became obsessed with this personage and would not leave the subject alone. I perceived an unhealthy attitude in his attention to the female, and advised *X* that his energy must be spent on the sole prize of [excised] his wife in her [eliminated].

After some deep consideration I altered my opinion; this phenomenon, I had come to realise, was hysteria induced by suggestion, which could, therefore, following Babinski's principle, be cured by persuasion. I divined that if *X* should so encounter a woman, covered in hair from top to toe, then the revulsion would be so complete that the cure would be instantaneous and a happy marriage might flower. Now here, one might be forgiven for supposing that my inclinations on this matter were correct. Not so.

X, upon meeting this hirsute female, did lose all feelings of revulsion when faced with this peculiar Nondescript. However, *X* did not go home at once and make up for time lost, so to speak. *X* became [withdrawn] fascinated with the Nondescript, and commenced an affair with same, and in so doing lost all interest, desire and what little passion he had so far achieved for his wife. It was some months before this fact became known to me, and, by that time, the obsession was intensely and irrevocably carved into his fevered brain.

Euphemia put the book and chinagraph pencil down on her desk to rub crumbs of sleep from the corners of her eyes. The cutting from the previous week's newspaper had been at her elbow, and now it fluttered noiselessly from her desk to the floor. She eyed it for some seconds where it had come to rest then stuck out her foot to retrieve it. She drew it close with her bare heel and kept it there, under her skirts.

A knock on the bedroom door made her start. Then she remembered that this was the day. 'Come,' she said, and the door swung wide. 'Susan,' she said, looking up.

'Ma'am, they are here.'

'All right. Is everything made ready?'

'Ma'am.'

‘And the room is completely empty now?’

‘Yes, ma’am. Just as you said. And Mr Pemberton says to give you this. I think it’s a letter, ma’am. But I couldn’t be sure.’

Susan handed over the small portfolio she had been keeping behind her back.

‘All right, Susan. You can see to the rest.’

‘Will you not be seeing them after all, ma’am?’

‘No. There’s no need. Just let me know when they have gone.’

‘Yes, ma’am,’ and the door swung shut behind her. From here, the house was utterly silent.

Euphemia untied the tapes at the sides and opened up the stiff covers. Inside, was a familiar document, slightly foxed, slightly dog-eared. With it were two letters which she tore open. The first was from Edward’s solicitor, Mr Bettlesham. She did not read it properly; there was nothing there that she did not already know. The other was from her sister. Carrick House is yours . . . She did not read it further. Euphemia took both letters to the fire and threw them in; she turned away from the sudden flare as the letters began to curl and open up again in the heat. Euphemia closed the covers of the portfolio over the fragile deeds to Carrick House and tied up the tapes.

CHAPTER LXII

BACKSTAGE, ROYAL OPERA HOUSE, LONDON.
FRIDAY, OCTOBER 5, 1866.

'You may come with me now, Mrs Pemberton.'

With tension rising in every part of her, Gwen followed the girl. Under her evening stole, she clasped her purse, which contained, as well as the programme for the evening's opera, her glasses and her fan, the incongruous inclusion of a certain very battered and hard-travelled book. Gwen passed sweaty people dressed in their costumes, and carrying parts of costumes, their greasy make-up running and smudged now after the efforts of their performances. They laughed under the yellow light and joked together, stepping aside to let her pass, not really noticing her. The girl stopped at the end of the long corridor and bowed her head outside the door, waiting for Gwen to catch up.

'Miss Jaspur will see you now, madam.' She leaned forward and tapped lightly on the door before opening it and stepping back to let Gwen go inside. Gwen murmured her thanks to the girl who bobbed a curtsey and would not raise her head. The door shut quietly behind her.

She was sitting with her shrouded profile to the door.

'Miss Jaspur, good evening. Congratulations on a magnificent performance.'

'Thank you. Please, come and sit down with me.'

Gwen looked about the room, and saw that it was furnished very comfortably, if rather elaborately with a lot of lace and ruffles. She sat down and felt a rush of heat flare through her body as a wave of nerves got the better of her.

'I don't mean to take up much of your time; thank you for agreeing to this interview.'

The little woman laughed and leaned back in her seat. 'Do you know, those were his exact words to me.' She suddenly leaned forward to peer through the dark veil. She lifted it away from her face. 'And he kept me awake all night. Though, of course, he did not come to see me any more once he had found you.' Miss Jaspur looked firmly into Gwen's eyes. 'You must have once loved him very much. Perhaps you loved him as much as I once did, to have found strength enough.' She turned her face away. 'Which performance did you mean, when you congratulated me?' She looked briefly into Gwen's eyes again before letting her gaze settle on Gwen's bare shoulder.

'This evening's, I'm sure.'

'Well, congratulations are also due to yourself, Mrs Pemberton. I must say that I like your style. You emerge, free, saved from the gallows and what do you do? Go to the opera, of course! But what do you want here? Aren't we both free now, of him and of each other?'

Gwen's pulse thudded in her throat as she kept her gaze steady. She gripped her purse. 'I have brought something with me—' Her voice broke. 'I have brought something, which I wondered—' She fumbled with the clasp on the purse and managed to bring out the book wrapped in its handkerchief. 'I wondered if you would be able to tell me anything about it.' She held the book out and her hand shook violently. Miss Jaspur took the book from her hands. Gwen watched her turn it over.

'It is in a bad way, I think, Mrs Pemberton.'

'That was all my fault.'

'This little volume has a tale to tell, Mrs Pemberton, I can see.'

Gwen's eyes pricked and welled. 'There is no one left, whom I might ask. Did you not write a book, Miss Jaspur, and publish it?'

'This?' She ran her fingers over the tooling on the spine as Gwen had once done. '*Eternal Blazon*,' she spelled out slowly. 'You won't find another like it on any book stall, Mrs Pemberton. What few were bound are locked away, I think.' Miss Jaspur sat back into her chair and held the stiff book in her lap. 'Mrs Pemberton, I would like to know where you found this.'

'It was sent to me an—'

'Anonymously.' She rose from her seat and turned to face Gwen. 'Mrs Pemberton, I can't tell you why she would have gone to the trouble of doing such a thing, when she might have just told you. Perhaps she was a little afraid.'

'Who was afraid?'

'Isobel Scales. Isobel, his first wife. I did not have the money, then, for books. I did not have the stomach for dangerous games. I learned of it all too late, Mrs Pemberton; after you had gone. My attempts to contact you had come to nothing, but when I met your sister I knew I had failed to stop him.' Miss Jaspur sat down again, and gave the book back to Gwen.

'Did you read it?' Gwen's question was a whisper.

'No.' Miss Jaspur flapped her small hands in the air as if to push it away. 'I had heard of it, of course, but I did not want to read it. The printer was imprisoned for it. And other books, not just that little thing.'

For a long while neither woman said anything. Gwen felt the precision of Miss Jaspur's gaze; she knew Miss Jaspur was trying to fix in her mind the scene of Edward's death. The book slipped from her hands and Gwen knelt on the floor to retrieve it.

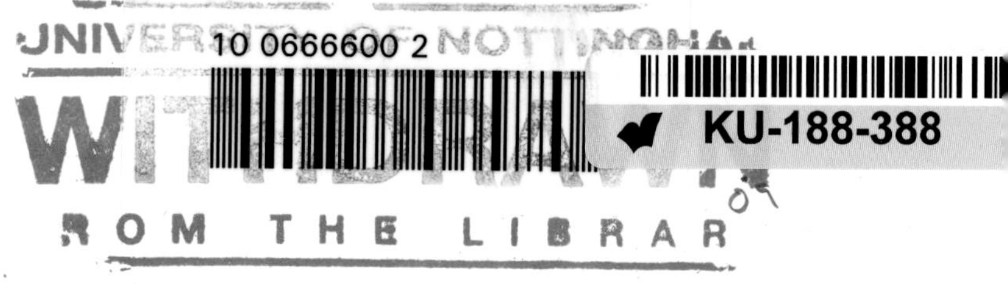

DEATH BY MODERATION

This book addresses an important but little-noticed phenomenon in the revolutionary world of military technology. Across a wide range of otherwise unrelated weapons programs, the Pentagon is now pursuing arms deliberately crafted to be less powerful, deadly, and destructive than the systems they are designed to supplement or replace. This direction is historically anomalous; military forces generally pursue ever-bigger bangs, but the modern conditions of counterinsurgency warfare and "military operations other than war" (e.g., peacekeeping and humanitarian assistance) demand a military capable of modulated force. By providing a capacity to intervene deftly yet effectively, the new generations of "useable" weaponry should enable the U.S. military to accomplish its demanding missions in a manner consistent with legal obligations, public relations realities, and political constraints. Five case studies are provided regarding precision-guided "smart bombs," low-yield nuclear weapons, self-neutralizing antipersonnel land mines, directed-energy antisatellite weapons, and nonlethal weapons.

David A. Koplow is a professor of law at Georgetown University Law Center and Director of the Center for Applied Legal Studies, where students represent refugees who seek political asylum in the United States due to persecution in their homelands because of race, religion, or political opinion. After graduating from Yale Law School in 1978, Professor Koplow served in the U.S. government in the Arms Control and Disarmament Agency (1978–1981), as attorney–adviser and as Special Assistant to the Director, and in the Department of Defense (1997–1999), as Deputy General Counsel for International Affairs. As the latter, he was the senior legal specialist for top Pentagon leadership on the full array of international legal issues, including the use of military force in the Persian Gulf and in Kosovo, the negotiation and implementation of treaties, the law of the sea, the programs of military cooperation and assistance, and the law of outer space. He has published many articles dealing with treaties and U.S. constitutional law in law journals and books on national security and arms control policy.

Death by Moderation

THE U.S. MILITARY'S QUEST FOR USEABLE WEAPONS

David A. Koplow
Georgetown University Law Center

CAMBRIDGE UNIVERSITY PRESS
Cambridge, New York, Melbourne, Madrid, Cape Town, Singapore,
São Paulo, Delhi, Dubai, Tokyo

Cambridge University Press
32 Avenue of the Americas, New York, NY 10013-2473, USA

www.cambridge.org
Information on this title: www.cambridge.org/9780521135344

First published 2010

Printed in the United States of America

A catalog record for this publication is available from the British Library.

Library of Congress Cataloging in Publication data

Koplow, David A., 1951–
Death by moderation : the U.S. military's quest for useable weapons /
David A. Koplow.
p. cm.
Includes bibliographical references and index.
ISBN 978-0-521-11951-1 (hbk.) – ISBN 978-0-521-13534-4 (pbk.)
1. Military weapons – United States – Case studies. 2. Weapons systems – United States – Case studies. 3. United States – Armed Forces – Weapons systems – Case studies. 4. Precision guided munitions – United States. 5. Tactical nuclear weapons – United States. 6. Land mines – United States. 7. Anti-satellite weapons – United States. 8. Nonlethal weapons – United States. I. Title.
UF503.K66 2010
355.80973–dc22 2009017285

ISBN 978-0-521-11951-1 Hardback
ISBN 978-0-521-13534-4 Paperback

To Mort and Marcy

Contents

Preface

"Paper tiger." That's how Mao Zedong famously derided the United States and its military muscle, including its burgeoning nuclear arsenal, during the 1940s and 1950s. There was no denying the devastating force of atomic power – and the Chinese leader was even then attempting to replicate it by enlisting scientific and materiel assistance from the Soviet Union to create a comparable inventory for Beijing. But Chairman Mao recognized that military tools alone were inadequate; even the most overwhelming weaponry can provide no guarantee of success on the battlefield or meaningful control over global political affairs.

The intervening decades have reinforced that message, repeatedly demonstrating that superiority in armaments – as valuable as it may be – hardly suffices to ensure victory, peace, stability, or even survival of a regime. From the jungles of Vietnam to the sands of Palestine to the collapse of the U.S.S.R., qualitative dominance in sophisticated military hardware has failed to translate into effective control of the situation on the ground and has left putative global or regional superpowers frustrated and hamstrung, if not outright defeated.

This book examines that conundrum – and the latest American efforts to overcome it. The focus here is on the ongoing U.S. quest to develop weapons that are more "useable" – weapons that would not merely adorn an arsenal and impress an audience, but that could actually be employed with telling effect on a modern battlefield. In particular, the book examines a series of proposed or emerging military technologies that are remarkable because they are deliberately *less* powerful, *less* deadly, and *less* destructive than their predecessors. Paradoxically, these new generations of armaments – featuring, in various measure, greater precision, shorter duration, less lethality, and reduced collateral damage – may provide more effective power than their larger and more destructive, but also more inexact and crude, predecessors.

This incipient understanding – reflected simultaneously but independently in a wide array of ongoing U.S. weapons programs – emphasizes that values other than sheer firepower matter a great deal and will become even more decisive in the future. The ability to apply organized violence with something of a deft touch will have to characterize U.S. military operations; success today depends on influencing people, inducing them to bend to our will, and that often requires a mixture of both brutality and subtlety. To adapt another line from Mao, if "power grows out of the barrel of a gun," it grows best if the gun is sufficiently focused, precise, and narrowly tailored to achieve a particular purpose – the blunderbuss approach alone will no longer suffice.

To explore that proposition, the book features five case studies – analyses of five vastly different sorts of new weapons embodying the full array of explosive power, technological sophistication, frequency of use, and deadly effect. What they all share in common, however, is a gravitation toward "useability" – they enable the possessor to target a particular person, place, or thing with greater precision and to project a hostile effect in a more discrete, temporary, circumscribed manner. By being less powerful, less apocalyptic than their predecessors, these new, more moderate armaments may accordingly alter the familiar grammar of international conflict and become invoked in combat more often and with greater success.

As background to those five cases, Chapter 1 describes the ongoing "revolution in military affairs," a multifaceted undertaking that augurs broad-gauged transformation in all aspects of U.S. military life, from the structure, organization, and operation of the forces to the next waves of weapons our troops will wield. Over a period of years, these new generations of arms technology will institute changes in military doctrine as fundamental as those occasioned by the introduction of the airplane, the satellite, or the atom. One fundamental hallmark of the current revolution is an unprecedented emphasis on the emergence of "useable" weapons – the goal is not just the accretion of more raw explosive power, but more deft, calibrated power. This development is surprising, if not historically unique, for it runs contrary to the general thrust of centuries of weapons development, which almost monotonically has pursued tools of ever-increasing lethality and destructiveness.

Chapter 2 places this transformation into context by elaborating on the concept of deterrence. The most prominent traditional application of deterrence involves precluding international military aggression by intimidating the opposition. When we lack a robust ability to prevent, to intercept, or to defeat an enemy's attack upon us (or even if we did enjoy that power) a desirable, and often plausible, alternative is to *persuade* the potential enemy not to launch a strike against us in the first place. Often, that persuasion comes in the form of threatening retaliation ("unacceptable damage") in response to any attack, convincing any putative aggressor that the gains from an onslaught would not be worth the losses suffered in return.

The flip side of deterrence is self-deterrence, describing, in this context, a situation in which a country is reluctant or unwilling to exercise its military power, not because of fear of retribution, but for other reasons. The most relevant inhibition here would be a sense that application of excessive or indiscriminate power would be inappropriate, politically and morally unacceptable, and illegitimate. The worst problems of Gulliver in Lilliput arise when a country (arguably, the United States today) possesses an overwhelming military ability to obliterate any foe in all-out combat but does not simultaneously possess a sufficiently refined military capability to wage effective wars at less than the all-out level. If we are self-deterred against using too much power, then we may wind up doing little or nothing at all in effective response to provocations that, although serious, do not warrant the massive use of overly crude weaponry.

Standards of international law reinforce that judgment, and Chapter 3 describes the relevant principles of the "law of armed conflict" that underpin military and diplomatic dealings. Although this body of widely accepted jurisprudence enjoys neither the precision we might like nor the universal adherence it deserves, it provides important principles that align well with the intuitive sense of what is appropriate and justifiable in hostilities. In particular, the hoary concepts of necessity and proportionality, derived from nineteenth-century international diplomatic correspondence, and the accompanying notion of a requirement for discrimination or distinction between combatants and nonbelligerents, retain their validity. Together, these privileged legal obligations channel armed combat into more tolerable, more civilized forms in the hope of avoiding the worst depredations, and they reinforce the progression toward increasing the useability of nascent weapon systems. The fundamental legal requirement to be proportional in our exercise of military force – to sufficiently graduate our applications of violence – constrains our military operations: doing too much is illegal; doing too little is feckless.

Five case studies then follow. Chapter 4 presents the most obvious illustration of a military transformation under way: the creation of precision-guided munitions (PGMs) of various sorts, especially smart bombs for air-to-surface operations. Promising – and already conveying – a genuine revolution in combat, modern bombs and projectiles can be targeted with hitherto unimaginable accuracy and reliability, zeroing in on a selected location while leaving neighboring sites unaffected. This capacity has accorded military planners a much more useable vehicle for projecting power; missions can now be undertaken in settings that would previously have been ruled off-limits out of fear of inflicting unacceptable collateral damage on the surrounding people and places. When we have the ability to do *less* damage by striking and destroying or disabling only the intended target, we gain more freedom of action.

Chapter 5 pursues that proposition in a very different setting: nuclear weapons. The history of the evolving U.S. nuclear arsenal reveals a persistent pressure toward the bigger bang, with modern nuclear leviathans exceeding by several times the explosive power of their forebears; a similar story can be told for the other nuclear countries. But in recent years, some strategists have opined that the hypertrophy of the nuclear arsenal has gone too far – by concentrating on developing such large and overwhelming devices, we have lost (or failed to pursue) the ability to apply lesser nuclear power with a sufficient degree of precision or finesse. They have suggested that a smaller, more restricted nuclear weapon might be the appropriate tool for selected missions, such as attacking an enemy's hardened or deeply buried command bunkers without inflicting massive cratering and widespread radioactive fallout on the surface. If, they reason, we possessed a calibrated nuclear arsenal capable of that kind of deft, localized destruction, we could undertake militarily valuable missions that, at present, remain outside our capacity.

Chapter 6 tests the arguments for useability in a very different setting. Antipersonnel land mines (APL) are much lower than nuclear weapons on the scale of explosive power and much higher on the scale of frequency of use. But in the past decade and a half – in reaction to the deployment of millions, perhaps hundreds of millions, of land mines in the field – the world has awoken to the humanitarian crisis caused by long-lived APL that remain lethally active for years (or decades) after the war has ended and the soldiers have moved on. Many countries, therefore, have responded by pledging to refrain from mine warfare and have negotiated a treaty to ban APL completely. The United States, however, has abstained from joining that instrument, favoring instead pursuit of a new technology of "smart" APL devices that self-destroy or self-neutralize in various measure after a short, predetermined period of time. That way, the Pentagon asserts, we can have the best of both goals: the nonpersistent smart mines enable us to employ the systems in situations in which there is a military advantage in doing so, without contributing to the humanitarian horrors of long-lived "dumb" mines. By making the mechanisms less robust and less durable, so they do not last as long in the field as did the earlier forms, the inventors achieve another dimension of useability.

Chapter 7 continues the exploration by investigating another very different genre of military programs: antisatellite (ASAT) weapons. The United States and the Soviet Union, as global superpowers and the major spacefaring states, explored various incarnations of ASATs throughout the cold war, and more recently, China has entered this insidious competition as well. But each of these ASAT schemes has suffered from inherent defects. Although several of the systems would likely have sufficed to obliterate enemy spacecraft, they would have accomplished that combat mission via crudely destructive explosions (nuclear or conventional) or debris-creating high-speed collisions that would simultaneously endanger the user's own satellites and perhaps inflict erratically widespread damage on the ground as well. Where any antisatellite warfare would be Pyrrhic in that way, the potential users were self-deterred. In contrast, the modern concept for ASAT – to destroy, damage, or disrupt an enemy's satellite via beams of nonexplosive directed energy – again undertakes to accomplish the assigned mission with more finesse and less collateral damage. The new technology – relying on high-energy lasers, microwaves, or subatomic particle beams – is less crudely destructive, again resulting in a more useable capacity while avoiding excessive self-deterrence.

Finally, Chapter 8 addresses one additional emerging technology, or a group of somewhat related technologies lumped under the heading of "nonlethal weapons" (NLW). Although some might see the concept of a nonlethal weapon as an oxymoron (the whole point of fighting, after all, is to inflict pain, incapacity, and death on an enemy force), there are, in fact, many situations in which it is preferable to disorient, disable, or constrain an enemy without killing, or to damage or disrupt enemy equipment without utterly destroying it. NLW advocates, therefore, have sponsored research into a bevy of novel mechanisms, and several of these nonlethal systems are now about to spill out of laboratories and research facilities. Again, the notion is that by providing an intermediate capability – less than invoking traditional lethal force, but more than doing nothing – these developments can scratch an itch in a place that's hard to reach, empowering the military where a forceful and deft presence is required.

Each of these chapters opens with an illustration – a historical (Chapters 1–3) or hypothetical (Chapters 4–8) scenario in which the principles and weapons are demonstrated in realistic settings. These illustrations, based on contemporary or near-term future contingencies, adduce in simplified form the factual predicates and strategic constraints confronting decision-makers in recent or plausible use-of-force imbroglios.

After those disparate case studies, Chapter 9 raises fundamental questions about what we should make of this broad-based, multisector drive toward useability in weapons. The headlong pursuit of useability is not the product of a central directive, emanating from senior Pentagon officials and directed uniformly at all arms programs; nor is it uniquely a hobby horse of the Bush administration or former Secretary of Defense Donald Rumsfeld. But it is now a clear trend, with applications across this wide array of quite different programs – is that a good or a bad thing?

On the one hand, we should welcome the progress toward useability. If it makes our forces more effective, if it enables them to carry out legitimate missions more surgically and to pursue valid national security goals with greater discretion and finesse, it should be welcomed. Reducing collateral damage – thereby validating the legal, political, and public affairs emphasis on avoiding unintended casualties among civilian persons and property – is desirable not only on humanitarian grounds, but also because it enhances the competence of the military as a tool of national policy.

On the other hand, there are profound reasons to be apprehensive about these new capacities, too, and Chapter 9 also outlines the case against useability in the abstract. First, if we come to possess the ability to apply force more deftly, reducing some of the inhibitions against the exercise of power, is it not predictable that we will inevitably come to apply that military force more often? When we shift the nation's traditional cost-benefit calculation about warfare by lowering some of the costs, we must anticipate that reduced self-deterrence will result in an increased willingness – perhaps increased too much – to go to war or to employ selected more deft weapons in ambiguous circumstances. Second, we must also be mindful that any unilateral pursuit of these advanced capabilities will not remain unilateral for long – if increased useability in weapons is advantageous to the U.S. military, then other countries may well reach similar conclusions for themselves, too, and pursue comparable capabilities. Before taking these first steps down the momentous path toward more useable weapons, we should contemplate whether a world filled with these more deft arms is truly to our advantage, because no monopoly can be perpetual.

This vast new armada – precision-guided munitions, low-yield nuclear weapons, smart antipersonnel land mines, antisatellite weapons, non-lethal weapons, and all the rest – carries profound implications for U.S. and global national security policies. Any transformation that enhances the effectiveness of a military force can be wielded for good purposes or for evil – even mechanisms that aim to reduce the frequency and severity of unintended collateral damage can be perverted to horrific ends. And when a new technology – or a revolutionary new approach to military weaponry across the board – influences such a wide array of capabilities, it bears special attention. If American weapons, with increased useability, are no longer "paper tigers," what, exactly, will they become?

Acknowledgments

I owe an enormous debt of gratitude to many individuals who have helped me refine and validate the thesis for this book, investigate and substantiate the evidence for it, and express it with whatever degree of clarity the current book provides. Among these generous individuals (who, of course, bear no responsibility for errors in the text, and who may not fully subscribe to the argument I present) are: Juergen Altmann, James Benoit, Irwin Binder, Michel Bourbonniere, Marshal Brown, Jim Burger, Craig Burton, Tom Cataldo, Ian Corey, Stacy Davis, George Fenton, Nathan Friedman, David Graham, Dick Haddad, Theresa Hitchens, Rob Hunt, Dave Jonas, Frank Kendall, Richard Kidd IV, Andrew Krepinevich, Michael Krepon, James Lawrence, Adam Lovinger, Andy Marshall, Mike Matheson, Murf McCloy, Jonathan Medalia, Steve Metz, Frank Miller, W. Hays Parks, Eric Patterson, Dmitry Ponomareff, John Rawcliffe, Chris Ryder, Stanley Sloan, Scott Smith, John Stevens III, Steve Tuttle, Mick Wagoner, and Sean Watts.

In addition, deep gratitude goes to my colleagues at the Georgetown University Law Center, including Dean T. Alexander Aleinikoff, who extended gracious support during the research and writing phases; the several participants in the faculty workshop, who helped vet the concepts developed here; and the research assistants at the Law Library, who relentlessly tracked down countless obscure documents.

Abbreviations and Acronyms

ABM	Antiballistic missile
ADS	Active denial system
APL	Antipersonnel land mine
ASAT	Antisatellite weapon
AVL	Antivehicle land mine
BW	Biological weapon
BWC	Biological Weapons Convention
C^3	Command, control, and communications
CALCM	Conventional air-launched cruise missile
CBU	Cluster bomb unit
CCW	Convention on Certain Conventional Weapons
CDEM	Collateral damage estimation methodology
CEP	Circular error probable
CW	Chemical weapon
CWC	Chemical Weapons Convention
DoD	Department of Defense
EMP	Electromagnetic pulse
EOGB	Electro-optical guided bomb
ExComm	Executive committee
GPS	Global positioning system
HDBT	Hard and deeply buried target
ICBM	Intercontinental-range ballistic missile
ICJ	International Court of Justice
IED	Improvised explosive device
JASSM	Joint air-to-surface standoff missile
JCS	Joint Chiefs of Staff
JDAM	Joint direct attack munition
JSOW	Joint standoff weapon

KE-ASAT	Kinetic-energy antisatellite weapon
kt	Kiloton
LGB	Laser-guided bomb
LoAC	Law of armed conflict
MAD	Mutual assured destruction
MHV	Miniature homing vehicle
MIRACL	Mid-infrared advanced chemical laser
MOAB	Massive ordnance air blast
MOOTW	Military operations other than war
MOUT	Military operations in urban terrain
MRE	Meal ready to eat
Mt	Megaton
NATO	North Atlantic Treaty Organization
NLW	Nonlethal weapon
OC	Oleoresin capsaicin
OST	Outer Space Treaty
PAROS	Prevention of an arms race in outer space
PGM	Precision-guided munition
RCA	Riot control agent
RMA	Revolution in military affairs
RNEP	Robust nuclear earth penetrator
SAINT	Satellite interceptor
SDB	Small diameter bomb
SIPRI	Stockholm International Peace Research Institute
SLBM	Submarine-launched ballistic missile
SPOT	Satellite Pour l'Observation de la Terre
START	Strategic Arms Reduction Treaty
TASER	Thomas A. Swift's electric rifle
TERCOM	Terrain contour matching
UAV	Unmanned aerial vehicle
UN	United Nations
UNGA	United Nations General Assembly
UNSC	United Nations Security Council
WMD	Weapon of mass destruction

1

Revolutionary Weapons and Transformed War

Scenario 1

During the second week of May 1972, two strategic bridges in war-torn North Vietnam provided the transportation – both literally and symbolically – into the modern era of aerial conflict.

Both bridges – the Long Bien in the city of Hanoi and the Thanh Hoa, about 150 kilometers south – were high-value targets for American bombers; they served as Ho Chi Minh's principal arteries for road and rail shipments to the south, and clogging those chokepoints would have greatly impeded his effort to reinforce and resupply North Vietnamese and Viet Cong brigades. At the same time, both bridges were frustrating and dangerous to attack; they were so well constructed and well defended that waves of U.S. bombs had failed to penetrate them, and scores of aircraft and crews had been lost in the attempt.

The Thanh Hoa Bridge proved to be an especially alluring target. It was 56 feet wide, 540 feet long, and 50 feet above the water, of steel construction with two spans resting upon a 16-foot reinforced concrete pier in the middle of the Song Me River. The central 12 feet of the bridge fed the main trunk rail line that ran down the Vietnam panhandle; two 22-foot-wide concrete highways that constituted Route 1 were cantilevered on the sides.

But the Thanh Hoa Bridge was also an extraordinarily vexatious target. Construction on the bridge was completed only in 1964; between 1965 and 1968, 800 American sorties had attacked it, unloading some 10,000 tons of high explosives. The bridge withstood all onslaughts and, even when damaged, repair crews had always been able to restore it swiftly to normal functioning. Volumes of near misses with inaccurate bombs produced a myriad of craters pockmarking the approaches to the bridge, giving it a vivid uninhabitable "Valley of the Moon" appearance. U.S. forces began to refer grudgingly to Thanh Hoa as "the bridge that would never go down."

Part of the reason for the bridge's resiliency was geographic: hills at either end of the span provided solid bracing for the concrete abutments that anchored it. But a bigger part of its stamina was due to the zealous defensive anti-aircraft installations that surrounded what the Vietnamese referred to as "the Dragon's Jaw." Some 104 American pilots were shot down in the 75-square-mile area around the site.

For example, on April 3–4, 1965, during the American "Rolling Thunder" bombing campaign, 77 determined aircraft deposited 504 750-pound bombs and 298 rockets against Thanh Hoa, yet it remained mockingly erect – charred, but still fully functional. Five U.S. aircraft were downed in the effort.

The Long Bien Bridge (also known as the Paul Doumer Bridge, after the French governor general of Indochina, who had conceived the transportation system for the country and had inaugurated the bridge in 1902) was a similarly critical transportation node over the Red River in the nation's capital. Four of the five major rail lines coming from the north (including those conveying all freight from China and the port city of Haiphong) converged to cross the Long Bien, as did much of the truck traffic. Twenty-six trains, carrying 6000 tons of supplies, transited the bridge daily.

To a casual observer, the Long Bien Bridge might have appeared vulnerable or even delicate. At 8500 feet in length, including its terminal viaducts, it was the longest bridge in North Vietnam, with a series of 19 graceful metal segments, and it was designed by the same architect who produced the Eiffel Tower. That stylishness, however, concealed the bridge's deadly aspect – the North Vietnamese defended this unique asset with 300 anti-aircraft guns, 85 surface-to-air missile sites, and several MiG fighters at surrounding bases.

Like the Thanh Hoa Bridge, the Long Bien site had been singled out as a priority target, and whenever the American rules of engagement permitted missions against urban targets in Hanoi, the bridge was struck hard – but never suffered more than temporary disruptions in service. Also like Thanh Hoa, Long Bien had been responsible for sending disproportionate numbers of American pilots to their deaths or to horrific prisoner of war camps.

Everything changed radically for these "indestructible" bridges in 1972. "Operation Linebacker" authorized increased pursuit of northern targets and – more critically – improved technology brought modern guided aerial bombs into widespread play for the first time.

On April 27, 1972, a flight of eight U.S. Air Force F-4 Phantoms attacked the Thanh Hoa Bridge with five 2000-pound Walleye II electro-optical guided munitions. These bombs were not notably larger than those that had been applied in earlier engagements, but the greater accuracy of their placement inflicted far more damage on the bridge and far less "collateral damage" on the surrounding locations. Additionally, the new weapons permitted safer tactics for the attacking aircraft, affording them a greater "standoff" capability rather than having them fly directly over the superdefended site, and no pilots were lost.

On May 13, the American crews revisited the Thanh Hoa, dropping 15 more electro-optical bombs, nine 3000-pound laser-guided bombs, and 48 conventional bombs. This time, the western span of the bridge was knocked off its struts, and the remainder of the structure was rendered unusable for months. Again, no aircraft were lost.

Between those two strikes, the May 10 action against the Long Bien Bridge was even more dramatic. Sixteen F-4s, accompanied by several other planes to suppress the North Vietnamese defensive fire, launched 29 precision bombs against the site. At least 12, perhaps 16, of these struck the bridge directly, destroying or damaging several of the spans. The next day, four more aircraft undertook a "mop-up" mission, delivering eight more precision bombs, ruining three more sections of the bridge – and again, losing no pilots. The Long Bien Bridge carried no further traffic until the end of the war.

The numerical "box score" of these engagements provides a stunning contrast with the earlier campaigns. In the 1965 raids on the Thanh Hoa, 77 aircraft were used and 189 tons of ordnance were dropped, all with little lasting effect. In 1972, with the debut of precision-guided munitions, only eight aircraft were employed in the two raids, and 33.5 tons of more deft munitions were expended – and this time, the bridge was knocked out of commission. Numerous other northern bridges also quickly fell under the weight of the improved U.S. weaponry and, for the first time – at the moment when the war was already effectively lost – American bombers were able to interdict vital traffic routes faster than the North Vietnamese could repair them.[1]

[1] A.J.C. Lavalle (ed.), The Tale of Two Bridges, US Air Force Southeast Asia Monograph Series, Vol. 1, Monograph 1, 1976; Melvin F. Porter, Linebacker: Overview of the First 120 Days, U.S. Air Force, Project CHECO Report, September 27, 1973; George Friedman and Meredith Friedman, The Future of War: Power, Technology, and American

The introduction of precision-guided aerial bombs in 1972 was a discontinuity – an abrupt break with prior technology – and it inaugurated distinctly new military capabilities and helped reform the way modern wars would be fought. The sudden innovation came too late to alter the outcome of the Vietnam War, but it illustrates the phenomenon of occasional, dramatic big bursts in revising weapons technologies and military operations. This chapter analyzes those episodic nonlinear moments and describes the current metamorphosis already under way.

WORLD AT WAR

War is a tragic but remarkably persistent fact of the human experience. Historians Will and Ariel Durant calculated in 1968 that the world had witnessed only 268 war-free years in the previous 3421.[2] Another leading authority, the Stockholm International Peace Research Institute (SIPRI), annually reports on the number of ongoing major armed conflicts: the tally for 2007 revealed 14 active wars, a relatively low number given that 33 miscellaneous conflagrations, many persisting for many years, had raged somewhere or another between 1998 and 2007.[3] Another source, the Friends Committee on National Legislation, applying slightly different criteria, found 14 significant current armed conflicts (each inflicting 1000 or more battle deaths) at the start of 2008 and another 21 precarious hot spots around the globe that could quickly slide into or revert to open war.[4]

One more sanguinary statistic helps us translate those overall numbers into a more human scale: during the twentieth century, there were more than 100 million warfare-related deaths.[5]

World Dominance in the 21st Century, 1996; Eduard Mark, Aerial Interdiction: Air Power and the Land Battle in Three American Wars, 1994; Michael Russell Rip and James M. Hasik, The Precision Revolution: GPS and the Future of Aerial Warfare, 2002.

[2] Will and Ariel Durant, The Lessons of History, 1968, p. 81. See also William Eckhardt, Civilizations, Empires and Wars: A Quantitative History of War, 1992.

[3] Lotta Harbom and Peter Wallensteen, Patterns of Major Armed Conflicts, 1998–2007, in Stockholm International Peace Research Institute, Yearbook 2008: Armaments, Disarmament, and International Security, p. 72. See also Lotta Harbom and Peter Wallensteen, Patterns of Major Armed Conflicts, 1997–2006, in Stockholm International Peace Research Institute, Yearbook 2007: Armaments, Disarmament, and International Security, p. 79; Lotta Harbom and Peter Wallensteen, Patterns of Major Armed Conflicts, 1990–2005, in Stockholm International Peace Research Institute, Yearbook 2006: Armaments, Disarmament, and International Security, p. 108.

[4] Daniel Smith, World at War, 37 Defense Monitor No. 1, Special Issue, January/February 2008, p. 3.

[5] Ruth Leger Sivard, World Military and Social Expenditures 1996 (16th ed.), 1996, p. 7.

To support that frenzied activity, nations of the world have routinely invested major slices of their respective treasuries in the various implements of war – research, development, and procurement of weapons have always been booming businesses. Global military spending now tops an inconceivable $1.3 trillion annually, and armaments production accounts for approximately one-quarter of that total.[6]

Not only have human beings demonstrated an enormously voracious appetite for the hardware of warfare, they have manifested an insatiable curiosity about developing new types of military toys – perhaps a creativity and persistence unparalleled in other aspects of human activity. As George Bernard Shaw put it in "Man and Superman" (speaking through the character of the devil):

> I tell you that in the arts of life, man invents nothing; but in the arts of death, he outdoes Nature herself, and produces by chemistry and machinery all the slaughter of plague, pestilence, and famine.... In the arts of peace, Man is a bungler... his heart is in his weapons.[7]

Most of the time, this energized inventiveness aims to promote weapons of ever-increasing lethality and destructive power. That is, the warfighters and their political masters seek augmented capacities for inflicting death and obliterating enemy property – that is often the whole point of fighting a war – and the combatants prize any tools that can accomplish those apocalyptic missions more effectively, more swiftly, and on a wider scale.

There are, of course, other desiderata in weapons design, too – defense establishments simultaneously prefer armaments that are inexpensive, simple to maintain, sufficiently rugged to withstand battlefield conditions, and easy to transport. And weaponry alone does not begin to tell the whole story of a nation's military effectiveness – British military historian J. F. C. Fuller argued in 1919 that weapons account for 99 percent of victory, but most other observers would contest that assessment, citing

[6] Peter Stalenheim, Catalina Perdomo, and Elisabeth Skons, Military Expenditure, in Stockholm International Peace Research Institute, Yearbook 2008: Armaments, Disarmament, and International Security, p. 175. See also Peter Stalenheim, Catalina Perdomo, and Elisabeth Skons, Military Expenditure, in Stockholm International Peace Research Institute, Yearbook 2007: Armaments, Disarmament, and International Security, p. 267; J. Paul Dunne and Eamon Surry, Arms Production, and Peter Stalenheim, Damien Fruchart, Wuyi Omitoogun, and Catalina Perdomo, Military Expenditures, in Stockholm International Peace Research Institute, Yearbook 2006: Armaments, Disarmament, and International Security, p. 387, 295; International Institute for Strategic Studies, The Military Balance, 2006.

[7] George Bernard Shaw, Man and Superman: A Comedy and a Philosophy, Act 3, pp. 142–43, 1903.

the centrality of training, discipline, morale, logistics, leadership, and other features.[8]

Still, efforts to increase the lethality of armaments are typically at or near the top of the military's "wish list." New generations of military hardware typically feature bigger bangs for the bucks, and the abilities to exert a lethal or destructive force over a wider area, strike more suddenly or for a longer time, or overcome defensive battlements are major sales points.

Attempts to document empirically this ever-increasing destructive power are doomed to frustration over the full array of definitional issues. (How does one measure lethality precisely? How does one interpolate antipersonnel and antimateriel devices?) But as Trevor Dupuy has demonstrated, even crude subjective judgments reflect a rising trend line, from ancient swords, pikes, and battle axes, to various adaptations of bows and arrows, to primitive firearms. The popularization of gunpowder makes his historical trend line of violence bow upward, with the emergence of a series of arquebuses, flintlocks, muskets, and rifles of increasing range, accuracy, and power, and a sequence of ever-more-devastating types of cannons and other artillery. In the twentieth century, this notional "lethality curve" arcs even more sharply upward, with relatively rapid injections of modern machine guns and automatic weapons, tanks, bombers, missiles, and, of course, nuclear devices.[9]

Even more dramatic, within each particular category of weaponry there seems to be an inexorable pressure for each new generation to outdo its predecessor in deadly effectiveness. New types of hand grenades, for example, or assault rifles, or battle tanks secure funding and earn the right to deployment and use when they command greater destructive force. Likewise, new bombers or new battleships are not necessarily larger than their forerunners, but in the effervescent international arms races, each new weapon seems almost automatically to advertise itself as possessing greater lethal firepower. In the same vein, it is no accident that as bad as mustard gas, lewisite, phosgene, and the rest of the witches' brew of chemical toxins were in the trenches of World War I, the next generation

[8] J.F.C. Fuller, Armament and History: A Study of the Influence of Armament on History from the Dawn of Classical Warfare to the Second World War, 1945, p. 18.

[9] See, for example, Trevor N. Dupuy, The Evolution of Weapons and Warfare, 1984, p. 92, 286–89; Max Boot, War Made New: Technology, Warfare, and the Course of History, 1500 to Today, 2006, p. 300 ("the lethality of weapons increased roughly two-thousand-fold between the Peloponnesian Wars and World War II, between the days of spears and those of tanks").

of chemical weapons – the nerve gases sarin, soman, and tabun pioneered (but not widely used) for World War II – were much worse.

It is unnecessary to be crudely reductionist in describing this progression – obviously, there is a lot more going on in the military–industrial complex. But one unmistakable tendency is the introduction, dissemination, and use of military artifacts of ever-increasing deadliness and destructiveness. Weapons capable of greater explosive power, inflicting their effects over a wider area or for a longer period of time or against more resistant targets, have continuously displaced their earlier, smaller, simpler, and less devastating antecedents.

REVOLUTIONS IN MILITARY AFFAIRS

These boosts in weapons technology do not necessarily occur at a smooth pace or a predetermined rate. To the contrary, it often appears that technological innovation in military matters is marked by episodic discontinuities – sudden jumps in weapons capabilities that inject radically new performance possibilities. These seismic shifts, characterized as "revolutionary moments," not only jumble the weapons inventories themselves, they also provide occasion for radical revisions in the organization of military structures, in the concepts of operation for the forces, and in the roles and missions assigned to them.

Important spurts of creativity of this kind do not occur often; historians disagree about which breakthroughs have achieved sufficient magnitude in opening new modes of military operation to qualify as genuine revolutions.[10] Among the most salient historic paradigm-shifting global

[10] Boot, supra note 9; Andrew F. Krepinevich, Cavalry to Computer: The Pattern of Military Revolutions, National Interest, Fall 1993/1994; Theodor W. Galdi, Revolution in Military Affairs? Competing Concepts, Organizational Responses, Outstanding Issues, Congressional Research Service Report for Congress, 95–1170 F, December 11, 1995; MacGregor Knox and Williamson Murray (eds.), The Dynamics of Military Revolution 1300–2050, 2001; Colin S. Gray, Strategy for Chaos: Revolutions in Military Affairs and the Evidence of History, 2002; Jeffrey McKitrick, James Blackwell, Fred Littlepage, George Kraus, Richard Blanchfield, and Dale Hill, The Revolution in Military Affairs, in Barry R. Schneider and Lawrence E. Grinter (eds.), Battlefield of the Future: 21st Century Warfare Issues, Maxwell Air Force Base, Air Chronicles, 1995; Dupuy, supra note 9, at 286–307; Williamson Murray, Thinking About Revolutions in Military Affairs, Joint Forces Quarterly, Summer 1997, p. 69; Stephen Biddle, Military Power: Explaining Victory and Defeat in Modern Battle, 2004; Michael J. Mazarr, Jeffrey Shaffer, and Benjamin Ederington, The Military Technical Revolution: A Structural Framework, Center for Strategic and International Studies, March 1993; Clifford J. Rogers (ed.), The Military Revolution Debate: Readings on the Military Transformation of Early Modern Europe, 1995.

transformations – the articulation of new things and ideas that interrupt preconceived notions of how to fight – we may plausibly include the following dramatic illustrations:

- The six-foot yew longbow, exploited by a vastly outnumbered English army in the Battle of Crecy in 1346 in northern France at the turning point of the Hundred Years' War. The archers employed this revolutionary technology – featuring longer range and double the rate of fire of existing crossbows – to devastate a vaunted French corps of armored knights, overnight displacing heavy mounted cavalry as the dominant force in land warfare.
- Sail-powered warships armed with cannons, which in the sixteenth century proved faster and more maneuverable than oared galleys and were capable of destroying an enemy fleet from afar without the peril of boarding the victim's vessel and engaging in hand-to-hand combat. Naval vessels and naval warfare, which had not evolved much in the two millennia since classical Greek archetypes, were suddenly transformed by French and Venetian leadership, converting ships from mere floating garrisons of soldiers to mobile artillery platforms.
- The Napoleonic revolution, through which the French were able to mobilize a vastly larger army than their opponents (via the *levee en masse* (mass uprising or conscription)), to motivate that populist cadre with the scent of patriotism, and to improve and standardize the organization and command structure of their formations.
- The adaptation to military operations of Industrial Revolution breakthroughs in communications, transportation, and manufacturing, such as the telegraph, the railroad, and the mass-produced rifled firearm. As illustrated during the American Civil War of 1861–1865, these advances enabled unprecedented speed and coordination in shuttling well-armed troops, equipment, and supplies rapidly to remote theaters of battle.
- A second naval revolution in the late nineteenth century and early twentieth century, as ironclad ships, steam turbine power, and large rifled cannons (and slightly later, submarines and torpedoes) radically altered the structure of engagements at sea and enabled new modes of combat, such as the strategic blockade. The British 1906 launch of the *HMS Dreadnought* triggered a naval arms race, as all major powers sought to mimic the breakthrough pulsed by the leading seafaring state of the day.

- The cluster of deadly innovations in World War I, in which different experts would identify tanks, aircraft, radios, or chemical weapons as the most important cutting edge of the modern implements of war. The popular image of stagnant armies mired in incessant trench warfare obscures appreciation of the novel military technologies introduced in that era.
- The even more deadly innovations of World War II, through which the debut of *blitzkrieg* (lightning war), aircraft carriers, amphibious warfare, radar, and long-range bombing vividly demonstrated the advantages of speed and the sudden assemblage of mass firepower.[11]
- The nuclear weapon, especially when mated to the long-range ballistic missile, which exposed enemy societies – indeed, the entire world – to the specter of mass annihilation within 30 minutes after the push of a button. Although earlier societies had often feared that military innovation would threaten to destroy all human life, by the 1960s or 1970s, that specter became a realistic possibility – and our utter defenselessness swiftly led to altered concepts of war, deterrence, and peace.
- The space age, which creates the conditions for instantaneous global reconnaissance and communications, improving leaders' abilities at command and control over the forces in the field and dissipating much of the "fog of war" that has always obscured battlefield conditions.
- The contemporary computer or information revolution and associated quantum leaps in microelectronics, sensors, laser- and other directed energy devices, and automated control technologies, which thoroughly alter both the strategic (big picture, long range) and tactical (localized) aspects of battlefield management and conduct.

These illustrations suggest that a true revolution in military affairs is a rare, complex phenomenon, without standardized features. Sometimes,

[11] William H. McNeill captures the spirit of the moment and the concomitant burst of military inventiveness, writing, "World War II was different. The accelerated pace of weapons improvement that set in from the late 1930s, and the proliferating variety of new possibilities that deliberate invention spawned, meant that all the belligerents realized by the time fighting began that some new secret weapon might tip the balance decisively. Accordingly, scientists, technologists, design engineers, and efficiency experts were summoned to the task of improving existing weapons and inventing new ones on a scale far greater than ever before." William H. McNeill, The Pursuit of Power: Technology, Armed Force, and Society Since A.D. 1000, 1982, p. 357.

multiple innovations occur nearly simultaneously, altering combat across a wide range of venues. Sometimes, the revolutionary moment is protracted, as decades are required for countries to recognize the value of the incipient transformation and to inculcate their fighting forces with new understandings and modified technologies. Sometimes, a revolution is driven by, or associated with, a particular agent or sponsor, as with Napoleon's eponymous innovations; at other times, the change benefits from multiple parents. Often a viable offset or countermeasure will spring up almost as soon as the novel breakthrough itself is registered, swiftly rebalancing offenses and defenses in new equilibria. Frequently, a revolution is not confined solely to the military apparatus, as relevant inventions bleed from the civilian sector into the arena of combat and back again.

Primacy in a revolutionary era can confer significant advantages upon the successful entrepreneur. By effectively marshaling a new weapon, a revised strategy, or a novel concept of operations, even a relatively small country can succeed against more formidable opposition – at least until the rivals also adapt, aping or even improving upon the innovation. Whoever first succeeds in exploiting the chariot, the stirrup, or the iron sword can acquire at least a transitory advantage over larger, wealthier foes – and even ephemeral advantages may be worth seizing.

In all of this, it is a mistake to focus exclusively on new weapons hardware; the novel equipment may be the most visible manifestation of a revolution in military affairs, but even more important is a transformed mode of thought or analysis, a reformation in understanding how modern armies, navies, and air forces can be wielded to maximum effect. Organization, structure, and missions must be revised to accommodate the new hardware, and it is frequently observed that the most important revolution in military affairs must occur in people's minds and not in their equipment. It is instructive to note, for example, that tanks, mobile artillery, and radios were generally available to many countries prior to World War II, but only in Germany did the leadership seize proper insight regarding revised operational concepts and the new culture of command necessary to create the devastation of the *blitzkrieg*.

TODAY'S REVOLUTION(S)

The application of precision-guided munitions (PGMs) in 1972 against the North Vietnamese bridges, as described in Scenario 1, provides a recent, handy illustration of a modern revolution, and it ushered in an era with implications as profound as those associated with the introduction of the longbow, gunpowder, and the airplane.

The United States pioneered this particular new PGM technology, as detailed in Chapter 4. The true depth of the revolution, however, lies not only in the dramatically increased accuracy of one country's laser-, optical-, or satellite-guided aerial bombs but also in the speed with which these capabilities can be assigned to their targets, the relative safety of the air crews that deliver them from standoff ranges, and the "economy of force" savings implicated by the exquisite reliability of a system in which, to a large extent, only one bomb is required to destroy one target.

These features imply not only that aerial bombardment is more powerful than ever before but also that the nature of the conflict is dramatically altered: we can undertake missions today that we may not have risked in earlier eras; we can intercept an enemy's efforts at movement, concealment, or reconstruction faster than he can initiate them; and we can minimize damage inflicted upon the enemy's civilians and infrastructure to spare them the worst ravages of conflict and to facilitate postwar recovery.

Other countries, of course, are pursuing the American edge in these technologies; laser-guided munitions have already proliferated, although no other military force has incorporated this aspect of the revolution in military affairs nearly as thoroughly as the Pentagon. As a general matter, it now appears that revolutions occur, and their effects spread, much more rapidly today than before. In the Information Age, technologies such as aerial precision guidance may ingratiate themselves to diverse military planners much more swiftly and comprehensively than the *HMS Dreadnought*.

The contemporary picture is rendered even more complicated by the fact that there are now multiple military innovations under way simultaneously – distinct revolutionary technologies are growing like so many ravenous cultures in a globalized Petri dish. As several chapters of this book illustrate, autonomous yet oddly similar processes are under way in a number of independent military sectors, each carrying the possibility of remarkable modification of prior warmaking processes. Former Secretary of Defense William Perry referred to this emerging weaponry synergy as developing a "system of systems."[12]

[12] James R. Blacker, Understanding the Revolution in Military Affairs: A Guide to America's 21st Century Defense, Progressive Policy Institute, Defense Working Paper No. 3, January 1997, p. 5.

More important, these revolutions seem irreversible. After the ratchet has been turned with the introduction of a novel technology, there is no going back. As Steven Metz and James Kievit have observed,

> the increase in combat effectiveness associated with revolutions in military affairs is cumulative. Since the collapse of the Roman Empire, there has been no instance of reversion to pre-revolutionary levels. While the aggregate change may vary, the trend in combat effectiveness has been steadily upward, with short periods of intense movement (revolutions) and longer periods of evolutionary development.[13]

In any event, the notion of a modern revolution has caught on within the U.S. military, among the top civilian leadership, and increasingly among the general public. Even before his first presidential election, George W. Bush spoke of the "tremendous opportunity... created by a revolution in the technology of war," noting that "our military and our nation are entering another period of consequences – a time of rapid change and momentous choices." Ambitiously, he added, "The real goal is to move beyond marginal improvements – to replace existing programs with new technologies and strategies. To use this window of opportunity to skip a generation of technology."[14]

BUREAUCRATIC STRUCTURES AND CONTROVERSIES

Three signs that revolutionizing the military has become mainstream: First, the concept has developed its own widely acknowledged abbreviation, RMA (revolution in military affairs), which can now be found in most standard glossaries of military vocabulary. Second, the U.S. Department of Defense has spawned not one but several distinct organizational subunits charged with at least part of the responsibility for moving the RMA forward.[15]

The first of these bureaucratic units, the Pentagon's Office of Net Assessment, has been led since 1973 by the redoubtable Andy Marshall. Functioning as the department's internal think tank, this office has long

[13] Steven Metz and James Kievit, Strategy and the Revolution in Military Affairs: From Theory to Policy, June 27, 1995, p. 11.

[14] George W. Bush, A Period of Consequences, address at the Citadel, South Carolina, September 23, 1999, p. 4.

[15] U.S. Department of Defense, Transformation Planning Guidance, April 2003; U.S. Department of Defense, Elements of Defense Transformation, October 2004; U.S. Department of Defense, Military Transformation: A Strategic Approach, Fall 2003; U.S. Joint Forces Command, Joint Transformation Roadmap, January 21, 2004.

been the catalyst for authoritative studies on military innovation and war gaming designed to provoke the military establishment to generate, evaluate, and pursue outside-the-box thinking. In January 1994, then-Deputy Secretary of Defense William Perry augmented this office by establishing a task force to coordinate a department-wide RMA project. More recently, then-Secretary of Defense Donald Rumsfeld chartered the Office of Force Transformation as the nidus to help focus additional attention on facilitating big jumps in technology and, just as important, on recognizing and incorporating that technology into the department's standard operating procedures. The Office of Force Transformation was renamed the Office of Force Transformation and Resources in 2007 as part of a general reorganization of policy-making bureaus,[16] and the proliferation of RMA units continues, with the Joint Chiefs of Staff and the individual military services sustaining offices and programs designed to look a couple of decades into the future to imagine the contributions that may be realized by weapons systems that are today not even on the drawing boards. In addition, of course, the "shadow government," comprising defense intellectuals in think tanks, consulting firms, nongovernment organizations, and academia, has elicited another corps of RMA analysts (both inside the United States and elsewhere) – espousing both pro and con viewpoints.[17]

[16] The "realignment" of the transformation office reportedly reflects an attitudinal change in the Pentagon bureaucracy: Originally, the notion of transformation was an "outside" idea, foist upon a largely recalcitrant department. Now, these alternative views have become welcome, even mainstream, and the need for a separate, dedicated transformation office has diminished. See Interview: Ryan Henry, Defense News, May 7, 2007.

[17] See, for example, Eliot A. Cohen, A Revolution in Warfare, 75 Foreign Affairs No. 2, March/April 1996, p. 37; Edward N. Luttwak, Toward Post-Heroic Warfare, 74 Foreign Affairs No. 3, May/June 1995, p. 109; Ralph Peters, The Counterrevolution in Military Affairs: Fashionable Thinking About Defense Ignores the Great Threats of Our Time, 11 Weekly Standard No. 20, February 6, 2006; Colin S. Gray and John B. Shelton, Spacepower and the Revolution in Military Affairs: A Glass Half-Full, in Peter L. Hays, James M. Smith, Alan R. Van Tassel, and Guy M. Walsh (eds.), Spacepower for a New Millennium, 2000, p. 239; Michael J. Vickers, The Revolution in Military Affairs and Military Capabilities, in Robert L. Pfaltzgraff, Jr. and Richard H. Shultz, Jr. (eds.), War in the Information Age, 1997, p. 29; Qiao Liang and Wang Xiangsui, Unrestricted Warfare, Beijing: PLA Literature and Arts Publishing House, February 1999; John Garstka, The Transformation Challenge, NATO Review, April 18, 2005; Andrew F. Krepinevich, Jr., The Military-Technical Revolution: A Preliminary Assessment, Center for Strategic and Budgetary Assessments, 2002; Michael O'Hanlon, Technological Change and the Future of Warfare, 2000; Lawrence Friedman, The Revolution in Strategic Affairs, Adelphi Paper No. 318, 1998.

A third and perhaps most imposing indicator of the political-military arrival of the concept of an RMA is the fact that it has already elicited its own counterrevolution. Without missing a beat, a number of defense intellectuals, perhaps most vivid among them Army Col. H.R. McMaster, have critiqued the transformation process as self-delusional, hubristic, and fundamentally flawed by overreliance upon technology. The unsatisfactory experiences in Iraq and Afghanistan, the revisionists argue, demonstrate the inherent limitations of new gadgets and gizmos in land warfare against a determined, indigenous, adaptive enemy. We cannot blithely rely upon transformational weaponry to allow us to fight the kind of war we would like to fight instead of the war that the enemy's tactics compel us to fight.[18]

Even with all this attention, the term "revolution in military affairs" still defies easy definition. The rhetoric of military-technical revolution was originally popularized in the 1970s by Soviet theorists such as Marshal Nikolai V. Ogarkov, chief of the Soviet General Staff, as shorthand for the quantum leaps in weaponry witnessed in World War I and World War II – and for the incipient next surge in armament inventiveness that Soviet strategists foresaw in the realms of electronics, sensors, directed energy, miniaturization, and computers. Today, references to RMA are sometimes displaced by the language of "defense transformation," and the terms are frequently used interchangeably to describe "large-scale, discontinuous, and possibly disruptive changes in military weapons, concepts of operations (i.e., approaches to warfighting), and organization."[19]

The vogue of defense transformation additionally implicates a variety of military science trends and controversies, reverberating well beyond the scope of this book: whether the U.S. military should focus more attention on high-technology long-range aerial weaponry or on traditional infantry grunts bearing "boots on the ground"; whether the apparatus should be reconfigured to feature more special operations and

[18] H.R. McMaster, On War: Lessons To Be Learned, 50 Survival No. 1, February-March 2008, p. 19.

[19] Ronald O'Rourke, Defense Transformation: Background and Oversight Issues for Congress, Congressional Research Service Report for Congress RL32238, August 30, 2006. Historians have used the term "military revolution" for at least 50 years to describe upheavals such as the transformation of the art of war in Europe during the 16th and 17th centuries. Clifford J. Rogers, The Military Revolutions of the Hundred Years War, in Clifford J. Rogers (ed.), The Military Revolution Debate: Readings on the Military Transformation of Early Modern Europe, 1995, p. 55.

low-intensity counterinsurgency capacities; whether the U.S. armed forces should strive to become even more "joint" (with even less emphasis upon autonomous operations by the separate military services); whether to embrace "effects-based operations" (the concept of swiftly circumventing, neutralizing, or avoiding concentrations of enemy power instead of engaging the enemy in traditional attrition warfare); and how to incorporate "network-centric warfare" (the emphasis upon speedy and reliable communications, surveillance, and identification throughout the battlefield to minimize combat uncertainties and confusion). Each of these controversies swirls around RMA, further complicating transformation efforts.

In all of this, the emphasis is upon creating a more agile, more multipurpose, and more connected force, on the understanding that something beyond the ordinary incremental evolution of weapons will be required to achieve the higher operational tempo and greater effectiveness demanded by modern military engagements.

Revolutionary Missions

The incentives for pursuing these multifarious transformed capabilities spring from several sources. In part, the RMA is driven by the fact that the American military is today being tasked to perform a much wider array of unorthodox missions than before. In addition to traditional major combat operations, which could be contested in a diverse range of geographic regions in coalition with (and against) a spectrum of other militaries, we must now confront the specter of sustained counterinsurgency operations. Less organized, but no less deadly, irregular, guerrilla, or terrorist opponents might attack American forces (and civilian populations under their protection) asymmetrically with tactics that avoid direct confrontations but that exploit vulnerabilities and frequently occur inside urban areas where civilian persons and property abound rather than in isolated battlefields or uninhabited forests.

These counterinsurgency and counterterrorism operations are now frequent enough, important enough, and different enough from the inherited portrait of World War II-style combat that they demand new means and methods of deployment. The stresses of adapting our tactics, personnel, and rules of engagement to awkward pressures (including the embarrassment of having to relearn the obscured lessons about the failure to win hearts and minds in Vietnam) provide a pressing incentive for crafting new weaponry, too.

In an even greater departure from the military's established roles and missions, U.S. forces these days engage in frequent "military operations other than war" (MOOTW). This ungainly term covers everything from peacekeeping in tumultuous regions, to counterdrug operations and resistance to international organized crime, to low-intensity counterterrorism forays, to humanitarian assistance missions in response to floods, famines, and other natural disasters, to a variety of other functions that assist civil law enforcement authorities.

These encounters can be of first-order importance, and although they may not inherently be military operations, often it is only the military that can provide the manpower, the logistics, and the modicum of force required to impose or maintain order. But obviously, something more deft than traditional armaments and bulk firepower will be required to achieve the objectives – we need to be able to act without overreacting, and that can be a most delicate game.

The point is that as our forces are injected into harm's way – into a variety of harms' ways – a range of irregular capabilities may be demanded to cope with the chameleon character of modern war. Troops must be organized, trained, and equipped to respond with finesse to these novel contingencies where something other than (or in addition to) the legacy systems' massive quantity of rockets, bullets, and overwhelming bombardment is required.

In addition, some of the impetus that makes the current force transformation chic percolates from a sober realization of failure or inadequacy: even with America's overwhelming military superiority, we do not always win. Despite access to unparalleled economic, diplomatic, and military superpower resources, the U.S. military was conspicuously unable to achieve national objectives in Vietnam in the 1970s, in Lebanon in the 1980s, in Somalia in the 1990s, and in Iraq and Afghanistan in the 2000s. Rogue regimes, failed states, and entrenched insurgencies frustrate us today, seemingly immune to our vastly superior armed muscle.

There are, of course, multiple explanations for each of those debacles, but one common feature is the humbling recognition that even Herculean military power does not always translate into political or diplomatic fortune. As Gen. David Petraeus has cautioned about the snarl in Iraq, "We cannot kill our way out of this endeavor." Apparently, then, we should be doing something differently today to harness our armed forces for more international effectiveness in pursuit of tomorrow's national goals – and that is where the revolution in military affairs comes in.

This is not surprising. History suggests that defeat (or at least frustration) in combat is frequently the cauldron within which RMAs are shaped. A country that is stressed on the battlefield is more likely to dedicate itself to pursuing transformation; adversity and apprehension can be the catalysts for generating a culture of innovation.

Revolutions in military affairs, after all, are inherently disquieting experiences – for the society as a whole and especially for leading members of the military establishment, who will have grown up in and been promoted for excellence through a particular structure now being challenged. It is rudely jolting for existing forces to be blasted out of old modes of thought and operation – especially during a time of ongoing combat, when the incentive to think about immediate problems is at its apex and when taking the opportunity to step back and reflect creatively upon longer-term challenges will seem a diversion.

We should therefore never be surprised when conservative instincts resist change; departing from the comfort zone of orthodox military traditions requires a psychic leap that is always difficult for some to accept. Many jaundiced observers have noted that the received wisdom of any established "religion" (e.g., the military's traditional ways of doing things) will not easily be changed as long as the established "priesthood" is still calling the shots.

The reluctance to embrace radical change is one reason why history is littered with examples of countries – including the leading dinosaurs of an era – that failed to anticipate or to respond with alacrity to an incipient RMA. China, for example, had developed gunpowder and functional firearms a century before Europe, but failed to take advantage of the innovation and fell behind. In the twentieth century, Great Britain squandered its naval supremacy by failing to recognize the advantages of carrier-based aviation. Stephen Biddle has calculated that through history, the bigger, wealthier state has prevailed in state-to-state warfare barely more than 50 percent of the time; effective marshaling of national resources, mating emergent technology with available assets, is often key.[20]

AN ODDITY IN THE ONGOING TRANSFORMATION

As Donald Rumsfeld put it, "A revolution in military affairs is about more than building new high-tech weapons – although that is certainly part of it.

[20] Biddle, supra note 10, at 21; McKittrick, *et al.*, supra note 10, at 4.

It is also about new ways of thinking and new ways of fighting... All the high-tech weapons in the world won't transform the U.S. armed forces unless we also transform the way we think, train, exercise, and fight."[21]

Concealed among those competing new modes of thought and action is one feature of the current RMA that seems historically peculiar and that provides the inspiration for this book. Many newly emerging military technologies, as surveyed in Chapters 4 through 8, share one surprising characteristic: they are designed to produce weapons that are noticeably less powerful, less deadly, and less destructive than the systems they are designed to supplement or replace.

This development – the conscious pursuit of paradigm-shifting armaments intended to inflict reduced levels of violence – is remarkable, counterintuitive, and contrary to the general trend of military history. For the first time, we are directing our defense laboratory wizardry along the azimuth of self-restraint, and it is important to tease out the reasons why this odd sort of revolution is occurring and what its implications may be.

One powerful motivating force is the recognition that in many situations, existing tools are simply too powerful for what we seek to accomplish: they are too crude, too imprecise, too overwhelming, last too long, and hurt too many people. By being excessive, they generate inhibitions – political, moral, and legal – that justifiably make us reluctant to commit them to the fray. Even when the proffered weapon might accomplish a valid military objective, and even when its application would provide a definite battlefield advantage, we will be deterred if the tactic foreseeably results in too much avoidable carnage.

Especially in an era when the victims of warfare are disproportionately civilians – and by some accounts, upwards of 90 percent of the casualties in today's wars are noncombatants – the desire to exercise some modicum of restraint is essential. As discussed in Chapter 3, the existing law of armed conflict mandates a proportionality judgment matching provocation and response, and political sensitivities to the globally televised specter of helpless civilian sufferings drive the same message. Civilized societies are, to an increasing extent, self-deterred against inflicting more harm than they have to – even in pursuit of a just war.

Increasingly, the goal of combat is not simply and crudely to destroy an enemy – we are uninterested in conquest, retribution, or exploitation – but

[21] Donald H. Rumsfeld, Transforming the Military, Foreign Affairs, May/June 2002, p. 20, 21, 29.

to restore (or create) a society we can coexist with under conditions of security, stability, and international peace. We hope (as with Germany and Japan a half-century ago) to facilitate the reemergence of a reasonable, functioning civil society in our enemy's state, fostering its participation in a harmonious political and commercial community. Utter devastation, even if helpful in winning the war, may disserve those long-term objectives.

At core, however, the inducement for pursuing less devastating weapons arises not from a naïve desire to be nicer to enemy civilians (or even to enemy soldiers) but from a hard-headed desire to become even more effective in operating in today's complex and confusing battle environment. The primary function of the military is still – as it is crudely but accurately phrased – to kill people and break things, but in the modern era, we do not want to break too many things or kill the wrong people. Instead, we now demand greater specificity in wreaking our havoc, and we pursue weapons that facilitate drawing precise lines along the battlements.

Laser-guided bombs, as applied against the Long Bien and Thanh Hoa bridges, provide a vivid illustration of the concept. They aim to produce a powerful effect upon a target, but inextricably associated with that goal is the objective of reducing the probability of harming others. We maintain, or increase, the likelihood of accomplishing the mission while harming the surrounding civilians less, wasting less ordnance in near-misses, and exposing air crews to less jeopardy.

As discussed in Chapter 2, increased military effectiveness carries an additional payoff as well: If our weapons are more deft in this way, and if they can be wielded with greater effectiveness and reduced collateral damage, we will less often be inhibited – less self-deterred – in applying them. That greater willingness to exert force should translate into greater credibility and enhanced effective power. Our enemies would then believe that we can and will exercise ourselves with discretion and precision, not artificially constrained by worries about overdoing it. The ability to project power with specificity should then also mean that we are called upon to carry out our implicit military threats less often.

DIMENSIONS OF USEABILITY

As a heuristic matter, it might be desirable to create a new metric – a device for combining into a single measurement all the ways in which a military tool could be less (or more) deadly and destructive. This assessment of precision or deftness would objectively evaluate all newly proposed arms as well as their predecessors already serving in the Pentagon's arsenal. However, each of the emerging systems described in this book presents distinct aspects or dimensions of power – and they thereby suggest different mechanisms for being more useable.

Precision-guided munitions (as presented in Chapter 4) provide the most obvious illustration – they offer the prospect of exquisitely accurate aerial bombardment, helping ensure that the targeted site, and only the targeted site, is struck. The advent of low-yield nuclear weapons (Chapter 5) provides an equally clear advantage: smaller bombs – even smaller nuclear bombs – will create a reduced lethal radius, restricting the zone of death and destruction. In contrast, smart antipersonnel land mines (Chapter 6) are not placed with greater accuracy than older types of mines nor do they carry less explosive power. Instead, they offer the prospect of less indiscriminate force because they contain self-neutralizing features that render them inoperable after a relatively short period of time. They may thus be less lethal in the temporal sense – they do not last as long in the field as existing types of mines. Therefore, they inflict less unintended carnage upon civilians and others who may come along years after the mines are strewn.

Modern or proposed antisatellite (ASAT) weapons (Chapter 7) present yet another version of useability. These directed energy systems are less destructive than prior or existing ASAT systems in two senses: First, when they attack a target, they generate no outer space debris from explosions or collisions – debris increasingly recognized as presenting a significant and growing hazard to our own and others' spacefaring vehicles. Second, directed energy systems might be capable of creating a temporary or partial impairment of satellite operations, not necessarily destroying or permanently disabling a target but allowing it to return to normal functioning after the crisis had passed. Finally, nonlethal weapons (Chapter 8) are designed to affect personnel or equipment in a partial or transitory manner, impeding, disrupting, or disabling the target without killing or obliterating it. In each instance, the suggestion runs, by inflicting less damage, the proffered weapon may be more useable – there are circumstances in which we might be willing to exert our power if we could effectively do so while minimizing the amount of death and destruction we inflict.

Current Department of Defense programs have adopted this strategy in these five distinct and dispersed weapons areas. This has not been the result of any single, deliberate top-down strategy; there has been no big-picture DoD Directive that has adopted the goal of reduced lethality or increased useability across the board. Nor is it the product of a single president or secretary of defense; some of the programs, such as laser-guided smart bombs, are decades old, whereas other inventions have yet to see the light of day. And this pursuit of reduced-power weaponry is manifestly not a system-wide or rationally calculated response to any particular provocation such as the end of the cold war or the emergence of global terrorism.

At the same time, it is surely not a coincidence that the same remarkable, historically anomalous trend is emerging simultaneously in such disparate sectors. Something peculiar is going on here that runs contrary to the general trends of military history and that responds to the unique threats and opportunities we confront in the twenty-first century.

We cannot know at this point how thorough and successful the current RMA earthquake will be or how zealously and quickly these less deadly components will be injected into it. The exponents of Department of Defense procedures continually stress that transformation is a "process," not an "objective," so there is no "finish line," no moment when the reform is completed and the operators can wipe their hands and declare success. Instead, the task of remaking America's warfighting machinery will be perpetual, and the need to adjust to rapidly evolving dangers and opportunities will always be with us.

BOTTOM LINE

The term "revolution in military affairs" has been used so often (at least inside the Washington, D.C., Beltway) and in so many different contexts that it has lost some of its rhetorical punch. It has emerged as an all-purpose buzz phrase to describe everything from high strategy and sudden modification in battlefield maneuvering to bookkeeping modifications in the way the Department of Defense conducts its internal budgeting, auditing, and procurement practices.

There is nonetheless something far more than empty sloganeering here. If my observation is correct, and if the U.S. military is now undertaking – across the broad array of five different types of military systems surveyed in subsequent chapters – the unprecedented effort to capitalize upon more useable weapons of reduced power and lethality, then this eccentric development has profound ramifications for the future of combat and international relations.

At various points in history, many people, recoiling against absurd horror of armed conflict, have suggested or at least hoped that evolving weaponry would render warfare obsolete. If the terror and wastage of combat were increased so much through the accumulation of ever-deadlier implements, would leaders and citizens awaken to the stunning reality that some other mechanism must be developed to resolve international disputes peacefully?

As recounted by Donald Kagan, a Polish entrepreneur, Ivan Bloch, published a late–nineteenth-century six-volume tract exposing the reality that war had become too awful to embark upon – it would be futile and suicidal to unleash the then-emerging gruesome implements of violence. "The dimensions of modern armaments and the organisation of society have rendered [war's] execution an economic impossibility," Bloch wrote. The symmetric development of modern tools of military mayhem would inevitably lead to stalemate and "increased slaughter on so terrible a scale as to render it impossible to push the battle to a decisive issue."[22]

Alfred Nobel, the Swedish polymath who combined expertise in chemistry, engineering, and manufacturing to invent and mass produce dynamite, also captured the notion that the trauma of modern weapons might "scare straight" all of mankind. Conversing with a prominent peace activist in 1892 after she had returned from an International Peace Congress in Berne, Switzerland, he projected, "Perhaps my [dynamite] factories will put an end to war even sooner than your congresses. On the day when two army camps may mutually annihilate each other in a second, all civilized nations will probably recoil with horror and disband their troops."[23]

Those hopeful (?) prognostications proved inexact – even nuclear weapons, the apotheosis of mankind's nefarious inventiveness, have failed to abolish warfare. Some weapons – not just atomic powered but others surveyed in subsequent chapters, too – have indeed become so mighty, and so awful to contemplate, that their utility has been reduced; there just are not very many circumstances in which it makes military sense to employ such limitless destructive weight.

But the world has so far responded to that reality not by abolishing warfare but by developing additional types of weapons, now including an increasing array of less powerful substitutes. The army, navy, air force, and marines of the future will not be constrained by possessing only a few categories of armaments and will not have to select among devices

[22] Quoted in Donald Kagan, On the Origins of War and the Preservation of Peace, 1995, pp. 2–3.

[23] Nicholas Halasz, Nobel: A Biography of Alfred Nobel, 1959, p. 241.

so overly powerful as to be unappealing. They will also possess, if the current RMA proceeds along its ordained trajectory, a complementary array of more deft, more useable weapons, too.

Revolutions in military affairs do not just happen; conscious, directed, and inspired human activity is required to imagine new tools, develop associated technologies, and incorporate them into revised military structures and battle plans. At the same time, the internal logic of an RMA and the permutations of military research and development cannot be fully controlled or even predicted. We can set goals, encourage certain types of discoveries, and foster a climate of inventiveness – most of all, we can decide rationally what (if anything) to do with the fruits of military inventions. But the power of unleashed creativity, in the military as in other endeavors, is unruly.

At the same time, we have to be sensitive to the fact that the United States does not operate in a global vacuum – the current RMA may start with a "Made in the USA" label, but it cannot indefinitely remain the province of any one power. NATO allies and other economically developed powers have been the first to jump onto the bandwagon, but China, Russia, and others have also been quick to acknowledge the potential of the full field of new methodologies. The nature of technology is to spread – and in the era of the Internet, it spreads much more rapidly than the English longbow or Napoleon's *levee en masse*.

The impossibility of forever maintaining a unilateral advantage in weapons applications reminds us that just because a technological turn of art makes an RMA possible, that does not necessarily make it desirable. At the moment, the laboratory inventiveness – in the five examples discussed, as well as in others – is outstripping our ability to think carefully through all their extended consequences. We are plunging ahead with defense transformation in some novel, surprising directions: What are its implications?

BIBLIOGRAPHY

A. J. Bracevich, Preserving the Well-Bred Horse, 37 National Interest, Fall 1994, p. 43

J. Marshall Beier, Discriminating Tastes: 'Smart' Bombs, Non-Combatants, and Notions of Legitimacy in Warfare, 34 Security Dialogue No. 4, December 2003, p. 411

Stephen Biddle, Military Power: Explaining Victory and Defeat in Modern Battle, 2004

Jeremy Black, War: Past, Present & Future, 2000

James R. Blacker, Understanding the Revolution in Military Affairs: A Guide to America's 21st Century Defense, Progressive Policy Institute, Defense Working Paper No. 3, January 1997

Max Boot, War Made New: Technology, Warfare, and the Course of History, 1500 to Today, 2006

Peter J. Boyer, Downfall: How Donald Rumsfeld Reformed the Army and Lost Iraq, The New Yorker, November 20, 2006

Bernard and Fawn M. Brodie, From Crossbow to H-Bomb, 1973

George W. Bush, A Period of Consequences, address at the Citadel, South Carolina, September 23, 1999

James Jay Carafano, Jack Spence, and Kathy Gudgel, A Congressional Guide to Defense Transformation: Issues and Answers, Heritage Foundation Backgrounder No. 1847, April 25, 2005

Eliot A. Cohen, A Revolution in Warfare, 75 Foreign Affairs No. 2, March/April 1996, p. 37

Jeffrey R. Cooper, Another View of the Revolution in Military Affairs, Proceedings of the Fifth Conference on Strategy, U.S. Army War College Strategic Studies Institute, April 1994

J. Paul Dunne and Eamon Surry, Arms Production, in Stockholm International Peace Research Institute, Yearbook 2006: Armaments, Disarmament, and International Security, p. 387

Trevor N. Dupuy, The Evolution of Weapons and Warfare, 1984

Will and Ariel Durant, The Lessons of History, 1968

William Eckhardt, Civilizations, Empires and Wars: A Quantitative History of War, 1992

James R. Fitzsimonds and Jan M. Van Tol, Revolution in Military Affairs, Joint Forces Quarterly, Spring 1994, p. 24

George Friedman and Meredith Friedman, The Future of War: Power, Technology, and American World Dominance in the 21st Century, 1996

Lawrence Friedman, The Revolution in Strategic Affairs, Adelphi Paper No. 318, 1998

J.F.C. Fuller, Armament and History: A Study of the Influence of Armament on History from the Dawn of Classical Warfare to the Second World War, 1945

Theodor W. Galdi, Revolution in Military Affairs? Competing Concepts, Organizational Responses, Outstanding Issues, Congressional Research Service Report for Congress, 95–1170 F, December 11, 1995

John Garstka, The Transformation Challenge, NATO Review, April 18, 2005

Colin S. Gray, The Influence of Space Power upon History, 15 Comparative Strategy 293, 1996

Colin S. Gray, Strategy for Chaos: Revolutions in Military Affairs and the Evidence of History, 2002

Colin S. Gray, How Has War Changed Since the End of the Cold War?, 35 Parameters, Spring 2005, p. 14

Colin S. Gray and John B. Shelton, Spacepower and the Revolution in Military Affairs: A Glass Half-Full, in Peter L. Hays, James M. Smith, Alan R. Van

Tassel, and Guy M. Walsh (eds.), Spacepower for a New Millennium, 2000, p. 239
Nicholas Halasz, Nobel: A Biography of Alfred Nobel, 1959
Lotta Harbom and Peter Wallensteen, Patterns of Major Armed Conflicts, 1990–2005, in Stockholm International Peace Research Institute, Yearbook 2006: Armaments, Disarmament, and International Security, p. 108
Lotta Harbom and Peter Wallensteen, Patterns of Major Armed Conflicts, 1997–2006, in Stockholm International Peace Research Institute, Yearbook 2007: Armaments, Disarmament, and International Security, p. 79
Lotta Harbom and Peter Wallensteen, Patterns of Major Armed Conflicts, 1998–2007, in Stockholm International Peace Research Institute, Yearbook 2008: Armaments, Disarmament, and International Security, p. 72
B.H. Liddell Hart, The Revolution in Warfare, 1946
Ronald Haycock and Keith Neilson (eds.), Men, Machines, and War, 1988
Human Security Centre, Liu Institute for Global Issues, University of British Columbia, Human Security Report, 2005
International Institute for Strategic Studies, The Military Balance, 2006
International Institute for Strategic Studies, Strategic Survey 1995–1996, 1996, p. 29
Interview: Ryan Henry, Defense News, May 7, 2007
Donald Kagan, On the Origins of War and the Preservation of Peace, 1995
Frederick W. Kagan, Finding the Target: The Transformation of American Military Policy, 2006
John Keegan, A History of Warfare, 1993
Zalmay M. Khalilzad and John P. White (eds.), The Changing Role of Information in Warfare, 1999
MacGregor Knox and Williamson Murray (eds.), The Dynamics of Military Revolution 1300–2050, 2001
Andrew F. Krepinevich, Cavalry to Computer: The Pattern of Military Revolutions, National Interest, Fall 1993/1994
Andrew F. Krepinevich, The Military-Technical Revolution: A Preliminary Assessment, Center for Strategic and Budgetary Assessments, 2002
A.J.C. Lavalle (ed.), The Tale of Two Bridges, U.S. Air Force Southeast Asia Monograph Series, vol. 1, Monograph 1, 1976
Robert Leckie, Warfare, 1970
Adrian R. Lewis, The American Culture of War: The History of U.S. Military Force from World War II to Operation Iraqi Freedom, 2007
Qiao Liang and Wang Xiangsui, Unrestricted Warfare, Beijing: PLA Literature and Arts Publishing House, February 1999
Martin Libicki, Information & Nuclear RMAs Compared, National Defense University Strategic Forum No. 82, July 1996
Edward N. Luttwak, Toward Post-Heroic Warfare, 74 Foreign Affairs No. 3, May/June 1995, p. 109
Douglas A. MacGregor, Transformation Under Fire: Revolutionizing How America Fights, 2003
Robert Mandel, Security, Strategy, and the Quest for Bloodless War, 2004

Eduard Mark, Aerial Interdiction: Air Power and the Land Battle in Three American Wars, 1994
Michael J. Mazarr, Jeffrey Shaffer, and Benjamin Ederington, The Military Technical Revolution: A Structural Framework, Center for Strategic and International Studies, March 1993
Anthony D. McIvor (ed.), Rethinking the Principles of War, 2005
Jeffrey McKitrick, James Blackwell, Fred Littlepage, George Kraus, Richard Blanchfield, and Dale Hill, The Revolution in Military Affairs, in Barry R. Schneider and Lawrence E. Grinter (eds.), Battlefield of the Future: 21st Century Warfare Issues, Maxwell Air Force Base, Air Chronicles, 1995
William H. McNeill, The Pursuit of Power: Technology, Armed Force, and Society Since A.D. 1000, 1982
Phillip S. Meilinger, Precision Aerospace Power, Discrimination, and the Future of War, 15 Aerospace Power Journal No. 3, Fall 2001, p. 12
Steve Metz, Non-Lethality and the Revolution in Military Affairs, in Malcolm Dando (ed.), Non-Lethal Weapons: Technological and Operational Prospects, Jane's On-Line Special Report, November 2000
Steven Metz and James Kievit, Strategy and the Revolution in Military Affairs: From Theory to Policy, June 27, 1995
Williamson Murray, Thinking About Revolutions in Military Affairs, Joint Forces Quarterly, Summer 1997, p. 69
National Defense Panel, Transforming Defense: National Security in the 21st Century, December 1997
Robert L. O'Connell, Of Arms and Men: A History of War, Weapons, and Aggression, 1989
Michael O'Hanlon, Technological Change and the Future of Warfare, 2000
Ronald O'Rourke, Defense Transformation: Background and Oversight Issues for Congress, Congressional Research Service Report for Congress RL32238, August 30, 2006
William A. Owens, A Report on the JROC and the Revolution in Military Affairs, Marine Corps Gazette, August 1995, p. 47
William A. Owens, The Once and Future Revolution in Military Affairs, Joint Force Quarterly, Summer 2002, p. 55
Geoffrey Parker, The Military Revolution: Military Innovation and the Rise of the West, 1500–1800, 1988
Ralph Peters, The Counterrevolution in Military Affairs: Fashionable Thinking About Defense Ignores the Great Threats of Our Time, 11 Weekly Standard No. 20, February 6, 2006
Melvin F. Porter, Linebacker: Overview of the First 120 Days, U.S. Air Force, Project CHECO Report, September 27, 1973
Richard A. Preston and Sydney F. Wise, Men in Arms: A History of Warfare and its Interrelationships with Western Society (4th ed.), 1991
Michael Russell Rip and James M. Hasik, The Precision Revolution: GPS and the Future of Aerial Warfare, 2002
Clifford J. Rogers (ed.), The Military Revolution Debate: Readings on the Military Transformation of Early Modern Europe, 1995

Ian Roxborough, From Revolution to Transformation, Joint Forces Quarterly, Autumn 2002, p. 68

Donald Rumsfeld, 21st Century Transformation, address at National Defense University, Fort McNair, Washington, D.C., January 31, 2002

Donald H. Rumsfeld, Transforming the Military, Foreign Affairs, May/June 2002, p. 20

George Bernard Shaw, Man and Superman: A Comedy and a Philosophy, 1903

Ruth Leger Sivard, World Military and Social Expenditures 1996 (16th ed.), 1996

Daniel Smith, World at War, 37 Defense Monitor No. 1, Special Issue, January/February 2008, p. 3

Peter Stalenheim, Damien Fruchart, Wuyi Omitoogun, and Catalina Perdomo, Military Expenditures, in Stockholm International Peace Research Institute, Yearbook 2006: Armaments, Disarmament, and International Security, p. 295

Peter Stalenheim, Catalina Perdomo, and Elisabeth Skons, Military Expenditure, in Stockholm International Peace Research Institute, Yearbook 2007: Armaments, Disarmament, and International Security, p. 267

Peter Stalenheim, Catalina Perdomo, and Elisabeth Skons, Military Expenditure, in Stockholm International Peace Research Institute, Yearbook 2008: Armaments, Disarmament, and International Security, p. 175

Alvin and Heidi Toffler, War and Anti-War: Survival at the Dawn of the 21st Century, 1993

U.S. Department of Defense, Transformation Planning Guidance, April 2003

U.S. Department of Defense, Military Transformation: A Strategic Approach, Fall 2003

U.S. Department of Defense, Elements of Defense Transformation, October 2004

U.S. Government Accountability Office, Military Transformation: Clear Leadership, Accountability, and Management Tools Are Needed to Enhance DOD's Efforts to Transform Military Capabilities, report to congressional committees, GAO-05-70, December 2004

U.S. Joint Chiefs of Staff, Joint Vision 2010, 1996

U.S. Joint Chiefs of Staff, Joint Vision 2020, June 2000

U.S. Joint Chiefs of Staff, Peace Operations, Joint Publication 3–07.3, October 17, 2007

U.S. Joint Forces Command, Joint Transformation Roadmap, January 21, 2004

Martin van Creveld, Technology and War: From 2000 B.C. to the Present, 1989

Martin van Creveld, The Transformation of War, 1991

Michael J. Vickers, The Revolution in Military Affairs and Military Capabilities, in Robert L. Pfaltzgraff, Jr. and Richard H. Shultz, Jr. (eds.), War in the Information Age, 1997, p. 29

Simon P. Worden and Martin E.B. France, Towards an Evolving Deterrence Strategy: Space and Information Dominance, 20 Comparative Strategy, 2001, p. 453

Quincy Wright, A Study of War (2nd ed.), 1965

2

Deterrence and Self-Deterrence

Scenario 2

Events in and around Cuba in October 1962 brought the planet closer to World War III than at any time before or since. The superpowers ratcheted up their cold war nuclear and conventional weapons to the highest state of readiness; the diplomats stumbled through imperfect communications, misunderstood motivations, and outright deceit; and President John F. Kennedy later remarked that he personally calculated the odds on nuclear war breaking out as "between one out of three and even."

The queasy path toward that precipice began in 1959, when Fidel Castro's revolution ousted the former dictator, Fulgencio Batista, and turned the country sharply leftward. There followed, in short order, a series of uncompensated expropriations of privately owned property, a comprehensive trade embargo imposed by the United States, and an ill-fated invasion at the Bay of Pigs – all of which drove Castro into the willing arms of the Soviet Union's Premier Nikita Khrushchev and propelled Cuba to the pinnacle of the American domestic political agenda.

In the summer of 1962, the U.S.S.R. and Cuba secretly and rapidly began construction of an elaborate set of installations across the island for a series of air fields, ground bases, surface-to-air missile sites, and – most ominous of all – launchers for nuclear-armed ballistic missiles. Up to 42 medium-range (2000 km) SS-4 missiles and 24 intermediate-range (4000 km) SS-5 missiles were planned; these would be capable of holding at risk most of the population of the continental United States, with flight times of only 20 minutes or less.

This covert encroachment of the muscular Soviet presence only 90 miles from American territory was laden with both military and political freight. First, the addition of the planned warheads would greatly increase Moscow's capacity for inflicting horrifying carnage on the United States, at a time when the U.S.S.R.'s home-based intercontinental-range missile force was greatly inferior to that of the United States. Even with that augmentation, Khrushchev's missile fleet would remain numerically and qualitatively behind Kennedy's – but inadequate intelligence-gathering capabilities kept the American administration largely in the dark about the true extent of the U.S. advantage, and in Washington, D.C., it felt as if a seismic shift was occurring in the delicate balance of deliverable nuclear weapons.

Second, in political terms, the Soviets' sudden acquisition of a Cuban nuclear outpost would have significant repercussions in the propaganda and public-relations competition in the Western Hemisphere and throughout the world. Again, however, the underlying reality was not quite so dramatic: Although it might seem that Khrushchev was undertaking a dramatic and unprecedented incursion into the American "sphere of influence," in fact, the opposite type of juxtaposition had already occurred. The United States had long maintained medium- and intermediate-range nuclear missiles and bombers in Western Europe on the doorstep of the Warsaw Pact nations and had recently introduced a squadron of 15 Jupiter missiles into Turkey. Still, the abrupt change in the status quo – and the fact that Soviet leaders blithely insisted in both public and private conversations that they were not installing any offensive missiles in Cuba – seemed of critical importance.

It was not until October 16, 1962 that an American U-2 spy plane acquired high-altitude photographs unambiguously revealing the Soviets' preparation of an SS-4 missile site near San Cristobol. Over the next few days, feverish construction activity on the island was matched by feverish aerial reconnaissance by the U.S. Air Force and the CIA. American intelligence officials also monitored 20 large ships en route from the U.S.S.R. to Cuba, presumably transporting additional missile-related cargo, and analysts estimated that some of the controversial bases could be fully operational within a few days – by the end of October at the latest.

President Kennedy's innermost circle of advisors convened in an "Executive Committee" (ExComm) of the National Security Council to assess the unraveling crisis and advise the president. Five options were on the table. First was the possibility of doing nothing: The United States could calmly acknowledge that it, too, had disseminated military bases and nuclear arms around the world and assert that there was nothing illegal or improper about doing so; we had nothing to fear from the U.S.S.R. adopting a parallel course. This rationalization would have preserved the peace and sustained what had become a substantial U.S. lead in the nuclear arms race. However, passive acquiescence would surely have been interpreted by Khrushchev, Castro, and other global leaders as spineless irresolution on the part of the young president, with long-term implications for future controversies; it also would have constituted political suicide domestically. A second option was to rely exclusively on diplomatic pressures. Kennedy could have (in confidential exchanges and/or in public) requested, argued, and demanded withdrawal of the missiles, soliciting the support of European and other allies and engaging the United Nations in the tumult. This option, like the first, would have avoided warfare but would likewise, almost certainly not have resulted in the removal of the missiles, thereby dealing the United States a significant public humiliation.

Turning to forceful options, the ExComm considered the notion of launching a preemptive air strike against the missile sites to destroy them before they could become operational. The Air Force cautioned, however, that such an attack could not be undertaken with "surgical" precision – there would doubtless be many Cuban and Soviet casualties, perhaps triggering escalation into a wider war – nor could the generals guarantee that all of the offending missiles would be destroyed by an initial bombing salvo. Accordingly, a fourth option was also developed: a full-scale land, sea, and air invasion of Cuba. The ExComm considered this course – projecting more than 1000 air sorties on the first day backed up by an amphibious force of more than 180,000 troops – to have a greater likelihood of obliterating the missiles before they could be used. (Unknown to the Americans, however, some of the nuclear weapons were already operational by mid-October, and the Soviets might well have launched them against American invaders at the first sign of aggression from the north.) The invasion force would also have taken as part of its mission the defeat and overthrow of Castro, but as the scope of the operation crept upward, the risk of inciting general war in the Caribbean, and most likely well beyond it, rose concomitantly.

Finally, an intermediate option called for the United States to declare and enforce an immediate partial naval blockade of Cuba. This maneuver would have intercepted the Soviet ships carrying additional offensive nuclear materials to the island, impeding the completion of the provocative installations, but would not have, by itself, compelled the abandonment of construction or removal of the hardware already installed.

As the unprecedented crisis deteriorated over the next few fateful days, the Americans attempted behind-the-scenes diplomacy, but to no avail, as the mendacious Soviets continued to deny that they had dispatched anything other than modest defensive support to Castro.

Kennedy then rejected the ExComm's preemptive surprise attack scenarios as an immoral "Pearl Harbor in reverse" and selected the blockade option (changing the name to "quarantine," which sounded less provocative). On October 22, he announced to the breathless American public the discovery of the missile construction sites and his imposition of the quarantine, adding a proclamation that "it shall be the policy of this nation to regard any nuclear missile launched from Cuba against any nation in the Western Hemisphere as an attack by the Soviet Union on the United States, requiring a full retaliatory response on the Soviet Union."

Tensions then reached fever pitch. The U.S. Navy moved quickly to demarcate the quarantine line, three Marine battalions were dispatched to reinforce the base at Guantanamo Bay, the Army surged to position 125,000 troops in Florida, 20 nuclear aircraft were scrambled, and the nation's nuclear missile alert level was raised to DEFCON 2 for the first time ever. Castro likewise mobilized his military forces in anticipation of an invasion, and the Soviets, both in Cuba and around the globe, precipitously heightened their battle readiness. The CIA reported that five of the missile sites appeared to be fully operational.

In one of the most celebrated diplomatic maneuvers of the cold war era, Khrushchev responded to Kennedy with public bluster and private pragmatism. The Soviets in fact sent two overlapping proposals to resolve the crisis: the first promised withdrawal of the contentious missiles if the Americans would promise not to invade Cuba or support any invasion by others. The second, delivered the next day, upped the ante by demanding, in addition, the withdrawal of the American missiles from Turkey as a compensatory offset.

Kennedy strategically decided to respond only to Khrushchev's first, more conciliatory, message, and undertook not to invade Castro – as well as issuing an even more strident ultimatum for the immediate withdrawal of Soviet missiles. Behind the scenes, the president also authorized his brother, Attorney Gen. Robert F. Kennedy, to inform the Soviet embassy that the U.S. missiles in Turkey would be quietly withdrawn within 4 or 5 months.

On October 28, the apocalyptic deal worked. The Soviet ships unilaterally stopped dead in the water as they approached the American quarantine line, and Khrushchev announced that the contentious missiles would be removed from Cuba and the offending installations dismantled. The world then collectively exhaled in relief, and U.S. Secretary of State Dean Rusk famously commented, "We were eyeball to eyeball, and the other fellow just blinked."

No one was completely satisfied with the outcome of the Cuban Missile Crisis. Those thirteen white-knuckled days humiliated Khrushchev, leading to his ouster two years later by a Soviet Politburo embarrassed by his "hare-brained schemes" – both his initiation of the showdown and his forced retreat from it. Castro felt betrayed by the Soviets – set up for a confrontation and then abandoned when things got tough. Many in the U.S. military felt that Kennedy, too, had displayed insufficient resolve – the opportunity to attack Castro and remove a thorn in America's side should not have been missed.

But cooler heads prevailed. The offensive missiles were verifiably removed from Cuba within two months, the U.S. Navy stood down from the quarantine, and the fifteen American Jupiter missiles (already obsolete by that time) were withdrawn from their base near Izmir, Turkey. The showdown also inspired the two superpowers to craft a Hotline Agreement, to establish a reliable direct communications link between Moscow and Washington, D.C., to facilitate timely resolution of future diplomatic contretemps.

The Cuban Missile Crisis has spawned a cottage industry in political science analysis – as the world's closest brush with Armageddon, it has provided fertile ground for analysis, introspection, and recommendation.[1] For our purposes, the incident also establishes the most vivid and focused illustration of the principle and practice of the arcane science of deterrence.

WHAT IS DETERRENCE?

Deterrence is essentially a psychological phenomenon: the effort to create in someone else's mind a compelling incentive to do (or, more precisely, to refrain from doing) a particular action for fear or distaste of the consequences we would impose. In military terms, the strategist attempts to manipulate other parties' calculations of their individual and national options – to persuade them (without firing a shot or inflicting a casualty) that the course of action that we favor is, all things considered, the most attractive open to them. By adjusting the other side's perceived gains and losses, we hope to make them see that resistance to, or violation of, our

[1] See, inter alia, Graham T. Allison, Essence of Decision: Explaining the Cuban Missile Crisis, 1971; Elie Abel, The Missile Crisis, 1966; Dino A. Brugioni, Eyeball to Eyeball: The Inside Story of the Cuban Missile Crisis, 1991; Abram Chayes, The Cuban Missile Crisis: International Crises and the Role of Law, 1974; Robert F. Kennedy, Thirteen Days: A Memoir of the Cuban Missile Crisis, 1971; U.S. Department of State, Foreign Relations of the United States, 1961–1963, vol. XI; Thinkquest.org, Fourteen Days in October: The Cuban Missile Crisis, http://library.thinkquest.org/11046/.

preferred path would incur unacceptable risks or consequences for them. As the U.S. Department of Defense defines it, "Deterrence is a state of mind brought about by the existence of a credible threat of unacceptable counteraction."[2]

At a higher level of abstraction, deterrence is a prosaic phenomenon of daily life, with applications in penology (cautioning potential miscreants, "don't do the crime if you can't do the time"); in business competition (warning that if one firm cuts its prices, others will follow, triggering a price war that could harm them all); in road rage (intimidating other drivers with the threat that if you cut me off in traffic, I'll switch lanes and cut you off worse); and, perhaps most pervasively, in parenting (establishing, or attempting to establish, a logical and transparent system of rewards and punishments for guiding a growing child's pattern of socially acceptable behavior.)

International relations, however, is the field in which the notions of deterrence have become most prominent, especially regarding the still-primitive sector of reciprocal military relations, where more sophisticated forms of communications and bargaining have yet made few inroads. The cold war antipathy between the superpowers, in particular, provided the locus for the articulation of the guiding concepts of these imposed restraints. As expressed by the U.S. Joint Chiefs of Staff "Doctrine for Joint Nuclear Operations,"

> Strategic deterrence is defined as the prevention of adversary aggression or coercion that threatens vital interests of the United States and/or our national survival. Strategic deterrence convinces adversaries not to take grievous courses of action by means of decisive influence over their decision making.[3]

Deterrence came to play this central role in U.S.-U.S.S.R. relations accidentally, only because of the absence of better alternatives. The preferred strategy would ordinarily be to *prevent* an enemy from attacking us successfully, through construction of adequate defensive fortifications that could blunt, repel, or defeat any onslaught – we would rather rely upon physical interdiction instead of the precarious restraints in the "state of mind" of a Manichean rival. But the odious dynamics of the nuclear age – the awesome destructiveness of even a single nuclear weapon, coupled with the speed of ICBMs, which defy reliable antimissile interception – make those impregnable defenses largely impractical. Even

[2] Department of Defense Dictionary, http://www.dtic.mil/doctrine/jel/doddict.

[3] U.S. Joint Chiefs of Staff, Doctrine for Joint Nuclear Operations, Joint Publication 3–12 (Final Coordination Draft), March 15, 2005, p. viii.

today, proponents of a ballistic missile defense system are careful not to claim too much – they argue only that, if all goes well with a series of cutting-edge technological breakthroughs, a novel system might someday be able to interdict a small number of relatively primitive missiles from a lesser nuclear power such as North Korea. No one believes that a true "Astrodome" shield could be erected to provide airtight defense against a massive nuclear onslaught from a technologically adept near-peer nation such as the former U.S.S.R.

So if we cannot count on truly preventing or intercepting a nuclear attack on our homeland (or even if, hypothetically, we could) the next best available strategy is to try to convince or intimidate the adversary not to launch or threaten such an attack in the first place – and that is where deterrence comes in. Our military strategy becomes an effort to persuade the leadership of another country that it would not be in their interest to strike us, because our retaliatory counterstrike against their military apparatus, population centers, industrial capacity, and other sites of value would inflict so much pain on them that it would obliterate any possible gains they might have sought from the initial act of aggression.

This geopolitical gamesmanship reached its morbid apotheosis as the dominant nuclear strategy of the cold war. The United States and the Soviet Union each threatened the other with massive retaliation as the knee-jerk response to an attack, and each structured its thousands of nuclear weapons in a posture for instant and overwhelming reprisal for its rival's provocations. Each fervently hoped, of course, never to have to unleash that paroxysm of death and destruction – the nuclear exchange would surely devastate both countries and perhaps jeopardize all human life on earth – but each became convinced that the only way to avoid *having* to employ its nuclear arsenal was by perpetually *threatening* to do so if challenged. As Thomas Schelling emphasizes, this sort of strategy "is not concerned with the efficient *application* of force but with the *exploitation of potential force*" – if the threat actually has to be carried out, then the deterrent has failed.[4]

That entrenched relationship – characterized as "mutual assured destruction," with the appropriate acronym MAD – proved marvelously successful through the decades of the cold war. (At least, it was successful in preserving a measure of strategic stability and avoiding nuclear holocaust, but that accomplishment came at the price of massive expenditures of money, global political stalemate, cataclysmic risk, and immense psychic

[4] Thomas C. Schelling, The Strategy of Conflict, 1980, p. 5.

stress.[5]) The United States initially scaled its robust nuclear arsenal to meet the arbitrary criteria established by Secretary of Defense Robert McNamara, under which the ability promptly to destroy one-third of the Soviet population and half of its industrial base would qualify as unacceptable damage to Moscow, establishing reliable deterrence.[6]

Subsequent buildups on both sides far surpassed those levels, generating the nightmarish phenomenon of "overkill," whereby each nation had ample nuclear resources to obliterate the other many times over. This was the true "balance of terror," in which each country tiptoed around the other to avoid a direct confrontation that could spiral horrifyingly out of control. Even in later years, as MAD morphed into doctrines of "flexible response," envisioning the possibility of something less than an all-out spasm of nuclear war, deterrence remained the centerpiece of U.S.-Soviet strategic thinking, vigilantly threatening excruciating retribution for untoward acts.

The shift from traditional defense (as represented by weapons intended to engage and defeat an enemy's military forces) to deterrence (as embodied in weapons designed to hold hostage the enemy's cities and industrial resources) is monumental. Alexander George and Richard Smoke have suggested that the modern "correlation of forces" (to use a Soviet term) introduces a sharp, novel distinction between the power to hurt an enemy society and the power to defeat its military forces – between punishment and victory. As they describe the transformation, into the twentieth century it was largely impossible to harm an enemy seriously – to burn his cities, enslave his population, or seize his property – until after one had defeated his military forces. But with the advent of strategic bombing, it suddenly became feasible to reach over the fielded forces and strike the foreign population directly, before routing or even fully engaging the enemy's troops. With the opening of this possibility, the threat to ruin an enemy could be delinked from the threat to confront and destroy his forces. "Deterrence was conceived in its modern sense when it became possible to threaten vast damage and pain while leaving opposing military forces intact."[7]

The Cuban Missile Crisis, as depicted in Scenario 2, reveals the superpowers waging deterrence at its apex. Both Kennedy and Khrushchev

[5] Patrick M. Morgan, Deterrence Now, 2003, pp. 34–5.
[6] Robert McNamara, Mutual Deterrence, address in San Francisco, September 18, 1967.
[7] Alexander L. George and Richard Smoke, Deterrence in American Foreign Policy: Theory and Practice, 1974, p. 21.

were aware that neither side could win a nuclear war in any meaningful sense – regardless of who held a tactical advantage in the local theater or who counted more deliverable warheads at his disposal, each country wielded sufficient power to devastate the other. Each was deterred from striking the other, and each had abundant incentives to nudge the standoff toward resolution. As Khrushchev wrote to Kennedy on October 26, when the crisis was at its worst,

> You and I should not now pull the ends of the rope in which you have tied a knot of war, because the harder you and I pull, the tighter the knot will become. And a time may come when this knot is tied so tight that the person who tied it is no longer capable of untying it, and then the knot will have to be cut. What that would mean I need not explain to you, because you yourself understand perfectly what dread forces our two countries possess.

The absurdity of mutual assured destruction lies in the fact that national leaders – Kennedy's ExComm and its counterpart inside the Kremlin – are called upon to undertake casualty calculations worthy of Dr. Strangelove, to project the "expected value" from various war games and to steer a path along the brink that runs such immense risks. Gen. Lee Butler, former head of the U.S. Strategic Air Command, summarized the precariousness of MAD this way in 1997:

> Deterrence was our shield and, by extension, our sword. The nuclear priesthood extolled its virtues and bowed to its demands. Allies yielded to its dictates, even while decrying its risks and costs. We brandished it at our enemies and presumed they embraced its suicidal corollary of mutual assured destruction. We ignored, discounted, or dismissed its flaws and even today we cling to the belief that it remains relevant in a world whose security architecture has been transformed.[8]

In short, with the axioms of deterrence as the guidepost, neither country wanted war over Cuba or anyplace else. Neither side could possibly benefit in any meaningful sense from such a cataclysm, but each side had to prepare for war, each side had to appear resolute in its willingness to risk such a self-destructive outcome, and neither side could appear to be afraid of peering over and even teetering upon the precipice.

VARIATIONS UPON DETERRENCE

In that sense, deterrence is hardly a modern aberration or an artifact of a bilateral nuclear stalemate. Thucydides recounts Peloponnesian War

[8] Quoted in Robert D. Green, Re-thinking Nuclear Deterrence: Summary of Arguments from The Naked Nuclear Emperor, 2001, p. 5.

brinksmanship in which the Spartan and Athenian alliances would each undertake strategic diplomatic and military maneuvers to attempt to persuade the other that initiating or expanding a conflict would prove unremunerative. Likewise, the eighteenth-century Westphalian concept for the European balance of power relied upon construction of a delicate series of equilibrium-enhancing alliances intended to ward off continental warfare through negative feedback about likely consequences.[9] Today, the precarious mixture of conflict and cooperation between, say, India and Pakistan, or among the various stakeholders in the Middle East, also partakes of the leitmotif of deterrence – although the game of contingent threat and counterthreat grows precariously more complicated and less stable in the chaotic multilateral version.

Nor is nuclear deterrence necessarily confined to the single goal of precluding all-out war. Even during the height of the superpower antagonism, the mystique of deterrence was regularly expanded to try to persuade potentially hostile countries (again, especially the Soviet Union) not to undertake actions that, although not directly threatening U.S. national survival, nonetheless jeopardized our perimeter allies, undercut our foreign policy, or disserved our interests. This notion of "extended deterrence," in which the mighty U.S. nuclear umbrella would be unfurled against a range of lesser provocations, tests the resolve and leverage of the affected actors in perilous ways: Would we really launch a nuclear attack (knowing that a counterattack against us was forthcoming) if provoked by something short of the most extreme circumstances?

An associated notion, sometimes referred to as "compellence," turns deterrence on its head. Compellence is the effort to marshal the threat of the nuclear cudgel to inspire, scare, or otherwise motivate another state to take affirmative action we desire. (The distinction between deterrence as persuading a state *not* to do something vs. compellence as persuading it to *do* something may be elusive, but sometimes it does make a difference in international life.)[10]

Both extended deterrence and compellence required yet another adjustment in the traditional notion of superpower nuclear relations: the possibility of a "limited" nuclear war. Gallons of ink (but fortunately, no blood) were shed over the possibility that a superpower conflict might escalate only slowly and incrementally through a series of stages (like

[9] Noted in George and Smoke, supra note 7, at 12–21.

[10] Raymond L. Garthoff, Deterrence and the Revolution in Soviet Military Doctrine, 1990; Colin S. Gray, Maintaining Effective Deterrence, Strategic Studies Institute Monograph, U.S. Army War College, August 2003; Thomas C. Schelling, Arms and Influence, 1966, pp. 70–86.

climbing the rungs on a wobbly ladder), with intensifying conventional combat perhaps leading to use of a small number of relatively small-sized nuclear weapons on the periphery of a battlefield, but perhaps stopping (again, because of the central role of deterrence) before engaging the main strategic nuclear weapons in a true global holocaust.

Western Europe provided the most prominent locus where these scenarios were imagined to play out. There, a feared Soviet and Warsaw Pact invasion might be too powerful for the United States and NATO to contain on a conventional level. The threat of tactical nuclear weapons (smaller, more discrete – and therefore more useable than the giant globe-spanning ICBMs) might deter the aggressors, defeat their assault, and subside before escalating to Armageddon.

If limited, protracted nuclear war of that sort was conceivable – and many analysts concluded, on balance, that the whole concept was nonsensical – then a more sophisticated, step-by-step form of deterrence might still operate, even after the initial threshold of nuclear weapons use had been crossed. Smaller, more useable weapons thus became the handmaidens of an extended deterrence.[11]

The multiplicity and adaptability of deterrence, its persistent hardiness even in the post cold war world, and its adaptability for other pairs or groups of states that have studied the U.S.–U.S.S.R. model, learned from it, and bought into its precepts, are all quite remarkable. These features suggest that the orthodoxy of pursuing national defense through deterrence has become something of a self-fulfilling prophesy, a self-reinforcing belief system. As the deterrence dogma is perpetuated and elaborated in additional contexts, it further intensifies its adherents' support, channeling their thinking, their strategizing, and their weapons procurement decisions into avenues that fit the concept – making deterrence approximate to what some would call "a self-licking ice cream cone."

SELF-DETERRENCE

That analysis brings us to an associated concept we could label "self-deterrence." This phenomenon is characterized by a national reluctance to engage in military action, but not principally because we fear the retaliation that our target may inflict upon our homeland population centers in response (in this advanced lexicon of war, that would count

[11] Herman Kahn, On Escalation: Metaphors and Scenarios, 1965.

as "ordinary" deterrence). Rather, a range of other, secondary inhibiting factors now comes into play.[12]

All deterrence is, in some sense, self-deterrence, because we are dealing here with a phenomenon of psychology or social psychology in which a country decides, for a variety of reasons, not to undertake an action or range of actions that it is physically capable of pursuing. But to parse the inhibitions one step further, self-deterrence focuses upon our hesitancy to *inflict*, not only to *receive*, the pains of war.

There are, of course, many valid reasons to be circumspect about using military force. Prominent among them is the understandable reluctance to cough up the money and accept the casualties that warfare inevitably imposes. Some argue that American policy has become *too* casualty-averse, too inhibited about exposing our troops to mortal danger. During NATO's Kosovo intervention in the spring of 1999, for example, there was great caterwauling that an unspoken American insistence upon "zero body bags" would unreasonably restrict military operations, undercutting the effectiveness of the enterprise. Some commentators of that era elaborated the thesis, complaining that the "great powers" (European and North American alike) were behaving in an unduly nongreat, introspective fashion, ignoring their responsibilities to lead, fight for, and if necessary die for, a just global cause.[13]

Waves of introversion, isolationism, and "foreign policy fatigue" have periodically characterized many countries, not just the United States. Coupled with the hope (and sometimes with the experience) that non-forceful options – diplomacy, United Nations and other multilateral "good offices," litigation in the World Court, or the currently fashionable choice, economic sanctions – will succeed, it is rational not to be too quick on the trigger finger or too profligate with soldiers' lives.

[12] Stanley R. Sloan, The United States and the Use of Force in the Post-Cold War World: Toward Self-Deterrence? Congressional Research Service Report for the U.S. House of Representatives Committee on Foreign Affairs, August 1994 (identifying diverse causes and consequences of American self-deterrence during the 1990s). See also Stansfield Turner, Caging the Genies: A Workable Solution for Nuclear, Chemical, and Biological Weapons, 1999, Chapter 3, "Points of Self-Deterrence," pp. 51–64; John Lewis Gaddis, The Long Peace: Inquiries into the History of the Cold War, 1987, pp. 104–46.

[13] See, for example, Edward N. Luttwak, Where Are the Great Powers? At Home with the Kids, 73 Foreign Affairs No. 4, p. 23, July/August 1994; Hugh Smith, What Costs Will Democracies Bear? A Review of Popular Theories of Casualty Aversion, 31 Armed Forces & Society No. 4, p. 487, Summer 2005; Jeffrey Record, Collapsed Countries, Casualty Dread, and the New American Way of War, 32 Parameters No. 2, Summer 2002, p. 4; International Institute for Strategic Studies, Strategic Survey 1995–1996, 1996, p. 48.

What many of these "casualty allergy" considerations boil down to is the judgment that in some circumstances, whatever we might gain from military entanglement is not worth the price. Sometimes, as in the standard model of deterrence, the primary focus is on the excesses of the cost side of the equation (what we might lose in battle or in retaliation); other times, more attention is paid to the shortfalls on the benefit side (where we have insufficient national interests at stake, even a relatively small price tag is disproportionate).

For the United States, the hesitancy to engage in half-baked "wars of choice" was reflected most vividly in the Weinberger-Powell Doctrine, articulated by President Ronald Reagan's Secretary of Defense Caspar Weinberger in 1984 and elaborated by Colin Powell as Chairman of the Joint Chiefs of Staff in 1990–1991 – and further reified in Presidential Decision Directive 25, issued by the Clinton Administration in May 1994.[14] These proclamations established stringent conditionality against intervention in overseas conflicts, mandating that the United States would consider a long list of factors in deciding whether to participate in multilateral peacekeeping operations or other types of foreign conflicts. These factors included many that resonate with the concerns of deterrence and self-deterrence, such as: the true financial cost of the mission; the need for clear political and military objectives, an adequate plan, and sufficient resources for accomplishing the specified mandate; the contemplated duration of the mission and realistic criteria for ending it (an "exit strategy"); and the presence of domestic public and congressional support. These inhibitory standards were deliberately crafted to avoid the insidious "mission creep" that had ensnared the United States in unrewarding quagmires in Vietnam, Lebanon, Somalia, Haiti, and elsewhere – and ultimately compelled the Americans to withdraw, sometimes in humiliation and sometimes after suffering relatively low numbers of casualties.

ENEMY CASUALTIES

One special aspect of self-deterrence is particularly relevant to the revolution in military affairs and the contemplation of more useable weaponry.

[14] Caspar W. Weinberger, U.S. Defense Strategy, 64 Foreign Affairs, Spring 1986, p. 675, 686; U.S. Department of State, Clinton Administration Policy on Reforming Multilateral Peace Operations (PDD 25), February 22, 1996, available at http://www.fas.org/irp/offdocs/pdd25.htm; Kenneth J. Campbell, Once Burned, Twice Cautious: Explaining the Weinberger-Powell Doctrine, 24 Armed Forces & Society No. 3, Spring 1998, p. 357; Jeffrey Record, Back to the Weinberger-Powell Doctrine?, Strategic Studies Quarterly, Fall 2007, p. 79.

That is, the United States now feels, in addition to all the previously noted inhibitions, a profound reluctance to engage in military operations where doing so would inflict too many casualties, too much property loss, and excessive associated damage *on the other state*. We are concerned not only with our own expenses in treasure and blood but also with the extent and nature of the agony we inflict upon the putative enemy society – its civilians and even its combatants. It is "casualty aversion squared": We worry about losses on *all* sides.

Why not enforce high costs on the enemy? Why should there be any ceiling on making their society sacrifice things of value if they are foolish enough or evil enough to engage us in mortal combat? The natural instinct to despise, even to demonize, one's opponents in battle is understandable, and familiar grisly logic stretching back to Machiavelli and Clausewitz asserts that the more excruciating war becomes, the sooner the enemy will capitulate, and the less likely the next aggressor will be to initiate hostilities against us. But even that cold logic has bounds.

First, simple considerations of morality play a restraining role. Although death and destruction are inherent parts of warfare, they are subject to some limits of conscience. Exceeding those norms by inflicting more suffering than is necessary or more than is warranted by the provocation is cruel, degrading, and dehumanizing. Even if our enemy has committed grievous acts, we do not want to denigrate ourselves and our society by denying the common bonds of humanity and forsaking all mercy and sympathy. The deeper legitimacy of combat requires, upon mature reflection, that we abstain from doing more than is necessary to prevail; our use of force can justifiably be overwhelming, devastating, and immensely destructive, but it cannot be wanton, wasteful, or disproportionate.

Second, practicality contributes to self-deterrence. History demonstrates that even bitter enemies need not remain so – the perpetual enmity between Rome and Carthage is not the only, or most satisfactory, model for interstate rivalry. In contrast, decent treatment after the barbarity of World War II helped convert Japan and Germany into America's close allies, peaceful friends, and trading partners, to the lasting benefit of all. And these days, when the United States routinely helps reconstruct vanquished enemies, it makes financial sense to maintain their human and physical capital. If we are going to bankroll the postwar recovery, as in Yugoslavia in 1999, Afghanistan in 2001, and Iraq in 2003, then we have an incentive to win the war at the lowest cost to the enemy, not further alienating and disempowering the vanquished with unnecessary carnage.

Image also plays an important role in moderating our conquests – both self-image and preservation of the portrait of us that we want others to hold. Our sensibilities dictate that we do not want to "look bad," even when we are performing the dirtiest, most gruesome tasks of combat. Part of looking bad – fortunately, an escapable part – is overdoing things, inflicting punishment on the helpless, and making the horror of war even more horrible than it absolutely must be. Perhaps it is inevitable that a big, powerful nation will run a risk of looking bad in war – the shadow of the Vietnam fiasco casts the clumsy, increasingly desperate foreign interventionists into the role of a bumbling Gulliver, vacillating between applying immense, overwhelming, excessive power in a manner that seems unfair and being slowly bled to death by a thousand pinpricks.

The importance of image is magnified these days by the so-called "CNN effect," as the trauma of distant warfare is telecast instantly to living rooms around the world. Vivid scenes can be readily distorted or manipulated. Even when presented accurately, they are susceptible to multiple interpretations, many of which naturally highlight the human dimension of warfare, evoking sympathy for the dead, injured, and displaced victims, and reinforcing the incentive to restrain the violence.

Modern aerial bombardment can sometimes seem antiseptic – the operational equivalent of a loathsome live-action video game, with the attacker far removed physically and psychologically from the impact upon the target. But today's omnipresent news media can capture every moment of suffering, beaming it back to a domestic audience that learns compassionately not to stand the sight of blood – our own, or even the enemy's.

One vivid illustration of the power of this principle comes from Gulf War I in 1991, in which American and coalition forces quickly routed Saddam Hussein's army, ejected the aggressors from Kuwait, and began to press the offensive north toward Baghdad. However, as soon as televised images of smoldering Iraqi tanks and desperately fleeing soldiers along the "Highway of Death" began to circulate, the leadership in Washington, D.C., instructed Gen. Norman Schwarzkopf to call off the "turkey shoot" pursuit, even at the price of allowing large elements of the Republican Guard to escape and permitting the Ba'athist regime to remain in power. President George H.W. Bush explained that America had pulled its toughest punch because we were not in the business of wanton slaughter.[15]

[15] Harvey M. Sapolsky and Jeremy Shapiro, Casualties, Technology, and America's Future Wars, 26 Parameters No. 2, Summer 1996, p. 119; Colin Powell with Joseph E. Persico, My American Journey, 1995, pp. 519–28; H. Norman Schwarzkopf with Peter Petre,

Image does matter in international military affairs, more so than ever before. Incompetent management of the public relations aspect of an armed campaign can be disastrous, corrupting support for the enterprise among the public and national legislatures at home and abroad. If our democracy fights badly – using excessive or disproportionate force, inflicting more casualties than public opinion finds acceptable – we soon call into question the justice of our cause and undercut our ability to sustain it. If we sacrifice the precious resource of public support, the battle cannot be won; increasingly, the U.S. military is reluctant even to begin a major engagement if the American population is not sufficiently behind the undertaking for the long haul.

The point here is not simply to be nicer to an enemy's soldiers or even to its domestic population as a magnanimous humanitarian gesture. There is more at stake than mere effete sensibilities or a syndrome of subtle psychic guilt we might experience over inflicting pain upon another people. At a basic level, our society's evolving norms of civilized behavior will inevitably deeply and appropriately influence the behavior of our armed forces.

The more hard-headed point is that deft application of limited military power is often more successful – use of precise, limited, circumscribed force is a more effective mechanism for waging a war. If we confine ourselves to what is appropriate under common notions of warfighting ethics, then the operation is more sustainable. Conversely, if we routinely violate the norms that will be dissected in the next chapter as the legal principles of necessity and proportionality, then the public, and even the military forces themselves, will not long tolerate it. We simply will not be willing, over the long term, to apply more destructive force than required to accomplish a valid mission. Even where we have the physical and fiscal capacity for invoking overly great destructive power, our own inhibitions will often, and sensibly, preclude that option.

CAPABILITY AND RESOLVE

Deterrence and self-deterrence are therefore linked. If American forces are ultimately going to be unwilling or unable to apply "too much" power to

It Doesn't Take a Hero, 1992, pp. 468–72. See also Christopher B. Puckett, In This Era of 'Smart Weapons,' Is a State Under an International Legal Obligation to Use Precision-Guided Technology in an Armed Conflict? 18 Emory International Law Review 645, 709, Fall 2004.

a given military situation, and if our adversary knows and understands those *de facto* constraints, then the viability of any proclaimed threat to act in that overwhelming fashion dissipates.

Effective deterrence depends upon the putative target accurately assessing (a) our genuine physical capability to inflict pain upon him, and (b) our unwavering willingness to do so. If either condition fails – if we lack either the capacity or the resolve to implement the threats – then deterrence loses its credibility.

Ironically, there may be times when an increase in factor (a) can cause a perceived decrease in condition (b). That is, if we have the ability to inflict terrible harm, but *only* the ability to inflict terrible harm (i.e., we lack a more refined capacity to visit less-than-overwhelming force) then the target may believe that we might not, in fact, pull the trigger – we might, if forced to a showdown, be reluctant to overrespond to the provocation. If we hesitate to enforce our will out of antipathy toward unleashing an unreasonably excessive response, then our threat loses much of its impact.

Nuclear weapons – capable of inconceivably devastating power – may provide the best illustration of this ominous dilemma. During the Cuban Missile Crisis, both the United States and the Soviet Union brandished impressive nuclear armadas, and each registered a series of explicit and implicit threats – Kennedy's October 22 commitment could hardly have been more direct that any nuclear attack on the United States from Cuba would result in a cataclysmic retaliatory strike against the U.S.S.R. At a lower level, each superpower wanted the other to believe that even lesser actions – Moscow's continued efforts to emplace SS-4s and SS-5s in Cuba, or Washington, D.C.'s blockade, air strike, or invasion – would likewise run a grave risk of triggering a full-scale ballistic bombardment.

But were those barbarous threats credible? Would either side rationally initiate World War III over this provocation? Was it fully believable that the ExComm and its Soviet counterpart would deliberately take steps resulting in the deaths of millions of people in an October fit of pique or misguided resolve?

In the same way, the concept of extended deterrence, critics argue, hinges upon the willingness of a superpower to undertake actions that might be rational to *threaten* but not to *carry out*. For example, if the United States had used military force against Cuba, and if the Soviet Union had responded (as many anticipated) with an invasion or other attack on West Germany, would NATO and the United States have replied with the first use of nuclear weapons? Doing so might have succeeded in blunting the Warsaw Pact aggression but might well have plunged both countries into the vortex of an unimaginable nuclear war. But frank, public recognition of the horror of that outcome could subtly undercut the credibility of the threat. In the parlance of the day, would the United States really sacrifice New York to protect Berlin? Would the Soviet Union believe that an American president would implement that deadly, sterile plan?

The horror of nuclear war – the specter of an overkill that would vastly exceed anything we might gain from escalating to that level – calls into question the utility of the whole category of weaponry. As Colin Powell has observed, "The monstrous devastation and radioactive pollution created by nuclear weapons render them useless to achieve any rational military objective."[16] Indeed, in Vietnam and in Korea, to cite just two examples, the United States refrained from crossing the nuclear threshold – preferring defeat or protracted stalemate to the most cosmic form of escalation, even when the opposing state was wholly incapable of retaliating against us in kind.

International relations, of course, is not exclusively a rational game, and the nature of a "threat that leaves something to chance" promotes deterrence even when it is not 100 percent clear that we would actually carry out our promised counteraction. A mere probability can have an impact – even just a substantial danger that physical coercion will apply can inject qualms into a risk-averse target. And the tradition of brinksmanship is for the eyeball-to-eyeball superpowers to undertake actions that *might* lead to a horrific outcome that neither side wants, but that it is now up to the *other* side to avoid – a high-stakes game of "chicken," played not by juvenile delinquent hot-rodders but by John F. Kennedy and Nikita Khrushchev.

PROPORTIONAL RESPONSE

Self-deterrence thus provides a primary reason why these traditional notions of national deterrence sometimes falter. It is a widely shared view that there should be some reasonable relationship between a provocation and a response, reflected in the aphorism that we should "let the punishment fit the crime." If we threaten to do vastly more than that – if our articulated deterrent threat is distinctly out of synch with what would

[16] Quoted in Donald C. Whitmore, Revisiting Nuclear Deterrence Theory, March 1, 1998, p. 5, available at http://www.abolishnukes.com/short_essays/deterrence_theory_whitmore.html.

be a proportionate retaliation – then the other side may not fully believe it would actually be carried out.

This disjunct between threat, provocation, and response is not exclusively the province of strategic nuclear weapons. In any wartime application – including the five categories of precision-guided munitions, low-yield nuclear weapons, smart antipersonnel mines, antisatellite weapons, and nonlethal weapons surveyed in Chapters 4–8 – the same relationships obtain. If we have only weapons that are large, powerful, deadly, and longlasting, then we may well be inhibited about using them in marginal cases. That self-restraint will be known, or at least suspected, by the potential provocateur as well as by outside observers, and it may strongly affect their resistant behaviors.[17]

In the general sense, if country X possesses only the ability to overreact (using a weapon or tactic that is disproportionate to the challenge) or to underreact (doing nothing effective), then country Y might rationally conclude that X would be unwilling to exercise the big option in response to small misdeeds. Y might then gamble to get away with those low-level provocations, testing X's self-deterrence limits. The classic case is where X *could* punish Y, but X *elects* not to do so because it cannot fine-tune its response and prefers to tolerate minor violations instead of overdoing things.

This is the sort of malign paradox that now confronts the United States daily. Uncle Sam is the global hegemon (the United States' annual military budget is now nearly half the world's combined total and far greater than any combination of our potential rivals'[18]), but the effective global reach of that power is fraying around the edges. There is a manifest mismatch between America's formidable military, economic, and diplomatic muscle and our ability to accomplish national goals in the chaotic

[17] Morgan, supra note 5, at 48.

[18] Peter Stalenheim, Catalina Perdomo, and Elisabeth Skons, Military Expenditure, in Stockholm International Peace Research Institute, Yearbook 2008: Armaments, Disarmament, and International Security, p. 175; Peter Stalenheim, Catalina Perdomo, and Elisabeth Skons, Military Expenditure, in Stockholm International Peace Research Institute, Yearbook 2007: Armaments, Disarmament, and International Security, p. 267, 299; Peter Stalenheim, Damien Fruchart, Wuyi Omitoogun, and Catalina Perdomo, Military Expenditures, in Stockholm International Peace Research Institute, Yearbook 2006: Armaments, Disarmament, and International Security, p. 295; International Institute for Strategic Studies, The Military Balance, 2006; Center for Arms Control and Non-Proliferation, U.S. Military Spending vs. the World, February 5, 2007, available at http://www.armscontrolcenter.org/archives/002279.html.

international arena. The objectives of deterring, or responding effectively to, aggression, terrorism, insurgency, proliferation, and other threats to public order are not adequately supported by the weapons currently in our arsenal – a self-deterred Goliath lacks the ability to respond with deft, agile, and effective power.

The Bush Administration reacted to the new security realities by evoking a doctrine of "tailored deterrence," suggesting that more discrete packets of military force could be doled out, measure for measure, in response to varying provocations. At the same time, it is far from clear whether the existing inventory of nuclear and other weapons would actually support such hand-crafted retaliatory measures or whether the "tailoring" remains at this point mostly a rhetorical device.[19]

Not just the United States, however, is constrained or even paralyzed by inadequate tools and beleaguered by a simultaneous, generic reluctance to overreact. French President Jacques Chirac warned in early 2006 that "his country's nuclear arsenal had been reconfigured to include the ability to make a tactical strike in retaliation for terrorism."[20] Most experts, in rebuttal to this declaration, would opine that it is far from clear that nuclear weapons play any useful role at all in counterterrorism; except for state-sponsored terrorists, these actors, almost by definition, lack the high-value targets and infrastructure that nuclear weapons are designed to obliterate. But Chirac's frustration is understandable – what *can* we do to lash out at this new threat; and if nuclear weapons are inutile in combating this new insidious threat to our society, what good are they?

ORIGINS OF SELF-DETERRENCE

Where does our notion of this judicious self-restraint come from? Perhaps some of it is a predictable byproduct of civilization, democracy, rule of law, and respect for human rights. As we increasingly seek to avoid and to constrain battlefield violence, we may also inevitably grow soft in our distaste for inflicting excessive casualties, and we have no stomach for systematic brutality. Gruesome totalitarian regimes, in contrast, may not suffer so much of this particular disability – the Nazis, to take

[19] Amy F. Woolf, Nuclear Weapons in U.S. National Security Policy: Past, Present, and Prospects, Congressional Research Service Report for Congress, RL 34226, December 30, 2008.

[20] Molly Moore, Chirac: Nuclear Response to Terrorism Is Possible, Washington Post, January 20, 2006, p. A12.

an extreme example, might not have bowed before Mahatma Gandhi's nonviolent resistance campaign for Indian independence in 1947, as the British ultimately did. Likewise, today's most vicious al-Qaeda terrorists exhibit no compunction about generating large numbers of casualties among defenseless civilians, a freedom of conscience that may further asymmetrically embolden them in confrontations with law-abiding opponents. In a sense, these despicable cadres have "weaponized" our own moral restraints, turning our self-deterrence against us in today's deadly competition.

Another contributing source of advancing self-deterrence is the advent of mesmerizing new military technology – in a sense, we seek to reduce the hellishness of warfare simply because we now (for the first time in history) have some real ability to do so. No longer does it seem so inevitable that such large numbers will suffer – our soldiers, our civilians, enemy civilians, and even enemy soldiers can be spared some of the worst ravages of combat, and the revolution in military affairs can still empower us to press the battle forward effectively.

In fact, the ongoing technological transformation may become the leading mechanism for resolving the dilemma of self-deterrence – enabling us to fight (and to threaten to fight) effectively while still respecting our loathing for generating excessive casualties and property damage. Weapon systems that are more deft – more accurate, more localized, more controllable, less lethal, and of shorter duration – are therefore more useable. We seek a "rheostatic" ability in combat, to be able to mete out pain and suffering *quid pro quo*, in appropriate response to intolerable provocation, without crossing unacceptable lines. That way, our threats become more credible, we will become more willing to carry them out, and we will accordingly be less frequently called upon to do so.

Much in these desiderata is far from new. The ancient Chinese strategist Sun Tzu surely appreciated the occasional value of a massive "shock and awe" campaign in particular contexts, but he also observed the considerable advantages of deliberate moderation in combat 2500 years ago:

> Generally in war the best policy is to take a state intact; to ruin it is inferior to this. To capture an enemy's army is better than to destroy it; to take intact a battalion, a company or a five-man squad is better than to destroy them. For to win one hundred victories in one hundred battles is not the acme of skill. To subdue the enemy without fighting is the acme

> of skill.... Thus, those skilled in war subdue the enemy's army without battle. They capture his cities without assaulting them and overthrow his state without protracted operations.[21]

We are therefore in pursuit not only of a "just war," but of "adjustable war" – that is, we want to fight for the right reasons, and also to fight in the right way, responding appropriately and effectively across the entire spectrum of combat and near-combat possibilities without inflicting more death and destruction than necessary.

BOTTOM LINE

The epochal revolution in military affairs is occurring at full tilt, generating profound consequences for the traditional modes of equipping U.S. troops and conducting military operations. This transformation also has important implications on the psychological side – it promises to alter the historic norms of deterrence and self-deterrence that have dominated American and global strategic thinking for decades.

As subsequent chapters detail, we are thus crossing an important threshold, entering an era of sharply increased useability in a wide range of new weapons programs, with an associated erosion in self-deterrence. One of the important inhibitions against the application of force – the apprehension about avoiding excessive, indiscriminant, or disproportionate destruction – is markedly abating.

To some, the whole notion of self-deterrence will automatically seem wooly-headed, pacifist, decadent, or dysfunctional; macho fortitude in the application of military power, in contrast, is depicted as unvaryingly admirable, zealous, and effective. But there is more to self-deterrence than merely pulling our punches – it is about fighting in a more legitimate, more effective, and more sustainable manner.

In any event, increasing the deftness and useability of modern weapons is hardly an unmixed blessing. In fact, as elaborated in Chapters 4–8, one leading caveat must be the concern that as self-deterrence is reduced

[21] Sun Tzu, The Art of War, c. 400–320 B.C., p. 77. The official guidance from the U.S. Marine Corps in 1940 reached strikingly similar conclusions: "A Force Commander who gains his objective in a small war without firing a shot has attained far greater success than one who resorted to the use of force" and "In small wars, caution must be exercised, and instead of striving to generate the maximum power with forces available, the goal is to gain decisive results with the least application of force and the consequent mimumum loss of life." U.S. Marine Corps, Small Wars Manual, 1940, p. 18, 32.

(through the advent of more pinpoint weaponry) the restraints against a headlong rush into international combat might be lowered *too much*.

That is, any time an important constraint is relaxed, we should expect – as a corollary to the law of supply and demand – to observe an automatic increase in the behavior in question. If national leaders, both civilian and military, conclude that the use of force is now incrementally easier and cheaper – because we can worry less about the adverse consequences of misdirected, inaccurate, or overly powerful armaments – then we should anticipate increased pressures to apply that more deft force more frequently.

We may thus be nationally lulled into a false sense that warfare can become relatively safe, innocuous, brief, and decisive. With our newfound weapons prowess, we may be tempted to systematically underestimate the true long-term and big-picture costs of engagement. In short, if the vaunted revolution in military affairs makes weapons more useable, we will use them more often – it's not just hubris that will make us miscalculate, becoming too quick on the trigger. If the fear of cataclysm had been abated just a bit in 1962, perhaps the odds would have been even worse that Kennedy and Khrushchev could have found a safe way to climb down from the precipice of war.

Around the world, most people, when contemplating the planet's political and military miseries, do not reach the judgment that twenty-first-century American leaders have become too prudent, too reluctant to use force – that is not "The Problem" that most countries would identify for global peace and security today. The prospect of further reductions in U.S. self-deterrence, and perhaps a concomitant tendency to plunge into combat even more readily, will be greeted with grim alarm in many quarters – but that is the direction that useability and diminished self-deterrence are now taking us.

BIBLIOGRAPHY

Elie Abel, The Missile Crisis, 1966

Graham T. Allison, Essence of Decision: Explaining the Cuban Missile Crisis, 1971

Richard K. Betts, What Will It Take to Deter the United States? 25 Parameters, Winter 1995, p. 70

Wyn Q. Bowen, Deterrence and Asymmetry: Non-State Actors and Mass Casualty Terrorism, 25 Contemporary Security Policy No. 1, April 2004, p. 54

Dino A. Brugioni, Eyeball to Eyeball: The Inside Story of the Cuban Missile Crisis, 1991

V.M. Burenok and O.B. Achasov, Non-Nuclear Deterrence, 17 Military Thought No. 1, 2008, p. 1

Kenneth J. Campbell, Once Burned, Twice Cautious: Explaining the Weinberger-Powell Doctrine, 24 Armed Forces & Society No. 3, Spring 1998, p. 357

Center for Arms Control and Non-Proliferation, U.S. Military Spending vs. the World, February 5, 2007, available at http://www.armscontrolcenter.org/archives/002279.html

Abram Chayes, The Cuban Missile Crisis: International Crises and the Role of Law, 1974

John T. Correll, Casualties, 86 Air Force Magazine No. 6, June 2003, p. 48

Sidney D. Drell and James E. Goodby, What Are Nuclear Weapons For? Recommendations for Restructuring U.S. Strategic Nuclear Forces, Arms Control Association Report, October 2007

Lewis A. Dunn, Deterrence Today: Roles, Challenges and Responses, IFRI Security Studies Department, Proliferation Papers, Summer 2007

Karl W. Eikenberry, Take No Casualties, 26 Parameters No. 2, Summer 1996, p. 109

Andrew P.N. Erdmann, The U.S. Presumption of Quick, Costless Wars, 43 Orbis No. 3, Summer 1999, p. 363

Lawrence Freedman, Deterrence, 2004

John Lewis Gaddis, The Long Peace: Inquiries into the History of the Cold War, 1987

Adam Garfinkle, Culture and Deterrence, August 30, 2006, available at http://www.realclearpolitics.com/articles/2006/08/culture_and_deterrence.html

Raymond L. Garthoff, Deterrence and the Revolution in Soviet Military Doctrine, 1990

Scott Sigmund Gartner and Gary M. Segura, War, Casualties, and Public Opinion, 42 Journal of Conflict Resolution No. 3, June 1998, p. 278

Alexander L. George and Richard Smoke, Deterrence in American Foreign Policy: Theory and Practice, 1974

Colin S. Gray, Maintaining Effective Deterrence, Strategic Studies Institute Monograph, U.S. Army War College, August 2003

Robert D. Green, Re-thinking Nuclear Deterrence: Summary of Arguments from The Naked Nuclear Emperor, 2001

Peter Grier, In the Shadow of MAD, 84 Air Force Magazine No. 11, November 2001

Roger G. Harrison, Deron R. Jackson, and Collins G. Shackelford, Space Deterrence: The Delicate Balance of Risk, Eisenhower Center for Space and Defense Studies, 2009

Darryl Howlett, The Emergence of Stability: Deterrence-in-Motion and Deterrence Reconsidered, 25 Contemporary Security Policy No. 1, April 2004, p. 18

International Institute for Strategic Studies, Strategic Survey 1995–1996, 1996, p. 48

International Institute for Strategic Studies, The Military Balance, 2006

Robert Jervis, Deterrence Theory Revisited, 31 World Politics No. 2, January 1979, p. 289

Herman Kahn, On Thermonuclear War, 1961
Herman Kahn, On Escalation: Metaphors and Scenarios, 1965
Robert F. Kennedy, Thirteen Days: A Memoir of the Cuban Missile Crisis, 1971
Charles Krauthammer, The Obsolescence of Deterrence, Weekly Standard, December 9, 2002, p. 22
Adrian R. Lewis, The American Culture of War: The History of U.S. Military Force from World War II to Operation Iraqi Freedom, 2007
Tod Lindberg, Deterrence and Prevention, 8 Weekly Standard No. 20, February 3, 2003
Edward N. Luttwak, Where Are the Great Powers? At Home with the Kids, 73 Foreign Affairs No. 4, p. 23, July/August 1994
Robert Mandel, Security, Strategy, and the Quest for Bloodless War, 2004
Max G. Manwaring (ed.), Deterrence in the 21st Century, 2001
Robert McNamara, Mutual Deterrence, address in San Francisco, September 18, 1967
Molly Moore, Chirac: Nuclear Response to Terrorism Is Possible, Washington Post, January 20, 2006, p. A12
Patrick M. Morgan, Deterrence Now, 2003
John Mueller, Retreat from Doomsday: The Obsolescence of Major War, 1989
National Research Council, Naval Studies Board, Post-Cold War Conflict Deterrence, 1997
National Security and Nuclear Weapons: Maintaining Deterrence in the 21st Century, Statement by the Secretary of Energy, Secretary of Defense, and Secretary of State, July 2007
National Security Archive, The Cuban Missile Crisis (documents and photographs), http://www.gwu.edu/~nsarchiv/nsa/cuba_mis_cri/index.htm
Keith B. Payne, The Fallacies of Cold War Deterrence and a New Direction, 2001
Colin Powell with Joseph E. Persico, My American Journey, 1995
Christopher B. Puckett, In This Era of 'Smart Weapons,' Is a State Under an International Legal Obligation to Use Precision-Guided Technology in an Armed Conflict? 18 Emory International Law Review 645, Fall 2004
Michael Quinlan, Is Deterrence Dead? Stockholm International Peace Research Institute, Yearbook 2003, p. 639
Jeffrey Record, Failed States and Casualty Phobia: Implications for Force Structure and Technology Choices, Center for Strategy and Technology, Air War College, Maxwell Air Force Base, Occasional Paper 18, October 2000
Jeffrey Record, Collapsed Countries, Casualty Dread, and the New American Way of War, 32 Parameters No. 2, Summer 2002, p. 4
Jeffrey Record, Back to the Weinberger-Powell Doctrine? Strategic Studies Quarterly, Fall 2007, p. 79
John Renaker, Dr. Strangelove and the Hideous Epoch: Deterrence in the Nuclear Age, 2000
C. Paul Robinson, Pursuing a New Nuclear Weapons Policy for the 21st Century, Sandia National Laboratories, White Paper, March 22, 2001
Paul Robinson, 'Ready to Kill but Not to Die,' 54 International Journal, Autumn 1999, p. 671

A.P.V. Rogers, Zero-Casualty Warfare, International Review of the Red Cross No. 837, March 31, 2000, p. 165
James A. Russell and James J. Wirtz, United States Nuclear Strategy in the Twenty-first Century, 25 Contemporary Security Policy No. 1, April 2004, p. 91
Harvey M. Sapolsky and Jeremy Shapiro, Casualties, Technology, and America's Future Wars, 26 Parameters No. 2, Summer 1996, p. 119
Thomas C. Schelling, Arms and Influence, 1966
Thomas C. Schelling, The Strategy of Conflict, 1980
H. Norman Schwarzkopf with Peter Petre, It Doesn't Take a Hero, 1992
Stanley R. Sloan, The United States and the Use of Force in the Post-Cold War World: Toward Self-Deterrence? Congressional Research Service Report for the U.S. House of Representatives Committee on Foreign Affairs, August 1994
Hugh Smith, What Costs Will Democracies Bear? A Review of Popular Theories of Casualty Aversion, 31 Armed Forces & Society No. 4, p. 487, Summer 2005
Glenn H. Snyder, Deterrence and Defense: Toward a Theory of National Security, 1961
Theodore C. Sorensen, Kennedy, 1965
Peter Stalenheim, Damien Fruchart, Wuyi Omitoogun, and Catalina Perdomo, Military Expenditures, in Stockholm International Peace Research Institute, Yearbook 2006: Armaments, Disarmament, and International Security, p. 295
Peter Stalenheim, Catalina Perdomo, and Elisabeth Skons, Military Expenditure, in Stockholm International Peace Research Institute, Yearbook 2007: Armaments, Disarmament, and International Security, p. 267
Peter Stalenheim, Catalina Perdomo, and Elisabeth Skons, Military Expenditure, in Stockholm International Peace Research Institute, Yearbook 2008: Armaments, Disarmament, and International Security, p. 175
Paul C. Stern, Robert Axelrod, Robert Jervis, and Roy Radner (eds.), Perspectives on Deterrence, 1989
Nina Tannenwald, The Nuclear Taboo: The United States and the Normative Basis of Nuclear Non-Use, 53 International Organization No. 3, Summer 1999, p. 433
Thinkquest.org, Fourteen Days in October: The Cuban Missile Crisis, http://library.thinkquest.org/11046/
Stansfield Turner, Caging the Genies: A Workable Solution for Nuclear, Chemical, and Biological Weapons, 1999
Sun Tzu, The Art of War, c. 440–320 B.C.
U.S. Department of Defense Dictionary, "deterrence," http://www.dtic.mil/doctrine/jel/doddict
U.S. Department of Defense, National Defense Strategy, June 2008
U.S. Department of Defense, Report of the Secretary of Defense Task Force on DoD Nuclear Weapons Management, Phase II: Review of the DoD Nuclear Mission, December 2008
U.S. Department of State, Foreign Relations of the United States, 1961–1963, vol. XI
U.S. Department of State, Clinton Administration Policy on Reforming Multilateral Peace Operations (PDD 25), February 22, 1996, available at http://www.fas.org/irp/offdocs/pdd25.htm

U.S. Joint Chiefs of Staff, Doctrine for Joint Nuclear Operations, Joint Publication 3–12 (Final Coordination Draft), March 15, 2005

U.S. Marine Corps, Small Wars Manual, 1940

Caspar W. Weinberger, U.S. Defense Strategy, 64 Foreign Affairs, Spring 1986, p. 675

Donald C. Whitmore, Revisiting Nuclear Deterrence Theory, March 1, 1998, available at http://www.abolishnukes.com/short_essays/deterrence_theory_whitmore.html

Amy F. Woolf, Nuclear Weapons: Changes in Policy and Force Structure, Congressional Research Service Report for Congress, RL31623, August 10, 2006

Amy F. Woolf, Nuclear Weapons in U.S. National Security Policy: Past, Present, and Prospects, Congressional Research Service Report for Congress, RL 34226, December 30, 2008

3

The Law of Armed Conflict

Scenario 3

The specter of revolution loomed over Canada in 1837. William MacKenzie's abortive uprising against British rule had been quashed in what is now the province of Ontario, but the remnants of his rebel band retreated into the United States, especially into upstate New York, to regroup and resupply, as well as to recruit new members.

On December 11–13, 1837, in a series of rousing mass meetings in Buffalo, MacKenzie issued a new proclamation for insurrection and earnestly solicited private American citizens to join his quest to oust the British overlords. He established a makeshift headquarters on Navy Island, a small British possession in a narrow portion of the Niagara River. Rallying to his support, an eager American, Rensselaer Van Rensselaer, who had been appointed a general by MacKenzie, raised a "Patriot Army" of 300 and advanced to Navy Island, unfurling a new Canadian flag. Within two weeks, the force had grown to 1000 well-armed men, encamped on Navy Island and also at Black Rock on the American side of the river.

The Caroline was a small steamer (46 tons displacement, 71 feet long), owned by an American and chartered by the rebel force to shuttle men and materiel. On the morning of December 29, the Caroline left Buffalo, called at Black Rock and then at Navy Island, and discharged a quantity of men and freight. The ship then progressed on to Ft. Schlosser, but it made two more trips back to Navy Island that afternoon before tying up for the night at the port at Ft. Schlosser. The captain and a crew of ten men stayed with the steamer, and they also accommodated another 23 random visitors who asked to spend the night onboard because they had been unable to obtain lodging elsewhere in the wintry city.

Meanwhile, Colonel Allan Napier McNab, the commander of the British forces in the region at Chippawa, had become apprised of the threatening activities of MacKenzie, his new American colleagues, and the Caroline. He calculated that prompt destruction of the ship would impede additional efforts to reinforce the rebels on Navy Island and would also deprive them of the means to cross the river and invade Canada.

Under the cover of a frigid darkness on December 29, McNab dispatched a force of 45 armed men in five small boats under Commander Andrew Drew of the Royal Navy. They had expected to ambush the Caroline on Navy Island, but when they rounded the point of that island, they realized that the ship was moored on the American shore instead, so they then decided to extend their mission, breaching U.S. territory to attack and seize the vessel.

About midnight, the invasion force, armed with muskets, swords, and cutlasses, assaulted the ship. The skirmish lasted only a short time; few of those aboard the vessel offered any resistance, and most sought only to escape. In the fighting, one or two men (Amos Durfee and possibly the cabin boy, "Little Billy" Johnson) were killed, several rebels were wounded, and two were taken prisoner.

The British forces then cut the Caroline loose from her moorings, towed her into the middle of the river, and set her afire. In full flames, the ship then drifted downstream, ultimately cascading to destruction over the Niagara Falls, only 5 kilometers away.

MacKenzie's revolution eventually fizzled, but the controversy ignited by the British invasion of American sovereignty and the destruction of the Caroline defied easy resolution. A series of tight-jawed diplomatic exchanges between U.S. Secretary of State John Forsyth and the British minister in Washington, Henry S. Fox, only escalated the tensions. The British complained about the manifest failure of federal and state authorities to prevent U.S. territory from being exploited by the rebels and claimed that this American infringement of the principles of neutrality and friendly relations justified the forceful British exercise of self-defense. American interlocutors just as rigidly asserted that the British incursion was unjustified and illegal and demanded a full apology and reparations.

By 1841, the redoubtable Daniel Webster had succeeded Forysth as secretary of state and was eager to resolve the matter that had vexed his predecessor. Webster renewed a detailed correspondence with Fox and with British ambassador Alexander Baring (Lord Ashburton), who had been dispatched from London to attempt to resolve this and other nagging Anglo-American controversies.

In his key letter to Ashburton, on July 27, 1842, Webster adduced the central legal principles at stake, reiterating that Britain's position regarding the use of military force inside the United States could be justified only upon a showing of

> *Necessity of self-defense, instant, overwhelming, leaving no choice of means, and no moment for deliberation. It will be for it to show, also, that the local authorities of Canada, even supposing the necessity of the moment authorized them to enter the territories of the United States at all, did nothing unreasonable or excessive; since the act justified by the necessity of self-defence, must be limited by that necessity, and kept clearly within it.*

Ashburton responded by accepting Webster's articulation of the guiding legal principles, but he asserted that the British action had, in fact, satisfied these strict criteria defining reasonable self-defense: The invading force had not originally intended to touch American soil but had advanced that far only on the spur of the moment, when they realized where the Caroline had docked. The river current was so strong that they were unable to tow the vessel safely to the Canadian side, so they did no more than was necessary to destroy it. They had deliberately chosen to attack at night to minimize the loss of life in any battle; they had brought the ship into the river channel before lighting her on fire to avoid endangering the port of Ft. Schlosser.

Nonetheless, Ashburton wrote, Her Majesty's government regretted the incident and apologized for not resolving it sooner. Webster, deftly responding to the closing portion of Ashburton's letter, pocketed the British "apology" and considered the matter closed.

In the ensuing years, the two conditions specified by Webster in his July 27 epistle have come to underpin the fundamental principles of the modern international law of armed conflict. A use of military force, to be considered valid as an exercise of national self-defense, must now be (a) necessary, in the sense of a "last resort" – no diplomatic or other non-violent measures would suffice to resolve the matter peacefully, and (b) proportional, meaning that the invading force responds in a measured fashion, doing nothing in scope or duration beyond what is narrowly tailored to accomplish the legitimate objective. Countries and commentators around the world and through the centuries have come to accept these standards – which arose from the wreckage of the Caroline – as binding international law.[1]

[1] The leading sources regarding the Caroline affair include John Bassett Moore, A Digest of International Law, volume II, sec. 217, 1906; Kenneth R. Stevens, Border Diplomacy:

LAW OF ARMED CONFLICT

Many people still deride the whole notion of a law of armed conflict as absurd – an oxymoron equivalent to "military intelligence" or "military music" – because warfare represents the ultimate breakdown of law and social order. The image of battlefield violence being hamstrung by cool jurisprudence seems so far-fetched that there is even a hoary Latin aphorism (often attributed to Cicero) on point: *inter arma silent leges* (in time of war, law is silent).

Nonetheless, law does, in fact, happen – even when the bullets are flying and the cutlasses swirling. Since the Egyptians and the Sumerians in the second millennium B.C., countries have attempted to rein in their violent instincts with the strands of international law. Today, the United States, along with virtually all other members of the world community, has joined in choreographing rules to constrain warfare, and the participants take those rules seriously. A series of canonical treaties has codified and elaborated Webster's principles; an enormous literature has commented upon them; and severe diplomatic and public relations repercussions – as well as criminal prosecutions – may attend any substantial deviation from agreed codes of conduct.

To operationalize the standards, military service members are trained to know, understand, and apply the fundamental principles of the law of armed conflict (LoAC – also referred to as the law of war, or as international humanitarian law). Likewise, commanders at all levels are enjoined to adhere to binding legal principles, and legions of lawyers – uniformed judge advocates or their civilian counterparts – are comprehensively injected into strategic planning, war games exercises, and operational actions.

Even weapons procurement decisions are guided by law. Pursuant to treaty arrangements and to internal U.S. directives, each new armaments technology – including all those surveyed in Chapters 4–8 of this

The Caroline and McLeod Affairs in Anglo-American-Canadian Relations, 1837–1842, 1989; R.Y. Jennings, The Caroline and McLeod Cases, 32 American Journal of International Law 82, 1938; Louis-Philippe Rouillard, The Caroline Case: Anticipatory Self-Defence in Contemporary International Law, 1 Miskolc Journal of International Law No. 2, p. 104, 2004. See also James A. Green, Docking the Caroline: Understanding the Relevance of the Formula in Contemporary Customary International Law Concerning Self-Defense, 14 Cardozo Journal of International and Comparative Law 429, Fall 2006. But see Maria Benvenuta Occelli, 'Sinking' the Caroline: Why the Caroline Doctrine's Restrictions on Self-Defense Should Not Be Regarded as Customary International Law, 4 San Diego International Law Journal 467, 2003 (arguing against expansive use of the Caroline precedent).

book – must be reviewed for its consistency with international arms control and other legal obligations at the stage of initial engineering and development, at the stage of procurement authorization, or both.[2]

Of course, there are notorious violations of this body of law – just as there are deliberate, conspicuous, and seemingly perpetual violations of all legal systems, including the internal criminal law of the United States. Some rogue international actors seem to "get away with" their violations, in the sense that the global legal apparatus appears congenitally incapable of apprehending them or inflicting meaningful punishment upon them. Again, the comparison to domestic legal systems, even in law-intensive societies such as the United States, is illustrative. Here, too, some miscreants (pick your favorite sociopath: petty street criminals, organized crime families, white collar corporate swindlers, corrupt politicians) seem to evade effective law enforcement for long periods of time – but that's a story for another book!)

In every modern war, American service members have committed crimes, sometimes serious, sustained misdeeds, in violation of the applicable LoAC. And in each of those wars, the United States has investigated, prosecuted, and punished guilty parties. For example, the 1968 My Lai massacre during the Vietnam War, and the subsequent court martial of Lt. William Calley, galvanized public attention and emotion regarding the operation of the military justice system; a generation later, the same sorts of war crimes allegations are on display regarding Abu Ghraib, Haditha, and other horrors in Iraq. The record of military law enforcement is, of course, imperfect – but perhaps it approximates the record of zeal, success, and honor accumulated by domestic U.S. criminal law enforcement agencies at the same times.

WHY OBEY THIS LAW?

Why do countries articulate LoAC rules? Why do they obey and enforce those rules, even in "fog of war" situations where a violation might

[2] U.S. Department of Defense Directive 5000.1, The Defense Acquisition System, May 12, 2003, sec. E1.1.15; Protocol Additional (No. I) to the Geneva Conventions of August 12, 1949, and Relating to the Protection of Victims of International Armed Conflicts, June 8, 1977, 1125 U.N.T.S. 3, 16 I.L.M. 1391 (1977) [hereinafter Protocol I] (United States not a party), art. 36; Justin McClelland, The Review of Weapons in Accordance with Article 36 of Additional Protocol I, International Review of the Red Cross, No. 850, June 2003, p. 397; Isabelle Daoust, Robin Coupland, and Rikke Ishoey, New Wars, New Weapons? The Obligation of States to Assess the Legality of Means and Methods of Warfare, International Review of the Red Cross No. 846, June 2002, p. 345.

be perceived as advantageous or even irresistible under life-and-death pressures of conflict?[3] One type of explanation lies in simple honor or ethics, derived from the ancient codes of chivalry and religion – there are some things that respectable people and countries simply do not do, even in the most extreme circumstances, and even if the enemy, for whatever reasons, is not similarly morally self-restrained.

Another category of rationales supporting the dynamic notion of LoAC sounds in national self-interest. First, we follow the laws of civilized behavior to encourage our enemies to do likewise. Setting a good example in this way does not, of course, guarantee reciprocity, but the inverse proposition does seem to be true: if we deviate from lawful practice, the probability goes up that the other side will, too. Second, a disciplined, well-regulated military is a more effective fighting force; if our soldiers concentrate their energies on the valid operational tasks at hand, without being distracted by lawless pillaging and raping, they are more likely to succeed in battle. Third, adherence to law can encourage our enemies to surrender: if they know we treat our prisoners of war and our defeated enemies decently and with respect, they will be less prone to fight to the bitter end, as they would logically do if they believed that surrender would inevitably result in monstrous mistreatment. Fourth, compliance with fundamental codes of humanity will help build and sustain vital public support for military operations – at home, among the population of the host country, and in the world at large. Fifth, humanitarian moderation in combat and avoiding excessive damage can help reduce postwar bitterness, facilitate recovery, and promote the restoration of normal relations with a defeated – but not ravaged – enemy, improving prospects for long-term peace and security.

Finally, service members adhere to legal constraints because they know they can be prosecuted – in their own country's military justice system or in an international war crimes tribunal of some sort – if they fail to live up to those standards. The leadership up the chain of command, likewise, is increasingly aware of the prospect of intrusive after-the-fact judicial review and of severe criminal sanctions if they or their subordinates fall conspicuously short of established law.

In short, countries train their troops, they expect to fight, and they do in reality wage war in a law-bound fashion – not always, but routinely. People sometimes say that "All's fair in love and war" – but at least the combat part of that assessment is no longer quite so true.

[3] This discussion is drawn from the work of David E. Graham, as presented in his guest lectures in my International Law class at the Georgetown University Law Center.

MODERN STRESSES ON LoAC

The traditional international legal principles regulating battlefield violence have fallen under unusual stresses in recent years. Three factors in particular, paralleling certain salient characteristics of the "revolution in military affairs," stand out.

First, the awesome destructiveness of modern weaponry challenges all precedents. Nuclear, biological, and chemical weapons carry the potential to inflict such catastrophic damage that our forebears' notions of decent self-restraint may seem unacceptably risky. When modern "delivery systems" – strategic bombers and especially swift long-range missiles – are added to the mix, the modern era is categorically different from everything that has come before. Perhaps each generation, as it experiences its own revolutions in military affairs, is apprehensive about the newfound prowess that threatens all of humanity in jaw-dropping ways – the longbow, gunpowder, and the Gatling gun surely seemed to augur a possibility for mass slaughter that imperiled their civilizations. But the twenty-first century has genuinely achieved unthinkable doomsday capabilities – we truly have invented, and have proliferated, the capacity to end all human life on earth – and there is no guarantee that earlier laws of war will suffice to protect us from our species' own short-sightedness.

Second, the onslaught of modern superterrorism throws an additional monkey wrench into the gears of LoAC. International law arose in a state-centric era, and, unsurprisingly, most articulated rules deal with state-to-state behavior. That, after all, was where the world's principal security problems arose for several centuries, so that is where the law-makers concentrated their attention. Today, however, the cast of relevant characters has enlarged significantly, and perhaps the rules of the game need to be altered, too, to accommodate more effectively the emerged threat from nonstate actors. Where twenty-first century conditions on the world's battlefields – and in the world's subways, office buildings, and airports – no longer approximate the nineteenth century's pitched engagements between professional corps of uniformed national combatants, perhaps the inherited legal wisdom must be revisited, too.

Third, the traditional international legal structure has lately been strained in a different way by the manifest disrespect shown for international law in general, and LoAC in particular, by the George W. Bush Administration. This chapter is not the place to revisit the controversies about the preemptive invasion of Iraq, the detention camp at Guantanamo Bay, the secret practice of "rendition," or the use of "waterboarding" and other near-torture techniques in interrogation. But it is obvious that any legal structure depends in a basic way upon support and reaffirmation from its key participants. When the largest and most influential player, the planet's sole remaining military superpower, conspicuously distances itself from established precedent, the system will be stressed. When senior White House leadership refers to the Geneva Conventions (widely regarded as the foundation stone for all LoAC) as "obsolete" and "quaint,"[4] it becomes much easier for other actors around the globe to disparage other aspects of the international legal structure, too. Not only particular rules of LoAC, but the whole edifice of national self-restraint in combat, become jeopardized by that level of disrespect.

Still, despite all these diverse pressures, the core principles of LoAC retain their validity. Individual rules, of course, will be amended and supplemented to respond to new circumstances – in any healthy legal system, some degree of change is a positive indicator of the ability to adapt in an appropriate fashion to alterations in the external environment. But the underlying fundamentals received from Daniel Webster and his heirs are not out of line with modern circumstances; they may need to be bolstered, edited, and applied in new ways because of the new stimuli, but they need not be overborne.

Four traditional LoAC principles in particular remain central to our analysis and ought to constrain American and other military adaptations to the modern challenges. These doctrines undergird both military professionalism and enduring social notions of decency, and they should apply, *mutatis mutandis,* to and through the contemporary revolution in military affairs. The next sections of this chapter, therefore, introduce and explain the unequivocal normative notions of arms control, discrimination, necessity, and proportionality, as they will apply in different ways to the weapons technologies surveyed in subsequent chapters.[5]

[4] Alberto R. Gonzales, Counsel to the President, Memorandum for the President, Decision Re: Application of the Geneva Convention on Prisoners of War to the Conflict with Al Qaeda and the Taliban, January 25, 2002 (noting that the war against terrorism is "a new kind of war," placing a premium on quickly obtaining information from captured terrorists, and asserting, "In my judgment, this new paradigm renders obsolete Geneva's strict limitations on questioning of enemy prisoners and renders quaint some of its provisions. . . . ")

[5] On applicable LoAC principles, see generally Jean-Marie Henckaerts and Louise Doswald-Beck, Customary International Humanitarian Law, 2005; Dieter Fleck (ed.), The Handbook of Humanitarian Law in Armed Conflicts, 2008; Marie Anderson and Emily Zukauskas (eds.), Operational Law Handbook, U.S. Army Judge Advocate General's Legal Center and School, International and Operational Law Department, 2008; Judith Gardam, Necessity, Proportionality and the Use of Force by States, 2004; A.P.V. Rogers, Law on the Battlefield (2nd ed.), 2004.

ARMS CONTROL LIMITATIONS ON SPECIFIC WEAPONS

A cardinal principle of the international law regulating the use of military force is the proposition that countries are not free to use any and all weapons and tactics in fighting – there are some important, ascertainable limits, and the corpus of law from time to time creates additional constraints. As expressed in the 1868 Declaration of St. Petersburg (the first modern arms control treaty, designed to outlaw exploding or inflammable bullets, which caused much worse injuries than ordinary projectiles of that era):

> The only legitimate object which States should endeavor to accomplish during war is to weaken the military force of the enemy . . . for this purpose it is sufficient to disable the greatest possible number of men . . . this object would be exceeded by the employment of arms which uselessly aggravate the sufferings of disabled men or render their death inevitable . . . the employment of such arms would, therefore, be contrary to the laws of humanity.[6]

From this seed has sprouted a general accord on the principle of "humanity": countries must refrain from employing weapons or tactics that create "unnecessary suffering" or "superfluous injury." Those pregnant terms, of course, do not lend themselves to easy definition – in the miasma of warfare, it may be difficult to differentiate between "necessary" and "excessive" violence. One relevant touchstone expunges weapons or actions that inherently result in the otherwise-avoidable death or permanent serious injury of the victim. Where lesser levels of power would readily suffice to disable an enemy temporarily (effectively making him *hors de combat*, out of any further action), anything beyond that accomplishment is "superfluous."

In addition, a series of agreements has fleshed out specific prohibitions on particular categories of unacceptable weapons and ploys, including some that might otherwise be of potential interest in the ongoing U.S. revolution in military affairs. There is little inherent logic in the list of armaments and tactics that have so far been explicitly outlawed as inhumane by treaty or by customary international law. These are not necessarily the deadliest, the most powerful, the most painful, or the most horrifying to the imagination, but they are devices and modes of fighting

[6] Declaration Renouncing the Use, in Time of War, of Explosive Projectiles Under 400 Grammes Weight, adopted at St. Petersburg by the International Military Commission, December 11, 1868, Preamble.

that, for whatever reason, have attracted the attention of the public, the military leadership, and the disarmament negotiators, who have cast them beyond the pale of legitimate warfighting apparatus.

The earliest examples of these prohibitions intended to reduce war's torment and toil included bans on serrated-edge bayonets, on lances or spears with barbed heads, and on expanding bullets (such as the dum-dum variety), all of which needlessly inflict more grievous injuries than their "ordinary" counterparts. Likewise, weapons that injure primarily through glass or plastic fragments not detectable in the human body via x-rays provide no additional military advantage but do compromise medical treatment efforts. More recently, certain types and applications of booby trap mechanisms, incendiaries, and lasers designed to cause total, permanent blinding have been proscribed by treaties.[7]

Closer to the concerns of this book, widely adopted treaties have stigmatized chemical and biological weapons. The unspeakable horrors of chlorine, phosgene, mustard, and a noxious potpourri of other lethal chemicals killed nearly 100,000 and injured more than 1 million during World War I and sparked a public revulsion that led to the 1925 Geneva Gas Protocol and (much later) to the 1972 Biological Weapons Convention and the more comprehensive 1993 Chemical Weapons Convention. These instruments establish a comprehensive prohibition against toxic chemicals on the battlefield, although a curious exception allows the use of "nonlethal" riot control agents for domestic law enforcement purposes. As elaborated in Chapter 8, certain nonlethal chemical concoctions have attracted renewed interest for military applications as well.

Antipersonnel land mines (APL), too, have drawn the attention of treaty drafters, and not one, but two competing legal regimes are now in place, as discussed in Chapter 6. One of these bans, for its 156 parties, all APL; the other, supported by 91 countries (including the United States), is less categorical, allowing some types of mines while prohibiting the very longlasting varieties that contribute most directly to a humanitarian crisis.

The antisatellite weapons addressed in Chapter 7 are only partially constrained by international law, prominently the 1967 Outer Space Treaty, but at least some versions and some applications of space weapons would not be lawful under widely accepted jurisprudence. Even more complicated are the low-yield nuclear weapons discussed in Chapter 5.

[7] Convention on Prohibitions or Restrictions on the Use of Certain Conventional Weapons Which May Be Deemed to Be Excessively Injurious or to Have Indiscriminate Effects, Oct. 10, 1980, 1342 U.N.T.S. 137, 19 I.L.M. 1523 [hereinafter CCW].

On that subject, the International Court of Justice (ICJ; a.k.a. the World Court) ruled in 1996 that international law neither expressly permits nor expressly prohibits the threat or use of nuclear weapons, but that these most devastating armaments would be governed by the same generally applicable legal principles noted in the sections to follow. There are numerous treaties relevant to nuclear weapons – banning or regulating their proliferation, testing, and deployment numbers – but not declaring them to be *per se* invalid agents of "unnecessary suffering."

So the point for this first step in the application of LoAC to revolutionary new weapons technologies is the observation that some types of arms are regulated or outright banned by international law as uselessly aggravating the inevitable suffering caused by warfare. The scope and operation of these specific arms control instruments may not always be crystal clear (especially in considering their application to newly emerging devices), and the web of legal constraints they have so far managed to weave is porous. But the weaponeers will have to aim for those (admittedly rather large) gaps in the understanding of "unnecessary suffering" and prohibited weaponry and tactics.

DISCRIMINATION

The second vital LoAC principle is discrimination (or distinction). Warring parties are required at all times to differentiate between combatants and other legitimate military objectives (who may be attacked) versus civilians and other protected persons, property, and locations (who are immune from direct targeting). A military force must undertake all feasible precautions in selecting the means and methods of its attacks to minimize civilian losses. Belligerents are further mandated to separate themselves from concentrations of noncombatants and not to intermingle military and civilian assets, in order to enable enemy forces to direct their power only against lawful targets.

Legitimate military targets are "objects which by their nature, location, purpose, or use make an effective contribution to military action and whose total or partial destruction, capture or neutralization, in the circumstances ruling at the time, offers a definite military advantage."[8] All other persons and objects are protected against attack unless they take a direct or active part in hostilities.

[8] Protocol Additional (No. 1), supra note 2, article 52.2. The United States is not party to this protocol, but has accepted article 52 as declaratory of binding customary international law.

An indiscriminate weapon – a cloud of chemical gas cast onto a capricious wind, for example – is banned by this principle. Because the lethal agent cannot be effectively steered toward a specific, valid military target or its effects reliably directed away from off-limits civilian areas, it fails the test of discrimination. Inaccurate, unguided missiles are likewise suspect; random luck, rather than a targeteer's controlled and deliberate choice, determines what sites are exposed to shrapnel. Large nuclear weapons may be the ultimate indiscriminate "ecocide" device; as the ICJ declared in the 1996 case, their catastrophic power "cannot be contained in either space or time."[9]

The modern invocation of precision guided munitions (PGMs) as surveyed in Chapter 4 provides today's best elaboration of the principle of distinction. An offensive force equipped with these exquisitely accurate "smart bombs" becomes able to select targets individually and to have high confidence in striking the designated aimpoints – and only those locations. To the extent that protected persons and sites can reliably be avoided, PGMs enable an enormously effective and still fully lawful, discriminating application of air power.

In practice, of course, this sharp segregation between civilian and military assets is often impossible. Bombs (even smart bombs) still go astray, and damage is rarely neatly confined to a single designated strike location. And even a precise weapon may be employed in an illegitimately indiscriminate fashion. Laser or other directed energy antisatellite weapons, for example, as surveyed in Chapter 7, could be capable of exquisite specificity, zooming in on a particular satellite or even a specified *part* of a particular satellite. But an unrepentant ASAT user could also endanger the greater outer space environment with indiscriminate malice, arbitrarily pumping disrupting electromagnetic energy into space, where it could wreak havoc upon civil and military satellites of many random countries.

Moreover, it is often devilishly difficult to characterize an object as strictly civilian or military. The Caroline, as described in Scenario 3, was clearly performing a militarily valuable function for MacKenzie's rebels in shuttling between rebel encampments on Navy Island and Black Rock, but many of its other operations involved concurrently serving ordinary commercial customers in Ft. Schlosser, Buffalo, and other benign locations.

In the twenty-first century, the dividing line between military and civilian entities and activities has often been stretched so thin as to be nearly

[9] International Court of Justice, Legality of the Use by a State of Nuclear Weapons in Armed Conflict, (Advisory Opinion), ICJ Reports, July 8, 1996, p. 66, 243, para. 35.

invisible. As elaborated in Chapter 7, for example, modern fleets of orbiting satellites are multifunction: they serve alternately, or simultaneously, both sets of applications. Communications, remote sensing, and meteorology, after all, are needed by both the Pentagon and civilians; it is virtually impossible to tease apart the interwoven aspects of these dual purpose birds. More prosaically, common terrestrial assets such as roads, railroads, bridges, electrical power plants, telephone stations, and radio transmitters are all multitasking and ambiguous – they are essential for both military and civilian users – and their vulnerability to attack becomes controversial.

Moreover, the tactics and harsh realities of modern warfare increasingly confound the neat discrimination contemplated by earlier law. As combatants intrude into densely populated areas – MOUT (military operations in urban terrain) is the new buzzword for the now-prevailing form of conflict – the burden of separation becomes much more difficult than it was in the relatively simple era of massed armies engaging across static trench lines, open fields, or isolated woodlands. Partly for these reasons, the statistical documentation is striking: in recent conflicts, upwards of 90 percent of wartime casualties have been civilians.

That story is unlikely to improve soon. In fact, to the extent that ongoing operations in Iraq, Afghanistan, and elsewhere are harbingers, the nature of much future warfare may be predominantly counterinsurgency campaigns. These typically involve relatively low-intensity operations in built-up communities, attempting to win the hearts and minds of the citizenry, as well as to defeat the guerrilla armed bands operating in their midst, and the difficulty of identifying and separately targeting enemy fighters, and *only* enemy fighters, is a defining characteristic of the enterprise.

The United Nations Security Council has recently noted the increasingly horrible toll that armed conflict now inflicts upon civilians, stressing the importance of full compliance with the principles of humanitarian law and suggesting that widespread or flagrant violations of LoAC principles could constitute a "threat to international peace and security," triggering the Security Council's own responsibilities to redress the breach.[10]

Associated with the requirement for discrimination is the principle of respect for the rights of neutral or nonbelligerent countries. If a nation wishes to absent itself from a particular international or internal armed conflict, it is ordinarily permitted to do so as long as it impartially refrains from assisting or favoring either side in the fighting. In response, the

[10] United Nations Security Council Resolution 1674, April 28, 2006.

belligerents are required to honor the neutral's status, not attacking it or using it as a base for military operations. In the Caroline case, it was the inability or unwillingness of authorities in New York and Washington, D.C., to enforce true neutrality that provided the occasion and partial justification for British anger and action.

As indicated in subsequent chapters, the ability to respect the isolation of neutral countries is increasingly suspect in many circumstances today. Nuclear weapons, as indicated in Chapter 5, are enormously powerful; even a relatively small, low-yield nuclear weapon packs a Hurricane Katrina-like punch that disregards political boundaries. Likewise, the subsequent fallout and other deadly contaminating effects can hardly be confined to a legitimate military target caught in the cross hairs, or even to a single victimized country. In the same vein, many of the antisatellite weapons addressed in Chapter 7 operate via exoatmospheric explosions or collisions that generate quantities of debris. This "space junk," traveling at enormous orbital speeds, inevitably creates an enduring hazard for the spacecraft of other nations, even those who sought to preserve strict neutrality between the warring parties.

Still, the notion of distinction, along with the core of the other LoAC principles – which the ICJ has labeled "intransgressible"[11] – retain their vitality. Indiscriminate weapons and tactics are prohibited; an attack that is not directed against a specific military objective is illegitimate. A weapon that, because of its nature and design, is incapable of distinguishing between military and civilian objects, or a method or means of combat operated in a fashion that ignores these time-honored requirements of differentiation, is illegal.

MILITARY NECESSITY

The basic principle of military necessity is, in a sense, derived from the other principles adduced previously. In wartime, a country is justified in wreaking a great deal of havoc on the enemy – but the legitimate scope of death and destruction must be confined to what is militarily necessary. Attacks that confer a definite military advantage in pursuit of compelling the enemy to submit are valid; anything beyond that objective is, by definition, unnecessary, and therefore proscribed.

Soldiers are not required to be nice to an enemy and may apply deadly, devastating, and overwhelming force – but only where it is necessary to

[11] ICJ, supra note 9.

do so. Both the scale of the violence and its duration are assessed under this criterion; if too much power is applied, or if it lasts too long, the operation is suspect.

The standard of necessity is admittedly imprecise; it is often painfully difficult to parse "essential" and "excessive" force. Moreover, necessity may be an elastic measuring stick. That is, as our military technology improves – as we acquire the capacity to behave in a more accurate, more deft, more nuanced fashion – the evolving legal standard may eventually grow to *require* that heightened degree of care. Today, this jurisprudential creep is most evidenced regarding precision-guided munitions. That is, some scholars suggest that where a country (i.e., the United States) possesses the ability to employ ordnance of greater precision than traditional types, and where there are sufficient smart bombs in the inventory, it may eventually become *mandatory* to use them instead of deploying old-fashioned, less accurate "dumb" bombs, to avoid inflicting what has then become "unnecessary" damage. Moreover, a country so equipped may be subject to this heightened legal exactitude, even if its adversary (because of inferior technology, lesser financial resources, or simple bad military judgment) is not similarly constrained.[12]

In comparable fashion, it is predictable that before too long, the array of nonlethal weapons considered in Chapter 8 may invoke a parallel controversy. If a country (again, the United States is the pioneer in the field) is able to parlay its inventory of tasers, pepper spray, millimeter wave heat rays, and other devices to accomplish its military objectives without killing people or destroying property, should it be *required* to do so, to avoid fatalities and property losses that are no longer, because of these technological marvels, necessary? To date, the United States and its NATO allies have righteously rejected any such interpretation, and any asymmetrical imposition of a requirement for using nonlethal weapons, in an environment in which the opponents are equipped only with traditional lethal force, does seem problematic. But this example,

[12] For the debate about whether the United States may be required to use only precision-guided munitions, see Stuart Walters Belt, Missiles Over Kosovo: Emergence, Lex Lata, of a Customary Norm Requiring the Use of Precision Munitions in Urban Areas, 47 Naval Law Review 115, 2000; Danielle L. Infeld, Precision Guided Munitions Demonstrated Their Pinpoint Accuracy in Desert Storm; But Is a Country Obligated to Use Precision Technology to Minimize Collateral Civilian Injury and Damage? 26 George Washington Journal of International Law and Economics 109, 1992; Christopher B. Puckett, In This Era of 'Smart Weapons,' Is a State Under an International Legal Obligation to Use Precision-Guided Technology in Armed Conflict? 18 Emory International Law Review 645, Fall 2004.

too, illustrates the fundamental LoAC point: nothing more than necessary force is authorized.

Conceivably, even the antisatellite weapons analyzed in Chapter 7 could witness a comparable development: If the United States becomes capable of negating enemy spacecraft without destroying them (e.g., by crafting laser beams that could temporarily disrupt or confuse a hostile satellite without totally or permanently destroying it, and without spewing a cloud of pernicious debris that could prove lethal to other space systems that wander into the same orbit), could that degree of self-restraint eventually become mandatory?[13]

In the more general sense, LoAC practitioners have long recognized that even international law can be a weak reed in the face of revolutions in military technology – the painstaking step-by-step accomplishments of diplomats in crafting new treaties are regularly lapped by the effervescence of weapons designers and the creativity of laboratories. Accordingly, a generic sort of "savings provision," known as the "Martens Clause" after its original exponent, underpins the legal principles. As expressed in the 1907 4th Hague Convention, which articulated many of the rules still applicable to war on land today,

> Until a more complete code of the laws of war has been issued, the High Contracting Parties deem it expedient to declare that, in cases not included in the Regulations adopted by them, the inhabitants and the belligerents remain under the protection and the rule of the principles of the law of nations, as they result from the usages established among civilized peoples, from the laws of humanity, and the dictates of the public conscience.[14]

This provision functions as a sort of permanent customary law "precautionary principle," suggesting that even in the absence of specific regulation of a newly emerging weapon program, the established corpus of general LoAC principles and the dictates of the public conscience will extend to provide coverage; there should be no unrestrained lacuna, no totally unfilled gaps in the fabric of law.

PROPORTIONALITY

The criterion of proportionality is where all the LoAC principles come together. In short form, in launching an attack, a combatant is required to

[13] Elizabeth S. Waldrop, Weaponization of Outer Space: U.S. National Policy, 26 Annals of Air and Space Law, p. 329, 2004.

[14] Convention (No. IV) Respecting the Laws and Customs of War on Land, concluded at the Hague, October 18, 1907, U.S.T.S. 539, 36 Stat. 2277, preamble.

weigh or balance two admittedly incommensurate variables: the concrete and direct military advantage to be gained from the attack (which provides the legitimate justification for undertaking it) versus the predictable collateral damage it will incur in the form of incidental death or injury to civilians or damage to protected objects. A warfighter is not required to avoid all collateral damage – that would be impossible in any realistic engagement – but is required to assess how much unintended harm the attack is likely to generate, to do everything feasible to avoid or minimize those spinoff losses, and to refrain from launching a disproportionate attack.

Law provides no quantitative guidance in construing this proportionality edict – there is no simple *a priori* formula for judging whether X number of civilian casualties or Y amount of property damage is worthwhile or excessive compared to the capture of a particular location or the destruction of a targeted enemy military asset. Judgments proffered in advance and after the fact will inevitably differ as to whether this subjective calculation has been done correctly. But that is the LoAC challenge – to determine whether an otherwise valid operation must be modified or aborted because it will inflict "too much" harm on protected persons and locations.

This ineffable proportionality calculation is one reason why the job of military planners has become so complex: they must consider how the balance between military effectiveness and collateral damage would be affected by variations in the means and methods of warfare, such as by adjusting the number, size, and type of ordnance applied, the time of day and day of the week of the attack, and the azimuth, angle, and height of burst of the bombs. A formalized Collateral Damage Estimation Methodology (CDEM) relies upon both computer modeling and human intelligence and analysis to predict likely civilian personnel and property losses from proposed strikes, and directs operators to consider techniques for minimization (and for bucking the decision further up the chain of command, if the projected adverse consequences are seen as substantial).

During Gulf War II, American targeteers adopted an informal rule of thumb that if a contemplated attack was likely to result in more than 30 Iraqi civilian casualties, approval from the Secretary of Defense was required. LoAC itself imposes no such absolute strictures (and in any event, twenty such missions were authorized and carried out in 2003), but instituting procedures for high-level approval constitutes an acknowledgment that mature judgment is required in making this excruciating proportionality determination.[15] Leaders' self-restraint, it should not go unnoticed, can carry a performance cost: Secretary Rumsfeld asserted that some three dozen high-priority Iraqi targets, mostly in Baghdad, had been removed from strike lists because of apprehensions about excessive civilian casualties – including some instances in which the danger of high collateral damage had been created deliberately by Saddam Hussein, cynically emplacing human shields in the midst of otherwise legitimate targets.[16]

This is the maddening task of all commanders who order military operations – will this proposed air strike, even when carried out with precision-guided munitions, prove too deadly to use in a crowded neighborhood? Would use of a nuclear weapon – arguably the only effective way to dig out an enemy's hardened, deeply buried command bunker and thereby shorten the war – generate an unacceptable level of immediate destruction and long-lived fallout, jeopardizing far-distant civilians and neutral states? Will application of a modern antisatellite weapon be justified because it disrupts an enemy's military command and control nodes, even if it does so at the cost of polluting the outer space environment, to the long-term disadvantage of all spacefaring states?

An authentic proportionality judgment requires attention not just to the raw numbers of civilian persons, property, and places adversely affected, but also to the extent and nature of the harm inflicted. That is, a death counts for more than a temporary incapacitation; total and irreversible destruction of a protected object or site requires more justification than a partial or transitory disruption or denial of service. Moreover, consideration of indirect or "second-order" effects can become exceedingly complicated. In the 1991 Gulf War I, for example, coalition bombing of Iraq's electrical power generating facilities (a classic dual use infrastructure) succeeded in crippling Saddam Hussein's military command and control apparatus, but it also, predictably, led to a shutdown of Baghdad's civilian water purification and sewage treatment plants, resulting in epidemics of cholera, typhoid, and other communicable diseases, and the deaths of hundreds of civilians. The exact scale, type, and duration of the weapon's effects must be therefore assessed for a valid proportionality judgment.

[15] Mark Benjamin, When Is an Accidental Civilian Death Not an Accident? Salon.com, July 30, 2007.

[16] Eric Schmitt, Rumsfeld Says Dozens of Important Targets Have Been Avoided, New York Times, March 24, 2003, p. B12.

Disproportionate harm to other bystander countries and to the global natural environment, too, is taken into account. For example, the sorts of wanton antisatellite weapons that generate excessive quantities of space debris, harmful over the long term to the peaceful outer space activities of other countries, would be vulnerable under this principle. Likewise, nuclear weapons, even if directed against a valid military target, might inevitably cause the sort of "widespread, long-term and severe" damage to the environment prohibited by a 1977 protocol to the Geneva Conventions.[17]

Daniel Webster's 1842 notion of proportionality requires that we not "go overboard" in responding to another country's provocations. We need not exactly match the aggressor's tactics, weapons, or timing, but neither can we expand without limit the scale of hostilities. Law cannot demand an exquisite calibration of the violence in accomplishing a valid mission – French resistance poet Rene Char referred to war as a "time of damned algebra."[18] But law can require careful, considered judgment in the application of force: exercising enough power to deal effectively with the situation, but not going beyond it to inflict raw punishment, vengeance, or disproportionate suffering on noncombatants.

Finally, it should be noted that the four legal factors outlined previously are independent and possibly antagonistic in some situations. For example, nonlethal weapons, such as acoustic waves, slippery foam, or heat rays described in Chapter 8, are designed to inflict less harm (and less longlasting harm) than ordinary munitions – which should privilege them on the proportionality scale. On the other hand, some of these same nonlethal systems are designed to be used in a widespread, broadcast fashion, directly targeting, or at least simultaneously affecting, a large crowd or general area – which makes them more problematic on the discrimination variable. Similarly, some military use of nonlethal weapons (especially the chemicals, such as mace or pepper spray used as "riot control agents") may run afoul of particular arms control treaties, even if their use might, in fact, save some lives and would continue to be lawful and reasonable in domestic applications. So each of the LoAC considerations must be judged both separately and in combination.

[17] Additional Protocol 1, supra note 2, arts. 35.3 and 55.1. The United States is not party to this protocol and has not explicitly accepted this provision as declaratory of customary international law.

[18] Quoted in Kenneth Anderson, Who Owns the Rules of War? Crimes of War Project, April 24, 2003.

A point of comparison: Much of internal U.S. law is traditionally informed by the notion of a "reasonable man," an imaginary device that enables law students, practitioners, judges, and juries to contemplate what a hypothetical prudent person would, or should, do in the circumstances of a specific case. The companion concept of a "reasonable warrior" may seem even more artificial, but that is what Daniel Webster's 1842 notions of necessity and proportionality demand: We must do "nothing unreasonable or excessive." Even in the midst of conflict, we need to balance the competing considerations of military value versus civilian harms, and we are privileged to do only what is reasonable.

BOTTOM LINE

The modern principles of the law of armed conflict align well with most people's considered notions of common sense, fairness, and legitimacy. They also align well with the "revolution in military affairs'" focus on "effects-based operations" – the insight that we do not necessarily have to kill a person or obliterate a target to negate its military value to an enemy; we may merely have to prevent it from functioning in its usual mode.

More to the point, these LoAC principles dovetail well with the emerging notions of "useability." That is, as we acquire a more refined warfighting capability – the knack for applying force in discrete, measured packets, to the right target, in the right way – it becomes more justified for us to exercise our military muscle.

In the opposite circumstances, where we lack the deft power to inflict pain and suffering with appropriate finesse, we are "self-deterred," reluctant to engage in excessive force that generates too much collateral damage to innocent civilians. That self-restraint is appropriate, and it is strongly reinforced by prevailing legal norms: where a weapon or a tactic is too powerful, where its use would inflict disproportionate, indiscriminate losses upon neighboring protected persons and places, we should refrain from using it, even against a lawful target.

Moreover, where technology changes – and this is the central thesis of this book – the calculations about useability change, too. If the next generation of weapons – for aerial bombardment, nuclear strikes, antipersonnel land mines, antisatellite weapons, and nonlethal weapons – provides an increasing range of capabilities, it offers the promise of empowering us to act with greater military effectiveness. If the emerging weapons are less powerful, less deadly, less destructive, and will generate reduced levels of long-term collateral damage, the proportionality balance is struck differently. Missions formerly scrubbed because they would go beyond military necessity or because they would generate unacceptable harm to unintended victims might now become valid.

If we can create armaments featuring a smaller amount of explosive or greater precision in their placement, or less lethality and shorter duration of their effects, those alterations should change the application of LoAC restrictions. The more useable weaponry thus ameliorates the legal impediments and shifts the morality of self-deterrence.

BIBLIOGRAPHY

Marie Anderson and Emily Zukauskas (eds.), Operational Law Handbook, U.S. Army Judge Advocate General's Legal Center and School, International and Operational Law Department, 2008

John Bellinger III and William J. Haynes, letter to Dr. Jakob Kellenberger, regarding Red Cross Customary International Law Study, November 3, 2006, 46 ILM 511, 2007

Stuart Walters Belt, Missiles Over Kosovo: Emergence, Lex Lata, of a Customary Norm Requiring the Use of Precision Munitions in Urban Areas, 47 Naval Law Review 115, 2000

Mark Benjamin, When Is an Accidental Civilian Death Not an Accident? Salon.com, July 30, 2007

Michel Bourbonniere, Law of Armed Conflict (LOAC) and the Neutralisation of Satellites or *Ius in Bello Satellitis*, 9 Journal of Conflict & Security Law No. 1, 2004, p. 43

Antoine Bouvier, Protection of the Natural Environment in Time of Armed Conflict, International Review of the Red Cross, No. 285, December 31, 1991, p. 567

John T. Correll, Casualties, 86 Air Force Magazine No. 6, June 2003, p. 48

J.W. Crawford, III, The Law of Noncombatant Immunity and the Targeting of National Electrical Power Systems, 21 Fletcher Forum of World Affairs No. 2, Summer/Fall 1997, p. 101

Isabelle Daoust, Robin Coupland, and Rikke Ishoey, New Wars, New Weapons? The Obligation of States to Assess the Legality of Means and Methods of Warfare, International Review of the Red Cross No. 846, June 2002, p. 345

Charles J. Dunlap, Jr., Technology: Recomplicating Moral Life for the Nation's Defenders, 29 Parameters No. 3, Autumn 1999, p. 24

Charles J. Dunlap, Jr., The End of Innocence: Rethinking Noncombatancy in the Post-Kosovo Era, 28 Strategic Review, Summer 2000, p. 9

Dieter Fleck (ed.), The Handbook of Humanitarian Law in Armed Conflicts, 2008

Judith Gardam, Necessity, Proportionality and the Use of Force by States, 2004

Alberto R. Gonzales, Counsel for the President, Memorandum to the President, Decision Re: Application of the Geneva Convention on Prisoners of War to the Conflict with Al Qaeda and the Taliban, January 25, 2002

James A. Green, Docking the Caroline: Understanding the Relevance of the Formula in Contemporary Customary International Law Concerning Self-Defense, 14 Cardozo Journal of International and Comparative Law 429, Fall 2006

Jean-Marie Henckaerts and Louise Doswald-Beck, Customary International Humanitarian Law, 2005

Michael Howard, George J. Andreopoulos, and Mark R. Shulman (eds.), The Laws of War: Constraints on Warfare in the Western World, 1994

Human Rights Watch, Off Target: The Conduct of the War and Civilian Casualties in Iraq, 2003

Danielle L. Infeld, Precision Guided Munitions Demonstrated Their Pinpoint Accuracy in Desert Storm; But Is a Country Obligated to Use Precision Technology to Minimize Collateral Civilian Injury and Damage? 26 George Washington Journal of International Law and Economics 109, 1992

R.Y. Jennings, The Caroline and McLeod Cases, 32 American Journal of International Law 82, 1938

Colin H. Kahl, How We Fight, 85 Foreign Affairs No. 6, November/December 2006, p. 83

Frits Kalshoven and Liesbeth Zegveld, Constraints on the Waging of War: An Introduction to International Humanitarian Law, 2001

Karen Lawand with Robin Coupland and Peter Herby, A Guide to the Legal Review of New Weapons, Means and Methods of Warfare: Measures to Implement Article 36 of Additional Protocol I of 1977, International Committee of the Red Cross, January 2006

Justin McClelland, The Review of Weapons in Accordance with Article 36 of Additional Protocol I, International Review of the Red Cross, No. 850, June 2003, p. 397

John Bassett Moore, A Digest of International Law, volume II, sec. 217, 1906

John Norton Moore and Robert F. Turner (eds.), National Security Law (2nd ed.), 2005

John F. Murphy, Some Legal (and a Few Ethical) Dimensions of the Collateral Damage Resulting from NATO's Kosovo Campaign, in Andru E. Wall (ed.), Legal and Ethical Lessons of NATO's Kosovo Campaign, Naval War College, vol. 78, 2002

Maria Benvenuta Occelli, 'Sinking' the Caroline: Why the Caroline Doctrine's Restrictions on Self-Defense Should Not Be Regarded as Customary International Law, 4 San Diego International Law Journal 467, 2003

Mary Ellen O'Connell, International Law and the Use of Force: Cases and Materials, 2005

W. Hays Parks, Air War and the Law of War, 32 Air Force Law Review p. 1, 1990

Jean Pictet, Development and Principles of International Humanitarian Law, 1985

Christopher B. Puckett, In This Era of 'Smart Weapons,' Is a State Under an International Legal Obligation to Use Precision-Guided Technology in Armed Conflict? 18 Emory International Law Review 645, Fall 2004

John T. Rawcliffe, Changes to the Department of Defense Law of War Program, Army Lawyer, August 2006, p. 23

Jefferson D. Reynolds, Collateral Damage on the 21st Century Battlefield: Enemy Exploitation of the Law of Armed Conflict, and the Struggle for a Moral High Ground, Air Force Law Review, Winter 2005

Kenneth R. Rizer, Bombing Dual-Use Targets: Legal, Ethical, and Doctrinal Perspectives, Air & Space Power Chronicles, May 1, 2001

Paul Robinson, 'Ready to Kill but Not to Die,' 54 International Journal, Autumn 1999, p. 671

Dwight A. Roblyer, Beyond Precision: Issues of Morality and Decision Making in Minimizing Collateral Casualties, Program in Arms Control, Disarmament, and International Security, University of Illinois, April 28, 2003

A.P.V. Rogers, Zero-Casualty Warfare, International Review of the Red Cross No. 837, March 31, 2000, p. 165

A.P.V. Rogers, Law on the Battlefield (2nd ed.), 2004

Martin A. Rogoff and Edward Collins, Jr., The Caroline Incident and the Development of International Law, 16 Brooklyn Journal of International Law No. 3, p. 493, 1990

Louis-Philippe Rouillard, The Caroline Case: Anticipatory Self-Defence in Contemporary International Law, 1 Miskolc Journal of International Law No. 2, p. 104, 2004

Dakota S. Rudesill, Precision War and Responsibility: Transformational Military Technology and the Duty of Care Under the Laws of War, 32 Yale Journal of International Law 517, Summer 2007

Marco Sassoli, Legitimate Targets of Attacks under International Humanitarian Law, International Humanitarian Law Research Institute, Harvard University, January 2003

Marco Sassoli and Antoine A. Bouvier, How Does Law Protect in War? Cases, Documents, and Teaching Materials on Contemporary Practice in International Humanitarian Law, 1999

Eric Schmitt, Rumsfeld Says Dozens of Important Targets Have Been Avoided, New York Times, March 24, 2003, p. B12

Michael N. Schmitt, *Bellum Americanum:* The U.S. View of Twenty-First Century War and Its Possible Implications for the Law of Armed Conflict, 19 Michigan Journal of International Law 1051, 1997–98

Michael N. Schmitt, War, Technology, and International Humanitarian Law, Program on Humanitarian Policy and Conflict Resolution, Harvard University, Occasional Paper No. 4, Summer 2005

Michael N. Schmitt, Precision Attack and International Humanitarian Law, International Review of the Red Cross No. 859, September 2005, p. 445

Michael N. Schmitt, Effects-Based Operations and the Law of Aerial Warfare, 5 Washington University Global Studies Law Review 265, 2006

Kenneth R. Stevens, Border Diplomacy: The Caroline and McLeod Affairs in Anglo-American-Canadian Relations, 1837–1842, 1989

Gabriel Swiney, Saving Lives: The Principle of Distinction and the Realities of Modern War, 39 International Lawyer No. 3, Fall 2005, p. 733

Ward Thomas, The Ethics of Destruction: Norms and Force in International Relations, 2001

U.S. Air Force Intelligence Targeting Guide, Air Force Pamphlet 14–210, February 1, 1998
U.S. Army, Field Manual 27–10, The Law of Land Warfare, July 18, 1956
U.S. Department of Defense Directive 5000.1, The Defense Acquisition System, May 12, 2003
U.S. Department of Defense Directive 2311. 01E, DoD Law of War Program, May 9, 2006
Martin van Creveld, The Transformation of War, 1991
Elizabeth S. Waldrop, Weaponization of Outer Space: U.S. National Policy, 26 Annals of Air and Space Law p. 329, 2004
David A. Wallace, Battling Terrorism Under the Law of War, Military Review, September/October 2007, p. 101
Catherine Wallis, Legitimate Targets of Attack: Considerations When Targeting in a Coalition, Army Lawyer, December 2004, p. 44
Matthew C. Waxman, International Law and the Politics of Urban Air Operations, RAND Project Air Force, 2000
Thomas C. Wingfield, The Law of Information Conflict: National Security Law in Cyberspace, 2000

TREATIES

Declaration Renouncing the Use, in Time of War, of Explosive Projectiles Under 400 Grammes Weight, adopted at St. Petersburg by the International Military Commission, December 11, 1868
Convention (No. IV) Respecting the Laws and Customs of War on Land, concluded at the Hague, October 18, 1907, U.S.T.S. 539, 36 Stat. 2277, 1 Bevans 631 (entered into force January 26, 1910)
Protocol Additional (No. I) to the Geneva Conventions of August 12, 1949, and Relating to the Protection of Victims of International Armed Conflicts, June 8, 1977, 1125 U.N.T.S. 3, 16 I.L.M. 1391 (1977) (United States not a party)
Convention on Prohibitions or Restrictions on the Use of Certain Conventional Weapons Which May Be Deemed to Be Excessively Injurious or to Have Indiscriminate Effects, Oct. 10, 1980, 1342 U.N.T.S. 137, 19 I.L.M. 1523

4

Precision-Guided Munitions

Scenario 4

The United States is preparing to fight a limited war in Belovenia – a very limited war. The motivation for entering the conflict is noble enough, with pure, generous humanitarianism at its core. Over the past year, Americans have been shocked and outraged as the Belovenian government has undertaken a particularly rapacious program of repression against its own ethnic minority. The government has stripped members of the minority of many of their fundamental human rights, depriving them of civil and political freedoms and degrading their social and cultural identity. Most recently, the government has undertaken an even more vigorous program of "ethnic cleansing," expelling minority families from their homes in the southern province of the country, revoking their citizenship, firing them from their jobs, expelling their children from schools, and generating a flood of vagabond refugees. Their property has been confiscated, their personal effects and official papers have been destroyed, and their cultural icons obliterated. At length, horrifying violence has erupted, arousing the conscience of the world to the specter of genocide: there are widespread reports of government-orchestrated mass killings and rapes targeted at the minority populations.

Many members of the United Nations have expressed their alarm and demanded immediate, forceful action, but Belovenia still enjoys the stalwart support of one of the permanent members of the Security Council. The threat of a veto has therefore blocked any meaningful Resolution authorizing international military action under Chapter VII of the United Nations Charter. Diplomatic pressure and economic sanctions have proven unavailing; while the world searches in vain for some means to gain traction on the problem, the government of Belovenia continues its daily carnage.

The president of the United States has stepped into the breach and cobbled together a "coalition of the willing," an assembly of countries volunteering to contribute to an effective military operation to halt the genocide. But the coalition is not really all that willing; because the values at stake are "merely" humanitarian, without implicating hard-line national security or essential economic interests, the participating states are hesitant to devote too much treasure or blood to the operation. They want the rescue operation to succeed, of course, but their lukewarm support for the enterprise imposes two important kinds of constraints.

First, the participating states (and their domestic populations) share a general reluctance to jeopardize their own soldiers by inserting them directly into large-scale hostilities on the ground. This means, in effect, a veto against deploying the infantry – there will be no grand invasion of Belovenia by the coalition – even if that might be the quickest and most effective mechanism for derailing the government's onslaught. Instead, air power alone will have to do the job, bombing the Belovenian national leadership into submission. Even then, the air campaign will have to be conducted in a manner that minimizes danger to pilots and crew, because the coalition members' collective will to fight is likely to degrade as soon as their young officers become converted into casualties or prisoners of war.

Second, the political realities of the situation further inveigh against the most vigorous forms an air campaign could assume. General "carpet bombing" of Belovenia is ruled out by three considerations: First, it's expensive and wasteful. Second, the Belovenian government has procured and deployed an effective air defense system, capable of detecting, tracking, and targeting even modern and sophisticated aircraft, thereby placing at risk crews that overfly and bomb. Third, the physical configuration of the country's infrastructure often intermingles civilian and military sites – army buildings are typically located proximate to ordinary commercial establishments; military installations are frequently surrounded by dwellings, schools, hospitals, and historic places of worship; and the Belovenian government has recently exacerbated this problem by deliberately moving tanks, antiaircraft installations, fighter planes, and other military assets into civilian neighborhoods to complicate the task of the coalition bombers and to deter air strikes.

The essential technical problem, the senior military advisors inform the president, is the accuracy – or, rather, the inaccuracy – of coalition bombs. We cannot be sure that the deadly payloads will be delivered exactly on the intended targets. There is always some margin of error, some probability that bombs will fly long or short, left or right, and the deviations from the projected trajectory may be substantial. Although we have more than sufficient firepower to strike a telling blow against the Belovenian government and military and to obliterate the enemy's fighting force and its ability to continue to perpetuate the genocide, we cannot be sure of striking only the government and military; there will inevitably be some degree of collateral damage to civilians, including to the members of the very minority groups we are intending to protect. The only viable way to improve the accuracy of the bombs is to drop them from lower altitudes, because shorter range generally connotes less error, but that tactic would exacerbate the risk to our strike force by prolonging their exposure to Belovenian air defenses.

How, then, can the United States and its partners wield their awesome air power effectively? How can the president accomplish valid military and political objectives without excessively jeopardizing both Belovenian civilians and coalition pilots?

Accuracy may be the single most important and most elusive factor in armed conflict. No matter how big, destructive, and deadly a bomb you build, if you cannot deposit it reasonably close to the intended target, it will not do the enemy much harm or you much good. The history of human combat – from thrown stones to bows and arrows to bullets to Intercontinental Ballistic Missiles (ICBMs) – is largely the history of incremental success in discovering means to deliver a payload with greater accuracy, and of the frustration that accrues when contemporary targeting technology is too imprecise to support our military ambitions. "Ever since military men began shooting things at enemies," James Digby has observed, "most shots have missed or been ineffective."[1]

CONSTRAINTS ON ACCURACY

For most of that history, insurmountable difficulty arose from the fact that after a projectile was released, it was "uncontrolled." That is, once a spear is thrown, a cannonball fired, and a bomb dropped from a plane, they all follow a "ballistic" trajectory, free from further human influence. The person discharging the weapon can aim it with great skill, trying to take into account all the relevant factors, but after the projectile has received its initial thrust, nature takes over and the payload simply coasts toward its impact point, influenced by inertia, gravity, aerodynamic lift, wind, and other unregulated and largely unpredictable factors. The human agent

[1] James Digby, Precision-Guided Weapons, Adelphi Paper No. 118, International Institute for Strategic Studies, 1975, p. 1.

has no residual power, no ability to insert midcourse corrections to compensate for an imperfect starting impetus.

Generations of weapons designers attempted to improve accuracy by better understanding the natural phenomena that would affect the flight patterns, by improving the design of the projectiles to minimize their susceptibility to those disruptions, or by ever-greater finesse in controlling the initial burst of energy that directed the payload toward the target. Impressive improvements in accuracy were registered for almost every type of weapon through the ages, but even for the most skilled practitioners, as soon as the implement was fired, there was little to do but wait, watch, hope, and reload.

Among the first meaningful successes in surmounting these limitations was Fritz X, an aircraft-dropped bomb developed by Germany during World War II. After releasing this device, the bombardier would visually monitor its flight and, by manipulating a joystick, send instructions via radio signals to a receiver in the tail of the bomb. Control mechanisms onboard the bomb would then adjust the position of external fins or vanes, slightly changing the wind resistance and thereby adjusting Fritz X's descent path.

On September 9, 1943, this system was employed to attack the Italian battleship *Roma* off Sardinia to prevent it from defecting to the Allies at Gibraltar after Mussolini's ouster. Dornier aircraft released two Fritz Xs from 18,000 feet, well above the ceiling that Italian antiaircraft guns could reach, and deftly guided the 3000-pound armor-piercing explosive toward the target. The *Roma* was completely destroyed and more than 1000 crewmen were lost. Eighty other vessels, including at least four British and American cruisers and battleships, were similarly victimized by Fritz X's accuracy and firepower during the war.[2]

Later in World War II and continuing into the Korean conflict, the United States and its allies successfully mimicked the Nazi development with successively larger and more maneuverable radio-guided bombs such as AZON, RAZON, and TARZON. Some of these devices were also equipped with flares in the tail, facilitating the bombardier's task of tracking and then adjusting the weapon's descent.

Any system that depends upon maintaining visual contact with a rapidly falling bomb has obvious limitations – clouds, smoke, and

[2] George and Meredith Friedman, The Future of War: Power, Technology, and American World Dominance in the 21st Century, 1996, p. 270; James F. Dunnigan, Digital Soldiers: The Evolution of High-Tech Weaponry and Tomorrow's Brave New Battlefield, 1996, pp. 126–27.

darkness would obviate the whole control apparatus. A very different concept was to make the bomb self-guiding, surging automatically toward its target without further human intervention. On May 12, 1943, Britain deployed perhaps the first such self-correcting weapon, an aircraft-dropped acoustic homing torpedo designated Mark 24, which locked onto and seriously damaged a German submarine by tracking and automatically responding to the noise it generated.[3]

Other types of active homing weapons – designed to seek heat, magnetism, radar emanations, or other energy emitted by a target – were developed during the cold war era. Even these relatively primitive iterations demonstrated the potential power of the revolution in precision guidance, and a multitude of technologies came to populate the battlefield. A major watershed, U.S. application of laser-guided bombs against the Thanh Hoa and Long Bien bridges during the closing phases of the Vietnam War, has already been described in the opening scenario of Chapter 1. Other indicia of the dramatically changing nature of war – and the changing standards for successful accuracy in bombing – quickly emerged. During World War II – the Allies' 1943 raid on the Czech city of Pilsen, for example – strategists were satisfied when 95 percent of the bombs landed within three miles of the aiming point. In Desert Storm in 1991, in contrast, nearly 85 percent of the U.S. smart weapons detonated within a mere 10 feet of their targets.[4]

MODERN PRECISION-GUIDED MUNITIONS

Today, a casserole of precision-guided munitions (PGMs) has been introduced into military competition, creatively exploiting a number of different technologies. They have been embraced by land and sea forces – the Government Accountability Office estimated that by 1995 the United States had 19 different types of PGMs in the inventory and another 14 types under development, for a total investment of almost $60 billion.[5] To date, the most advanced adaptations of the precision guidance revolution have been expressed by the Air Force, and four kinds of air-to-ground PGMs deserve description.

[3] Richard P. Hallion, Precision Guided Munitions and the New Era of Warfare, Air Power Studies Centre, Royal Australian Air Force, Working Paper No. 53, 1995.

[4] Stuart Walters Belt, Missiles Over Kosovo: Emergence, Lex Lata, of a Customary Norm Requiring the Use of Precision Munitions in Urban Areas, 47 Naval Law Review 115, 117, 2000.

[5] U.S. General Accounting Office, Weapons Acquisition: Precision Guided Munitions in Inventory, Production, and Development, GAO/NSIAD-95-95, June 1995.

First, an electro-optical guided bomb (EOGB) relies upon a miniature television camera built into the nose of the weapon that transmits an image in real time back to the launching airplane. As the EOGB approaches the target, the weaponeer in the plane selects a particular aim point – a specific site with high contrasts in reflected light – and designates it as the bull's eye. The bomb then locks onto that point and automatically guides itself toward it, using inertial energy and adjustable external vanes.

Although the EOGB concept was a great step forward in the pursuit of accuracy, it carried inherent limitations. It could function only in daylight, and in relatively clear skies, at that, because the continuous visual image was crucial. Moreover, focusing on a high-contrast point was problematic: sometimes the high-contrast point is not the most important or most vulnerable spot on a target, and sometimes the contrasts change with the movement of the bomb (or the target), meaning that the EOGB could lose its lock during flight.

Still, electro-optical and related systems have been used extensively and with great effect. During the Vietnam War, American pilots employed the GBU-15 EOGB, the AGM-62 Walleye, and the AGM-65 Maverick missile. The Maverick, which has remained a mainstay of the arsenal for decades, is available in variants that rely upon either visual or infrared guidance systems (for use at night) and can be adapted for striking tanks, ships, or troop formations. Mavericks cost only about $50,000 each, and despite their relatively small explosive charge, some 5100 were fired during Desert Storm in 1991 and were credited with decimating Iraqi armor. The most modern incarnation of EOGB, the AGM-130, costs $450,000; it has a range of more than 25 miles, ensuring a standoff safety zone for the pilot who deploys it.

A second type of PGM, the laser-guided bomb (LGB), depends upon a different type of nosecone sensor unit, which detects coded laser beams reflected off the target. To generate those invisible, low-power laser beams, a target designator must be pointed at the desired site; the designator can be housed on the airplane that drops the LGB or on another aircraft nearby, or it can be carried by troops on the ground (for example, special forces units concealed within sight of the target). Responding to those reflected light waves, the LGB's onboard computer continuously recalculates the bomb's course and adjusts a rear wing assembly to effectuate necessary corrections.

The concept of laser guidance was introduced in the 1960s with the Paveway system used by the United States in Vietnam. A great advantage of LGBs is that the essential components (the sensor, computer, wings, etc.) can be retrofitted onto existing types of "dumb" bombs, quickly and inexpensively transforming them into PGMs. A Paveway conversion kit can cost as little as $10,000–25,000 per bomb.

The first drawback of the LGB arises from the limitations on laser beam propagation through the atmosphere. The beam functions just as well at night as during the day (an advantage over the EOGB), but it dissipates in difficult air – an overcast, dusty, smoky, or debris-ridden sky (all common features of a battle environment) will cause the laser to lose its coherence, and the message to the bomb will be compromised. In addition, the designator must keep the target constantly illuminated until the bomb lands – but loitering in the area may jeopardize the aircraft or the ground forces engaged in "painting" the target with the laser.

More than 9000 Paveways, assisted by an improved infrared navigation and targeting system denominated LANTRIN, were dropped against Iraq during the 1991 Gulf War I. Thirty or more other countries, including Canada, France, Israel, Saudi Arabia, and South Korea, are now also equipped with Paveway or modifications or knock-offs of it.

A third distinct PGM concept creates a self-contained attacking instrument not requiring any ongoing human input. The best examples are the sea-launched Tomahawk cruise missile and its Air Force equivalent, the Conventional Air Launched Cruise Missile (CALCM). These missiles are long range (500 miles or more) unmanned aircraft, continuously powered throughout the journey to a target (unlike a glide bomb, which basically just drops) – essentially, they are robotic Kamikaze vehicles. The principal guidance mechanism for the cruise missile is a "terrain contour matching" (TERCOM) radar, which continuously reads the ground it is flying over and compares elevation features with a digital map stored in the missile's computer memory. Where the altimeter indicates a deviation from the planned course, the engine and the wings are automatically adjusted to swing the weapon back onto course.

Tomahawk missiles are capable of breathtaking accuracy in all weather and light conditions, and they can approach the target from any azimuth, even following a squiggly flight path to avoid known defense systems. Moreover, the crew launching the weapon can remain far distant, out of harm's way, whereas only the hardware itself is exposed.

On the other hand, the Tomahawk is expensive (originally $1.4 million each, although a newer, shorter-range version costs about $575,000), it carries a relatively small 1000-pound warhead, and it depends upon that very detailed radar mapping of the target and all intended approaches toward it. If the map is inaccurate (or if the terrain changes, such as through extensive bomb damage), the missile may go astray.

Tomahawk cruise missiles were famously used on August 20, 1998, against six of Osama Bin Laden's terrorist training camps in Afghanistan and against the alleged al-Shifa chemical weapons plant in Khartoum, Sudan. The weapons (13 against Sudan; 66 against Afghanistan) obliterated the targets swiftly and suddenly, without exposing American pilots to danger.[6]

Finally, the newest category of precision weapon relies upon guidance from 24 global positioning satellites (GPS). Here the only input data the bomb receives in flight come from the same ubiquitous Navstar satellite system that helps retrieve off-course automobiles. By comparing its current location (derived with exquisite accuracy from the timing of several arriving satellite signals) with the location of the target (inserted into the weapon before release), the bomb can adjust its course independent of weather, light, or other factors. Importantly, GPS-guided bombs are truly "fire and forget" arms – the aircraft need not loiter in the area to help steer the weapon on its approach to the target, and nothing tethers a ground observer to the site (and to the attendant dangers).

On the other hand, this sort of prior programming is applicable only to strikes against fixed targets – anything mobile (e.g., vehicles or troops) may quickly stray from known coordinates. In addition, a plausible countermeasure for the enemy would be to disrupt the low-power GPS signals, interfering with satellite communications service in the vicinity of the target. Jamming and spoofing technology of that sort is now inexpensive and widely available, and the United States worried that Iraq might be able to make effective use of it during the 2003 Gulf War II fighting. However, newer GPS receivers and filters can also be made more powerful and more resistant to that sort of electronic disruption.

Numerous subspecies of GPS-guided weapons are now being introduced into the American arsenal, among them the Joint Direct Attack Munition (JDAM), the Joint Standoff Weapon (JSOW), and the Joint Air to Surface Standoff Missile (JASSM). The JDAM, first deployed in 1999, is not really a new weapon; instead it is a kit (consisting of GPS sensors, data processors, and a tail assembly) that can be fitted onto various types of existing bombs for about $20,000 each to create a very accurate,

[6] Michael Russell Rip and James M. Hasik, The Precision Revolution: GPS and the Future of Aerial Warfare, 2002, pp. 365–73.

all-weather, fire-and-forget bomb. In the 2001 fighting in Afghanistan, the Air Force dropped 6650 JDAMs at ranges up to 15 miles and reported that fewer than 10 percent missed their targets.[7] JDAM is expected to become the workhorse of the bomber fleet; the U.S. Air Force has already made plans to purchase some 240,000.

The JSOW, which is truly a new weapon, entered into service in 1998. Its range is about 50 miles; like a Tomahawk cruise missile, it is powered continuously throughout its flight, so it can maneuver over a wide range to attack from odd angles. That augmented capability carries a hefty price tag, about $200,000 per missile. The JASSM offers a comparable operational flexibility, with an extended range up to 230 miles.

In addition, these emerging guidance capabilities can be mixed and matched almost at will to provide synergistic benefits. A Tomahawk, for example, can be equipped with both TERCOM and GPS guidance systems to provide greater precision even if one of the programs fails. Another hybrid, grafting a laser seeker onto a GPS-guided JDAM, enables the munition to pinpoint even targets moving at 70 mph. Likewise, other mechanisms, relying upon inertial guidance algorithms in flight and on additional sophisticated terminal guidance devices just before impact, can be incorporated into many of the designs to perfect the weapon's accuracy.

GROWTH IN PGM USE

The revolution in precision guidance has been spectacularly successful; this aspect of the ongoing transformation of the U.S. military has already been substantially completed, and it is now difficult to imagine modern warfare with only old-fashioned "dumb" munitions. Statistical assessments about the increased use of PGMs in recent wars vary somewhat, depending upon exactly what variables are being measured and what sources are employed, but the general picture is unmistakable: an exponential growth in American exploitation of smart technology.

One useful calculation juxtaposes the four most recent major U.S. and allied military campaigns: Operation Desert Storm in Iraq in 1991 in Gulf War I; Operation Allied Force in the former Yugoslavia during the Kosovo fighting in 1999; Operation Enduring Freedom in Afghanistan

[7] Robert Mandel, The Wartime Utility of Precision Versus Brute Force in Weaponry, 30 Armed Forces & Society No. 2, Winter 2004, p. 171, 186.

against the Taliban and al-Qaeda in 2001–2002; and Operation Iraqi Freedom in Iraq in Gulf War II in 2003.[8]

Location	Date	Sorties flown	Bombs dropped	Precision bombs dropped	Percent precision bombs
Iraq	1991	118,700	265,000	20,450	8%
Yugoslavia	1999	37,500	23,000	8,050	35%
Afghanistan	2001	38,000	22,000	12,500	57%
Iraq	2003	41,400	29,199	19,948	68%

These statistics reflect the totals for the entire U.S.-led coalition or alliance; if the American role were isolated, the growing reliance upon precision would be even more pronounced because the overwhelming majority of the smart munitions have been used by American forces. In Desert Storm, for example, 89 percent of the precision ordnance was dropped by the United States, and in Operation Enduring Freedom, 99 percent of the PGMs were American. Even close American allies have not yet made the same wholehearted leap to PGMs; they have not fully trained or equipped their forces for such heavy reliance on smart warfare.

Recent combat has continued to display the full armada of PGM types available to targeteers – as well as their dazzling effectiveness. In Gulf War I, for example, laser-guided GBU-12 bombs destroyed 200 Iraqi tanks per night, and GBU-15 electro-optical bombs were employed to disrupt the mechanisms that Saddam's forces had adapted to force polluting oil to discharge into the Persian Gulf. Although LGBs constituted only a fraction of the PGM total in that campaign, they were credited with inflicting 75 percent of the serious damage suffered by Iraqi strategic and operational forces. A few years later, in the Kosovo fighting, U.S. and British surface ships fired 218 Tomahawk cruise missiles while B-2 bombers registered the first combat use of GPS-guided JDAMs. By the time of the Afghanistan campaign, U.S. ordnance was so accurate that as few as 200 sorties per day were dispatched, yet they succeeded in hitting the same number of targets as the 3000 sorties per day that had consumed coalition energies during Desert Storm. In the 2003 Iraq fighting, by one

[8] Mandel, supra note 7, at 181–82.

estimate, about 30 percent of the U.S. munitions were LGBs, 22 percent were GPS-guided JDAMs, and 3 percent were Tomahawks.[9]

The U.S. armed services have jumped aboard the PGM bandwagon with such alacrity that the users have sometimes outpaced the suppliers. The Navy, for example, almost ran out of JDAMs during the Afghanistan war and had to borrow weapons from the Air Force. Production was quickly ramped up, to 1500–2000 per month, but a lag persisted (exacerbated somewhat by simultaneous sales of JDAMs to Italy, Israel, and other countries).

ADVANTAGES OF PRECISION

Precision guidance offers several distinct advantages to warfighters in situations such as those portrayed in Scenario 4. The first benefit is "economy of force." Simply put, it is cheaper to drop a small number of smart bombs than a large number of dumb bombs. Even when the old-fashioned ordnance can cost as little as $2 per pound of explosive, there is a great deal of waste in the form of devices that never come near their assigned targets. During the Vietnam War era, for example, the United States dropped some 8 million tons of (mostly unguided) bombs on Southeast Asia; in contrast during the (much shorter) Desert Storm air campaign, only 85,000 tons of (often smart) bombs were expended.[10]

In Scenario 4, if we were confident in the ability of our PGMs to strike accurately and effectively at key Belovenian targets, we could efficiently devote fewer bombs and missiles to each aimpoint and undertake fewer sorties overall. That savings, in turn, rewards us by reducing the exposure of our aircraft and crews – they will have to put themselves into harm's way less often.

A longitudinal study that posed a standard sort of military mathematics puzzle reveals a crude indicator of the revolutionary effect of accuracy: How many ordinary 2000-pound bombs would be required to be 90 percent confident of destroying a typical target measuring 60 by 100 feet? During World War II, with the prevailing conditions of (in)accuracy, the answer would have been that such a mission would have necessitated 9070 bombs delivered by 3024 aircraft. By the Korean

[9] John A. Tirpak, Precision: The Next Generation, 86 Air Force Magazine No. 11, November 2003.

[10] Benjamin S. Lambeth, The Transformation of American Air Power, 2000, p. 13.

War, improvements in sighting, aiming, and delivering ordnance reduced the quota to 1100 bombs from 550 aircraft. In the Vietnam era, 176 bombs and 44 aircraft would have sufficed.[11] Today, only 1 or 2 bombs, carried by a single aircraft, would be assigned to such a mission – almost a 10,000-fold increase in military effectiveness.

But the benefits of PGMs go beyond economics – smart weaponry is also more effective. By depositing an electro-optically guided explosive charge with exactitude on one of Belovenia's radar suites, we ensure that it will be knocked out of commission in a way that hordes of larger but less accurate munitions might not accomplish. By hitting a Belovenian tank directly with a Maverick LGB, we can verify its destruction and obviate the need to revisit it as a target. A single JDAM that bursts through a preselected window of a Belovenian military headquarters is a more reliable mechanism for disrupting the nation's war effort than imprecise ordnance could ever be. A 1993 Defense Science Board study concluded that, overall, a ton of PGMs could replace 12–20 tons of unguided munitions on a "tonnage per target kill basis" – and that was even before the most splendid modern smart bombs came on board.[12]

The 1999 fighting in the former Yugoslavia provided a stunning illustration of this precision and economy of force. In April 1999, during a single pass at Serbia's Obrva airfield, a single B-2 bomber "placed a 2000 pound JDAM squarely on each of the airstrip's six runway-taxiway intersections, thereby precluding any operations by Serb fighters until repairs had been made to all six bomb craters."[13] Each of these weapons had been released from approximately 40,000 feet, and each was impervious to adverse weather conditions.

Longer-range PGMs also provide another margin of safety: Tomahawks, air-launched cruise missiles, and satellite-guided JASSMs enable the launching crews to remain far beyond the reach of Belovenia's anti-air and antiship fire. Even laser-guided and EOGB systems, which are shorter range and do not enable the bombing crew to flee the scene immediately, put fewer of our pilots at risk than ordinary massive bombing campaigns.

Moreover, the accuracy of PGMs carries an important correlate: the bombs can be smaller and still get the assigned job done. Through smart

[11] Hallion, supra note 3, at 4 (citing a 1990 Air Force Study, Air Power Lethality and Precision: Then and Now); Rip and Hasik, supra note 6, at 214.

[12] Cited in Lambeth, supra note 10, at 160.

[13] Barry D. Watts, The Military Use of Space: A Diagnostic Assessment, Center for Strategic and Budgetary Assessments, February 2001, pp. 42–43.

weaponry, we can inflict less overall devastation and create a reduced zone of lethality because we can effectively concentrate a lower volume of explosive on the exact Belovenian location intended.

Pursuing that logic, the next generation of precision-guided munition will be even smaller. Currently designated as the Small Diameter Bomb (SDB), the GBU-39 weighs about 285 pounds (about half the size of the previous smallest bomb in the regular Air Force quiver) and carries only about 50 pounds of explosive – giving it a correspondingly reduced lethal radius. It operates on an advanced GPS system, immune to local jamming, and has a standoff range that can be extended up to 50 miles via pop-out wings. This incarnation of "PGM Lite" allows a single aircraft to carry many more bombs so it can attack more targets on a single flight, and the weapon's reduced blast area enables use in cramped circumstances where a larger bomb might generate unacceptable collateral damage and fratricide.

The first operational use of SDB came in October 2006, when F-15 Strike Eagles employed it in close air support of U.S. ground troops in Iraq, and it has been used extensively in Afghanistan, too. The Air Force's initial purchase order calls for a production run of 24,000 SDBs, and others estimate a program of 150,000 of the creatures over the next 10 years.

Future iterations of SDB and other munitions may become even more precise in their effects by incorporating novel components to provide even more sharply focused lethality. They may be outfitted with reformulated Dense Inert Metal Explosives (DIME) (designed to concentrate an even stronger blast effect at short range but not to carry that power beyond 100 feet, or even 25 feet) and they will be shaped by carbon filament casings, instead of steel, to generate less high-velocity shrapnel.[14]

This reduction in collateral damage is exceptionally important in modern warfare. If our forces can accomplish their valid military objectives without imposing so much unintended death and destruction on nearby civilian persons and objects, there are enormous benefits for all concerned. As noted in Chapter 3, the political, moral, and legal considerations all align here: the humanitarian roots of the law of armed conflict insist upon proportionality between the force applied in pursuit of militarily necessary objectives and the unnecessary suffering inflicted upon noncombatants.

[14] David Hambling, Blast Reduction, Defense Technology International, September 2007, p. 54.

The nasty, and so far unavoidable, fact (as reflected on the classic antiwar T-shirts) is that war is unhealthy for children and other living things. In almost every modern large-scale conflict, casualties among civilians have exceeded those inflicted upon fighting forces as unintended byproducts of weapons that were aimed at point X but went astray and landed at point Y. By one estimate, some 2 million noncombatants were killed by insufficiently precise aerial bombardment between 1900 and 1970.[15]

The PGM era promises to rewrite those historic statistics. Compared to the Allies' massive carpet bombing of German and Japanese cities during World War II, for example, when more than 1 million noncombatants perished, the modern application of force is extremely restrained. As Colin Kahl summarizes the arcane statistics, "All told, the number of civilian deaths per ton of air-delivered munitions during major combat in Iraq was about 19 times lower than that in Dresden and 162 times lower than that in Tokyo."[16]

Excessive bomb damage would undermine a U.S. military campaign in Belovenia in multiple ways. History (the Battle of Britain during World War II or the bombing of North Vietnam) suggests that an air force imposing these unnecessary costs rarely breaks the will of the population or causes the leadership to submit; instead, it often unites the country against the outsiders, stiffening the collective will to resist. The specter of massive civilian casualties may also generate a political backlash in other countries, perhaps especially where there is a racial, religious, or political identification with the victims. And in the long run, violations of the norms of legitimate combat will sap the strength of the violator, too – at least in a democracy, the population will not indefinitely sustain a war based upon illegal and excessive tactics that needlessly victimize civilians. Especially, as in Scenario 4, where the motivation leading to the intervention was humanitarian in nature, wanton destruction of nonmilitary assets would be worse than ironic.

Finally, another critical aspect of the useability benefits of precision guidance arises from the ability to undertake particular missions that would otherwise remain off-limits. When we can be more confident that our bombs will strike the exact target intended and will thereby minimize collateral damage, even to very proximate buildings, our targeteers' inhibitions are reduced accordingly. The prowess to prosecute a more

[15] Phillip S. Meilinger, A Matter of Precision, Foreign Policy, March/April 2001, p. 78.

[16] Colin H. Kahl, How We Fight, 85 Foreign Affairs No. 6, November/December 2006, p. 83, 88.

effective campaign against Belovenia increases when the enemy's military assets cannot escape exposure to attack even when they are sited near protected locations that we would not want to jeopardize.

For example, during the 2003 Gulf War II fighting, the United States and its partners undertook a variety of delicate aerial missions – and accomplished them with breathtaking success – in circumstances that would not have been tolerated just 12 years earlier in Gulf War I. The increasing accuracy and reliability of the newer PGMs unleashed modern air power from the prior inhibitions of excessive self-deterrence.

To cite one instance: in the March, 2003, conflict in and around the southern Iraqi city of Basra, the British and American forces felt constrained not to undertake a frontal assault, fearing that prolonged house-to-house combat would devastate the city and sacrifice many lives (civilian and military alike). But doing nothing throughout a prolonged stalemate was also unacceptable at a time when the allies' "shock and awe" strategy emphasized a speedy sweep toward Baghdad. Precision-guided munitions provided a mechanism for deft applications of telling force: on one occasion, U.S. bombers destroyed the local headquarters of the ruling Ba'ath party with two GPS-guided JDAMs while preserving basically unharmed a neighboring school on one side of the building and a hospital on the other. A few days later, American F-15E fighters directed two laser-guided PGMs to a building where the local resistance forces were meeting; the ordnance killed some 200 *fedayeen* fighters without unduly harming the neighbors. Shortly thereafter, British aircraft battered the Basra home of the regional commander of Saddam's forces, the notorious Lt. Gen. Ali Hassan al-Majid, a cousin of the dictator, who had earlier earned the nickname "Chemical Ali" because of his brutal campaign featuring illegal use of chemical weapons against the rebellious Kurds in the northern part of the country. This sort of strike into a densely populated civilian section of the city might well not have been authorized during Gulf War I, but by 2003, PGMs opened the way for an effective blow while leaving most nearby residences intact.[17]

Equally dramatically, PGMs provided the mechanism for attacking the elusive Abu Musab al-Zarqawi, the notorious leader of al Qaida in Iraq, on June 7, 2006. When local intelligence sources finally located

[17] Human Rights Watch investigators have concluded that this attack, in the al-Tuwaisi section of downtown Basra, did succeed in destroying the targeted building, but the laser-guided bombs also destroyed two next-door homes, killing 17 civilians. Human Rights Watch, Off Target: The Conduct of the War and Civilian Casualties in Iraq, 2003.

al-Zarqawi in a particular two-story house in Baqouba, two F-16C fighter jets on patrol were diverted to the mission. One of them (staying 4–5 miles away from the house to remain undetected) fired a laser-guided GBU-12 and a GPS-guided GBU-38 JDAM, each carrying 500 pounds of explosive. Both bombs slammed into the house, killing al-Zarqawi and four others (including one child) and triggering a series of 17 raids in the vicinity that yielded what officials called a treasure trove of intelligence.

In the same vein, American urban counterinsurgency tactics in Iraq in 2008 have included efforts to adapt even the smallest bombs into more precise sniper's weapons by offloading some of the explosives and replacing them with ordinary cement. By reducing the ordnance package to 30 pounds or less of explosive, Air Force crews now undertake calibrated missions to target particular known individuals, with much less collateral damage to surrounding persons or structures.[18]

That sort of useability is particularly important in an era in which some U.S. opponents have conspicuously intermingled their civilian and military assets. Their deliberate failure to differentiate themselves from civilians – to allow the warmakers to distinguish between combatants and innocents – is a clear violation of the law of armed conflict as outlined in Chapter 3, and can deter attacks by law-abiding forces unwilling to jeopardize protected persons and places. But such honorable self-restraint has the perverse effect of rewarding the enemy's illegal tactic and placing out of reach what would otherwise be important and legitimate targets. Precision can provide the mechanism for squaring that circle, enabling our forces to attack the military asset efficiently without disproportionate collateral damage.

MEASURING PRECISION PRECISELY

No weapon can ever be 100 percent accurate and reliable; there will always be some quantity of unintended consequences in wartime. In fact, the principal measuring stick for assessing the accuracy of an armament illustrates clearly the defects in judging precision. Traditionally, the key statistic is "circular error probable" (CEP), defined as the radius of a circle within which half the bombs would be expected to fall. Thus, a device (such as the unguided "dumb" bombs of decades ago) with an assessed CEP of, say, 50 meters, is considerably less accurate than a

[18] Mark Benjamin, Killing "Bubba" from the Skies, Salon.com, February 15, 2008.

more modern smart munition with a CEP of 20 meters. By recalling the familiar algebraic formula for the area of a circle (*pi* times r squared), for the former weapon, half the bombs will be expected to fall within an area of 7850 square meters, whereas for the latter, the area is only 1256 square meters, about one-sixth as large. Still, in each case, fully half the explosions would be expected to fall further off target than that.

CEPs for American bombs have been steadily decreasing. In rough terms, from 1945 to 1975, CEPs dropped by an order of magnitude, from 1000 meters to 100 meters; even more impressive was a second order-of-magnitude reduction, from 100 meters to 10 meters between 1975 and 2000.[19] Today, the satellite-guided JDAM is rated with a CEP of 13 meters (although the actual performance is often better than that); the laser-guided Paveway has a CEP of 8 meters; modern cruise missiles have a CEP of about 5 meters; and the electro-optical GBU-15 has a CEP of 3 meters. The next generation of Small Diameter Bomb is likely to have a CEP of 4 meters or less, and one version will include a terminal seeker that can automatically recognize and follow its prey, suitable for attacking mobile targets.

No single statistical measurement of dispersal is perfect, of course, and CEP alone does not tell us everything we would like to know about a PGM's likely pattern of impacts. For most weapons, the spread of actual hits around the aimpoint will, very roughly, approximate a normal distribution, with more "close misses" and fewer weapons that wander far astray. But, in general, more error occurs in range (the weapon deviates long or short) than in azimuth (missing left or right), so the actual pattern of hits may be more elliptical than circular.

With precision-guided weaponry, however, more of the errors are caused by a major system failure – a computer snafu, a missing GPS or laser input, or a damaged steering fin – so there is a higher probability that a miss will become a wild miss. During Desert Storm, for example, some otherwise excruciatingly accurate Tomahawk cruise missiles flew many miles away from their targets, meandering even into neighboring Iran.

This residual inaccuracy of even the most sophisticated PGMs can have tragic consequences – human beings are injured and killed when bombs go astray. Even when the vast bulk of armaments now hits the intended targets, it is important not to overstate their accuracy – no

[19] Michael Mok, Precision Guided Munitions, 2002.

one should be lulled into a false sense that accidents can always be avoided. In the 1999 Kosovo fighting, for example, one leading analyst concluded:

> To be sure, errant bombs and shrapnel caused civilian casualties in Yugoslavia. Out of 10,000 strikes, there were 90 incidents in which civilians were killed because of technical failures, or because they were too close to military targets, or because of errors in judgment by pilots or targeters. In all, there were some 500 civilian deaths and a few hundred injuries from the bombing.[20]

Moreover, the vaunted precision of modern weaponry is predicated upon adequate military intelligence to identify and characterize a proposed target and its milieu. The choreography of modern combat demands that we know with unprecedented accuracy where the enemy is, how to get there, and what sorts of protected sites are located nearby. But good intelligence is a perishable commodity, often with a very short shelf life before obsolescence – and lacking comprehensive, truthful, and still-timely information, even smart weapons can wind up looking very stupid, indeed. According to Human Rights Watch, of the 50 air strikes launched by U.S. forces against senior Iraqi leadership figures in 2003, none succeeded in killing the intended targets, while dozens of civilians were struck.[21]

The infamous accidental May 7, 1999, U.S. bombing of the Chinese embassy in Belgrade during the Kosovo fighting demonstrates even more vividly what can happen when smart bombs are fed poor data. The CIA and Department of Defense experts who nominated targets for the airstrikes mistakenly thought that the building in question was a Yugoslavian military headquarters for the Federal Directorate for Supply and Procurement. They were relying upon outdated maps and an inadequate database of buildings and occupants, and they did not realize that the Chinese embassy had moved there some years earlier. The real Yugoslavian military headquarters was some 300 meters away, but no one in the chain of review caught the error in time. A B-2 bomber expertly dropped five GPS-guided JDAMs on the site, and the precise weapons performed their assigned mission with exactitude, killing three people, injuring

[20] William Arkin, Smart Bombs, Dumb Targeting? 56 Bulletin of the Atomic Scientists No. 3, May/June 2000, p. 46; Human Rights Watch, Civilian Deaths in the NATO Air Campaign, vol. 12, no. 1, February 2000.

[21] Human Rights Watch, Off Target: The Conduct of the War and Civilian Casualties in Iraq, December 11, 2003, p. 6, http://www.hrw.org/en/reports/2003/12/11/target-0.

20 others, and severely damaging the facility. There was nothing wrong with the PGMs themselves – they performed just as they were supposed to do (at night and in bad weather, to boot) – but human error in inputting an appropriate aimpoint ruined the operation and created a stark international crisis.

Similarly, on February 13, 1991, during the first Gulf War, the United States infamously attacked the Al Firdos command and control bunker in west Baghdad with two GBU-27 laser-guided bombs, not realizing that it had been adapted for nightly use as a bomb shelter by the local populace. When 300–400 civilians were killed, the reaction was justified outrage on an international scale; precision-guided bombs in inexpert hands can result in precise catastrophe.

Other cases of fatally mistaken identity arose when U.S. pilots interpreted as hostile fire the bullets that a wedding party was shooting into the air in celebration, and when they misconstrued a convoy of fleeing refugees as a column of enemy troops. Sometimes, even excellent intelligence and exquisite precision cannot prevent lethal collateral damage; in an agonizing tragedy, a pilot released a bomb against a bridge in Serbia in 1999 only moments before a passenger train unexpectedly attempted to cross it.

FUTURE DEVELOPMENTS

Precision guidance has the effect of altering the customary tradeoff between accuracy and firepower. That is, in the stereotypical competition between a cannon (great volume of fire but low accuracy) and a rifle (precise targeting but low aggregate destruction), each component could fill a specialized niche, and neither would be judged to be generically superior for all purposes. PGMs, however, now allow us to combine both elements: the pinpoint accuracy of super-effective guidance with overwhelming mass explosive power.

The forced marriage of the two features is perhaps best displayed in a new PGM, the GBU-43 Massive Ordnance Air Blast (MOAB – an acronym that also suggests the weapon's nickname: Mother Of All Bombs). MOAB will have GPS guidance, offering a CEP of perhaps 10 meters or better, great maneuverability, and a bigger warhead than any other conventional U.S. bomb: almost 20,000 pounds. The combination is imagined to provide a new capability for striking the most difficult targets, such as well-defended caves or tunnel complexes in Afghanistan, which are too tough for even JDAMs or LGBs to crack.

Now, in fact, the emerging political and legal question is whether there is any remaining role at all for "dumb" bombs – when the United States is capable of combining such great accuracy and such overwhelming firepower, should we rely *exclusively* on PGMs? Should we procure enough kits to convert all our bombs into modern laser-, satellite-, or video-guided hybrids?

Some have argued that with the capacity for greater accuracy comes a corresponding obligation to refrain from falling back to imprecise ordnance. They assert that the ethical and legal standards identified in Chapter 3 – especially the mandate to avoid inflicting "unnecessary" suffering – require us to abjure inaccurate weaponry altogether. If we have the ability to behave in a more deft fashion, perhaps the law of armed conflict now *requires* that we do so; it is no longer "necessary" for us to inflict the additional array of civilian losses that accompany the use of dumb munitions.

Moreover, some argue, the evolving sensibilities continuously ratchet up the self-restraint that must be exercised – even if the opposing force is not similarly impeded. That is, if the United States is engaged in combat against a less wealthy country or a country that simply made different decisions about whether to research, develop, and deploy a full arsenal of PGMs, then perhaps the American forces would still be obligated to use only PGMs, even if the other country were asymmetrically free to exercise its less technologically sophisticated arsenal.[22]

American military leaders reject any such interpretation, maintaining that there is still a valid role for more primitive weaponry. In attacking large, soft targets (such as Belovenian military warehouses, rail yards, industrial plants, or truck farms in Scenario 4) in isolated locations where collateral damage is not such a pressing concern, massive quantities of dumb bombs may be the weapon of choice – they are cheaper, larger, and more efficient, and the premium on delivery accuracy is less important. Moreover, in attacking concentrations of Belovenian troops, the psychological "shock and awe" effects of saturation bombing may be compelling: the noise, vibration, and smoke from a flotilla of dumb

[22] See Danielle L. Infeld, Precision-Guided Munitions Demonstrated Their Pinpoint Accuracy in Desert Storm; But Is a Country Obligated to Use Precision Technology to Minimize Collateral Civilian Injury and Damage? 26 George Washington Journal of International Law and Economics 109, 1992; Christopher B. Puckett, In This Era of 'Smart Weapons,' Is a State Under an International Legal Obligation to Use Precision-Guided Technology in an Armed Conflict? 18 Emory International Law Review 645 (Fall 2004).

bombs may create an even greater disruption in enemy troops' morale and cohesion than would a more precise and limited-scale PGM strike.

Sometimes, therefore, the optimal tactic might be to reserve the precision munitions for more well-defended targets or for targets located closest to civilian sites that ought to be off-limits or for initial strikes at the outset of a military campaign (before reliable air superiority has been attained), and to allocate the residual inventory of dumb bombs to the simpler, cruder subsequent aspects of the operation. Still, it is predictable that as the PGM revolution proceeds, and as the capability to function with that deft touch spreads around the world, the collective sense of what is appropriate and legitimate in warfare will evolve, and the tolerance for imprecise ordnance will fall. Sooner or later, the preference for smart munitions will likely harden into a more compulsory aspect of the calculation of "unnecessary suffering."

The suggestion that a modern PGM capability will, sooner or later, more or less percolate to other countries around the world also implies that one other consideration must be surveyed in this chapter: the danger of proliferation. Recent wars – Gulf War I and II, the fighting in Kosovo and in Afghanistan, etc. – have been one-sided affairs, at least as far as technology is concerned. The United States has enjoyed a near-monopoly in advanced weaponry, especially in sophisticated PGMs. But what the Soviet Union used to call "the correlation of forces" may not always be so favorable.

At the moment, other nations – even our closest allies in NATO – lag seriously behind the United States in the incorporation of precision-guided mechanisms into their armed forces, but the gap may be narrowing. JDAM kits have been shipped to Australia, Belgium, Chile, Israel, Pakistan, Saudi Arabia, and South Korea, among others. China and Russia have developed indigenous laser-guided or electro-optical systems, or both; and several European nations have taken steps toward inaugurating a continental version of the JASSM standoff missile. Ironically, because complete Navstar signals are now freely available to customers around the world on a nondiscriminatory basis, other countries may be able to exploit that precision against us, incorporating our GPS advances into their own weapons.

In the long run, nothing is more predictable than the inexorable pressure toward dispersion of weapons technology. If the United States finds benefits in revolutionary precision guidance, it should not be surprised when other nations reach similar conclusions. Profit-seeking activity by public and private actors will surely endeavor to expand the market (open or black) for PGM capabilities. Someday these dynamic weapon systems will inevitably be used against, not only by, us and our allies.

BOTTOM LINE

This first case study of a revolutionary weapon ratifies many of the themes introduced in Chapters 1 through 3, applying them to what is probably the clearest and easiest case of a new military system becoming more useable than its predecessors. As expressed by a 1993 Center for Strategic and International Studies exploration of the Revolution in Military Affairs,

> Technologies and doctrines representative of the MTR [military technical revolution] will also have a profound effect on *the balance between destructiveness and lethality*. The trend in warfare over at least the last 200 years has been dominated by the increasing destructiveness of warfare and weapons. Greater lethality was achieved through the application of overwhelming firepower. This trend began in the Napoleonic war, intensified through the Civil War and World War I and II, and culminated in the development and use of nuclear weapons. The advent of precision weapons represents a break in this trend as it allows greater degrees of lethality to be achieved without corresponding increases in destructiveness, as both collateral damage to civilians and as the requirement to annihilate the enemy's forces in detail. This fact carries dramatic implications for the use of force as an instrument of a U.S. foreign policy.[23]

One of those implications arises from the fact that it is almost axiomatic that if a military force (or its civilian leadership) is more confident in the ability to strike a particular target accurately, it will be more willing to undertake the mission – precision guidance reduces the danger of disproportionate collateral damage and thereby relaxes one of the key inhibitions against employment of force. But if that self-deterrence is eroded too far – if we are lulled into a false sense that PGMs can provide a reliably surgical capability – then the pursuit of more useable weapons has progressed too far. As A.J. Bacevich and Lawrence F. Kaplan have observed,

> Ultimately, a doctrine that relies on antiseptic methods of warfare may prove dangerously seductive. Seemingly tailor-made for an era of post-modern politics, precision weapons also have the potential to increase the propensity of political leaders to resort to violent means. The ready

[23] Michael J. Mazarr, Jeffrey Shaffer, and Benjamin Ederington, The Military Technical Revolution: A Structural Framework, Center for Strategic and International Studies, March 1993, p. 26 (italics in original).

> availability of such weapons may tempt them to conclude that force need no longer remain the option of last resort, and induce them to employ their arsenal casually and without due reflection.[24]

A real-world expression of that tendency, expressing the confounding and sometimes pernicious effect of greater useability in PGM weapons, comes from the memoirs of Colin Powell. Recalling a 1993 incident in the impending showdown with Yugoslavia's Slobodan Milosevic, Powell reports a terse comment from Madeleine Albright, then the U.S. ambassador to the United Nations. Seeking to compel greater restraint by Belgrade, Albright had argued in favor of a judicious application of military force, a course that Powell, as chair of the Joint Chiefs of Staff, had counseled against. Frustrated by her colleague's reticence, Albright wondered aloud, "What's the point of having this superb military that you're always talking about if we can't use it?"[25] Stephen Wrage aptly summarized the lesson of this dialogue, in terms as applicable to PGMs as to anything else: "If there are unusually useable weapons in the arsenal, there will be unusual pressures to use them."[26]

BIBLIOGRAPHY

William Arkin, Smart Bombs, Dumb Targeting? 56 Bulletin of the Atomic Scientists No. 3, May/June 2000, p. 46

A.J. Bacevich and Lawrence F. Kaplan, The Clinton Doctrine, The Weekly Standard, September 30, 1996, p. 16

Stuart Walters Belt, Missiles Over Kosovo: Emergence, Lex Lata, of a Customary Norm Requiring the Use of Precision Munitions in Urban Areas, 47 Naval Law Review 115, 2000

Frank Colucci, Small Precision Bomb Program on Fast Track, 89 National Defense, No. 608, July 2004, p. 40

J.W. Crawford, III, The Law of Noncombatant Immunity and the Targeting of National Electrical Power Systems, 21 Fletcher Forum of World Affairs 101, 1997

James Digby, Precision-Guided Weapons, Adelphi Paper No. 118, International Institute for Strategic Studies, 1975

Charles J. Dunlap, Jr., Technology and the 21st Century Battlefield: Recomplicating Moral Life for the Statesman and the Soldier, U.S. Army War College, Strategic Studies Institute, January 15, 1999

James F. Dunnigan, Digital Soldiers: The Evolution of High-Tech Weaponry and Tomorrow's Brave New Battlefield, 1996

[24] A.J. Bacevich and Lawrence F. Kaplan, The Clinton Doctrine, The Weekly Standard, September 30, 1996, p. 16, 20–21.

[25] Colin Powell, My American Journey, 1995, p. 576.

[26] Stephen Wrage, When War Isn't Hell: A Cautionary Tale, 102 Current History No. 660, January 2003, p. 32.

Karl W. Eikenberry, Take No Casualties, 26 Parameters No. 2, Summer 1996
Sandra I. Erwin, Threat to Satellite Signals Fuels Demand for Anti-Jam Products, National Defense, June 2000
Thomas J. Fiscus, Requested Legal Review of the Massive Ordnance Air Blast (MOAB) Weapon, U.S. Department of the Air Force memorandum, March 21, 2003
George and Meredith Friedman, The Future of War: Power, Technology, and American World Dominance in the 21st Century, 1996
Norman Friedman, A Problem with Precision? 127 Proceedings of the U.S. Naval Institute No. 4, April 2001, p. 4
David A. Fulghum, What a Blast, 159 Aviation Week and Space Technology No. 20, November 17, 2003, p. 68
Richard P. Hallion, Precision Guided Munitions and the New Era of Warfare, Air Power Studies Centre, Royal Australian Air Force, Working Paper No. 53, 1995
David Hambling, Blast Reduction, Defense Technology International, September 2007, p. 54
Human Rights Watch, Civilian Deaths in the NATO Air Campaign, vol. 12, no. 1, February 2000
Human Rights Watch, Off Target: The Conduct of the War and Civilian Casualties in Iraq, December 11, 2003, http://www.hrw.org/en/reports/2003/12/11/target-0
Danielle L. Infeld, Precision-Guided Munitions Demonstrated Their Pinpoint Accuracy in Desert Storm; But Is a Country Obligated to Use Precision Technology to Minimize Collateral Civilian Injury and Damage? 26 George Washington Journal of International Law and Economics 109, 1992
Greg Jaffe, To Fight Terrorists, Air Force Seeks a Bomb With Less Bang, Wall Street Journal, April 6, 2006, p. 1
Colin H. Kahl, How We Fight, 85 Foreign Affairs No. 6, November/December 2006, p. 83
Harold Kennedy, Precision Weapons Command More Attention, Resources, National Defense, March 2003, p. 36
Benjamin S. Lambeth, The Transformation of American Air Power, 2000
Robert Mandel, The Wartime Utility of Precision Versus Brute Force in Weaponry, 30 Armed Forces & Society No. 2, Winter 2004, p. 171
Robert Mandel, Security, Strategy, and the Quest for Bloodless War, 2004
Michael J. Mazarr, Jeffrey Shaffer, and Benjamin Ederington, The Military Technical Revolution: A Structural Framework, Center for Strategic and International Studies, March 1993
Phillip S. Meilinger, A Matter of Precision, Foreign Policy, March/April 2001, p. 78
Phillip S. Meilinger, Precision Aerospace Power, Discrimination, and the Future of War, 15 Aerospace Power Journal No. 3, Fall 2001, p. 12
David R. Mets, The Long Search for a Surgical Strike: Precision Munitions and the Revolution in Military Affairs, CADRE Paper No. 12, Air University Press, College of Aerospace Doctrine, Research and Education, October 2001
Michael Mok, Precision Guided Munitions, 2002

Colin Powell, My American Journey, 1995
Project on Defense Alternatives, Operation Enduring Freedom: Why a Higher Rate of Civilian Bombing Casualties, Briefing Report No. 11, January 18, 2002, revised January 24, 2002
Christopher B. Puckett, In This Era of 'Smart Weapons,' Is a State Under an International Legal Obligation to Use Precision-Guided Technology in an Armed Conflict? 18 Emory International Law Review 645, Fall 2004
Michael Russell Rip and James M. Hasik, The Precision Revolution: GPS and the Future of Aerial Warfare, 2002
Ward Thomas, The Ethics of Destruction: Norms and Force in International Relations, 2001
John A. Tirpak, The First Six Weeks, 82 Air Force Magazine No. 6, June 1999
John A. Tirpak, Precision: The Next Generation, 86 Air Force Magazine No. 11, November 2003
U.S. Air Force, Fact Sheets, http://www.af.mil/factsheets/index.asp
U.S. General Accounting Office, Weapons Acquisition: Precision Guided Munitions in Inventory, Production, and Development, GAO/NSIAD-95-95, June 1995
Barry D. Watts, The Military Use of Space: A Diagnostic Assessment, Center for Strategic and Budgetary Assessments, February 2001
Stephen Wrage, When War Isn't Hell: A Cautionary Tale, 102 Current History No. 660, January 2003, p. 32

5

Low-Yield Nuclear Weapons

Scenario 5

Relations between the United States and the People's Republic of East Chuan have gone from terrible to worse. Decades after the brutal civil war that serrated the east and west halves of the Chuan peninsula into independent, mutually suspicious states, no lasting peace accord has been reached and irredentist sentiments on both sides of the still-tense demilitarized zone perpetually generate nasty border incidents and a genuine fear of renewed hostilities.

The United States ally, West Chuan, has developed into a functioning democracy, reasonably prosperous and stable. In contrast, East Chuan has retrogressed into a xenophobic dictatorship, a hermit fiefdom, isolated from international commerce and the civilizing influences of globalism. Worse, East Chuan has vigorously pursued every form of modern weaponry; although its exact capabilities remain a tightly guarded state secret, United States intelligence estimates that the East Chuanese have stockpiled functioning arsenals of both chemical and biological weapons (CW and BW). With the burgeoning threats of proliferation and terrorism now at the top of the international agenda, East Chuan is suspected of industriously selling its unconventional weapons expertise on the international black market, including perhaps offering CW and BW devices to nonstate actors intent upon wreaking havoc upon the United States and its allies.

Conventional aggression is also a live fear: In recent weeks, the saber-rattling from the East has increased in intensity, troops have been mobilized, weapons have been placed on alert, and the rhetoric has turned increasingly bellicose. Any full-scale attack from East to West Chuan would be disastrous today – the capital cities of the two regimes are barely

200 kilometers apart, and heavily urbanized development would expose millions of civilian residents to the worst ravages of modern combat.

The United States president is therefore considering the possibility of a preemptive or preventative strike against East Chuan, with the goals of disabling its capability for aggression against the West, destroying its chemical and biological weapons before they can be deployed, and short-circuiting its threatened proliferation of weapons of mass destruction (WMD). American military planners have already constructed contingency plans for such an attack, emphasizing the need to suppress East Chuan's air defenses (radars and surface-to-air missile installations), to knock out bridges, roads, and railyards to impede enemy force mobility, and to disrupt command, control, and communications links – the now-familiar tactics to "prepare the battlespace" at the outset of combat. Two special factors, however, complicate the planning process.

First, East Chuan has succeeded, over a period of years, in "hardening" its most important military headquarters by burrowing deep into the solid rock of its massive central mountain range. It has entrenched its senior leadership in these tunnels, afforded them reliable means for two-way communications with troops in the field, and ensured them an adequate supply of food, water, air, and other essential services. U.S. military strategists calculate that these deeply buried bunkers are impervious to conventional military strikes – even our largest and most accurate ordnance would probably be insufficient to collapse the granite caverns or even to interrupt their functioning.

But such a "decapitation" mission would be very valuable – if the United States could succeed in destroying those leadership figures, it might trigger a massive uprising against the incumbent regime, precipitously ending the threat; short of that, such a blow would greatly impede the East Chuanese ability to attack the West, or even to wage defensive war effectively. Some U.S. experts postulate that only a nuclear weapon – perhaps a very small-yield explosion (on the order of a few kilotons) – could dig the opponents out of their bunker. The experts also opine that such a limited nuclear strike could be conducted in a manner that would avoid most collateral damage to civilians in East Chuan and elsewhere.

Second, the East Chuanese CW and BW inventories pose another special problem. The depots where those weapons are now stored could be attacked – indeed destroyed – with relative ease, but only with a risk of daunting collateral consequences. Conventional explosives would obliterate the buildings, but in so doing may well compromise the integrity of the munitions, casks, barrels, and tanks that contain the deadly chemical and biological agents, allowing pathogenic plumes to leak into the atmosphere. Those noxious excursions would be predicted to scatter the worst imaginable toxins; depending on that day's weather, civilians downwind – including our allies in West Chuan and in other countries in the region – could be severely jeopardized.

Again, some U.S. experts recommend assigning a small-scale nuclear weapon to the task. They posit that the extreme heat of a nuclear explosion (reaching over 10 million degrees) could instantaneously and completely incinerate the CW and BW materials, preventing their dissemination. The experts also caution that the time for any such proactive strike is at the very outset of a military campaign, because otherwise the East Chuanese leadership is likely to disperse the CW and BW arms broadly to their deployed troops in the field, and no single bomb could then destroy them before they could be used against American or allied forces and civilians.

Nuclear bombs carry incredible power. Six decades after their only two wartime explosions, they remain the ultimate weapon, with a destructive force impossible for most people to conceptualize. Even the yardstick for measuring the power of these blasts is unprecedented: a kiloton (kt) of nuclear yield means that the bomb (which might be quite compact and weigh only several pounds) packs an explosive force equivalent to *1000 tons* of TNT. The bomb that destroyed Hiroshima at the end of World War II was roughly 12.5-kt yield – it killed 80,000 or more people instantly and perhaps 150,000 over time, and it clear-cut five square miles of the city center, evaporating about two-thirds of the urban development. Remarkably, a 12.5-kt weapon today would be considered quite small.

VARIETIES OF NUCLEAR WEAPONS

Technically, there is an important difference between "atomic" and "nuclear" or "hydrogen" weapons, although colloquial speech frequently uses those cataclysmic terms interchangeably. An atomic device, the only sort available in 1945, relies upon fission – the release of immense quantities of energy from the splitting of the nucleus of atoms of a heavy element such as uranium or plutonium. In contrast, a nuclear (or "thermonuclear" or "hydrogen") device, of the sort first tested by the United States in 1954, operates via fusion – the release of even greater energy from the forced joining of small elements such as atoms of hydrogen to create helium. The most sophisticated modern types of weapons utilize both processes sequentially: an initial fission explosion (the so-called "primary"), which creates the heat and pressure conditions necessary to trigger a "secondary" fusion explosion, which accounts for most of the power of the bomb.

Nuclear weapons release several distinct forms of energy, resulting in four principal "kill mechanisms." First, about half the weapon's energy is typically expressed as a shock wave, a blast force that digs a crater, flattens buildings, and spreads flying debris into a lethal radius that varies depending upon the magnitude of the explosion, whether the detonation occurs in the air, on the ground or underground, and other factors. Second, a flash of intense heat accounts for approximately one-third of the bomb's power, generating an incandescent fireball of immense proportions; flammable materials in the area ignite, and a broad firestorm may ensue, consuming everything within its reach. Prompt radiation is the third consequence of a nuclear explosion, emitting an array of gamma rays, neutrons, x-rays, and ionizing particles hazardous to all life. Finally, delayed radiation, in the form of fallout containing perhaps 300 types of radioactive products, spreads a lethal shroud over a wide area, perhaps the entire globe, depending upon the exact characteristics of the weapon, the height of the burst, and the weather patterns.

For example, a relatively standard nuclear weapon, detonated in a typical warfighting mode, could create, instantaneously, a crater 300 feet deep and 1200 feet in diameter at ground zero. The blast wave would expand three miles in the first 12 seconds, destroying even heavy industrial buildings with winds of 250 miles per hour. Within the first second, the atmosphere would ignite into a fireball half a mile in diameter, generating three times the light and heat of a comparable area of the sun. Half the people in the vicinity would likely die immediately, and severe burns and injuries from flying debris would afflict thousands more, out to approximately three miles from the detonation. The long-term consequences (cancers, genetic abnormalities, psychic wounds, economic disruption, etc.) from the fallout and other pernicious effects could spread over an immense, unpredictable span of time and space.[1]

Human inventiveness now allows weaponeers to design bombs with specialized effects, to optimize the mixture of different forms of released energy to perform particular missions. Bombs with reduced blast, or enhanced radiation, for example, or with even more fine-grained permutations, can now be concocted. Moreover, the size, shape, and character of the device will vary, depending upon the need to mate it with an

[1] Lynn Eden, Whole World on Fire: Organizations, Knowledge, and Nuclear Weapons Devastation, 2004.

appropriate delivery system: nuclear explosives are configured differently for different types of bombs, missiles, artillery shells, land mines, and other applications. Perhaps the most obvious variable in nuclear weapons design, however, is simply the magnitude of the explosive yield.

After the 12.5-kt Hiroshima weapon and the 21-kt bomb that obliterated Nagasaki three days later, the United States developed, tested, and often deployed a ghastly inventory of nuclear weapons of all sizes. The W58 warhead for the Polaris A-3 submarine-launched ballistic missile (SLBM), for example, was introduced into the stockpile in 1964; it carried 150 kt yield. The W78 warhead for the Minuteman III intercontinental ballistic missile (ICBM) was first produced in 1979; its yield is 335 kt. The B61 "free-fall" bomb, dating back to 1966, came in a variety of modifications, ranging from 10 kt to 1 megaton (Mt), the equivalent of an incredible 1 million tons of TNT (or 1000 kt). The B28 bomb, created in 1958, was larger still, up to 1.45 Mt, and the W53 warhead, from 1962, for the Titan II ICBM was among the largest ever deployed by the United States, at 9 Mt.[2]

At the opposite extreme, some other nuclear devices featured yields that were quite small (at least when measured with this absurd yardstick of Armageddon). The Mk 57 nuclear depth charge from 1963, for example, was 5–10 kt. The W30 warhead produced in 1959 for the TALOS shipborne surface-to-air missile was 5 kt and the W25 warhead from 1957 for the Genie air-to-air missile was 1.25 kt. There was a W48 artillery projectile first manufactured in 1962 with a yield of 0.1 kt and a W54 atomic land mine from 1964 with a yield as low as 0.01 kt.

During the cold war, the United States manufactured an estimated 66,500 nuclear devices of 100 major types; at the peak (in 1966) as many as 32,000 nuclear weapons of various genres were deployed.[3] The Soviet Union demonstrated equivalent creativity and enthusiasm in constructing its nuclear arsenal; Moscow's inventory reached its zenith in 1986 with

[2] Data regarding nuclear weapons are taken from Christopher Campbell, Nuclear Weapons Fact Book, 1984; Chuck Hansen, US Nuclear Weapons: The Secret History, 1988; Thomas B. Cochran, William M. Arkin, and Milton M. Hoenig, Nuclear Weapons Databook, Volume 1: U.S. Nuclear Forces and Capabilities, 1984; and Robert S. Norris and Hans M. Kristensen, U.S. Nuclear Warheads, 1945–2009, Bulletin of the Atomic Scientists, July/August 2009, p. 72.

[3] Stephen I. Schwartz, Four Trillion Dollars and Counting, 51 Bulletin of the Atomic Scientists No. 6, November/December 1995, p. 32; Robert S. Norris and Hans M. Kristensen, The U.S. Nuclear Stockpile, Today and Tomorrow, 63 Bulletin of the Atomic Scientists No. 5, September/October 2007, p. 60. The United States deployed 120 different types of nuclear weapon systems (missiles, gravity bombs, artillery shells, etc.), most of which had a unique type of explosive dedicated to it.

45,000 deployed bombs. One artifact – the Tsar Bomba, from 1961 – was designed as a 100-Mt bomb. Other nuclear weapons-possessing countries (the United Kingdom, France, China, India, Pakistan, Israel, and North Korea) configured their own, much smaller arsenals.

CURRENT NUCLEAR WEAPONS INVENTORIES

In recent years, the stockpiles of deployed nuclear weapons deployed by the superpowers have shrunk considerably, both in raw numbers and in range of types. The United States has ceremoniously dismantled hundreds of land-based and sea-based missiles, withdrawn most of its nuclear weapons from Europe, denuclearized the Army, and removed nuclear arms from its Navy surface ships. What is referred to as the "enduring stockpile" includes, as of January 2009, about 5200 operational and reserve bombs of eight major types (and several submodifications), mated to a variety of ICBMs, SLBMs, cruise missiles, and gravity bombs. Russia retains about 15,000 nuclear weapons, many of which are awaiting dismantlement, and about 6000 of which are considered functional.

With the dramatic reductions in nuclear arsenals since the fall of the Berlin Wall, as codified in the 1991 START I Treaty, the 1993 START II Treaty (which did not enter into force), and the 2002 Moscow Strategic Offensive Reductions Treaty, the number of treaty-accountable U.S.- and Russian-deployed strategic nuclear warheads is expected to tumble further. From inventories of roughly 2700 operational treaty-covered bombs today, the two erstwhile competitors are racing downward, toward retaining stocks of between 1700 and 2200 strategic weapons apiece in 2012 – and the United States has already reached that target level, well ahead of schedule. In addition to those totals, however, thousands more warheads of various sizes and types will be warehoused in an inactive reserve rather than being promptly dismantled, and many of them could be returned to the active arsenal relatively quickly. Hundreds of shorter range nuclear weapons systems are also excluded from these treaty limitations.[4]

The Pentagon (and the Department of Energy, which is responsible for designing, testing, and building the nuclear bombs before certifying them to the Department of Defense) have realized that bigger isn't always better when it comes to nuclear explosions. The very biggest, as well as the very smallest, nuclear weapons have been phased out of the active inventory.

[4] Robert S. Norris and Hans M. Kristensen, U.S. Nuclear Forces, 2008, Bulletin of the Atomic Scientists, March/April 2008, p. 50.

What remain are disproportionately the most modern, effective, reliable, and destructive variants, most of which have yields in the range of 100 to 475 kt.

This revised posture comports well with the principal themes of classic deterrence theory: Insofar as the main (or the sole) purpose of nuclear weapons is to deter a nuclear attack upon the United States by any other country, then, as the likelihood of that danger recedes in the post-cold war world, it becomes appropriate to field fewer such weapons – and the nuclear arms that we do retain could principally be of larger varieties, to continue to effectuate an updated policy of mutual assured destruction. Only if one contemplates additional missions for nuclear weapons – for example, the notion of "extended deterrence" introduced in Chapter 2, to dissuade other countries from undertaking various other hostile activities well short of a nuclear strike against us – would there be much interest in retaining legions of smaller, more multipurpose nuclear arms.

USEABLE NUCLEAR WEAPONS: CAVES

Some in the U.S. defense establishment have been gravitating in exactly that direction as part of the revolution in military affairs: pursuit of diverse (principally smaller) nuclear weapons, optimized to perform a variety of more restricted, limited-scale missions, such as those outlined in Scenario 5. A number of advanced concepts for newer, especially smaller and precisely delivered, nuclear weapons have bubbled to the surface of strategic thinking in the United States. The first such application would be to root enemy forces out of their elaborately constructed underground bunkers.

In an era in which the United States has demonstrated the ability to undertake increasingly accurate and therefore deadly aerial assaults with conventional weapon PGMs, as discussed in Chapter 4, many potential opponents are seeking refuge underground, hoping that thick earthen "overburden," reinforced by layers of concrete and steel, can negate the revolutionary effect of super-precise U.S. bombing. The Soviet Union (years ago), Vietnam, and North Korea (more recently) have excavated the most famous and well-regarded subterranean fortifications; those in China and Iran today may be almost equally large and impregnable. In other battle zones, such as eastern Afghanistan, partisans have taken advantage of much simpler and cheaper techniques, exploiting existing warrens of relatively shallow and primitive ancient caves – and enlarging and reinforcing them as necessary – to hide from attackers and ensnare them in costly battles.

In a 2001 report to Congress, the Department of Defense defined and described these installations broadly:

> The term "hard and deeply buried target" (HDBT) refers to an adversary's threatening and well protected assets in structures ranging from hardened surface bunker complexes to deep tunnels. These facilities are typically large, complex structures incorporating the attributes of concealment, self-sustainment, multifaceted communications, strong physical security, modern air defenses, and siting in protective (often mountainous or urban) surroundings. In many countries, HDBTs are elements of a well-connected network of operational capabilities with duplication – a very important factor for both intelligence and strike planning. These facilities are protected for good reason – they are an essential element of any likely battle or crisis action. Such facilities routinely serve as: leadership shelters; command, control, and communications (C^3) centers; weapons production, assembly, storage and deployment facilities, especially for weapons of mass destruction (WMD); missile operations tunnels and garrisons; and point or integrated area defense system facilities.[5]

Upward of 70 countries are now thought to be pursuing defense-related activities underground, and modern excavation technology greatly accelerates the speed of exploitation and the size and stability of the resulting constructions. Some of these sanctuaries are quite shallow (only several meters deep), but many have been painstakingly hollowed out down to 250 meters, and a few are intact structures as much as 700 meters beneath the surface. Already, perhaps 100 of these HDBTs in potential adversary states have been identified as potential priority targets; other estimates put the number of underground WMD and command bunker sites at 1400. As inexpensive mining innovations and machinery continue to spread, more countries will be able to take advantage of natural features such as narrow canyons or steep mountain ridges to construct hideouts that can frustrate opposing strategists.

Existing offensive weapons and tactics are largely inadequate to meet this new challenge. Even the largest and most sophisticated precision-guided conventional munitions cannot puncture far enough to strike these sites effectively. The most advanced U.S. conventional "bunker buster" bombs, even when equipped with novel "burrowing" capability allowing them to penetrate the soil for some additional distance before detonation, simply do not carry sufficient power to collapse the deep

[5] Secretary of Defense in conjunction with Secretary of Energy, Report to Congress on the Defeat of Hard and Deeply Buried Targets, July 2001, p. 8.

underground caverns. A better strategy, usually, is to attack the adits (the cave's entrances and exits), the air vents and other support conduits, the power supplies, and the communications links, but these are usually redundant and difficult to locate.

The obvious alternative, to take out the caves manually via infantry on the scene, is both difficult and slow. Putting "boots on the ground" can be the surest mechanism for overcoming local defenses, but it is extremely hazardous work, even after the invading force has fought its way to the site. Where the attackers cannot see where they are going, where the defenders have had the opportunity to construct their redoubt and booby traps with foresight, and where each turn of the cave may have multiple unknown offshoots, the onslaught is perilous – as spelunkers dating back to Tom Sawyer can testify. The continuing ability of al-Qaeda remnants to frustrate American and allied efforts to root them out of Afghanistan's Tora Bora tunnel complexes demonstrates the difficulty of the task.

Another conceivable mechanism would be to attack those HDBT fortifications with existing (i.e., large) nuclear weapons, counting on the devastating shock wave and heat to crush or disable even buried installations. Although that tactic might suffice to get the job done, partisans on all sides agree that a 200-kt warhead is simply too large – it's the wrong tool for the job. As then-Secretary of Defense Donald Rumsfeld put it, responding to the challenge posed by other countries' advances in tunneling:

> At the present time, we don't have a capability of dealing with that. We can't go in there and get at things in solid rock underground. The only thing we have is very large, very dirty big nuclear weapons. So . . . do we want to have nothing and only a large, dirty nuclear weapon, or would we rather have something in between?[6]

The hole suddenly excavated by a standard nuclear weapon would be too large; the firestorm would reach too far; the prompt and delayed radiation would imperil too many friendlies. Even if a nuclear weapon were the only feasible way to accomplish valid, important military objectives, we would not use it. We would be self-deterred, some experts argue, unwilling to resort to such disproportionate force, unprepared to

[6] U.S. Senate Committee on Appropriations, Subcommittee on Defense, Hearings on Fiscal Year 2006 Defense Department Appropriations, April 27, 2005, testimony of Secretary of Defense Donald Rumsfeld.

contradict the legal, political, and public relations barriers against use of vastly excessive power.

The East Chuanese, being well aware of these inhibitions, would thus enjoy a confidence that we would refrain from initiating that type of nuclear attack against their HDBT. Their freedom of action would grow accordingly, and their underground command bunkers would rise to near-invulnerability. America's possession of a vast nuclear arsenal, therefore, and the enormous asymmetric advantage in the most prominent and high-visibility form of modern weaponry, drop entirely out of the military calculation between the United States and East Chuan. A threat that is not credible – that we would not, in fact, have the resolve to execute – is no threat at all.

To avoid that dilemma, some in the U.S. defense establishment now argue, we need a capacity for reacting effectively, without overreacting. We seek an improved ability to hold at risk certain realistic target sets that now remain essentially out of reach. In short, we need nuclear weapons that are more useable – that is, smaller, capable of performing more deft missions without automatically generating such an excessively widespread swath of death and destruction. As one military official expressed it, "What's needed now is something that can threaten a bunker tunneled under 300 meters of granite without killing the surrounding civilian population."[7]

The Bush Administration's December 2001 Nuclear Posture Review explicitly adopted this perspective for programming the nation's future nuclear weapons development efforts: where a precise touch is required, the nuclear devices in the current arsenal are simply too big to be useable, whereas the extant conventional weapons are too small to be adequate for the task. "Greater flexibility is needed with respect to nuclear force and planning than was the case during the cold war," the report commented. "Nuclear attack options that vary in scale, scope and purpose will complement other military capabilities."[8]

In the same vein, the December 2002 National Strategy to Combat Weapons of Mass Destruction also contemplates the possibility of preemptive strikes against an enemy's hard-to-reach WMD programs, including those secreted away underground. Likewise, the 2005 draft revisions

[7] Quoted in Walter Pincus, Senate Bill Requires Study of New Nuclear Weapons, Washington Post, June 12, 2000, p. A2.

[8] U.S. Government, Nuclear Posture Review (excerpts), submitted to Congress on December 31, 2001, excerpts released January 8, 2002, p. 7, available at www.globalsecurity.org/wmd/library/policy/dod/npr.htm.

to the key Joint Chiefs of Staff document, the Doctrine for Joint Nuclear Operations, concludes, "Deterrence of potential adversary WMD use requires the potential adversary leadership to believe the United States has both the ability and will to preempt or retaliate promptly with responses that are credible and effective."[9] Most vividly, the July 2001 DoD Report to Congress on the Defeat of Hard and Deeply Buried Targets described numerous Army, Navy, Air Force, and other programs necessary to redress important shortfalls in the U.S. ability to locate, characterize, attack, and assess damage to HDBTs.

Advocates suggest, as part of the revolution in military affairs, that a well-crafted "nuclear earth penetrator" could be developed to burrow ruggedly into the ground – perhaps several meters or even further – before detonating. In that way, the nuclear kinetic energy would be "coupled" into the earth more efficiently and the seismic shock wave would propagate toward the target with enhanced might. Studies indicate that a buried nuclear explosion could be much smaller than a detonation at the surface – perhaps by a factor of 15 or 25 times – and still be adequate to shatter or cripple an enemy's underground installation. A single-stage device relying exclusively on fission might suffice, perhaps with a yield on the order of 10 kt. Furthermore, advocates contend, the effects of a relatively small nuclear detonation, buried even that short distance, might be largely contained underground, minimizing the cratering effects on the surface and reducing the collateral fallout damage to people and other assets above ground. In this way, the argument runs, a nuclear earth penetrator can achieve the desired finesse: it can be effective in attacking the target, without being so overly powerful that we would be unduly inhibited about using it where necessary.

USEABLE NUCLEAR WEAPONS: WMD DEPOTS

The second leading source for the surge in interest in low-yield nuclear weapons concerns the difficulty in dealing with the possible accretion of chemical, biological, and nuclear weapons materials in other countries. Although U.S. intelligence proved grossly faulty on this point regarding Saddam Hussein immediately prior to the second Gulf War in 2003, it

[9] U.S. Joint Chiefs of Staff, Doctrine for Joint Nuclear Operations, Joint Publication 3–12, Final Coordination (2) draft, March 15, 2005, p. I-6. Notably, this document was never issued in final form; after public exposure and debate, the document was cancelled, but its contents reportedly remain effective and operational.

is not just "crying wolf" to call attention to this danger. Disquieting reports continue to surface about the possibility of secret inventories of unconventional arms or the facilities necessary to develop them in a number of parlous countries. The CIA and leading nongovernmental authorities estimate that no fewer than a dozen countries possess illicit nuclear, CW, or BW programs or stockpiles or are assiduously working in that direction.[10]

Obviously, the United States possesses a wide range of diplomatic, economic, and political tools to attempt to deal with the problem of WMD proliferation, but just as obviously, it is also prudent to consider how we might eventually respond if those less forceful policy alternatives prove inadequate. In particular, how could such sites be attacked, in the event of hostilities? Is there any reliable way to preemptively destroy these weapons instantly *in situ*, as in the East Chuan scenario, without the byproduct risk of spewing them into the atmosphere, in a manner that would jeopardize everyone nearby, including our own troops and neighboring countries as well as local civilians?

The concern about accidental atmospheric releases of chemical and biological pathogens during wartime is real and may well intensify in future conflicts. One illustration of the exacerbated dangers is given by the continuing uncertainty over the origins of Gulf War Illness, an insidious syndrome consisting of a variety of conditions, such as fatigue, muscle and joint pain, memory loss, sleep disturbances, and gastrointestinal problems experienced by numerous American veterans of Desert Storm. One hypothesis, neither confirmed nor disproven, associates some cases of the mysterious ailment with inadvertent exposure to Iraqi CW, such as when the U.S. Army XVIII Corps attacked and explosively destroyed the weapons cache at Khamisiyah in March 1991.[11]

[10] U.S. Central Intelligence Agency, Unclassified Report to Congress on the Acquisition of Technology Relating to Weapons of Mass Destruction and Advanced Chemical Munitions, 1 January through 30 June 2003; Joseph Cirincione, Jon B. Wolfsthal, and Miriam Rajkumar, Deadly Arsenals: Nuclear, Biological, and Chemical Threats (2nd ed.), 2005.

[11] For similar reasons, during the December 1998 Operation Desert Fox (when the United States struck several targets in Iraq to try to pressure Saddam Hussein's regime toward compliance with international inspection demands) the Pentagon was reluctant to include on the target list any facilities that were suspected of containing Iraqi CW and BW stocks. Secretary of Defense William Cohen cautioned, "We're not going to take a chance and try to target any facility that would release any kind of horrific damage to innocent people." Quoted in Steven Lee Myers, The Targets: Jets Said to Avoid Poison Gas Sites, New York Times, December 18, 1998, p. A1.

If even short-duration, inadvertent exposure to moderate levels of leaked sarin or other nerve gases can be so hazardous, and if ordinary bombs are insufficient to denature the chemicals or biologicals, then it may be mandatory to develop a more expeditious and safer mechanism for handling such arsenals in the future. The germicidal heat of nuclear explosions – more than 10 million degrees – some argue, offers a feasible solution. The 2001 Nuclear Posture Review points in that direction, saying, "Desired capabilities for nuclear weapons systems in flexible, adaptable strike plans include options for variable and reduced yields, high accuracy, and timely employment. These capabilities would help deter enemy use of WMD or limit collateral damage, should the United States have to defeat enemy WMD capabilities.... Nuclear weapons could be employed against targets able to withstand non-nuclear attack (for example, deep underground bunkers or bio-weapon facilities."[12] However, the Pentagon has also noted that the existing nuclear weapons inventory "was not developed with this mission in mind," and the stockpiled bombs are not optimally sized and configured for the proposed new tasking.[13]

EARLIER EARTH PENETRATION PROGRAMS

Pursuit of small and specialized nuclear weapons for these demanding functions is not new – in the United States, work on nuclear earth penetration technology dates back to the early 1950s. National weapons laboratories have undertaken more than 3000 tests, evaluating variations in the physical characteristics (size, shape, weight, etc.) of the penetrator, the impact velocity and angle, and the geological features of the target site.[14]

In principle, nuclear earth penetrator devices could be delivered either via missiles or via air-to-surface bombs. For example, in the 1980s, the United States developed and tested, but did not deploy, a W86 nuclear warhead for the Pershing II intermediate range missile, designed to penetrate 10 meters of granite or hardened concrete. However, missile warheads typically travel so fast that the impact with the earth's surface is extremely violent, shattering the casing and the bomb before it can burrow very far. So aircraft delivery of penetrating bombs is generally the preferred mode.

[12] Nuclear Posture Review, supra note 8, at 48. 12–13.

[13] Report on HDBT, supra note 5, at 19.

[14] Greg Mello, New Bomb, No Mission, Bulletin of the Atomic Scientists, May/June, 1997, p. 28.

Currently, the leading U.S. nuclear earth penetrator is the B61–11 bomb, which the Clinton Administration entered into the stockpile in 1997. This device incorporates a hardened steel casing and a new nose cone for the older B61–7 bomb; its yield can be adjusted from 0.3 to 340 kt, and it has shown an ability to penetrate two or three meters into frozen soil. At its minimum yield, that degree of penetration ability is assessed as being capable of destroying a target buried under 15 meters of hard rock or concrete; at maximum yield, it could dig out a hardened target 70 meters beneath the surface. Approximately 50 of these devices are now in the inventory. Concepts for future nuclear earth penetrators usually begin with various additional redesigns or further repackagings of the B61 or the B83, which is the largest device currently in the U.S. stockpile, at 1–2 Mt.

The military is also developing earth penetrators that would carry conventional explosives. The most advanced of these systems are the laser-guided GBU-28 and the GPS-guided GBU-37. Both carry 300 kilograms of high explosive and have demonstrated the capability for digging themselves through six meters of concrete or 30 meters of dirt – enough to destroy shallow, but not deep, underground targets. During Desert Storm, for example, the U.S. Air Force used the GBU-28 to destroy a bunker north of Baghdad, which had been covered by more than 30 feet of earth, concrete, and steel.[15] The next generation of conventional penetrators is now under development, designed to delve even further; some of these may be equipped with thermobaric explosives, such as the BLU-118B, which generate extremely high sustained heat and blast pressures in confined spaces such as underground chambers.[16]

CRITICS CONTEST THE HYPOTHESIS

These hypotheses about the potential utility of small nuclear weapons have been vigorously challenged by critics who doubt both the feasibility and safety of nuclear arms for either of the posited functions.

First, as revealed most vividly by an authoritative 2005 study from the National Academy of Sciences, even bombs and missiles of the best design and construction will inherently have only a limited ability to penetrate

[15] Charles D. Ferguson, Mini-Nuclear Weapons and the U.S. Nuclear Posture Review, Center for Nonproliferation Studies, April 8, 2002.

[16] Lisbeth Gronlund, David Wright, and Robert Nelson, Global Security Backgrounder: Earth Penetrating Weapons, May 2005; Amy Butler and Douglas Barrie, Dig for Victory, Aviation Week & Space Technology, September 11, 2006, p. 52.

into the earth.[17] The maximum depth that a bomb could reach will vary significantly with the type of medium (soil, competent rock, concrete, etc.) being transited, and it is possible that future technology will enhance the ability to punch into even deeper strata, but the terminal stresses of high-velocity impact are unavoidable. Experts conclude that it is implausible to predict that even well-crafted missile or bomb warheads could effectively puncture beyond about 12 meters in medium-strength rock, 30 meters in softer rock, or 140 meters in soil. Because some of the underground bunkers of greatest interest are located at such extreme depths (up to 700 meters below the surface) a rather large nuclear explosion would be required to ensure a kill. For example, the National Academy of Sciences experts assess that it would require a 300-kt nuclear penetrator to have a high probability of destroying a target buried 200 meters beneath it, and even a 1-Mt weapon would be unable to defeat a target covered by more than 300 meters.

The explosive effects of a weapon of such size could not be effectively contained at such shallow depths. For comparison, it is useful to note that when nuclear weapons are tested (e.g., to validate the effectiveness of a new design), an explosion as large as 300 kt would be undertaken at a depth of 800 meters in a precisely drilled and carefully backfilled emplacement hole. Even a miniature 1-kt event would ordinarily be buried and sealed at least 100 meters beneath the surface. Experience has shown that at shallower locations, the blast, heat, fallout, and other deadly sequelae would erupt to the surface in intense proportions and would inflict far-flung casualties. The fact that many underground bunkers of greatest interest are located near population centers further ensures that the notion of a benign, "clean" earth-penetrating nuclear strike, with only limited collateral damage on the targeted country, remains an illusion. According to one analysis,

> The blast of even a very low-yield, one-kiloton earth penetrator, detonated at its maximum penetration depth of 15 meters into dry hard rock, will eject more than one million cubic feet of radioactive debris from a crater about the size of ground zero at the World Trade Center.[18]

[17] Effects of Nuclear Earth-Penetrator and Other Weapons, National Research Council, National Academies Press, 2005. See also Michael A. Levi, Fire in the Hole: Nuclear and Non-Nuclear Options for Counter-proliferation, Carnegie Endowment for International Peace, Global Policy Program, Non-Proliferation Program, Working Paper No. 31, November 2002; Robert W. Nelson, Low-Yield Earth-Penetrating Nuclear Weapons, 10 Science and Global Security No. 1, 2002, p. 1.

[18] Sidney D. Drell and James E. Goodby, What Are Nuclear Weapons For? Recommendations for Restructuring U.S. Strategic Nuclear Forces, an Arms Control Association Report, April 2005, p. 20.

The National Academy of Sciences group concluded that, "For the same yield, and weather conditions, the number of casualties from an earth penetrator weapon detonated at a few meters depth is, for all practical purposes, equal to that from a surface burst of the same weapon yield." The only reduction in death and destruction arises from the fact that, with an earth penetrator, a smaller device can be used and still have a chance to destroy the underground bunker.[19]

U.S. government officials have (perhaps belatedly) conceded this point. As Linton Brooks, then the administrator of the National Nuclear Security Administration, testified to Congress in 2005:

> I really must apologize for my lack of precision if we in the administration have suggested that it was possible to have a bomb that penetrated far enough to trap all the fall-out. I don't believe the laws of physics will ever let that be true. It is certainly not what we're trying to do now. . . . There is a nuclear weapon that is going to be hugely destructive over a large area. . . . I do want to make it clear that any thought of . . . nuclear weapons that aren't really destructive is just nuts.[20]

Moreover, nuclear weapons may not be able to perform as advertised in the other posited Scenario 5 application, either. When attacking a WMD storage facility, whether located on the surface or buried, the key to effective neutralization of the deadly agents is sustained, intense heat. (Nuclear radiation can provide a secondary tool for negating chemical and biological weapons agents in some situations.) Unless the chemical and biological substances are thoroughly sanitized by the thermal energy, there is a grave danger that the shock wave and wind will spread them into the surrounding countryside – or beyond. Although nuclear weapons do generate terrifying heat, the temperature spike lasts for only the briefest of periods – the most extreme temperatures are present for less than 1 second – and the inferno of an underground explosion does not spread very far through the earth.

In contrast, the complete incineration of chemical weapons agents usually requires prolonged exposure to intense heat. The U.S. Army, for example, is currently in the process of destroying many of its existing obsolete chemical weapons via newly constructed, state-of-the-art incinerators. The standard operating procedure calls for cooking the liquid

[19] National Academy of Sciences, supra note 17, at S-2.

[20] Linton Brooks, quoted in Peter Wilk, Sarah Stanlick, Martin Butcher, Michael McCally, Ira Helfand, Robert Gould, and John Pastore, Projected Casualties among U.S. Military Personnel and Civilian Populations from the Use of Nuclear Weapons Against Hard and Deeply Buried Targets, Physicians for Social Responsibility, May 2005, p. 5.

agent (sarin, mustard gas, etc.) at 1400 degrees for 50 minutes to ensure full consumption of the noxious chemicals – and, even then, critics have challenged the safety of the system, worrying that some lethal agents or residues might escape through the smokestack.

The National Academy of Sciences and at least two other expert analyses[21] have cast doubt upon the concept of instantaneous destruction of WMD inventories via nuclear detonation. Some conclude that unless the placement of the incoming warhead were so accurate to detonate the bomb in the exact same underground chamber where the chemical and biological agents were stored, there could be no assurance of complete incineration. Even with modern PGMs, that degree of precision (and of intelligence in identifying the precise location and characteristics of the target) is a tall order, and the consequences of missing the mark by even several meters could be grave. Moreover, some argue, if that level of exquisite accuracy were attainable, a nuclear explosion would be unnecessary – depositing a large thermobaric or fuel air explosive (nonnuclear weapons designed to maximize heat) precisely into the midst of the CW or BW stash could also accomplish the sterilization task.

In addition, in any comprehensive calculation of comparative dangers, we would have to consider the effects of the nuclear explosion itself in causing casualties to civilians and to our own troops who might come on the scene later. In most scenarios, the prompt and delayed nuclear effects would be even more deadly and prolonged than those associated with the sudden release of chemicals or biologicals that might escape from an attack by conventional weapons.

Physicians for Social Responsibility has carefully assessed the likely consequences of hypothetical nuclear earth penetrator attacks against selected plausible target locations around the world. For example, in a typical strike scenario against a suspected Iranian underground nuclear materials storage site at Isfahan, 3 million people would die and 35 million more (including 20,000 U.S. troops, intelligence officers, and diplomatic personnel) in Iran, Afghanistan, and Pakistan would be exposed to radiation levels that would carry significant health dangers. In a second hypothetical attack, against the provocative Yongbyon facilities in North Korea, where plutonium has been produced and processed for weapons,

[21] Robert W. Nelson, Nuclear 'Bunker Busters' Would More Likely Disperse Than Destroy Buried Stockpiles of Biological and Chemical Agents, 12 Science and Global Security No. 1–2, 2004, p. 69; Michael May and Zachary Haldeman, Effectiveness of Nuclear Weapons against Buried Biological Agents, 12 Science and Global Security No. 1–2, 2004, p. 91. See also Levi, supra note 17.

500,000 people would die instantly, and there would be some 2 million other casualties.[22]

THE DANGERS OF NUCLEAR USEABILITY

But would we, in any case, really want nuclear weapons to become more useable? If the United States were to initiate (or, in view of the facts of 1945, to reinitiate) the battlefield use of nuclear weapons, would that take the world in a direction we want to go? Even if the prompt destruction of enemy leadership bunkers and WMD warehouses were a valuable and legitimate military mission, and even if nuclear arms were uniquely suited to the task, and even if a new type of small nuclear device could be fashioned to perform those functions in a manner that satisfied the law of armed conflict demands of necessity and proportionality, it would still be a momentous step to cross the threshold from conventional into nuclear war.

Opponents of new generations of nuclear armaments assert that any short-term gain in accomplishing these military objectives via nuclear bombs would be swamped by the adverse consequences from violating the six-decade-long taboo. Our nuclear nonproliferation objectives would surely be among the first casualties of such a measure – how could the United States hope to persuade other nations to abandon their nuclear weapons ambitions when our own actions validate the continuing centrality of those devices on the battlefield? The message to the world would be that even the United States, with its overwhelming superiority in conventional weaponry of every stripe, has to rely upon nuclear weapons to accomplish its military goals. If the sole remaining superpower needs, and uses, nuclear weapons, why should lesser powers exercise greater self-restraint?

Advocates of useable nuclear weapons rebut those apprehensions by asserting that the notion of a qualitatively different threshold separating nuclear and conventional weaponry is now obsolete. A very small nuclear device, they point out, could be engineered to have less destructive power than some very large conventional ordnance; there is an overlapping continuum of explosive force, and so-called tinynukes, mininukes, and micronukes could be configured with mere tons (not kilotons) of yield. It shouldn't matter to the victims of an explosion what specific physical principle was used to shatter their world – a bomb is a bomb is a bomb. We

[22] Wilk et al., supra note 20.

should focus instead, with greater rationality and pure logic, on the scale of the destruction, the imposed loss of life and property, and the efficiency and effectiveness of the operation – not on the outmoded symbolism of the nuclear/conventional distinction – and we should make use of whatever armaments can best accomplish the assigned mission.[23]

As the Pentagon's "Doctrine for Joint Nuclear Operations" puts it, in discussing the integration of U.S. nuclear and conventional forces:

> For many contingencies, existing and emerging conventional capabilities will meet anticipated requirements; however, some contingencies will remain where the most appropriate response may include the use of US nuclear weapons. Integrating conventional and nuclear attacks will ensure the most efficient use of force and provide US leaders with a broader range of strike options to address immediate contingencies.[24]

But stepping across the nuclear threshold is not exclusively a symbolic act, either in terms of the revolution in military affairs or in the broader context. In some confrontations (unlike Scenario 5), where both sides are equipped with nuclear arms, any first use – of even limited numbers of small nuclear arms for purely tactical purposes – may quickly cascade out of control. As elaborated in Herman Kahn's celebrated 1965 study, *On Escalation*, it is sometimes useful to conceptualize a "ladder" of international crises, comprising many increasingly hostile "rungs" of interstate tension, hostility, threats, and combat. As opponents climb up the ladder, toward the most apocalyptic spasm of all-out nuclear holocaust, there are certain stages where they may be more likely to pause – boundaries that differentiate qualitatively different categories of conflict. A most salient of these escalation thresholds involves the first use of nuclear weapons; no other "resting point" has such clarity and historic force, and violating the "no nukes" rule is a most provocative and consequential step.[25] To switch metaphors, once the firebreak against all nuclear weapons *per se* has been breached, the war knows no other logical stopping point.

Robert McNamara, perhaps the leading architect of the concept of mutual assured destruction as Secretary of Defense in the Kennedy and Johnson administrations, recently criticized "the fundamentally

[23] Thomas W. Dowler and Joseph S. Howard II, Countering the Threat of the Well-Armed Tyrant: A Modest Proposal for Small Nuclear Weapons, 19 Strategic Review No. 4, Fall 1991, p. 34.

[24] Joint Doctrine, supra note 9, at II-8.

[25] Herman Kahn, On Escalation: Metaphors and Scenarios, 1965.

flawed assumption that nuclear weapons could be used in some limited way."[26] These weapons, he wrote, are simply too powerful for any plausible use – and hypothesizing a small-scale, single shot against a particular fixed target only perpetuates a dangerous illusion and fuels further proliferation. In 2005, McNamara joined eight retired generals and admirals publicly urging Congress to reject pursuit of new nuclear weapons, writing,

> The United States currently enjoys unparalleled conventional military superiority. Efforts to expand the usability of nuclear weapons would lower the threshold for using nuclear weapons and risk blurring the bright line that has existed for sixty years between conventional and nuclear weapons. These efforts might also indicate a dangerous and misplaced increased reliance on nuclear weapons.[27]

Leading experts in the People's Republic of China express similar apprehensions. As several of them reported to Joanne Tompkins in 2002, the American effort to adapt even small nuclear weapons for attacks against buried bunkers or CW/BW installations "would lower the threshold for their use and blur the distinction between conventional and strategic weapons. It would become easier to think about fighting and possibly winning a nuclear war, and nuclear conflict would therefore become more likely."[28]

But the advocates of useable nuclear weapons do not relent, and they press the argument that a deterrent weapon, to have its intended persuasive effect, must be credible; it must not be so overly destructive that we would never actually resort to it. "Most of the nuclear options at our disposal now are so gross that their use is not credible," writes Loren Thompson. "To deter, we must have options that the enemy believes we will use."[29] Keith Payne elaborates, "Our existing arsenal's generally high yields and limited precision could inflict so many casualties that enemies may believe the U.S. president would be paralyzed by 'self-deterrence.'"[30]

[26] Robert McNamara, Apocalypse Soon, Foreign Policy, May/June 2005.

[27] Former Military and Civilian Leadership Oppose Nuclear Bunker Buster Funding, armscontrolcenter.org, July 26, 2005.

[28] Joanne Tompkins, How U.S. Strategic Policy Is Changing China's Nuclear Plans, 33 Arms Control Today No. 1, January/February 2003, p. 11, 13.

[29] Loren Thompson, defense expert at the Lexington Institute, quoted in Ann Scott Tyson, Nuclear Plan Changes Calculus of Deterrence, Christian Science Monitor, March 12, 2002, p. 1.

[30] Keith B. Payne, The Nuclear Jitters, National Review, June 30, 2003, p. 22, 24.

THE INTERNATIONAL LAW OF NUCLEAR WEAPONS

International law poses a challenge to the notion of a first use of a nuclear weapon in the conditions outlined in Scenario 5. In 1996, the International Court of Justice (ICJ or the "World Court," established as the judicial organ of the United Nations) issued an advisory opinion in response to the question posed by the General Assembly: Is the threat or use of nuclear weapons in any circumstance permitted by international law? (Under ICJ rules, an "advisory opinion" is not legally binding on states, but it can nonetheless provide a persuasive, authoritative statement of the global legal community.)

In a judgment rightly characterized as both groundbreaking and ambiguous, the ICJ declared (a) that international law did not contain "any comprehensive and universal prohibition of the threat or use of nuclear weapons"; (b) that the threat or use of a nuclear weapon would "generally" be unlawful; and (c) that the court could not "definitively" conclude that nuclear weapons would be outlawed "in an extreme circumstance of self-defense, in which the very survival of a State would be at stake." The split decision also reaffirmed the continuing centrality of the law of armed conflict principles identified in Chapter 3 and the undisputed applicability to nuclear weapons of the core criteria of "necessity" and "proportionality." The court's analysis was predicated on the proposition that nuclear weapons are uniquely destructive, with effects that "cannot be contained in either space or time. They have the potential to destroy all civilization and the entire ecosystem of the planet."[31]

That premise – that nuclear weapons are inherently so cataclysmic and indiscriminate that their use would automatically be excessive and disproportionate in all but the most extreme cases – is now challenged anew by the concept of low-yield weapons poised for more discrete, limited operations. Perhaps a single (or a few?) nuclear detonations of small (or not so small?) scale against East Chuan would not necessarily trigger a paroxysm of planet-jeopardizing violence.

The U.S. Department of Defense has interpreted the ICJ's pronouncement as a green light for existing military strategies, asserting bluntly that "no customary or conventional international law prohibits nations

[31] International Court of Justice, Legality of the Use by a State of Nuclear Weapons in Armed Conflict (Advisory Opinion), ICJ Reports, July 8, 1996, p. 66, 243, para. 35.

from employing nuclear weapons in armed conflict."[32] But the extreme conditions that escaped ICJ censure – a last, desperate act of self-defense by a country threatened with losing a major war, where sheer national survival was at stake – seem rather distant from Scenario 5's portrait of preemptive strikes against the command bunkers and WMD depots of a lesser enemy like East Chuan.

THE LEGISLATIVE DEBATE OVER USEABLE NUCLEAR WEAPONS

In recent years, the notion of developing new types of small nuclear weapons, optimized for applications such as those in Scenario 5, has run into a buzzsaw (perhaps a sputtering buzzsaw) of opposition in Congress. In 1993, Congress enacted the Spratt-Furse Amendment, prohibiting research and development that could lead to a precision nuclear weapon of less than 5 kt, finding that "Very low-yield nuclear weapons threaten to blur the distinction between conventional and nuclear conflict, and could thus increase the chances of nuclear weapons use by another nation."[33]

A decade later, at the behest of the Departments of Defense and Energy, Congress repealed that amendment, and the national nuclear weapons design laboratories sprinted to take advantage of the opportunity, in pursuit of earth penetrators and other purposes. A three-year feasibility study was initiated; the effort was confined to merely exploratory research and development, without any commitment to constructing and procuring any hardware, but the departments' long-term budget planning processes already contemplated the more ambitious follow-on steps. Two competing teams began to explore whether the major components of existing types of weapons – the B61–7 and the B83 – could be repackaged to hold at risk deeper targets than can be reached by existing penetrators.

Congress approved this funding for the Robust Nuclear Earth Penetrator (RNEP) program in the 2003 and 2004 fiscal year budgets, and the enterprise surged forward. But the legislature zigzagged the other way for FY 2005. Concluding that the research protocol "sends the wrong

[32] Joint Doctrine, supra note 9, at ix.

[33] U.S. Congress, House of Representatives, Committee on Armed Services, National Defense Authorization Act for Fiscal Year 1994, House Report 103–200, 1993, p. 427; Public Law 103–160, 107 Stat. 1946.

signal to the rest of the world" about the utility of nuclear weapons and about the United States' fidelity to its nonproliferation obligations, Rep. David L. Hobson (R-Ohio), then the chair of the House appropriations subcommittee that oversees the program, led a successful campaign to "zero out" all such funding.

The Bush Administration again championed the research program, proposing an $8.5 million allocation for FY 2006 to resume work on the RNEP. (About $4 million of this total would be devoted to pursuit of the revised nuclear device itself; the remainder would fund a study of how to adapt existing strategic aircraft to accommodate transport and delivery of the altered weaponry.) Hobson again resisted, leading his subcommittee to transfer all the funding from studies of *nuclear* earth penetrators into *conventional* penetrators instead. When the Democrats took control over both houses of Congress following the November 2006 midterm elections, the immediate prospects for RNEP seriously dimmed, and a chastened Department of Energy did not request any budgetary support for the program for fiscal years 2007 or 2008. Still, the concept has not disappeared, and depending on the gyrations of future politics, the RNEP funding controversy may yet reemerge as an annual legislative minuet.[34]

The amount of money at stake, when measured as a percentage of the overall defense budget, is trivial, and the proposed program at this point is still merely a study, with no commitment to future procurement or deployment. But the principle being contested is of the greatest significance, and it reflects the gravitational pull toward useable weapons, as reflected in other chapters of this book.

The RNEP and other low-yield nuclear weapons would surely be mated, at some point, with precision-guided munitions, as elaborated in Chapter 4, to ensure that the neatly calibrated bomb was reliably delivered to the exact target intended. Two distinct forms of "useability" are

[34] Jonathan Medalia, Nuclear Weapon Initiatives: Low-Yield R&D, Advanced Concepts, Earth Penetrators, Test Readiness, Congressional Research Service Report for Congress, RL32130, October 28, 2003; Amy F. Woolf, Congress and Nuclear Weapons: Review and Oversight of Policies and Programs, 14 Nonproliferation Review No. 3, November 2007, p. 499. Related to, but distinct from, the RNEP program is another proposal to develop a "reliable replacement warhead," (RRW) which would provide a modern successor (safer, more secure, and less prone to deterioration through aging) for existing weapons in the United States arsenal. RNEP raises many of the same issues as RRW, and the two proposals are sometimes linked. See Jonathan Medalia, The Reliable Replacement Warhead Program: Background and Current Developments, Congressional Research Service Report for Congress, RL32929, September 18, 2007.

therefore in play simultaneously.[35] But it is important to note that the two are proceeding independently – there is no overall Pentagon directive instructing weapons designers to move in lock step in that direction. Instead, what we observe is parallel but separate pursuit of the same underlying concept, the reinforcing effort to minimize excessive self-deterrence.

BOTTOM LINE

As with all the other weapons systems discussed in other chapters of this book, there is a case for, and a case against, the effort to procure more useable nuclear arms. The dangers of Scenario 5 are not merely speculative; there may be situations in which a small nuclear device carries an urgent, important, and unique advantage – the ability to perform a localized task and help win a war, without catastrophic excess. As Keith Payne asks, "Do we want rogue leaders to believe that they can create a sanctuary for themselves and their WMD just by digging?"[36]

There is no "silver bullet" solution to the problems of hardened and deeply buried targets or WMD depots, but if our military forces are going to be charged with accomplishing hazardous and vital missions under difficult circumstances, they should be equipped in a fashion that facilitates success. If our existing weapons are so cumbersome, so overly powerful that we are conclusively inhibited against using them, then future hostilities will be even more perilous, prolonged, and costly than they have to be. Paul Robinson, director of the Sandia National Laboratories, captures this worry, saying that "the yields of the weapons left over from the Cold War are too high for addressing the deterrence requirements of a multipolar, widely proliferated world. Without rectifying the situation, we would end up being self-deterred."[37]

On the other hand, useability carries great hazards, too – especially in the nuclear realm – because nuclear arms cannot be considered as just another tool in the military toolbox. It is almost axiomatic that if a weapon is more "useable," it will be used more often or at an earlier point – and using, or even threatening to use, nuclear weapons is a particularly provocative and short-sighted posture. Rep. Hobson put it most

[35] Elaine M. Grossman, More Accurate U.S. Nuclear Trident Faces Controversy, Global Security Newswire, August 17, 2007.

[36] Payne, supra note 30, at 22.

[37] C. Paul Robinson, Maintaining a Viable Nuclear Weapons Program in a Test Ban Environment: A Strong Technical Foundation in the Laboratories, March 28, 2000, http://www.sandia.gov/media/speeches/NSDMF2000.doc.

pointedly, "Other than a Cold War 'Russia gone bad' scenario, I don't believe our nuclear stockpile is useful against our new foes. What worries me about the nuclear penetrator is that some idiot might try to use it."[38]

The same features that make small (or any) nuclear devices attractive for the United States may exert a similar allure for other countries; if we pioneer the way, proliferant states are likely to follow. If they successfully ape the American pursuit of new generations of devices, and if our actions serve to legitimate not only possession, but hostile first use of the small, deft bombs, then the long-term consequences will surely undercut, rather than enhance, our security.

BIBLIOGRAPHY

Graham Allison, Nuclear Terrorism: The Ultimate Preventable Catastrophe, 2004

William M. Arkin, Nuclear Junkies: Those Lovable Little Bombs, Bulletin of the Atomic Scientists, July/August 1993, p. 22

William M. Arkin and Robert S. Norris, Tinynukes for Mini Minds, Bulletin of the Atomic Scientists, April 1992, p. 24

William J. Broad, Call for New Breed of Nuclear Arms Faces Hurdles, New York Times, March 11, 2002

Tim A. Bullman, Clare M. Mahan, Han K. Kang, and William F. Page, Mortality in US Army Gulf War Veterans Exposed to 1991 Khamisiyah Chemical Munitions Destruction, 95 American Journal of Public Health No. 8, August 2005, p. 1382

Amy Butler and Douglas Barrie, Dig for Victory, Aviation Week & Space Technology, September 11, 2006, p. 52

Christopher Campbell, Nuclear Weapons Fact Book, 1984

Joseph Cirincione, Jon B. Wolfsthal, and Miriam Rajkumar, Deadly Arsenals: Nuclear, Biological, and Chemical Threats (2nd ed.), 2005

Thomas B. Cochran, William M. Arkin, and Milton M. Hoenig, Nuclear Weapons Databook, Volume 1: U.S. Nuclear Forces and Capabilities, 1984

Thomas W. Dowler and Joseph S. Howard II, Countering the Threat of the Well-Armed Tyrant: A Modest Proposal for Small Nuclear Weapons, 19 Strategic Review No. 4, Fall 1991, p. 34

Sidney D. Drell and James E. Goodby, What Are Nuclear Weapons For? Recommendations for Restructuring U.S. Strategic Nuclear Forces, an Arms Control Association Report, April 2005

Sidney Drell, James Goodby, Raymond Jeanloz, and Robert Peurifoy, A Strategic Choice: New Bunker Busters Versus Nonproliferation, 33 Arms Control Today No. 2, March 2003, p. 8

[38] David Hobson, remarks to National Academy of Sciences 2004, quoted in Daryl G. Kimball, Nuclear Bunker-Buster (As We Know It) Is Dead, Arms Control Association Analysis, October 26, 2005.

Lynn Eden, Whole World on Fire: Organizations, Knowledge, and Nuclear Weapons Devastation, 2004
Charles D. Ferguson, Mini-Nuclear Weapons and the U.S. Nuclear Posture Review, Center for Nonproliferation Studies, April 8, 2002
David Fisher, Army Trains for Combat in a New Kind of Battlefield: Afghan Caves, Seattle Post-Intelligencer, December 1, 2001
Former Military and Civilian Leadership Oppose Nuclear Bunker Buster Funding, armscontrolcenter.org, July 26, 2005
James D. Fry, Contextualized Legal Reviews for the Methods and Means of Warfare: Cave Combat and International Humanitarian Law, 44 Columbia Journal of Transnational Law 453, 2006
Samuel Glasstone and Philip J. Dolan, The Effects of Nuclear Weapons, 1977
Michael R. Gordon, Nuclear Arms: For Deterrence or Fighting? New York Times, March 11, 2002, p. A1
Lisbeth Gronlund, David Wright, and Robert Nelson, Global Security Backgrounder: Earth Penetrating Weapons, May 2005
Elaine M. Grossman, More Accurate U.S. Nuclear Trident Faces Controversy, Global Security Newswire, August 17, 2007
Chuck Hansen, US Nuclear Weapons: The Secret History, 1988
International Court of Justice, Legality of the Use by a State of Nuclear Weapons in Armed Conflict (Advisory Opinion), ICJ Reports, July 8, 1996, p. 66
Herman Kahn, On Escalation: Metaphors and Scenarios, 1965
Daryl G. Kimball, Nuclear Bunker-Buster (As We Know It) Is Dead, Arms Control Association Analysis, October 26, 2005
James Kitfield, Ban the Bomb? Heck No, It's Too Useful, National Journal, September 12, 2001
Michael A. Levi, Fire in the Hole: Nuclear and Non-Nuclear Options for Counterproliferation, Carnegie Endowment for International Peace, Global Policy Program, Non-Proliferation Program, Working Paper No. 31, November 2002
Andrew M. Lichterman, Sliding Towards the Brink: More Useable Nuclear Weapons and the Dangerous Illusions of High-Tech War, Western States Legal Foundation Information Bulletin, March 2003
Michael May and Zachary Haldeman, Effectiveness of Nuclear Weapons against Buried Biological Agents, 12 Science and Global Security No. 1–2, 2004, p. 91
Robert McNamara, Apocalypse Soon, Foreign Policy, May/June 2005
Jonathan Medalia, Nuclear Weapon Initiatives: Low-Yield R&D, Advanced Concepts, Earth Penetrators, Test Readiness, Congressional Research Service Report for Congress, RL32130, October 28, 2003
Jonathan Medalia, 'Bunker Busters': Robust Nuclear Earth Penetrator Issues, FY2005–FY2007, Congressional Research Service Report for Congress, RL32347, February 21, 2006
Jonathan Medalia, The Reliable Replacement Warhead Program: Background and Current Developments, Congressional Research Service Report for Congress, RL32929, September 18, 2007
Greg Mello, New Bomb, No Mission, Bulletin of the Atomic Scientists, May/June, 1997, p. 28

Steven Lee Myers, The Targets: Jets Said to Avoid Poison Gas Sites, New York Times, December 18, 1998, p. A1
National Research Council, Effects of Nuclear Earth-Penetrator and Other Weapons, National Academies Press, 2005
Robert W. Nelson, Low-Yield Earth-Penetrating Nuclear Weapons, 10 Science and Global Security No. 1, 2002, p. 1
Robert W. Nelson, Nuclear 'Bunker Busters' Would More Likely Disperse Than Destroy Buried Stockpiles of Biological and Chemical Agents, 12 Science and Global Security No. 1–2, 2004, p. 69
Robert S. Norris and Hans M. Kristensen, The U.S. Nuclear Stockpile, Today and Tomorrow, 63 Bulletin of the Atomic Scientists No. 5, September/October 2007, p. 60
Robert S. Norris and Hans M. Kristensen, U.S. Nuclear Forces, 2008, Bulletin of the Atomic Scientists, March/April 2008, p. 50
Robert S. Norris and Hans M. Kristensen, U.S. Nuclear Warheads, 1945–2009, Bulletin of the Atomic Scientists, July/August 2009, p. 72.
Keith B. Payne, The Nuclear Jitters, National Review, June 30, 2003, p. 22
Keith B. Payne, The Nuclear Posture Review: Setting the Record Straight, 28 Washington Quarterly No. 3, Summer 2005, p. 135
Keith B. Payne, On Nuclear Deterrence and Assurance, Strategic Studies Quarterly, Spring 2009, p. 43
Walter Pincus, Senate Bill Requires Study of New Nuclear Weapons, Washington Post, June 12, 2000, p. A2
Thomas E. Ricks, Tender Bombs? U.S. Military Mulls Weapons That Disable Bunkers, Save People, Wall Street Journal, July 1, 1999, p. A1
C. Paul Robinson, Maintaining a Viable Nuclear Weapons Program in a Test Ban Environment: A Strong Technical Foundation in the Laboratories, March 28, 2000, http://www.sandia.gov/media/speeches/NSDMF2000.doc
Donald Rumsfeld, testimony to U.S. Senate Committee on Appropriations, Subcommittee on Defense, Hearings on Fiscal Year 2006 Defense Department Appropriations, April 27, 2005
Stephen I. Schwartz, Four Trillion Dollars and Counting, 51 Bulletin of the Atomic Scientists No. 6, November/December 1995, p. 32
Eric M. Sepp, Deeply Buried Facilities: Implications for Military Operations, Occasional Paper No. 14, Center for Strategy and Technology, Air War College, Maxwell Air Force Base, May 2000
Derek D. Smith, Deterring America: Rogue States and the Proliferation of Weapons of Mass Destruction, 2006
Roger Speed and Michael May, Dangerous Doctrine, 61 Bulletin of the Atomic Scientists No. 2, March/April 2005, p. 38
Nina Tannenwald, The Nuclear Taboo: The United States and the Normative Basis of Nuclear Non-Use, 53 International Organizations No. 3, Summer 1999, p. 433
Joanne Tompkins, How U.S. Strategic Policy Is Changing China's Nuclear Plans, 33 Arms Control Today No. 1, January/February 2003, p. 11
Ann Scott Tyson, Nuclear Plan Changes Calculus of Deterrence, Christian Science Monitor, March 12, 2002, p. 1

U.S. Central Intelligence Agency, Unclassified Report to Congress on the Acquisition of Technology Relating to Weapons of Mass Destruction and Advanced Chemical Munitions, 1 January through 30 June 2003

U.S. Congress, House of Representatives, Committee on Armed Services, National Defense Authorization Act for Fiscal Year 1994, House Report 103–200, 1993, p. 427; Public Law 103–160, 107 Stat. 1946

U.S. Department of Defense and Department of Energy, National Security and Nuclear Weapons in the 21st Century, September 2008

U.S. Government, Nuclear Posture Review (excerpts), submitted to Congress on December 31, 2001, excerpts released January 8, 2002, p. 7, available at www.globalsecurity.org/wmd/library/policy/dod/npr.htm

U.S. Government, National Strategy to Combat Weapons of Mass Destruction, December 2002

U.S. Joint Chiefs of Staff, Doctrine for Joint Nuclear Operations, Joint Publication 3–12, Final Coordination (2) draft, March 15, 2005

U.S. Secretary of Defense in conjunction with Secretary of Energy, Report to Congress on the Defeat of Hard and Deeply Buried Targets, July 2001

Peter Wilk, Sarah Stanlick, Martin Butcher, Michael McCally, Ira Helfand, Robert Gould, and John Pastore, Projected Casualties among U.S. Military Personnel and Civilian Populations from the Use of Nuclear Weapons Against Hard and Deeply Buried Targets, Physicians for Social Responsibility, May 2005

Amy F. Woolf, Congress and Nuclear Weapons: Review and Oversight of Policies and Programs, 14 Nonproliferation Review No. 3, November 2007, p. 499

6

Smart Antipersonnel Land Mines

Scenario 6

The United States is preparing to assist remote Kafiristan in its defense against an imminent invasion. Kafiristan is small, underdeveloped, and vulnerable; it is likely to be seriously outgunned and outmanned on the battlefield, and the most effective component of its resistance to the aggression is likely to be sheer geography – its mountainous terrain affords the attacker few easy routes for invasion, and most natural conduits are pockmarked by chokepoints and possibilities for ambush.

A hastily drawn strategic plan incorporates as many diverse military elements as the United States, Kafiristan, and a handful of other supporting states are able to cobble together. Air superiority will be crucial, but there is not much time to build up the infrastructure necessary to sustain full-scale aerial operations. Still less feasible is any immediate massive insertion of heavy ground-based equipment – it is not easy to transport large quantities of tanks and artillery into this isolated theater of battle. Even the task of assembling an appreciable pool of military manpower and supplies will consume time and logistics energies. The initial concept of operations, therefore, necessarily emphasizes defensive stalling – a holding operation, to cede ground to the aggressor only slowly, hoping to buy time to permit major reinforcements to arrive.

Land mines figure into the plan in three ways. First, Kafiristan over the years had taken the precaution of erecting solid defensive barriers along its most tempestuous borders. These battlements include expansive fields of emplaced automatic explosives, both antitank mines and antipersonnel mines, designed to complicate the task of an attacker and to slow any advance. The minefields are well maintained and conspicuously marked (to prevent Kafiristan's civilians from wandering into them); they could "channelize" the invading forces, compelling them to concentrate on fewer lines of approach.

Second, the defending armies intend to apply a quantity of remotely delivered land mines to further disrupt the invasion. Once it is clear which route the attackers are following, aircraft and long-range howitzers will blanket the area with scatterable ordnance, intended to slow, harass, and confine the aggressors, or at least to turn them away from their preferred avenues. Importantly, these particular mines will be "self-neutralizing," capable of destroying themselves or otherwise becoming inactive within a short, fixed period of time – probably two weeks in this case. That interval should be enough to blunt the attack and allow our reinforcements to build up further; a programmed counterattack could then safely traverse the mined area without so much "fratricide" danger of our forces triggering our own mines.

Finally, small units of "special operations forces" are standing by to perform especially hazardous covert missions behind enemy lines: rescuing a downed pilot, for example, or deftly attacking a sensitive, hard-to-target antiaircraft installation. Sometimes, the riskiest element in these missions is the withdrawal – after a special forces unit has completed its mission and is sneaking back to a rendezvous point for helicopter extraction, it may be trailed by enemy forces or even curious (and still-dangerous) enemy civilians. Small antipersonnel land mines known as "pursuit deterrent munitions" can impede the chasers; the special forces may toss these devices over their shoulders as they retreat, allowing them a margin of time to reach safety. The land mines selected for these purposes would have very short lifetimes, self-deactivating within only a few hours.

In almost every respect, land mines occupy the opposite end of the military spectrum from the nuclear weapons discussed in Chapter 5. Land mines are small (weighing only several ounces or a few pounds; many types will fit comfortably in the palm of a hand); cheap (commonly costing as little as $3 each); and low-technology (incorporating simple, easily replicated designs and tried-and-true mechanics). Although land mines carry an explosive power that is infinitesimal compared to the kilotonnage of nuclear weapons, land mines have been used in combat with much greater frequency, being deployed by the millions in scores of countries over the years. Further, unlike nuclear weapons, land mines continue to extract a daily human toll of deaths and injuries – year after year, land mines have claimed some 10,000–20,000 casualties.

DEFINITION AND TYPES OF LAND MINES

A land mine is defined by treaty as "a munition designed to be placed under, on or near the ground or other surface area and to be exploded by the presence, proximity or contact of a person or vehicle."[1] Notably, this definition concentrates on devices that operate autonomously or automatically whenever an enemy approaches, without requiring a human user to decide affirmatively to pull a trigger at a particular moment – devices that, instead, keep a soldier "in the loop" to detonate the device on command, are excluded from coverage.

Land mines come in two general varieties: antivehicle (AVL) and antipersonnel (APL).[2] The former are employed to immobilize or destroy tanks, trucks, or troop transports, or at least to deter them from moving swiftly through a mined area. AVL are relatively large (one common type weighs 30 pounds and contains 20 pounds of explosives, but they can also be much smaller) and therefore conspicuous; it would be relatively easy for the oncoming force to spot and then to disable them, and thereby to clear a pathway for vehicles to transit the contested area. Often, therefore, a field of AVL would be surrounded and protected by a larger quantity of APL – smaller and nearly invisible mines that will deter soldiers or others from approaching the AVL to disarm them. Antipersonnel mines may also be used independently, without AVL, to impede troop movements – or, these days, to terrorize civilian populations.

Mines vary enormously in their size, shape, explosive power, and other characteristics. The triggering mechanism, for example, might be a tripwire (detonating the mine when someone steps into a taut hidden filament), a tilt rod (a slender pole, obscured by tall grass, that a tank might run over and knock down), a pressure plate (sensitive, in the case of an APL, to the weight of a person stepping on it, or, in the case of

[1] 1997 Convention on the Prohibition of the Use, Stockpiling, Production and Transfer of Anti-Personnel Mines and on Their Destruction, signed December 3, 1997, entered into force July 3, 1998, 36 I.L.M. 1507, 1997 (U.S. not a party) [Ottawa Mine Ban Treaty], art. 2.2. Essentially the same definition is included in the Convention on Prohibitions or Restrictions on the Use of Certain Conventional Weapons Which May Be Deemed to Be Excessively Injurious or to Have Indiscriminate Effects, Oct. 10, 1980, 1342 U.N.T.S. 137, 19 I.L.M. 1523 [hereinafter Convention on Certain Conventional Weapons or CCW], Protocol II, art. 2.1.

[2] Regarding American land mine inventories and combat operations generally, see U.S. Army Headquarters, Mine/Countermine Operations, Field Manual 20–32, October 1, 2002; U.S. General Accounting Office, Military Operations: Information on U.S. Use of Land Mines in the Persian Gulf War, GAO-02–1003, September 2002.

an AVL, activated only when the greater mass of a vehicle drives over it), or another sensor of some sort (responding to the noise, heat, seismic pressure, or magnetic signature of a tank).

Some APL remain on the ground and exert their explosive force directly upward when stepped upon; depending on the size of the charge, such a mine could blow off a toe, foot, or leg, or could kill the victim outright. Even more insidious are "bounding" mines that pop a few feet up into the air before detonating in order to spray lethal shrapnel over a larger area.

Mines may be laboriously buried or emplaced by hand, one by one, to best conceal or camouflage their positions, compounding the task for clearance operations. Alternatively, an effective minefield may be established remotely, via aircraft dropping quantities of APL and/or AVL, or via artillery projecting the mines 10 miles or more forward. In that mode, the user has much less control (or even knowledge) about exactly where the mines will fall, and more of the individual mines may be inactive or useless because they happen to land in inapt locations or alignments. But remote delivery allows the user to create a deadly barrier relatively quickly and safely.

HISTORICAL PATTERNS OF MINE USE

For decades, mines have occupied a small but noticeable niche in the world of military affairs. Modern iterations, especially AVL, were introduced during the static trench warfare of World War I to combat the new developments in tank warfare. In the greater mobility of World War II, mines played a much more prominent role – 300 million AVL were employed during the conflict, including in locales such as North Africa where the battle lines surged back and forth erratically. Mines were considered an especially rapacious tool, feared and reviled by soldiers on all sides – but they carried an undeniable military effect. As explained by American Lt. George Wilson, who encountered the buzzsaw of APL in the German Siegfried Line in Belgium in 1944,

> By now I had gone through aerial bombing, artillery and mortar shelling, open combat, direct rifle and machine gun firing, night patrolling and ambush. Against all of this we had some kind of chance; against mines we had none. The only defense was not to move at all.[3]

[3] Stephen Ambrose, Citizen Soldiers, 1997, p. 143.

According to chilling Department of Defense statistics, some 100,000 Americans were killed or injured by land mines during the twentieth century.[4]

For strategists, land mines were an efficacious "force multiplier," magnifying the power of other ordnance, especially in aid of a defender confronting an onslaught by an enemy possessing superior numbers, mobility, or technologies. Mines could help restrict or shape the battlefield, creating "keep out" zones and confining the enemy to a smaller array of attack routes or sanctuaries. Mine barriers could channelize a *blitzkrieg* attack or turn it away from its preferred vector, enabling the defending force to concentrate firepower more effectively. Mines could protect an army's flanks, allowing it to mass its firepower against the direct frontal assault.

In other scenarios, a perimeter of APL and AVL could create a protective barrier that attackers would traverse only slowly and at great peril. At the macro level, the safety band could seek to insulate an entire country from attack. For example, the 1 million or more land mines strewn along the demilitarized zone between North and South Korea, and the 2 or 3 million more held in reserve for placement during a crisis or war, all serve as a "task complicator" for any aggressor.[5] At a smaller scale, mines could provide a buffer zone around an otherwise vulnerable military base or installation. For example, for many years the United States and Cuba each surrounded the American naval station at Guantanamo Bay with mines; for diametrically opposite reasons, each side wanted the base to be isolated from contact with the mainland. At the smallest level, an encampment of soldiers temporarily isolated in hostile territory might seek the shelter of an APL picket fence as a safeguard against surreptitious incursions.

In all these scenarios, mines by themselves were not expected to win a battle or turn the tide of a war. At most, they could compound the enemy's problem, reducing the speed of an attack, compromising the preferred avenues for the application of power, and preventing secrecy or surprise. Importantly, for most of this era, land mines were not viewed as more ethically problematic or inhumane than any other ordnance; they

[4] Harry N. Hambric and William C. Schneck, The Antipersonnel Mine Threat: A Historical Perspective, Symposium on Technology and the Mine Problem, Naval Postgraduate School, Monterey, CA, November 18–22, 1996, cited in Human Rights Watch Arms Project, Exposing the Source: U.S. Companies and the Production of Antipersonnel Mines, vol. 9, No. 2, April 1997, p. 6.

[5] But see Caleb Rossiter, Winning in Korea Without Landmines: Alternatives to Speed Victory and Reduce Allied Casualites, 1 Vietnam Veterans of America Foundation Monograph Series No. 3, Summer 2000.

were weapons of war, tactical tools of mayhem, vehicles – as are any other weapons – for inflicting fear, pain, injury, and death upon an enemy.

THE PARADIGM SHIFTS

In the 1990s, the world's general attitude toward land mines, especially antipersonnel land mines, began to shift radically. The global community awoke to a humanitarian crisis caused by the most familiar forms of mines, and a consensus emerged that APL were suddenly a profound problem that we had to do something about.

The crisis sprouts from the fact that land mines, as a breed, are remarkably hardy instruments. Once deployed, they may typically remain active in the field for years or even decades. The mechanics of an APL or AVL are relatively simple, the components are constructed of robust materials, and there is little to deteriorate or degrade. A mine emplaced today can remain silently on duty for a very long time, vigilantly guarding its turf until some unlucky presence triggers the firing mechanism – an event that may be many years delayed. In contrast, mine clearance operations, to remove the lethal charges from the field, are very difficult, dangerous, and expensive. Depending on the terrain, the types of mines employed, and other factors, the price tag for removal operations can run between $300 and $1000 per mine. New technologies are being adapted to the task, but it remains slow and laborious, and in many widespread areas, thickets of aged but still active APL linger in place indefinitely.

That persistence means that all too often, APL are triggered not by enemy combatants executing a timely attack but by civilians who happen along much later, long after the soldiers have marched away or even after the war has ended. In fact, these days, the overwhelming majority of land mine victims (80 percent of the estimated 1 million APL casualties suffered over the past 20 years) are civilians – farmers tilling their fields, peasants walking along a roadway to a well or market, or children playing innocently in a pasture. Active mines from World War I still occasionally crop up in fields along the Maginot Line in Europe; mines from World War II routinely surface in North Africa; and, in much larger quantities, APL sewn during contemporary conflicts in Afghanistan, Cambodia, Angola, and many other countries exert their deadly explosive force against unsuspecting civilians. As recently as 10 or 15 years ago, an estimated 2.5 million new APL were being laid annually, and only a paltry few were being removed. Today, upwards of 60–100 million mines, most long forgotten by the armies that initially deployed them, may remain in the field in some 60–80 unfortunate countries, steadfastly performing their stealthy round-the-clock duty, with unwitting civilians now the primary prey.

That unintended and indiscriminate force – driving some to label land mines as "weapons of mass destruction in slow motion" – inflicts horrible costs on individuals, communities, and whole nations. For individuals, the consequences range from sudden injuries to traumatic amputations to deaths. Accurate statistics are impossible to collect about the full effect of what the U.S. State Department has labeled insidious "hidden killers." But estimates suggest that during the 1980s, leftover APL inflicted as many as 25,000 casualties per year (probably one-third of them children) – the continuing, accidental but foreseeable legacy of this deadly detritus. Even today, after a variety of "mine action" programs (noted below) has helped mitigate the toll, some 5000–6000 people per year – almost one an hour, around the clock, every day of the year – will fall victim to persistent, leftover mines. In the most pervasively afflicted countries, the social consequences are immense; in Cambodia, for example, postconflict mine explosions have resulted in 35,000 amputees, very few of whom can afford adequate prostheses.

The ramifications for a community run even further. APL infestation – or even the misplaced fear of unmarked minefields – can inhibit normal access to village centers, water sources, schools, and crop lands. The risks of accidental detonations can impede plowing, woodcutting, and irrigation, further undercutting the local economy. Even travel to a hospital, such as to seek necessary treatment for land mine injuries, can be treacherous. The social, psychic, and economic costs of caring for mine victims – many of them grotesquely disabled – are immense; worldwide, there may be 350,000 to 400,000 people living with long-term mine-caused impairments.[6]

At the national level, uncleared land mines can deter the return of refugees who were displaced by a conflict and scare away potential capital investment, postponing any recovery. In Afghanistan, for example, the massive Aynak copper deposit, estimated to contain $30 billion in recoverable ore, lies beneath a landscape peppered with still-active mines, forestalling exploitation efforts.[7] Disruptions in transportation services can reverberate across the community; in Angola, for example, 70 percent of the country's roads have been blocked by persistent antivehicle mines, a sure formula for economic chaos.

[6] International Campaign to Ban Landmines, Landmine Monitor Report 2006, p. 5.
[7] Rex Dalton, Geology: Mine Games, 449 Nature p. 968, October 22, 2007.

DEBATING THE MILITARY UTILITY OF LAND MINES

Is this carnage worthwhile? Is there any valid military rationale for continuing to use APL and AVL? Some experts maintain that, at least in selected applications, land mines retain a unique defensive value. The most commonly cited illustration concerns the defense of South Korea. In that theater, it is frequently asserted, the outnumbered defenders would prudently seek any viable means for slowing a possible sudden North Korean advance; the penumbra of mines (already emplaced, or to be projected into the aggressors' path, once their intentions are manifest) would materially assist that effort. No one imagines that a South Korean mine barrier would be impenetrable; a variety of breaching techniques would enable an attacker to advance through even the densest emplacements sooner or later. But later is better than sooner, the mine advocates maintain, and even a short delay (a 30-minute penalty is commonly cited as the worst speed bump that a minefield could impose on the peninsula) would be valuable in allowing South Korean and American military units to mobilize and respond in a more organized fashion.

For that reason, the senior American military leadership has persistently maintained that land mines must remain an available option; on July 10, 1997, an unusual "64-star" letter (signed by 16 active duty four-star generals and admirals) to Congress asserted that precipitously abolishing mines would "endanger US military forces and significantly restrict the ability to conduct combat operations successfully."[8] As in the Kafiristan scenario at the outset of this chapter, judicious application of antipersonnel and antivehicle mines may stall an aggressor, multiply the power of our own forces, and protect the extraction of isolated units. Military history provides corroboration; by various accounts, for example, AVL accounted for 70 percent of American armor losses in Vietnam and 60 percent in Gulf War I. In World War II and in Korea, mines accounted for 3 to 10 percent of U.S. combat personnel casualties, but in Vietnam and Gulf War I, the fraction of American losses attributed to mines rose to 33 to 35 percent.[9] And of greatest current interest, the modern variant

[8] Joint Chiefs of Staff, letter to Strom Thurmond, Chair, Senate Armed Services Committee, July 10, 1977, available at http://www.security-policy.org/papers/1997/97-D97at.html.

[9] C.E.E. Sloan, Mine Warfare on Land, 1986, p. 2, cited in John F. Troxell, Landmines: Why the Korea Exception Should Be the Rule, 30 Parameters No. 1, Spring 2000, p. 82; Military Consequences of Landmine Restrictions, Dupuy Institute Research Study, 1 Vietnam Veterans of America Monograph Series No. 2, Spring 2000, p. 56.

of mines, "improvised explosive devices," continue to bedevil our troops in Iraq and Afghanistan.[10]

Still, the proposition remains contested, and on May 19, 2001, six retired generals and two admirals – several of whom had previously commanded elements of the American forces in the Korean theater – wrote a competing letter to President Bush, in which they concluded that APL "are not in any way critical or decisive in maintaining the peninsula's security. In fact, freshly scattered mixed systems would slow a US and ROK counter-invasion by inhibiting the operational tempo of friendly armor and dismounted infantry units.... It is our understanding that the standing response plan to a North Korean attack does not call for these weapons to be used to counter an initial attack."[11]

A historical study of 26 military conflicts, conducted for the International Committee of the Red Cross, doubts the utility of APL, finding that "even when used on a massive scale, they have usually had little or no effect on the outcome of hostilities. No case was found in which the use of anti-personnel mines played a major role in determining the outcome of a conflict. At best, these weapons had a marginal tactical value under certain specific but demanding conditions."[12]

At the same time, another form of debate has emerged regarding APL: whether our military is (or should be) self-deterred against deploying them, for fear of fratricide. In modern combat, U.S. forces have stressed high maneuverability; our troops and equipment have been configured to be able to transit the battlefield with unparalleled speed, and American war planners have learned to exploit that unmatched mobility to surprise, outflank, and overwhelm the opposition. Arguably, anything that impedes that rapid transportation – such as static minefields, including APL and AVL sewn by our own forces – undercuts that often decisive advantage.

Reportedly, U.S. commanders were reluctant to deploy longlasting mines widely in Iraq during the 1991 Desert Storm fighting for fear

[10] Robert Bryce, Man Versus Mine, Atlantic Monthly, January/February 2006, p. 44. As noted, devices triggered by an operator, instead of automatically, do not meet the legal definition of a "mine."

[11] Rear Adm (Ret.) Eugene Carroll, Lt Gen (Ret.) Henry Emerson, Lt Gen (Ret.) James Hollingsworth, Lt Gen (Ret.) Harold Moore, Lt Gen (Ret.) Dave Palmer, Vice Adm (Ret.) Jack Shanahan, Lt Gen (Ret.) DeWitt Smith, Lt Gen (Ret.) Walter Ulmer, Letter to President George W. Bush, May 19, 2001, quoted in International Committee to Ban Land Mines, Land Mine Monitor Report, 2001.

[12] International Committee of the Red Cross, Anti-Personnel Landmines: Friend or Foe? 1996, p. 7.

that they would become obstacles to our own forces, which might want to criss-cross the terrain in unpredictable ways. Likewise, a technology that pollutes the battlespace in Kafiristan with passive APL and AVL impediments would more likely work to the disadvantage of American freewheeling counterattacks. Something like an infantry "Hippocratic Oath" operates: our forces are loathe to deploy weapons that will quickly make things worse for their own operations.

Researchers are also pursuing transformational alternatives to traditional land mines, especially systems that would incorporate television cameras or other advanced sensors to permit enhanced "situational awareness" for commanders. These devices would enable a controlling authority to decide intelligently, on a case-by-case basis, whether to trigger a particular mine because it was clear that the person who was then attempting to traverse the minefield was an armed combatant, not a hapless, wandering farmer or woodcutter. Such systems could better satisfy the law of armed conflict principle of "discrimination" by intelligently treating civilians differently from belligerents. They could thus mitigate both the humanitarian problems and the fratricide issues associated with APL, but progress to date on these alternatives has been disappointing.

Recent U.S. policy and battlefield experience are equivocal regarding APL. In Gulf War I, the United States dispatched no fewer than 2.2 million land mines of varying types to Kuwait and Saudi Arabia and contemplated employing them in a wide variety of tactical applications. During the fighting, some 117,634 mines – all of them equipped with self-destructing or self-neutralizing features, as discussed below – were scattered via artillery and other means for a variety of missions, such as protecting a vulnerable U.S. Marine Corps defensive position and attacking Iraqi Scud missile transporters. Reportedly, concerns over fratricide and the associated loss of battlefield mobility impeded commanders' more widespread use of mines.

On the other side of the ledger, Iraq laid an estimated 9 million mines in Kuwait and may have developed a false confidence in the integrity of its defensive lines. The U.S. Army concluded, "Instead of needing 18 hours to break through Iraqi positions as originally calculated, the 1st Infantry Division successfully breached them in 2." An estimated 6 percent of U.S. battle casualties were attributed to Iraqi mines.[13]

In subsequent military campaigns in Kosovo (1999) and in Afghanistan (2001), the United States did not use any antipersonnel or antivehicle land

[13] Red Cross, supra note 12, at 40–41; U.S. General Accounting Office, supra note 2.

mines. In Gulf War II (2003), the United States transported 90,000 APL to Iraq, but did not deploy any into operation.

THE INTERNATIONAL LAW OF LAND MINES

The world has responded to the challenges of land mines by negotiating not one, but two, competing treaty arrangements. The larger and more ambitious regime, the 1997 Ottawa Mine Ban Treaty, incorporates a complete prohibition: its parties agree never under any circumstances to develop, produce, acquire, stockpile, retain, or use any APL; not to assist or encourage others to do so; and to destroy promptly all the mines they possess. This instrument was generated by a sudden burst of grassroots enthusiasm from committed individuals (notably, the United Kingdom's Princess Diana) and nongovernmental organizations worldwide (the International Campaign to Ban Landmines embraced some 300 organizations; it was awarded the Nobel Peace Prize in 1997 for its efforts to midwife the treaty).

The Ottawa Treaty captured the public imagination almost overnight and ignited the leadership energies of selected foreign ministries with stunning speed. The treaty has attracted the adherence of a majority of the world's countries, including almost all of the NATO allies except the United States; it currently has 156 parties.

The competing regime actually predates the Ottawa accord but is of more limited scope. The Convention on Certain Conventional Weapons (CCW) encompasses a series of independent protocols on miscellaneous discrete nasty problems, such as incendiary weapons and blinding lasers; a country may opt to join any of these protocols separately, *a la carte*. Protocol II, which originally entered into force in 1983 and was modified in important ways in 1998, covers APL. This treaty limits – but does not completely ban – the use of mines. Under this structure, parties may not employ mines that generate plastic or glass fragments that are not detectable in the human body via x-rays; in addition, minefields laid by hand (i.e., not delivered remotely by aircraft or artillery) must be marked and maintained (to ward off civilian traffic) or must consist of mines that automatically self-neutralize after a fixed period of time (as described further in the following section).

Some 91 states, including the United States and the other large mine-producing and mine-using countries such as Russia, China, India, and Pakistan, have joined this treaty and accepted these obligations. (Many countries are party to both CCW Protocol II and the Ottawa Treaty;

they would effectively be held to the tougher Ottawa standards.) The United States has recently proposed extending some of the Protocol II obligations – specifically, the prohibitions on persistent mines and on nondetectable mines – to AVL as well as APL.

This one-two punch of treaties has dramatically altered the world's attitude toward land mines. No longer "just another weapon" in the warfighter's quiver, APL have suddenly been delegitimized. These devices are no longer manufactured in anything near the previous quantity; international sales of mines have likewise essentially dried up; scores of millions of stockpiled mines have been destroyed; and only a handful of countries (and a few rebel bands) admit to having emplaced new APL in recent years. Instead, the world's energies have turned toward "mine action," a series of peaceful measures such as educating local populations for awareness about the dangers of persistent mines in their neighborhoods, training and equipping legions of de-miners, developing improved mine clearance techniques, destroying excess mines from national stockpiles, and providing assistance to APL survivors.

SMART AND DUMB MINES

Nonetheless, the United States – while becoming by far the largest financial contributor to global mine action strategies – has not joined the cavalcade of Ottawa Treaty parties. Instead, the United States policy, propounded by President Bush on February 27, 2004, seeks to differentiate between two types of APL: "smart" and "dumb" mines.[14]

By this vocabulary, a smart antipersonnel mine is one that becomes inert or inactive within a relatively short, predetermined period of time. Three different types of mechanisms can accomplish this. A "self-destructing" mine would literally blow itself up (usually with less than the mine's full explosive charge) when an internal timer so instructed. Second, a "self-neutralizing" mine contains an internal structure that switches the device off after the passage of time – there is no explosion, but the device would no longer detonate when stepped on. Finally, a "self-deactivating" mine incorporates into the mine's internal circuitry a component such as a battery that will wear out or lose power after an

[14] Official U.S. government policy does not adopt the vocabulary of "smart" and "dumb" mines, but refers to the ordnance as "non-persistent" or "persistent," and acknowledges that there is, in fact, no such thing as a "smart" mine. Nonetheless, the vocabulary of smart/dumb has stuck in popular usage.

interval, precluding the mine from operating. With each of these devices, the duration of the timer or the deteriorating components may be fixed during the weapon's manufacturing process, or in other instances, the user can select the mine's duration (commonly four hours, 48 hours, or 15 days) just before deploying it.

The advantage of the third type, a self-deactivating system, is reliability: both self-destructing and self-neutralizing mines rely upon an active mechanism inside the weapon's casing that must operate properly to ensure safety. Sometimes, of course, those precautionary mechanisms will fail, and the result will be a mine that remains deadly past its intended expiration date – one that reverts, in effect, into a standard long-lived dumb mine. Statistics have suggested a failure rate of 3–5 percent in these components, which, when mines are deployed by the thousands, translates into an unacceptable level of lingering hazard. (A contractor working to clean up the post–Desert Storm battlefield in Kuwait uncovered 1700 mines that had failed to self-destruct on schedule.[15]) A self-neutralizing mine, on the other hand, is "fail-safe," in the sense that we can be certain that the battery will run down – there may be some variation in exactly how long the battery's life can be sustained, but inevitably the mine will become inert with well over 99 percent reliability. Some modern mine types incorporate more than one of these safety features, assertedly generating a failure rate that is "statistically too low to measure."

The Bush Administration, accordingly, argued that the availability of reliable self-deactivating technology frees smart APL from the charge of contributing to a humanitarian crisis. The problem, military spokespersons assert, is not with APL *per se*; instead, the problem is with persistent dumb mines, which do not render themselves safe after a decent interval. In contrast, smart mines can play a vital role in certain carefully defined military operations, but then effectively disappear. They allow the U.S. military to perform essential operations – such as covering the withdrawal of special forces from enemy territory, as in the Kafiristan example – while not incurring the perpetual adverse consequences associated with older, less sophisticated dumb APL.

The rest of the world, however, generally refuses to buy this distinction. To champions of the Ottawa Treaty, "a mine is a mine is a mine," and the distinctions between smart and dumb variants are inconsequential. Only by prohibiting *all* APL, they argue, will the world gain any real traction on the humanitarian problem. Because smart mines are more

[15] Red Cross, supra note 12, at 57.

expensive (the devices necessary to ensure reliable self-neutralization or self-deactivation would greatly inflate the cost of what are otherwise dirt-cheap weapons), they would, in all likelihood, be procured only by wealthy states, such as the United States. But poorer countries would exploit the American retention of smart mines as political cover for their own continuing possession and use of old-fashioned dumb mines. Only by stigmatizing – and ridding the world of – *all* mines can the problem be solved, they maintain.

Still, the United States has argued for a critical differentiation between persistent dumb mines, which are so hardy that they outlive their military utility, and smart mines, which can be more precisely confined. The self-deactivation feature, the American position maintains, makes mines more "useable" in that they offer the military advantages traditionally associated with APL, without the adverse humanitarian consequences we have now come to recognize and abhor. No one – a local civilian or a U.S. service member who came along after the enemy left – has ever been harmed by an American mine when the self-destructing and self-deactivating features failed to operate as intended.

CURRENT INVENTORIES

Land mines are as diverse as they are hardy; 50 countries have produced, stockpiled, and operationally deployed at least 675 different types. The United States, the world's third-leading mine-possessing country (after Russia and China), holds an inventory of some 18 million land mines, including about 10.4 million APL. About 15 million of the total incorporate modern self-destruct or self-neutralizing features, and under current policy, by 2010 all the persistent mines will have been destroyed – the United States will thereafter employ only smart APL and AVL. The United States has not manufactured any new antipersonnel mines since 1997, and has not exported any to other countries since 1992.

Most U.S. mines these days are "scatterable," to be delivered or dispensed quickly and at standoff range by aircraft or artillery, albeit with some degradation in accuracy and accountability. Prominent among the U.S. antipersonnel munitions are the Gator (air delivered, via cluster munitions; most of the APL the United States employed in Gulf War I were of this type); Volcano (adapting the Gator mine, and emplacing it by helicopter or truck); ADAM/RAAM (artillery delivered, first fielded in 1983); and M86 Pursuit Deterrent Munition (a favorite of special forces, using a one-pound explosive device that ejects seven 20-foot trip wires when armed).

Some noteworthy systems can be configured to operate either as land mines (i.e., firing automatically when a tripwire or other mechanism is activated) or in "command detonation" mode (i.e., an operator, informed by data from on-site sensors, makes a deliberate decision to fire or not to fire – so the weapon escapes the legal definition of "land mine" contained in the two relevant treaties). The Claymore is the most well-known such apparatus; it fires 700 steel balls across a 60-degree arc to a range of 50 meters. Matrix is a soldier-in-the-loop system (i.e., it is not legally a "land mine") that can fire either traditional lethal or novel nonlethal pellets; it is remotely and wirelessly controlled via laptop computer. A follow-on system, denominated Spider, is principally designed for command detonation but may also be capable, through a "battlefield override" feature, of firing automatically, as a classic APL. Overall, the Department of Defense has requested $688 million for research and $1.08 billion for procurement of new nonpersistent antipersonnel and antivehicle land mines by 2011.[16]

BOTTOM LINE

Smart antipersonnel land mines provide a distinct dimension in the study of "useability." These weapons are less powerful and less destructive than their forebears, but not because they utilize any smaller, less deadly explosive charge (as is the case with the low-yield nuclear weapons surveyed in Chapter 5) and not because they are delivered with any greater accuracy (as with the precision-guided weapons of Chapter 4). Instead, smart APL incorporate a unique *temporal* limitation: these revolutionary nonpersistent mines are deadly for a much shorter period of time than dumb mines.

By remaining active for only those fixed, selected durations, the smart mines are, arguably, more useable than the standard genres of APL. Smart mines – at least if the self-deactivating or other self-negating function is reliable – do not jeopardize noncombatants to nearly the same extent. They should not inhibit our own forces from rapidly and safely transiting the previously mine-infested areas. They should not terrorize civilian communities or deter resettlement after the conflict. We should not, therefore, be as "self-deterred" against applying smart APL in situations where they might offer a military advantage.

[16] Human Rights Watch, Back in Business? U.S. Landmine Production and Exports, briefing paper, August 2005, p. 7.

Land mines, as a category, are on the way out – fated to join dum-dum bullets, chemical weapons, and biological weapons on the scrap heap of international combat. Although 160 million APL remain available in the inventories of the United States, Russia, China, India, Pakistan, South Korea, and other non-Ottawa countries, the world's revulsion against this particular form of weaponry will, sooner or later, reduce them to only occasional use, and the scourge of postconflict APL injuries will diminish over time. Advancing technology may, however, provide facile work-arounds that enable military forces to continue their operations essentially unchanged while still complying with the terms of the treaties and with the world community's evolving sense of legitimacy in combat. One such adaptation – grafting sensors onto the munitions, and requiring an affirmative command from a knowledgeable observer in order to fire the weapon – would suffice to escape the definition of "land mine" in the relevant conventions. Another modification – to graft onto the explosive some of the self-destructing, self-neutralizing, or self-deactivating mechanisms, would pass muster under the CCW Protocol II, but not under the Ottawa Treaty.

In either case, however, the commonality is an increase in "useability," in two dimensions. First, as these novel weapons enable the operators to dodge the humanitarian criticisms that have punctured the prior tolerance for persistent "dumb" antipersonnel land mines, it is predictable that the ordnance would be used more often. Scenarios such as the Kafiristan example – marshaling smart APL to impede an aggressor's onslaught or to deter pursuit of a small, isolated squad of our service members – become more tolerable if we are confident that the hazards will not linger indefinitely to the detriment of generations of local civilians. Indeed, that is the point of the innovations: to allow new breeds of nonpersistent smart APL to continue to be used on important military missions, even when the older, dumb types would be unacceptable.

Second, the military's self-deterrence against introducing land mines into a complex, shifting battlefield will be mitigated if we know that the smart mines we strew today (to impede an enemy's advance) will deactivate quickly and reliably enough that they will not pose a dangerous obstacle for our future counterattack. As in Kafiristan, American mobility is a significant advantage in modern combat; we would be foolish to jeopardize that signal strength through use of dumb permanent APL.

In short, the new smart mine technology – as with emerging generations of PGMs and low-yield nuclear weapons – offers the promise of a more useable capacity. By being less deadly – in the sense of remaining deadly for a much shorter period of time – smart APL seek to erode the humanitarian and tactical reservations that deter land mine use. Accordingly, the United States has maintained that smart mines can continue to be employed safely, legitimately, and strategically in many more situations.

BIBLIOGRAPHY

Stephen Ambrose, Citizen Soldiers, 1997

Lincoln P. Bloomfield, Jr., New Developments in U.S. Approach to Landmines, Department of State briefing, February 27, 2004

Robert Bryce, Man Versus Mine, Atlantic Monthly, January/February 2006, p. 44

Rear Adm (Ret.) Eugene Carroll, Lt Gen (Ret.) Henry Emerson, Lt Gen (Ret.) James Hollingsworth, Lt Gen (Ret.) Harold Moore, Lt Gen (Ret.) Dave Palmer, Vice Adm (Ret.) Jack Shanahan, Lt Gen (Ret.) DeWitt Smith, Lt Gen (Ret.) Walter Ulmer, Letter to President George W. Bush, May 19, 2001, quoted in International Committee to Ban Land Mines, Land Mine Monitor Report, 2001

Center for Security Policy, Hold That Line: JCS Objections Appear Crucial to Retaining American Right to Use Landmines to Save U.S. Troops' Lives, Decision Brief No. 97-D 81, June 18, 1997

Bill Clinton, New U.S. Land Mine Policy, 11 Defense Issues No. 40, May 16, 1996

Mike Croll, The History of Landmines, 1998

Rex Dalton, Geology: Mine Games, 449 Nature p. 968, October 22, 2007

Andrew C.S. Efaw, The United States Refusal to Ban Landmines: The Intersection Between Tactics, Strategy, Policy, and International Law, 159 Military Law Review p. 87, 1999

Robert G. Gard, Alternatives to Antipersonnel Landmines, 1 Vietnam Veterans of America Monograph Series No. 1, Spring 1999

Human Rights Watch Arms Project, Exposing the Source: U.S. Companies and the Production of Antipersonnel Mines, Vol. 9, No. 2, April 1997

Human Rights Watch, Position Paper on 'Smart' (Self-Destructing) Landmines, 2004

Human Rights Watch, Back in Business? U.S. Landmine Production and Exports, briefing paper, August 2005

International Campaign to Ban Landmines, Landmine Monitor Report 2006, 2007, and 2008

International Committee of the Red Cross, Anti-Personnel Landmines: Friend or Foe? 1996

Military Consequences of Landmine Restrictions, Dupuy Institute Research Study, 1 Vietnam Veterans of America Monograph Series No. 2, Spring 2000

Caleb Rossiter, Winning in Korea Without Landmines: Alternatives to Speed Victory and Reduce Allied Casualites, 1 Vietnam Veterans of America Foundation Monograph Series No. 3, Summer 2000

William C. Schneck, The Origins of Military Mines: Parts I and II, Engineering Bulletin, July and November 1998

C.E.E. Sloan, Mine Warfare on Land, 1986, p. 2, cited in John F. Troxell, Landmines: Why the Korea Exception Should Be the Rule, 30 Parameters No. 1, Spring 2000, p. 82

Baker Spring and John Hillen, Why a Global Ban on Land Mines Won't Work, Heritage Foundation Executive Memorandum 466, January 17, 1997

U.S. Army Headquarters, Mine/Countermine Operations, Field Manual 20–32, October 1, 2002

U.S. Defense Science Board Task Force on Munitions System Reliability, September 2005

U.S. Department of Defense, Report to the Secretary of Defense on the Status of DoD's Implementation of the U.S. Policy on Anti-Personnel Landmines, May 1997

U.S. Department of Defense, Inspector General Report D-2008–127, Spider XM-7 Network Command Munition, August 29, 2008

U.S. Department of State, Landmine Policy White Paper, Fact Sheet, February 27, 2004

U.S. Department of State, New United States Policy on Landmines: Reducing Humanitarian Risk and Saving Lives of United States Soldiers, Fact Sheet, February 27, 2004

U.S. General Accounting Office, Military Operations: Information on U.S. Use of Land Mines in the Persian Gulf War, GAO-02–1003, September 2002

U.S. Joint Chiefs of Staff, letter to Strom Thurmond, Chair, Senate Armed Services Committee, July 10, 1977

TREATIES

1997 Convention on the Prohibition of the Use, Stockpiling, Production and Transfer of Anti-Personnel Mines and on Their Destruction, signed December 3, 1997, entered into force July 3, 1998, 36 I.L.M. 1507, 1997 (U.S. not a party) [Ottawa Mine Ban Treaty]

Convention on Prohibitions or Restrictions on the Use of Certain Conventional Weapons Which May Be Deemed to Be Excessively Injurious or to Have Indiscriminate Effects, Oct. 10, 1980, 1342 U.N.T.S. 137, 19 I.L.M. 1523 [CCW]

7

Antisatellite Weapons

Scenario 7

The upcoming war between the United States and Iralia is going to be high-tech. Iralia, a medium-size and more than medium-power country, is even attempting for the first time to exploit outer space for specialized military operations. Although it cannot hope to match the American war fighters in overall satellite technology, Iralia calculates that in three novel applications, turning to the heavens might prove advantageous.

First, although Iralia has no remote sensing satellites of its own, it fully recognizes the value of modern overhead reconnaissance, and it now intends to acquire militarily useful photographic and related data from the satellites of other cooperating countries and foreign private consortia. Some of the contemplated satellite surveillance products are commercially available on the global market; others may be obtainable as concessions from more advanced spacefaring countries that will be officially neutral in the war, but are sympathetic to the Iralian cause.

Iralia figures that these augmented intelligence capabilities may be useful in several ways. As a most obvious example, enhanced meteorology information from space would bolster the ability of the national leadership to know, and to predict, local and regional weather patterns with greater precision and specificity. The Americans, of course, already collect and exploit this kind of information; Iralia hopes to achieve something of a balance in similarly adapting its military operations to the prevailing conditions – and, not incidentally, in being able to forecast better when and where the Americans will decide to undertake their military strikes, too.

At a higher level of sophistication, Iralia also hopes to obtain satellite imagery – ideally, in real time – that will reveal the positions and movements of local American forces. Depending on the resolution of the photographs, Iralia might be able to track U.S. ships, aircraft, vehicles, and troop concentrations as they rove through the theater of battle. Again, the United States already obtains this overhead surveillance information about Iralia, but perhaps the tables can be at least partially turned.

As a second aspect of the contemplated outer space operations, Iralia intends to disrupt the operation of the U.S. global positioning system (GPS). As noted in Chapter 4, some of the most shocking and awesome American air-delivered precision-guided munitions obtain their excruciating accuracy through GPS orientation, enabling them to home in on discrete targets and therefore to undertake delicate and demanding missions even in the midst of other sites that are off-limits to the targeteers. If Iralia can find a way to jam or distort the relatively low-powered GPS signals, then the JDAMs, JSOWs, JASSMs and other ordnance would be compromised; American war planners might be forced to revert to other, presumably less effective, devices.

Iralia hopes that ground-based jamming mechanisms would suffice to interrupt the flow of GPS signals to any particular locality. If appropriate, Iralia would also be prepared to invest money in alternative technologies – an airborne or even rocket-powered electromagnetic disruption system that could be dispatched to a strategic position high above a particular region just before the GPS bombs started to fall. Thinking even further outside their traditional boxes, the Iralian leaders also wonder whether similar jamming, spoofing, or disrupting technologies could be adapted to harass other types of U.S. satellites, interfering with normal communications, remote sensing, and battle management uplinks and downlinks.

Finally, and most ambitiously, Iralia contemplates acquiring at least a primitive ability to target U.S. outer space assets directly. The most plausible antisatellite system in the near term would be a modified intercontinental ballistic missile (ICBM) configured with some sort of radar guidance apparatus and an explosive (possibly a nuclear) warhead. Such a kluge would probably not be capable of reaching GPS or other satellites operating in the highest orbits, but it might be effective against other targets (including U.S. photoreconnaissance birds) that fly much closer to earth.

It is far from clear that Iralia, in the midst of ongoing hostilities, would be able to assemble, maintain, and operate the delicate antisatellite infrastructure – ICBM launching facilities, radar guidance suites, and command and control installations would be vulnerable to preemptive U.S. attacks. But if Iralia somehow managed to strike the first blow, sucker-punching the American satellites as the initial stroke of the war, the tactic just might succeed in suddenly blinding an important U.S. military capability.

Satellites have become ubiquitous in both civilian and military life; the diversity and importance of modern society's reliance upon outer space have grown dramatically in recent years and show no signs of abating. One factor contributing to this upward trend has been the stability of the security environment – so far, even the earth's military superpowers have been reluctant to extend their hegemony into space. Their antisatellite (ASAT) weapons technologies have remained relatively primitive and underdeveloped, and space has traditionally been preserved as a relatively safe place for expensive and vulnerable operational assets of all countries.

In contrast to the other chapters of this book, therefore, the story of the weaponization of outer space is mostly the saga of a dog that has not quite yet barked – we are exploring here a form of inchoate military competition that still looms, literally, over the horizon. But a number of different types of ASAT systems have been explored in the past, and the notion of "Star Wars" competition is again erupting as a modern possibility.[1]

Notably, the existing or contemplated U.S. programs in the field do describe yet another, very different sort of weapons engineering where a three-step progression toward more "useable" devices – systems that could deftly accomplish a narrowly tailored mission without excessive destructiveness – has been palpably under way, step by step, for a period

[1] Regarding antisatellite weapons in general, see: Paul B. Stares, The Militarization of Space: U.S. Policy, 1945–1984 (1985); John M. Logsdon and Gordon Adams (eds.), Space Weapons: Are They Needed?, Space Policy Institute, George Washington University, October 2003; Ashton Carter, Satellites and Anti-Satellites: The Limits of the Possible, 10 International Security No. 4, Spring 1986, p. 46; U.S. Congress, Office of Technology Assessment, Anti-Satellite Weapons, Countermeasures, and Arms Control, OTA-ISC-281, September 1985; Michael Krepon with Christopher Clary, Space Assurance or Space Dominance? The Case Against Weaponizing Space, Henry L. Stimson Center, 2003; David Wright, Laura Grego, and Lisbeth Gronlund, The Physics of Space Security: A Reference Manual, 2005; Michael O'Hanlon, Neither Star Wars Nor Sanctuary: Constraining the Military Uses of Space, 2004; John Pike and Eric Stambler, Anti-Satellite Weapons and Arms Control, in Richard Dean Burns (ed.), Encyclopedia of Arms Control and Disarmament, 1993, vol. 2, p. 991; Richard L. Garwin, Kurt Gottfried, and Donald L. Hafner, Antisatellite Weapons, 250 Scientific American No. 6, June 1984, p. 45; Steven Lambakis, On the Edge of the Earth: The Future of American Space Power, 2001; Peter L. Hays, James M. Smith, Alan R. Van Tassel, and Guy M. Walsh (eds.), Spacepower for a New Millennium: Space and U.S. National Security, 2000; William L. Spacy II, Does the United States Need Space-Based Weapons? CADRE Paper, College of Aerospace Doctrine, Research, and Education, Air University, September 1999.

of decades. Here we are dealing with the highest technology of the five case studies surveyed in this book, but the basic parameters of the story are now familiar.

CIVIL AND MILITARY EXPLOITATION OF OUTER SPACE

Space programs are now so thoroughly interwoven into modern American life that it is almost impossible to parse out the distinct contribution that satellite assets offer to the full range of the civilian economy and military programs. On the commercial side, we may be only vaguely aware of the role that satellites routinely play in trunk communications (routing Internet searches, emails, television programming, and cellphone conversations around the world); in meteorology (enabling the CNN viewer to discern timely weather conditions, hurricane tracks, and local forecasts wherever her travels might take her); in navigation (facilitating travel by aircraft, ships, and increasingly by private automobiles); in resources management (assessing future crop harvests, rain forest disappearances, and even the likelihood of subterranean mineral deposits); in banking (empowering instantaneous ATM and credit transactions); and in more adventuresome applications such as harrowing search and rescue missions for wayward boaters (satellite-enabled location and retrieval operations were credited with saving 1500 people worldwide in 2004).

Annual commercial space revenues have topped the $100 billion mark, and satellite nodes have become an indispensable component of the nation's – and the world's – critical infrastructure. Satellites are now so prosaic and so reliable that it is only their absence or interruption that makes the news: when a single Galaxy IV satellite malfunctioned in 1998, blacking out service for 80 percent of U.S. pagers, the public was aghast. Some estimate that within the next few years, the U.S. direct financial investment in space could reach $500–600 billion, equaling the value of American capital investment in Europe.[2]

On the military side, the incorporation of space assets into security operations is comparably comprehensive and vital. Early warning satellites serve the function of detecting a distant enemy's missile launches, granting the national command authority precious moments to evaluate and respond. U.S. and Soviet/Russian reconnaissance satellites provide the capability to reliably count each other's ICBMs and other strategic assets, to verify compliance with SALT and START nuclear weapons

[2] James Oberg, Space Power Theory, 1999, p. 16; Helen Caldicott and Craig Eisendrath, War in Heaven: The Arms Race and Outer Space, 2007, p. 84.

treaties. Satellites monitor electromagnetic pulses and measure minute earth movements that might be evidence of clandestine nuclear weapons test explosions. An alphabet soup of spy satellites collects vital SIGINT, COMINT, and ELINT (intelligence from signals, communications, and electronics – various forms of eavesdropping on conversations and data). The cluster of GPS satellites enables a nuclear submarine, a strategic bomber, a guided missile, or an infantry patrol to know exactly where they are in three dimensions, without having to compromise their silence. At the tactical level, satellite-aided optical and electronic surveillance tells weaponeers precisely where the enemy is located and helps guide smart bombs to their destinations; moments later, satellite-aided "battle damage assessment" enables them to discern promptly which targets have already been destroyed and which must be revisited.[3]

As well as supplying the "eyes and ears" of the national security structure, satellites also serve as the central nervous system. They enable the full range of secure, instantaneous, and reliable two-way communications that have revolutionized modern combat. Physical mobility does not do you much good if you cannot tell what is over the next hill, what is happening down the road, where the friendly forces are located, and how to coordinate your efforts. The time cycle for identifying, selecting, approving, and striking targets of interest has shrunk, due in large part to swift communications and the ability to issue commands and integrate responses through the ether.

One vivid example of satellite-enabled military heroism: On June 2, 1995, U.S. Air Force Captain Scott O'Grady was patrolling at 6000 meters altitude over Bosnia in his F-16 Falcon, to help enforce NATO's declared "no-fly zone." He was shot down by a Serbian SA-6 surface-to-air missile, and after he parachuted, dense cloud cover prevented other friendly aircraft from identifying his exact location, inside hostile territory. Radio contact was intermittent and indecipherable. O'Grady evaded Serbian patrols for six days and was finally able to contact NATO through the PRC-112 two-way radio, with an integrated GPS receiver, in his survival kit. The device fixed his position in a central Bosnian forest, enabling combat search-and-rescue helicopters (aided by their own GPS receivers) to swoop in and rescue him.[4]

[3] Barry D. Watts, The Military Use of Space: A Diagnostic Assessment, Center for Strategic and Budgetary Assessments, February 2001; Michael Russell Rip and James M. Hasik, The Precision Revolution: GPS and the Future of Aerial Warfare, 2002. See O'Hanlon, supra note 1, at 40–46 for a roster of major current U.S. military satellite systems.

[4] Rip and Hasik, supra note 3, at 221–22.

Moreover, the civilian and military satellite systems are closely intertwined. Gulf War I is frequently referred to as "the first space war" because U.S. combat forces drew so heavily upon satellite support, and much of that support, of necessity, came from civilian space systems. For example, the U.S. military relied extensively upon commercial satellite imagery from the LANDSAT and SPOT orbiters for rapid mapping, targeting, and change detection.[5] The civil/military integration has only grown since that time: During Gulf War I, commercial satellites supplied 45 percent of the bandwidth used for international communications by the U.S. military; by the time of the Kosovo campaign, the figure was up to 80 percent.[6] In Gulf War II, the U.S. military employed no fewer than 50 satellites, including many not owned or operated by the Department of Defense itself, in the war effort.[7] Realistically, there is now no other way these essential services can be provided. By one count, the U.S. military now fields some 65 dedicated military satellites and routinely employs 200 additional civilian platforms.[8]

In addition, it almost goes without saying that the technology is improving dramatically. To cite just one illustration: levels of overhead photographic intelligence that were jealously guarded military secrets only a couple of decades ago are now collected, processed, and widely disseminated by multiple commercial operations. The ground resolution (a measure of the smallest object on the surface of the earth that a satellite can discern) of publicly available earth-imaging satellites has fallen from 80 meters in 1972, to 30 meters in 1982, to 10 meters in 1986, to 5 meters in 1997, to 2 meters in 2003, and to 0.4 meters today.[9]

Other countries, too, have turned to satellite technology for civil and military applications – even the beginnings of a space tourism industry (at least for the extremely wealthy). Today, 14 states own satellites that routinely apply space capabilities to support their military operations, and in 2006, Kazakhstan became the 47th country to engage in its own civil space activities. Competition has intensified for the most desirable orbital slot allocations (there are more than 800 operational satellites jostling for position in orbit today) and for the most functional satellite radio frequencies (avoiding electronic overlaps in the key spectrum

[5] Rip and Hasik, supra note 3, at 138–42.

[6] Krepon and Clary, supra note 1, at 16.

[7] O'Hanlon, supra note 1, at 4, 38–40.

[8] Steven M. Kosiak, Arming the Heavens: A Preliminary Assessment of the Potential Cost and Cost-Effectiveness of Space-Based Weapons, Center for Strategic and Budgetary Assessments, 2007, p. 56.

[9] O'Hanlon, supra note 1, at 39.

regions has already become a major challenge – hundreds of satellite radio frequency interference incidents are recorded annually). The commercial space industry is now robust, multinational, and diverse, and every prediction is that exoatmospheric traffic of all sorts, by an ever-broadening array of nations, corporations, and ambitious individuals, will continue to swell.

USE OF SPACE BECOMES DEPENDENCE

The dark side of that increasing exploitation of space, however, is a parallel social vulnerability. As we *use* outer space more, and as we reap the myriad benefits of those operations, we eventually come to *expect* these services from our satellites, and then we start to *depend* on them. Perhaps inevitably, our alternative systems will atrophy, and we will lose the ability to perform those vital functions in the "old-fashioned" way. Traditional land lines, fiber optic cables, and other terrestrial communications links are hardly becoming dinosaurs, but in an era of high-speed digital communications, it often seems unnecessary to sustain the investment in redundant back-up devices. For the military especially, budgeting for and training personnel to operate multiple systems applicable to a global battlefield will often seem wasteful. Especially in times of peak demand, such as warfighting emergencies, there is only a narrow array of assets available to perform surging government and private functions. But without those fallbacks, our sensitivity to any perturbations in satellite services is magnified – once we put all our eggs into outer space, that one basket becomes quite important, indeed. Gen. Kevin P. Chilton, head of U.S. Strategic Command, acknowledged this stark reality, recently testifying to Congress that "our adversaries understand our dependence upon space-based capabilities."[10]

This emerging vulnerability is exacerbated because of the "soft" nature of satellites themselves. To minimize launch costs, satellites are ordinarily designed to be as lightweight as possible. This standard typically precludes outfitting them with anything like the thick skins, defensive armaments, evasive maneuverability, or other countermeasures capabilities that characterize naval vessels, ground vehicles, or aircraft. Instead, most satellites are quite delicate, designed to withstand the immense rigors of launch and of operation in the void of space, but not crafted with an eye to rebuffing

[10] Kevin P. Chilton, statement to Strategic Forces subcommittee of House Armed Services Committee, February 27, 2008, quoted in Walter Pincus, The New Art of War, Washington Post, March 3, 2008, p. A15.

hostile human action. Most satellites do not even incorporate sensors that could detect an enemy's attempt to interfere; an attack might be misidentified as natural phenomena or not attributed to the true author. Some high-value military satellites are now more hardened against potential disruption and more capable of local situational awareness, but similarly shielding the array of civilian orbiters would impose substantial financial and performance penalties.

Moreover, a satellite usually follows a known, predictable route, with minimal ability to adjust its orbital parameters – it is, therefore, a perpetual "sitting duck." And satellites are so expensive that owners and operators typically do not maintain fleets of redundant "spares," able to substitute for one that fails; there is only a modest "surge capacity" to reconstitute a satellite architecture quickly in times of sudden need. Finally, the infrastructure supporting satellite operations is fragile, too: the launch facilities and ground stations that enable space operations are few in number, well known, and vulnerable to attack; likewise, the communications mechanisms – the uplinks and downlinks that sustain the vehicles and transmit their intelligence back to earthbound users – may be susceptible to disruption.

Even seemingly small perturbations can be serious. When the Iraqi Republican Guard attempted in 2003 to interfere with GPS signals – a move that could have threatened the mechanisms that would guide American aircraft and PGM bombs – the jamming equipment instantly became priority targets for U.S. strikes. B-1 bombers quickly destroyed the offending jammers (ironically, by using GPS-guided munitions to accomplish the mission). The fact that the jammers were small, inexpensive and readily available (in that case, from Russian sources) only compounded the potential danger.[11]

Despite efforts to shield the system, the relatively weak GPS signals may be inherently vulnerable to interference, even 150–200 km away, via simple homemade jammers (with instructions available on the Internet). A more adventurous country like Iralia in Scenario 7 might also undertake more sophisticated (but potentially even more effective) jamming or spoofing via electromagnetic means deployed on aircraft or spacecraft – and these, too, would then have to become prime candidates for vigorous retaliatory attack.[12]

[11] Michael Krepon and Michael Katz-Hyman, Space Weapons and Proliferation, 12 Nonproliferation Review No. 2, July 2005, p. 323; Mike Moore, Space War – Now We're Jammin'! 61 Bulletin of the Atomic Scientists No. 2, March/April 2005, p. 6.

[12] Wright, Grego, and Gronlund, supra note 1, at 119–20, 168.

(Conversely, during the 2001 fighting in Afghanistan, the United States itself jammed some GPS signals, utilizing a new ground-based counter-communications system, to deny GPS service that local Taliban and al-Qaeda fighters were attempting to poach and exploit for their own purposes.)

PROLIFERATION OF SATELLITE CAPACITIES

As more and more countries gain access to outer space, the monopoly advantages enjoyed by the first two entrants, the United States and the Soviet Union, are distinctly reduced. Those pioneer nations may welcome newcomers in the peaceful exploration of space, and they may at least tolerate increased economic competition – but the proliferation of military advantage will be harder to swallow.

Today, a handful of additional nations – notably including France, China, India, Israel, Canada, Japan, Iran, Ukraine, and the United Arab Emirates – have begun to operate reconnaissance and other types of satellites of military significance.[13] Private companies, too, now command remote sensing capabilities that were the exclusive province of Moscow and Washington, D.C. only a decade or so previously. Space Imaging (a U.S. company), SPOT (French), and other commercial outfits now routinely provide prompt, high-resolution images that carry obvious military applications, and a new service, just coming online, offers such spectacular imagery that the U.S. government itself has already contracted to purchase $200 million worth of its products. If Saddam Hussein had enjoyed access to that sort of overhead intelligence, the famous "left hook" maneuver that caught the Iraqis by surprise at the outset of Operation Desert Storm in 1991 might not have succeeded, and a country such as Iralia could readily seek to exploit these products today during crisis or conflict.

Even more sophisticated satellite products, including synthetic aperture radar and hyperspectral imaging, may not be far behind in reaching the global marketplace. Likewise, the European Union's new Galileo satellite system and Russia's older but now revivified GLONASS array both seek to provide a competitor to GPS – an independent (i.e., not subject to U.S. control) source of reliable, accurate global positioning and navigation data.

[13] Jeffrey T. Richelson, The Whole World Is Watching, Bulletin of the Atomic Scientists, January/February 2006, p. 26.

The U.S. government retains the legal right of "shutter control" over American firms, ensuring the ability to regulate the images acquired and the distribution of the products during a time of national security crisis. But that authority does not extend to any of the dozen or so foreign companies and consortia possessing comparable reconnaissance skills. During Operation Enduring Freedom, therefore, the Pentagon resorted to its market power (contracting to buy up, for $1.9 million per month, exclusive rights to all the possibly relevant high-resolution imagery of Afghanistan that private sources could generate) or suasion (convincing the French government not to allow SPOT imagery of Afghanistan to reach the open market). It is anyone's guess, however, whether those tactics would be similarly availing in a future contingency, such as against Iralia, where global politics might be configured less favorably.

In today's worldwide political and economic alignment, America's predominance in space programs has never been greater. The United States government spends $36 billion per year for outer space activities, accounting for more than 70 percent of the global total. In military spending, the balance sheet is even more lopsided: the U.S. $20 billion per year is almost 95 percent of the world's combined defense-related expenditures in space.[14]

That one-sided American advantage, however, seems likely to wane, as France, India, and others step up their participation in space; in 2009, Iran, too, launched its first wholly indigenous satellite. By one count, 1100 companies in 53 countries now exploit space in some measure.[15] As space analyst Barry Watts puts it, "space systems and capabilities to which only the United States and a few other developed nations had access during the 1990s will be available to many smaller nations, including prospective American adversaries."[16]

EARLY ANTISATELLITE WEAPONS

These inherent characteristics – the high value of satellites and the growing civilian and military dependence upon a small number of vulnerable assets – combine to generate a seemingly irresistible allure for the concept

[14] Henry L. Stimson Center, Space Security or Space Weapons? A Guide to the Issues, 2005.

[15] Theresa Hitchens, Weapons in Space: Silver Bullet or Russian Roulette? The Policy Implications of U.S. Pursuit of Space-Based Weapons, in Logsdon and Adams, supra note 1, at 87, 107.

[16] Watts, supra note 3, at 71.

of antisatellite weaponry. To protect or defend our satellites, and to deny the enemy the use of comparable resources during a conflict, may seem like obvious military objectives – the application into the new environment of the most traditional concepts and functions of military forces.

The leading space nations – principally the United States and the Soviet Union – did, in fact, explore a series of ASAT concepts in fits and starts during the cold war. Today the American program may be heating up once again, even as China has now entered the ASAT fray. Each sequential version of an antisatellite weapon held its advantages and disadvantages, and a quick review of the historical evolution of several devices is instructive for where the programs may be headed today. Notably, the clear trend line is, once again, toward greater "useability," defining ASATs that are distinctly less powerful, less deadly, and less crudely destructive than the earlier generations, so they can be wielded, or at least threatened, in combat with more finesse and discretion, and accordingly with less "self-deterrence."

The first serious notions for antisatellite weapons arose in the late 1950s, almost simultaneously with the first serious notions for satellites themselves – in fact, the U.S. Army's initial ASAT feasibility study was completed within six weeks of Sputnik's pathbreaking orbit. After some early missteps had fizzled, the first full-scale United States ASAT effort, denominated Project SAINT (for *Sa*tellite *Int*erceptor), contemplated locating, approaching, inspecting, and possibly damaging or destroying another country's satellites. Because great accuracy in the intercept could not be guaranteed with contemporary technology, the concept envisioned employing a nuclear weapon (up to 1 Mt yield) to ensure a kill. The large (1100 kg) SAINT vehicle would be launched by Atlas rockets, but the program was canceled by the Air Force in 1962, before its first test flight.

A U.S. Army follow-on effort, denominated Program 505 or Project Mudflap, fleshed out the concept of a nuclear ASAT and conducted a dozen flight tests, using Nike-Zeus ground-launched missiles, between 1962 and 1966. The Air Force's entry into this early ASAT competition, Program 437, used a larger Thor rocket, which could reach higher altitudes (up to 200 miles), although it could not respond as quickly as the smaller, solid-fueled Nike-Zeus. The Air Force's nuclear-tipped ASAT became operational in 1964, based on Johnston Island in the Pacific Ocean. It was tested 16 times between 1964 and 1970 before being retired in 1975.[17]

[17] Stares, supra note 1; Federation of American Scientists, Space Policy Project, Military Space Programs, http://www.fas.org/spp/military/program/asat/overview.htm; Clayton

This nuclear explosive power (1–1.5 Mt) would surely have sufficed to obliterate the offending satellite; the problem with the warfighting concept was the vast and unpredictable overbreadth of the deadly penumbra. The prompt nuclear effects (primarily x-rays and neutrons) would fan out to an enormous radius (possibly hundreds of kilometers), indiscriminately jeopardizing our own satellites as well as the enemy's.[18]

Even more ominous, the radiation effects of a nuclear weapon would linger in space for years to come, gradually dispersing into an orbiting radioactive cloud or belt, lethal to any satellites that traversed it. In fact, according to some calculations, if a desperate country such as Iralia were to detonate even a small nuclear weapon in low altitude space over its country, 90 percent of the world's low-earth-orbiting satellites would be severely degraded or destroyed within one month. Investments worth billions of dollars (including many of the most important military assets) would become useless – and it would not be safe to replace them for many months to come.

Moreover, a somewhat larger exoatmospheric nuclear explosion would generate a powerful surge of energy known as an electromagnetic pulse (EMP). That jolt would be disastrous on earth: it would be harmless to human beings, but cataclysmic for our electronic artifacts, sufficient to fry all unprotected electronic circuits, instantly incapacitating legions of automobiles, airplanes, and computers.[19]

Before the phenomena of EMP and artificial radiation were fully understood, the superpowers conducted about a dozen test explosions of nuclear weapons in the upper atmosphere and in near space. One of these, the American "Starfish Prime" event in July 1962, involved a 1.4-Mt blast 400 km above Johnston Island. The EMP effects triggered burglar alarms, burned out streetlights, and disrupted radio service in Hawaii (1300 km away), and compromised communications all across the Pacific. The nuclear radiation from that test also inadvertently (but

K.S. Chun, Shooting Down a 'Star': Program 437, the US Nuclear ASAT System and Present-Day Copycat Killers, CADRE Paper No. 6, Air University Press, Maxwell Air Force Base, April 2000.

18 O'Hanlon, supra note 1, at 68.

19 Clay Wilson, High Altitude Electromagnetic Pulse (HEMP) and High Power Microwave (HPM) Devices: Threat Assessments, Congressional Research Service Report for Congress, RL32544, April 14, 2006; Ian Steer, High-Altitude Nuclear Explosions: Blind, Deaf and Dumb, Jane's Defence Weekly, October 23, 2002; Nick Schwellenbach, Empty Threat? 61 Bulletin of the Atomic Scientists No. 5, September/October 2005, p. 50; John S. Foster, Jr. et al., Report of the Commission to Assess the Threat to the United States from Electromagnetic Pulse (EMP) Attack, 2004.

fatally) corrupted six U.S. satellites and one British satellite in subsequent weeks.[20]

NONNUCLEAR ASATs

The next iteration of antisatellite weapons, therefore, eschewed overly powerful nuclear explosions, aiming for more localized effects. In the Soviet Union's version, a 1400 kg hunter-killer satellite would be launched atop a rocket into an orbit that matched the characteristics of its prey. It would maneuver ever closer (completing one or two circuits of the earth, requiring 2 or 3 hours), using a radar tracking device. When it approached near enough – it was lethal to a range of 1 kilometer, although ordinarily, it would slide into much greater proximity – it would blow itself up. The blast and shrapnel fragments, powered by 300 kg of conventional high explosives, would destroy the target. Initially, the system would be effective only in relatively low altitudes, against satellites 230 to 1000 kilometers above the earth.

The Soviets conducted approximately 20 launches to test this device, about half of them successful. The first series of outer space tests, between 1968 and 1971, accomplished seven interceptions and five detonations. After a unilateral moratorium, Moscow resumed the development sequence between 1976 and 1982, to expand the range of the system (enabling it to engage targets from 150 to 1600 km altitudes), to shorten its speed of engagement (so it could rendezvous with and strike a target within a single orbit), and to supplement the radar guidance system with onboard optical and infrared seekers. By the end of the second test series, the Pentagon had assessed the Soviet co-orbital ASAT as achieving operational status; the program has been in hiatus since that time.[21]

The contemporary American variant was designated MHV (Miniature Homing Vehicle); it relied upon a high-speed direct impact between the interceptor and the target, rather than a suicidal explosion. The kill mechanism would be launched by a two-stage missile from a steeply climbing F-15 Eagle jet fighter, instead of from a ground-based rocket. This procedure would allow the ASAT to be deployed from almost any airport location rather than only from fixed missile sites. It would also permit the interceptor to ascend directly and immediately to the target

[20] Krepon and Clary, supra note 1, at 20.

[21] Stares, supra note 1; Laura Grego, A History of US and Soviet ASAT Programs, Union of Concerned Scientists, April 9, 2003.

without having to achieve a gradual co-orbit; theoretically, the MHV could strike a satellite within 10 minutes of launch. Eight infrared sensors and telescopes would vector the ASAT cylinder toward its target; 64 small steering jets provided the maneuverability, enabling the 15.9-kg projectile to ram into its target at up to 24,000 km/hr, with devastating effect.

The Air Force tested the MHV system (against an unoccupied designated "point in space" rather than against a target satellite) twice in 1984. The first and only test against a satellite – the obsolete Solwind solar observation vehicle at 555 km above the earth – came on September 13, 1985; it was completely successful in obliterating the unfortunate target. Further testing against points in space continued in 1986, and the Air Force proposed to procure 112 of the ASAT missiles, but the program was essentially abandoned in 1987. There were reports that the Soviet Union, too, was pursuing a similar system, based on a MIG-31 aircraft, but there is no evidence of advanced work.

More recently, the U.S. Army has sustained, but never flight tested, a similar program, denominated KE-ASAT (for Kinetic Energy ASAT). To be launched by a Minuteman ICBM booster from a site in the western United States or the Pacific Ocean, the interceptor would seek, acquire, and track the target with onboard sensors and maneuver toward it with small thrusters. It would collide with the victim at high speed, spanking it with a giant mylar flyswatter attachment, to disable or destroy the offending satellite. More than $350 million was devoted to the KE-ASAT concept in the 1990s, despite the Army's distinctly ambivalent attitude toward the project. In December 2005, the Government Accountability Office found the entire program to be "in a state of disarray"; the enterprise has since been reorganized and renamed, surviving on the barest life support of modest funding. Three weapon prototypes were constructed, but reportedly two of them have already been cannibalized for other projects.[22]

Most recently, the United States exercised yet another form of emergent ASAT technology with different nomenclature. On February 20, 2008, the Navy's USS Lake Erie fired a modified Standard Missile-3

[22] See George C. Wilson, Mr. Smith's Crusade, National Journal, August 11, 2001, p. 2542 (noting that Sen. Bob Smith (R-N.H.) had been the primary moving force behind the KE-ASAT for many years, insisting that the Army proceed with the program, when military officials would have preferred to devote their energies (and funding) elsewhere); Theresa Hitchens, Michael Katz-Hyman, and Jeffrey Lewis, U.S. Space Weapons: Big Intentions, Little Focus, 13 Nonproliferation Review No. 1, March 2006, p. 35, 43.

(which had been developed to intercept incoming ballistic missiles rather than satellites) against the National Reconnaissance Office's USA-193 satellite. That radar intelligence satellite had failed catastrophically shortly after its December 2006 launch, and efforts to regain control – to return it to its assigned mission or just to bring it gracefully back to earth – had been frustrated. American authorities were worried that if the satellite slipped into an uncontrolled deorbit, it was large enough (the size of a school bus) and solid enough (weighing 5000 pounds) that substantial sections might survive the stresses of reentry and impact the earth. Of particular concern, the satellite's fuel tank carried 1000 pounds of noxious hydrazine, a potential health risk if the impact occurred in any populated area.

Accordingly, top military officials proposed, and President Bush approved, modifications to the interceptor missile, which then successfully collided with USA-193 at over 22,000 miles per hour and shattered it (and the fuel compartment) into thousands of small pieces, which were all expected to incinerate promptly and completely upon reentry.

On the other side of the world, on January 11, 2007, China became the third country to conduct a destructive ASAT experiment. A mobile, solid-fueled two-stage ballistic missile was launched from the Xichang Space Center, and shortly thereafter its kinetic kill vehicle (not containing an explosive conventional or nuclear warhead) rammed into China's aging Fengyun-1C weather satellite at 8 kilometers per second. The head-on collision, occurring about 860 kilometers up in space, obliterated the satellite in spectacular fashion. China had conducted two or three earlier tests of this SC-19 ASAT, either deliberately or accidentally just missing the target satellites, and the devastating interception now demonstrates a third country's capability to hold at risk all satellites in low earth orbit, including many of the world's most important and sensitive spacecraft.[23]

The most recent drawing board innovation in hunter-killer ASAT concepts is the notion of miniature "space mines." Swarms of these inexpensive microsatellites, each weighing only a few pounds, could be efficiently launched in quantity and surreptitiously scattered, to remain aloft (either near the potential targets or parked far away), virtually invisible, until activated. When called upon, they would suddenly maneuver close to

[23] Shirley Kan, China's Anti-Satellite Weapon Test, Congressional Research Service Report for Congress, RS22652, April 23, 2007; David Isenberg, The Newest Anti-Satellite Contender: China's ASAT Test, British American Security Information Council, BASIC Notes, Occasional Paper, March 16, 2007; Michael R. Gordon and David S. Cloud, U.S. Knew of China Missile Test, But Kept Silent, New York Times, April 23, 2007.

their intended victims and detonate with deadly force (or perform less cataclysmic blinding, jamming, or interfering functions). The first two prototypes in the U.S. Air Force's experimental series to explore this concept, XSS-10 and XSS-11, were launched in 2003 and 2005. By 2009, the Pentagon was employing its highly maneuverable MiTEx microsatellite to approach and inspect a disabled orbiter.

Without understating the technological or financial problems that would have to be overcome, it is clear that many of these variations upon conventional explosive ASAT interceptor concepts would work – they would suffice to destroy the soft, easy-to-find, and defenseless satellites – and they would do so without the cataclysm of a nuclear explosion. But even these devices are primitive compared to what might soon be available – and two limiting features of particular importance stand out.

First, the Soviet, Chinese, and American kamikaze interceptors are all aimed at achieving a total destruction of the target satellite; it is an all-or-nothing proposition (in contrast to the more deft systems noted next). The only effect these weapons can pursue is a complete, permanent breakage.

Second, an inevitable side effect of the testing and operation of these exploding or colliding ASATs is the creation of an immense quantity of debris – when the ASAT and its target are blown to smithereens, those smithereens can remain in orbit for a very long time, posing an enduring hazard to other satellite traffic, including by our own or allied craft. For example, the U.S. 1985 Solwind ASAT test generated some 286 trackable fragments; some of that breccia later came within 1 mile of the International Space Station, and it took 19 years for the last pieces of hazardous junk to decay out of orbit. The Chinese 2007 ASAT test spawned a hailstorm of 2600 pieces of trackable debris, and perhaps 150,000 smaller (but still dangerous) shards – a perilous cloud stretching from 200 to 3850 kilometers altitude, through which at least 100 vital earth observation satellites must repeatedly tread over the next few decades before the new debris settles out of orbit. Two U.S. satellites and one French craft have already been forced to alter their normal orbital course to avoid the Fengyun 1C danger zone.[24]

[24] Theresa Hitchens, Code Red? Chinese ASAT Test Raises Debris Threat to EO Sats, Imaging Notes, Summer 2007, p. 36. Because this ASAT test occurred at a relatively high altitude, the debris fragments will remain in orbit even longer than did the junk produced by the earlier U.S. and Soviet ASAT interceptor tests. See also Union of Concerned Scientists, Space Weapons and Technical Issues: Debris from China's Kinetic Energy ASAT

The February 2008 U.S. Navy downing of the failed USA-193 reconnaissance satellite erupted in some 3000 pieces of trackable debris, but that intercept was accomplished at a much lower altitude (only 150 miles). Few satellites operate so close to the atmosphere, and most of the debris from the collision precipitated out of orbit within a few days or a few weeks. The last noticeable fragment reentered the earth's atmosphere in October 2008. Even so, some experts worried that the violence of the intercept could cause some of the wreckage to kick unpredictably into higher orbits, and the American authorities were careful to ensure that the space shuttle would return to earth before the ASAT activity began, and that the International Space Station would not be in the endangered neighborhood at the time.

In fact, the problem of space debris is increasingly recognized as a substantial impediment to the continued exploitation of space. Even tiny fragments of a pulverized satellite or interceptor, when traveling at enormous orbital speeds, can inflict catastrophic damage upon another spacecraft that wanders by. The windows on the space shuttle, for example, have repeatedly been pockmarked by a high-speed collision with a tiny fleck of dried paint traveling at ten times the speed of a high-powered rifle bullet. The impact with a hypervelocity particle even one centimeter in diameter – the size of a marble – can have an effect comparable to a one-ton safe falling from the top of a five-story building.

The U.S. Air Force Space Command at Cheyenne Mountain in Colorado now uses 30 sensors worldwide to track nearly 17,000 orbiting items larger than 10 centimeters, most of which is space junk discarded by earlier launches. There may also be 300,000 additional orbiting items of potentially deadly wreckage between 1 and 10 centimeters in size, and perhaps 35 million scraps of debris in total – an inventory of 3–5 million kg of human-created space trash seems plausible. The unwanted material at lower orbits will eventually fall back to earth, mostly burning upon reentry, but the detritus at higher altitudes will likely stay there essentially

Test, May, 2007, http://www.ucsusa.org/assets/documents/global_security/Debris-from-China-ASAT.pdf (calculating that more than 50 percent of the debris larger than one centimeter will remain in orbit for more than 20 years, and noting that the Chinese weather satellite was relatively small (mass just under one ton); an ASAT attack on a larger satellite could generate an even bigger cloud of hazardous debris); Nicholas L. Johnson, Eugene Stansbery, David O. Witlock, Kira J. Abercromby, and Debra Shoots, NASA History of On-Orbit Satellite Fragmentations (14th ed.), June 2008, p. 1 (the PRC 2007 ASAT test now accounts for 17 percent of all catalogued debris in orbit).

forever – a gauntlet of continuous danger, reminding us of the enduring costs of 50 years of human littering in space.[25]

An average small satellite in a popular low orbit now has a 1 percent chance per year of failing because of collision with a fragment in this mosh pit of discarded rubbish, and NASA estimates that the space shuttle has a 1-in-200 chance of being seriously damaged by space debris (and other authorities calculate the odds as being four times as dangerous). Three accidental collisions between space objects were catalogued between 1991 and 2005, and in February 2009, the first full-scale outer-space catastrophe occurred, as a fully operational U.S. communications satellite, operated by the Iridium corporation, smashed into the defunct, but intact, Russian Cosmos 2251 satellite, obliterating both blindsided vehicles. Moreover, because each of those cosmic fender-benders has the potential to create much more trash, the possibility arises of a chain reaction of accidental debris generation, irretrievably polluting important zones of space.[26]

Since 1988, official U.S. government space policy has directed both military and civilian entrepreneurs to minimize further contributions to the debris hazards; the procurement of spacecraft and launch vehicles, and the design and operation of space tests, experiments, and systems are to avoid further intensification of the problem.[27] Likewise, international space policy has come to recognize the impending debris crisis, and the U.N.'s Inter-Agency Space Debris Coordination Committee has urged all spacefaring countries to adopt measures to avoid, to the extent possible, additional contributions to the cloud of space junk that threatens to encircle the earth. Still, the pollution continues, with a 2.1 percent increase in space objects in 2005 and a 5.5 percent bump in 2006 – most of

[25] Joel R. Primack, Debris and Future Space Activities, in James Clay Moltz (ed.), Future Security in Space: Commercial, Military, and Arms Control Trade-Offs, Monterey Institute, Center for Nonproliferation Studies, Occasional Paper No. 10, July 2002, p. 18; Leonard David, The Clutter Above, 61 Bulletin of the Atomic Scientists No. 4, July/August 2005, p. 32; NASA History, supra note 24.

[26] J.-C. Liou and N.L. Johnson, Risks in Space from Orbiting Debris, 311 Science p. 340, January 20, 2006.

[27] The White House, National Science and Technology Council, Fact Sheet: National Space Policy, September 19, 1996; U.S. Air Force Space Command, Satellite Operations, Instruction 10–1204, June 1, 2006, p. 10; The White House, Office of Science and Technology Policy, Interagency Report on Orbital Debris, November 1995; NASA Procedural Requirements for Limiting Orbital Debris, NPR 8715.6A, February 19, 2008; NASA Handbook for Limiting Orbital Debris, 8719.14, July 30, 2008.

which came from the United States. Because of the Chinese ASAT test and some other unlucky malfunctions, experts consider 2007 to be "the worst year for new debris creation ever." A further 2.2 percent increase was registered in 2008.

Explosive ASATs could add immeasurably to the debris problem,[28] but even the most inexpensive and crude nonexplosive and nonhoming satellite-killers could be devastating to the space economy. In fact, one very low-tech ASAT scenario posits a desperate country such as Iralia simply ejecting into space a quantity of sand, gravel, or nails, which would disperse into a lethal shroud, indiscriminately jeopardizing all satellites within range.[29] Such a "scorched earth" (or "scorched space") tactic would be as destructive as it is imprecise – even a BB traveling at orbital speed would carry the punch of a bowling ball impacting at 100 km/hr. At least 28 countries now possess missiles that could put that sort of primitive ASAT payload into low orbit.

DIRECTED ENERGY ASATs

In response to those limitations and hazards, the current American notions for a "third-generation" ASAT system would rely on a very different sort of technology: beams of directed energy (microwaves, high-energy lasers, radio-frequency transmissions, or columns of subatomic particles). Unlike kinetic energy systems (which rely on tangible objects colliding with, or exploding near, enemy satellites) the directed energy would burn a hole in the satellite, or interfere with its internal circuits, or befuddle its sensors and onboard computers – allowing a much more deft array of ASAT concepts of operations. Operating at the speed of light, unencumbered by gravity, able to span great distances, capable of engaging multiple targets rapidly, and perhaps even able to function surreptitiously (so the target might not even realize that it had been subjected to a deliberate attack, or by whom), beam weapons offer – at least in principle – revolutionary advantages, as "the mother of all ASATs."

First, there would simply be no issue of widespread nuclear blast, radiation, or electromagnetic pulse; likewise, the concern about creating long-duration debris would be moot, because the target satellite would

[28] Notably, some concepts for the Army's KE-ASAT system would include outfitting the interceptor with a sheet of mylar plastic, a "kill enhancement device," which would strike the target satellite and render it inoperative, but without shattering it, to minimize debris creation. FAS, supra note 17.

[29] Wright, Grego, and Gronlund, supra note 1, at 157–65.

not fragment. Third, and even more intriguing, a laser or microwave ASAT might allow a more sophisticated mission: perhaps we could damage, but not destroy, the target; perhaps we could inflict only a temporary disability, enabling the satellite to return to its routine operations at a later time; perhaps we could interrupt only part of its normal functions, permitting the others to continue undisturbed; perhaps we could commandeer the satellite, bending it (again, temporarily) to our will instead of its owner's.

To date, these images of precisely calibrated ASAT operations are mostly pipe dreams – but they have an obvious appeal to the warfighter. According to U.S. Air Force Lt. Gen. Daniel P. Leaf, when it comes to offensive counterspace operations, "Our priority is on temporary and reversible means, not destruction."[30]

In the Iralia scenario depicted at the outset of this chapter, the United States might contemplate both offensive operations in space (to attempt to deny Iralia the benefits of satellite data for weather forecasting, tactical reconnaissance, or any other missions) and defensive operations (to protect the integrity of our GPS signals and to rebut the threat of a crude Iralian ASAT). If our only ASAT tools were the "old-fashioned" types of kinetic interceptors, they might suffice, but would we be willing to use them? In Scenario 7, doing so would entail attacking a commercial or national sensing satellite owned and operated not by Iralia but by some other nation or private company we were not engaging as a belligerent, and self-deterrence could be a powerful inhibiting factor.

If our only option were a total, permanent destruction of the satellite, that would be a most provocative choice. If, instead, a directed energy system allowed us to "anesthetize" the satellite, interfering only temporarily with its operations, permitting it to return to normal functioning as soon as the war was over (or, even more deftly, prohibiting it from undertaking regular activities during the portion of its orbit when it was circling above Iralia, but allowing unencumbered operations for the rest of its circuit), that might be seen as appreciably less obnoxious.

Likewise, a directed-energy ASAT would avoid the valid and growing inhibition against generating new volumes of space debris. The United States would be justifiably self-deterred about invoking a modern version

[30] Seven Questions: Space Weapons, Part II, Foreign Policy, August 1, 2005. See also Report of the Commission to Assess United States National Security Space Management and Organization (Rumsfeld Commission Report), January 11, 2001, at 28 ("The preferred approach to negation is the use of effects that are 'temporary and reversible in their nature.'")

of the MHV or KE-ASAT to attack an enemy's reconnaissance or other satellites, even if Iralia were exploiting them for military advantage. The short-term gain from inhibiting Iralia's warfighting abilities might well be swamped by the longer-term debris inflicted upon decades of U.S. and allied spacecraft.

Any hostile action against space assets of a neutral state, of course, would be both risky and threatening. But if the newer technology allows us to fine-tune the provocation to the minimum necessary, if it is exactly sized to accomplish the valid military mission and nothing more, then that should be a more tolerable tactic. If our forces know that they could accomplish the ASAT operation with that smaller, softer, reversible measure of force, perhaps they would be more inclined to undertake the operation. Directed energy ASATs, therefore, become more "useable" than traditional ASATs.

The focal point to date for the exploration of a ground-based anti-satellite energy beam has been America's most powerful laser, designated MIRACL (Mid-InfraRed Advanced Chemical Laser). Built in 1980 and now housed at the Army's White Sands missile range in New Mexico, MIRACL is capable of generating a prodigious 2 megawatts of power. In October 1997, the Air Force commissioned a test of the system against a defunct MSTI-3 satellite orbiting at 420 kilometers altitude. The avowed purpose of the event was defensive – to assess the vulnerability of American satellites to hostile laser illumination – but the value in helping to develop an offensive U.S. ASAT capability was obvious, too.

In any event, the outcome of the test was remarkable: although the MIRACL laser itself basically failed, a lower-powered companion laser, intended merely to align the system and track the satellite, proved sufficiently powerful to blind the target satellite temporarily without destroying or damaging the onboard sensors. Few had anticipated that what was essentially a piece of commercially available apparatus could have such militarily significant effects.[31]

The U.S. Air Force has continued its investigation of laser ASATs, spending $4.9 million in 2006 and budgeting $5.7 million for 2007 – in addition to research into airborne versions of the equipment.[32] In the same vein, the Air Force has also sustained a $75 million program to procure a next-generation mobile ground-based jamming capability, denominated the Counter Satellite Communications system, intended to

[31] Grego, History, supra note 21.

[32] Jeff Hecht, US Plans Anti-Satellite Lasers, New Scientist, May 3, 2006.

interfere with links between other countries' satellites and their ground stations.[33]

The Soviet Union, too, had tinkered with a ground-based laser ASAT system, and its installation at Sary Shagan in Kazakhstan aroused considerable agitation in the West during the 1980s. In 1989, however, a U.S. delegation was invited to tour the facility, and its inspection revealed that the fears were greatly exaggerated; the apparatus was much less capable than the Department of Defense had estimated. Subsequently, Russia essentially abandoned the entire enterprise.

China, too, has apparently delved into the directed energy ASAT business, although the details remain classified and shrouded from public view. Reportedly, in September 2006 (or earlier), China employed a high-powered ground-based laser to illuminate a U.S. spy satellite, as one of several tests of a possible blinding system. No real information is available regarding the impact of this lasing or the frequency with which it has been undertaken, but the performance of the targeted satellites reportedly declined precipitously while they were overflying China. Alternatively, less profound interpretations of the events have also been proposed (some suggest that China may have merely been testing a laser device for monitoring space activity, not an ASAT weapon), but the incident surely underscores the increasing vulnerability of the American satellite fleet.[34]

Chinese military writings do betray an interest in "soft killing" of enemy satellites, as well as "hard killing" – that is, in developing a capacity to interfere only temporarily with satellite operations and command and control, as well as to destroy an offending orbiter.[35]

Perhaps even more ominously, a group of space security experts reported in 2007 that "as many as 30 states may have low-power lasers to degrade unhardened satellite sensors."[36] Iran and Libya, among others, have reportedly already exercised the ability to jam or interfere with satellites operated by the United States and others.[37]

[33] Kosiak, supra note 8, at 83.

[34] Warren Ferster and Colin Clark, NRO Confirms Chinese Laser Test Illuminated U.S. Spacecraft, Space News, October 2, 2006, p.10; Space Security 2007, spacesecurity.org, p. 18; Union of Concerned Scientists, Satellite Laser Ranging in China, UCS Technical Paper, January 8, 2007.

[35] Center for Naval Analyses, China's Space Program: Civilian, Commercial, and Military Aspects, 2006, p. 12.

[36] Space Security 2007, supra note 34, at 134.

[37] Terry Everett, Arguing for a Comprehensive Space Protection Strategy, Strategic Studies Quarterly, Fall 2007, p. 20, 23.

Of course, numerous hurdles must be overcome to weaponize a high-energy laser or other directed energy system for concerted antisatellite purposes. For any ground-based installation, the earth's atmosphere poses a severe constraint: propagating the energy through the air will cause the beam to dissipate and lose its lethal punch. To avoid that problem, the apparatus might be placed inside a high-flying airplane or into the void of outer space; to date, however, engineers have been unable to craft power sources, mirrors, and other equipment that are small and light enough to make the laser weapon that mobile.[38]

Similar attractions and impediments also characterize another related weapons technology, notably programs that pursue antiballistic missile (ABM) capabilities. Indeed, as demonstrated by the U.S. Navy's February 2008 shootdown of the failing USA-193 satellite, there are substantial overlaps between symbiotic ABM and ASAT notions, and any effective device in one realm is likely to have at least some residual capacity in the other. The Standard Missile-3 employed to kill the failed reconnaissance satellite had been reconfigured from its original ABM mission with only three weeks' notice, by modest modifications in the seeker software and guidance systems (accomplished at a cost of $100 million), to extend the missile's range from 100 to 150 miles.

Any breakthroughs in the effort to shoot down incoming ICBMs (currently, ABM systems enjoy much stronger funding than ASAT initiatives, and therefore may drive the technological advances) will probably have latent ASAT implications, too. In fact, because the ASAT mission is appreciably easier (the defense would have to engage larger, fewer, softer targets, with more advance warning) any land-, air-, or space-based ABM energy beam systems could probably be readily adapted for ASAT applications, too.[39]

CURRENT U.S. ASAT PROGRAMS

The formidable military logic advocating ASAT development is, of course, intensely controversial, and the programmatic support for antisatellite initiatives has sputtered, both on Capitol Hill and within the executive branch. Congress had statutorily prohibited MHV tests against target

[38] William Spacy, II, Assessing the Military Utility of Space-Based Weapons, in Logsdon and Adams, supra note 1, at 121; Matthew Mowthorpe, The Revolution in Military Affairs and Directed Energy Weapons, Air & Space Power Chronicles, March 8, 2002.

[39] David Wright and Laura Grego, Anti-Satellite Capabilities of Planned US Missile Defence Systems, 68 Disarmament Diplomacy, December 2002-January 2003.

satellites from 1985 to 1988, and had likewise barred employing the MIRACL laser against an object in space from 1991 to 1995. As the political winds shifted, however, Congress in 1996–1997 provided funding for the Army KE-ASAT that the Clinton Administration had not even requested, and low levels of budgetary ASAT support were foist upon a reluctant Pentagon through 2002.

Within the executive branch, too, the competing interests of space control and self-restraint have likewise fluctuated. The National Space Policy of 1996 (the overarching framework for guiding federal satellite activities) reflected both these instincts when it intoned:

> Consistent with treaty obligations, the United States will develop, operate and maintain space control capabilities to ensure freedom of action in space and, if directed, deny such freedom of action to adversaries. These capabilities may also be enhanced by diplomatic, legal or military measures to preclude an adversary's hostile use of space systems and services. The U.S. will maintain and modernize space surveillance and associated battle management command, control, communications, computers, and intelligence to effectively detect, track, categorize, monitor, and characterize threats to U.S. and friendly space systems and contribute to the protection of U.S. military activities.[40]

However, when the Bush Administration entered office in 2001, only the shards of the former ASAT programs remained. Prior testing may have generated some residual capability, but the hardware had mostly been discarded, and the intellectual expertise dissipated.

Incoming Secretary of Defense Donald Rumsfeld, however, brought a very different agenda. Having just finished leading the Commission to Assess U.S. National Security Space Management and Organization, Rumsfeld joined the commission's conclusion that "an attack on elements of U.S. space systems during a crisis or conflict should not be considered an improbable act." To avoid the possibility of a "Space Pearl Harbor" – such as a sudden Iralian poke at vulnerable American military reconnaissance and communications assets – the United States should reinvigorate its programs to deploy both defensive and offensive weapons in space. "[T]he U.S. must have the capabilities to defend its space assets against hostile acts and to negate the hostile use of space against U.S. interests."[41]

40 1996 National Space Policy, supra note 27.

41 Rumsfeld Commission Report, supra note 30, at 8–11 of Executive Summary. The Commission also recommended "live fire" ASAT tests in outer space, Id. at 29.

Official doctrine from the U.S. Air Force now speaks in similar tones. Gen. Lance W. Lord, former commander of the Air Force Space Command, affirmed, "Space superiority is our imperative – it requires the same sense of urgency that we place on gaining and maintaining air superiority over enemy air space in times of conflict."[42] The Counterspace Operations guidance, issued in August 2004, boldly asserts that "space superiority provides freedom *to* attack as well as freedom *from* attack." It seeks the capability to deceive, disrupt, deny, degrade, and destroy an adversary's civilian or military space capabilities.[43] Likewise, the Air Force Space Command's "Strategic Master Plan" cautions that "we cannot fully exploit space until we control it."[44]

Most vividly, the Bush Administration adopted a new U.S. National Space Policy on August 31, 2006. Although not radically departing from the language of the predecessor policy statement (established 10 years earlier), the newer pronouncement rhetorically strikes a more assertive posture, more emphatic about the principle of "space control" and more forward-leaning regarding the intention to deny potential enemies the opportunity to exploit outer space in a hostile fashion, and to dissuade and deter them from even attempting to develop the capacity to jeopardize U.S. space assets.

The 2006 space policy rejects new treaties that might inhibit the creation of ASAT capabilities, asserting, "The United States will oppose the development of new legal regimes or other restrictions that seek to prohibit or limit U.S. access to or use of space. Proposed arms control agreements or restrictions must not impair the rights of the United States to conduct research, development, testing, and operations or other activities in space for U.S. national interests."[45]

Accordingly, the Bush Administration attempted to start, or to restart, a constellation of ASAT technologies, with a (largely secret) budget of scores of millions of dollars annually. Although the plans are obscure

[42] U.S. Air Force, Counterspace Operations, Air Force Doctrine Document 2–2.1, August 2, 2004, p. 19.

[43] Air Force, Counterspace Operations, supra note 42, at 1 (italics in original), 2–3, 31.

[44] U.S. Air Force Space Command, Strategic Master Plan FY04 and Beyond, November 5, 2002, p. 5.

[45] U.S. National Space Policy, authorized August 31, 2006 (released to public October 6, 2006); Robert G. Joseph, Remarks on the President's National Space Policy, December 13, 2006, http://www.state.gov/t/us/rm/77799.htm; Sam Black, The Rhetoric of the Rumsfeld Space Commission, Center for Defense Information, January 24, 2007; Theresa Hitchens, Testimony before National Security and Foreign Affairs Subcommittee of the House Oversight and Government Reform Committee, May 23, 2007.

and the programs are highly classified, the available tea leaves indicate a Pentagon interest in the "full spectrum" of ground-based and space-based antisatellite weapons, both kinetic interceptors and directed energy systems. The immediate funding objectives would be only for preliminary experiments, but the goals in the "out years" (i.e., 2016–2028) would include deployment of defensive and "shoot-back" capabilities, seeking to afford the United States control over all altitudes of outer space.[46]

Unsurprisingly, one of the Obama Administration's first acts was to navigate in a starkly different direction regarding space policy. Within moments of the January 20, 2009, inauguration, the White House Web site displayed a new defense agenda, including the following pledge:

> The Obama-Biden Administration will restore American leadership on space issues, seeking a worldwide ban on weapons that interfere with military and commercial satellites. They will thoroughly assess possible threats to U.S. space assets and the best options, military and diplomatic, for countering them, establishing contingency plans to ensure that U.S. forces can maintain or duplicate access to information from space assets and accelerating programs to harden U.S. satellites against attack.[47]

It is premature, at this writing, to speculate exactly how this new direction in space policy will play out, but it is evident that the prior American encouragement for ASATs, and the resistance to new measures of space arms control, will be modified if not directly reversed.

OTHER COUNTRIES' ASAT PROGRAMS AND ATTITUDES

No other country has yet jumped wholeheartedly into an ASAT arms race. Russia, historically the only nation to rival the American presence in outer space, has been crippled by budgetary constraints; until a recent revival, its space operations have been a deteriorating shell of their former glory. Still, Russian Deputy Defense Minister Gen. Valentin Popovkin, observing American and Chinese ASAT exercises, commented, "We can't sit back and quietly watch others doing that; such work is being conducted in Russia."[48]

[46] Hitchens, Katz-Hyman, and Lewis, supra note 22; Bryan Bender, Pentagon Eyeing Weapons in Space, Boston Globe, March 14, 2006, p. 1; John A. Tirpak, Space and Counterspace, 89 Air Force Magazine No. 6, June 2006.

[47] The Agenda: Defense, http://www.whitehouse.gov/issues/defense/. See also Obama '08, Advancing the Frontiers of Space Exploration (campaign statement about space policy).

[48] Russia Pursuing Antisatellite Capability, Global Security Newswire, March 6, 2009.

China certainly seems to be on the precipice of an expanded role in outer space; in 2003, it became the third country to send astronauts into orbit, and by 2020 (if not sooner), China could be the world's number 2 space nation. Beijing's 2007 ASAT interceptor test came as a surprise, but not a shock; in 2005, the U.S. Department of Defense had already concluded that "China is working on, and plans to field, ASAT systems.... China is also conducting research to develop ground-based laser ASAT weapons."[49]

Certainly, Beijing's ambitious civil and commercial space programs will generate or spin off projects, including high-energy lasers, with worrisome military capabilities. Significantly, Chinese defense analyst Wang Hucheng published an article in July 2000 observing that, "For countries that can never win a war with the United States by using the method of tanks and planes, attacking the U.S. space system may be an irresistible and most tempting choice. Part of the reason is that the Pentagon is greatly dependent on space for its military action."[50]

Indeed, not-so-fanciful scenarios about a coming Sino-U.S. confrontation in space have become a staple for prognosticators. They posit that if a future contretemps, such as over Taiwan, turns into a shooting war, Chinese reconnaissance satellites could detect, identify, and track U.S. aircraft carriers and other vessels steaming into the region; satellite guidance could then direct long-range land-to-sea missiles against the fleet. In those circumstances, would the United States feel compelled to protect our forces by attacking the offending Chinese space assets? And would the Chinese, conversely, resist striking American satellites that were assisting the U.S. intervention?[51]

Speculation about a coming space arms race posits that India, for example, might feel compelled to mimic China's emerging ASAT capabilities, and if New Delhi proceeds in that direction, Pakistan might follow – as could Japan and others. Private parties, too, now provide

[49] U.S. Department of Defense, Annual Report to Congress, The Military Power of the People's Republic of China, 2005, p. 36.

[50] Wang Hucheng, The US Military's 'Soft Ribs" and Strategic Weaknesses, Beijing Xinhua Hong Kong Service, July 5, 2000, quoted in China Reform Monitor No. 331, September 12, 2000; see also Hui Zhang, Action/Reaction: U.S. Space Weaponization and China, 35 Arms Control Today No. 10, December 2005, p. 6.

[51] O'Hanlon, supra note 1, at 91–104 (noting that American strikes against the Chinese ground control facilities might be inadequate to prevent ocean surveillance, and that electronic jamming might not fully foreclose China's access to targeting information, so direct attacks (temporarily disabling or permanently destroying) the satellites in orbit might be the most effective U.S. option.

another, novel source of potential antisatellite activity. Hackers, terrorists, or diverse other troublemakers of quixotic motivation may attempt to interfere with normal satellite operations and may occasionally succeed. In the most notorious example, the Falun Gong spiritual group has repeatedly jammed Chinese governmental television broadcasting satellites, inserting several hours of the group's own images and messages to tens of millions of surprised viewers – during the June 2002 World Cup soccer championships, during the October 2003 coverage of China's first manned space mission, and repeatedly since then.

THE LAW OF OUTER SPACE

For such a vast expanse, outer space is populated by relatively little international law.[52] The most important security-related instrument, the 1967 Outer Space Treaty (OST), establishes key "constitutional" principles (e.g., outer space is not susceptible to national claims of sovereignty; international law, including the Charter of the United Nations, applies to outer space; and the peaceful exploration and use of outer space are available to all nations without discrimination).[53]

But the weapons-related aspects of the OST are relatively modest. It establishes two key principles potentially relevant to ASAT operations. First, treaty parties undertake not to place in orbit around the earth, or otherwise to station in outer space, nuclear or other weapons of mass destruction. (Notably, a nuclear weapon making only a temporary *transit* of outer space, as on a direct-ascent ASAT or ICBM en route to its target, is not governed by this provision – it applies only to orbital or long-term deposit of nuclear weapons in space.)

Second, the OST specifies that parties may use the moon and other celestial bodies "exclusively for peaceful purposes" and may not establish military bases, test weapons, or conduct military maneuvers in those locations. Again, however, what is omitted from that ban is as significant

[52] See generally Joanne Gabrynowicz, Space Law: Its Cold War Origins and Challenges in the Era of Globalization, 37 Suffolk University Law Review 1041, 2004; Francis Lyall and Paul B. Larsen, Space Law: A Treatise, 2009; Michel Bourbonniere, Law of Armed Conflict (LOAC) and the Neutralisation of Satellites or *Ius in Bello Satellitis*, 9 Journal of Conflict & Security Law No. 1, 2004, p. 43; Christopher M. Petras, The Debate Over the Weaponization of Space: A Military-Legal Conspectus, 28 Annals of Air and Space Law p. 171, 2003; Francis Lyall and Paul B. Larson (eds.), Space Law (2007).

[53] Treaty on Principles Governing the Activities of States in the Exploration and Use of Outer Space, Including the Moon and Other Celestial Bodies, opened for signature January 27, 1967 (United States is a party).

as what is covered: parties are not restricted from conducting the specified military activities in the void of space, only on the moon or other celestial bodies. An ASAT weapon – ground based or orbital – may therefore lawfully be tested, deployed, and operated in open space (as long as it does not contain a nuclear weapon and is not operated inconsistently with the principles of the U.N. Charter).

The Outer Space Treaty is a remarkably successful instrument; it has now been joined by 98 countries, including all the major spacefaring nations, including the United States, Russia, and China.

Three other bits of treaty law must be noted. First, the 1963 Limited Test Ban Treaty (now accepted by 117 countries, including the United States, Russia, and most of the other nuclear weapons-possessing countries) bans nuclear explosions in outer space. Testing or operation of the original U.S. SAINT program, therefore, would no longer be lawful.

Second, a number of bilateral and multilateral arms control treaties, beginning with the since-abandoned 1972 U.S.-U.S.S.R. Anti-Ballistic Missile Treaty, provide a measure of protection for certain reconnaissance and other satellites embraced within the category of "national technical means of verification." To promote mutual confidence that the disarmament provisions of the treaties are being respected, the parties have agreed to prohibit deliberate interference with those monitoring assets. A party's ASAT strike – whether via kinetic energy or directed energy mechanisms, whether aimed to accomplish a total destruction or merely temporary disruption – against any of those treaty-monitoring satellites, therefore, would be illegal.

Third, the Outer Space Treaty, supplemented by the 1972 Liability Convention, establishes a definitional rule that a state is financially liable for injury or damage inflicted by space objects it launches. For harm to objects on earth or in the air, the liability is absolute (meaning that no excuses will suffice); for harm to satellites in space, the responsibility is based on "fault." In either event, financial liability for accidents inflicted by debris created by a launching state's ASATs could be substantial.

Additionally, it is noteworthy that the leading spacefaring countries have attempted, with singular lack of success, to emplace other, more meaningful, treaty restraints on ASAT activities. In 1978 and 1979, the United States and the Soviet Union danced through three exploratory rounds of ASAT treaty negotiations. They confronted (but never quite resolved) vexing issues such as what should count as an ASAT system (e.g., what to do about the U.S. space shuttle program, which, despite its civilian character, undoubtedly has some ability to undertake hostile action against enemy satellites) and how to verify compliance with a treaty (e.g., tests of ground-based laser ASAT weapons would be hard for the other side to monitor). Talks foundered with the general deterioration in U.S.-Soviet cold war relations. Subsequent efforts during the Reagan Administration to address some of the same issues in the Defense and Space talks similarly sputtered.

The United Nations General Assembly annually adopts, by overwhelming vote, a nonbinding resolution addressing the "Prevention of an Arms Race in Outer Space" (PAROS), to encourage diplomatic initiatives that would resist the trend toward ASATs. The United States has traditionally abstained from this resolution, and in 2005 it became the first government to vote against it. The United Nations also sustains a diplomatic infrastructure in the Geneva-based Conference on Disarmament, standing by to elaborate the principles that could lead to an additional formal treaty; both Russia and China have repeatedly tabled draft PAROS treaties that would embrace ASAT issues. The United States, however, has traditionally demurred (and thereby vetoed the project), arguing that there is no ongoing arms race in space, so the effort to articulate any additional international legal constraints would be premature. In view of the incipient intensification of ASAT activities, however, others consider this judgment unduly sanguine, and again, it remains to be seen how far and how fast the Obama Administration may tack in another direction.[54]

Finally, the fact that terrestrial international law applies, *mutatis mutandis,* to outer space mandates that the law of armed conflict provisions explored in Chapter 3 be construed for ASAT applications. In particular, military forces may not directly target civilian space assets as such unless they take a direct part in hostile activities. Similarly, neutral states' property and other rights in outer space must be respected. Where unintended "collateral damage" may be inflicted upon commercial satellites as a byproduct of a valid attack against enemy military space vehicles, a "proportionality" assessment must weigh the legitimate military value of the strike against the foreseeable losses to noncombatants. Moreover, the legal regime outlaws "indiscriminate" ASAT attacks that cannot differentiate between valid targets and protected civilian or neutral assets; this principle would surely bar the crude nuclear ASAT schemes of the

[54] Vitaly A. Lukiantsev, Enhancing Global Security Through Improved Space Management: A Russian Perspective; Cheng Jingye, Treaties as an Approach to Reducing Space Vulnerabilities; and Eric M. Javits, A U.S. Perspective on Space, in Moltz, supra note 25; Donald A. Mahley, The State of Space Security, address to Space Policy Institute conference, George Washington University, January 24, 2008.

1950s and might also inveigh against any nonnuclear kinetic interceptor that irresponsibly generates massive quantities of longlasting, potentially lethal space debris.

IS SPACE A SANCTUARY?

Many people reject the notion of ASATs or other weaponization of outer space for two complementary sorts of reasons.[55] First, on the philosophical level, many want to sustain a romantic notion that outer space is different from other regions – a little closer to heaven, perhaps – and it ought to be retained as a refuge from earthborne military competition. Other "special areas" – Antarctica, the ocean seabeds – have been carved out by treaty as weapons-free sanctuaries, and perhaps the world can continue to cling to the vision of outer space, too, as a locale that reflects only the noblest, cooperative side of humanity.

Second, on the level of hard-headed practicality, opponents of ASATs observe that the United States currently benefits from and depends upon satellites for both military and civilian operations far more than any other society. We therefore have the most to lose if satellites are exposed to new kinds of threats, and the most to gain if a reliable regime of reciprocal restraint can be created. They concede that if the United States pursues ASAT technology, and opens that cosmic Pandora's Box, we might be able to achieve a temporary unilateral advantage over less technologically advantaged countries, such as Iralia. But the history of the diffusion of all other previous types of weapons technologies suggests that in the longer term, the increasingly useable ASAT capabilities we pioneer today will sooner or later proliferate to our rivals – to our serious disadvantage. It is short-sighted in the extreme, they argue, for the United States to lead the charge into a destabilizing arms race cycle that would turn outer space into a shooting gallery.

On the other side of the argument, ASAT enthusiasts dismiss the philosophical longing for a pristine sanctuary in outer space as just so much wistful wooly thinking. Space, they assert, is just a place – a place that cannot be preserved as virginal. In the words of the modern Johnny Appleseed of ASATs, the Rumsfeld Space Commission,

> [W]e know from history that every medium – air, land and sea – has seen conflict. Reality indicates that space will be no different. Given this

[55] See Karl P. Mueller, Totem and Taboo: Depolarizing the Space Weaponization Debate, in Logsdon and Adams, supra note 1, at 1, for a depiction of six different attitudes toward space as a sanctuary or otherwise.

> virtual certainty, the U.S. must develop the means to deter and to defend against hostile acts in and from space. This will require superior space capabilities.[56]

Moreover, in this view space is not "just another" venue; it may in the future become the decisive medium – the "new high ground" for future conflict. Accordingly, dominance of outer space will be as important in the Information Age as dominance of air and sea was in the Industrial Age. Given the heavy American investment in satellites for peaceful and military applications, it makes sense to protect those satellites against the possibility of hostile action and to prepare to deny an enemy the opportunity to use space effectively against us. In view of the enormous potential advantages of space, even high-minded American self-restraint could provide no guarantee that China or other emerging space powers would be similarly inhibited; they might assiduously pursue secret ASAT programs, seizing an important, useable advantage while we sleep.

In addition, ASAT proponents argue, if the United States ostentatiously develops an effective, reliable ASAT system – one we would not be overly self-deterred against using – that "unbeatable ace" could deter other countries from attempting to enter a space weapons competition. By making that initial investment and effectively occupying the field, the United States might foreclose what could otherwise develop into a more dangerous and destabilizing arms race.

BOTTOM LINE

The peculiar biorhythms of modern life mean that at the same time that some engineers are rapidly developing new civilian devices that enable us to exploit space even more profitably, other engineers are pursuing weapons technologies that could undercut the stability of the space environment. The right hand may know what the left hand is doing, but each is undaunted in pursuing its contradictory solo mission.

To date, the technology of antisatellite weaponry is relatively undeveloped and the world has not yet gotten close to real warfare in space. But that age of innocence is threatened again, and zealous pursuit of ASAT capabilities is high on the agenda for China and for a more assertive U.S. military. At the same moment that Secretary Rumsfeld was wondering whether the U.S. military was "overly dependent" on space, the Pentagon

[56] Rumsfeld Commission Report, supra note 30, p. 100.

was also zealously investigating options that would severely penalize that sort of reliance by others.

A reasonably techno-savvy Iralia, it would seem, might attempt to exploit the American commitment to its cluster of fragile, exposed satellites through nuclear, conventional explosive, electronic, or other means. Disrupting a U.S. military superstructure that has grown accustomed to massive data flows for navigation, communication, targeting, and other indispensable purposes might not swing the tide of war, but it could ensure that the United States pays an unaccustomed cost. Even more predictable, American warfighters would find themselves less self-deterred and more inclined to pull an ASAT trigger if Iralia, too, attempted to exploit satellite links in a fashion that jeopardized U.S. troops and missions.

If space warfare becomes more deft – if third-generation directed energy ASAT mechanisms allow us to challenge a particular enemy satellite without the overkill of nuclear weaponry and without generating plumes of space debris that would jeopardize our own space operations – it automatically becomes more likely. If we have the capability to accomplish a partial or temporary effect on a target, rather than obliterating it completely, the action becomes more acceptable – or, at least, it abates some of the most serious arguments against proceeding.

The ironic result – following the pattern depicted in other chapters – is that a less powerful, less destructive, less lethal weapon offers a more desirable, more useable capability. The kinder, gentler ASAT, accomplishing a soft kill, or even a soft wounding, of an enemy satellite may thus carry us unwittingly into the next era of space competition and warfare.

BIBLIOGRAPHY

Bryan Bender, Pentagon Eyeing Weapons in Space, Boston Globe, March 14, 2006, p. 1

Sam Black, The Rhetoric of the Rumsfeld Space Commission, Center for Defense Information, January 24, 2007

Michel Bourbonniere, Law of Armed Conflict (LOAC) and the Neutralisation of Satellites or *Ius in Bello Satellitis*, 9 Journal of Conflict & Security Law No. 1, 2004, p. 43

William J. Broad, Administration Conducting Research into Laser Weapon, New York Times, May 3, 2006, p. 22

Helen Caldicott and Craig Eisendrath, War in Heaven: The Arms Race and Outer Space, 2007

Ashton Carter, Satellites and Anti-Satellites: The Limits of the Possible, 10 International Security No. 4, Spring 1986, p. 46

Clayton K.S. Chun, Shooting Down a 'Star': Program 437, the US Nuclear ASAT System and Present-Day Copycat Killers, CADRE Paper No. 6, Air University Press, Maxwell Air Force Base, April 2000

Commission to Assess United States National Security Space Management and Organization (Rumsfeld Commission) Report, January 11, 2001

Leonard David, The Clutter Above, 61 Bulletin of the Atomic Scientists No. 4, July/August 2005, p. 32

Everett Dolman, Astropolitik: Classical Geopolitics in the Space Age, 2002

Daniel G. Dupont, Nuclear Explosions in Orbit, Scientific American, June 2004, p. 100

Sandra I. Erwin, Threat to Satellite Signals Fuels Demand for Anti-Jam Products, National Defense, June 2000

Terry Everett, Arguing for a Comprehensive Space Protection Strategy, Strategic Studies Quarterly, Fall 2007, p. 20

Federation of American Scientists, Space Policy Project, Military Space Programs, http://www.fas.org/spp/military/program/asat/overview.htm

Warren Ferster and Colin Clark, NRO Confirms Chinese Laser Test Illuminated U.S. Spacecraft, Space News, October 2, 2006, p. 10

Geoffrey Forden, After China's Test: Time for a Limited Ban on Anti-Satellite Weapons, 37 Arms Control Today No. 3, April 2007, p. 19

John S. Foster, Jr. et al., Report of the Commission to Assess the Threat to the United States from Electromagnetic Pulse (EMP) Attack, 2004

Joanne Gabrynowicz, Space Law: Its Cold War Origins and Challenges in the Era of Globalization, 37 Suffolk University Law Review 1041, 2004

Richard L. Garwin, Kurt Gottfried, and Donald L. Hafner, Anti-Satellite Weapons, 250 Scientific American No. 6, June 1984, p. 45

Bill Gertz, Moscow, Beijing Eye Space Weapons, Washington Times, January 17, 2007, p. 6

Michael R. Gordon and David S. Cloud, U.S. Knew of China Missile Test, But Kept Silent, New York Times, April 23, 2007

Laura Grego, A History of US and Soviet ASAT Programs, Union of Concerned Scientists, April 9, 2003

Eric Hagt, China's ASAT Test: Strategic Response, China Security, Winter 2007, p. 31

Roger G. Harrison, Deron R. Jackson, and Collins G. Shackelford, Space Deterrence: The Delicate Balance of Risk, Eisenhower Center for Space and Defense Studies, 2009

Peter L. Hays, James M. Smith, Alan R. Van Tassel, and Guy M. Walsh (eds.), Spacepower for a New Millennium: Space and U.S. National Security, 2000

Jeff Hecht, US Plans Anti-Satellite Lasers, New Scientist, May 3, 2006

Theresa Hitchens, Michael Katz-Hyman, and Jeffrey Lewis, U.S. Space Weapons: Big Intentions, Little Focus, 13 Nonproliferation Review No. 1, March 2006, p. 35

Theresa Hitchens, Testimony before National Security and Foreign Affairs Subcommittee of the House Oversight and Government Reform Committee, May 23, 2007

Theresa Hitchens, Code Red? Chinese ASAT Test Raises Debris Threat to EO Sats, Imaging Notes, Summer 2007, p. 36
Theresa Hitchens, Space Wars: Coming to the Skies Near You? 298 Scientific American No. 3, March 2008, p. 78
Herman Hoerlin, United States High-Altitude Test Experiences, Los Alamos Scientific Laboratory Monograph, October 1976
David Isenberg, The Newest Anti-Satellite Contender: China's ASAT Test, British American Security Information Council, BASIC Notes, Occasional Paper, March 16, 2007
Joan Johnson-Freese, China's Space Ambitions, IFRI Security Studies Department, Proliferation Papers, Summer 2007
Robert G. Joseph, Remarks on the President's National Space Policy, December 13, 2006.
Shirley Kan, China's Anti-Satellite Weapon Test, Congressional Research Service Report for Congress, RS22652, April 23, 2007
Marc Kaufman and Dafna Linzer, China Criticized for Anti-Satellite Missile Test, Washington Post, January 19, 2007, p. A1
Alane Kochems and Andrew Gudgel, The Viability of Directed-Energy Weapons, Heritage Foundation Backgrounder No. 1931, April 28, 2006
Steven M. Kosiak, Arming the Heavens: A Preliminary Assessment of the Potential Cost and Cost-Effectiveness of Space-Based Weapons, Center for Strategic and Budgetary Assessments, 2007
Michael Krepon with Christopher Clary, Space Assurance or Space Dominance? The Case Against Weaponizing Space, Henry L. Stimson Center, 2003
Michael Krepon and Michael Katz-Hyman, Space Weapons and Proliferation, 12 Nonproliferation Review No. 2, July 2005, p. 323
Jon Kyl, China's Anti-Satellite Weapons and American National Security, Heritage Lectures No. 990, January 29, 2007
Steven Lambakis, On the Edge of the Earth: The Future of American Space Power, 2001
Jeffrey Lewis, What If Space Were Weaponized? Possible Consequences for Crisis Scenarios, Center for Defense Information, July 2004
J.-C. Liou and N.L. Johnson, Risks in Space from Orbiting Debris, 311 Science p. 340, January 20, 2006
John M. Logsdon and Gordon Adams (eds.), Space Weapons: Are They Needed? Space Policy Institute, George Washington University, October 2003
Francis Lyall and Paul B. Larsen (eds.), Space Law, 2007
Francis Lyall and Paul B. Larsen, Space Law: A Treatise, 2009
Donald A. Mahley, The State of Space Security, address to Space Policy Institute conference, George Washington University, January 24, 2008
James Clay Moltz (ed.), Future Security in Space: Commercial, Military, and Arms Control Trade-Offs, Monterey Institute, Center for Nonproliferation Studies, Occasional Paper No. 10, July 2002
Mike Moore, Space War – Now We're Jammin'! 61 Bulletin of the Atomic Scientists No. 2, March/April 2005, p. 6
Matthew Mowthorpe, The Revolution in Military Affairs and Directed Energy Weapons, Air & Space Power Chronicles, March 8, 2002

Vago Muradian, China Tried to Blind U.S. Sats with Laser, Defense News, September 25, 2006, p. 1

James Oberg, Space Power Theory, 1999

Michael E. O'Hanlon, Neither Star Wars Nor Sanctuary: Constraining the Military Uses of Space, 2004

Steven R. Petersen, Space Control and the Role of Anti-Satellite Weapons, Air University Press, Maxwell Air Force Base, Research Report No. AU-ARI-90–7, May 1991

Christopher M. Petras, The Debate Over the Weaponization of Space: A Military-Legal Conspectus, 28 Annals of Air and Space Law p. 171, 2003

John Pike and Eric Stambler, Anti-Satellite Weapons and Arms Control, in Richard Dean Burns (ed.), Encyclopedia of Arms Control and Disarmament, 1993, vol. 2, p. 991

Walter Pincus, The New Art of War, Washington Post, March 3, 2008, p. A15

Jeffrey T. Richelson, The Whole World Is Watching, Bulletin of the Atomic Scientists, January/February 2006, p. 26

Michael Russell Rip and James M. Hasik, The Precision Revolution: GPS and the Future of Aerial Warfare, 2002

Phillip C. Saunders and Charles D. Lutes, China's ASAT Test: Motivations and Implications, Institute for National Strategic Studies, National Defense University, Special Report, June 2007

Nick Schwellenbach, Empty Threat? 61 Bulletin of the Atomic Scientists No. 5, September/October 2005, p. 50

Seven Questions: Space Weapons, Part II, Foreign Policy, August 1, 2005

Bao Shixiu, Deterrence Revisited: Outer Space, China Security, Winter 2007, p. 2

Jeremy Singer, USAF Interest in Lasers Triggers Concerns About Anti-Satellite Weapons, 17 Space News, May 1, 2006

Space Security 2007, spacesecurity.org

William L. Spacy II, Does the United States Need Space-Based Weapons? CADRE Paper, College of Aerospace Doctrine, Research, and Education, Air University, September 1999

Paul B. Stares, The Militarization of Space: U.S. Policy, 1945–1984 (1985)

Ian Steer, High-Altitude Nuclear Explosions: Blind, Deaf and Dumb, Jane's Defence Weekly, October 23, 2002

Henry L. Stimson Center, Space Security or Space Weapons? A Guide to the Issues, 2005

Arjun Tan, Gautam D. Badhwar, Firooz A. Allahdadi and David F. Medina, Analysis of the Solwind Fragmentation Event Using Theory and Computations, 33 Journal of Spacecraft and Rockets No. 1, January/February 1996, p. 79

Michael W. Taylor, Orbital Debris: Technical and Legal Issues and Solutions, thesis at Institute of Air and Space Law, McGill University, August 2006

Ashley J. Tellis, Punching the U.S. Military's 'Soft Ribs': China's Anti-Satellite Weapon Test in Strategic Perspective, Carnegie Endowment for International Peace Policy Brief No. 51, June 2007

Ashley J. Tellis, China's Military Space Strategy, 49 Survival No. 3, Autumn 2007, p. 41

John A. Tirpak, Space and Counterspace, 89 Air Force Magazine No. 6, June 2006

Union of Concerned Scientists, Space Weapons and Technical Issues: Debris from China's Kinetic Energy ASAT Test, May, 2007

United Nations, Technical Report on Space Debris, Report adopted by the Scientific and Technical Subcommittee of the Committee on the Peaceful Uses of Outer Space, A/AC.105/720, 1999

U.S. Air Force, Counterspace Operations, Air Force Doctrine Document 2–2.1, August 2, 2004

U.S. Air Force, Space Operations, Doctrine Document 2–2, November 27, 2006

U.S. Air Force Space Command, Strategic Master Plan FY04 and Beyond, November 5, 2002

U.S. Air Force Space Command, Satellite Operations, Instruction 10–1204, June 1, 2006

U.S. Congress, Office of Technology Assessment, Anti-Satellite Weapons, Countermeasures, and Arms Control, OTA-ISC-281, September 1985

U.S. Department of Defense, The Military Power of the People's Republic of China, 2005, Annual Report to Congress

U.S. Department of Defense, Military Power of the People's Republic of China, 2007, Annual Report to Congress

U.S. National Space Policy, authorized August 31, 2006

Elizabeth S. Waldrop, Weaponization of Outer Space: US National Policy, 26 Annals of Air and Space Law p. 329, 2004

Barry D. Watts, The Military Use of Space: A Diagnostic Assessment, Center for Strategic and Budgetary Assessments, February 2001

The White House, Office of Science and Technology Policy, Interagency Report on Orbital Debris, November 1995

The White House, National Science and Technology Council, Fact Sheet: National Space Policy, September 19, 1996

The White House, The Agenda: Defense, http://www.whitehouse.gov/issues/defense/

Christopher D. Williams, Space: The Cluttered Frontier, 60 Journal of Air Law & Commerce p. 1139, 1995

Clay Wilson, High Altitude Electromagnetic Pulse (HEMP) and High Power Microwave (HPM) Devices: Threat Assessments, Congressional Research Service Report for Congress, RL32544, April 14, 2006

George C. Wilson, Mr. Smith's Crusade, National Journal, August 11, 2001, p. 2542

David Wright and Laura Grego, Anti-Satellite Capabilities of Planned US Missile Defence Systems, 68 Disarmament Diplomacy, December 2002-January 2003

David Wright, Laura Grego and Lisbeth Gronlund, The Physics of Space Security: A Reference Manual, 2005

Hui Zhang, Action/Reaction: U.S. Space Weaponization and China, 35 Arms Control Today No. 10, December 2005, p. 6

Peter D. Zimmerman and Charles D. Ferguson, Sweeping the Skies, 59 Bulletin of the Atomic Scientists No. 6, November/December 2003, p. 57

TREATIES

Treaty Banning Nuclear Weapons Tests in the Atmosphere, in Outer Space and Under Water, signed August 5, 1963, 14 U.S.T. 1313, 480 U.N.T.S. 43, T.I.A.S. No. 5433 (entered into force October 10, 1963) [LTBT]

Treaty on Principles Governing the Activities of States in the Exploration and Use of Outer Space, Including the Moon and Other Celestial Bodies, January 27, 1967, 18 U.S.T. 2410, 610 U.N.T.S. 205, T.I.A.S. No. 6347 (entered into force October 10, 1967) [Outer Space Treaty or OST]

8

Nonlethal Weapons

Scenario 8

The beautiful but desperately poor and long-tumultuous nation of Ethalia is in chaos again. The previous government, whose grasp on control was always tenuous at best, collapsed in disarray months ago, ceding practical authority to half a dozen thuggish warlords; their ill-defined clan-based rivalry now erupts in daily bloodshed. The ubiquitous competing gangs – they are hardly organized or coherent enough to be characterized as forces engaged in a civil war – wreak perpetual havoc in the capital city and much of the surrounding countryside. The armaments of choice, mostly small arms and light weapons, have proliferated widely, and squads of irregular, nonuniformed fighters intermittently patrol the main streets, setting up roadblocks to search for rivals, to recruit or impress new members, and to extort money from civilians. The national economy has ground virtually to a halt and the civilian infrastructure is crumbling, resulting in widespread hunger, now approaching starvation levels. Outbreaks of infectious diseases, especially malaria, are also surging, as massive flows of refugees collect in ad hoc, poorly administered, and increasingly squalid encampments.

Pursuant to an emergency resolution by the United Nations Security Council, the United States has undertaken a limited intervention mission, with an expeditionary force of 2200 Marines dispatched to Ethalia in pursuit of three articulated goals: (a) to protect the skeleton staff of U.S. and U.N. diplomats who remain at their posts and the few hundred private citizen foreigners (mostly Americans, but several European and other nationals, too) who have chosen not to evacuate; (b) to safeguard the American embassy, which now serves as the Marines' own base, and to the extent possible, protect other nations' embassies and foreign-owned private corporate and nongovernmental organization properties, too; and (c) to establish and operate a relief center for the distressed population, providing life-sustaining food, water, shelter, and medicine to displaced persons within a circumscribed safety zone.

The Marines deploy into the capital without incident, swiftly secure their position inside embassy grounds, and define the perimeter of a safe haven nearby. The next day, the first trucks bearing quantities of "MREs" (meals ready to eat) and tankers laden with potable water are scheduled to arrive, beginning the process of emergency assistance to the locals. When word of the impending relief leaks out, huge crowds instantly assemble; it immediately becomes obvious that the proffered supplies will be vastly insufficient to meet the demand.

Shortly after noon, the first two relief trucks arrive in the scorching summer heat of the parched city. As they inch their way through traffic into the city's central plaza, hordes of distraught civilians clamor for food and water. The mass of humanity quickly forces the drivers to stop the trucks, and people begin to climb onto and into the vehicles, intent on ripping into the desperately needed supplies. The American drivers and the few accompanying guards attempt to restore order, but the hungry crowd largely disregards their instructions. Several unintimidated young men are the first to reach the MREs, and they begin tossing them to their friends on the ground – some of whom brandish rifles and machetes to keep the other people at bay – and loading quantities of them into their own jeeps.

At the same time, another crowd of several hundred Ethalians approaches the U.S. embassy site, now guarded by a contingent of wary Marines. The crowd seems to contain a broad cross-section of the local population – men, women, children of all ages – and they ignore the Marines' megaphone instructions to stay back. Some in the crowd shout their pleas for immediate, large-scale humanitarian assistance; others demand that the Americans and other foreigners immediately go home. When the embassy offers no response, the crowd becomes, in increasing measure, frustrated, agitated, emboldened, and downright hostile. Angry chanting begins, and a few rocks are thrown, ineffectually, against the embassy gates, while the Marines apprehensively look on. Suddenly, two shots of rifle fire ring out from the crowd.

What should U.S. military forces do in these compromised predicaments? Obviously, it is unacceptable to stand by and do nothing when valuable assets are jeopardized, when relief supplies intended for the population generally are stolen and appropriated by gangs, and when an embassy or base comes under hostile fire. On the other hand, it is just as unacceptable to loose lethal gunfire on a civilian crowd, killing or injuring the very people we are there to aid, and inflicting mass casualties in response to what might be a small number of truly hostile armed antagonists. But when the Marines are so outnumbered, and when the indigenous population mob refuses to obey even the most emphatic and reasonable orders to desist, what level of force (in self-defense, or to protect supplies and property) is warranted? What means do our troops have to diffuse these bewildering "Escalation of Force" scenarios in which the application of lethal power appears both imminent and disastrous?

NONLETHAL WEAPONS

New technology may now (or soon) offer at least a partial solution to this oft-repeated dilemma. A family of so-called "nonlethal weapons" (NLW) is emerging, as yet another aspect of the ongoing revolution in military affairs, to promise a more refined military capability for dealing with low-level but highly unstable threats such as those depicted in Scenario 8, allowing a response calibrated to be intermediate or moderate, landing somewhere "between bullhorns and bullets."

To many people (both inside and outside the defense establishment), the very concept of nonlethal weapons may appear as self-contradiction, or even as apostasy – the traditional role of the military, they assert, is "to kill people and break things," and any "softer" approaches will soon degrade the fighting force and detract from its capability to perform those core missions.

Nonetheless, NLW are for real; millions of dollars of research and development are poured annually into inventing and procuring them, and no less than the U.S. Marine Corps has been designated as the Pentagon's lead authority (the "executive agent") for overseeing and coordinating the myriad joint nonlethal weapons development programs. All this activity is in recognition of the fact that, often, it is possible – and perhaps it is even more advantageous – to defeat an opponent without killing him and to neutralize enemy equipment and property without totally ripping it asunder. A soldier who has been temporarily disabled or disarmed, or an irregular streetfighter who has been disoriented, isolated, or captured, may no longer be so much of a threat; NLW may thus spare a life while still accomplishing the military objective of defeating or counteracting the opposition. Likewise, a troop transport, an urban bridge, or an oil refinery (all of which have undoubted military utility, making them valid targets in warfare) might be effectively denied to the opposing army via advanced NLW without catastrophically destroying them – thereby preserving them for benign civilian applications during a postwar peacetime recovery period.[1]

TRADITIONAL NONLETHAL TECHNOLOGIES – STRENGTHS AND WEAKNESSES

Some types of NLW are already familiar, having been incorporated over a period of decades into the arsenals of military units around the world (or, even more frequently, used by domestic police forces in many countries for local law enforcement and riot control purposes).[2]

Water cannon, for example, will be familiar from the civil rights demonstrations and antiwar protests in the United States (and their counterparts elsewhere) during the 1960s and 1970s. The concept was to use blasts from high-pressure fire hoses to disperse a crowd, to drive the participants away from prominent city squares and other high-value locations, and to douse the participants' spirits as well as their bodies. Generations of tear gas have served much the same function; law enforcement uses noxious sprays and canisters to sow confusion (as well as pain), to disaggregate mobs, and to deter the more faint-hearted from persisting in the group activity. At shorter ranges, authorities have applied other types of systems to control particular individuals: snarling police guard dogs, for example, or electric shock "cattle prods" can compel people to move away (or to stay put) and to comply with shouted orders.

In each case, the concept was for the police to exert their influence in a deliberately nonlethal fashion. That is, infliction of pain, nausea, fear, isolation, or confusion was the tactic; some measure of temporary injury

[1] Regarding the evolution of nonlethal weapons, see generally: Bradford NonLethal Weapons Research Project, Centre for Conflict Resolution, Department of Peace Studies, University of Bradford (U.K.), http://www.brad.ac.uk/acad/nlw/; U.S. Department of Defense, Joint Non-Lethal Weapons Directorate, https://www.jnlwp.com/; and Council on Foreign Relations, Nonlethal Weapons and Capabilities, Report of an Independent Task Force, Graham Allison and Paul X. Kelley, Co-Chairs, Richard L. Garwin, Project Director, 2004.

[2] Neil Davison and Nick Lewer, Bradford Non-Lethal Weapons Research Project, Centre for Conflict Resolution, Department of Peace Studies, University of Bradford (U.K.), Research Report No. 8, March 2006; Neil Davison, The Contemporary Development of 'Non-Lethal' Weapons, Bradford Non-Lethal Weapons Research Project, Centre for Conflict Resolution, Department of Peace Studies, University of Bradford (U.K.), Occasional Paper No. 3, May 2007; Greg R. Schneider, Nonlethal Weapons: Considerations for Decision Makers, University of Illinois at Urbana-Champaign, Program in Arms Control, Disarmament, and International Security, ACDIS Occasional Paper, January 1997.

might result, but, at least ordinarily, not death or severe bodily harm. All too often, of course, that moderate expectation was frustrated, as the devices were too crude and too powerful, or as authorities wielded them in an inexpert or malicious fashion, and lethal effects were inflicted. In the United States, in Northern Ireland, in the Middle East, and elsewhere, the articulated goal was "the 5 Ds": to deter, dissuade, disrupt, disorient, and defeat – but more than a few deaths resulted, too.

Perhaps the largest category of traditional police NLW comprises blunt impact or trauma devices. These include the truncheon or nightstick (and any other apparatus that could be swung in like manner, such as a heavy metal flashlight); more exotic applications include nunchakus (weapons of Japanese origin, consisting of two hard wooden sticks connected by a short chain or rope). For longer-range NLW impact functions, firearms (handguns as well as rifles) could be outfitted to shoot, instead of the usual deadly bullets, rubber, plastic, or wooden plugs or cloth "beanbags" of various configuration, designed to surprise, impress, and hurt, but not to kill. Again, however, there could be no guaranties: if the munition struck a particularly vulnerable (old, young, or frail) person, or if it impacted a sensitive body part (such as the face or neck), serious harm or death could occur. (For many firearms, a critical variable is the distance the ballistic projectile is expected to fly before it hits the target: to be effective and accurate at long range, the slug has to be traveling at high velocity when it first leaves the muzzle of the gun – but then, if the impact happens to occur at less than the intended distance, the speed (and accordingly the kinetic power of the punch) will be much higher than necessary, perhaps resulting in greater, unintended consequences.)

These early manifestations of nonlethal weaponry have been regularly supplemented and improved over the years. Tear gas, mace, and comparable chemical concoctions gave way to pepper spray (technically, *oleoresin capsaicin* or OC), derived from natural pepper plants (or artificial analogues). Pepper spray is much faster-acting and more powerful than tear gas, inflaming the mucous membranes so quickly and thoroughly as to overcome even the most determined resistors (including those under the influence of alcohol or drugs that might put them beyond the reach of tear gas).

Exploiting a different NLW mechanism – electricity – are stun guns of various design. For example, the Taser brand (a playful acronym for Thomas A. Swift's Electric Rifle) fires two small barbed darts from a handheld device resembling a pistol. The darts trail very thin wires back to the handset, which contains a powerful battery. When the darts hit a target, the barbs affix to clothing or skin and 50,000 volts are released, coursing through the victim for up to five seconds. A charge of this sort momentarily paralyzes the skeletal musculature, causing the person to lose physical control and usually to collapse in a heap. Again, even strong and highly motivated people, and those under the influence of drugs, are unable to fight through the taser's neuromuscular incapacitation and pain. The victim may regain strength and composure within a few seconds after the electric charge ends, but by that point the police should have been able to take custody (and the user can reinitiate a second jolt, if necessary). Current versions of the weapon are effective only to about 35 feet, the length of the darts' wires; longer-range alternatives (including possibly wireless "area denial" variants capable of stopping groups of people within a range of 100 meters) are under development. According to the manufacturer, 390,000 tasers have been sold to 13,900 law enforcement, corrections, and military agencies in the United States and 40 other countries, as well as to the U.S. military, including for operations in Iraq.[3]

Again, critics vigorously contest whether OC, tasers, and the rest of these gizmos actually deserve the title "nonlethal," and hundreds of instances have been identified in which an individual died following exposure to pepper spray or electric stun guns. The manufacturers have vigorously rebutted those allegations, asserting that most or all of the fatalities should properly be ascribed to other causes, especially alcohol, illegal drugs, or excited delirium, and in virtually all cases, medical examiners have ruled that the law enforcement tools were not the primary cause of death. Tasers, in particular, have been scrutinized in reams of independent scientific research reports from governmental and private laboratories in the United States, Canada, the United Kingdom, and elsewhere. Still, critics such as Amnesty International are not satisfied with the existing level of safety-related research and testing, which has not incorporated all the rigorous human effects assessments that the Department of Defense has applied in other contexts. Too much of the "research" so far has involved police and other volunteers shooting the device at each other, observing ruefully that, "It sure hurts, but I'm still alive," and concluding that the weapon should therefore be suitable for use on the streets.[4]

Other deficiencies plague existing NLW, too. Many systems, for example, are effective only at short range – police have to come within arm's reach to use a baton or a cattle prod – and that proximity could be

[3] Occasional Paper No. 3, supra note 2, at 30.

[4] Amnesty International, United States of America: Excessive and Lethal Force? Amnesty International's Concerns About Deaths and Ill-Treatment Involving Police Use of Tasers, 2004.

dangerous in situations such as Scenario 8, in which military or law enforcement authorities are vastly outnumbered. A weapon's "rate of fire" is an issue, too. Taser devices might work to keep a particular individual under control – a specific young man who was climbing onto a truck to steal supplies – but would not be capable of sufficiently wide coverage to deal simultaneously with large clusters of onrushing people.

Other tools are indiscriminate or imprecise – chemical sprays, for example, can dissipate in the rain or drift with the breeze, erratically contaminating innocent bystanders or even blowing back onto the police or military themselves. In the hypothetical case of Ethalia, for example, it might be effective to pepper spray the crowd around the relief trucks or the assemblage outside the embassy gates – but only if wind, temperature, and humidity could be counted upon to remain favorable. In addition, in response to some traditional nonlethal weapons, the putative target can adopt simple self-protective measures, such as gas masks, to evade or blunt the effect. Rudimentary shields, perhaps available even in Ethalia, may be able to negate the force of a water cannon, or even of low-impact bullets, dissipating the kinetic energy with minimal effect.

NEW GENERATIONS OF NONLETHAL WEAPONS – SOMETHING NEW UNDER THE SUN

Weapons designers have taken these challenges to heart and have begun to respond with a cornucopia of dazzling new NLW technologies. No one of them can solve all the problems – there is, and probably never can be, a perfect weapon suitable for all situations. But the eclectic mechanisms now emerging from design laboratories will greatly amplify the effective power of the military in these sensitive and urgent situations.

Among the first NLW innovations to capture 15 minutes of fame were slippery foam and sticky foam. The former would be projected as a liquid or gel from a hose or spray tank; it would quickly spread over a flat surface, such as the Ethalian plaza in front of the American embassy, to form a super-slick coating. The glaze would be durable, and much, much more slippery than the shiniest ice sheet. People could not walk or stand on it; vehicles, too, would lose all traction. The crowd could hardly advance against the embassy under those conditions (they would have a hard time withdrawing, too); concerted and coordinated opposition activities would quickly break down. Sticky foam would utilize the opposite principle – it would shoot out from a nozzle (probably to a relatively short range) and quickly harden upon contact. It would envelop the targeted person with a polymer goo that promptly solidified into a rigid, Styrofoam-like immobilizing straightjacket, precluding movement.

Unfortunately, both these concepts still need work. Sticky foam, for example, is too uncontrollable; as it expands over the targeted person, it might flow into the nose and mouth, choking off airways. It still has promise for antimateriel and antivehicle operations (spraying it into the engine block or the driver compartment would disable the jeeps driven by the young hotheads stealing the MREs, for example). Slippery foam is more promising – researchers still consider the superlubricant a viable mechanism for putting a railyard, dock, airstrip, or bridge out of commission temporarily without permanently destroying it. But the interruption on pedestrian and vehicle traffic may be *too* temporary – the slippery sheen could be washed away or covered with dirt or sand to restore traction quickly.

Other novel chemicals might be of use in Scenario 8. One promising concept for "malodorants" would unleash upon the crowd a witches' brew of the foulest smells imaginable – the aromas of fecal material, rotting flesh, burning sulfur, and anything else calculated to most annoy, offend, and repel the target. Unlike tear gas or OC, these malodorants would not have a direct disabling physical effect (and they should, therefore, generate fewer concerns about physical safety). But they could be concocted to be incredibly, irresistibly annoying, and would surely have the effect of driving away anyone not absolutely committed to the enterprise and not equipped with special breathing apparatus.

NLW systems undertake antivehicle, as well as antipersonnel, missions. Novel barrier systems, for example, feature rapidly installed barbed or concertina wire fencing or a carpet of caltrops (spiked pyramids that can puncture vehicle tires). Projectile netting of various sorts can likewise be used to capture and immobilize their prey. To halt a person (either fleeing or advancing) a small rope net can be fired from a shotgun-like weapon; it tightly ensnares the individual, effectively inhibiting movement without inflicting serious injury. For cars and trucks (e.g., those approaching a contested checkpoint on a highway), a larger, stronger system can be embedded in the roadway. The current version, denominated Portable Vehicle Arresting Barrier, is capable of safely stopping within 200 feet a 7500-pound truck traveling 45 miles per hour. Soldiers positioned in front of an embassy or military base in Ethalia may not know whether an oncoming vehicle is driven by a suicidal terrorist or by an innocent civilian. If the driver fails to obey signs, signals, and verbal warning to stop or turn away, the guards may not know whether the intent is hostile (and lethal action would be warranted, even demanded, to stop it) or whether the driver was simply inattentive, uncomprehending, scared, or drunk. A netting mechanism that reliably but safely captures the vehicle before it can reach a danger zone may allow the guards the luxury of time for additional investigation.

A different sort of nonlethal technology for comparable applications is provided by a "dazzling laser," which projects an intense beam of focused green light to 200 meters to arrest a driver's attention when approaching a checkpoint too rapidly. Unmistakably threatening and impossible to ignore, the laser glare forces the driver to reveal his or her intentions – either slowing and changing course or alerting the soldiers to a significant threat. These vehicle checkpoint confrontations are a genuine problem in Iraq today; according to coalition military sources, some 250 innocent Iraqis have been killed at those locations due to soldiers reacting vigorously to the ambiguity of their behavior, and in 2006, an average of eight times per day American soldiers were forced to shoot lethal firearms to attempt to stop vehicles that advanced too closely. Laser dazzlers are designed to ward off and clarify those types of provocations without causing permanent damage to eyes – but even if there were some level of danger to sight, as Lt. Gen. Peter Chiarelli, the commander in Iraq put it, "I have no doubt that bullets are less safe."[5]

Perhaps the most intriguing new nonlethal weapons technology is the Active Denial System (ADS), an antipersonnel device that projects a millimeter wave energy beam from a parabolic dish mounted on top of a Humvee or comparable flatbed combat vehicle. The beam – invisible and inaudible, traveling at the speed of light – causes everyone it hits to feel as if they're being intensely burned. But because the millimeter wave penetrates the skin so shallowly (only 1/64 of an inch) it does not, in fact, burn or cause any other damage. The heat sensation is so intense (comparable to touching a glowing light bulb with your bare finger) that no one can resist – the targeted person must reflexively withdraw or buckle under the pain – but the sensation ceases almost immediately after the waves are aimed elsewhere.

The ADS device is capable of a remarkable range – a kilometer or more – enabling the user to achieve a "standoff" capability, that is, to have a powerful effect while remaining outside the reach of an opponent's small arms fire. The beam effectively penetrates even heavy clothing or other types of cover. It has been thoroughly tested for safety, too – 10,000

[5] James Rainey, A Safer Weapon, With Risks, Los Angeles Times, May 18, 2006.

people have been exposed to the heat rays over 12 years of research – and it does not damage skin, genitals, eyes, or internal organs.

The first ADS, perhaps mounted on multifunction transports denominated Sheriffs or Silent Guardians, has been slated for deployment in Iraq, but the operation has been repeatedly delayed – the system now may not have its initial operating capacity until 2010. In a setting such as Scenario 8, the ADS could enable the Marine guards around the embassy to keep rioters at bay; they could respond to the two gunshots not with a return of lethal fire but by slewing the beam across the crowd and inflicting temporary pain. Even if some of the most determined antagonists could find a way to shelter themselves from the millimeter wave, most innocent bystanders could not; the ordinary civilians would flee, uninjured, thereby isolating the hostiles and simplifying the situation.[6]

Other novel nonlethal systems are also under development – enough to overfill a futuristic weapons bazaar. In the chemical realm, many have expressed special interest in the concept of a "calmative" potion – a gaseous knockout formula that could be surreptitiously introduced into hostage or barricade situations. (The 2002 seizure of the Moscow theater by Chechen terrorists comes to mind.)[7] The chemical would slow, sedate, or render unconscious everyone – terrorists and victims alike – allowing the rescuers to swoop in without gunfire. Of course, finding a concoction that quickly depresses hostile functioning without simultaneously endangering human life processes has, to date, proven to be an insurmountable barrier, but scientists are not giving up.

[6] Joint Non-Lethal Weapons Program, Active Denial System (ADS) Fact Sheet, March 2007; Associated Press, Pentagon Nixes Ray Gun Weapon in Iraq, August 29, 2007.

[7] On October 23, 2002, approximately 50 Chechen terrorists seized the Dubrovka Theater in Moscow during a performance, took nearly 800 audience, cast and crew members hostage, and emplaced deadly explosives in their midst. After three days of fruitless negotiations, Russian special forces units injected quantities of sedative gases (probably fentanyl) through the ventilation system and mounted an explosive assault, retaking the theater and killing all the terrorists. In the process, some 125 hostages succumbed to the respiration-suppressing effects of the fentanyl – and analysts still debate whether the loss of 15 percent of the hostages was a success or failure, in view of the terrorists' apparent determination to play the script to an explosively lethal conclusion. See Robin M. Coupland, Incapacitating Chemical Weapons: A Year After the Moscow Theatre Siege, 362 Lancet p. 1346, October 25, 2003; David P. Fidler, The Meaning of Moscow: 'Non-lethal' Weapons and International Law in the Early 21st Century, 87 International Review of the Red Cross No. 859, September 2005; Monterey Institute of International Studies, Chemical and Biological Weapons Nonproliferation Program, The Moscow Theater Hostage Crisis: Incapacitants and Chemical Warfare, November 4, 2002; Nikolaus von Twickel, Unmasking Dubrovka's Mysterious Gas, Moscow Times, October 23, 2007, p. 1.

Another candidate technology is acoustic: audible or inaudible sound waves that could (under various concepts) disturb internal organs with nausea-inducing (but not harmful) frequencies; pack a shock wave punch, comparable to that of a nonlethal impact munition; or simply use volume and pitch to annoy and drive away unprotected rioters (systems evocatively named "Screamer" and "Curdler" are already in use). Again, most of these concepts are not yet ready for prime time; in particular, the unmet challenges include making the sound waves sufficiently controllable and directional so they can be selectively steered toward the target without impacting our own forces.[8]

Other proposed antimateriel NLW systems would employ microwave projectors to shut down the microprocessors essential to the operation of modern cars and trucks, enabling security guards to intercept oncoming vehicles at the flick of a switch. Perhaps even tanks and armored personnel carriers could be swiftly and nondestructively halted in their tracks this way. Other scientists have also investigated supercaustic chemicals that could be clandestinely sprayed onto enemy vehicles to render them (unbeknownst to the owner) more fragile and more vulnerable in combat. The biological equivalent would be the genetic engineering of novel bacteria that could invisibly attack and corrode or contaminate an enemy's military resources; strategic petroleum reserves might be be particularly vulnerable to this sort of sabotage, as well as perhaps the tires, gaskets, and insulated wires of vehicles.

The next generation of NLW systems, mated with the incipient products of other military-technical innovation, could be even more jaw-dropping. Robotics, for example, has already given us inquisitive mobile devices that can help detect, identify, and disarm improvised explosive devices (IEDs) in Iraq. Likewise, miniature unmanned aerial vehicles (UAVs) and their underwater submersible cousins can unostentatiously monitor suspicious activities and dispense sudden weapons. As the devices become even smaller and more stealthy – the next frontier will be nanotechnology, building weapons bit by bit from the atomic scale – the horizons for NLW, as for lethal effects, will be revolutionary.

The United States military, under the aegis of the Marine Corps' Joint NonLethal Weapons Directorate is vigorously exploring a full roster of possible NLW innovations. The Pentagon now devotes approximately $65 million per year to the Joint Directorate, and kicks an equal amount to the individual military services' NLW research and development

[8] Caroline Graham, Blitzed, The Mail (U.K.), November 13, 2005.

programs. A nascent "military-industrial complex" has arisen in nonlethal weapons as a growing number of companies (especially small entrepreneurs) invent or refine the NLW tools for the trade. Then-Secretary of Defense Donald Rumsfeld called in 2006 for his staff to prepare a new investment plan for future NLW technologies, which could lead to a doubling of current spending levels. Outside the military sector, the U.S. Department of Justice has long served as the catalyst for law enforcement experimentation with NLW, and the Department of Homeland Security has also begun to invest increasingly in nonlethal devices for domestic applications.[9]

Other countries, too, are dipping cautious toes into the realm of NLW. NATO members have been swept along with the U.S. enthusiasts, and Russia has also announced that selected antiterrorism and other Army and Navy units will henceforth be equipped with indigenously produced NLW, as well as traditional Kalashnikov automatic rifles.

Still, critics assert that progress has been slow in bringing new NLW forward from the drawing board into the operational field. Advocates have touted diverse acoustic, microwave, chemical and other NLW candidate technologies for years, but it remains a boutique industry, carrying relatively little impact upon the actual patterns of combat. The Government Accountability Office vividly displayed the shortcomings, finding that the Department of Defense had spent $817 million in various nonlethal weapons programs between 1997 and 2008, with almost nothing (other than a few commercially available products) showing up on the battlefields.

To gain acceptance, nonlethal weapons need promptly to demonstrate a special ability to supplement traditional military tools by offering a new capability: the ability to intervene in delicate situations with sufficient power to influence the outcome, but also with sufficient deftness to be useable where conventional – that is, lethal – force is just too much.

MILITARY OPERATIONS OTHER THAN WAR

Occasions such as those in Scenario 8 are ineffably complicated because of their mixed character – civilians and belligerents, looters and refugees, all occupy the same space; forceful action by the Marines risks killing or injuring hostages, victims, and noncombatants. This is a most uncomfortable posture for the traditional military units – it is certainly a far

[9] Jason Sherman, DoD: Spend More on Non-Lethal Weapons, InsideDefense.com, May 23, 2006.

cry from the familiar missions of large-scale force-on-force combat that characterized World War II, the Korean War, and even much of the Vietnam conflict.

Although that kind of "old-fashioned" warfare has not disappeared – there are plenty of combat zones around the world that still resemble, to some extent, the isolated and relatively static battle lines of prior eras – a new genre of military mission has frequently displaced it. The vocabulary of Military Operations Other Than War (MOOTW) is Pentagon-speak for a variety of situations in which the fighting force has been tasked with a more complicated mandate. And the frequency of MOOTW is increasing.

Peacekeeping, for example, may require some of the same weapons and tactics as conventional warfighting – but there are profound differences, too. Peacekeepers (under the auspices of the United Nations or otherwise) are inserted into a recently quieted zone at the (perhaps grudging) request of the erstwhile warring forces. The mandate of the peacekeepers is usually to maintain a physical buffer, separating the combatants, keeping a lid on the situation, and interrupting the cycle of violence. The peacekeepers must ordinarily be at least lightly armed, for self-defense – it can be quite a dangerous mission – but the goal is to avoid gunplay and any escalation of force. NLW such as tasers and ADS may permit intervening forces to respond to dangerous provocations without "upping the ante" by invoking more firepower than necessary.

The pilot program for this sort of operation was undertaken by Lt. Gen. Anthony C. Zinni in Somalia in 1995. Tasked with protecting the withdrawal of United Nations peacekeeping troops from Mogadishu – and wary about inciting the locals to further levels of violence against departing foreigners – Zinni outfitted his Marines with an array of novel NLW (in addition, of course, to their full complement of lethal force). Sticky foam, laser dazzlers, beanbag or wooden bullets, chemical riot-control agents, and similar accoutrements were marvelously successful in keeping at bay the curious and dangerous indigenous gangs, enabling smooth, essentially nonviolent completion of the mission. Reflecting on this precedent-setting accomplishment, Zinni commented, "I think the whole nature of warfare is changing."[10]

Rendering humanitarian assistance to the victims of a natural or man-made disaster is another increasingly frequent MOOTW. Again, it is not quite a military mission, but, again, often only the military can perform it.

[10] Quoted in Rick Atkinson, Lean, Not-So-Mean Marines Set for Somalia, Washington Post, February 25, 1995, p. A22.

American armed forces have unique access to the personnel, airlift resources, and organizational talent to be able to reach remote locations swiftly and provide life-sustaining assistance to the victims of flood, famine, or disease. But, as in Scenario 8, even these aid missions may require some element of force, at least to protect against the most venal elements who would siphon assistance away from those most in need. Machine guns and rifles (to say nothing of tanks and aircraft) are simply too powerful to play much of a role in these contexts, and we would rightly be self-deterred against using them. In addition to "precision," the weapons of choice should offer less deadly approaches, and NLW may provide a capacity for doing something meaningful against the looters without doing too much.

Other types of MOOTW include international counterterrorism operations and counterdrug missions. Both are of increasing importance and frequency for the American military these days, and both require a careful mixture of finesse (because there may be civilians, hostages, or others who need protection in the midst of the bad guys) and armed force (because the bad guys might shoot back). Again, nonlethal weapons can provide some of that more useable combined capability, allowing operations of the requisite deftness.

One recent illustration (drawn from police rather than military action as part of the broad antiterrorism campaign) demonstrates the attraction of NLW in contested, controversial settings. In 2005, in response to horrific terrorist bombings on the London subway and bus system, U.K. police felt compelled to act with greater vigor and dispatch against anyone who might pose a suicide bomb threat on the Underground. So they armed themselves with an array of lethal weaponry and adopted an unaccustomed "shoot to kill" policy. Predictably, a tragic mistake soon followed, as an undercover surveillance team and its marksman colleagues failed to communicate properly, and 27-year-old Jean Charles de Menezes, an innocent Brazilian with no connections to or intentions toward terrorism, was mistakenly shot to death on July 22, 2005.[11]

In the aftermath, British officials skeptically reviewed their new policies regarding use of force, and questioned, in particular, whether nonlethal weapons (existing or to be developed) could be applied to quickly and

[11] Doubt Over Shoot-to-Kill Policy, The Independent (U.K.), August 21, 2005; David Williams and Stephen Wright, Tragic Trail of Police Blunders Over Shooting, Daily Mail (U.K.), August 17, 2005; Jean Charles de Menezes: In the Wrong Place. At the Wrong Time, The Independent (U.K.), July 25, 2005.

reliably incapacitate a suspected suicide bomber without resorting to deadly force – rescuing the police from their dilemma and providing a margin of safety to the public. In the absence of that sort of less deadly capacity, what should authorities do when confronting an ambiguous situation? Traditional police tools are either too powerful (resulting in tragedies like Mr. de Menezes's when misused) or too weak (resulting in other catastrophes when real terrorists strike). Inadequate military weaponry can pose the same type of Hobson's choice: self-deterrence (an underreaction to the stimulus) or application of excessive force (overreaction).

NONLETHAL WEAPONS IN LARGE-SCALE COMBAT

Even in traditional, large-scale combat, new nonlethal weapons can play a valuable role. One application, concerning "military operations in urban terrain" (MOUT), has already been introduced, in Chapter 3's discussion of the international law applicable to armed conflict. Whenever a battle intrudes into built-up areas, civilians will be imperiled; it may be impossible to fight effectively in urban neighborhoods without inflicting substantial civilian casualties and property losses. Still, perhaps the danger to the populace can be reduced without sacrificing military effectiveness by partially substituting NLW for lethal bombs and guns. Instead of vigorously shooting up an urban neighborhood and further victimizing the residents – but without ceding the enemy a sanctuary amidst the local population – NLW such as ADS or acoustic waves may allow the military to accomplish the legitimate mission with requisite proportionality.

A similar calculation applies to assaults upon public buildings and other urban properties. Many civil works installations – bridges, electric power plants, telecommunications facilities, airports, and the like – are "dual purpose," used by both military and civilian customers. During time of war, they may become legitimate targets for hostile forces, aiming to interrupt the benefit that their normal operation confers upon the enemy warmakers. But sometimes, total destruction of those installations is more than the attacker really needs. Especially if the superior force anticipates that the war might be short, and especially if (as seems to be the case in wars America fights these days) the victor will, upon successful termination of the fighting, help rebuild the vanquished, then full-scale destruction (even if legitimate under the applicable law of armed conflict) seems wasteful. If a less powerful mechanism could be found – providing the possibility of temporarily neutralizing the military function of the offending facility while preserving the opportunity to restore it relatively quickly and easily after the war to promote peaceful reconstruction – that flexibility would be a boon for all concerned.

NLW can sometimes provide the ability to eat the cake now and still have it later. For example, during the 1999 fighting in the former Yugoslavia, the United States and its NATO allies were eager to force Serbia to succumb quickly, to terminate the genocide of Kosovar Albanians. At the same time, the outsiders wanted to avoid laying waste to Belgrade – they knew that civilians would suffer, not only during the war, but for years thereafter, if the country's infrastructure were damaged beyond repair.

Part of the solution was to inflict only a "soft kill" on selected electrical switching installations. The United States developed a novel CBU-102 cluster bomb in which each bomblet carries 147 tiny spools of glass-like, highly conductive aluminum fibers. When these packages, instead of explosive ordnance, were dropped onto some of the transformer stations, they caused massive short circuits. These disruptions sufficed to put the facilities out of service for hours or days, depriving the Serbian military of electrical power but allowing the grid to come back online relatively quickly thereafter.[12] In the same vein, similarly less destructive, more deft attacks were sometimes launched against comparable Iraqi electrical yards during Gulf War II in 2003.

If other nonlethal weapons could likewise substitute for other conventional bombs, perhaps more missions could be undertaken with equal military effectiveness and fewer long-term adverse consequences. Many of Serbia's bridges over the Danube River, for example, were bombed as military targets in 1999 and suffered total destruction. Even years thereafter, some had not been restored or replaced, to the continuing disadvantage of the civilian population (and of NATO's efforts to help reconstruction, reconciliation, and resumption of normal economic activity). If nonlethal weapons (e.g., slippery foam) had been able to preclude tanks, trucks, and other military vehicles from crossing those bridges during the war without dropping the spans into the river, could those less powerful, but more deft, devices have served us better?

NONLETHAL DOES NOT REALLY MEAN NONLETHAL

The ethos of the NLW revolution was aptly expressed by Admiral Arthur Cebrowski, head of the Pentagon's Office of Force Transformation,

[12] William M. Arkin, Smart Bombs, Dumb Targeting? 56 Bulletin of the Atomic Scientists No. 3, May/June 2000, p. 46.

"The general rule is fewer dead people is better than more dead people."[13] Unfortunately, even these more useable NLW weapons are not yet always fully useable. Although routinely advertised as "nonlethal," the devices – OC, tasers, slippery foam, ADS – carry no guarantees against occasional excesses. The objective, as defined by the U.S. Department of Defense regulation establishing the NLW program, is "minimizing fatalities," not necessarily eliminating them altogether.[14]

Because human beings vary widely in their strength, health, vulnerability, and resilience, a dose (of a calmative chemical, a beanbag munition, or anything else) that would be sufficient to inflict the desired disabling effect on one person might simultaneously be *too much* for someone else (killing or seriously injuring an old, infirm person who had been taken hostage) and *not enough* for someone else (failing to incapacitate a young, strong, highly motivated person, such as a terrorist).

Likewise, antimateriel or antivehicle NLW may not be completely temporary or readily reversible in their effects. As long as the intention is to inflict less than complete or permanent damage, the NLW moniker can be applied.

For those reasons, many people refuse to endorse the term "nonlethal weapon," deriding it as false advertising for a type of armament that can still result in unwanted fatalities. Moreover, the critics assert, by lulling us into the expectation that these devices can be wielded with complete safely in complex situations (such as Scenario 8), the reassuring vocabulary may promote facile overreliance upon a form of violence that, as with any other weapon, should be applied only with the greatest care and restraint.

[13] Stephen Mihm, The Quest for the Nonkiller App., New York Times Magazine, July 25, 2004.

[14] Department of Defense Directive No. 3000.3, Policy for Non-Lethal Weapons, July 9, 1996, specifies the definition of nonlethal weapons:

> 3.1. Nonlethal Weapons. Weapons that are explicitly designed and primarily employed so as to incapacitate personnel or materiel, while minimizing fatalities, permanent injury to personnel, and undesired damage to property and the environment.
>
> 3.1.1. Unlike conventional lethal weapons that destroy their targets principally through blast, penetration and fragmentation, nonlethal weapons employ means other than gross physical destruction to prevent the target from functioning.
>
> 3.1.2. Nonlethal weapons are intended to have one, or both, of the following characteristics:
>
> 3.1.2.1. They have relatively reversible effects on personnel or materiel.
>
> 3.1.2.2. They affect objects differently within their area of influence.

If military officials or soldiers in the field rely too much on the over-promoted NLW nomenclature, they may wrongly come to expect that a particular nonlethal weapon carries no appreciable risk. Overconfident national leadership, too, may be seduced by the utopian concept of "bloodless" nonlethality, believing that the devices magically can be fired without reservation even in the fog of battle because the worst harm they might inflict, even upon a mistaken target, would be a headache or a bruise. Being too "quick on the trigger," however, can carry fatal consequences, even for so-called nonlethals.

Disturbing evidence of that "mission creep" phenomenon has already emerged in the domestic police environment. In several instances – Orange County, Florida, is the most well publicized – when a local U.S. police force becomes comprehensively armed with tasers, the first effect is a noticeable and welcome reduction in the number of lethal shootings of civilians by law enforcement officers. Cops quickly come to rely on the lesser but still effective power of electricity instead of bullets in situations that are dangerous, but perhaps not the *most* dangerous. A second effect, however, is often a sharp rise in the overall incidence of the use of force by police. Although they use their guns less often, they use their new tasers much more often, including in situations where they earlier would have found some way to resolve the problem without resorting to any use of force at all.[15]

That is, the availability of NLW has reduced the adverse consequences of using force – it has made it easier for the gung-ho user to "shoot first and ask questions later." Mistaken uses of the weapon, it is felt, are less costly and more tolerable; self-deterrence is abated. No one should be surprised if future soldiers on the battlefield, similarly equipped with more useable tasers, ADS, or other NLW, respond with similarly increased resort to their more deft power. The illusion that NLW could enable us to fight sanitized, bloodless wars with minimal casualties on all sides may obscure some of the inherent costs and dangers of any realistic military engagement.

THE LAW OF NONLETHAL WEAPONS

International law already imposes noteworthy constraints upon nonlethal weapons. To begin, NLW, like all other weapons, are automatically

[15] Regarding this form of "mission creep" for tasers, see Amnesty International, supra note 4, pp. 3–7, 18. See also Sylvia Moreno, In Houston, Questions of Bias Over Tasers, Washington Post, December 18, 2006, p. A3.

subject to the full corpus of the law of armed conflict (LoAC) as elaborated in Chapter 3. This means that the novel armaments must be wielded only in pursuit of militarily necessary objectives, that civilians and other protected objects must not be deliberately targeted, and that excessive collateral damage must be avoided.

Importantly, the "proportionality" judgment lying at the heart of the LoAC calculations should ordinarily favor NLW. The reduced force of a rubber bullet, the pepper spray that incapacitates or deters a target instead of killing or even wounding, and the filament bombs that accomplish a temporary "soft kill" rather than an obliteration of an enemy electrical power station all cause less damage than their explosive forebears. These devices should all satisfy the cost-benefit calculation more readily than traditional means that result in death or long-term physical distortion – that is, in essence, what it means for a weapon to be more "useable."

In fact, some have questioned whether the reduced collateral damage of NLW might impose a legal *requirement*, not merely an opportunity, to apply these devices instead of traditional lethal force. That is – as with precision-guided smart bombs studied in Chapter 4 – if the military is now able to exert itself with more restraint and with equal effectiveness, should it be *obligated* to try NLW before resorting to traditional means? To date, the United States and NATO have both resolutely rejected any such interpretation, maintaining that NLW is strictly an option, not a mandate, but the point will remain debatable into the future.

Regarding a second LoAC principle, some NLW might be more suspect in the customary legal assessment of "discrimination" or "distinction." Systems such as ADS that might be slewed across a crowd, or riot control chemical concoctions that cannot be targeted with precision against specific individuals, or acoustic devices that disturb anyone within haling distance are, by definition, not applied exclusively against combatants. Any mechanism that exerts its influence broadly against an entire area raises unsettling questions about the user's obligation to differentiate lawful targets from protected persons and sites.

Ironically, most of the other revolutionary weapons in this book acquire greater useability by *reducing* the exposure of civilians: smart bombs zoom in more reliably on intended targets, sparing even proximate civilians; low-yield nuclear weapons are intended to carve a substantially smaller lethal radius, accomplishing their assigned missions while sparing the surrounding communities; smart antipersonnel land mines, by becoming inert relatively quickly, would target enemy forces and then disarm themselves before they morph into a continuing hazard for unarmed passersby. Some nonlethal weapons, in contrast, will actually *increase* the exposure of civilians – they function as broad area-coverage devices, intended to drive away less committed or less protected individuals, clearing the field for easier identification and engagement of the genuine opponents. NLW seek to accomplish this sorting-out function in a relatively less offensive fashion, inflicting only temporary pain, disorientation, incapacitation, fear, or blockage – but the fact that they operate across the entire spectrum of the population is different from the other systems surveyed in this book, and is legally more problematic.

Treaty law imposes important additional constraints upon specified candidate NLW mechanisms. In particular, the 1993 Chemical Weapons Convention (CWC) commits its parties (including the United States) broadly not to develop, produce, acquire, stockpile, retain, transfer, or use chemical weapons. The treaty does not prohibit the use of chemicals for "law enforcement including domestic riot control purposes" but does forbid the application of riot control agents "as a method of warfare."[16] The oddity of this construction (we can use noxious chemicals against our own civilian population to resist civic disruptions that we could not legally use against enemy troops in international warfare) and the ambiguity of the terms (what counts as a toxic chemical, where is the dividing line between "law enforcement" and "war" in complex counterterrorism environments) have led to considerable confusion and contradiction.

Further complicating the legal situation, the United States government has long espoused an unusually permissive interpretation of when riot control agents may lawfully be employed in near-combat situations – an interpretation explicitly not shared by our allies and CWC treaty partners. The U.S. military's general response, therefore, has been to stay away from anything smacking of chemical warfare, including the application of nonlethal chemical incapacitants on or even near the battlefield.[17] The military has generally eschewed the use of temporary disrupters such as

[16] Convention on the Prohibition of the Development, Production, Stockpiling and Use of Chemical Weapons and on Their Destruction, concluded in Paris, January 13, 1993, entered into force April 29, 1997, S. TREATY DOC. No. 103–21, 31 I.L.M. 800 (United States is a party) [hereinafter CWC], arts. II.9, I.5.

[17] See Testimony of Donald Rumsfeld before House Armed Services Committee, on FY 2004 Defense Authorization, February 5, 2003. ("With respect to the use of nonlethal riot agents, I regret to say that we are in a very difficult situation. There is a treaty that the United States signed, and there are existing requirements that, without getting into details, require – let me put it this way, absent a presidential waiver, in many instances, our forces are allowed to shoot somebody and kill them but they're not allowed to use a nonlethal riot control agent, under law. It is a very awkward situation.")

OC even on the periphery of warfare; future generations of immediate disabling or disorienting potions would likely also be treated as dubious chemical hot potatoes.

Even more pronounced is the legal prohibition against biological weapons. The 1972 Biological Weapons Convention is definitive in barring all hostile uses of disease agents and other germs and contains no explicit exception for domestic law enforcement. NLW concepts such as biologically engineered microbes that could surreptitiously attack an adversary's stockpiles of food or fuel, or that could corrupt enemy vehicles' tires or belts, are therefore categorically banned.[18]

Outside the realm of the life sciences, laser weapons have fallen under international legal scrutiny. Protocol IV of the Convention on Certain Conventional Weapons bars lasers intended to cause permanent blindness, reflecting the world's general revulsion with that form of admittedly very precise (only one person is attacked at a time) nonlethal force. (Again the anomaly is that it remains legal to *kill* an enemy combatant, even though blinding – surely a lesser harm – would be impermissible.) The "dazzling" lasers discussed previously, because they cause only temporary disruption rather than permanent loss of vision, would not be covered by this proscription.[19]

DISADVANTAGES OF NLW

There are other kinds of legitimate apprehensions about nonlethal weapons, too, paralleling concerns identified in previous chapters. If these kinds of additional deft NLW powers carry substantial appeal for U.S. military and law enforcement officials, the same sorts of attractions might soon inspire other potential users; this aspect of the revolution in military affairs may soon spawn a broad and troubling array of imitators.

Other countries' military forces would be one obvious proliferation danger, and it is far from clear who would benefit most in a future

In Gulf War II, President Bush did authorize the use of tear gas in Iraq, but there have been no authoritative reports of actual use. Nicholas Wade and Eric Schmitt, Bush Approves Use of Tear Gas in Battlefield, New York Times, April 2, 2003.

[18] Convention on the Prohibition of the Development, Production and Stockpiling of Bacteriological (Biological) and Toxin Weapons and on Their Destruction, Apr. 10, 1972, 26 U.S.T. 583, 1015 U.N.T.S. 163, T.I.A.S. No. 8062 (entered into force Mar. 26, 1975) [hereinafter BWC].

[19] Convention on Prohibitions or Restrictions on the Use of Certain Conventional Weapons Which May Be Deemed to Be Excessively Injurious or to Have Indiscriminate Effects, Oct. 10, 1980, 1342 U.N.T.S. 137, 19 I.L.M. 1523, Protocol IV.

"mixed" battlefield in which all forces were armed, probably asymmetrically, with both lethal and nonlethal capabilities. One should also anticipate the likely effect of an emergent black market in nonlethal technologies, through which terrorists would acquire knockoff versions of the ADS capability to inflict searing heat at a kilometer's distance, or the microwave mechanisms enabling them to arrest moving vehicles without firing a shot. Already we have suffered the effects of domestic "nonlethal crime," as neighborhood malefactors armed with inexpensive and readily available pepper spray or electric stun devices have been further emboldened in petty street crime and robberies. Human rights abusers could also provide a market for something like the ADS system, seeing it as a mechanism to inflict torturous pain on prisoners or political opponents without leaving any telltale scars that subsequent investigators could monitor.

In short, the nature of technology, even transformative technology, is to spread, and it is unrealistic to suppose that any American monopoly in NLW could be long sustained – if we pioneer the field, others will come.

BOTTOM LINE

Nonlethal weapons, like other categories of more useable weapons surveyed in prior chapters, aim to enhance the effectiveness of military forces (and, in the case of NLW, of police forces, too) by providing more useable, more deft power, ensuring the ability to act decisively without overreacting. Law enforcement officials today sometimes complain that their arsenals have not improved appreciably since the era of Wyatt Earp – if the person or persons they confront are unwilling or unable to comply with forceful instructions, the immediate alternatives too often turn out to be firearms or nothing.

NLW add finesse through the sophistication of targeting the "functionality" of a person, vehicle, or location. That is, if our weapon can inhibit the movement of a truck, or the normal operation of a television tower, or the ability of a person to shoot back at us, then perhaps a sufficient purpose has been accomplished – even if the target is not destroyed or killed. NLW may thus be said to effectuate a "mission kill" – preventing the target from functioning in its normal or hostile fashion – even without accomplishing a complete "kill" in the traditional sense. These are, in the vernacular of the Pentagon office responsible for leading the ongoing Revolution in Military Affairs (RMA), "effects-based operations." The objective is not to win a military campaign through crude destruction or physical attrition of the enemy, but to prevail by effectively inducing the opponent to submit to our will.[20]

No one would assert that NLW should displace traditional weapons across the board in all applications; at best, they would merely *supplement* deadly firearms and other tools wielded by military and police units in specified circumstances. There is no "one size fits all" weapon; instead, the expectation (or hope) is that particular devices – characterized by significantly lower levels of violence, destruction, and death – could fill a niche, adding a new element to the authorities' existing arsenals. Sometimes, of course, lethal force is necessary – but sometimes we will be appropriately self-deterred about jumping precipitously to that level, and invoking a smaller quantity of violence will be more appropriate to the task. In short, sometimes, less (force) is more (effective).

By avoiding lethal or destructive power, NLW are not merely more humane (although that value is important, too); they are more successful. Deft NLW can be applied in situations where the normal dollop of military force would be excessive; they enable a military to undertake, and to complete, delicate operations in which too much power ought to be avoided. By mitigating one of the key impediments against the application of organized coercion (the apprehension about the adverse consequences of a mistake), NLW enable a transformed military to use force more quickly, more decisively – and more frequently.

BIBLIOGRAPHY

Steven Aftergood, The Soft-Kill Fallacy, Bulletin of the Atomic Scientists, September/October 1994, p. 40

John B. Alexander, Future War: Non-Lethal Weapons in 21st Century Warfare, 1999

John B. Alexander, The Role of Nonlethal Weapons in Future Military Operations, in Anthony D. McIvor (ed.), Rethinking the Principles of War, 2005, p. 401

Amnesty International, United States of America: Excessive and Lethal Force? Amnesty International's Concerns About Deaths and Ill-Treatment Involving Police Use of Tasers, 2004

William M. Arkin, Smart Bombs, Dumb Targeting? 56 Bulletin of the Atomic Scientists No. 3, May/June 2000, p. 46

Associated Press, Pentagon Nixes Ray Gun Weapon in Iraq, August 29, 2007

Rick Atkinson, Lean, Not-So-Mean Marines Set for Somalia, Washington Post, February 25, 1995, p. A22

[20] U.S. Department of Defense, Military Transformation: A Strategic Approach, Fall 2003, p. 34.

William P. Bozeman et al., Safety and Injury Profile of Conducted Electrical Weapons Used by Law Enforcement Officers Against Criminal Suspects, 20 Annals of Emergency Medicine No. 10, January 2009, p. 1

John M. Collins, Nonlethal Weapons and Operations: Potential Applications and Practical Limitations, Congressional Research Service Report for Congress, 95-974 S, September 14, 1995

Committee for an Assessment of Non-Lethal Weapons Science and Technology, Naval Studies Board, Division on Engineering and Physical Sciences, National Research Council, National Academies, An Assessment of Non-Lethal Weapons Science and Technology, National Academies Press, 2003

Margaret-Anne Coppernoll, The Nonlethal Weapons Debate, 52 Naval War College Review 112, Spring 1998

Council on Foreign Relations, Independent Task Force Report, Non-Lethal Technologies: Military Options and Implications, Malcolm Wiener, Chair, 1995

Council on Foreign Relations, Independent Task Force Report: Nonlethal Technologies: Progress and Prospects, Richard Garwin, Chair, 1999

Council on Foreign Relations, Independent Task Force Report, Nonlethal Weapons and Capabilities, Graham Allison and Paul X. Kelley, Co-Chairs, Richard L. Garwin, Project Director, 2004

Robin M. Coupland, 'Calmatives' and 'Incapacitants': Questions for International Humanitarian Law Brought by New Means and Methods of Warfare with New Effects? 19th Workshop of the Pugwash Study Group on the Implementation of the Chemical and Biological Weapons Conventions, April 26–27, 2003

Robin M. Coupland, Incapacitating Chemical Weapons: A Year After the Moscow Theatre Siege, 362 Lancet p. 1346, October 25, 2003

Malcolm Dando, A New Form of Warfare: The Rise of Non-Lethal Weapons, 1996

Malcolm Dando (ed.), Non-Lethal Weapons: Technological and Operational Prospects, Jane's on-line special report, November 2000

Neil Davison, The Contemporary Development of 'Non-Lethal' Weapons, Bradford Non-Lethal Weapons Research Project, Centre for Conflict Resolution, Department of Peace Studies, University of Bradford (U.K.), Occasional Paper No. 3, May 2007

Neil Davison, 'Off the Rocker' and 'On the Floor': The Continued Development of Biochemical Incapacitating Weapons, Bradford Science and Technology Report No. 8, Bradford Disarmament Research Centre, Department of Peace Studies, University of Bradford (U.K.), August 2007

Neil Davison, 'Non-Lethal' Weapons, 2009

Neil Davison and Nick Lewer, Bradford Non-Lethal Weapons Research Project, Centre for Conflict Resolution, Department of Peace Studies, University of Bradford (U.K.), Research Report No. 8, March 2006

Defense Science Board Task Force on Directed Energy Weapon Systems and Technology Applications, Report, December 2007

Doubt Over Shoot-to-Kill Policy, The Independent (U.K.), August 21, 2005

Raymond L. Downs, Less Lethal Weapons: A Technologist's Perspective, 30 Policing No. 3, 2007, p. 358

James C. Duncan, A Primer on the Employment of Non-Lethal Weapons, 45 Naval Law Review, 1998, p. 1

George P. Fenton, Current and Prospective Military and Law Enforcement Use of Chemical Agents for Incapacitation, for Symposium on Biochemical Weapons: Scientific, Military, Legal and Policy Perspectives and Prospects, July 15, 2005

David P. Fidler, The International Legal Implications of 'Non-Lethal' Weapons, 21 Michigan Journal of International Law 51, Fall 1999

David Fidler, Law Enforcement under the Chemical Weapons Convention: Interpretation of Article II.9(d) of the Chemical Weapons Convention in Regard to the Use of Toxic Chemicals for Law Enforcement Purposes, memorandum to Federation of American Scientists Working Group, April 24, 2003, presented to the Open Forum on Challenges to the Chemical Weapons Ban, The Hague, May 1, 2002

David P. Fidler, The Meaning of Moscow: 'Non-lethal' Weapons and International Law in the Early 21st Century, 87 International Review of the Red Cross No. 859, September 2005

David A. Fulghum, Silent Launch; New Directed-energy Weapon Balances Strength, Low Cost and Portability, 165 Aviation Week & Space Technology No. 4, July 24, 2006, p. 66

Martin Furmanski, Military Interest in Low-lethality Biochemical Agents: The Historical Interaction of Advocates, Experts, Pragmatists and Politicians, background paper for Symposium on Biochemical Weapons: Scientific, Military, Legal and Policy Perspectives and Prospects, Geneva, Switzerland, June 11, 2005

David C. Gompert, et al., Underkill: Scalable Capabilities for Military Operations Amid Populations, 2009

Caroline Graham, Blitzed, The Mail (U.K.), November 13, 2005

International Institute for Strategic Studies, Strategic Survey 1995–1996, 1996, p. 40

Jean Charles de Menezes: In the Wrong Place. At the Wrong Time, The Independent (U.K.), July 25, 2005

John M. Kenny, Sid Heal, and Mike Grossman, The Attribute-Based Evaluation (ABE) of Less-Than-Lethal, Extended-Range, Impact Munitions, Pennsylvania State University, February 15, 2001

Lynn Klotz, Martin Furmanski, and Mark Wheelis, Beware the Siren's Song: Why 'Non-Lethal' Incapacitating Chemical Agents Are Lethal, March 2003

David A. Koplow, Non-Lethal Weapons: The Law and Policy of Revolutionary Technologies for the Military and Law Enforcement, 2006

Mark W. Kroll and Patrick Tchou, How a TASER Works, IEEE Spectrum, December 2007

F. Kruger-Sprengel, Innovative Legal Effects of Non-Lethal Weapons (NLW) for Political and Military Strategy and for Humanitarian Intervention, 38 Military Law and Law of War Review p. 383, 1999

Timothy J. Lamb, Emerging Nonlethal Weapons Technology and Strategic Policy Implications for 21st Century Warfare, thesis, US Army War College, Carlisle Barracks, PA, 1998

Nick Lewer (ed.), The Future of Non-Lethal Weapons: Technologies, Operations, Ethics, and Law, 2002
Nick Lewer and Steven Schofield, Non-Lethal Weapons: A Fatal Attraction? Military Strategies and Technologies for 21st Century Conflict, 1997
Frederick M. Lorenz, 'Less-Lethal' Force in Operation UNITED SHIELD, Marine Corps Gazette, September 1995, p. 68
F.M. Lorenz, Nonlethal Force: The Slippery Slope to War? 27 Parameters No. 3, Autumn 1996, p. 52
Douglas C. Lovelace, Jr., and Steven Metz, Nonlethality and American Land Power: Strategic Context and Operational Concepts, U.S. Army War College, Strategic Studies Institute, June 15, 1998
Robert Mandel, Security, Strategy, and the Quest for Bloodless War, 2004
Robert M. McNab and Richard L. Scott, Non-lethal Weapons and the Long Tail of Warfare, 20 Small Wars and Insurgencies No. 1, March 2009, p. 141
M.S. Meselson and J.P. Perry Robinson, 'Non Lethal' Weapons and Implementation of the Chemical and Biological Weapons Conventions, paper for the 20th Pugwash Workshop Study Group on the Implementation of the CBW Conventions, November 8–9, 2003
Stephen Mihm, The Quest for the Nonkiller App., New York Times Magazine, July 25, 2004
Monterey Institute of International Studies, Chemical and Biological Weapons Nonproliferation Program, The Moscow Theater Hostage Crisis: Incapacitants and Chemical Warfare, November 4, 2002
David A. Morehouse, Nonlethal Weapons: War without Death, 1996
Sylvia Moreno, In Houston, Questions of Bias Over Tasers, Washington Post, December 18, 2006, p. A3
'Non-Lethal' Weapons, The CWC and the BWC (editorial), The CBW Conventions Bulletin, No. 61, September 2003, p. 1
Omega Foundation, Crowd Control Technologies: An Assessment of Crowd Control Technology Options for the European Union (an Appraisal for the Technologies of Political Control) EP/1/1V/B/STOA/99/14/01, Section C, Technical Annex, May 2000
W. Hays Parks, Non-Lethal Weapons: Musings from Experience, presentation to Council on Foreign Relations NLW Task Force, September 8, 2003
Alan M. Pearson, Marie Isabelle Chevrier, and Mark Wheelis, Incapacitating Biochemical Weapons: Promise or Peril? 2007
The Pentagon's Ray Gun, CBS News Sixty Minutes, March 2, 2008
James Rainey, A Safer Weapon, With Risks, Los Angeles Times, May 18, 2006
Brian Rappert, Scenarios on the Future of Non-lethal Weapons, 22 Contemporary Security Policy No. 1, April 2001, p. 57
Brian Rappert, Non-Lethal Weapons as Legitimizing Forces? Technology, Politics and the Management of Conflict, 2003
Barbara Rosenberg, Nonlethal Weapons May Violate Treaties, Bulletin of the Atomic Scientists, September/October 1994, p. 40
Donald Rumsfeld, Testimony before House Armed Services Committee, on FY 2004 Defense Authorization, February 5, 2003

Vincent Sautenet, Legal Issues Concerning Military Use of Non-Lethal Weapons, 7 Murdoch University Electronic Journal of Law No. 2, June 2000
Greg R. Schneider, Nonlethal Weapons: Considerations for Decision Makers, University of Illinois at Urbana-Champaign, Program in Arms Control, Disarmament, and International Security, ACDIS Occasional Paper, January 1997
Jason Sherman, DoD: Spend More on Non-Lethal Weapons, InsideDefense.com, May 23, 2006
Martin N. Stanton, What Price Sticky Foam? 26 Parameters No. 3, Autumn 1996, p. 63
Ronald G. Sutherland, Chemical and Biochemical Non-Lethal Weapons, SIPRI Policy Paper No. 23, November 2008
Alvin and Heidi Toffler, War and Anti-War: Survival at the Dawn of the 21st Century, 1993
US Aims to Use Heat-Beam Weapon by 2010, New Scientist, January 25, 2007
U.S. Department of Defense Directive No. 3000.3, Policy for Non-Lethal Weapons, July 9, 1996
U.S. Department of Defense, Military Transformation: A Strategic Approach, Fall 2003, p. 34
U.S. Department of Defense, Joint Non-Lethal Weapons Program, Active Denial System (ADS) Fact Sheet, March 2007
U.S. Department of Defense, Air, Land, Sea Application Center, NLW: Multi-Service Tactics, Techniques, and Procedures for the Tactical Employment of Nonlethal Weapons, FM 3–22.40, October 2007
U.S. Department of Defense, DoD Non-Lethal Weapons Program Annual Report 2008: Expanding Warfighter Capabilities
U.S. Government Accountability Office, DoD Needs to Improve Program Management, Policy and Testing to Enhance Ability to Field Operationally Useful Non-lethal Weapons, Report to Congressional Requesters 09-344, April 2009
U.S. Joint Chiefs of Staff, Peace Operations, Joint Publication 3–07.3, October 17, 2007
Nikolaus von Twickel, Unmasking Dubrovka's Mysterious Gas, Moscow Times, October 23, 2007, p. 1
Nicholas Wade and Eric Schmitt, Bush Approves Use of Tear Gas in Battlefield, New York Times, April 2, 2003
Mark Wheelis, 'Nonlethal' Chemical Weapons: A Faustian Bargain, 19 Issues in Science and Technology No. 3, Spring 2003, p. 74
Mark Wheelis, Will the New Biology Lead to New Weapons? and The Danger of 'Nonlethal' Weapons, 34 Arms Control Today No. 6, July/August 2004, p. 6
David Williams and Stephen Wright, Tragic Trail of Police Blunders Over Shooting, Daily Mail (U.K.), August 17, 2005
Richard Winton, The Long, Safer Arm of the Law, Los Angeles Times, September 18, 2007, p. A1

TREATIES

Convention on the Prohibition of the Development, Production, Stockpiling and Use of Chemical Weapons and on Their Destruction, concluded in Paris,

January 13, 1993, entered into force April 29, 1997, S. TREATY DOC. NO. 103–21, 31 I.L.M. 800 (United States is a party) [hereinafter CWC]

Convention on the Prohibition of the Development, Production and Stockpiling of Bacteriological (Biological) and Toxin Weapons and on Their Destruction, Apr. 10, 1972, 26 U.S.T. 583, 1015 U.N.T.S. 163, T.I.A.S. No. 8062 (entered into force Mar. 26, 1975) [hereinafter BWC].

Convention on Prohibitions or Restrictions on the Use of Certain Conventional Weapons Which May Be Deemed to Be Excessively Injurious or to Have Indiscriminate Effects, Oct. 10, 1980, 1342 U.N.T.S. 137, 19 I.L.M. 1523 [Convention on Certain Conventional Weapons, or CCW], Protocol IV

9

What to Do about Useability

"We knew that no single bomb would win the war, but also that one wayward bomb could lose it."[1] That melancholy insight, from an anonymous senior instructor at a 2002 U.S. Air Force training course, neatly summarizes the warfighter's current conundrum, and it encapsulates much of the unsettling motivation animating the American pursuit of "useable" weapons. In contemporary combat – even as the "global war on terror" morphs into "the long war" – no one battle, no single engagement, still less any individual bomb, can decisively turn the campaign in our favor. But one erroneous munition – inaccurately placed, too large in its effects, lasting too long, or otherwise failing to discriminate between valid targets and protected civilians – could potentially so poison the political atmosphere that the support of the population (at home, in the theater of battle, and around the world) could be irretrievably compromised, sacrificing an indispensable element in winning the war. That spirit – driving the military to be, in equal measure, both effective and deft – is responsible for the current fascination with weapons that are less deadly, less destructive, and less powerful than their predecessors.

Still, a skeptical reader might ask, "What's the big deal here? The Pentagon always buys new weapons – for offense and for defense; for air, sea, and land. If ever there were a 'dog bites man' story, it would be a recital about the U.S. Department of Defense trying to develop new generations of advanced armaments."

[1] Anonymous speaker at U.S. Air Force training course, quoted in Dwight A. Roblyer, Beyond Precision: Issues of Morality and Decision Making in Minimizing Collateral Casualties, Program in Arms Control, Disarmament, and International Security, University of Illinois, April 28, 2003, p. 5.

But there *is* something generically different going on here, well beyond the perennial Easter egg hunt for new military hardware. In two senses, one general and one specific, the current era is distinct, if not unique, and the activities we now observe defy close historical precedent.

First, on the big picture level, there is indeed a Revolution in Military Affairs (RMA) under way. These are rare and epochal phenomena, laden with barely controllable consequences both profound and broad – we are altering the organization and structure of the military, the roles and missions assigned to the troops, the concepts of operations and rules of engagement for deployments, and, of course, the weapons technology. In response to novel global threats and opportunities, the Pentagon is zealously shifting paradigms all over the place – and exciting (and dangerous) capabilities are emerging. And we are also spending money at a frenetic pace; by one estimate, the ongoing defense transformation will ultimately carry a price tag well north of $100 billion.[2]

A revolutionary era is consequential for another, deeper reason, too. When the military *status quo* is jostled, there is no guarantee that the currently dominant countries will retain their leadership roles. As Max Boot has demonstrated,

> History is full of examples of superpowers failing to take advantage of important Revolutions in Military Affairs: the Mongols missed the Gunpowder Revolution; the Chinese, Turks, and Indians missed the Industrial Revolution; the French and British missed major parts of the Second Industrial Revolution; the Soviets missed the Information Revolution. The warning that appears at the bottom of mutual fund advertisements applies to geopolitics: *Past performance is no guarantee of future returns.*[3]

In fact, national complacency and natural military inertia may make it even more likely that the leading states of one era (who, after all, have achieved their prominence at least partially through success in the then-prevailing formats of military competition) may fall asleep at the switch when a new era of defense transformation begins. For those reasons, Jeremy Shapiro has suggested that a "revolution by the strong" is not only relatively rare, but a bit illogical.[4] A superpower – especially one

[2] Patrick M. Morgan, Deterrence Now, 2003, p. 233, note 19.

[3] Max Boot, War Made New: Technology, Warfare, and the Course of History, 1500 to Today, 2006, p. 455 (italics in original).

[4] Jeremy Shapiro, Information and War: Is It a Revolution?, in Zalmay M. Khalilzad and John P. White (eds.), The Changing Role of Information in Warfare, 1999, p. 113, 139.

suddenly lacking a near-peer competitor – may be particularly vulnerable to surprise if opponents' rapid alterations in tactics and tools (such as adapting jetliners into flying bombs) catch it unprepared for abrupt change.

Second, this particular RMA carries an additional special feature not characteristic of earlier revolutions and not hitherto much noticed. That is, some of the new weapons being deployed, developed, debated, or at least imagined today are remarkable because they depart from the previously near-unanimous pattern of ever-increasing lethality and destructiveness. For the first time, across a range of otherwise unrelated weapons programs, we are pursuing arms that are deliberately less powerful than their predecessors – that was decidedly not the originators' concept with the introduction of the longbow, the machine gun, the dreadnought, or the tank.

The attraction of more useable weapons – the ability to overcome self-deterrence and to apply a deft quantity of meaningful force – enables a modern military to act without overreacting. That newfound finesse is categorically different from the traditional pursuit of ever-bigger bangs for the bucks and qualifies as metarevolutionary, even by RMA standards.

Some aspects of useability, of course, have always been on the agenda. Militaries have frequently sought to procure weapons that were more accurate, for example. Likewise, sometimes a smaller weapon can be cheaper and lighter, both longstanding military desiderata. And, of course, these five case studies hardly describe everything going on in the Pentagon today, where a great conglomeration of weapons developments and advances in warmaking theory always coexist and simultaneously pursue multiple, competing approaches, many having nothing much to do with useability. Nonetheless, the zeitgeist in pursuit of useability has accelerated and broadened so rapidly that, following Lenin's famous epigram, we observe that the *quantity* of incipient change has a *quality* all of its own.

This notion of weapons of deliberately modulated killing power must swim upstream against the centuries-old current of military thought long dominated by the notion that war is not only Hell, it is unlimited Hell, in which any restrictions, moderation, or restraints are illusory. Carl von Clausewitz, the luminary dean of Western military strategy, sponsored the barnacled notion that "war is an act of force, and there is no logical limit to the application of that force," and "to introduce the principle of moderation in war itself would always lead to logical absurdity," explaining,

> Kind-hearted people might of course think there was some ingenious way to disarm or defeat an enemy without too much bloodshed, and might imagine this is the true goal of the art of war. Pleasant as it sounds, it is a fallacy that must be exposed: war is such a dangerous business that the mistakes which come from kindness are the very worst.[5]

Antoine-Henri Jomini, the celebrated nineteenth-century Swiss intellectual (and general in both the French and Russian armies) was perhaps second only to Clausewitz in crafting Western military thought and in shaping what he called "the poetry and metaphysics of war." Jomini's first maxim of combat instructed that "the art of war consists in bringing into action upon the decisive point of the theater of operations the greatest possible force" – he hesitated not at all on soft notions such as proportionality, self-restraint, or economy of force.[6]

The "total wars" of the twentieth century revealed the absurd costliness of that approach to the maelstrom of international combat. As B.H. Liddel Hart observed in 1946, the atom bomb and long-range aircraft "may tear away the veil of illusion that has so long obscured the reality of the change in warfare – from a *fight* to a process of *destruction*."[7] The folly of that metamorphosis – and the hope that perhaps the world can change it back again – reflects the desire that the unlimited warfare strategies of Clausewitz and Jomini can be at least partially cabined into their own eras. More useable weapons, supporting more restrained and partial versions of international combat, can evolve to support that desire.

WHY USEABILITY IS ATTRACTIVE

Why is this peculiar form of defense transformation ripe today? What is it about modern circumstances that has evoked a sudden flourishing of less deadly and less destructive armament, after millennia of zealous arms racing in the other direction?

At the outset, it must be stressed that no single one-size-fits-all decision or deliberate overarching strategy was responsible for the movement.

[5] Carl von Clausewitz, On War (Michael Howard and Peter Par, eds. and trans., 1984) pp. 75–77.

[6] J.D. Hittle (ed.), Jomini and His Summary of the Art of War, 1947, 1958, pp. 80–81.

[7] B.H. Liddell Hart, The Revolution in Warfare, 1946, p. 32 (emphasis added).

We observe a trend toward useable weapons, but not a coherent, self-conscious trend, not a Pentagon-wide directive that pushes engineers in lock step. There is parallel movement in the five widely disparate weapons programs surveyed in this book, but it has largely been the product of independent action – not uniquely the vision of the Bush Administration, former Secretary of Defense Donald Rumsfeld, or any other centralized mandate. This aspect of the process of defense transformation is not specifically attributable to the ending of the cold war (the movement toward precision-guided munitions, for example, emerged long before that) or to the catastrophe of 9/11 (antisatellite weapons and low-yield nuclear bombs, for example, would hardly be applicable to the global war on terrorism). Instead, this feature of the emergent revolution in military affairs is a more general and elusive phenomenon, a calculated response to what Alexander Solzhenitsyn once called "the pitiless crowbar of events."[8]

Still, the pursuit of more useable weapons is not five independent stories – it is one story, with five illustrations. The several programs are at least partially "stovepiped," in the classic Department of Defense tradition, with relatively little interaction among them, and relatively few people who are involved in, or even knowledgeable about, more than one of them. But there is a common animating spirit, a shared desire to move beyond the hamstrings of self-deterrence – it is not just coincidence that so many programs are now simultaneously tilting into the same headwind of history. And the responsibilities for the different manifestations of useability have certainly been spread around the Pentagon and the U.S. government as a whole: precision-guided munitions (PGMs) are mainly the responsibility of the Air Force and the Navy; low-yield nuclear weapons have been promoted by both the Secretary of Defense and the Secretary of Energy; antipersonnel land mines are mostly within the purview of the Army; antisatellite weapons have been pursued by the Air Force and the Army; and the lead agent for the concept of nonlethal weapons (NLW) has been the Marine Corps. There seems to be plenty of Kool-Aid to go around when more useable weapons are being discussed.

Eight factors help account for the national security community's contemporary gravitation toward these less deadly, more useable weapons.

1. *Loss of faith in deterrence.* Many of America's most dangerous potential enemies these days – rogue states and terrorist groups – seem to

[8] Alexander Solzhenitsyn, address at Harvard University Class Day Afternoon Exercises, June 8, 1978.

be at least partially beyond the reach of the "normal" deterrence strategies described in Chapter 2. President Bush cautioned that "deterrence – the promise of massive retaliation against nations – means nothing against shadowy terrorist networks with no nations or citizens to defend."[9] The authors of the Carnegie Endowment's *Deadly Arsenals* reference book, in sizing up nuclear, chemical, and biological threats, concur, "Although *states* can be deterred from using nuclear weapons by fear of retaliation, *terrorists*, who do not have land, people, or national futures to protect, may not be deterrable."[10]

It is not just misguided nostalgia for the cold war – an era of immense, but at least somewhat simpler, threats – that accounts for these sentiments. For much of the post–World War II era, there was at least a valid reason to hope (but, unfortunately, not to be truly confident) that we would not have to actually *use* the massive inventories of nuclear and other weapons that the United States and the Soviet Union had so laboriously compiled. Even in the most white-knuckled moments (e.g., the Cuban Missile Crisis, as analyzed in Chapter 2) one side or the other would blink as the world approached the apocalyptic intersection. The horrific notion that "nuclear war cannot be won, and must not be fought" seemed to have resonated up and down the national security apparatus in both countries, and the unsteady architecture of mutual assured destruction prevailed.

Today, in contrast, we face repeated provocations in which "they" (al-Qaeda, North Korea, Iran) do not seem so predictable, or so rational, or at least quite so susceptible to the familiar forms of communication and bargaining. What worked with Khrushchev, Brezhnev, and Gorbachev does not appear to be as availing in reaching a *modus vivendi* with Osama Bin Laden, Kim Jong Il, or Mahmoud Ahmadinejad. As deterrence becomes a less steady principle, and as the probability of actual combat rises, the premium also rises on weapons that not only *look* good for deterrence purposes, but that would actually *work* well in combat.

2. *Casualty aversion.* At the same time, when confronting the prospect of frequent and sustained combat against persistent, undeterrable foes, the United States and its key allies may have lost some of their appetite (or, to be fair, their tolerance) for operations so costly in blood and treasure.

[9] George W. Bush, Commencement address at West Point, June 1, 2002, 38 Weekly Comp. Pres. Docs. 944, 946

[10] Joseph Cirincione, Jon Wolfsthal, and Miriam Rajkumar, Deadly Arsenals: Nuclear, Biological, and Chemical Threats (2nd ed.), 2005, p. 16 (emphasis in original).

The first manifestation of this inhibition, not surprisingly, is the reluctance to consign our own soldiers to a grisly fate – body bags returning to the mortuary at Dover Air Force base will always incite controversy, opposition, and combat reluctance. As the International Institute for Strategic Studies editorialized in 1996 about the immediate post-cold war experience,

> The promise that either the United Nations or rapidly formed *ad hoc* coalitions would be able to stamp out regional and inter-ethnic conflict withered almost as soon as it flowered. Instead of order there is disorder; instead of containment there is withdrawal.[11]

In this postmodern era, an additional, new consideration (or an old consideration of renewed vigor) emerges: a general social squeamishness about imposing unnecessary casualties upon an enemy state's civilians, or even upon its soldiers. Whether we label this an ennobling expression of our common humanity or an effete reluctance to get our hands dirty in the often unpleasant business of international turmoil, it seems to be a force of genuine and growing political weight. Either way, the psychic eddy of casualty aversion creates strong incentives to develop new modes of conflict, to provide an ability to operate internationally without incurring – and without inflicting – so much death and destruction. As our national character evolves, along with our perceptions of national self-interest, so must our military tactics and tools.

3. *Mission expansion.* Complicating the military task these days is the expansion of assigned missions. The international environment remains a hazardous forest, inhabited by a wide variety of dragons and demanding a diverse array of responsive capabilities. The United States, as the sole remaining superpower, shoulders a disproportionate responsibility for readiness for traditional major combat; for lower-intensity counterinsurgency operations; for antiterrorist missions; for counterdrug, antipiracy, and anticrime contingencies; and for peacekeeping and the whole host of other Military Operations Other Than War (MOOTW) – and these could be contested in jungles, mountains, deserts, cities, or the high seas. The price of having to defend so many scenarios simultaneously includes the obligation to innovate in weapons technology.

As Michael Mullen, Chairman of the Joint Chiefs of Staff, explained in responding to a reporter's question about the U.S. military

[11] International Institute for Strategic Studies, Strategic Survey 1995–1996, 1996, p. 48.

needing to be prepared to respond to both the threat of future conventional warfare and the ongoing counterinsurgency warfare in Iraq and Afghanistan,

> Well, we definitely need to continue the focus on irregular warfare and counterinsurgency. We're not far enough down that road by any means, despite having come a long way in a very short period of time. I think irregular warfare will be with us for the foreseeable future, and we need to invest in that and make sure we get it right. We can't take our eye off the long-term ball, however, and fail to invest in traditional and conventional kinds of capabilities as well. In the world we're living in today, we've got to deliver both an exceptional irregular-warfare capability, and an exceptional conventional capability. That's a big challenge.[12]

Michele Flournoy, Undersecretary of Defense for Policy, characterized the dilemma as pulling the U.S. military "in two very different directions" to respond both to low-intensity irregular combat and to high-end threats. In his 2009 budget submission, Secretary of Defense Robert M. Gates proposed to split the pie three ways, allocating half the department's fund to dealing with traditional conflicts, 40 percent to dual-purpose capabilities, and the remaining 10 percent to irregular warfare.

If our defense establishment is to be charged with that cornucopia of responsibilities, it will have to be equipped with more refined, flexible tools – the legacy weapon systems were simply not optimized for many of the current jobs. To be effective in unusual, hybrid missions – situations that are undoubtedly dangerous, but not soluble with "mere" overwhelming force – sometimes requires a subtle, precise, proportionate, discriminating, and nonlethal touch.

4. *Asymmetric warfare.* One pernicious form of modern combat requires special attention. Because the United States today has accumulated such a formidable, perhaps insurmountable, lead in most categories of nuclear and advanced conventional weaponry, some potential opponents – being intelligent and adaptive characters – have opted to respond asymmetrically. They do not directly challenge American superiority in the customary "bean count" of weapons statistics, but instead prepare for and conduct novel operations to detect and challenge weak points and to exploit untraditional vulnerabilities.

[12] The Admiral's Agenda (interview with JCS Chairman Michael Mullen), National Journal, June 21, 2008.

Insurgency operations, especially those conducted in urban areas, are foremost among these asymmetric challenges today. Military Operations in Urban Terrain (MOUT) is a most baffling assignment – even a state possessing clearly predominant military muscle has a hard time bringing to bear the familiar assets of air superiority or heavy artillery when the enemy fighters are intermingled with civilians. A mighty Gulliver is crudely hamstrung when the enemy – instead of foolishly massing his forces and presenting himself for a traditional formal battle – eludes detection and destruction.

Jason Lyall and Isaiah Wilson III have presented a provocative empirical assessment of the frustration of counterinsurgency warfare. After analyzing 286 insurgencies between 1800 and 2005, they conclude that the Great Powers have recently suffered a significant slump – they have prevailed in only 27 percent of these wars in the past quarter century. The authors blame increasing "mechanization" for the decline in effectiveness – as the heavy-handed counterinsurgents operate large, cumbersome military machinery, they become more distant from the local population, more likely to wield their awesome firepower indiscriminately, and more prone to push fence-sitters into the camp of the rebels.[13]

The U.S. military has now seen a similar light; a rejection of simple-minded overwhelming force is key to the startling 2007 Counterinsurgency Manual (prepared by a team led by Gen. David H. Petraeus, who thereafter was tasked to implement the newfound strategy in Iraq). The opening chapter of this Army-Marine Corps manual now cautions practitioners to ponder several "paradoxes" about asymmetric and hybrid warfare, including "Sometimes, the More Force Is Used, the Less Effective It Is," and "Sometimes Doing Nothing Is the Best Reaction."[14] The newly evolving threat of protracted irregular warfare negates some of the technological and numerical advantages the United States has enjoyed and requires the creation of new, smarter tools and tactics.

The extreme version of the danger arises when the opposing force is not only creative and clever, but willing to act in a blatantly illegal and inhumane manner, violating some of the key law of armed conflict precepts identified in Chapter 3. By refusing to separate themselves from civilians and civilian property, but instead deliberately mingling their

[13] Jason Lyall and Isaiah Wilson III, Rage Against the Machines: Explaining Outcomes in Counterinsurgency Wars, 63 International Organization No. 1, Winter 2009, p. 67.

[14] Department of the Army, Counterinsurgency, Field Manual 3–24, December 15, 2006, pp. 1–27.

assets, insurgents of varying stripe in Iraq hope to escape effective counteraction. More broadly, when the opponents park their tanks next to mosques, or emplace snipers in hospitals, or adapt schools for weapons depots, the law-abiding side faces a terrible dilemma. Any attack on those sites risks inflicting unacceptable collateral damage – but allowing the enemy a sanctuary simply rewards cynical use of human shields.[15]

Useable weapons – precision-guided munitions and nonlethal weapons, for example – may offer one partial mechanism for surmounting this Hobson's choice, to enable MOUT operations that are effective yet adroit, respectful of local populations, and not crudely handing the enemy a vivid propaganda triumph.

5. *Effects-based operations.* More than just the latest military-babble slogan, "effects-based operations" offers a genuine insight. For most purposes, inflicting death or destruction may not be necessary; "mission kill" can be sufficient. If the legitimate goal of armed conflict is to compel or persuade the enemy to submit to your will, or to frustrate the accomplishment of his objectives, then putting his military assets out of commission may suffice – and sometimes, even temporary suspension of effective operations may do the trick.

Nonlethal weapons, as depicted in Chapter 8, offer the most vivid illustration of this sound bite. In some confrontations (MOOTW and other), "death is overkill"; we can accomplish our antipersonnel function amply by disarming a potential aggressor, dispersing a hostile crowd, temporarily disabling a troublemaker, capturing a leader, or scaring off the faint of heart. Likewise, antimateriel weapons can sometimes preserve the targeted country's infrastructure while effectively removing it from combat use – permitting bridges, railroads, TV broadcasting installations, government buildings, and the like to serve the postwar civilian economy even while we attempt to repair normal diplomatic relations. A constellation of useable weapons can thus assist in both wartime and postwar phases: denying the enemy the opportunity to apply these "dual-use" assets effectively against us during the fighting, while retaining the ability to husband national resources for peaceful applications during the subsequent recovery.

6. *Limited budgets.* Although the United States now spends annually as much on defense as does the rest of the world combined, even the American military budget knows limits. We cannot purchase every item

[15] Mathew C. Waxman, International Law and the Politics of Urban Air Operations, 2000, pp. 48–51.

that would be nice to have; we often run short even of equipment that turns out to be essential. Transformation of a military force is especially challenging when the country is engaged in not just one, but two, ongoing international conflicts – the public fisc can accommodate only so many claimants.

The long lead time between a procurement decision and the eventual deployment exacerbates this tension – a clairvoyant's skill is demanded for foreseeing military needs into the next decades of a new weapon's lifespan. As then-Secretary of Defense Donald Rumsfeld reminds us, judicious choices must be made – and they carry long-term consequences, "[Y]ou go to war with the Army you have. They're not the Army you might want or wish to have at a later time."[16]

This process of choosing wisely means that a sensible transformation is much more complex than simply jettisoning the inherited weapons systems and plunging wholeheartedly into the newly configured armada. The novel weapons dissected in Chapters 4–8 would be intended, for the most part, to supplement, not to totally replace, their bigger, heavier, more devastating predecessors – the thesis that useability, in some circumstances, offers distinct advantages does not imply that deft, small, precise, or short-duration arms are optimal in *all* applications.

7. *Proportionality.* The American leadership has recently been compelled by circumstances to learn some hard lessons about Daniel Webster's nineteenth-century concept of proportionality. Both the public affairs/political realities and the legal criteria reinforce these judicious messages, dating back to the *Caroline* case noted in Chapter 3.

For both the domestic and international audiences, military overreaction is no longer so tolerable; sustainable policy must be more nimble, and if we exceed reasonable restraints, even in pursuit of a just cause, we look ham-handed and inhumane. As provocative and gory images are instantaneously broadcast worldwide, legislators and ordinary citizens will recoil with horror at the blunderbuss application of "ordinary" weapons. No one these days should understate the "soft power" of this public imagery in evoking self-deterrence – as the elusive jihadist insurgent Ayman al-Zawahiri sees it, "We are in a battle, and more than half of this battle is taking place in the battlefield of the media."[17]

[16] U.S. Department of Defense, News Transcript, Secretary Rumsfeld Town Hall Meeting in Kuwait, December 8, 2004, p. 3.

[17] David Hambling, Blast Reduction, Defense Technology International, September 2007, p. 54; Peter Brookes, The Newest Trends in Terror, New York Post, June 3, 2008.

On the legal side, the law of armed conflict is of growing importance and visibility. Lawyers have insinuated themselves into the decision-making process at all levels of the U.S. national security community – choices about procurement, target selection, and rules of engagement must all now partake of Chapter 3's concerns, which push in the same direction about not overdoing things. As Ward Thomas has observed about precision-guided munitions, where the legal and the moral imperatives combine, access to more useable weaponry makes it "easier to be good."[18]

Treaty law has already foreclosed some traditional lines of military competition, narrowed others, and threatened still more. The 1993 Chemical Weapons Convention, for example, broadly prohibits a particularly reviled breed of combat; loophole-finders are reduced to scavenging any remaining role for "riot control agents" or malodorants as being something other than a "method of warfare."[19] Antipersonnel land mines are hemmed in by two rival treaties; under the pact joined by the United States, the devices are not banned altogether, but the most notorious versions and their most horrifying applications are outlawed. International law, it must be acknowledged, is typically a lagging factor – treaty negotiators routinely fall far behind the pace set by weapons innovators – but legal principles may incrementally help lock down some otherwise alluring options.

Customary international law, too, threatens to impinge combat operations in the name of reasonableness. If a combatant creatively develops precision-guided munitions or nonlethal weapons of such exquisite refinement that they can perform a military mission with a discrete touch, obviating the need for previous versions of deadly and destructive explosives, does that newfound prowess ratchet up the legal obligations? It may no longer be truly "necessary" to kill and to obliterate to accomplish legitimate objectives – at some point, that reality, even if one-sided, will work its way into the Judge Advocate General (JAG) attorney's calculations.

On the operational side, too, concerns about fratricide can also compel the "reasonable warrior" to be temperate in the application of deadly force. Where long-lived antipersonnel land mines (APL) might jeopardize our own troops who mount a freewheeling counterattack, or where

[18] Ward Thomas, The Ethics of Destruction: Norms and Force in International Relations, 2001, p. 172 (building on the analysis of Robert Tucker).

[19] Kyle M. Ballard, Convention in Peril? Riot Control Agents and the Chemical Weapons Ban, 37 Arms Control Today No. 7, September 2007, p. 12.

debris-creating antisatellite weapons might threaten our own (or our allies') orbiters, or where radioactivity from even a small-yield nuclear bunker buster might imperil downwinders of many nations, the exercise of overly large power can be both unwise and ineffective. As one pithy Marine put it, "It's easy to be hard; it's hard to be smart."

8. *Faith in technology.* Finally, observers have suggested that America's fascination with the latest military technology results in a hardy, if ahistorical, belief that war can be perfected – it can be rendered spotlessly clean (and therefore, quick, cheap, successful, and relatively bloodless) if we just had enough of the right know-how. The contemporary incarnation of that aspiration – the pursuit of transformational remote, robotic, smart means of warfighting – simply reflects that American persona. Colin S. Gray writes, "American culture . . . loves the latest technology, believes it enjoys a long lead in exploiting that technology, and yearns to find clean, discriminate, (American) casualty-minimal modes of war."[20] Harvey M. Sapolsky and Jeremy Shapiro identify the same tendency (or shortcoming), writing, "Technology is our first answer to the lethal hazards of waging war."[21] Andrew Bacevich adds his cautionary note, too, "Americans must also be disabused of the notion . . . that technology is sanitizing war or paving the way for an era when technologically advanced countries such as the United States will employ the military instrument bloodlessly."[22]

This American affinity for technology is rational – it plays to our current comparative advantage, as no other military force can afford to invest so much money into weapons research and development, and no potential enemy can now match the Yankee ingenuity in inventing new tools of mayhem and applying them to the battlefield.

Just as surely, however, some current techno-fetishism reflects American hubris – the baby boom generation, in particular, has demanded that even problems that have afflicted humanity for centuries should now be amenable to quick-fix solutions. We earnestly solicit and expect magic pharmaceutical correctives for communicable diseases, perfect air conditioning to overcome heat and humidity, new eco-friendly transportation

[20] Colin Gray, quoted in Morgan, supra note 2, at 232; see also Colin S. Gray, The American Way of War, in Anthony D. McIvor (ed.), Rethinking the Principles of War, 2005, pp. 27–33.

[21] Harvey M. Sapolsky and Jeremy Shapiro, Casualties, Technology, and America's Future Wars, 26 Parameters No. 2, Summer 1996, p. 119.

[22] A.J. Bacevich, The Use of Force in Our Time, 19 Wilson Quarterly No. 1, Winter 1995, p. 50, 62.

systems to mitigate the effects of distance. If perennial scourges such as male pattern baldness, sagging facial wrinkles, and erectile dysfunction now admit of technological solutions, why not apply the same sorts of creative energy to the warfighter's requirements for weapons that are simultaneously efficacious and discriminating?

At the same time, even the most starry-eyed aficionados have to admit that technology cannot solve everything – that sometimes modern innovations do not deliver all they have promised, and sometimes even the simplest, low-tech responses frustrate the scientist. It is noteworthy, for example, that sand – simple, plentiful, cheap sand, with no additives or electronic wizardry – can be noted in Chapter 7 as a possible low-tech antisatellite weapon and in Chapter 8 as an antidote to the nonlethal antitraction concoction "slippery foam." Sometimes, as the Shaker hymn celebrates, "'tis a gift to be simple."

In sum, a perfect storm of transformative factors has led to this extraordinary RMA occurring at this time, in this place. The United States today

a. confronts a dramatically challenging array of potential conflicts, including large-scale conventional war as well as asymmetric, irregular, and hybrid military threats requiring an assertive, adaptable, multifunctional military;
b. possesses an unrivaled technological capacity for inventing new tools of the military trade, as well as a willingness to devote significant funding to those creations; and
c. proclaims a national character of adherence to law and avoidance of excess and overreaction, resulting in a susceptibility to self-deterrence against the infliction of unnecessary suffering.

Other countries, too, face similar challenges and opportunities, and may be reacting in similarly revolutionary ways, but today the conditions creating the evangelism for, and the practice of, the RMA have emerged in most conspicuous form in Washington, D.C.

CYBER WEAPONS – THE NEXT USEABLE WEAPON

Peering dimly into the future, we can already begin to discern the broad outlines of some of the next, imminent revolutions in military affairs. Robotics would be one such innovation: when the United States military went to war in Iraq in 2003, it took along a bare handful of unarmed drone aircraft; today there are 5300 unmanned aerial vehicles in the inventory (many of them equipped with bombs as well as cameras) and

12,000 ground-based robots.[23] These remotely controlled apparatus have earned a valued place in the field of battle, performing duties that are too dirty, dangerous, or dull for humans; foreseeable further enhancements in sensors, batteries, and control algorithms will surely multiply androids' warfighting importance in the coming years, allowing the military to accomplish important functions without exposing troops to quite so much risk.

The world of computer warfare, however, may be the next realm within which the progression toward useable weapons is most strongly expressed. The National Intelligence Council, while avoiding the hyperbole that has led some to warn of an impending "Cyber Pearl Harbor," has identified electronic attacks as a factor that "will become more prevalent in conflicts over the next two decades," and "will constrict US freedom of action."[24] Likewise, Gen. Kevin P. Chilton, head of the U.S. Strategic Command, has spoken of cyberspace as an "emerging war-fighting domain"[25] – the fifth such locus of combat, joining the more familiar environments of land, sea, air, and space. President Barack Obama trumped even those rhetorical apprehensions, warning that "this cyber threat is one of the most serious economic and national security challenges we face as a nation."[26]

Even if this ominous foreshadowing is correct, the emerging realm is still remarkably opaque and ill-defined. The term "cyber warfare" can include any mechanism for attacking (especially via electronic means, rather than via traditional kinetic ordnance) enemy computers, and through them, the multiple, diverse systems they coordinate and control. It is sometimes lumped within a broader category of "Information Operations," which can embrace propaganda efforts, as well as "Psychological Operations," aimed to influence enemy soldiers' and civilians' states of mind – but the clear trend is to treat the cyber sector as sufficiently important and distinct to merit its own category and a corresponding, autonomous bureaucratic structure.[27]

[23] P.W. Singer, Robots and the Rise of 'Tactical Generals,' Defense News, March 9, 2009.

[24] National Intelligence Council, Global Trends 2025: A Transformed World, November 2008, p. 71, xi.

[25] Walter Pincus, The New Art of War, Washington Post, March 3, 2008, p. A15.

[26] Remarks by the President on Securing Our Nation's Cyber Infrastructure, May 29, 2009, available at http://www.whitehouse.gov/the_press_office/Remarks-by-the-President-on-Securing-Our-Nations-Cyber-Infrastructure/.

[27] See Walter E. Richter, The Future of Information Operations, Military Review, January-February 2009, p. 103; U.S. Joint Chiefs of Staff, Information Operations, Joint Publication 3–13, February 13, 2006.

The goals of computer network operations are similarly just beginning to be defined, but can include (in attacking or exploiting computer systems of an enemy military force, its nonmilitary government counterpart, or wholly civilian and commercial operations): denial of service, corruption or exfiltration of data, interruption of communications capabilities, usurping control over the operations, reconnaissance, and the surreptitious insertion of "trap doors" that could allow future undetected reentry.[28]

The capabilities, as well as the vulnerabilities, of the United States government in conducting these sorts of covert programs are necessarily highly classified, and precious little authoritative data has yet leaked into the public arena, obscuring the effort to assess current activities and foresee future revolutionary enhancements. The December 2006 National Military Strategy for Cyberspace Operations has now been declassified and published; it affords at least some insight into the arc of development of computer warfare capabilities. In it, the chairman of the Joint Chiefs of Staff asserts that "the United States must have cyberspace superiority to ensure our freedom of action and deny the same to our adversaries through the integration of network defense, exploitation, and attack.... DOD will execute the full range of military operations (ROMO) in and through cyberspace to defeat, dissuade, and deter threats against U.S. interests."[29] Numerous other task forces and command authorities have been established inside the Pentagon and elsewhere in the executive branch, as well as in the private and think tank sectors, to study the newfound problem and develop doctrine and tools for the anticipated surge in activity, but this is such a fast-moving field that strategies

[28] See generally, Alexander Melikishvili, Recent Events Suggest Cyber Warfare Can Become New Threat, WMD Insights, December 2008/January 2009; William T. Lord, USAF Cyberspace Command: To Fly and Fight in Cyberspace, Strategic Studies Quarterly, Fall 2008, p. 5; Greg Bruno, Backgrounder: The Evolution of Cyber Warfare, New York Times, February 27, 2008; Thomas C. Wingfield, The Law of Information Conflict: National Security Law in Cyberspace, 2000; Shane Harris, China's Cyber-Militia, National Journal, May 31, 2008; CSIS Commission on Cybersecurity for the 44th Presidency, Security Cyberspace for the 44th Presidency, December 2008; David A. Fulghum, Cyber-Attack Operations Near, Aviation Week, January 18, 2009; Marching Off to Cyberwar, Economist, December 4, 2008; Keith Epstein and Ben Elgin, Network Security Breaches Plague NASA, Business Week, November 20, 2008.

[29] Chairman of the Joint Chiefs of Staff, The National Military Strategy for Cyberspace Operations, December 2006, p. 1, 2. See also Department of Homeland Security, Fact Sheet: Protecting Our Federal Networks Against Cyber Attacks, April 8, 2008; Wyatt Kash, Details Emerge about President's Cyber Plan, Government Computer News, November 21, 2008.

and recommendations become obsolete almost before they can be implemented.

The legal guidance, too, is thin. Is a computer attack a "use of force," as that pregnant term is expressed in the Charter of the United Nations? Only electrons are moved in the process, rather than bullets, bombs, or even laser beams, but the effects could be catastrophic. Attribution of the source of a cyber offensive remains a most elusive task – often, it is far from clear whether a particular computer malfunction is the result of a deliberate onslaught or just an unlucky failure in a critical component, and the ability of an attacker to cover his tracks can make it impossibly difficult to determine the true source and to do so with the certainty and transparency that might be necessary to convince a skeptical public. Even then, the appropriate allocation of responsibilities for countering or retaliating after an intrusion – with suitable roles for both law enforcement authorities and military actors – has not been worked out, in part because the traditional law of armed conflict applies mainly to state actors or state-sponsored actors, whereas individual cyber hackers, like terrorists, can operate independently of national direction.

Are cyber weapons more useable than others? In some senses, virtual offensives may offer the most humane, barrier-free mechanisms imaginable for warfare: they can be precisely targeted and of rheostatically controlled magnitude, striking only a designated computer work station or a specific portion of a particular program; they can be wholly nonlethal and reversible, facilitating quick recovery and return to normalcy after the war; they can be covert and instantaneous; and they can also be appealingly cheap and easy to mount, with all the necessary equipment being anonymously procurable at the neighborhood consumer electronics store. The manipulation of ones and zeros might enable a savvy cyber power to undress its opponent's military forces (as well as its communications, transportation, and economic systems) without firing a lethal shot. No blood would be spilled, no buildings demolished, no casualties inflicted on either side, yet the attacker may be able to achieve at least an important semblance of an immediate and decisive victory.

On the other hand, some forms of cyber warfare would not meet the criteria established by the five case studies in this book. Computer viruses or worms, for example, are typically indiscriminate, spreading to strike intended targets and widespread collateral victims alike. Much of the damage inflicted is extensive, unforeseeable, and irreversible, such as the permanent corruption of a database or the usurpation of a computer's function. In one publicized March 2007 test, the Department of

Energy's Idaho laboratory experimented with simulating a cyber attack on a power plant, leaving "a smoking self-combusting diesel generator incapacitated by nothing more than keystrokes."[30] Computer warfare could also be fully lethal, employed to attack aircraft in flight or to shut down the operation of an electrical system, which could lead to blackouts at hospitals and other critical infrastructure. If the author of a computer network attack is unable to control, or even reliably to predict, the future trajectory and range of effects of the virus or other malware it unleashes, then no law of armed conflict proportionality test could be passed.

What we can say with confidence is that the era of computer warfare is already upon us, with conspicuous – indeed, daily – illustrations. An early prominent victim was Estonia in April 2007. There, the government decided to relocate a prominent monument celebrating the Soviet army's World War II liberation of the country, transferring the icon from the center of the capital city to a military cemetery on the outskirts – a move that the Russian government and citizens considered blatantly disrespectful. Two weeks of coordinated computer onslaughts followed, during which the Web sites of the Estonian Ministries of Foreign Affairs and of Justice had to shut down (under the pressure of receiving some 2000 visits per second), and the national emergency toll-free number was likewise disabled. The direct role of the Russian government in the barrage is still obscure, but the scale, scope, and coordination of the challenge belie the notion that it was simply a spontaneous eruption among disparate private actors. The fact that Estonia is an especially cyber-enabled country, more integrated into the electronic era than any of its neighbors, underscores the vulnerability that inevitably accompanies a society's heavy reliance upon the computer.

Georgia was next to feel the pressure of a Russian-originated virtual blitzkrieg. The confrontation in August 2008 over the breakaway regions of Abkhazia and South Ossetia was the first occasion when online warfare and physical warfare were conducted jointly on a wide scale. Again, denial-of-service techniques (with the Russian government again preserving a thin veneer of plausible deniability) afflicted the email and other computer operations of the Georgian president, parliament, leading ministries, the national bank, and the predominant news services. Malicious software inserted into dozens of computers inflicted little permanent harm, and may not have gravely affected Tbilisi's ability to respond to the crisis, but surely amounted to more than simple mischief. Kyrgyzstan, too,

[30] Bruno, supra note 28.

has felt the sting of Russian hackivists, in January 2009, when Moscow wanted to pressure its neighbor regarding renewal of a U.S. military base there. Reportedly 80 percent of the country's operational bandwidth was affected – but, notably, Kyrgyzstan is a much less Internet-oriented country than Estonia, so the denial of service may have had less potential impact.

The United States, too, has long been a favorite target of computer intruders. James E. Cartwright, former head of the U.S. Strategic Command, has declared that in view of the hundreds of computer network probes that bombard Pentagon and other firewalls daily, "America is under widespread attack in cyberspace." The Department of Homeland Security reported 37,000 attempts to breach government and private computer systems in 2007, and assaults on federal agencies increased 152 percent from the prior year.[31] Different scorekeeping by the Department of Defense found an astonishing 360 million attempts to break into its networks in 2007; the Pentagon spent $100 million in six months alone trying to rebuff the incursions.

All told, cybercrime has cost Americans an estimated $8 billion in the past two years; losses of intellectual property from data theft in 2008 could be as high as $1 trillion. The Federal Bureau of Investigation now ranks cybercrime as the third-greatest threat to U.S. national security, after nuclear war and proliferation of weapons of mass destruction.

A prominent source of these encroachments (at least as far as we can determine a "return address" for some of them) is China. The People's Liberation Army has overtly formed information warfare units to develop viruses and other aggressive mechanisms, and is suspected of insinuating its electronic tentacles into government and commercial targets in Germany, France, and the United Kingdom, as well as the United States. One especially noteworthy raid on the Pentagon systems in 2007 lasted several weeks, afflicting 1500 computers; it succeeded in surmounting determined defensive efforts, including those surrounding the unclassified systems supporting the immediate office of Secretary of Defense Robert Gates. Equally dramatic, unknown cyberspies succeeded in hacking into networks leading the development work on the F-35 Joint Strike Fighter, a $300 billion project to create a state-of-the-art combat aircraft; they apparently pilfered data that could reveal the fighter's performance

[31] Dave Montgomery, Military Planners Mull Possibility of Cyber War, Kansas City Star, November 26, 2007, p. 1. See also Ben Bain, Number of Reported Cyber Incidents Jumps, Federal Computer Week, February 17, 2009.

specifications and potential vulnerabilities. The White House, the Department of State, and the National Aeronautics and Space Administration (NASA), among others, have also been targets of this e-snooping, as were both the Obama and McCain presidential campaigns in 2008.

The United States government has refrained from officially charging the Chinese government with authorship of these attacks – again, attribution can be cleverly dodged by the same hacking techniques that enable the intrusions in the first place. But Joel Brennan, the top U.S. cyber detective, points the finger of blame directly at Beijing, assessing that Chinese hackers are "very good and getting better all the time.... What makes the Chinese stand out is the pervasive and relentless nature of the attacks that are coming from China."[32]

The U.S. government's nascent response to these vulnerabilities has been slow to start, and still sputters – but the community has clearly begun to appreciate the scope of the threat and the size, complexity, and cost of the effort necessary to protect this Achilles heel. In January 2008, the Bush Administration launched a multipronged Comprehensive National Cybersecurity Initiative to address current vulnerabilities and anticipate future challenges, and the Director of National Intelligence has highlighted cyber dangers in his annual "Threat Assessment" – but the power of this newfound high-level attention is yet to be fully demonstrated.[33]

Among the bureaucratic missteps was confusion over designation, bureaucratic location, and identity of a "cyber czar" to exercise central authority over a concerted national prophylactic effort that could command $5–6 billion annually. The U.S. Air Force, the Department of Homeland Security, and the National Security Agency each initially claimed a lead role, but each was forced to take a step back when other stakeholders resisted that assertiveness. Under the Air Force's vision, cyber operations would be about 85 percent defensive (to protect U.S. networks from attack and disruption) and 15 percent offensive (to target potential adversaries' computer capabilities).[34]

[32] Harris, supra note 28. See also U.S.-China Economic and Security Review Commission, Report to Congress, November 2008, p. 165 ("China is targeting U.S. government and commercial computers for espionage.")

[33] Dennis C. Blair, Annual Threat Assessment of the Intelligence Community, March 10, 2009; John Rollins and Anna C. Henning, Comprehensive National Cybersecurity Initiative: Legal Authorities and Policy Considerations, Congressional Research Service Report for Congress, March 10, 2009.

[34] Erik Holmes, Donley Sets Out Structure for Cyber Command, Air Force Times, February 25, 2009.

Immediately upon taking office, the Obama Administration signaled its appreciation for the seriousness of the problem, undertaking a 60-day review of the "plans, programs, and activities underway" in the field.[35] A new Cybersecurity Office is being established in the White House, to be complemented by a new operational military Cyber Command. There is the promise of tens of millions of dollars of new research into computer security operations, and officials pledge to create a coordinated national "incident response plan" for cyberattacks and to develop "best practices" controls for protecting agencies' networks.

Again, consistent with a theme noted in Chapters 4 through 8, it is the United States that simultaneously possesses both the greatest ability to engage in this incipient form of warfare (having the most sophisticated capacity to invade, disrupt, and commandeer other nations' computer systems) and the greatest vulnerability if others should decide to attack us in that way (because the American economy depends so extensively on a relatively open, difficult-to-shield cyber infrastructure).

But as we have seen with other components of the revolution in military affairs, the National Research Council warns, "enduring unilateral dominance in cyberspace is neither realistic nor achievable by the United States."[36] Our ability to engage in cyber warfare, and our need to gird ourselves against electronic incursions may be outstripping our ability to think carefully about the proliferating opportunities and dangers. The next chapter of the story of useable weapons, therefore, may spin out in cyberspace, as we determine whether the principles of self-deterrence operate in the virtual world comparably to the real world, and what – if anything – can be done to foreclose yet another dangerous and destabilizing arms race.

WHAT TO DO ABOUT USEABILITY – BIG PICTURE

A complex phenomenon such as a general increase in the useability of revolutionary weapons cannot be abruptly adjudged as a good or bad thing *per se*. Just as this wrinkle in the RMA is not a manifestation of any

[35] The White House, The Agenda: Homeland Security, http://www.whitehouse.gov/agenda/homeland_security/ 2009; Top Brass Launch Manpower Study for Cyberspace Operations, Inside the Pentagon, March 5, 2009.

[36] William A. Owens, Kenneth W. Dam, and Herbert S. Lin (eds.), Technology, Policy, Law, and Ethics Regarding U.S. Acquisition and Use of Cyber Capabilities, National Research Council, 2009, pp. 1–19.

conscious, overarching national strategy, it does not admit of universal top-down policy prescription. Subtle analysis requires a more detailed assessment of the pros and cons of each weapon, the circumstances under which it may be pursued and applied, and the intelligence and good will of the leaders who will command it. Nonetheless, it is useful to start with some big-picture thinking, first adducing some generic benefits from this RMA process, and then some dangers.

Mission accomplishment. The first appeal of useable weapons is sheer effectiveness – if they work as advertised, these new generations of military hardware can better enable our forces to accomplish their assigned missions in operations that are diverse, dangerous, and far-flung. As long as the United States is going to sustain a superior military apparatus, and as long as we are going to task that apparatus with fulfilling a variety of roles – involving formal warfare, less-than-formal warfare, and Military Operations Other Than War alike – we should equip it to perform those functions as efficiently, cleanly, and cheaply as possible.

If precision-guided air-to-surface bombs, to take one example, empower our forces to exert a more nimble clout – to attack an enemy with devastating effect yet with greatly reduced collateral damage – that augmentation should reduce the self-deterrence constraints that arise from possessing only overly powerful military tools that are too crude for the contemplated task. To venture into the more controversial proposed weapons, the chief arguments in favor of third-generation antisatellite weapons or low-yield nuclear weapons also arise from similar calculations: if we are going to perform (or even to threaten) a particular action, we should have the capability to undertake that action – and the more dexterous and nuanced our capability, the more credible it will be. If we can fight better and win more quickly – and if the putative enemy understands that prowess – we will be called upon to exercise our capabilities less often.

The cost of *preparing* for war, too, must be taken into account; another form of wastage is mindless pursuit of glitzy armaments that do not, in fact, contribute materially to a genuine military function. As Martin van Creveld summarizes it, "From the point of view of society at large it simply makes no sense to produce weapons that are too expensive, too fast, too indiscriminate, too big, too unmaneuverable and too powerful to use in real-life war."[37]

[37] Martin van Creveld, The Transformation of War, 1991, p. 210.

We can argue, of course, about the wisdom and legality of past, present, and contemplated U.S. military operations. And prudential considerations may well inveigh against applying any particular quantity or type of force in any particular situation. But the general argument here is simply in favor of competence: useable weapons support a more capable military.

Humanitarianism. A very different sort of rationale for useable weapons sounds in ethics: warfare is so horrible, so costly to so many people, that we should privilege any mechanism for mitigating that carnage. Smaller yields in the explosives, greater accuracy in their placement, and shorter duration in their effects – all can help reduce the incidence of death and injury for our own forces, for enemy fighters, for bystanders, and for the infrastructure of whatever unlucky country the combatants are tearing up.

In this vein, useable weapons make a claim to greater humanity: PGMs, for example, spare civilians from the historically favored alternative of broad-gauged "carpet bombing"; nonlethal weapons enable counterinsurgency operations to incapacitate possibly threatening individuals and to sort out the real enemies later. Nonexplosive antisatellite weapons could perform a military function while inflicting less debris upon the space activities of nations that were neutral in a conflict; smart APL mitigate the long-term hazards that their robust, persistent predecessors pose to civilians and postwar societies.

Even from the perspective of the target, this nudge toward greater civility in warfare should be welcome. If force is going to be used against you, you would in general prefer that it be small, accurate, temporary, and nonlethal – anything that reduces the mindless wastage of war is a common boon to mankind. For the user, too, less deadly and destructive weapons can provide a less degrading way of fighting. Recall Golda Meir's famous statement to Anwar Sadat before one set of Middle East peace talks, "We can forgive you for killing our sons. But we will never forgive you for making us kill yours."

Ending war quickly. Uniting these first two elements is the notion that the only truly humanitarian step in warfare is ending it as soon as possible. In this vein, the most efficacious force, capable of decisively defeating the enemy promptly, will best accomplish the national objectives and reduce casualties on all sides; half-hearted or ineffective measures merely prolong the suffering. The famous Lieber Code – promulgated by Abraham Lincoln as legal and practical guidance for Union armies during the

Civil War – recognized this grim reality: "The more vigorously wars are pursued the better it is for humanity. Sharp wars are brief."[38]

In pre-RMA wars, this vigorous pursuit of warfare usually required the application of overwhelming force; with today's transformed capabilities, a more subtle approach sometimes complements that relationship – useable weapons, deftly applied, can enable an even more effective form of warfare, truncating the combat more quickly on favorable terms. As Rupert Smith notes, there is a distinction between a use of force and the utility of force – and we must focus intelligently on the latter.[39]

Will it help or hinder deterrence? If useable weapons make warfare more tolerable for the United States and its opponents alike, will that evolution be good or bad for deterrence? On the one hand, transformation could be helpful in sustaining a climate of peace: if a potential opponent realizes that the United States and its allies possess a genuine, efficacious, and useable capacity to respond effectively to aggression, then his calculations about the imagined fruits of victory will turn sour. Revolutionary weaponry from APL to NLW to low-yield nuclear bombs can deny opponents the glimpse of success that encourages their adventuresomeness. As "hard liners" traditionally argue, "weakness is provocative," and a prominent display of American preparedness and capacity to short-circuit others' aggressive designs may inhibit future wars. Winston Churchill likewise explained it a generation ago, saying, "The way to make war impossible is to make victory certain."[40]

On the other hand, if useable weapons indeed lower the adverse consequences of warfare for both the high-tech user and the low-tech target, might they not inadvertently reinforce any instinct toward petty aggression? Patrick Morgan has observed that if force is limited enough to make it "useable," it also becomes more "bearable" for the challenger.[41] When the potentially hostile state knows that its action is likely to be met with judicious, humane restraint from others – that they will endeavor to avoid collateral damage to its civilians, will undertake only a temporary "soft kill" of its infrastructure, and will refrain from massive retaliation – might the leadership conclude that the gamble was worth taking? Any humanitarian gesture in warmaking creates a potential "moral hazard" – if a

38 General Order 100, Lieber Code, Instructions for the Government of Armies of the United States in the Field, April 24, 1863, art. 29.

39 Rupert Smith, The Utility of Force: The Art of War in the Modern World, 2007, p. 41.

40 Quoted in Norman Angell, Peace Theories and the Balkan War, 1912.

41 Morgan, supra note 2, at 223.

party is even partially insulated from the negative effects of a risk, it may rationally respond by becoming less conscientious about avoiding that risk.

Jean Pictet, a leading exponent of humanitarian law, identified similar perverse incentives throughout the evolution of the law of armed conflict, beginning with the creation of the International Committee of the Red Cross. Any efforts to reduce the agony of war, he noted, will inevitably also mitigate the incentive to avoid it. He labeled that syllogism "absurd" regarding the Red Cross's campaign to institute moral and legal restraints on combat, but in the instance of useable weapons, the danger cannot be lightly dismissed.[42]

Counterpoised to these "big picture" arguments in favor of useability in the abstract – and partially derived from them – are two primary rejoinders: useable weapons may increase the frequency of warfare, and useable weapons may proliferate to other parties. Both considerations require careful inspection.

Increasing the propensity for war. A simple cost-benefit calculation applies here: if the adverse consequences of war are *reduced* for the United States via development and application of revolutionary useable weapons, we should then expect an *increase* in the frequency of combat. That is what it means to diminish self-deterrence: in close cases, where America in the past may have refrained from applying military force, we will in the future have less incentive to exercise that restraint – with both good and bad consequences.

The most stark danger, of course, is that self-deterrence will be relaxed too much – that leaders will be lulled into a false sense that war can be waged cheaply and quickly (and successfully), and they will miscalculate about when the initiation of hostilities would serve U.S. interests.

Precision air power provides a handy illustration of this hazard. Smart bombs are both more effective and more humane than their predecessors; they enable the sophisticated military to undertake missions that would have been scrubbed only a decade or two ago and to accomplish pinpoint destruction of enemy targets even when intermingled with civilian assets – and they do so without exposing U.S. ground troops to the vagaries of an assault. But we have to be careful about not overpromising – warfare is always dangerous and expensive, and it carries no guarantees. If we enter a

[42] Jean Pictet, Development and Principles of International Humanitarian Law, 1985, pp. 81–82.

war on the false premise that air power alone can accomplish any task, we may be rudely surprised by a rising local resistance and by the occasional off-target munition – because even the smartest bombs cannot root out all opposition and will sometimes result in horrific collateral damage. The PGMs discussed in Chapter 4 exacerbate any tendency toward precipitous action; by conjuring the illusion of 100 percent deft application, they will reinforce an instinct to overrely upon air power, emboldening us to inject our forces into tasks that ultimately prove costly to finish by other means.

From the global perspective, after all, few would argue that the main problem confronting the world in the security realm these days has been an America that has been *too much inhibited* in the use of military force or too constrained by an inadequate quiver of weaponry at its disposal. In Moscow, New Delhi, Berlin, or Johannesburg, observers worry much more that the global hegemon is too prone to act too quickly – not that excessive self-deterrence has been the defining hallmark of contemporary decision-makers in Washington, D.C. Further curtailment of one of the key factors inhibiting military adventures would tend toward even more "wars of choice" – not precisely the prescription that most global doctors would order these days. The 2008–2009 "Guidance" memorandum from the chairman of the Joint Chiefs of Staff recognizes this risk, cautioning against "further militarization of our foreign policy."[43] In an environment that provides such a rich set of stimuli and such an impoverished array of possible responses, there is a perpetual danger of overreliance upon useable military force.

At the tactical level, too, there is a legitimate worry that individual soldiers, equipped with seemingly less portentous arms (e.g., nonlethal acoustic beams or short-lived smart antipersonnel land mines), might be quicker on the trigger than they are when wielding traditional firepower – and perhaps quicker on the trigger than they should be. Anecdotal evidence suggests that local law enforcement agencies bearing nonlethal pepper-ball guns, for example, are more prone to shoot first (confident that no lasting injury will be inflicted) and ask questions later – a sequence that sometimes proves disastrous when the supposedly nonlethal mechanisms suddenly prove too powerful. Better training and discretely crafted rules of engagement can ameliorate those dangers, of course, but sometimes only a blanket rule can provide real security. The United Nations has recently imposed a total ban on the use of rubber bullets in Kosovo,

[43] Michael G. Mullen, CJCS Guidance for 2008–2009, November 17, 2008.

for example, following the deaths of two protesters there who were shot by police who had been overly persuaded about the advertised nonlethal nature of those implements.

The dispiriting result of all this may be a play on the old aphorism that "if all you have is a hammer, everything begins to look like a nail." Here the situation is even worse: If we now have a wider array of sizes and types of hammers, we become even more confident that what we are seeing is a variety of kinds of nails – and we will be more likely to overlook the possibility that perhaps we should not be using blunt force implements at all. As we elaborate our already-impressive arsenals of PGMs, APLs, NLWs, and the rest, we are similarly likely to become reinforced in our estimates of the utility of those instruments and correspondingly less disposed to appreciate the scope for the application of diplomacy, economic sanctions, and simple patience.

We must also remember that these new tools are not, and can never be rendered, truly safe – the title of this book is intended as an abrupt warning flag that even moderate weapons cause death. The revolutionary arms are intended to inflict fewer human and property casualties – or, at least, to generate fewer losses to the *wrong* people – but warfare is inevitably a grisly and grim prospect. A.A. Milne made this point decades ago, emphasizing the notion that war is inherently poisonous, so "we should not roll it meditatively round the tongue and wonder how to improve the taste."[44]

Jeffrey Record warns that the dividing line between "prudent caution" and "crippling timidity" is elusive;[45] the law of unintended consequences suggests that it may be too easy to get into a war that we think we can fight on the cheap, and too hard to get out when the initial level of commitment proves unavailing. The pithy remark of nineteenth-century Prussian Field Marshal Helmuth von Moltke is to the same effect: "No plan survives contact with the enemy" because unforeseen events inevitably intervene.[46]

This is not to suggest that any and all relaxation of self-deterrence would be catastrophic – plenty of vivid inhibitions remain that would deter a too-facile resort to the abyss of war. Everyone appreciates at some level that international conflict is a third-rail scourge to be painstakingly avoided; all sensate leaders hesitate before jumping onto it.

[44] A.A. Milne, Peace with Honor: An Enquiry into the War Convention, 1934, p. 8.

[45] Jeffrey Record, Back to the Weinberger-Powell Doctrine? Strategic Studies Quarterly, Fall 2007, p. 79, 80.

[46] Quoted in John M. Collins, How Military Strategists Should Study History, Military Review, August 1983, p. 32, 38.

Moreover, special taboos operate with enduring power in some of the most important RMA realms: any use of nuclear weapons, for example, even a small, accurate, and militarily necessary blast, would be a monumental departure from six decades of forbearance and would not be undertaken lightly. Marine Gen. James Cartwright, the vice chair of the Joint Chiefs of Staff, confirmed that judgment, labeling the justification for a low-yield nuclear "bunker buster" merely "a good academic argument," and asserting that virtually no U.S. president would resort to such a weapon in combat.[47]

Likewise, any hostile application of antisatellite weapons (ASAT), or even overt development and deployment of such a threatening system, would be a most provocative action. Even if the particular directed energy antisatellite weapon were designed to accomplish a temporary and partial disruption of satellite operations, it would constitute a radical violation of the hallowed nonweaponization ethos of outer space. Still, the whole point of the exercise – the reason why Pentagon authorities are interested in pursuing these revolutionary weapons – is precisely to craft more useable weapons, to mitigate some of the self-deterrence that operates today. The danger of reducing those inhibitions too much, and making the threshold of combat too easy to cross, is inescapable.

One other important set of restraining factors must be noted, deriving from the modern practice of fighting in international "coalitions of the willing." As that type of collaboration becomes more commonplace, revolutionary weapons pose additional practical challenges. First, because some emerging U.S. weapons are so sophisticated, so high-tech, and so costly, many of our allies cannot afford to procure them (even if we were willing to transfer to them the relevant technology). Interoperability with even close foreign colleagues is therefore impeded – the technology gap on PGMs, for example, reduces opportunities for effective burden-sharing partnerships.

Second, conflicting legal obligations – or disparate interpretations of shared legal commitments – may muddle attempts to fight in a fully integrated manner. For example, the United States, virtually alone among NATO allies, has refrained from joining the Ottawa Mine Ban Treaty, and the American military is therefore less constrained than the others regarding the strewing of self-deactivating antipersonnel land mines, as discussed in Chapter 6. But Ottawa parties are also strictly forbidden from

47 Elaine M. Grossman, Senior U.S. General Sees High Nuclear Threshold, Global Security Newswire, October 22, 2007.

"using" mines and from "assisting" anyone else in doing so.[48] In combined operations, how far could our British, Dutch, or other colleagues extend themselves in collaborative support operations such as transportation, refueling, or even mission planning without running afoul of their Ottawa commitments?[49]

Likewise, the Chemical Weapons Convention prohibits use of "riot control agents (RCAs)" as a method of war, as discussed in Chapter 8. The United States has traditionally adopted a narrow or restricted understanding of that obligation, purporting to retain the legal authority to disperse disabling nonlethal gas in particular near-combat circumstances. Most of our allies, however, consider the American interpretation excessively crabbed, and they have espoused much more expansive views about prohibiting RCAs on or around the battlefield. If our forces are to operate productively in coalition, these additional legal restrictions would have to be factored into any analysis of American propensity to resort quickly to new, revolutionary weapons.

Proliferation of the revolutionary arms. It is not plausible to suggest that the United States will indefinitely retain a monopoly in these emerging capabilities; if a transformed military offers significant advantages, others will, sooner or later, ape our accomplishments. We need, therefore, to think dynamically about international peace and security, pursuing our goals not only in the short term, but also for a time when others have had the opportunity to respond to the moves we make today. Winston Churchill, once again, said it best, "However absorbed a commander may be in the elaboration of his own thoughts, it is sometimes necessary to take the enemy into account."

To some extent, useable weapons have already proliferated. Precision-guided munitions, a most conspicuous example, have won popularity around the world; imported versions and indigenous knock-offs can now be found in the arsenals of a dozen or more countries. Land mines, too, had spread like kudzu, at least until the Ottawa treaty process marked them as illegitimate – although the "smart" varieties, incorporating self-neutralization features, remain basically an American taste. Rudimentary nonlethal weapons are likewise already a global phenomenon, and the more advanced iterations are swiftly catching attention in NATO as well

48 1997 Convention on the Prohibition of the Use, Stockpiling, Production and Transfer of Anti-Personnel Mines and on Their Destruction, signed December 3, 1997, entered into force July 3, 1998, 36 I.L.M. 1507, 1997 [Ottawa Mine Ban Treaty], art. 1.

49 U.S. Army, Center for Law and Military Operations, Forged in the Fire: Legal Lessons Learned During Military Operations 1994–2006, September 2006, pp. 152–53.

as in the United States – and the Russian deputy interior minister, noting the fad, boasted that modern NLW would shortly be introduced in his country and he opined that "Russian non-lethal weapons are considerably better than similar weapons produced in foreign and CIS [Commonwealth of Independent States] countries." More ominously, there are now nine countries generally understood to possess a nuclear weapons capability and three that have tested antisatellite devices.

As important as it may be to arrive first with a revolutionary new weapons technology, therefore, an equally important question, as Colin Grey notes, has always been, "For how long would 'first' mean 'only'?"[50] Frederick Kagan is even more fatalistic about dissemination of new weapons, calling it "the universal fate of revolutions in military affairs. The end result of every RMA to date has been the possession by all major powers of the technology and capabilities originally pioneered by one. This RMA will be no different."[51]

The near-certainty of proliferation of weapons technology is underscored by another bizarre reality: the United States is by far the world's leading arms merchant. In 2007, the United States sold roughly $25 billion worth of conventional armaments, far outpacing the nearest competitors (Russia and the United Kingdom) in a thriving market that totaled $60 billion. All told, weapons deliveries in 2007 reached the highest volume ever recorded.[52] Although the most high-tech and revolutionary weaponry does not yet sport a cynical "For Sale" sign, economic and political factors do drive the innovating countries and companies to solicit profitable international marketing opportunities.

Of course, other states may pursue revolutionary technologies anyway, even if the United States does not lead in that direction. As in every potential arms race, there can be no guarantee that American self-restraint will elicit reciprocal temperateness. But the converse is likely iron-clad: if we build it, others will follow. As the first entrant, the United States may indefinitely retain an edge in the technological competition, but as Andrew Krepinevich observes, prolonged monopoly in these endeavors does not seem sustainable.[53]

[50] Colin S. Gray, Strategy for Chaos: Revolutions in Military Affairs and the Evidence of History, 2002, p. 153.

[51] Frederick W. Kagan, Finding the Target: The Transformation of American Military Policy, 2006, p. 390.

[52] Richard F. Grimmett, Conventional Arms Transfers to Developing Nations, 2000–2007, Congressional Research Service Report for Congress RL 34723, October 23, 2008.

[53] Andrew F. Krepinevich, Cavalry to Computer: The Pattern of Military Revolutions, National Interest, Fall 1993–1994.

And once the dogs of RMA are unleashed, there is no certainty about who will benefit the most. Patrick Morgan posits that the developing states, rather than the most advanced military powers, might accrue larger advantages.[54] Indeed, it may seem paradoxical that the United States – which could be conceptualized as a paradigmatic "status-quo power" in view of the enormous strategic advantages it enjoys under current military alignments – would be at the forefront of the race away from the existing weapons lineup.

Certainly, the consequences of any global arms race in some of these RMA technologies could be starkly adverse – both for American security and for global peace and stability. It would be folly incarnate for a U.S. pursuit of low-yield bunker busters to validate the military and political importance of nuclear weapons, leading to further proliferation of the one technology that could truly pose an existential threat to American life. In the same vein, it is hard to imagine how a world characterized by readily available ASAT technologies would be better for the United States than is the current arrangement, given our overwhelming space superiority and the prospects for its continuation.

Moreover, it is not just use of these emerging weapons against the United States that should be of concern. If useable weapons proliferate, we might well anticipate a substantial *global* reduction in self-deterrence and a corresponding uptick in the incidence of violence around the world. As additional countries, equipped with increasingly deft weaponry, confront each other in their traditional antagonisms, we should anticipate that their access to PGMs or NLWs might make them, too, a bit quicker on the trigger against each other, a degree more prone to imagine that they could fight a quick, cheap, successful war with acceptable damage on all sides. If RMA inventions succeed only in making the world safer for more frequent warfare, that would be a most dubious accomplishment.

The virtue of a useable weapon, after all, depends not solely upon the innate character of the device itself but even more on the character of the putative user. We must ponder not only how these dynamic new implements might be advantageously wielded by our own troops, but how, over time, they might be turned against us by malefactors including enemy states, terrorists, and street criminals. It might be easier and safer to ban or otherwise preemptively foreclose a new technology altogether, rather than to forecast or control a future user's bona fides.

[54] Morgan, supra note 2, at 233.

Other imponderables also complicate any judgment about the desirability of jumping feet first into an RMA. Even without proliferation, the new technologies may drive our increasingly desperate foes to respond to American weapons superiority with unpredictable, asymmetric, or disproportional force. If we employ smart bombs that they cannot match, will they respond with terrorism? If we exploit disabling chemicals on the battlefield, stretching the bounds of the Chemical Weapons Convention, may others up the ante and deploy lethal nerve agents against us?

Charles Dunlap has explored the possibility that unilateral U.S. access to precision-guided munitions may have inspired Iraqi opponents in Gulf War I to torch their oil fields to generate thick plumes of smoke that would obscure laser guidance, and may likewise have driven Serb defenders of Belgrade to mobilize human shields to take high-value sites off American target lists.[55] Even worse, David Markov reported a decade ago that

> Many Russian military theorists believe nuclear weapons provide the best answer to the challenge posed by conventionally armed precision guided munitions, which have become such an important part of Western military strategies. Russian generals fear that, in a general war, Western nations could employ such "smart munitions" to degrade Russian strategic nuclear forces, without ever having to "go nuclear" themselves. Consequently, said Gen. Volkov, Russia "should enjoy the right to consider the first [enemy] use of precision weapons as the beginning of an unrestricted nuclear war against it."[56]

These pressures are exacerbated by the accelerating pace of change. Revolutions in military affairs are still rare episodes, but they come with increasing swiftness these days, and they accomplish their insidious effects in fewer years. As John Collins calculates it, the various components of warfare "have undergone greater revision in the last 50 years than during the previous 50 centuries. Acceleration not only continues but is also rapidly increasing."[57] With the dangers metastasizing at that frenetic pace, the current RMA in useable weapons must be approached only with the greatest caution.

[55] Charles J. Dunlap, Jr., Technology: Recomplicating Moral Life for the Nation's Defenders, 29 Parameters No. 3, Autumn 1999, p. 24.

[56] David R. Markov, The Russians and Their Nukes, 80 Air Force Magazine No. 2, February 1997.

[57] Collins, supra note 46, at 31, 42.

WHAT TO DO ABOUT USEABILITY – SMALL PICTURE

My own policy preferences, after examining the five emerging useable weapons studied in Chapters 4–8, is to support the further development of precision-guided munitions and nonlethal weapons; to oppose the pursuit of new antisatellite systems and low-yield nuclear weapons; and I'm frankly still not sure about smart antipersonnel land mines. Here's why.

Precision-guided munitions. The precision revolution has been so successful that it is now impossible to imagine modern armed conflict without it, and only a King Canute could try to order a reversal in this tide of battle. And if any weapon of warfare could ever be called both "strategic" and "humanitarian" in its effects, it would be the PGM – by incorporating greater accuracy, it enables an attacker to employ fewer bombs and smaller bombs. Smart ordnance thereby facilitates mission accomplishment, exposes fewer air crews to hostile fire, and conserves assets – and it inflicts far less collateral damage upon the targeted state.

We should not overstate the magic of smart bombs. Even the Pentagon has admitted that in the early phases of Gulf War II, over 50 hand-crafted air strikes attempted to "decapitate" Iraq's military hierarchy, but failed to kill a single leader – while inflicting an average of 30 civilian casualties each.[58] There will always be important limitations upon what air power alone can accomplish, and there will always be bombs that go astray or that wreak devastating punishment upon innocent victims. Still, if a war is going to be fought, it should be fought with this degree of accuracy and reliability.

Nonlethal weapons. NLW are still, for the most part, more promise than performance. The image of reliable, temporary incapacitation of enemy soldiers, terrorists, civilians, and hostages is tantalizing; the notion that we could craft antimateriel systems to preclude hostile use of a country's infrastructure during wartime while still preserving it for postwar civilian recovery is just as alluring. Self-interest, as well as empathy, align here – if we can win a war while sparing the innocent and facilitating a return to normalcy, we all benefit.

But the dream of NLW has stalled somewhere between the drawing board and the theater of battle. As Col. Kirk Hymes, Director of the Pentagon's NLW program ruefully observes: "Lethal systems have an

[58] Human Rights Watch, Off Target: The Conduct of the War and Civilian Casualties in Iraq, December 11, 2003, pp. 22–23, http://www.hrw.org/en/reports/2003/12/11/target-0; Robert A. Pape, Pape Replies, 83 Foreign Affairs No. 5, p. 162, 163.

easier time getting into our system."[59] The Active Denial System (ADS), to take the most conspicuous example, promises to create an effective "keep-out zone" of appreciable range, via heat rays that inflict pain but no somatic harm. It has been successfully tested thousands of times, but the public affairs mavens at the Department of Defense have kept it largely under wraps, perpetually alluding to its availability soon but still refraining from deploying it in Iraq, where it might actually do some good.

The novelty of ADS and other candidate nonlethal systems is surely problematic – there is a substantial task to craft an approach that will not alienate public opinion in the United States and around the world as mysterious new technologies are unleashed on human beings. But the only way to deal with that potentially adverse imagery is to get into the game – to display what the NLW are, what they are capable of, and what their effects may be. I would therefore support a much more vigorous NLW program, including a substantial public relations outreach component for those creations, such as ADS, that are virtually "shovel ready," to reduce the foot-dragging in this aspect of the RMA.

Antisatellite weapons. Antisatellite weapons, on the other hand, threaten to initiate a needless new form of arms racing. This is a complicated situation, because the security of the space environment is already under increasing threat, and because the capability for weaponizing the heavens is likely to proliferate even if the United States does not spark the competition. And there is some merit to the Rumsfeld notion that "weakness is provocative... Weakness invites people into doing things they wouldn't otherwise think of."[60]

But the greater insights lie in the awareness that America has the most to lose from this nascent competition and that a world characterized by reciprocal ASAT fleets could offer only scant protection for the expensive and vulnerable assets we are now so fully dependent upon for the vast array of civilian and military applications. If others were to inaugurate an ASAT steeplechase, the United States may well have to follow, and a modest, low-level research program might constitute a prudent hedge. But why would we want to lead in a direction that we do not want others to go? Even third-generation directed energy weapons, largely free

[59] Quoted in Robert M. McNab and Richard L. Scott, Non-Lethal Weapons and the Long Tail of Warfare, 20 Small Wars and Insurgencies No. 1, March 2009, p. 141, 143.

[60] Donald Rumsfeld, testimony to Senate Armed Services Committee, quoted in Jim Garamone, Rumsfeld Details DoD Goals, Objectives in Testimony, Armed Forces Press Service, January 12, 2001.

from the specter of debris generation, would constitute a most unwelcome development. Only a few states (predominantly Russia and China) offer current threats; the better mechanism for dealing with them would be via diplomacy, and the United States should immediately abandon its longstanding absurdist opposition to the articulation of new international restraints against ASAT innovations.

Low-yield nuclear weapons. Comparable prudential considerations inveigh with even more force against violating the nuclear taboo – even in a "small" way. Nuclear weapons offer the only truly apocalyptic threat to the United States; the nation's top security priority therefore ought to be to ensure against the proliferation and use of this most devastating weapon of mass destruction. Again, other countries may pursue nuclear weapons for their own purposes regardless of what self-restraint we exhibit. But how could we hope for any other response if the world's sole remaining superpower, vastly superior to any conceivable alignment of potential foes in all manner of conventional weapons confrontations, nonetheless validated the supremacy of nuclear ordnance by crafting, brandishing, and even using new generations of nukes?

Even when the United States enjoyed its brief nuclear monopoly immediately after World War II, and even when the rugby scrum of cold war relations offered multiple occasions to contemplate the reapplication of the ultimate weapon, cooler heads always prevailed. When President Harry Truman was reminded by an aide in late 1945 that although rapid demobilization proceeded, he still held an atomic weapon up his sleeve, Truman replied, "Yes, but I am not sure it can ever be used."[61] That insight is even more valid today, and it is a cruel illusion to suppose that a precise, small-yield, earth-penetrating nuclear weapon could solve more problems than it would create.

The (deserved) international opprobrium that would surely follow any American first use of a nuclear weapon, even for legitimate war-fighting aims, would obliterate any gains sought; we cannot, as the Romans did in ancient Britain, create a wasteland and call it peace. Any invention that would reduce the self-deterrence against nuclear weapons and expand their range of missions would be a horrible mistake.

As with ASAT systems, self-restraint is a necessary but not entirely sufficient policy prescription for nuclear weapons. In addition to refraining from pioneering these fields, the United States should devote its

[61] John Lewis Gaddis, The Long Peace: Inquiries into the History of the Cold War, 1987, p. 106.

considerable diplomatic strengths to the effort to globalize an enduring norm against possible arms racing. Strengthening the 1967 Outer Space Treaty and the 1968 Nuclear Non-Proliferation Treaty will require creativity, persistence, and focused leadership, based upon an understanding that sometimes seizing a transitory military advantage, at the cost of sparking a global proliferation of revolutionary capabilities, disserves our long-term interests.

Antipersonnel land mines. Smart APL is the category of useable weapons that causes me the most uncertainty. Two irreconcilable truths collide here. First, mines equipped with reliable self-neutralizing or self-deactivating features do not contribute to the humanitarian crisis that lies at the core of the world's revulsion with long-lived mines that outlast their legitimate purposes. It is therefore overinclusive to sweep them in with other properly reviled Ottawa Treaty ordnance. On the other hand, it is an equally valid truth of global politics that only a genuinely comprehensive antimine posture that embraces all the disparate franchises of this phenomenon would have a realistic chance of attracting widespread adherence. Any treaty that protected the particular brand of mines that the United States would seek to retain while requiring abandonment of other countries' cheaper alternatives would be a nonstarter in any negotiations.

The avulsive change in global attitudes toward APL has been remarkable; these once-ubiquitous weapons have now been generally stigmatized as illegitimate, and the manufacture, sale, and use of mines have dramatically diminished. The United States, too, while remaining aloof from the Ottawa Treaty, has become much less profligate in its strewing of mines – in part because the modern scheme of highly mobile warfare offers fewer occasions for advantageous use. As alternative systems come online (incorporating advanced sensors that keep a discerning human trigger-puller in the loop, rather than relying upon automatic detonation) the military rationale for preserving this option will diminish, and the political premium from joining so much of the rest of the world, including our NATO allies and traditional coalition partners, in walking away from even smart APL will appreciate.

BOTTOM LINE

The stakes are high here. Within the catchment area of the ongoing revolution in military affairs will lie billions of dollars, long-term decisions about training, equipping, and organizing modern military forces, implications for employing those troops and materials in diverse combat missions for decades to come, and, of course, consequences for many lives potentially saved or lost by increasingly useable weapons. The momentous and largely unnoticed gravitation toward armaments that are more precise, smaller, of shorter duration, and of limited lethality will characterize American and other defense establishments for the next generation – or at least until the next, unforeseeable RMA unravels much of the current thinking.

At the same time, we should not oversell. Most of the weapons systems addressed in this book have little or nothing to do with some of the most pressing, confounding contemporary security problems: suicide bombers, improvised roadside explosive devices, and other low-intensity operations are immune to the application of low-yield nuclear weapons or directed-energy antisatellite mechanisms. No matter how precise our weaponry, we cannot effectively target an evildoer if we cannot identify and locate him, if he has no assets to hold at risk, and if he can anonymously slink back into the civilian crowd with impunity. Suicidal terrorist footsoldiers willing to walk or drive up to an unprotected civilian gathering point can achieve a degree of precision that aerial bombs, even with the smartest guidance mechanisms and smallest circular error probable (CEPs), will never match.

Deterrence and effective combat require a careful match between our capacities and our commitments. It is not always about having the largest weapons, the deepest pockets, or the snazziest technology; victory in modern battle does not automatically flow to the protagonist with the mightiest accumulation of raw power. Instead, what counts is being able to wield *appropriate* force, properly sized and deftly located, to achieve a legitimate military objective efficiently and without excess.

By designing and scaling our weapons with a realistic eye to how they actually could be wielded in combat, the advocates of useable weaponry promise to mitigate the paralyzing effects of self-deterrence. No longer stuck between the dangers of applying too much or too little force, the American military would enjoy greater credibility and improved clout. We do not get to decide what tactics or implements an enemy might use against us – generals and admirals are often castigated for planning to fight the "last" war, rather than the "next" one, but today there are several distinct types of warfare that might arrive next on our doorstep, and we have to be ready for any of them. If we are prudent, we will have to contemplate an array of asymmetric approaches from different azimuths, probing for diverse soft spots in our defenses. But we do get to decide how we will equip, train, and deploy our forces, and both competence and humanitarianism now drive us toward favoring more discrete packets of power.

In fact, the existing array of modern American weapons has already grown so powerful, so swift, and so deadly that there is little room left for improvement at the top of the traditional hierarchies. Even if we could imagine weapons more energetic than nuclear bombs, faster than intercontinental ballistic missiles (ICBMs) or laser beams, more accurate than GPS guidance, or hardier than existing antipersonnel land mines, any such improvements would surely be marginal. The only remaining growth area, the place where revolutions are still possible, involves "weapons in-fill," moving smartly in the opposite direction by crafting arms that are less powerful, less devastating to property, and less deadly to enemy personnel and civilians.

I do not mean to suggest that the deft weapons will "complete" the arsenals or create an immutably perfect inventory of weapons. As long as human creativity and avarice exist, we will never reach the end of history in the pursuit of decisive military innovations. But the future arms race gets more complicated than a simple-minded search for an ever more rippled military musculature. Martin van Creveld has even invented an apt acronym for the phenomenon, writing that we should no longer fetishize weapons that have become "TOO6EFIBUP": Too expensive, too fast, too indiscriminating, too big, too unmaneuverable, and too powerful to be very useful in real-life war.[62]

It can be disconcerting at first to contemplate mixing self-restraint with military force, leavening muscle with humility. And even with the most useable weapons, we should not fool ourselves into believing that technology can evade the horror of warfare – that illusion leads only to military misadventures, squandering our power by sliding into combat that then proves hopelessly difficult to limit or escape. Still, as Shankar Vedantam puts it, we shouldn't send a lion to catch a mouse. "If you want to catch a mouse, you need a cat. If you hire a lion to do the job because it is bigger and stronger, the very strength and size of the lion can get in the way of getting the job done."[63]

[62] Martin van Creveld, Technology and War: From 2000 B.C. to the Present, 1989, p. 67.

[63] Shankar Vedantam, Don't Send a Lion to Catch a Mouse, Washington Post, March 5, 2007, p. A3.

With its pursuit of more useable weapons in the five categories described in previous chapters, the U.S. military is now applying that lesson of moderation – for better and for worse.

BIBLIOGRAPHY

The Admiral's Agenda (interview with JCS Chairman Michael Mullen), National Journal, June 21, 2008

Norman Angell, Peace Theories and the Balkan War, 1912

A.J. Bacevich, The Use of Force in Our Time, 19 Wilson Quarterly No. 1, Winter 1995, p. 50

Ben Bain, Number of Reported Cyber Incidents Jumps, Federal Computer Week, February 17, 2009

Kyle M. Ballard, Convention in Peril? Riot Control Agents and the Chemical Weapons Ban, 37 Arms Control Today No. 7, September 2007, p. 12

Dennis C. Blair, Annual Threat Assessment of the Intelligence Community, March 10, 2009

Max Boot, War Made New: Technology, Warfare, and the Course of History, 1500 to Today, 2006

Peter Brookes, The Newest Trends in Terror, New York Post, June 3, 2008

Greg Bruno, Backgrounder: The Evolution of Cyber Warfare, New York Times, February 27, 2008

George W. Bush, Commencement address at West Point, June 1, 2002, 38 Weekly Comp. Pres. Docs. 944

Chairman of the Joint Chiefs of Staff, The National Military Strategy for Cyberspace Operations, December 2006

Joseph Cirincione, Jon Wolfsthal, and Miriam Rajkumar, Deadly Arsenals: Nuclear, Biological, and Chemical Threats (2nd ed.), 2005

John M. Collins, How Military Strategists Should Study History, Military Review, August 1983, p. 32

CSIS Commission on Cybersecurity for the 44th Presidency, Security Cyberspace for the 44th Presidency, December 2008

Sidney D. Drell and James E. Goodby, What Are Nuclear Weapons For? Recommendations for Restructuring U.S. Strategic Nuclear Forces, An Arms Control Association Report, October 2007

Charles J. Dunlap, Jr., Technology: Recomplicating Moral Life for the Nation's Defenders, 29 Parameters No. 3, Autumn 1999, p. 24

Keith Epstein and Ben Elgin, Network Security Breaches Plague NASA, Business Week, November 20, 3008

Michael Fabey, NGA Chief Says Cyberspace Intel Faces Growing Security Threat, Aerospace Daily & Defense Report, September 27, 2007

David A. Fulghum, Cyber-Attack Operations Near, Aviation Week, January 18, 2009

John Lewis Gaddis, The Long Peace: Inquiries into the History of the Cold War, 1987

Jim Garamone, Rumsfeld Details DoD Goals, Objectives in Testimony, Armed Forces Press Service, January 12, 2001

Nikolas Gardner, Resurrecting the 'Icon': The Enduring Relevance of Clausewitz's On War, 3 Strategic Studies Quarterly No. 1, Spring 2009
Robert M. Gates, A Balanced Strategy: Reprogramming the Pentagon for a New Age, Foreign Affairs, January/February 2009
General Order 100, Lieber Code, Instructions for the Government of Armies of the United States in the Field, April 24, 1863
Siobhan Gorman, NSA to Defend Against Hackers, Baltimore Sun, September 20, 2007
Colin S. Gray, Strategy for Chaos: Revolutions in Military Affairs and the Evidence of History, 2002
Richard F. Grimmett, Conventional Arms Transfers to Developing Nations, 2000–2007, Congressional Research Service Report for Congress RL 34723, October 23, 2008
Elaine M. Grossman, Senior U.S. General Sees High Nuclear Threshold, Global Security Newswire, October 22, 2007
David Hambling, Blast Reduction, Defense Technology International, September 2007, p. 54
Shane Harris, China's Cyber-Militia, National Journal, May 31, 2008
B.H. Liddell Hart, The Revolution in Warfare, 1946
J.D. Hittle (ed.), Jomini and His Summary of the Art of War, 1947, 1958
Erik Holmes, Donley Sets Out Structure for Cyber Command, Air Force Times, February 25, 2009
Human Rights Watch, Off Target: The Conduct of the War and Civilian Casualties in Iraq, December 11, 2003, http://www.hrw.org/en/reports/2003/12/11/target-0
International Institute for Strategic Studies, Strategic Survey 1995–1996
Frederick W. Kagan, Finding the Target: The Transformation of American Military Policy, 2006
Wyatt Kash, Details Emerge about President's Cyber Plan, Government Computer News, November 21, 2008
Zalmay M. Khalilzad and John P. White (eds.), The Changing Role of Information in Warfare, 1999
Andrew F. Krepinevich, Cavalry to Computer: The Pattern of Military Revolutions, National Interest, Fall 1993–1994
William T. Lord, USAF Cyberspace Command: To Fly and Fight in Cyberspace, Strategic Studies Quarterly, Fall 2008, p. 5
Jason Lyall and Isaiah Wilson III, Rage Against the Machines: Explaining Outcomes in Counterinsurgency Wars, 63 International Organization No. 1, Winter 2009, p. 67
Marching Off to Cyberwar, Economist, December 4, 2008
David R. Markov, The Russians and Their Nukes, 80 Air Force Magazine No. 2, February 1997
Anthony D. McIvor (ed.), Rethinking the Principles of War, 2005
Robert M. McNab and Richard L. Scott, Non-lethel Weapons and the Long Tail of Warfare, 20 Small Wars and Insurgencies No. 1, March 2009, p. 141
Alexander Melikishvili, Recent Events Suggest Cyber Warfare Can Become New Threat, WMD Insights, December 2008/January 2009

A.A. Milne, Peace with Honor: An Enquiry into the War Convention, 1934
Dave Montgomery, Military Planners Mull Possibility of Cyber War, Kansas City Star, November 26, 2007, p. 1
Patrick M. Morgan, Deterrence Now, 2003
John Mueller, Retreat from Doomsday: The Obsolescence of Major War, 1989
Michael G. Mullen, CJCS Guidance for 2008–2009, November 17, 2008
National Intelligence Council, Global Trends 2025: A Transformed World, November 2008
Barack Obama, Remarks on Securing Our Nation's Cyber Infrastructure, May 29, 2009, available at http://www.whitehouse.gov/the_press_office/Remarks-by-the-President-on-Securing-Our-Nations-Cyber-Infrastructure/
William A. Owens, Kenneth W. Dam, and Herbert S. Lin (eds.), Technology, Policy, Law, and Ethics Regarding U.S. Acquisition and Use of Cyber Capabilities, National Research Council, 2009
Robert A. Pape, Pape Replies, 83 Foreign Affairs No. 5, p. 162
Jean Pictet, Development and Principles of International Humanitarian Law, 1985
Walter Pincus, The New Art of War, Washington Post, March 3, 2008, p. A15
Jeffrey Record, Back to the Weinberger-Powell Doctrine? Strategic Studies Quarterly, Fall 2007, p. 79
Walter E. Richter, The Future of Information Operations, Military Review, January–February 2009, p. 103
Dwight A. Roblyer, Beyond Precision: Issues of Morality and Decision Making in Minimizing Collateral Casualties, Program in Arms Control, Disarmament, and International Security, University of Illinois, April 28, 2003
John Rollins and Anna C. Henning, Comprehensive National Cybersecurity Initiative: Legal Authorities and Policy Considerations, Congressional Research Service Report for Congress, March 10, 2009
Harvey M. Sapolsky and Jeremy Shapiro, Casualties, Technology, and America's Future Wars, 26 Parameters No. 2, Summer 1996, p. 119
P.W. Singer, Military Robots and the Laws of War, New Atlantis, Winter 2009, p. 25
P.W. Singer, Robots and the Rise of 'Tactical Generals,' Defense News, March 9, 2009
Rupert Smith, The Utility of Force: The Art of War in the Modern World, 2007
Alexander Solzhenitsyn, address at Harvard University Class Day Afternoon Exercises, June 8, 1978
Nina Tannenwald, The Nuclear Taboo: The United States and the Normative Basis of Nuclear Non-Use, 53 International Organization No. 3, Summer 1999, p. 433
Ward Thomas, The Ethics of Destruction: Norms and Force in International Relations, 2001
Top Brass Launch Manpower Study for Cyberspace Operations, Inside the Pentagon, March 5, 2009
U. S. Army, Counterinsurgency, Field Manual 3–24, December 15, 2006
U.S. Army, Center for Law and Military Operations, Forged in the Fire: Legal Lessons Learned During Military Operations 1994–2006, September 2006

U.S.–China Economic and Security Review Commission, Report to Congress, November 2008

U.S. Department of Defense, News Transcript, Secretary Rumsfeld Town Hall Meeting in Kuwait, December 8, 2004

U.S. Department of Homeland Security, Fact Sheet: Protecting Our Federal Networks Against Cyber Attacks, April 8, 2008

U.S. Government, Cyberspace Policy Review: Assuring a Trusted and Resilient Information and Communications Infrastructure, 2009, available at http://www.whitehouse.gov/assets/documents/Cyberspace_Policy_Review_final.pdf

U.S. Government, National Strategy to Secure Cyberspace, February 2003

U.S. Joint Chiefs of Staff, Information Operations, Joint Publication 3–13, February 13, 2006

Martin van Creveld, The Transformation of War, 1991

Martin van Creveld, Technology and War: From 2000 B.C. to the Present, 1989

Shankar Vedantam, Don't Send a Lion to Catch a Mouse, Washington Post, March 5, 2007, p. A3

Carl von Clausewitz, On War (Michael Howard and Peter Par, eds. and trans.) 1984

Mathew C. Waxman, International Law and the Politics of Urban Air Operations, 2000

The White House, The Agenda: Homeland Security, http://www.whitehouse.gov/agenda/homeland_security/2009

Thomas C. Wingfield, The Law of Information Conflict: National Security Law in Cyberspace, 2000

TREATIES

Convention on the Prohibition of the Development, Production, Stockpiling and Use of Chemical Weapons and on Their Destruction, concluded in Paris, January 13, 1993, entered into force April 29, 1997, S. TREATY DOC. NO. 103–21, 31 I.L.M. 800 (United States is a party) [CWC]

1997 Convention on the Prohibition of the Use, Stockpiling, Production and Transfer of Anti-Personnel Mines and on Their Destruction, signed December 3, 1997, entered into force July 3, 1998, 36 I.L.M. 1507, 1997 [Ottawa Mine Ban Treaty]

Convention on Prohibitions or Restrictions on the Use of Certain Conventional Weapons Which May Be Deemed to Be Excessively Injurious or to Have Indiscriminate Effects, Oct. 10, 1980, 1342 U.N.T.S. 137, 19 I.L.M. 1523 [CCW], Protocol II

Index